THE
WOMAN
WHO PLEADS

Love Can Not Be Measured By Words

ANTONIO FLEMING

Distributed by:
Iqra Publishing Inc.
157 Sunset Avenue
Atlanta, GA 30314
http://iqrapublishing.com

Edited by: Vittorio Triofano & Lori McCaskill

DEDICATION

The achievement of this book will always be dear to me, because I just didn't write this novel to remind women of their significance to life or the importance of them never allowing the blessing they are to be taken for granted merely to be accepted by someone who don't appreciate them. I wrote this book initially to impress a woman who gives meaning to the word: *EXTRAORDINARY*. She didn't just challenge and inspire me to unlease potential I sheltered, while at the same time ARGUING to ensure I upheld the integrity of **"ALL"** women in my writing. In my pursuit to gain her acceptance, she allowed me to learn through her grace the honor and appreciation of true love. I dedicate this book to the woman who made it her own personal work of art, though the words are my collection of thoughts. Renesha Acosta, I thank Allah ta'ala for allowing my mind, eyes, heart, and soul to be nurtured by the spectacular essence of your love. Without you, this emotional rollercoaster novel would not be. You are magnificent in so many ways, yet indescribable as a whole. "Demi," is my reflection of you for the world, though she still fall short of truly defining your worth.

It is also imperative that I give appreciation and love to Aya and Cadence - *IRREPLACEABLE* the both of you are.

IN THE NAME
ALLAH
COMPASSIONATE,
ALL MERCIFUL

All praise and thanks are due to Allah ta'ala, alone, the Sustainer and Creator of existence. May the choicest blessings and peace be upon the last of the righteous messengers and prophets, Muhammad ﷺ his family, Companions and all those who follow in his footsteps till the blowing of the trumpet.

قُلْ إِنَّمَا أَنَا بَشَرٌ مِّثْلُكُمْ يُوحَى إِلَيَّ أَنَّمَا إِلَهُكُمْ إِلَهٌ وَاحِدٌ فَمَن كَانَ يَرْجُو لِقَاء رَبِّهِ فَلْيَعْمَلْ عَمَلًا صَالِحًا وَلَا يُشْرِكْ بِعِبَادَةِ رَبِّهِ أَحَدًا ﴿١١٠﴾

Say: "I am only a human being like you. It is revealed to me that your God is One God, therefore whoever wishes to reach Allah (before death) let him do improving deeds (the soul's cleansing) and let him not associate anyone with Him in the worship of his Lord".
(Surah Al-Kahf: 110)

The Prophet (PBUH) stated the following:
"The mother is in the middle of the doors of Paradise."
(Ibn Hanbal, V, 198);
"Paradise is under the feet of mothers."
(Nasai, Jihad, 6)

TABLE OF CONTENTS

CHAPTER 1

With the soothing sounds of raindrops beating rhythmically, and the cool mystic breeze seeping through the window on an autumn morning, Randle laid in bed holding his pillow with a semblance of intimacy. Existing in a dream that seemed so real, he basked in the ambiance of Lo Jones and Alice Braga feeding him honey grilled flamingo rolls on the luxury sundeck of the chartered superyacht, Eclipse, drifting on the currents of the Mediterranean.

Startled, by the music of Nikki Minaj blasting by his ear, he strained to open his eyelids and looked around, disoriented as the phone rang unwantingly. Randle struggled to reach for the phone in pure frustration. Deeply immersed in a soothing dream, he wasn't ready to wake up from it's pleasantries, especially given the fact that he had a throbbing headache from his excessive drinking at Club Erotic, prior to staggering home to close his eyes.

"Yeah?" Disgruntled, he pressed the phone to his ear answering in a tone of pure rebuke. "Who the fuck is this?"

"Good morning, Randle. May I speak to Sheri, please?"

With his eyes glancing at the clock on the nightstand to clearly distinguish the time, he spoke with open distaste, not surprising to Naomi. "Haven't I advised your stupid trifling ass not to call my house before twelve o'clock?" He growled. "Instead of disturbing my fuckin' sleep, why not utilize this time to decontaminate your throat and body, given its no more than a playground for STD's?"

Naomi had no practical idea what her girlfriend actually saw in this sorry life of trash, but given an associate was leaving her office, she responded without losing any sense of her composure. "Randle, will you please give the phone to Sheri?! The matter is very urgent. And may I remind you, the house you are currently breathing in belongs to her father, a man of prestige and character which you certainly are not. I can't fight my girl battles nor stop her from loving you, though I have begged her to stop having compassion for stray animals. But if you ever disrespect me again, I promise with all the life inside of me that you will regret the day you ever desired to experiment with a black woman."

Randle's anger intensified while hearing that statement. Deep down inside, he knew so well that he was crossing the wrong line disrespecting Naomi, but the

1

thought of her checking him and abruptly waking him from a jewel of a dream he may never visit again only fueled what was already thumping inside of his throbbing head. In his inner thought, he wished he could sit on her chest and pluck out her eyebrows with two rusty nails welded together. With nothing but air filling his chest, and the alcohol still affecting his emotional state, Randle exploded, "Bitch, I wouldn't care if you were on your last breath or you were calling to warn that there's a hurricane outside the fuckin' door. If I tell you not to call my damn house before a certain damn time, then respect it!! Even though you too trifling to have respect for yourself. Your girl is my hoe, and wherever she lay her head, I'm the man of that mutha-fucka!"

With all intentions of hanging up the phone following his last words, Randle couldn't help but glance at Sheri as he removed the phone from his ear, not concerned with any rebuttal that Naomi may slam him with. The sight of her resting peacefully in the sun's glow before his eyes insanely aggravated him, especially considering what he had subconsciously lost. Without pondering upon the thought or hesitating on his action, Randle slammed the phone against Sheri's face as if he was crushing an irritating mosquito.

Startled in immeasurable disbelief, Sheri quickly sprang up in the bed, completely covering her face while screaming in shock and aggravation, not knowing if another blow would follow or if he was just exercising as he does sometimes. "Aiiiiiiiii!!" With blood starting to ooze into the palm of her hand firmly pressed against the throbbing and squirting cut, Sheri peered through her fingers and asked, "What the hell was that for?!"

"Your lame ass girlfriend is on the phone, slut." He replied, staring intensely into her visible eye. "Now get the fuck up! Because if you get a drop of blood on these sheets, you gon' have a muthafuckin' problem."

Witnessing the cold look of anger that ran in his eyes and knowing fully well of his unpredictable rage, Sheri lowered her gaze, quickly eased off the bed while picking up the phone in fear, simply placing it against her face while stepping into the bathroom. Closing the door behind her, Sheri shook her head in complete disgust while observing the reflection of the gash in the mirror. She pretty well knew from the wavering pain starting to be felt that another black eye was imminent due to this idiot's abuse and it would have people gossiping about how he had abused her yet again. This was the last thing she needed on a day as prominent as this one. "Girl, let me call you back," Sheri insisted. Before nonchalantly whispering, "I love you," and placing the disconnected phone on the countertop without inquiring the purpose of Naomi calling.

The streaming blood on her face had her suddenly thinking about her late grandfather and wishing she was a child in his arms again — no worries, no cries, just laughter and love. At 26, Sheri was already an honor graduate from Spellman University, a successful CEO of the art gallery "Art of Life," as well as "Art Annex," her web based service which electronically connects novice art buyers to professional art sellers around the world. Impressively, she was also founder and CEO of Unity After School Center (Unity), a program for heightening the scholastics and critical thinking skills of inner-city kids. Driven by ambition to be more than just another beautiful black face in a sexist world, Sheri initially started the art companies to expose her late grandfather's secret collection to more than the stale air of his secluded gallery exiled in the basement of his home and to fill his void in her life. Later, she would host a private showing of art for some high echelon art buyers and couldn't believe she was now looking like she'd been slapped by an elephant's trunk across the eye. If only Randle could control his temper.

"Sheri! Sheriiiiii! I'm hungry!" Randle yelled. "Slut come fix me something to eat, cause I know you hear me calling you."

"I'm coming right out bae!" She yelled without hesitation.

"Bitch, I don't see you! And, since your dumb-ass girlfriend woke me up from my dream, I also need you to bring me two Advils for my damn headache." Fueled with anger, that tasting the sensuous soft fingers and lips of Lo Jones was no longer a virtual reality for him, Randle's impatience spawned new and increased anger as his headache caused him to became even more agitated.

"Slut, it doesn't take that fuckin' long to wipe your face. If you don't bring your ass now, imma get outta bed and really give you a reason to spend time playing with a first aid kit — I'm your first priority bitch, and don't you forget it."

The annoying sound of his voice was the last thing she desired at the moment, but aggravating his flaring insensitivity and slave owner rage, she didn't desire either. "Okay, baby!" She hollered back like a woman with no self-worth and scurrying into the room.

"I didn't hit your soft ass that hard." Randle shouted, as she walked over and handed him two Advil, before going downstairs and quickly returning with a bottle of water.

Observing her walk away, Randle couldn't help but admire how unfathomably sexy she was. Her luscious skin resembled bee's honey, and the Victoria's Secret Pink boy-shorts were fitting her body as if spandex gained it's origin from the way they accentuated every curve and seemingly melted onto her flesh. Sheri's walk was so graceful and seductive that the most faithful of married men, or woman, wouldn't be able to resist staring in lust.

"Fuck them stank whores!" Randle yelled out while cackling in between his self-centered comments. "My President is a gangster and boss pimp."

Lost in the political controversy being broadcast on CNN, Randle had forgotten about his command to Sheri and notice when she walked back into the room with breakfast in hand — two fried turkey sausages, scrambled eggs with melted cheddar cheese, toast with apple jelly and a glass of orange juice.

"Baby," Sheri called out enticingly, while standing beside the bed, extending the breakfast tray.

"Bitch, don't you see me watching my pimp tight President talking on TV. This is the second time I've been interrupted this morning, and it will definitely be the last," he threatened while turning to look at her square in her eyes, piercingly void of empathy with vile darts of hatred.

Not knowing if trying to be seductive would cause him to react abusively towards her as well, Sheri just stood there mildly trembling, and holding the tray while staring into his den of demons. Randle liked being in control and sensed her fear of him potentially punishing her. Reaching for the glass of orange juice of which he took just a few sips, Randle unexpectedly grabbed the glass rectangular serving tray from her hands then instructed her to take off her clothes. Leaning to the side of her as she slowly removed her white chiffon sleep shirt, he arrogantly releasing his hold of the Florentine designed crystal tempered, allowing it to fall to the floor.

The disgrace of his actions sparked a sense of fear and dampened even greater the ambiance. Sheri wanted to be alone but knew walking away would be physically detrimental. In a natural reaction to stimulate passion, after removing her bra to expose her peanut size nipples, Sheri lowered herself and tried to kiss Randle while maneuvering to slide out of her panties, assuming that a spark of heated affection would breathe sexual tranquility into the atmosphere. Yet, he surprised her by muzzling her face with his right hand, before their lips could connect, and stiff-arming backwards with a quick thrust.

"Bitch, I said take off your clothes, not touch me! And turn the fuck around before you drop them panties." Randle scoffed in a tone that was more so cold and empty of desire. "I wanna see that ass not your face."

Sheri had a strong adrenaline rush of uneasiness but turned her back to him and slowly wined as she slid her panties over her ass. Bonding her legs together as the descending fabric caressed her thighs, Sheri bent forward to expose her pretty, shaved pussy to him. Stepping out of her boy short panties, she separated her legs so he could see straight through her gap, then seductively bite into her fingernail while gazing at him over her shoulder. In her complete nakedness, Sheri knew for sure that responding in any way besides remaining silent was not in her best interest. So, she sensuously began caressing her clitoris with the fingers of her free hand and hoping that it would suppress his newfound attitude by turning him on instead of making her stand naked like a scarecrow.

"Trump! Trump! Come here boy!" Randle called out, seemingly paying her no further attention. Caught off guard, she jumped at the shock of Trump dashing in between her legs with the speed of a competition show dog on an obstacle course. Trump was a very active pit bull puppy that mysteriously vanished from his ex-girlfriend house who had bought the puppy for her nine-year-old autistic son. Randle presented him to Sheri as a gift of apology for slapping her in front of her cousin, Maria, at a jazz lounge a few weeks prior. His senseless excuse for the public embarrassment was that Maria wouldn't stop voicing disrespectful lies about the President, and Sheri never attempted to stop her, which eventually set him off.

"Hi boy... Hi boy..." Randle chuckled as he tickled Trump's face.

After lifting him to say, "I love you," while looking into Sheri's slanted left eye, he leaned over and placed Trump in front of his breakfast tray on the floor as she silently stared in disbelief, mildly shivering with her nipples hard and pussy dripping like a broken faucet. Leaning back onto his pillow without surrendering any affection to her nakedness, Randle began fantasizing of his moments with Lo Jones and Alice Braga, while admiring more of what the President was saying on CNN than his naked and supposedly irresistible girlfriend before him.

CHAPTER 2

Walking through Hartsfield-Jackson International Airport terminal with the swagger of an Arabian prince, exposing his pedicured toes in Fendi sandals and Ralph Laruen linen giving more attraction to the muscular curves of his Zulu warrior physique, Terry epitomized the male definition of sexy. The magnitude of unexpected attention he was receiving from the eyes of passing women had him smiling, and psychologically feeling as though he was shirtless on the shores of Zanzibar, especially when the four Russian bikini models standing a few feet in front of him on the escalator turned around and casually eased back down the ascending steps, merely to take a few selfies in his arms. Exiting with expansively animated smiles embellishing their exotic aura, they openly cajoled, strolling through the terminal.

Damn he's a lucky guy, Terry heard a passing traveler voice to an associate walking in the opposite direction with hm, as one of the foreign runway models seductively caressed his chest with a V.I.P entry pass to their upcoming fashion show and a separate piece of paper with all of their international cell phone numbers scribbled on it. The exotic beauty of each foreign model was hypnotic to the eyes of the onlooking strangers. Finally reaching their separation point in the airport, the models conjoined and whispered among themselves as Terry said good-bye, before attempting to walk away programming their numbers in his phone. Giggling after they all called out his name enticingly in unison, they then paraded behind him like a gang of hyenas. The tallest of the entourage spoke in a raspy, sexy accent, seductively asking if he would be their personal trainer, masseur, and tour guide during their weekend stay at the Ritz Carlton, while the others stood behind her, anxiously awaiting a response with shy poses and giggling.

"I'd be less than a gentleman if I allowed y'all to come and leave my city without exposing each of you to unforgettable memories in Hotlanta." Terry stated as they began to hug him again, and express their excitement and thanks, noisily, with heightened elation.

"Здорово!" He heard one utter as they strutted away, casually looking over their shoulders, giggling.

It had been six years since Terry was last seen in the city, and he knew that the discovery of his return was about to ignite fireworks among family and associates. With each step, he couldn't help but linger on all the years that he had lost by being away from his loved ones and how emotional he was getting by just breathing the southern air. A sacrifice that positively helped to mold him into a better man as a whole traveling the world as a philanthropist and an exceptional Playboy. The anticipation of hugging his mother and sister once again filled him with nothing shy of endless joy. Yet, it was momentarily critical not to expose the secret of his return, otherwise their constructed plan would crumble.

With his plane arriving thirty minutes ahead of schedule and his driver not scheduled for another forty-five minutes, Terry decided to kill some time by catering to his appetite, instead of waiting at the entrance. Surveying the area as he strolled admiring the airport's transformation, he walked into Annette's Bar and Grill restaurant after making eye contact with the gorgeous British bartender and incorrectly reading her body language. Electing to sit at the bar to bask in her ambiance, Terry ordered roasted chicken with pan drippings and mussels in a bourbon chile broth while admiring her hypnotic features, brushed with brown skin. Psychologically feeling himself, he assumed that the bartender was in awe of his sexiness and constantly stealing glances, but she was actually observing the lacrosse game, broadcasting on the wall mounted flat screen behind him. Seeking to nurture her attraction, Terry invaded her privacy by gaining her attention and asking, "If I was so fortunate to breathe life as your man, would you look at another man just as you are looking at me right now?"

"What? Excuse me sir?!" Shocked by such an unexpectedly forward question, the bartender could only smile out of politeness, given the fact that his words caught her completely off guard and she didn't want to deflate his ego by expressing her thoughts. "With all due respect, sir, I can't answer that question."

"Your smile reflects tranquility in an indescribable way." Terry conveyed, while indirectly lowering his gaze to caress the visible curves of her body.

"Thank You sir," she replied.

"My name is Terry, and yours?"

"Demi," she said with the most seductive and cocky accent he had ever heard, rivaling the tall Russian model, as she fixed a drink for another customer.

"Respectfully, I know we just met, but would you mind if I referred to you by what you are as a whole?"

Using her fingers, Demi combed the curly strands of fallen hair from her face as she obliged the request of a new customer at the bar, before allowing Terry to look into her eyes again. Slightly confused and taken aback by the stranger's second off the wall corny question, and clueless of whether or not he was about to be disrespectful or make an attempt to be appealing, Demi briefly stared at him with a puzzled look upon her face before politely uttering, while placing the brandy bottle back on the shelf, "I thank you sincerely for the Casanova charm sir, but it will be unprofessional and inappropriate for me to say yes."

Respecting her words but not trying to lose the opportunity of exploding the depths of her foreign wetness, while back in the city, Terry rained phrases in a charming French manner that wet her intellectual appetite. "*Tu es plus belle qu'une rose irresistible.*" By artistically teasing with words that made it quite impossible for her to hold back the radiant beauty of her smile, flattering images floated in thin air, causing her to lower her head in a shy effort to shield her blushing cheeks, walking away to assist another customer.

Observing the extraordinary book, "*Destruction of the Black Civilization,*" by William Chancellor, Demi had laying behind the counter. Terry took a new approach in his attempt to stimulate her interest once she returned and began sanitizing her work area. Gaining her attention by surprising her with an intellectual question regarding the book, they preempted the traditionally prescribed dialogue, foregoing the opportunity to discover each other in an orthodox fashion. Though they intrigued each other anticipatingly and overwhelmingly, Terry found himself hesitant for the first time as his prowess was arrested by her stature. Looking into her eyes, Terry felt an unexpected sense of vulnerability that had him wishing Demi had no moral standards but felt her religious beliefs would cause her to reject his request to exchange numbers.

Being internally groomed to always be a lady, she remained silent in anticipation of his desire to court, for it is the gentleman who pursues the woman and not the reverse. Surprised by the way Terry paid his bill, then walked away from the bar without granting them the pleasure of discovering more about one another beyond the given, Demi began to feel exposing her intellect and elements of her integrity may have intimidated him. She couldn't believe she had crossed the path of someone debonair enough to be mentally and physically attractive yet seemed to be afraid to pursue her. Before rising out of his seat Terry eloquently said, *"la vie est une fleur, et la beauté de votre sourire est ce qui la nourrit. Un plaisir inoubliable c'était."* Demi grabbed his plate and glass off the counter to be washed.

Attempting to leave the restaurant with suspense lingering in the air between them, Terry couldn't help but wonder who she was internally while selfishly fantasizing of how she may taste and how it would feel to be deep inside her hidden warmth as she bit passionately into his bottom lip.

"L'eau peut accorder à la vie les plaisirs les plus doux et les pires malheurs, Terry!" Demi vocalized in French, which caused him to turn his head and interlock their eyes in one last intimate stare exiting the restaurant.

Terry smiled without making any other bodily gestures, knowing fully well the true reference of her statement. Retrieving the cellphone from his pocket as he strolled through the terminal en route to the train, Terry started texting to discover the status of his driver and noticed a floral shop before the entrance of the concourse and decided to enter.

"Good afternoon, sir," the florist greeted with a foreign dialect as he walked in.

"Good afternoon," Terry replied while gazing at the exotic floral arrangements around the shop. "Do you deliver?" He asked.

"Yes sir," the florist answered.

"Excellent," Terry mumbled to himself, caressing a bouquet of Lady Slippers. Recognizing her Hakka dialect from his time in Taiwan, he unintentionally humored her with his diversity by trying to communicate in Mandarin, which caused her to hold her stomach while laughing, given he unknowingly said, he was a gay mud wrestler and wanted her to spank him with roses. After being enlightened of his statement and laughing with her in regards to his own stupidity, Terry spoke directly and requested, 47 red roses with 1 white rose inserted in the center, to be delivered to a blessing, while writing on a card:

'In traveling the world, I've discovered that not even this extra-fragrant bouquet of roses scratches the surface of the unparalleled beauty of your smile. You are a blessing that exceeds the boundary of, and I pray as we breathe apart, The Most High never erase the priceless glow of your imprint from my memory.'

Emotionally touched by an Angel,
Terry
404-555-8132.

"Awww, this is sooo sweet of you. Thank you for your generous purchase, sir," the florist stated. "I wish more men were as thoughtful as you."

"Truly, I thank you for assisting me in birthing a smile upon a phenomenal woman's face, which is far more appreciated. I ask that you be creative with the arrangement and give her a significant reason to think of me."

"I promise to arrange something unforgettably magnificent for you, sir," the florist assured.

Receiving a text message from his driver acknowledging that he was walking into the airport, Terry paid the florist then departed the shop. Bounding and exiting the train in the concourse, Terry kept pondering on the metaphor of Demi last words.

"Excuse me sir," the contracted security officer said to Terry in her bedroom voice as he strutted through the security exit and the traveler in front of him caused the gate sensor to beep, by brushing against it.

"Yes?" Terry replied, perplexed, slightly turning his head to give the officer his full attention as she walked up to him grinning mysteriously.

"Sir, I need you to come with me for a moment please." The officer advised grabbing the long head of his triceps, caressing it affectionately as she escorted him into an unguarded security section of the airport.

In complete confusion of what was transpiring, Terry walked without resistance while repeatedly asking her to elaborate on why he was being detained.

"TSA routine security check, given your presence caused the sensor to go off, sir."

"Security check! That sensor went off..."

Interjecting his explanation by using the hand gesture as though she cut her throat, Terry immediately stop talking. "Please don't agitate me with your questions right now, sir," the officer retorted sternly while silently praying that he didn't make a scene which would attract uninvited attention, undoubtedly causing her to be fired and possibly prosecuted if her prior actions came to be revealed as well. Trying to seem more convincing with her hidden intentions, she called a code into her walkie talkie and stated when someone responded, "I can request more officers to come assist me if need be, sir." The act of deception suspended him of resistance, and she noticed as she stared in his eyes.

Shaking his head in complete disbelief, Terry calmly replied no, while obeying her command to enter a door, he noticed she opened by jimmying the lock with her service knife, instead of using a key. Observing that the air in each room they entered lingering of a fetid smell and was dark, until she turned on the lights, Terry wondered should he just stop and request his lawyer. Stepping into an empty room with only a reciprocal mirror and no adjacent door, she handed Terry a drug urine cup and a grey tote box. Attempting to close the door as he stood eyeing her in bewilderment, she calmly instructed him to urinate inside, after removing all his clothes, and then stand on the metal plate in the center of the room.

He initially detested the officer's command out of audacity, given the fact that he has gone through numerous airport security screenings around the world without having to remove his clothes or submit a urine sample. Yet, realizing his objective for getting home clearly meant that he must remain incognito, and had nothing to hide, Terry obliged after the officer grabbed her radio and made it seem as if she was calling for additional assistance. "Code 6!"

Locking the room to secretly admire the articulated curves of his naked body on the other side of the two-way mirror, Debra couldn't believe that a man's skin could have the perfection of a marble sculpture and a body that out measured that of an Adonis. In her mind, Terry was undeniably sexy with his clothes on, yet with them off, he looked like a luxury sex toy made of rare, perserved To'ak chocolate.

"Code 6! Code 6!" Debra uttered into her walkie talkie.

Standing naked on the cold metal floor plate feeling slightly violated, Terry looked around dumbfounded not understanding why he was instructed to wait naked. The thought of hollering for the officer to bring her supervisor and contact his lawyer seeded his thoughts, but he didn't want them to think his impatience meant he had something to hide. A simple act of suspicion, that could warrant them to detain him longer and a cavity search was definite out of the equation.

"Gurrrl, dis butta be a code 6 dat cause me to fantasize when I'm with my man tonight," her co-worker Trina said sarcastically as she walked into the room behind two other female co-workers. "Yo last code 6 was cute, but he had a mustard seed dick, and I'm not in da mood to be strainin' me eyes right now. I was just about to take my damn lunch break and try out dis new vibrating tongue that ya insert on ya pantie liner. I bought it on da way to work."

"Oh, my fucking god, what is that?" Pam lustfully asked entering the room and staring through the two-way window in overwhelming awe. The sight of his nakedness caused her to teasingly fondle her breast with intimate affection and mildly stuck out her tongue desiring to massage every measure of his muscular body with it.

"Damn. Damn. Dammmmn — I've never climaxed by just looking at a naked man before, and I think I just did twice." Stacey admitted while starting to take picture of his body with her cell phone. "Gurl I'm beyond moist — I..I.. I can feel myself drippin'. They cut their fuckin' hand in the Bible over Joseph (may God be pleased with him), but I'll cut a nipple and a toe to feel his lips, fingers, and dick inside of me."

Laughing amongst themselves at her comment, Trina contemplated going to the supply room to retrieve her new vibrator and using it while staring at him. "Gurl ya talkin' 'bout cuttin' ya nipple. A man dat sexy can fuck me in my ass on my mama bed while her and my fuckin' daddy watch." Trina admitted while giggling, though everyone knew she was dead ass serious.

"Girl you stupid," Pam rifled. "And I literally mean that witcho nasty ass. Debra, I applaud you for this one, but I may never be able to fuck my man again without fantasizing about him the entire time," she confessed without cracking a smile. "I'll ride that dick until the vertebrates in my suspension cord lock up. I know that's ain't no soft dick! Damn he sexy as fuck!"

"Bitch, you need psychiatric treatment and yes that anaconda sleeping. You mean spinal column or spine, not suspension cord with your dumb ass. But gurrl, the three of you is playin'." Debra corrected while scrambling to reconnect the intercom. "When you're fortunate enuff to have a man in your life that will literally cause Michael Angelo's '*David*' to weep in envy, you comfort him by dedicating your throat to him in his grandma car if requested, at his fuckin' baby mama house, and all the ex's just to make a statement." Her stupidity caused them all to laugh. Realizing the system was now working, Debra pressed the intercom button and stated, "Turn to your right sir. Turn to your left sir. Turn around, spread your legs, and touch your toes sir. Squat and cough aloud three times please. Now turn back around sir."

Laughing uncontrollably until the shift supervisor called on the radio for Debra to reveal her location, her co-workers began scrambling and peeking out the door window while fearing the risk of being caught. They took one last lustful look before Debra pressed the intercom button to say, "Sir you may put your clothes back on and the door will be unlocked."

"Dammmn. I wish we could keep him forever." Trina cried. "I've neva seen a man wit bulging veins in a limp dick before. I can only imagine what it looks like hard and coated with my cum."

"You are the Queen Bitch, Debra," Pam cheered while squeezing her with a hug as Trina cracked the door and peeped out. "He is unmatchable in this life! I thank you for this one, but I'm glad I don't know his name because I would definitely call it out while straining to force a climax with my icepick dick ass boyfriend. I'm so tired of using a vibrator to stimulate myself when he get off me."

"I'm assisting an elderly woman through the terminal, sir. I'm en route back." Debra retrieved her walkie talkie and stated as Terry stepped into his boxers.

"Ya damn lie bitch! Ya back here wit me sweatin' dis fine ass nicca wit an anaconda dick." Trina piped, as Debra clipped the walkie talkie back onto her service belt, which caused everyone to laugh.

"His name is Terry," Debra blurted out, smiling "And I don't care who I'm with because my mind, my mouth, and my pussy belongs to me. Just because I'm married don't mean that I have to think of my husband or call his name in order to stimulate myself. I'm definitely going to fantasize about Terry sexy ass when my husband touches me tonight."

"Debra, did you say his name was Terry?" Pam asked for confirmation.

"Yes," she replied still smiling and envisioning climaxing on his mouth reverse rodeo style.

"Gurl have you lost your damn mind?" Pam screamed in an aggressive tone that caught everyone's full attention. "Yo hot ass has literally gone too fuckin' far this time. Are you fucking stupid?"

With everyone's mind now swirling in total confusion of who Terry is, Trina shook her head while allowing her hands to hide the emotional shock in her face until Pam allowed the movements of her tongue to cut through the silence that had begun to engulf the room. "Terry's my future baby daddy, bitches, because I'm going to find out where he lives and blackmail him with these pictures in my phone, for some of that dick."

Everyone burst into uncontrollable laughter while slightly pushing at Pam playfully because they seriously thought that she was about to say he was a killer that would look into this incident and hunt each one of them down once he discovers the truth.

With everyone giggling and continuing to stare at his every move, Debra lift out the office to unlock his room door. Completely oblivious to the truth of his violation of privacy, Terry quietly followed as Debra and her giggling coworkers escorted him through security. He wasted no time in walking towards the luggage area. Reaching to grab his designer bags from the baggage conveyor, Terry felt his phone vibrating and disregarded it for the moment because he wanted to leave the airport before another unexpected incident occurred.

"Terry," Marcus called out approaching from behind him. "Terry!"

Turning around to a smothering bear hug. "It's good to see you again, sir," Marcus grinned while patting him on the back. With both of them smiling, Terry handed Marcus two of his three his bags and said "Let's get out of here without hesitation."

"Yes sir," Marcus uttered, "I had to park in the garage because you took longer than 10 minutes, and I didn't want to miss you by driving around in circles."

"It's okay," Terry stated while laughing to himself at the thought of what just occurred. "Marcus, you wouldn't believe why I'm late if I literally wrote it down for you."

"Terry, coming from you, I'd definitely believe it," he replied simmering with a small chuckle. "Everything is unexpected regarding you!"

"Marcus, do you have everything situated as I asked?"

"Yes sir!" He replied opening the rear car door for Terry to enter. Everything is in place as you requested, and she left a message this morning asking me to instruct you to take your vitamins because you will definitely need them, given you couldn't get away to share the weekend with her Croatia."

Retrieving his vibrating phone from his right front pocket as the car exited the parking garage, Terry noticed he had a text message from an unknown number:

"If I were your woman, would you look at another woman as you looked so bright-eyed at me and submissive to me?"

Smiling at the anticipation of seeing her again, Terry responded to the text, *"I'll never take for granted a blessing that only God can bestow."*

CHAPTER 3

Screaming at the top of her lungs as though she were an opera singer trying to be soulful, Sheri gave new meaning to the Toni Braxton song, *"Just Be A Man About It"* even though she knew so well that her voice resembled the sound of a choking squirrel. Singing seemed to be the therapy that allowed her to mentally escape while blanketing her in tranquility. The audio system in her Lexus LC 500 had her grooving like she was part of the engineered sound, drifting through traffic without concern for the speed limit or police.

Pulling into the Art of Life parking lot, Sheri shook her head in amusement when she saw her mother's AMG S 63 parked sideways in three reserved spots. After backing into her slot, she gathered her things and took one last look in the rear-view mirror to assure herself that the foundation she applied to hide the discoloration had not faded away. "Flawless," she whispered to herself, sliding on her Cartier shades before exiting the car to meet her mom who was already approaching, gracefully.

Wearing a crepe ruffle front sheath dress that outlined her ebony curves with precision and an open toe pair of red bottoms, Mrs. Johnson couldn't help but give signature to the fact that she's the original, and Sheri was no more than a carbon copy of her sexiness.

"Good morning Ma," Sheri said smiling, silently adoring her shoes as she walked closer.

"Morning baby," she replied, expressing her affection with a gentle hug and an European style kiss greeting without their cheeks touching.

"Ma, how many times must I inform you that you cannot park your car like that? Those spots are reserved for my marketing employees," Sheri chastened.

"Well, I guess until you utilize your college degree and clearly comprehend the fact that I am Teflon to all that. Girl, men like to see the way I perch down in the seat like a swan when I enter the car and drag my legs inside with a slow grace of seduction. I cannot do that with another car parked tightly beside me."

"Ma!"

"Ma, nothing," Mrs. Johnson shot back. "You need to remind yourself of how sexy you are, and stop being a trailer park doormat for that sorry abusive white boy you consider your man."

Catching the glare in her mother's eyes as she spoke her words, Sheri knew pretty well that her mother was being direct, and in trying to avoid any form of confrontation, she kept silent as she followed her mother into the office building.

"Good morning, Mrs. Johnson and Ms. Johnson," Heidi, the receptionist, greeted as they entered the building.

"Good morning," they replied in unison.

"Ms. Johnson, with the showing that you have scheduled this morning with the buyers, I took the liberty of contacting Keyerra, and I asked her to fill in for the luncheon with the kids. She accepted. Novia Maori from the Beatriz Gallery called and said she felt offended that you didn't invite her to the private showing. She claims she doesn't love you right now because she's quite jealous. And Naomi is in your office eating your chocolate covered strawberries," she instigated with a giggle.

"What strawberries, Heidi?" Sheri inquired, shrouded with a confused look.

"A 48-count decorative arrangement that arrived about 10 minutes ago."

Without saying anything more than, "Thank you," Sheri turned and headed to her office with her mother in matching step. Opening the door, Naomi was sprawled across the sofa as though she was smizing for a glamour photoshoot. With 24 long stem purple roses on her desk in a Vera Wang crystal vase and two large decorated confectionery boxes, one containing chocolate covered strawberries and the other white chocolate covered strawberries, Sheri paid Naomi no mind because she was so in awe of the arrangement and dumbfounded as to who would possibly have sent them.

"You may actually be my daughter after all," Mrs. Johnson said, reaching to grab the card to see who sent the arrangements only to have her hand slapped and pushed away by Sheri.

"Stop being so nosy, Ma," Sheri jabbed. "The roses and confectionery inside the boxes are for your eyes and your tummy, but the card is off limits. It's for my eyes only, unless, of course, I choose to share. These flowers are so beautiful!"

"They truly are, but just because these may be the first flowers you have ever received, don't try to start acting so special. Naomi, what does the card say?" Mrs. Johnson asked while cutting her eyes in a catlike slant with attitude. "I know your nosy ass has already read the card, looked in the boxes, and probably went online to find out what the person sending them looks like," she voiced intuitively.

With Sheri and Mrs. Johnson staring at her with intense curiosity, Naomi just sat smiling and pondering the words that she read. Given that Naomi didn't reveal what they both were aware that she knew, Mrs. Johnson rolled her eyes while sarcastically stating, "And I was going to tell your bald headed, slue-footed ass you look cute in that Christian Dior outfit, but now I'm not going to lie." Sticking out her tongue to seal the gesture, thereby causing an outburst of laughter from all of them.

After taking a bite from one of the chocolate covered strawberries in the box and witnessing Sheri read the card, Mrs. Johnson demanded that someone should tell her what the card said and who the mystery man was because she knew without a doubt that it wasn't Randle's pathetic ass. He and Sheri had been dating for almost two years, and the only gifts he managed to give her were repeated black eyes and busted lips.

"These strawberries are really good," she blurted while reaching to secure three more between her fingers.

"Damn, can I at least have the pleasure of tasting one before you and Naomi eat them all?" Sheri barked.

"Girl, you can eat the whole damn box and swallow every drop of water in the vase to clear your throat for all I care," her mother retorted, "Just tell me what the note says. What the hell you being so secretive for?"

Retrieving her phone from her hand-made Louis Vuitton tote bag, to act as though she actually dialed a number, Mrs. Johnson placed the phone to her ear and voiced aloud. "Randle, Sheri has a gift in her office from another man and she won't tell me what the card attached to the flowers says," she conveyed while giggling.

Literally hearing his name sent an impulsive chill through Sheri's entire body, and she knew that he could never discover the gift because he'd take his jealousy out on her instead of being understanding. "Ma... that wasn't cool at all."

"Well, it sure was funny." Naomi assured, still laughing. "I wish you would have enlightened me of your intentions Mrs. Johnson, so that I could have recorded it and submitted it to Funniest Home Videos. Girl, you looked like you literally transformed into cement when you heard your mom mention his name, and you know that's physically impossible."

"Shut the hell up, Naomi!" Sheri shot back. "And Ma, the arrangement is from someone I'm absolutely clueless about, named Abdul Waahid, which is scary, because a stalker is dangerous, and that's not sexy."

"I'd rather have a romantic stalker than a southpaw fighter for a lover," Mrs. Johnson admitted sarcastically while grabbing another strawberry.

Sheri began rolling her eyes because she knew what her mom was implying, so she continued by reading the card aloud to alleviate her mom's suspense. "The card says, Miss Nosy — *You are more beautiful than a word and more precious than time. May you never forget that you're an irreplaceable blessing! A gift of God's true mercy upon life! Sincerely, Abdul Waahid.*"

"How come I can't meet a man with sensitivity and sweetness like that?" Naomi complained while rising from the sofa to hand Sheri a tablet detailing all the art scheduled for the showing that morning, and reaching across the desk to grab two more strawberries with crunchy bits of toffee attached, before blowing a kiss to Mrs. Johnson in her pursuit to exit the room. "Every man I meet only wants to buy me shots of hard liquor."

Holding in the sarcastic response she wanted to convey to Naomi's words, Mrs. Johnson rendered a teasing smile instead. "Sheri, I'm not going to open a discussion with you about this mysterious admirer, because I know how you are." Shaking her head in disgust and just thinking about Randle, but more so how she'd like to dip him in banana syrup and throw him into a lightless dungeon with three wild baboons. "Baby, you deserve the right to see who this Abdul Waahid is," her mom uttered with sincerity. "His message confirms it all. And in light of the fact that he just opened your eyes to three characteristics your unmannered toddler of a man never has — money to buy you a gift, thoughtfulness to appreciate you, and the essence of romance — I urge you to get his digits and coordinates."

"Mom, Randle would kill me if I looked at another man, let alone entertained open conversation, or accepted gifts." While leaning back in her chair, Sheri secretly mumbled while admiring the flowers.

"That's your problem Sheri. You're truly becoming complacent, entertaining fear and abuse instead of love and happiness. You are the property of God, and not a man you open your acceptance to. Your father has never disrespected me in public or in private. Nor has he ever raised his hand to me, and you've helped me to campaign for women of abuse. I just don't understand how, of all things, you accept it with endurance."

"Ma, I have some very important things to give my focus to this morning, and respectfully, I don't have the time to have a love life discussion with you. You can have these flowers and the strawberries."

"What?" Mrs. Johnson exclaimed in shock.

"You heard me," Sheri spat, "I cannot accept these gifts. So, you can have them or, rather, give them away to someone you think would like them."

In complete disbelief of the words spoken, Mrs. Johnson just looked at her daughter, momentarily, without saying a word while reaching for the boxes of strawberries with no sense of hesitation. For the life of her, she just didn't understand how her baby girl, who was molded to be a woman of strength and stature, allowed this freeloading boy to beat on her and destroy her self-esteem, and even more dangerously, how she considered it to be love.

"Well, I'm going to eat these strawberries with appreciation of God and Abdul Waahid, whomever this mysterious admirer is." Mrs. Johnson acknowledged candidly. "But I think the roses would signal a taste of class and elegance if we presented one rose stem to each of the guests attending the art exhibit."

Lifting her eyes away from the documents she was now reading and cutting them upon her mother, Sheri jokingly stated "I applaud the idea and think we should offer them one of the strawberries as well."

"You have lost your damn mind in more ways than I actually imagined." Mrs. Johnson said without any hint of humor in her tone. "I'm about to finish the remaining strawberries, but the only individuals who will be able to share in the untouched box with me are Zoe Kravitz, Iman, and Sanaa Lathan if they attend the exhibit. Otherwise, all your father will taste upon his tongue from my body tonight is liquid chocolate covered strawberries," Mrs. Johnson avowed humorously.

Laughing out loud to herself, Sheri paid her mom no mind as she giggled softly. She liked being in her atmosphere when time permitted them to merge their schedules and admired her aura far more than she knew. Her mom was not only the strongest woman she has ever been exposed to in her life but also the most courageous.

Raised by a single father due to her mother dying of triple negative breast cancer at the age of three, Mrs. Yara Johnson never knew the enduring warmth of a mother's love, only a father's protection, compassion, and sincerity. This is why she gives so much of herself to being a rock and pillow for her Sheri.

While working as a waitress at night to help support her way through college, at a once prestigious and prominent strip joint in Buckhead called the Gold Club, she met Sheri's father, Gip, whom at the time was one of Atlanta's most powerful drug kingpins. A king in his underworld, yet he chased her like the paparazzi seeking the mesmerizing glimpse of Jessica Moore's smile. After having Sheri and her brother, Yara gave Gip an ultimatum to give up the underworld life of crime and raise their kids to have worthy moral values or to continue a life of uncertainty and exist without all three of them. To her surprise, Gip left the house that night without saying a single word to her or the kids, only to return the following morning after the sun had risen with a six carat marquee cut diamond ring, with which he proposed and granted her request without ever looking back to the streets. Strategically, the Johnson's built a lucrative foundation off buying, selling, and developing real estate as their new hustle.

Unable to stop lifting her eyes to admire the roses from her mysterious sender, Sheri couldn't help but linger in thought of who he was and what it actually felt like to be appreciated by someone. Only her father and brother had given her flowers before.

With Mrs. Johnson sitting in her daughter's office trying to take the perfect sexy selfie for her social media page with a strawberry squeezed between her lips and Sheri vividly lost in thought of being romanced by a man, the intercom buzzed on her desk slightly startling both of them.

"Yes, Heidi?" Pressing the button, she answered.

"The cars are beginning to arrive, and a few of the guests have been escorted inside the gala event." Heidi advised.

"Thanks Heidi. Please advise Camila to serve the NV Veuve Clicquot instead of Dom Pérignon, and make sure that she doesn't pour it like she's serving at a house party even though it is non-vintage. The vintage champagne will be served to extra special guests who become customers. Mom and I will be down in a moment," Sheri acknowledged while looking to witness her mom still in model posture.

As she stood to gaze in the mirror fastened to the wall behind her desk, she attentively began checking that the nature of her eye color hadn't worsened and fluffing her hair to perfection. Sheri teasingly scolded, "Get yourself together and come on, Mom."

"Unlike you my child, I go to sleep resembling an angel. I wake up defined as a queen and spend every moment of my day reflecting a Boss Bitch.

So, know I'm always, in essence, perfection," Mrs. Johnson effused while snapping her last photo.

Shaking her head in amusement of her mom, Sheri grabbed the vase along with her tablet, and uttered, "Come on," once again while exiting the office.

CHAPTER 4

"**B**reaking News... Breaking News..."

Placing his grilled lobster tail back on the plate, Gip reached for the T.V remote so he could turn the volume up on the television. He then yelled, "Hussshhh," in an unintentional demanding manner to his mom, who was standing at the kitchen bar counter video chatting with a fellow church sister and admiring the assortment of autumn flowers and elephant's ears that he just bought for her to plant in the yard.

"Hold on sister Carolyn," Mama Lewis asked as she lowered the tablet and rotated her neck like an owl. "I know damn well that you didn't just tell me to hush like I'm a damn child!" she shouted in an alarming tone that would spark fear in a grizzly bear.

Chuckling, as though Mama Lewis shared a punchline to a joke, he replied "No, Ma! I apologize, and you know I didn't mean it that way. I'm asking you to hold your excitement for a moment, if you don't mind, please, so I can hear what Tamara Smith is reporting about this breaking news."

Grabbing the stem of one elephant's ear with her gloved hand, she walked over to her son, who was sitting on the sofa with his attention centered on the breaking story. After slapping him across the side of the face from behind with the elephant's ear, Mama Lewis walked around the sofa and began waving the leaf in his face as she gave clarity to her statement. "Don't allow that breaking news to be the reason you end up eating this plant raw. Matter of fact, every plant you just bought. And I promise you I could sell that story as BNN, 'Breaking News Now.' So, show me you 'bout that life! Go on! Build your nerves up to tell me to hush again."

Knowing damn well the inner strength and fierceness of his mom, Gip could do nothing but shake his head respectfully as he rubbed his face and glared at her attentively to make sure she didn't touch his lips with the plant and listened to the anchor woman as she spoke.

"Ma stop playing! You know I meant no disrespect by what I said." Gip uttered, while chuckling at how his mom stood before him waving the oversize leaf, being annoying, but as though she was trying to be intimidating. "Don't make me call Yara and tell her what you did."

"I don't give a fuck what you tell your nappy head ass wife. I'll make her literally eat every R.I.P bullet in my closet if she ever gets the audacity to try and check me 'bout mine." Mama Lewis boasted.

Gip leaned back into the sofa chuckling at her words, while paying her verbal threat no real attention. "Ma, are you listening to this? This makes no sense, I mean beyond the realm of senseless, even."

"No, what's going on?" She inquired while turning around to see the news report.

"A 15-year-old boy went to a candy festival dressed up as a pirate, and killed 9 people, wounding 33 others, claiming he was bullied into doing this and was told that it would make him famous. This literally don't make no sense. I'm so troubled by this. If that kid was tricked into doing this heinous crime, the perpetrators oughta pay for it as well. My heart feels so heavy for the victims and their families."

"Ooh my God," Mama Lewis cried in complete disbelief as she raises her free hand to cover her mouth. "Oooooh - my - God!"

Retrieving his phone from the sofa cushion beside him, Gip called his assistant, Keisha, instructing her to have a dozen white roses sent to every surviving victim of the tragedy with a compassionate message, and a dozen red roses to the families of the victims who died in the incident.

"That's so sweet of you, baby," Mama Lewis said as she walked back to the counter to replace the long-stemmed elephant ear with the others. Noticing her church sister's picture on her phone screen entering the kitchen, she suddenly remembered asking her to hold on. "I'm so sorry Carolyn. Carolyn. Carolyn?!" She expressed, beckoning after lifting the tablet from the counter. Pressing to disconnect after repeatedly calling her name and receiving no reply, Mama Lewis grabbed a tray of flowers to sit at her front door, then walked back into the kitchen and whispered, "I love you," peering at her son over the counter.

"God rewards us in life to see if we'll be ignorant misers and amass more sin to our scale of balance. He also grants us the ability to prove that not only are we grateful for the blessings of which He bestows, but loving Him is truly within our hearts, and not merely upon our tongue. Ma, growing up observing your life struggles taught me that having money means nothing if it's not well utilized to awaken the smile on someone else's face."

"I understand baby, and I applaud the man I've raised you to be." Mama Lewis concurred, attempting to lift all the remaining flowers at once.

"Ma, I'll take those trays outside for you. I don't want you hurting yourself by lifting them." Gip acknowledged, observing her actions.

"Boy, stop playing with me. Lifting these trays is no different than lifting one of my boyfriends to drive a tack in somebody's ass for violating my tranquility."

Leaning forward to scoop a chunk of lobster with his fork from the shell as Mama Lewis continued to rant in the background, Gip just shook his head while electing to remain silent.

"Gip, I'm going to give these Casablanca Lilies to Robin instead of planting them because they will look so beautiful next to the red tip Photinias in her flower bed." Mama Lewis professed, caressing the buds with her fingers. Walking over to open her front door, Mama Lewis looked over her shoulder and asked, "Did you truly mean it when you said that having money means nothing if it's not well utilized to awaken the smile on someone else's face?"

"I can't believe you seriously just asked me that question, Ma." Gip replied as he lifted his eyes from reading a text message.

Challenging his truthfulness, Mama Lewis said, "Well, it would truly make me smile and warm an old lady's heart this day if you were to come help me plant these flowers in the yard."

Slightly choking on his Poo Pu-Erh tea, due to her request causing him to laugh, Gip removed his left shoe and lifted it as he rose from the sofa to display it for his mom. "This is a thirty-five-hundred-dollar mink boot that was hand made by a blind woman of short stature in the Congo jungle with seven fingers and no legs. The fabric of my pants was imported from a lost tribe in Zimbabwe, and woven by a man using only his toes, secluded in a cave on the banks of a Libyan river. Ma, I can't disrespect those hard-working inspiring people like that. I'm far too sexy to be tilling soil on my hands and knees."

"Boy, you say some of the craziest shit. I don't care if you walked a hundred miles, naked and barefooted to skin a giraffe with your toe nail," Mama Lewis rifled without a hint of humor in her delivery, "I want to plant these flowers today before it gets too late because it's supposed to rain tomorrow."

"Seriously Ma, I can't because I have a meeting scheduled in a few hours. But I promise to get you some help if that's okay with you."

"Just as long as it's not your wife's sister," Mama Lewis shouted with a sense of aggression as she started to separate the flowers in the trays she placed on her front porch. "Because I'm not in the mood to hear everybody's business in Atlanta.

I honestly see why she doesn't have a man or a damn job. That woman would gossip in a confession booth with gorilla tape and a muzzle on her mouth."

After walking out to the porch to kiss his mom's cheek and assure her that he'd contract some landscapers to come assist her in the yard, Gip put his boot on again then walked back in the house to finish his meal and make a few calls. Family was the at the core of Gip's strength. There was nothing he wouldn't do to comfort his mom and assure her happiness, which centered on her flowers more than all other things. Gip was the most successful of his mom's five kids, and through his numerous investments, he made sure that everyone lived without the overwhelming struggles that often come with life.

Watching the ending of a classic rerun episode of Sanford And Sons and hearing the sound of doors slamming and conversation coming from outside, Gip knew that the landscape company he called to come plant the flowers for his mom had arrived.

Walking over to peer through the window in the foyer, Gip stood silently watching his mom dictate like Ledisi on a bass line. He could do nothing but smile while admiring her sense of serenity. Seeing the way she was waving her hand in the face of one of the workers, Gip had a mental flash back to when he was in the tenth grade, the torturing memory of how he boldly cut twelve of his mom's competition roses to give to a girl named Lisa Watkins, for whom he harbored a high school crush. Not only did Lisa give them to her so-called boyfriend after school, which was devastating after she told everyone they were from her soulmate, but she had the audacity to snatch the buds off each stem before sprinkling the petals on her boyfriend's head.

To add insult to injury for Gip's young ego, Mama Lewis made him attend school the following two weeks wearing a pair of knee high yellow water boots and an extremely unforgettable floral design outfit each day which she purchased from one of her church sisters' yard sale.

So engulfed by the excitement of having professional landscapers in the yard courting her vision and following her command, Mama Lewis paid no attention to the sound of the garage door opening.

"Ma! Ma!" Gip shouted out a second time after blowing the car horn before Mama Lewis turned her head and acknowledged her son calling out to her. "Can you come here for a moment please?" Gip beckoned as he walked to the rear of the car, texting.

Excusing herself from the workers, Mama Lewis approached, smiling and hugged her son at arm's reach. "Son, I love you so much." She stated. "You truly know how to surprise me with joy. They just told me that they can uproot that oak tree stump and build me a Koi Carp Fish pond encased with a costumed pond liner and #57 crushed rock, bordered with decorative slate supported by alder wood stakes and concrete, a water supply line with a sprinkler head in the middle, and a heavyweight filtration system and lights."

"Ma, you know I exist to show you how much I appreciate you for all you have given me in life and the sacrifices you made and endured for me."

"You getting ready to leave?" She inquired, making a sad face that caused both of them to laugh.

"Yes, and James is five minutes away. He will stay here until the workers leave."

"Boy, I don't need no bald-headed Asian man watching me. I'm from Atlanta, not Decatur. The R.I.P's in my boyfriend mouth are all the protection I need and everyone at the police department already knows I have a heavy trigger finger, boy."

"Whatever Harley Quinn! James will stay as I've asked him to. You need anything else?"

"Besides you finding the time to attend church with me, no, baby," Mama Lewis replied.

After hugging, kissing his mom on the forehead, and handing her ten one hundred-dollar bills from his pocket to pay the landscape workers, Gip stood at the door of his Quattroporte Maserati and just observed his mom's body structure as she walked back into the yard. He couldn't do anything but laugh to himself and shake his head as he got in the car because he could tell that Mama Lewis had her gun holstered in the back of her pants. He so loved his Harley Quinn imitator.

Backing out of the driveway, Gip chuckled because he knew those landscapers had no idea of the labor about to be imposed upon them. Seeing the text notification from James come across the Infotainment system screen as he pulled up to the traffic light, a sense of comfort blanketed Mr. Johnson because he knew his mom was a lot safer with James there than with her trying to be a modern-day gun slinger. Riding past a young couple at the bus-stop holding hands as they waited for the bus caused Gip to smile. The bond of their companionship brought to mind cherished memories of him with his wife and how, in his pursuit to gain her acceptance, he had to ride the public bus a few times and walk places with her, even though he had a car. Using voice commands with the Infotainment system, Gip called his wife, and once Mrs. Johnson answered, he commanded the system to play the Kevon Edmond's song, '24/7,' for her to listen to.

"I love you, baby," Mrs. Johnson sang once the song ended.

"I love you too, Boss Lady," he added openly with sincerity.

"Baby, we're just leaving the gala which, by the way, was a huge success. Every exhibit on display was purchased, except two, which she received promises from potential buyers. I'm so happy for Sheri right now."

"That's wonderful love. I'll call her in a moment to congratulate her, but right now I would appreciate your opinion on something."

"Yes, baby" Mrs. Johnson said rendering her full attention.

"There's a hundred acres for sale in Canton, GA. With the Texas green energy deal now official, I'd like to develop a horse park that includes a training facility, a stable, and a store to cater to all the needs of the horses. In order to gain approval of the land purchase, it must be approved by the community, of which is currently 50/50 due to me having no local roots. Do you think, as an incentive, I should elect to give the community ten percent of all proceeds to utilize towards their schools and parks to approve my bid of purchase?"

"No! Give them twenty percent baby, which in return will give them greater motivation to help make it a success."

"Awarding twenty percent would mean you'd have to trade in your Mercedes for a Ford Fusion, and you can only get your hair done once a month then," Gip teased, laughing with an acute sense of humor as he was imagining his wife going just a week without getting her hair done.

"What?!" Mrs. Johnson bellowed without finding his statement funny at all.

"Hold on love, I'm pulling into the gas station. Better yet, I'll call you back in a few minutes," Gip uttered before ending the call.

"Don't be trying to get off the damn phone now! Gip, don't play with me." She voiced before realizing her husband had already hung up the phone.

Given that the service station was slightly crowded, Gip used his debit card to pay at the pump instead of going inside. Being raised in the heart of Atlanta, he was always aware of his surroundings; a learned survival skill as opposed to instinct. He noticed that when he initially pulled into the station, three young teenagers stood at the telephone booth in front of the service building admiring his car. But when he started pumping gas, they split up, yet, all three were walking suspiciously in his direction, covertly glancing at each other for assurance.

While removing the gas nozzle from the car and closing the tank cover, Mrs. Johnson's text message ringtone started playing, which caused him to lower his head briefly as his eyes scanned her text, *"Guess what I taste like?"* Just the thought itself made him smile. In placing the phone back into his pocket and attempting to open the door to get in, one of the young men stepped from behind the gas pump fumbling as he pulled out a .38 and pointed it at Gip.

"Give me the keys, old man," he shouted. "Hurry da fuck up!"

Seeing the trembling in his hand, and the distinct essence of fear in the young man's eyes as he stood there, Gip initially started to take the gun using a technique he learned years ago when one is pointing a gun too close. But when the other two cohorts approached from opposite directions brandishing weapons as well, he thought about it and the last thing he wanted was for anyone at the gas station to get hurt.

"Produce those keys or get lit, shawty," the tallest of the three instructed as he approached from behind Gip waving his gun as though he was auditioning for a video.

Slowly reaching into his pocket to retrieve the Maserati's key fob after advising the robbers of his intentions, Gip turned his head from side to side, eyeing each perpetrator while distinctly inquiring with stern sincerity in his voice, opening his hand, revealing the key fob, "Y'all sure you really wanna make this mistake?"

"Damn straight, bitch!" The tall one said, now standing in Gip's face. "Do you want to die is the fuckin' question, shawty?" He retorted while lifting the AMT Hardballer to his chin in an attempt to instill fear within the heart of Gip. "I said give me the keys, not a remote, muther-fucker."

"This is the key," Gip informed while watching attentively as their nervousness began to govern them, thereby causing the new age robbers to look more around than at him. "It's keyless entry and push-to-start. All you need is this key fob to get in if the doors are locked, and once you're inside the car, you press and hold the brake pedal while pushing the start button then release the break when the car starts." Gip instructed them, given that the carjackers were ignorant of its operation.

Snatching the key fob out of his hand, the tall one threw it to one of his friends and told him to see if it works. Once the car started, the other two perpetrators jumped in without engaging Gip or observing others at the gas station as they sped off. Standing calmly as he retrieved his phone from his pocket, Gip called James.

"Yes sir?" He answered.

"I've just been carjacked."

"What?! Do you want me to come to get you? Are you hurt?"

"No, stay there, I'm good. Just a few misguided kids that have no sense of direction, right now. Have your boys initiate the tracker for the Quattroporte."

"Yes sir!"

"James, I want to be looking at my car and those boys before they have time to burn one gallon of gas." Gip stated with a sense of calmness which actually meant there's no option for anything less.

"On it Boss."

"And James, make sure the merchandise in the trunk is secure."

"Excuse me, sir," a woman approached Gip, holding her baby," I saw what happened, and I called the police. Are you okay?"

"Yes, I am. Thank you" Gip assured, respectfully, while casually walking away from the gas station and dialing his wife's number.

"I need you to pick me up." He stated the very moment she answered the phone.

CHAPTER 5

Noticing the front door open and the interior lights in the foyer on as she backed her car up the driveway into the garage, Sheri felt a sigh of relief knowing fully well that Randle was home. She had been calling him since leaving the gala to share the extraordinary news of the exhibit but kept being sent to his voicemail for some odd reason. Watching the garage door close to make sure no one entered, she couldn't help but find herself reminiscing as the Beyoncé's *"Dangerously In Love"* blasted through her speakers.

In the core fibers of her heart, Sheri loved Randle and appreciated him for being in her life. She liked the way he used to listen to her thoughts, take the time to help her see beyond the narrative in her vision, and make her feel as though her smile was a priority over all other things. But above all, it was the incredibly addictive way he bathed her body with his tongue that kept her yoked by his web. Everything that defined who he was as a man, initially, caused her to gravitate to him without pause or friction. The suaveness of his character, compassion for the detriment of others, sense of value regarding family, self-confidence, and integrity all turned her on and caused her to break through the mental glass ceiling that she had for dating outside her race. The reverse of Beyonce's smash hit had her missing the way he made her feel irreplaceable in the beginning. Yet, since allowing him to move in eleven months prior, all she seemed to feel was an elevated fear of being verbally or physically assaulted instead of being reminded of what true love is all about.

Opening her car door, Sheri was completely surprised at how loud the music was blasting inside the house. She wondered if he had company, even though there were no cars outside because Randle never listened to music at this volume. Walking into the house and seeing dripping beer cans scattered on the marble and hardwood floors, dog shit paw prints all over the cushions of her champagne cashmere sofa, and vomit floating in her aquarium, Sheri couldn't believe her eyes.

"Randle! Randle!" she yelled only to be heard by herself given that the music was so loud.

Trump stood at the top of the stairs shaking with excitement, seeing Sheri. Unfortunately, after witnessing tiny shit prints all over her sofa, the floor, and stairs, he was the last thing she wanted to play with or see right then. More than anything, she wanted to use him as the scrub brush to clean his nasty shit from her sofa. "You lucky dog, you. If it wasn't for the thought of PETA finding out about my actions, I promise, I would turn you into a permanent scrub brush! Arrrrgh!"

"ARF! ARF!" Trump barked while Sheri escalated the steps as though he was responding to her words.

Pushing her bedroom door open, Randle rendered no attention to Sheri as she stood in the doorway watching him in overwhelming disbelief. Glistening of baby oil, and dancing to the Bruno Mars song, *"That's What I Like,"* in a pair of raccoon printed speedos as if he was a private stripper.

"Randle!" Sheri shouted, pressing the power button on the surround sound system in order to turn the music off. Sheri never expected Randle to throw and hit her in the neck with the beer he was drinking, which caused her to lose her footing and fall.

"Bitch, I didn't tell you to turn that off," Randle scolded, slurring his words, "Now get your stupid ass up and turn it back on."

Suspended in disbelief of what he just did, Sheri found herself unable to move as she sat on the floor looking at him. All she wanted was to share the events of her day with him and attend the evening reception with her man by her side. But, standing right before her was someone she didn't recognize.

Tipsy from drinking nine double-deuce size beers throughout the day and feeling very disrespected by Sheri seemingly ignoring his command, Randle walked into the room from the bathroom. With his eyes totally empty of compassion, he kicked Sheri in the chest while she was down on the floor for not doing as he instructed. The thrust of the impact forcefully caused her to slide back, colliding with the gypsum wall, leaving a visible imprint denting the sheetrock kind of like the cartoon characters going straight through the wall leaving the complete outline of their shape. Only she didn't go all the way through, rather her upper body slid sideways to the floor with her holding her chest and starting to cry.

"Slut, when I say do something you do it without hesitation," Randle threatened after bending over to slap Sheri with the palm of his hand and then backhanded her. The adrenaline rush had him contemplating abusing her body even more, but he elected to point his finger and speak with fury fueled by the effects of the alcohol, "Now get your ass up and turn my mother-fucking music back on before I break my foot off in yo ass."

Scurrying to her feet to press the power button, Sheri wondered if every bone in her chest was broken. Every movement seemed to exacerbate the intensity of the throbbing pain. With the music back on and Randle finding solace with his movements, Sheri sat on the bed crying into the palms of her hand and wondering what she was doing wrong. Why can't she be more in tune with what makes him happy, rather than being selfish and agitating his anger?

Wiping away her tears, Sheri walked downstairs to retrieve a cold beer from the refrigerator and brought it to Randle. "I'm sorry, baby."

Hoping to bridge some chemistry between them, Sheri began dancing with him to share in the moment. Randle clearly indicated that he didn't want her in his presence by a stare of disgust that sent an undeniably clear signal of repudiation.

Leaving the room to go back downstairs, Sheri knew that she couldn't go to the reception without first making sure her house was no longer in disarray. Cleaning the aquarium and sofa took more time than she actually thought it would due to her mom's repeated calls demanding to know what she was wearing. Now with everything back in order, she smiled internally even though not telegraphed.

Not wanting to interfere with whatever Randle currently had going on, she tip-toed around him in the bedroom and took a shower. Yearning for affection, the thought of him turning the music off and showering with her had her nipples hard and sensitive to the touch of the wool sea sponge she used to lather her boobs. Sliding the glass door completely open and throwing a towel on the floor to absorb the water, Sheri had high hopes that Randle would take notice of her touching herself while watching him groove even without rhythm. Leaning her back against the porcelain tile as her fingers massaged her clitoris with just the right amount of pressure, the stimulation from the water peppering her body, cascading soap in all the right places, caused her climax to be intense and soothing with her seductive cries, calling out Randle's name.

"R-A-A-N-N-N-D-D-L-L-L-E!"

Stepping out of the shower to moisturize her body, Sheri observed her face and the redness of her chest in the mirror. She stared deeply into the retinas of her own eyes, gazing long and hard at her reflection, "Is this the sacrifice of true love? I will not fail you, love," she whispered with sincerity, before allowing the towel to fall from her body to the floor, and walking out of the bathroom while exposing the exotic beauty of her irresistible body.

Paying Sheri's naked caramel curvy body no mind, yet noticing the Christian Siriano dress she removed from the closet to lay across the bed and the sparkling Gucci skirt now in Sheri's hand, Randle stopped dancing and staggered to hit the power button on the surround system.

"Where the fuck you think you're about to go, bitch?" Randle asked harshly and spitting as he spoke.

"Baby, I'm hosting a reception tonight at the Georgia Aquarium, and I wanted us to attend it together. Remember?"

"How in the fuck you want us to go together, when you ain't said shit to me? Did you buy me an outfit? Did you ask my permission to host or go anywhere — well, attend as you put it?" He yelled, slinging beer as he talked.

"No baby, but I've been informing you all week of the exhibit and of the reception."

"Bitch, you calling me a liar?" Randle shouted while moving closer to Sheri, "You can put them clothes back in the closet and get yo dry pussy ass in bed 'cause you ain't goin' no mother-fucking where, and I drink to that."

"Randle, I have to be there," Sheri advised with a sense of pleading compassion in her voice, "I can't be a no show for my own reception."

Feeling as if his words meant nothing to her and fell upon deaf ears, Randle slapped Sheri with his right hand, causing her to drop the Gucci skirt that she was holding as her body twisted against the closet door and slid down to the floor. Enveloped with a burst of rage as he needed to prove a point, Randle repeatedly found the delicate softness of Sheri's face with the open palm of his right hand, while holding a hand full of her hair with his left. With every intoxicated swing, he struck with precision.

"Shut up, slut!" Randle yelled as she cried, screaming loudly with tear draining eyes. Forcefully tilting her head back with the grip of her hair, Randle lowered himself and began squeezing Sheri's neck with so much pressure that she was now screaming silently, gasping for air as her heart raced in one sixteenth tempo.

"Whore, you belong to me." Randle stated with emphasis. "You're mine! And don't you ever forget that. When I say do something, there is no alternative. If you ever disobey me again or try to leave me, I'll kill your black ass, bitch. Do you hear me? [Pause] DO...YOU...HEAR...ME?!"

With tears overflowing in Sheri's eyes, her lungs crying for oxygen, and new elements of fear blanketing her, she barely responded, nodding as best as she could with him pulling at her hair just to indicate that his words were well understood.

"Looks like we have an understanding after all. Trump!" Randle called out, letting her go and walking out of the room with him following.

Scrabbling to get to her feet, Sheri walked into the bathroom to view herself in the mirror. Discombobulated and horrified, she lowered her head and allowed her tears to fall repetitively into the sink after seeing the bruises and abrasions on her face. So distraught by her pulverized reflection staring back at her, Sheri was not aware that she had lost herself in time, standing there in a trauma induced state until she heard Randle's voice.

"I'm sorry, baby," Randle pathologically uttered, standing in the bathroom doorway looking and sounding more pathetic than a homeless beggar drinking another beer.

His words seemed to have landed upon deaf ears, for Sheri was mentally lost within herself. He had no idea she was standing there contemplating whether love and life was worth the constant abuse. Admiring the gorgeous beauty of Sheri's naked body, Randle staggered forward and slapped the soft curve of her right cheek. The sudden shock sent cold chills through her body that didn't just awaken her from her tormenting thoughts but instantly caused her to feel as though she was suspended in an ice chamber.

"Come here," he whispered grabbing her arm, escorting her back into the bedroom.

Trembling in her nakedness, Sheri closed her eyes once Randle stopped. Halting her at the foot of the bed then aggressively placing his hand between her shivering thighs, he forced his finger inside of her. His intoxication was void of affection as he slammed the beer can into her back. Wanting to scream but fearing the outcome, Sheri bent herself over the bed as numbness enveloped every fiber of her body. Mustering an erection by teasing the head of his limpness with the cold beer can while observing the way her wetness lubricated his finger, Randle then forced himself inside of Sheri's tightness.

After a few non-sensual, reckless strokes that Sheri could tell were void of passion and being sprinkled with droplets of beer like a filet mignon char-grilling, Randle removed his hardness from the warmth of her wetness then began to tease her by rubbing the head of his dick back-n-forth between her lips. Lowering himself to lick the droplets from Sheri's back, Randle stumbled in his intoxicated attempt to slide his hardness back into her tightness. In a clumsy effort to keep from tumbling to the floor, Randle released the beer and grabbed Sheri which caused them both to fall onto the bed. No whispers of passion were in the atmosphere, just the distinct sound of teardrops splashing on her comforter.

Feeling the intense urge to finish what he started while also defining his dominance, Randle instructed her to slide up in the bed to position himself between her legs. Forcing his finger back into the depth of her treasure, he massaged Sheri's tightness without arousing any measure of affection as she laid crying without sound. Seeking to satisfy his yearning without sharing it with Sheri, Randle began stroking himself until he ejaculated upon her back with selfish gratification. Removing his finger which had gruesomely caused her entire body to go numb, Randle arrogantly slid it along the entire length of her spinal column before verbal sewage slimed through his lips, "I love you, bitch."

Balling up like she was in a cocoon after Randle eased off the bed and walked out of the bedroom, Sheri felt highly molested and never knew that loving someone would have her feeling so grimy and empty inside. All she wanted was to build a promising life with someone who would help to nurture her and unleash her potential just as she would for them in return. Sacrifices, she knew for sure would come in time to strengthen their bond of union, but she never expected fear and abuse to become intrusive elements, especially, when everything in the beginning was centered upon respect, appreciation, and not taking a moment with one another for granted.

Observing Randle out of her peripheral vision, she saw him walk back into the room and enter the bathroom. Sheri never expected Randle to call out to her as she laid motionless while trying to understand what just transpired. Conjuring the strength to get off the bed and into the glass encased shower with him took every ounce of inner strength that Sheri could muster. Struggling with each step, she was so emotionally cold and physically numb that she felt no effects of the ice-cold water bashing her body entering the 3/4-inch glass door. His love and compassion were so desired yet void of evocation when Randle started stealing kisses from her nipples — her body didn't scream thief nor even dial 911 for assault.

"I'm going to let you go to the reception." Randle surprisingly said, while stepping out of the shower without drying off. He walked into the room dripping and returned with a strapless high-slit peplum gown with ruffle trim. "I want you to wear this," he instructed in a devilish tone that seemed to echo in Sheri's mind, while hanging it on the bathroom clothes rack and staring at her for approval.

Not believing the words she was hearing or the act, Sheri said nothing as she stood beneath the water nodding and wondered how she could wear such a beautiful gown and attend the reception with her face looking like she just disrespected Bi Nguyen by blowing a seductive kiss to her boyfriend.

Every moment of preparing herself seemed like torture. Not only did Randle watch as though he was fascinated with her sheer existence, but the thought of her being seen by so many prominent people this way was mortifying. Adding the Louis Vuitton white ceramic chain necklace her grandma gave her for her birthday, a single tear fell from Sheri's eye as she gazed upon herself in the mirror.

"Love will not break me." She whispered, while applying "Wide Awake" by Maison Francis Kurkdjian to her wrists.

Dressed and afraid to say she's not going due to her face telegraphing the effects of trauma, they left the house without saying a word to each other. Thought after thought swam through Sheri's mind while driving to the Georgia Aquarium. What will she say when asked about her face? The thought of them calling the police terrified her even more. What would happen to Randle? The silence allowed her to think and escape the reality of her nightmare. Yet, when Randle selected Jagged Edge on her car playlist and sang *'Walked Outta Heaven'* word for word with them, elevating his voice with emphasis when saying, *"Don't know what to do. Feel like I just walked outta heaven,"* she literally began to feel that she was losing her mind and dreaming a bad dream.

Pulling up to the entrance and seeing the security officers directing the guests, Randle grabbed her wrist and said, "Don't forget my words. I love you, Sheri!"

"I love you too, baby," Sheri, disgusted, whispered while leaning over and kissing his lips before exiting the passenger side of the car.

Walking into the building through security with her head down in an attempt to conceal her bruises which she could not camouflage, Sheri went into the women bathroom and locked herself in a stall. Her plan was to escape the reception and the embarrassment for the night, while Randle parked and waited for her in the parking garage. Inserting the ear buds she stored in her purse, Sheri selected H.E.R. on Pandora and listened. She sat in the sounds of familiarity leaning against the stall wall responding to several text messages of, "Where are you?"

With no attention given to those walking in and out of the restroom, Sheri gave no thought to the shadow standing in front of her stall door, until the heavy pounding on the door caused the side walls to vibrate.

Knock... Knock... Knock...

"I'm using this stall!" Sheri yelled out, removing the ear buds from her ear.

"Trick, you not using shit," Naomi responded, "Open this door before I kick it in, and you know I will. Don't no damn body shit that long without flushing the toilet!"

Hesitantly unlocking the door in complete disbelief, Sheri held her head down as Naomi squeezed inside and closed the door behind her.

"What's wrong Sheri? Why the fuck are you in this stall?"

With her best friend's head completely lowered, and *revealing nothing*, beside the strands of her hair, Naomi leaned down and placed her hand beneath Sheri's chin, gently lifting her head, *having everything revealed*. Tear drops began to merge with Naomi's hand. She squatted in shocking outrage and total anger, due to Sheri's ghastly appearance becoming the norm at T.H.O.R., *The Hands of Randle*.

"I'm tired of this shit! I'm about to call your grandma, I know she'll shoot that cowardly motherfucker!" Naomi screamed in a fit of rage.

"No!" Sheri shouted gripping her arm. "No! It was my fault!"

"What the hell you mean your fault? Bitch please! Sheri this bullshit has to stop. You are far too precious to be accepting this flagrant abuse and uncut disrespect from anyone. Especially from some freeloader who claims to love you! There is no love in abuse of any sort. You gonna tell somebody or I promise you, I will." Naomi averred.

"No, Naomi please! Promise me please! Do not tell anyone! Promise! Randle is just going through some things right now, but he has apologized and asked for my forgiveness."

Seeing her best friend so detached from reality caused tears to begin bursting from her eyes like a water sprinkler. While gently caressing Sheri's face with her fingers, Naomi agreed, "I promise. But why did you come here in this condition?"

"Randle made me, and I was afraid to challenge him. So, I decided to hide in the bathroom until it was over. He's waiting in the parking garage."

"What?! You should let me tell your father if you're not going to tell your grandma, Sheri."

"No Naomi you promised! Please let me handle this on my own. And how did you know I was here anyway?"

"Your iPhone location, Bellibone!"

"Yo nosy ass," Sheri fired a shot, rolling her eyes.

"Gurl, you are looking more fabulous than Lauren Cohan when she wore Vince Camuto. You can't be sitting in this stall hiding how magnificent you look and feeling sorry for loving some trailer park trash. Bitch, this is your night! Now let's go!"

Sheri couldn't do anything but blush at the words of her friend. "You are cute as well Naomi. But I'm not going out there looking like this."

"Hater, I got fashion game from your mom, and I know Brandon Maxwell has me looking like an exotic stunner. I'm too sexy to ever just be cute!" Naomi bolstered, causing them both to laugh as she turned around in the stall like a model. "Do you trust me, Sheri?"

Looking her friend in the eyes, "Yes," she responded without hesitation. "Why?"

"I'll be right back," Naomi insisted, making an attempt to leave the stall.

"Wait, don't leave me!"

"Gurl, I'm too mutha-fuckin' gorgeous right now to hide in a funky bathroom stall with you all night. I love you, but you are far too beautiful to be doing the same. Trust me, I will be right back. Plus, Julio Jones may be here and want me to spread my falcon wings on his mouth tonight."

"Stank, don't nobody want your nasty loose ass," Sheri mumbled, sparking an attempted laugh, jokingly.

Seeing Naomi walk away from the stall truly had her wondering about her intentions. When more than twenty-six minutes passed, Sheri found herself wondering even more what she was up to. Trust her in what regards? Was she breaking her promise and telling her father? The thought of her maybe telling the police or having something done to Randle in the parking lot became the only two things she could linger on until Naomi knocked at the door again.

"Where the hell you been?" She snapped while unlocking the door and allowing her to step back inside.

"This fine chocolate bowlegged gentleman who owns a platinum mining company in North Dakota wouldn't allow me to walk to the garage alone. He is so handsome girl, and he might get a bite of this snapper tonight. Forget Julio!"

Laughing uncontrollably loud, triggered by Naomi's naivety, Sheri had to hide her face in her hands to suppress the sound of almost hideous laughter.

"Trick, what's so damn funny?" Naomi asked, revealing a Beijing opera mask from a velvet bag.

"I'm in here losing my fuckin' mind and you're out there entertaining an uneducated con-artist. Heffa, you're stupid! There are no damn platinum mines in North Dakota. Fuck that mask, you should just write GULLIBLE around your whole face! " Crying laughing.

"Say what? Dammmn!" Naomi shouted with sincere sadness in her voice. "I been, I been, you mean ... Are you sure there's no platinum mines in North Dakota? I was truly fantasizing about going to sleep and waking up with a cold platinum bar or nugget in my mouth, or better yet, a fly ass platinum grill for these pearly whites." She said while giggling at her own painful gullibility and sense of humor.

"Sooo, what are you doing with ... with that mask anyway? Did he ... (giggling and trying to talk) ... did, di, did he give you that too and promise that you will become some Platinum Queen of Hollywood if you wear it while he's fucking and seeding you with his platinum sperm?" Sheri popped off, turning red in the face, truly out of control, and she needed that.

"I see that this bitch has come to life all of a sudden. But no, not saying that I wouldn't have gone for it, though, but the mask is for you, Sheri."

"Heffa Please! Have you lost your damn mind altogether? Do I look like a Chinese carnival clown to you? I'm not the one with pipe dreams of a platinum king."

"Sheri, just listen. All jokes aside. You are far too beautiful in that gown to be hiding in this stall, and I refuse to allow that coward to steal any measure of joy from you. This is a very prominent art reception, and everyone is waiting to see you, not hear a lie that you're at home with a stomach virus as you've been texting.

"What better way to be creative and to define the Art of Life than for you to be the art of all attraction tonight. Look how stunning you already look! This mask will cover all your bruises, but not the extraordinary woman that you are. It will add a sense of creative style that's mysterious and sexy. Own the night by allowing the conversation to be about the unforgettable woman in the Beijing opera mask who caused the auction of two phenomenal portraits to support a vital after school program and a classy display of other paintings to be a fleeting thought whisked away by the winds of a fabulous solo masquerade. They will remember you tonight in that dress, artfully disguised by this mask. You may never be Michelle Obama, but your worth as a woman would allow you to stand firmly in her shoes. If she can wear a mask for an elegant event, then you can as well. I plead with you, do this, and you won't regret it."

"I love you," Sheri professed to Naomi as she took the mask from her hand, "It's beautiful, and I like your concept. You sure it's not from your Platinum King?"

"Gurrl, please. I see you not gonna let that go. If I catch you laughing in the middle of your presentation, I'll know exactly where your gutter mind is, Stank."

Rising from the toilet, she placed the mask on her face, and viewed herself in her compact mirror before leaving the stall pacified and confident. Sheri hugged Naomi with sincerity after gazing at herself in the bathroom mirror, blotting the joyful tears from her face, then whispered, "I love you," once again.

As they walked through the aquarium, undoubtedly gaining the full attention of everyone they passed by, Sheri leaned into Naomi and asked, "Girl, I'm really curious, where did you get this mask from?"

"I collect them and keep a few in my car on reserve for unexpected purposes."

"Reserve purposes?" Sheri repeated questionably.

"Yes! When I have sex, I like to wear them to hide my facial expressions. If that dick is not causing my eyes to roll back in the socket or have me feeling like he's trying to puncture a new passageway through my rib cage, I can just close my eyes with the mask on and hum a Jill Scott song without him truly knowing that he's boring the fuck out of me. Girl, I literally went to sleep on a guy eating my pussy last month, and he keeps calling like he has that magic stick. Ha!"

With both of them laughing, Sheri secured Naomi's hand as they entered the ballroom and was very thankful that this hot, nasty ass freak was her friend.

CHAPTER 6

Swerving through interstate traffic as though they were auditioning for a NASCAR sponsorship; Moe, J-Roc and Lil Stunna had no idea that the Quattroporte they were momentarily flossin' the streets of Atlanta in was locked in on a GPS tracking system. They were being tailed by six ex-marines who work for Mr. Johnson's private security firm and following in two white Porsche Cayennes.

After rambling through the interior compartments and discovering a sealed envelope containing eighteen thousand dollars in unmarked hundred dollar bills stashed in the armrest console, all they were geeked up about was the clothes they intended to buy at Southlake Mall, the way they were going to ball out in V.I.P at the Playground Strip Club later that night, and renting a suite at the downtown Hilton. The thought of finessing a few women to the room and making it rain on them like real ballers had them psychologically hyped to the fullest.

With three unlicensed guns in the car and Moe driving recklessly without a valid permit, the thought of ditching the luxury hotbox for one more low-key or to board the public transit entered neither mind — only getting high on some exotic marijuana, spending at the mall, and chicks was there focus. This actually meant their first priority was going to the Bird to buy a few ounces of White Rhino or Gorilla Glue Kush from Haircut's spot.

Exiting the expressway ramp on University Ave., J-Roc instructed Moe to roll down all the windows so that everyone could see them as they cruised by. Even though he wasn't driving nor was the car his own, the attention it commanded from everyone made J-Roc feel like a boss and he intended to exploit every measure of it. Turning onto McDaniel Street from University Ave. at the light, J-Roc leaned forward to figure out how to increase the volume on the touch screen Infotainment system as T.I.'s *Check, Run It* came on the radio. Seeing a group of girls start to bounce on their porch to the music as they cruised by, J-Roc stood up in the sunroof to be more visible for the onlookers while telling his boys, "This how y'all know it's our time to shine, 'cause we young and fly."

Bouncing to the music and feeling like a self-made man, Moe pulled into the plaza of the Pittsburgh apartment complex. The assemblage of sexy ladies congregating by an Infiniti QX60 and a Rally Pink '68 Z/28 instantly instilled the desire for them to flex their status instead of going straight to the back of the apartments to cop some Kush as intended. Backing into the parking spot beside the Camaro, he noticed that all the street hustlers in the vicinity and ladies turned their heads to see who was driving.

Desiring to be completely visible to all the onlookers, Moe allowed the song *'Drip Too Hard'* by Lil Baby and Gunna to go off before he leaned forward a little in his seat to lower the volume. J-Roc and Lil Stunna maintained their newly discovered gangster lean posture as Moe spat, "What's up shawty?" Trying to sound appealing to the light skinned chick sitting on the hood of the Camaro in a deep V-neck, leopard, long sleeve jumpsuit with her legs crossed, taking selfies.

"You uncircumcised delinquent, who the fuck you calling shawty?" She stormed back with attitude in her voice and rolling her neck with the balance of a viper. "Didn't yo mama teach you any etiquettes on how to approach a grown mutha-fuckin' woman? 'Cause a shawty, I am not, boy."

Moe looked dumbfounded and embarrassed, given that everyone, including Lil Stunna, was laughing at how she just scolded him in his moment of imitating a boss Mack.

In trying not to squander the opportunity to gain their acceptance and maybe get at least one of them to the room tonight, J-Roc rose through the sunroof and spoke which extinguished the momentary laughter. "I apologize! My partna' didn't mean no disrespect by his gesture. Respectfully, you have some women who accept the slang greeting when chillin' in the hood as we are right now, because slang is the common tongue of our culture. Then, you have women such as yourself who demand a higher level of respect and to be approached with greater measure of intellect, regardless of the setting. Pretty lady, you can't fault him for trying to gain your attention, for only a fool wouldn't open their eyes to an enthralling Queen and not try to crawl for her acceptance. I apologize again on his behalf if he offended you in any way."

She rolled her eyes aggressively without a word spoken.

"So, who are you supposed to be, the game spitter for the crew?" One of the ladies inquired from the group, standing between the vehicles, lifting a cup of Hornitos Cristalino to her mouth while combing the loose hair from her face enticingly and eyeing him with great attraction.

"No, gorgeous! Just a man who has learned from the narrow-minded mistakes of his past and groomed to be a gentleman," J-Roc retorted with a degree of suaveness that she found appealing.

"Interesting rehearsed lie you tell," her girlfriend who was sitting in the passenger seat of the Camaro rolling blunts, and lip-syncing the Camila Cabello song, "Havana," objected as J-Roc dropped his line of game. "Are you and your overly excited homeboys going to guard y'all's father's car seats all night and drool like a Neapolitan mastiff over my sisters or get out and mingle like true gentlemen?" She queried, looking directly at Moe.

"Our dad's car?" Moe bellowed defensively while trying to reestablish himself.

"Okay then, your grandfather's car, cause ya definitely can't drive that off the lot when you're too young for a learner's permit." She tweaked and reasserted, snickering at his impulsive reaction while sliding the blunt wrap against her tongue seductively, just to assure it's sealed with perfection and to tease all three of the delinquents as they watched her movements in fascination.

"Shawty, this is my damn car," Moe rebuked with arrogance in his tone, stuffing unfolded bills in his pocket and stepping out of the car.

"Boy, didn't my damn sister just address your non-comprehending, flexin' ass about calling a woman shawty?" She scoffed while shaking her head and passing one of the finished blunts to a street hustler standing at the car window. "But if you say it's yours, then I have to accept your word, big balla," she recanted.

So entranced by the ladies' beauty, voluptuous figures, and the attention they were receiving for the first time in their lives, not one of them noticed the two Porsche Cayenne's pull into the parking lot and park in the adjacent section. Equally, they were completely oblivious to Aaron getting out of the SUV, walking past them, and taking pics with his phone, which he immediately forwarded to Mr. Johnson for confirmation.

With so many individuals walking and socializing in the parking lot, Aaron walked over and stood amongst a group of street hustlers who were smoking, drinking, and shooting dice against the curb. Realizing after observing the three targets and the scenery for a few minutes that securing them and the car would not require the assistance of the APD, he advised two of his team members on the wireless intercom system that they were using to communicate amongst themselves to step out of the SUV and congregate. With no need to add fuel to the adrenaline already flowing through each of them, he instructed them to blend in and gain cooperation of at least one of the women. Successfully linking in with the female entourage, they could move in without being viewed as robbers in this setting while the others wait for further instructions. Some warfare type action is what each of them wanted, but there were too many bystanders in the vicinity to engage in a gun fight. Noticing a few women leaving the gathering to grab something to eat from the BBQ grill, One Eye and Mike exited the vehicle and pursued.

Crossing the street and walking at a steady pace until they were a few feet from the secluded cooking area of the parking lot, "Excuse me," Mike said, standing behind the three ladies in line at the grill, causing them to turn their heads to him attentively.

"You excused if you're paying for our plates." One of the ladies cajoled with a sense of humor in her tone and allowing her eyes to linger at his crotch area without hiding her interest.

"Then, order whatever you and your friends desire because he's definitely going to pay for it," One Eye affirmed while chuckling and gaining smiles from all three ladies.

"Hmm, a man who takes control and caters to a lady. You're cute wit yo one eye ass," effused her girlfriend who sultrily eyed him before turning back to the grill to pick out the meats she wanted.

"Even though you were genuinely forced to pay for our plates by your friend, I thank you, cutie, and my name is Tina, by the way." Arching her back a little to add extra definition to her booty curve, hoping that Mike liked what he saw and solicited her number.

Retrieving the money from his pocket to pay for the plates, without saying a word, One Eye laid his head on Mike's shoulder and jokingly asked while disguising his voice as a woman and snickering to himself, "Do I get to order a plate also, cutie pie?"

"Yes, if you promise to move your hair shedding, bare mouth sister out my house," he barked, causing laughter to erupt between them.

"Well, on that note, I'll pass," One Eye countered as they continued to laugh between them. "She not about to be laying up in my house naked and farting all day." Getting their plates and turning away from the grill, One Eye politely asked while jumping in their conversation, "May we have the pleasure of walking with the three of you once my partner finishes paying the bill?"

Shifting her eyes up and down his body and admiring how sexy he was looking in his tailored black suit, "Sure," Cindy beamed, introducing herself with emphasis on the vowel pronunciation to highlight her Asian accent. "As long as neither of you are married, 'cause we empower our sisters, not disrespect them."

"No, we're not married." One Eye affirmed, lifting his left hand to assure confirmation of no ring or ring line circling his finger.

"Good," Tina mumbled to herself, sipping a cup of Patrón while seductively eyeing Mike. "My kids need a new babysitter."

Walking back to the gathering, laughing and flirting heavily amongst themselves, One Eye informed the ladies of their purpose for being in the plaza. They assured the ladies that they were not trying to use their guns to apprehend them because a shootout could cause innocent people to get hurt. Holding Tina's hand like a soulmate, Mike promised that no one in their entourage would be harmed as a result of them assisting with their plan, and neither of the ladies tipped them off. Respectfully, as a bonus incentive for their participation, Mr. Johnson was generously awarding everyone a full day spa treatment and dinner at his wife's log cabin mountain resort, and they were also invited to his cookout tomorrow at Grant Park.

Blowing on the Kush, the ladies passed among themselves, and sipping on cups of tequila that they poured, Moe, J-Roc and Lil Stunna had gotten completely lost in the moment, so engulfed in the ideal image of the self-made men they were trying to portray that the essential elements of street awareness seemingly became invisible and non-existent. With J-Roc generously paying the woman in the Camaro to roll another blunt of her Kush, Lil Stunna trying to impress a fat booty chunky sister by flashing his money, and Moe sponsoring a five hundred dollar twerking contest on the side of the Infiniti SUV, neither noticed the mysterious way the ladies were whispering among themselves after One Eye and Mike arrived to the gathering, nor did either of them render any attention to Cindy holding up the bottle of Cîroc and waving for the Marines sitting in the Cayennes to come over.

Spitting out her Patrón coaxed by the uncontrollable laughter that caused her to stop taking selfies, she screamed in amusement while wiping her mouth. "Will someone please come get this baby before the Feds indict me for allegedly exposing uranium pussy to a daycare student?!! Boy, even if I was to inject yo li'l dick with two Viagras, 500 mg apiece, and supported yo dick with two hands, yo diaper wearin' ass still couldn't stand up in this pussy." She stunted on Lil Stunna, sliding off the hood of the Camaro. "Girl, this nasty li'l delinquent just said he will give me a thousand dollars to lick a jolly rancher out my ass with my leopard jumpsuit on. Chil' get da fuck outta here!"

"George, I'll let you lick two jolly ranchers and a strawberry out my ass if you really 'bout that life!" One of her girlfriends offered as she walked over to stand in front of him and started rotating her stilettos as her booty started clapping with no hands like butterfly wings as she touched her toes and stuck out her tongue to solicit his unabated attention.

"My name Lil Stunna, not George," he announced, removing the money from his pockets without shifting his eyes away from the rotation of her hips.

His lack of street knowledge caused the women who heard his response to laugh. "Boy, it doesn't matter what yo name is. I'll call you my White Knight as long as you have the paper to capture my attention." She straightened, slapping her butt, then inserting a finger in her mouth, elevating her erogenous appeal. "

"Gurl, I believe he jes flexin' and can't afford to smell yo ass, let alone eat two Jolly Ranchers out of it," one of her girlfriends exclaimed, exhaling the Kush smoke as she leaned against the SUV.

"My folks got money," Lil Stunna mouthed, counting out a thousand dollars from his stash, and making it rain on her back as her erotic dance movements began to stimulate all of his erogenous zones. "What yo name is?" He asked.

"My name Cradle Robber right now." She answered, snickering, while starting to twerk as she grabbed the loose bills falling to the ground that he was serenading her body with.

"We have an uneducated balla makin' it rain in our midst ladies!" Tina shouted. "Get your umbrellas if you don't want to get your weave wet."

Lil Stunna felt like he was on top of the world, smoking and sipping on his cup of tequila. In a mindless stunt to truly impress the ladies, subconsciously influenced by Future blasting through the speakers saying, "Let's have a money shower," in the song, *'F*ck Up Some Comas,'* Lil Stunna tossed the remaining thousands in the air that he was loosely dangling merely for a few seconds of street cred. All the ladies and a few street hustlers in the vicinity stopped what they were doing on a dime to grab as many spiraling dead presidents their hands could rake in.

"You stupid as a fuck!" Moe hollered as he walked over and grabbed Lil Stunna's arm. "What the fuck you do that for?"

"Bosses make boss moves." Lil Stunna replied without taking his eyes off the ladies scrambling before them. The mirage in his mind had him fantasizing about how he was going to bathe one of their luscious, bangin' bodies with his tongue tonight in the room.

Puffing on a blunt and stepping around the ladies picking up the money from the ground to stand beside Moe and Lil Stunna. J-Roc held his intended words for Lil Stunna because, for the first time, he noticed all the guys standing around wearing black suits, inconspicuously watching their every move, and he knew something wasn't right.

"Both of y'all strapped, right?" J-Roc whispered.

"No." They both denied.

"Fuck!" he grumbled. "How in the hell can y'all not be strapped? How stupid can the two of you be, to leave y'all shit in da car?"

"Excuse me." Aaron said while walking up from behind all three of them and extending his hand to give them the phone.

"Who the fuck are you?" J-Roc sternly questioned, gripping the handle of his gun.

"I'm just someone advising you that you have a phone call, young blood." He evaded without lowering his arm.

Grabbing the phone nervously without saying anything, Moe noticed it was on video chat when he flipped it over in front of them. The sight of actually seeing the man they had just car jacked on the phone screen, suddenly engulfed him in fear and shock.

"You boy's look as though y'all just saw a ghost." Mr. Johnson said calmly, sitting at a private table inside Buckhead's five-star restaurant, Bones.

With all three staring at the screen in complete disbelief, the ex-marines motioned discreetly for the women to move out of the way, as they eased into striking distance by encircling them.

"You boys have cost me a lot of unnecessary money today trying to be what you are not." Mr. Johnson scowled. "Since y'all want to imitate street thugs instead of utilizing your time wisely to cultivate your inner potential, then y'all respect the consequences that come along with the streets when you violate. I'll see the three of you soon."

With the line of communication now disconnected, the fear of them maybe dying extracted every measure of gangsterism from the hearts of Moe and Lil Stunna.

Trying to maintain his sense of hardness, as Moe barely held onto the phone as if he was going into cardiac arrest, J-Roc managed to bellow out, "Fuck You," to the black screen while attempting to retrieve his gun from his back waist. He thought in his mind that going out in a shootout would give him street cred because surrendering only to be executed in secret non-disclosure was not an option for a thug. Unfortunately, before his arm could muster the strength to lift the gun from his waist, One Eye landed a bone crushing tomahawk bow to the base of his chin with such precision that J-Roc's legs became like wet Ramen Noodles at the exact engagement of impact, sound asleep before his face made contact with the asphalt.

"Damn, One Eye!" Aaron exclaimed shaking his head and crossing his arms in disappointment. "You could have let one of us video that shit for social media. Somebody stand that fool up so we can capture One Eye tomahawk bowing him one more time." He quipped jokingly.

Scared beyond reason, Moe and Lil Stunna stood there silent and attentive as three of the ex-Marines picked up J-Roc after securing the AMT Hardballer that he was holstering and the remaining funds he had in his front right pocket. After being searched by the ex-Marines and relieved of the money in his pocket as well, Moe was escorted to the back seat of the Quattroporte and secured, while J-Roc and Lil Stunna were escorted and seated in each of the Cayennes.

"Mike! Mike!" Tina yelled out, walking over to the Cayenne with more swing in her athletic hips as they secured an unconscious J-Roc in the seatbelt.

"Yes, sweetie?" He responded while switching on the child lock and closing the door.

"You better not have been lying to us about going to the spa." She said placing her left hand on her hip and the nail of her right index finger on her bottom lip.

"Mr. Johnson is a man of his word, I assure you. I will personally hand him the list with y'all's names and numbers, Tina. Confirmation may not be given tonight due to the circumstances, but I promise you that he will have his assistant contact each of you for a scheduling date. Hopefully, you will attend the cookout tomorrow so I can be a man of my word."

"And what word is that?" She asked, completely confused.

Getting into the driver seat of the Cayenne and closing the door, Mike started the ignition as Aaron instructed them on the intercom to follow him. Staring into her eyes, Mike said while putting the SUV in gear, "If you come to Grant Park tomorrow any time after five o'clock looking as sexy as you are right now, you'll definitely find out."

Smiling as though she just confirmed a new baby sitter for her kids, Tina waved goodbye as she turned and strutted back to her entourage who were individually standing around and counting the money Lil Stunna blessed them with, and watching the video Cindy recorded of J-Roc getting knocked out by One Eye's bow.

"Girl, look at his legs!"

"Mr. Johnson, we have secured all three of them and are en route to the loft as you instructed," Aaron assured while speaking into the phone. "The items in the trunk are also secure, sir."

Thank you, Aaron. Good work," Mr. Johnson replied. "After you drop the three of them off, locate their parents."

CHAPTER 7

Waking up to the low soothing melodies of India Arie's 'Brown Skin' playing on Alexa beside the bed, the enticing aroma of morning breakfast mixed with the intoxicating fragrance of Polo Red and the perspiration of a man, sexually, Sheri opened her eyes feeling like a woman of new worth and purpose. She was so surprised that Randle wasn't breathing beside her, but even more surprised when she noticed the pink and white rose petals that were sprinkled on her and the bed. Closing her eyes to bask in the serenity of her own ambiance, she lingered upon the enjoyment of last night's engagement. Remembering that she didn't eat or drink anything at the reception due to her mask, Sheri reopened her eyes to assure herself that no one drugged her and that she wasn't losing her mind by witnessing the romantic decor. Sitting up in bed, Sheri couldn't believe that rose petals were actually scattered across the floor in the room as well, and there was a heart shaped note card laying beneath a single white Calla Lily on Randle's pillow that read: "***Love is an action.***"

Unable to hide the smile expanding on her face, Sheri slid out of bed and into her slippers. The words on the card in her hand had her feeling vulnerable and desiring to be in Randle's arms. Admiring the rose petals, she entered the bathroom so that she could properly groom herself a little before going downstairs to thank Randle for his thoughtfulness toward her, discovering "***I love you***" scribbled across the bathroom floor in all pink rose petals, Sheri blushed with immeasurable joy flowing through her heart. The tub was filled with overflowing vanilla scented bubbles and another heart shaped note card laying beneath a Calla Lily on the counter that read: "***I'll never take you for granted again.***" Eyeing herself in the mirror, and seeing the reflection of the petals that lay on the floor instead of the bruises that were hiding the true essence of her irresistible beauty.

Sheri murmured, "I love you too."

Wanting to step into the tub to soothe herself before going downstairs, Sheri brushed her teeth instead and washed her face because the aroma of the breakfast was smelling too alluring to continue torturing her stomach by prolonging the anticipation of delicious indulgence. Following the carpet of petals out of the bedroom door and down the stairs, Sheri couldn't believe what her eyes were literally seeing, nor the words embedding them that her ears were hearing. White rose petals covered everything in every room, "*I love you*" was written before the fireplace, on the marble in the foyer, and across the entire length of the kitchen floor using pink rose petals. On the dining table, was a tray of homemade buttermilk biscuits with melted butter on top of them, a dish of scrambled eggs blended with shredded pepper jack cheese, a bowl of buttered grits, a plate of salmon and capers, a glass of orange juice submerged in ice, and a bowl of sliced white grapes.

At a loss for words, Sheri found herself subconsciously drifting in an unbelievable fantasy that was causing tears to fall within the core pillars of her heart at that very moment. The songs, 'Love' and 'Teach Me To Love' by Musiq Soulchild, serenaded her in rotation through her surround sound system in the living room, yet Randle was nowhere in sight as she sat at the table eating.

All this had Sheri feeling as though she was suspended in a fairy-tale, blanketed by emotions unknown to her heart. Never had Randle ever done anything like this before, nor the few men she dated prior to him. The blanketing rose petals turned her on. As she continued to look around the room, abstemiously masticating the salmon, she began to wonder how it would feel to make love to Randle with the velvety petals caressing her body. She wanted to be in his arms, to kiss his lips and whisper "I love you" over and over centimeters away from his ear as his heart beats against her body.

Disappointed, as there was no one there to share this beautiful romantic moment with besides Trump, of all God's creations, Sheri sat and ate her breakfast while lingering endlessly in thought of why Randle would do all of this and not be there to bridge a lasting memory with her. Did he expect her to sleep a little longer and stepped out to grab something else to add even more substance to the romantic ally phantasmal display? "Where is he?" She wondered. Finishing her breakfast with Trump and still no sign of Randle, Sheri cleaned up behind herself and decided to go relax in the rose petal hot tub of eroticism, while hoping that Randle would show up and walk in on her teasing her clitoris so she could climax staring into his eyes.

Laying back in the bubbles with her eyes closed, Sheri fantasized of Randle intimately bathing her body beneath the water while sitting on the edge of the tub kissing her. Yearning to explore the feeling of her fantasy, Sheri began caressing her clitoris with her fingers while imagining Randle slapping the inner wetness of her pussy with his tongue as she lay on her stomach, arching her ass in the air. So mentally engulfed in the fantasy, Sheri found herself climaxing with a measure of pleasure that seemed as if Randle's tongue was literally bathing the fibers of her precious treasure. But Randle still hadn't surfaced.

Gasping for breath and floating upon pillars of satisfaction, Sheri spent a few more minutes just encircling her nipple with her thumb, mystified by the mystery of the missing mysterious stranger she had opened her heart to.

Donning her Victoria's Secret panties after stepping out of the shower and moisturizing her body with cocoa butter lotion, Sheri stood in front of the mirror admiring how perfect her titties looked, and envisioned a tattoo of Randle's name scribbled across her heart with rose petals beneath it. She slid on her bra and walked into the bedroom to discover a vase with Calla Lilies sitting in the center of her bed and a newly appearing heart shaped note card that read: "*I may not be worthy of you, but I'm sorry. I'll never stop proving I love you.*"

"Randle! Randle! Randle where are you baby?" Sheri yelled, walking through the house, looking for him in every room. "Randle, why are you torturing me with this hide-n-seek fantasy, when you know I want to hug and kiss you right now?"

Walking in circles throughout the breadth and depth of her house, calling Randle's name to no avail, Sheri looked down at Trump who was following her every step like an infatuated stalker and said, "Go find Randle, Trump. Go find Randle, boy!"

"Arf! Arf!" Barking as though he understood what Sheri said, Trump began sniffing the floor all the way into the laundry room. Sheri followed, hoping to see Randle and expose his hiding spot. Instead, she discovered one of her new Giuseppe stilettos that Trump had been gnawing in secret, dampening the odd fantasy slightly more than Randle's aloofness.

She scooped a handful of petals from the sofa's seat cushion after walking back into the living room and threw them in the air as a gentle breeze found its way in through an open window assisting them in floating like snowflakes and some whirling and spiraling like whirlybirds. Sheri couldn't keep herself from whispering "I love you Randle," while taking in the entirety of the majesty and pressing the power button on the entertainment system so as to stop the Musiq Soulchild songs' infinite loop. She decided to put on some clothes, since Randle seemingly didn't want to see her in the Victoria's Secret blue lace bra and panties set that she was adorning. Sheri headed for her bedroom smiling like a mother embracing her baby for the first time and then taken aback by the vase of Calla lilies which she had taken off her bed and sat on the fireplace mantle, now sitting at the top of the stairs with, magically, another heart shaped card resting against the vase that read: "**How deep is your love?**"

Submerged in so much joy while lingering upon his words and utterly surprised that "*Make It Last Forever*" by Keith Sweat was coming from her bedroom and increasing in volume, Sheri yelled, "Randle, wherever you are, I love you!"

Opening her bedroom door, she expected to see Randle laying across the bed in a sexy, provocative manner, which would grant her the pleasure of jumping on top of him and allowing their heartbeats to become one rhythm as she kisses him with all of her passion. Instead, she found their bed made to perfection as the rose petals initially sprinkled everywhere now arranged into a big heart with a Gordon's ring box placed in the center, and another heart shaped note that read: "*I'll die proving I love you.*"

Feeling as though the arctic wind was blowing upon her skin as she held the ring box in her hand, Sheri could not believe her eyes when she opened it and witnessed the Betteridge 5 carat cushion cut diamond Halo ring sitting inside.

"I've made unforgivable mistakes, trying to be a man I'm not," Randle said while stepping out of the closet and startling Sheri. "But I know I love you, and I know the woman you are is irreplaceable. Will you marry me Sheri?" Randle asked lowering to kneel as Sheri turned to envelope him in her arms.

"Yes," she said without hesitation and sincerely whispering "I love you too," as tears of endless joy began to caress her face.

"Baby, nothing I say or do will ever be able to erase the way I've disrespected you." Randle said rising to his feet, grabbing a hold of Sheri's hand while looking into her eyes without blinking, and speaking with a typical sincerity in his voice. "The greatest measure of dishonor a man can offer a woman is raising his hand and obliterate her smile. Sheri, I'll spend the rest of my life defining that you are my irresistible breath of life, love, and the air that I breathe before ever raising my hand to you again. I make no excuse for my selfish arrogance and animalistic ignorance, but with this ring, I promise to surrender my soul to you and devote every aspect of my heart to proving that my every action defines that I am worthy of your very presence. I'm sorry for how I've hurt you, but with this ring, I'm acknowledging that failure and causing you to lose yourself in the demonic cloak which I have so egregiously thrown over your purity is not an option. Please forgive me."

Using her lips to express her words, Sheri leaned forward and kissed Randle with every measure of love within her body. While his hands caressed her back affectionately, Sheri jumped into Randle's arms and wrapped her legs around him. Lowering his hands beneath her butt cheeks, Randle laid her on the bed and lifted her bra to expose her thick, hard nipples to his mouth. Spreading her legs as his tongue elevated her cries of pleasure, Sheri grabbed Randle's hand and guided it straight into her panties. Already moist, his finger invaded her wetness with explicit intentions that caused her back to arch immensely. She wanted all of it inside of her. Rotating her hips with his strokes as he lifted himself off of her body to remove his pants while gazing upon her, her smile, her nipples, and the way her pretty, tight pussy was coating his finger with golden nectar. Randle removed his finger while saying, "I love you," and placing it into his mouth to taste her hidden sweetness.

"I love you, too," Sheri purred.

Stroking his hardness, Randle pulled Sheri to the edge of the bed and started patting her clitoris with his erection.

"I forgive you, Randle," Sheri confessed, looking squarely into his eyes as he held her ankles suspended together behind her head with his left hand and eased inside of her wetness while squeezing his erection with the right.

"Hmmmmmm!" Sheri cried, unleashing her passion as his hardness slowly expanded her walls. With each thrust of their hips, she could feel her sexual peek heightening, as she peered into his eyes, and all she wanted was to climax on that hard stick, hypnotizing her entire body. And just then, demonic, animalistic growls emanated from Randle as his eyes went blood red, inundating Sheri's phantasmic world with shock and hysteria consuming her subconscious state of embarking upon a bright amber and new beginning.

"Arf-arf, grrrrr, whimper." The urge to release his bloated bladder of amber urine inside was at a critical point. Potty trained by Randle to go outside to handle his business instead of making a mess in the house, there was no doggy door, and without assistance in getting out to relieve himself, Trump jumped repeatedly against the bed on Sheri's side, barking for her to let him out.

Startled, horrified but unable to escape the terror while trapped in her subconscious fantasy turned nightmare, Trump barked, growled and whimpered more urgently having reached an inflection point of disaster. Finally breaking the veil of darkness, her eyelids finally and suddenly peeled back as she gasped bending forward, free of the chains of terror, looking around frantically, only to see Randle breathing and snoring beside her while Trump growled, barked, and jumped despairingly in the amber glow of the rays of sun. Sheri wanted to just cry, realizing it was all a dream. This was so vivid, so real, so necessary at this psychological point in her life that she needed a reason to escape. Turning over and biting into her pillow, she screamed with overwhelming frustration at the top of her lungs. "Ughhhhhhh!" Why, of all times, would Trump wake her now? It literally had to be the very moment Randle was about to make her climax after she accepted his marriage proposal and a sincere promise not to physically abuse her anymore. Not only did he deny her the dick she so craved, but he even managed to deny her the pleasure of climaxing just once with him in her romantic fantasy.

Easing out of bed with frustration of having to go downstairs to open the patio door for Trump to go out, given Randle wouldn't and snapped at her for trying to wake him, Sheri lingered upon the fantasy of her dream and wondered if those moments would ever truly exist, but didn't take heed to the sustenance of the rude awakening. Just seconds ago, her heart was lost in the pillars of raw, uncut phantasmal love, and now she's leaning against the patio, watching a dog she didn't entirely like stream amber piss and shit turds on the lawn. Vanity. All in vain, it was all in vain. All of this is simply in the name of vanity, trying to be strong in imaginary love.

She checked her phone for missed calls and text messages as she walked over to clean up Trump's mess. The pictures Naomi sent of her in the Beijing mask last night were so beautiful, a spark of needed inspiration that birthed her smile. "*I thank God for you being in my life every day,*" Sheri texted her back.

After bagging and throwing Trump's poop in the outside trash, Sheri strolled into the house and retrieved her wireless ear buds that rested on the living room table. Inserting them into her ear so she could listen to her girl, Nicki Minaj's Queen album, she tried to imitate her grandma in the kitchen. Standing over the stove sprinkling diced onions into the skillet of eggs, a text notification ringtone caused her to reach for her phone. Seeing that it was from her father, she immediately scanned it with her eyes. "*You spread your wings as a woman of worth last night, and I applaud you. You were artistic and creative in wearing your mask. Beautiful, yet you're breaking my heart.*"

Sheri was her father's baby, and she knew so well that there wasn't anything in life he wouldn't sacrifice or do to ensure her happiness. His wisdom and love for her are two things Sheri didn't take for granted. Knowing her father wasn't a fool when it came to life but would often speak to her in riddles or metaphors to express himself without being direct as a way of pampering her feelings, she called him out of the curiosity of knowing how she was breaking his heart.

"Good morning Precious! You're up early. I didn't expect this."

"Good morning daddy! Yes, I'm up cooking breakfast."

"Do I need to alert the fire department chief of what you're doing without a permit or assistance?" Mr. Johnson questioned while laughing humorously.

"Ha daddy, so you're trying to do auditioning for a talent show I see. Ha! I can cook better than your wife and grandma while you're talking junk. I have skills!"

"Precious, your skills include spending my money and causing my blood pressure to rise. The only thing you can do better than my wife or mother in the kitchen is warm water in the microwave, and that's only because neither of them use one. Since you talkin' junk early in the morning, I'm about to call and share with my mom what you just professed, which you know may cause you to get punched through the phone, granddaughter or not. And I'm definitely not going to be your shield, messing with Harley Quinn. Ha!" Gip recoiled.

"Whatever Daddy, Randle will agree with me, and please don't mention it to grandma because you know I was just playing. I went to visit her the other day, and she was trying to get me to buy her some type of machine gun a solider on YouTube was shooting. Grandma is off the chain."

"Yes, she is, Precious. And had the nerve to tell me, she keep a very close eye on the new generation running rampant with no sense of direction or self-purpose beyond smoking to seem cool, robbing each other for iPhones, and senselessly shooting up schools as the new fad. What's even more sad is that she has seriously embraced the 50 Cent slogan," Get *the strap*." Texting me yesterday her new survival motto is, "Shoot first, Bond out later," I couldn't do nothing but shake my head and make sure the law firm was locked on her speed dial because I knew she was serious."

"Grandma Gangsta!"

"No, your grandma thinks she's Harley Quinn and she's definite not," Mr. Johnson asserted, causing them both to burst into laughter.

"Daddy, what did you mean by your text, I'm breaking your heart?"

"I texted that because you're my daughter, and you know I'll surrender my life for your own. It comforts no father to see his child hurting in any manner. Especially, when that child is a daughter and she accept being abused to feel loved or out of fear. Seeing you in that mask last night was beautiful, yet it wasn't the art you symbolized it to be. My heart is breaking because you're allowing your freeloading boyfriend to abuse you, and I raised you to be a woman of worth."

"Daddy, we are good. I aggravated him yesterday, being selfish, but he apologized to me. It's just a slight bruise, and I didn't want to overshadow my face with a lot of makeup and look like a clown trying to hide the bruise. So, I wore the mask to be mysterious and creative."

"Precious, don't lie to me or make excuses for that coward. You never have any reason to be dishonest with me. I love you no matter the circumstance. Trust is what we share, not deception. The only reason I have yet to have every bone in his body broken is because I know how blind and unstable young love is. I also know you would be sitting at his bedside in the hospital, which would mean all my works would be in vain. Just a veil of vanity. Everything would reveal itself meaningless. Never make an excuse for a man hitting you. Never! It takes a self-centered coward to hit a woman, whereas a man will appreciate and respect the blessing you are would never jeopardize losing you. If you allow a man to disrespect you once, then he will continue no matter how many times he cries, 'I'm sorry,' because you've allowed him to witness and exploit your weakness. Never surrender your integrity for acceptance, Precious."

"I understand Daddy, but every relationship has its growing pains. You didn't raise me to be a weak or naive woman, nor did Randle mean to do what he did to me yesterday. Daddy, I promise you that it will not happen again."

"Baby girl, you can't promise me what you don't have control over! You can never change a man, so never waste your time trying! How can you say he didn't mean to hit you when he did? That's just an excuse a co-dependent person would make out of fear of being alone. Precious, I've been with your mother for thirty years and I've never disrespected her honor once, and you know your mom is a challenging woman."

"Daddy! Don't badmouth her like that." Sherry protected.

"Whatever Precious, listen. I allow you to live your own life, but I'm not going to continue accepting him beating on you. It only takes one opportunity for it to go too far. I haven't said or done anything thus far for one other reason, and that's because I promised your mother, I would let you define your own strength. Plus, I promised myself that I won't have One Eye throw his pathetic body into an ant bed covered in pineapple juice until you have removed him from your life. So just know, One Eye is on standby awaiting my command. But last night, you disrespected the worth of your mom and yourself by wearing that mask for such a prestigious gathering, which is a clear indication it has already gone too far without me interceding."

"Daddy, please stop. I'm okay and we're okay. Please do not do anything to Randle. Daddy promise me that you will allow us to work on our relationship without you interfering," Sheri pleaded with deep sincerity in her request. Sheri was beginning to personify the woman who pleads, but to what end?

"I love you, Precious, and it's hard knowing that you're embracing this type of dangerous love of Russian Roulette. Your grandfather died because he was shot in the face for trying to stop his sister's boyfriend from beating on her. Now, here you are acting as though you will be the first woman of many to make a difference because of your beauty, intelligence, and success, I guess. Sheri, you are my daughter, and the last thing you have to live in is fear of anyone but God."

"Daddy, I have to go, but promise me before I hang up the phone that you will not interfere in our relationship." Sheri adamantly requested.

"Precious, I promise you that I will refrain from making a decision at this moment, but if he raises his hand to you again ... then, I promise to have his hands and feet broken to such an extent he can never use either of them again."

"Bye, Daddy," Sheri huffed.

"Bye, Precious."

Hanging up the phone on her father and pondering on his words, Sheri wondered how is it that her father is always able to recognize things that other people are not able to. Initially, she thought Naomi broke her promise, but given the fact that Randle wasn't snatched out of the car as he slept in the parking garage last night confirmed that the seal on her lips was still pressurized. Knowing that her father doesn't speak idle words, she allowed her mind to flash memories of when One Eye physically handled the stalker who tried to break into her room in college. Sheri walked to her bedroom to surprise Randle with breakfast in bed while literally contemplating getting pregnant, having Randle's baby, cradling the child hostage as an aegis to stave off her father's desire to inflict circumstantially deserving, unconscionably crippling wrath upon Randle. She bent and kissed Randle on the lips as she stood beside the bed holding the breakfast tray, imagining every bone in his body crushed.

"Good morning," Sheri said, deeply in thought as his eyes opened.

Turning his head to look at the clock without initially saying anything, Randle removed his arm from beneath the cover and motioned for Sheri to lower the tray to see what she had cooked. Without sitting up or reaching to taste anything, he arrogantly pulled the comforter back over his shoulder, while turning on his side and closing his eyes with the desire to go back to sleep.

"Give it to Trump, I'm not hungry."

Not believing his words, she placed the tray on the nightstand and contemplated giving him some morning head in order to stir some affection between them but didn't want to agitate him. After standing beside the bed, perplexed for a few minutes just staring at him, she walked out of the room without saying a word and went downstairs to lay on the sofa. Listening to Nicki Minaj, with her feet kicked up, Sheri suddenly realized that she hadn't had her cycle while lingering on the thought of having Randle's baby.

CHAPTER 8

Cruising through Atlanta in the new Gunmetal Pearl color SRT Demon that Terry purchased prior to his return, he was surprised at all the new development in the downtown area after six years of absence, but even more amazed to see that there were no major developmental changes in the Bankhead, Simpson Road, Vine City, Campbellton Road, or the West End areas of Atlanta.

"Whether black or white lives, does life in our community have a voice anymore?" He wondered.

It seems like the majority of the rich only focus on accumulating money for the benefit of increasing their Forbes status, rather than truly investing in beautifying life holistically.

While stopped at the traffic light on the corner of Sylvan Road and Dill Ave., he watched as a young boy pulled stolen food out of his pants as he left the convenient store, and a group of teenage boys selling drugs on the adjacent corner. Terry became a little frustrated thinking of all the thousands of dollars the street hustlers and wannabe ballers throw in the air every night at Playground and other strip clubs around the city, yet, no one has invested a single coin in building a recreation facility that centers around helping inner city kids to build greater life skills and values. And society wonders why the generation of today is lacking core morals and motivation.

So lost in thought while sitting there, Terry didn't even realize that the light had turned green, until his phone started vibrating due to an incoming message that said: "*If I were your woman, would I go to sleep and wake up feeling forgotten or unappreciated?*"

With Penélope surprising him by spending the night and waking him by sitting on his face while giving him some signature head, Terry was a little disappointed in himself for allowing so much time to pass without sending a single message to let Demi know that she was on his mind. But at least for the night and early morning, it seemed excusable since Penélope spent significant time rotating her hips on his hardness and face. After turning onto Dill Ave. and pulling up beside the young kid who stole a bag of chicken strips and some rice from the store, Terry leaned over after rolling down the passenger window. Reaching in his pocket for cash as he called the young teen over to the car, Terry then extended a hundred dollar bill with the agreement that he could keep the change if he went back into the store and paid for the items he took. Seeing the smile illuminate on the teen's face as he snatched the C-Note and ran back into the store, Terry grabbed his phone and decided it was time to call.

"Hello?" Demi answered.

"May I speak to Immeasurable please?" Terry asked.

"Who?"

"Immeasurably Beautiful."

Blushing at the sound of his flattery and recognizing his voice, "this is she," Demi purred while trying to sound a little more seductive in her reply.

"Oh! I'm sorry Demi, I didn't mean to dial your number," Terry teased, bursting into laughter. "My intentions were set on calling Janelle Monáe."

"Oh rubbish! But cute! I never took you for a comedian Anton Jackson — Ooh, I meant Terry," Demi said wildly giggling. "Don't try me, because I will have all my Muslim brothers pull up on you for disrespecting me."

Terry found great humor in her words, given he feared no one, yet respected them with understanding because he knew how protective he was for his sister. "Just so you know Demi, you can never be forgotten nor unappreciated whether you're my woman or an endless dream I have to spend my life lingering of."

"Don't try to be sweet now," Demi joked sarcastically. "So, I have to compete with Janelle Monáe for your attention?"

"Truthfully, you have to compete with no one. Janelle Monáe is a cherished dream I've surrendered my heart and soul too, but my attention is centered upon discovering who you are holistically."

"I don't share who I offer my time and open my acceptance to. UK women are very territorial, just like any real woman who values her worth." Demi asserted with intense inflection recognizable in her tone. "Nor, will I disrespect another woman by flirting with or chasing her man. I wouldn't want it done to me, so if she has your heart and soul, then, respectfully, there can be nothing between us but silent dreams, if that."

"I never took you for a woman who would be afraid of a challenge." Terry quipped while internally admiring the fact that she has integrity. "Just as your heart and soul is sealed in a protective box, guarded day and night, what's wrong with me submitting my heart to, saaaaay, Janelle until I discover a woman who's worthy of nurturing it, treasuring it, and feeding my soul better than I imagined she could? It's no question that I must offer far more than a single extravagant bouquet of roses to secure the softness of your hand in mine for a lifetime. So, it's quite understandable without thought that your accent and natural beauty alone will not have me seeking to bridge life with you as my last first kiss."

"Ha..ha..ha.. I hear you talking the talk, yet walking the walk is completely different, Mr. Wanna-be Casanova. There's a huge difference between challenge and dishonor. Invading another woman's privacy is blatantly disrespectful and beneath my character. What are you doing right now?"

"You're seemingly more intriguing than my initially imagined grandeur!"

"If only you knew, Terry. Now answer my question please"

"Well, given the fact that I kept typing your name into my GPS to no avail, I'm currently seeking to retain a private detective who will be able to reveal your address so that I can be granted the blessing of witnessing the mesmerizing beauty of your smile unexpectedly," Terry joked with cunning laughter in his tone.

"I never took you for a stalker, but life surprises us every day with unexpected things."

"Definitely not a stalker! But seriously, I'm just cruising through the city observing all that has changed in my absence and desiring to see you again. Are you free tonight?"

"No, I have to work, bills must be paid. For someone who spawned no thought of me until I texted, I can't tell you're interested in seeing me again. What do you have on right now?" '

'What?"

"Well, right now I'm sprawled across my bathroom floor wearing nothing but a pair of those ol' school granny panties extending from my waist to beneath my knees, an ankle length floral gown, and scrubbing the bathroom tile with the toothbrush I use to brush my teeth," Demi joked as seriously and seductively as she could before bursting into uncontrollable laughter. "Step out of the fantasy world for a moment Casanova, I asked what you were wearing because we can grab lunch if you're not too busy at the moment, and I don't want to be over-dressed and looking like I'm doing a goodwill gesture by feeding a homeless man." Demi elaborated while giggling.

"Is that so?"

"Yes, that's so!"

"Well, I can't wait to see how magnificent you look in something other than your work clothes, Bella. I have on a pair of black Bottega Veneta slacks, a butter brown Bottega Veneta mock neck shirt, and the Fendi loafers I'm wearing are black as well."

"Hopefully, you're not looking like recycled dead Presidents, yet smelling like you purchased your cologne from a Flea Market vendor." Demi said without humor in her voice. "I'm serious, 'cause cheap cologne gives me a headache. I will meet you in 30 minutes at the Watkins Crab House, and don't be late 'cause my time is valuable." Demi informed him.

"Where is this Watkins Crab House located?"

"Bloke, that's for you to find out if you truly desire to see my smile as your tongue insinuated," Demi advised, hanging up the phone leaving him fully in suspense.

Not wanting to pull to the side of the freeway to search the internet for Watkins Crab House nor to waste time trying to insert the restaurant's coordinates into his car GPS to direct him, Terry called Marcus who instructed him with perfection. Arriving to the surprise destination in a rapid fifteen minutes, courtesy of the 808 invisible horses under the hood, he contemplated searching the area for a florist shop but didn't want to be late. Turning into the parking lot of the Crab House, Terry struggled to find a decent parking space with the restaurant being so packed. Not trying to take the opportunity of being in her presence for granted, he jumped out of the car and scurried inside to secure a place in line for the next available table instead of waiting in the car for her to arrive. The new modernized restaurant with African artwork and several aquariums seemed like an interesting choice as he observed the interior structure while waiting for his table. Feeling like a kid anticipating a new toy as he patiently waited in the foyer hallway, seated on the thick, red cushioned bench, Terry constantly checked his watch, while scanning the parking lot like a trained sniper. With the restaurant's entrance door opening and closing to no avail of Demi's presence, Terry couldn't help but search the internet on his phone twice to make sure there was no other Watkins Crab House in the city.

Traveling to many parts of the world for the past six years, Terry had crossed the path of many fascinatingly beautiful women, especially in his conquest of South Africa. To him, none were more beautiful and mentally intoxicating than Penélope or Janelle Monáe. Yet, watching Demi walk across the parking lot and into the

Crab House, Terry couldn't believe that a creation of God was literally that breathtaking.

Demi's radiant brown skin seemed to illuminate like amber in the sun's glow, wearing her hair down in a Cleopatra bob instead of being pinned on her head as it was in the airport. The curls shaded portions of her face on the right side which highlighted the beauty of her eyes and cheekbone structure, and, oh, that walk — sassy, sensuous, demanding, flat out sexy.

Trying not to lustfully look at her gorgeous long legs as she stepped through the door in a black sleeveless halter A-line dress and ankle strap stilettos, Terry lowered his head and tried his best to act as though he had not noticed her prior to the moment she approached and greeted while lightly tapping his shoulder. Displaying a fake look of shock that did not fool Demi as he stood to greet her, he waved to let the hostess know that his guest had arrived.

Right this way, sir, the young female hostess uttered then led, them to a secluded booth next to a large shark aquarium. "Glad to see you back Ms. Laconette. Your usual table is currently occupied, so I took the liberty of placing you here given I know you like your privacy and it grants you all the options of sitting next to each other or just extra room."

"Thank you Crystalline," Demi effused approaching the booth as Terry observed her movements like a hypnotic puppet.

"You're welcome Ms. Laconette! Will you be ordering your usual dish, or will you be requiring a menu to order with the gentleman?"

"Just give us a moment please!"

"Sure! Well enjoy your visit, sir. And as always, it's a pleasure having you grace our presence Ms. Laconette. Your waitress will be with you shortly. Enjoy.

As a gentleman, Terry offered Demi the opportunity to be seated first, then he attempted to slide directly next to her, but she stopped him and motioned for him to sit on the opposite side of the booth.

"My mom raised a woman not a thot," Demi said openly. "And I will always demand my respect. Yet, since you want to act like you weren't watching me with hawkeye vision from the moment you saw me walking across the parking lot till I reached the entrance, I'll sit across from you and deduct a few cool points.

"Cool points," Terry repeated while shaking his head.

"Yes, you heard me, and just know, another deduction or two, and you will be forgotten," she said smartly while starting to giggle. The way she rolled her eyes caused them both to smile and laugh fondly.

"You may not know how to roll your eyes with the cut-throat attitude of a hood chick, but I see you're definitely a woman of awareness," Terry said.

"Whatever! Women naturally have the instinct of a cat. I'm a cross breed of a tiger and panther, so my awareness is always keen. If you don't mind, let's leave here and go to the Centennial Park. I asked you to come here because it's close to me and the food is fantastic, plus I wanted to see if you were all talk or not. With the weather being as nice as it is today, I desire to have a picnic for our first meeting out together, if you don't mind."

"Sure," Terry said while rising from his seat to escort her to the car, generously leaving a twenty-dollar tip for the waitress even though they only ordered water.

"Hold on for a minute," Demi said once they were standing in the parking lot. "I made us something to eat, so give me a moment to retrieve the basket from my trunk." Looking over her shoulder twice before reaching her car to see him watch her attentively, Demi smiled because she was genuinely feeling him and was hoping that he wasn't a waste of her time.

Riding through traffic doing not a single mile over the speed limit, Demi playfully grabbed her phone and asked Terry, sarcastically, "Do I need to call Dodge and tell them you driving this beautiful muscle car like my great grandmother's mother drove the church bus in the UK?"

Smirking while accelerating just a little, Terry gave her a taste of the power that allowed his Demon to blitz a quarter mile in a lightning quick, 9.65 seconds, dashing the short distance to the exit ramp. Marveling at her characteristics, "I didn't know you had a need for speed," Terry complimented surprisingly, pulling up to the light.

"Woooah, yeah! What an adrenaline rush, whewww," as she sighs. "There's a lot about me that you're clueless about, lad," Demi replied as he turned into the parking lot across from the park, astounded at her reaction. Smiling inside and out, he turned his body slightly to pay the foreign attendant for a parking space.

Reaching over the seat to grab the basket off the floor, Demi noticed Terry taking his shirt off out of her peripheral and attempting to step out of the car.

Turning back around in disbelief, she backhanded him in the chest as though she was the blood daughter of the legendary Ric Flair.

"Don't act as though you're dead from the neck up," Demi roared as Terry massaged the stinging sensation.

"It feels good out here, so given the fact that we were about to picnic. I'm going to enjoy the sun."

"Terry, you're not walking around with me, half naked, like you're some erotic striptease. We are not on the beach, so put your shirt on, please, because you're going to treat and respect me like the lady I am, no matter where we are," Demi asserted while defining herself with her finger pointed towards his face, "I'm not a side chick you're flaunting for entertainment. I'm looking far too amazin' right now for me to have to step out of character and knock one of your admirers out for trying to disrespect me out here in the park. If I sweat, looking like a Queen, then you sweat looking like a King," she huffed while getting out and closing the door behind her.

"Ain't nobody scared of you! And you're not my mother!" Terry yelled out while putting his shirt back on as he got out of the car.

Walking into the park, Terry couldn't help himself from stealing gazes at her body. The way the wind lifted, pressed, and teased the fabric of her dress seemed as if it was tailored for Terry to steal exclusive glimpses of her lower curves. She became even more alluring with every rapid click of her stilettos on the pavement. Her hips swayed like melodies in a jazz ballad. Wearing her work clothes, one could actually tell that she was hiding a nice-toned body, but Terry had no idea that she would be so magnificent.

Instead of sitting in the grass and picnicking, Demi elected to spread her blanket on the rocks close to the waterfall to make the atmosphere more tranquil with a hint of romantic gesture. Expecting light sandwiches, sliced fruit, and vegetables with dip, given that it was a picnic, Terry was completely surprised to see that Demi had actually cooked pan-fried salmon with pine-nut salsa, balsamic mushrooms with herbs, and rosemary glazed carrots for them to savor. He was even more surprised to learn that she brought bottles of Zamzam water to wash it down with instead of wine.

"I don't drink or smoke, Terry," Demi confessed when she noticed the way his pupils reacted to seeing the water. "The bouquet of roses you surprised me with are truly beautiful, and I truly never expected anything, nor to see you again. So, to reciprocate by showing my appreciation and respect for your genuinely shocking approach, I woke up this morning and cooked this with the intention of sharing it with you."

Unable to hide his smile, Terry stuck a spoon full of mushrooms in his mouth so that he could just stare into her eyes and linger upon how extraordinary he was finding her to be. Intrigued to discover that Demi's character and intellect was just as hypnotic as her beauty, Terry allowed himself to get lost in the moment, for it was rare to meet someone so diversified with world views and deprived inner city community issues.

Never one for politics, given the fact that it seemed to him like all politicians lied to the common people just to get elected for the sole purpose of entering the circle of collecting money from lobbyists, Terry listened with attentiveness as Demi spoke of the shame that both political parties are bringing to America, constantly bickering about petty issues for party title recognition instead of coming together as one body to cultivate the country for one common goal. She felt that if Government programs were being utilized properly, it would bring new life to inner city communities. Also, how sad it is that blacks who make it out of a poverty riddled upbringing will spend hundreds of thousands on cars, jewelry, and homes to impress others, coloring that as the signature of success. But what she seemed to find more of a cancer was how those who made it out of the hood would always come back to throw a party in the house they grew up in to remain relevant and feel like they've given something back.

Demi liked the way Terry looked at her, which was in the sense of being a woman of value to him and not as some object that he was constantly undressing in his mind. She found his compassion and calmness quite appealing but wondered if it was an initial persona he was presenting or his true attributes. With time being of essence, given the fact that Demi had to work that night, they took a stroll around the entire park before leaving because Demi wanted to take a few pictures. She refused to allow Terry to hold her hand or enter a single selfie due to the fact that he was stripped of a few more points for simply liking the Georgia Bulldogs over her Georgia Tech Yellow Jackets.

Crossing the street from the park as they attempted to leave, Terry noticed two homeless men searching through the trash can in the parking lot. He approached them, to Demi's surprise, and gave them both twenty dollars from his pocket. The unexpected gesture of compassion warmed Demi's heart because she knows God judges us by the sincerity of our actions. Righteousness to Him will always excel over boastfulness.

Smiling internally without saying a word as they turned around and walked to the car, Demi was overwhelmed by more shock when Terry opened the driver's door instead of her door first, instructing her to drive since she wanted to report his driving style to Dodge on the way down. Walking around the sleeping Demon with the distinct grace of Danica Patrick, Demi playfully snatched the red key fob from his hand and got in with a mischievous glow in her eyes. After adjusting the mirrors, lifting her seat, hitting the switch to drop the top, and connecting her phone to the audio system, Demi fastened her seat belt and pulled off gripping the steering wheel with both hands.

Her disposition was quite humorous to Terry, who sat beside her admiring more of her beauty than the fact that she was driving as though she was trying to pass the driver license road test on her seventh attempt. Demi didn't say a single word as Terry made jokes about her slow driving through the downtown traffic and trying to bet that he could beat her back to the Crab House by walking around I-285 entirely in the opposite direction, barefooted and blindfolded.

Still paying Terry no mind, nor even glancing in his direction, Demi grabbed her phone after easing off the ramp onto the interstate and selected the T. I. song *'More and More.'* With Terry acting like a comedian and paying no attention to the fact Demi had just leaned her seat back a little bit and cut her eyes devilishly at him. When the song started blasting through the speakers, Demi removed one hand from the steering wheel and completely put her stiletto on the neck of all 808 horses under the hood. Shifting her eyes from the road to Terry, she noticed his nervousness as the car accelerated to 100 mph while switching lanes. Demi pushed it to 110 mph before easing off the accelerator due to Terry asking her to slow down as she was finally approaching the Crab House exit.

"I didn't mean to scare you like that," Demi apologized. "But I could tell your car needed a woman's touch to expose the real Demons growling inside your motor," seductively stated, accentuated with her purring British accent but vividly laughing to herself as Terry tried to act unphased by the dare devil driving she just pulled off.

Silently admiring the way Demi brushed her hair from her face with her fingers as she teased the pistons and valves, exciting the demons, pulling into the restaurant parking lot as the quad-exhausts growled like gremlins. But the way she licked her lips after pausing in her sentences, Terry couldn't help but escape to how Penélope is going to be jealous of him sharing his attention with Demi, especially after she woke him by twerking her pussy lips on his mouth as breakfast in bed. He clearly understood and cherished the bond of union they shared, yet he wanted to know who she was internally, what she offered beyond God given beauty, and what it felt like to exist in her thoughts. Selfish desires had him wanting to advise her to take the day off, and he'd double what she earned just to continue basking in her ambiance. But he didn't want to lose any more points by making her feel disrespected by his gesture. Seeing her again was something he was already yearning for as she sat mere inches away from him, reminiscing about the good time she had in his presence.

Getting out of the car to walk Demi to her own, Terry fantasized about how he would hug her goodbye with a gentle squeeze and brush her neck with his lips. But after placing her basket in the back seat of her Honda Accord, Demi surprised him by kissing her hand and blowing the invisible kiss into the air.

"Terry, I can tell you're used to women losing their identity to be in your moment," Demi said. "Yet, my mom raised me to measure a man by his sincerity and not just the giving of his initial actions. I blew the kiss in the air instead of placing it upon your lips or cheek because no treasure of life is earned without effort and sacrifice. You said your heart and soul belongs to Janell Monáe. So, as a lady, I thank you for gracing my time with your presence. I will not cross the line by giving you a hug or kiss goodbye because I love and respect my sister. Hopefully, you'll find a way to catch the one I blew in the air before it hits the ground," Demi said while snickering as she got in her car, closing the door.

CHAPTER 9

Pacing through the loft with his jaw feeling like he'd been slapped with a sledge hammer and no visible way of escaping, J-Roc was getting more and more frustrated that Lil Stunna and Moe found so much comfort in being prisoners of the very individual they had carjacked hours earlier. The annoying sight of his boys sitting on the sofa eating the lemon pepper buffalo wings that the ex-Marines served them while undoubtedly losing their sense of reality with their PlayStation competition, only added fuel to J-Roc's internal frustration. Depleted of patience and voicing his anger for the umpteenth time to deaf ears, J-Roc stormed over to the nearest wall then started punching and kicking holes into the unpainted sheetrock.

"Get me da fuck outta here! I know y'all bitches hear me! I can't believe you two stupid fools acting like elementary kids right fuckin' now," J-Roc growled, precisely knocking the controller out of Moe's hand by throwing a broken piece of sheetrock he reached down and grabbed off the floor. "Our lives are in jeopardy, and the two of you are playing that fuckin' video game as if it doesn't even matter."

Raising his eyes from the TV to lock in a non-combative stare down with J-Roc, Moe wanted to speak the truth and say he wanted his mom, but he spoke nothing as tears began creating a wet passage on his face. The game allowed him to momentarily evade reality, yet J-Roc's words just brought the thought of them being killed, and it scared the fuck out of him. He wasn't a gangster, robber, nor a thug. Hanging around J-Roc and Lil Stunna made him feel cool, given that the kids at school taunted him for being a nerd, but at this very moment all he felt was fear of not seeing his mother smile again, eating her syrup covered boiled eggs, or hearing her voice say, "I love you Montavious," when she wants him to do something for her.

"Fall back, J-Roc," Stunna scowled aggressively. "We all know the situation we're in. Hell, it's your damn fault, so what you want us to do, walk back and forth worrying ourselves to death like yo suddenly scary ass? Look around if you haven't by now. There is no phone in this loft, no knives, no lifting furniture to use as a weapon, no one seems to hear us no matter how loud or how long we yell at the top of our lungs. Plus, there are two men with Rottweilers on the other side of that door — that we clearly know of. I'm not trying to get knocked out like yo stupid ass did, nor take my last breath being an unseasoned gourmet meal for those dogs unnecessarily. So, I'm going to ease my mind by playing this game which the big guard said is here for our entertainment, and if you don't like it, then inhale some extra wind in that bird chest of yours and go revenge your jaw against the one eyed guard who knocked you the fuck out with that tomahawk bow or shut the fuck up."

"Fuck you!" J-Roc roared back with complete anger in his voice, and kicking the sofa chair in disgust, for not shooting the man who now seemingly held their lives in the palm of his hand. Not knowing the intended plans of Mr. Johnson was actually driving him crazy. For the first time in his brief sixteen years of life, he was literally afraid as he was walking over to the window and gazing outside, yet his pride wouldn't allow him to expose that in front of Moe and Stunna.

After losing his father three years ago to a repeated DUI offender who was constantly looked over by the court because of his wealthy connections and his mom sustaining paralyzing injuries due to the accident, there was no one to help provide for his mom's medical bills or pay to maintain a roof over their heads after his father's insurance policy ran out. J-Roc dropped out of Magnet School and turned to the streets for guidance, identity, and a way to help support his mom. To him, selling drugs was too dangerous, and stealing out of stores brought upon too many risks, given the store cameras around and trying to run with things in his arms slowed him down. So, J-Roc adopted robbing as his occupational hustle because he felt that he controlled the narrative and could easily get away by the time the police would be notified without anyone ever getting hurt.

"I think I have a plan," J-Roc bellowed, turning away from the window to render his undivided attention to Moe and Lil Stunna, who seemingly cared not to hear him speak. "Did y'all hear what I just said, I have a plan," he reiterated, walking over and sitting in the chair beside the sofa.

"Instead of bustin' our ears wit sum mo' fuck shit, why can't you be like the soda, seven, and shut the fuck up?"

"A'ight man, but here me out, I got us into this shit, and I got a plan to get us out."

"What's the plan, fool, since you won' shut the fuck up?" Moe sought, not removing his eyes from the game.

"Moe, you make yourself vomit and lay on the ground acting like you having a seizure," J-Roc insinuated. "Lil Stunna will go to the door and notify the guard.

When he comes in to bend down and check on you, Lil Stunna and me, we go'n jump him. Hopefully, he has a gun that we can take and hold him hostage, then we can use him as leverage to escape and git the fuck on."

"You seriously are fuckin' stupid! Do you hear yourself? You straight slick on the bullshit. There's no way in hell that shit gonna work J-Roc," Moe countered.

"Why not? It's definitely worth a try unless he's got a fuckin' better idea."

"It's a stupid plan," Lil Stunna interrupted while pausing the game and turning to give his attention to J-Roc. "It won't work 'cause you're stupid. I guess you assume he'll be by himself all of a sudden. And if he was, then that big mouth Rottweiler he's been escorting by the leash and slobbering as it breathes is just going to lay down and close its eyes while we aggressively attack the one who feeds it. Not only is that a ridiculous idea but a clear indication that getting knocked the fuck out has affected your sense of thinking."

Realizing what Lil Stunna said made so much sense, J-Roc reached forward to grab a few French fries from the basket on the table, laid his head back into the seat cushion after stuffing them in his mouth, closed his eyes, and did the one thing he promised himself that he would never do ever since the fatal accident: prayed silently from his heart for God's help.

Unknown to Moe, J-Roc and Lil Stunna, it happened that Mr. Johnson had located their moms and had his security team secure them in the adjacent loft. Given that this high rise building is still under construction and in a secluded residential area, Mr. Johnson chose it from his many other properties because he knew so well that no one would hear a faint whisper of them screaming or take notice of them being there.

Growing up in the McDaniel Glen apartments in the southwest area of Atlanta, Mr. Johnson solidified the label "Jack of all trades" for himself in the streets at a young age by robbing, stealing, gambling, selling drugs, pimping, etc. If profit could be made selling air or mosquitoes, then Mr. Johnson wanted his cut without exception.

As a rising boxer with lightening quickness and knock out power in both hands, many who witnessed his performances considered him a natural cross breed of Muhammad Ali and George Foreman. But, with his early boxing earnings not able to support his young playboy antics and lifestyle, Mr. Johnson turned to selling cocaine, and by the age of nineteen, he had gone from serving nickel and dime bags on the corner, to dining with one of Columbia's cartel bosses and stashing thirty kilos a week in Mama Lewis' refrigerator panel without her knowledge. At the tender age of twenty-two, he controlled thirty-eight percent of all distribution coming in and out of Atlanta until his heart opened to love which was more precious than money and highly irreplaceable.

Not knowing if their final moment had arrived, and after hours of being tormented by silence while waiting in gruesome anticipation, hearing the door open caused Lil Stunna, J-Roc, and Moe to lift their eyes with full attentiveness. The suspense was so intense that the sound of rhythmic heartbeats was all that one could hear. When the first Rottweiler entered without a leash, no muzzle on its mouth, or guard following behind it, their eyes in disbelief as if they physically saw the angel of death himself. With three more Rottweilers unexpectedly following with mics clamped to their ears and the door being pulled closed by someone, the fear of death caused Moe to urinate on himself. As each dog approached growling with no teeth hidden and the look of malice in their eyes, one would think that J-Roc, Moe, and Lil Stunna were frozen in time because each became a statue that inhaled and exhaled without moving their chest.

For four minutes, which seemed like ten slow dreadful years, all four Rottweilers stood side by side as a united force of terror growling footsteps away from Lil Stunna, J-Roc, and Moe seemingly daring each to blink, before becoming silent and sitting in front of them mimicking four attentive students. Afraid to move in their seats or even dare to think, each just stared as they were being consumed by fear and hoping that the irregular sounds of their heartbeat didn't cause the dogs to suddenly attack.

Never in his life has Lil Stunna been this afraid. Robbing was supposed to be a quick way to elevate his status by putting some fast money in his pockets to impress the schoolgirls without anyone ever getting hurt. But, to lose his life over some material items wasn't worth it. They were mentally engulfed by so much fear that they all anticipated a grim ending in minutes or seconds. Lil Stunna didn't even feel the tears flooding the fabric of his face as he sat there staring into the dogs' eyes and thinking of how horrific his death would be for the dogs to bite him while snatching away chunks of his skin over and over and over again until his heart stopped.

So concentrated on the awareness of the four Rottweilers breathing in front of them, no one heard the door open nor noticed Mr. Johnson standing in the doorway looking like a corporate executive with his suit and tie fitting with craftsmanship, until he said, *"Mguu sawa!"* The dogs stood at attention, facing Mr. Johnson. Then he made hand signals that caused the dogs to come sit in front of him. With the executive looking gentleman whom they carjacked earlier lifting the immediate threat, they all expelled a huge sigh of relief. Lil Stunna found the strength to wipe the tears from his face without breaking his stare from Mr. Johnson and the dogs.

"What are you going to do with us?" J-Roc inquired nervously, "I should have shot your ass."

Motioning with his hand to two of the dogs that turned around and went back to standing in front of J-Roc, growling with seemingly more desire to attack. "If you had killed me, Jamal Luther Campbell, then, what do you think would have happened to Ms. Pamela Campbell?" Mr. Johnson asked.

J-Roc was completely shocked and dumbfounded as to how this stranger knew his name and his mom's name. With the two Rottweilers growling at him as though he resembled a char-grilled filet, moving his lips was the very last thing he was about to do.

"Where are you from Montavious Demarcus Jones?" Mr. Johnson asked Moe, noticing the wetness of his pants and urine dripping off the leather sofa cushion onto the floor.

Parting his lips to speak while seeing in his peripheral vision, the dog closest to him turn his head as though to say, *"I dare you to utter a sound,"* Moe said nothing until Mr. Johnson commanded the two of them to sit by saying, *"Kaa chini,"* and motioning again with his hand, all four Rottweilers immediately complied.

"I'm from McAfee, in Decatur, sir, where Kenny Man from," Moe confessed sniffling and trembling in compounded fear. "How do you know my name, sir?"

"Ms. Susan Jones told me."

Hearing the sound of his mother's name whose arms he wished he could hide in right now, blanketed him with even more confusion and fear. Did he kill his mother for information? Did he kill his mom as retaliation for robbing him? Was she being tortured by one of his men while he stands here intimidating us with his presence? With concerning thoughts of his mom overwhelming the channels of his mind, Moe laid his face into the palm of his hands and cried of true sorrow while repeating over and over in between sobs, "I'm sorry."

"Given that the three of you desire to be robbers instead of going to school and unleashing the potential inside of you, thinking not of how the selfishness of your actions may affect the one you are taking from, nor respecting any of the street codes in y'all's pursuit to gain weed, money, and party fair, I've taken the liberty of taking something from the three of you as well." Mr. Johnson said sternly. "So, I'm convinced that you'll understand without ever forgetting that there are certain consequences to every action."

Without completely understanding the magnitude of Mr. Johnson's words, Lil Stunna asked as he watched him use another hand signal to command the two dogs to come back to him and turned to the door, "Sir, what do you mean by that? What have you taken from us?"

"Your mothers, Travis Leonard Armstrong," Mr. Johnson acknowledged with calmness reaching for the doorknob. "You took my car and money, so out of respect, I took your mothers."

"I'll kill you," J-Roc jumped out of the chair, shouting with uncontrollable anger and waving his hands, which caused the dogs to snap instantly into attack mode, standing between them as a barrier grinding their teeth together, visually locked in on their prey and waiting attentively for their command. "I'll kill you if you touch my mom. I swear, I'll kill you!" Devastated, yet fueled by the thought of something happening to her, J-Roc unleashed every ounce of anger he could muster in a verbal assault.

"Boy, shut up and sit down," Mr. Johnson commanded so authoritatively that Moe had to raise his head out of his palms just to take notice. Observing all three of them while motioning with his hands for the dogs to stop and sit. "You talk too much! There's nothing you can do to me even if you dreamed of it. Look at yourself! If I've already had your mom killed or was about to have her killed, what could you do? I'm standing a few steps away from you right now, yet you can't even touch me. The art of war is strategically conquered by using your mind and not your tongue. Something you seem to have stopped utilizing since the accident that happened to your parents. You took from me and I respected the game. So, why are you now taking it so personal, Jamal, given that I now have the platform of control?" Mr. Johnson asked calmly. "How can you be a gangster, yet a sensitive hypocrite?"

Huffing and puffing as a deranged adolescent, J-Roc sat confused, yet realizing that he was speaking the truth. There was nothing he could do.

Sniffling as he wiped a tear from his face, Lil Stunna stood up without canting his eyes from Mr. Johnson or the dogs. Straining to firmly hold his composure and very afraid of saying the wrong thing, he asked the only thing that mattered. "Have you killed my mom, sir?"

"Does it matter?" Mr. Johnson replied with calmness in his voice and demeanor.

Uncertain of what to think or how to truly respond to him, Lil Stunna took a step forward without lowering his awareness of the dogs. "Well, if you're going to kill me for what I did, then kill me as a man, and not as a coward, muthafucka." Lil Stunna demanded.

"And how is a man killed?" Mr. Johnson inquired while mildly massaging the head of one of the dogs with his right hand.

"Look me in my eyes and shoot me, bitch," Lil Stunna mentioned wiping at his nose. "Don't be a coward and shoot me in the back. I'm not afraid to die, just kill me as a man, and I'm sorry, if it matters."

"Interesting! My father died by being shot in the face, Travis," Mr. Johnson shared, "But many men have died unfortunately by other reasons that still constitute them dying as men and not cowards."

Motioning with his hand without saying another word, the dogs barked viciously while springing into attack stance so unexpectedly and precise in union that J-Roc, Moe, and Lil Stunna jumped because of alarming fright. With every hand signal, a command was executed in unison. The sounds of hard nails clicking against wood as they stepped forward on instruction, was almost more frightening than the visibility of their teeth and slobber as they growled. Not seeing the dogs in this manner of rage before, J-Roc, Moe and Lil Stunna sat while being unable to breathe, blink, or move out of fear of causing a fatal reaction.

"Jamal, when I close my hands, my dogs will attack you after looking at you intently in your eyes as they are now, and if I make no further command, then you will die as a man or boy which would fulfill your request, given the fact that they did not attack you from the back." Motioning them to take another step forward and completely in front of Lil Stunna looking and sounding like a nightmarish terror. Mr. Johnson signaled for them to sit." A man can only die as a man if he existed as a man, Jamal," Mr. Johnson voiced. "Many cowards have died by the hands of individuals who looked them in the eye. You stood, puffed up your chest a second ago, and uttered you're not afraid of dying, yet you didn't stand as a man when my dogs confronted you."

Noticing the way Moe was sitting on the sofa trembling in fear. Mr. Johnson signaled for the dogs as he turned around and walked out of the room.

For an hour and twenty minutes, Mr. Johnson sat in his office conducting business affairs by phone and observing J-Roc, Moe, and Lil Stunna from the surveillance monitor on his desk. They repeatedly screamed at the top of their lungs, kicked the thick reinforced windows to no avail, prayed together on one occasion, but never stopped scouring the loft for any type of opening that would grant them a way out, even though they knew very well that their actions were futile, granting no reward of escape.

Grabbing the machete off the table, Mr. Johnson walked out of his office and signaled to one of the guys on his security team that he was ready. Stepping out of the elevator in his pursuit to the loft, Mr. Johnson couldn't help but reflect on how gangsters J-Roc, Moe, and Lil Stunna were when they all palmed handguns, finger on the trigger, at the scene of the carjacking, yet rendered no backbone, barely a navel when the tables were turned: From big cojones to spineless in 66 minutes. Pushing the door open with the machete, Mr. Johnson walked inside the loft and commanded them to come stand in front of him with their arms stretched forward. Having to raise his voice due to Moe crying, Mr. Johnson twirled the machete mimicking a Japanese technique while asking Jamal, given the fact that he was the first in line and the closest to him, "Do you choose to keep your left hand or right hand? Choose one."

Trembling from a fear great that he lost feeling in his legs and crumbed to the floor, crying and asking forgiveness, "I'm sorry! I'm sorry! Please forgive me sir! I'm sorry!"

"One moment you're a gangster, and the very next your sincerity can award you with an Oscar nomination!" Mr. Johnson exclaimed, while dragging the tip of the machete against J-Roc's body. "Get up Jamal," he instructed, mildly pressing the point of the machete into his chest. "Get up, and all three of you, sit — down!" Gip dictated.

Straining to gain his composure as he crawled and lifted himself onto the sofa, the fear of having his hand chopped off was so traumatizing that he had no knowledge he had crapped on himself until he sat on the sofa and felt his pants sticking to his thighs.

"As a young man at your age, I made countless bad decisions," Mr. Johnson said while sitting on the sofa lounge chair staring at them. "Yet, my mother always kept me grounded and God extended His mercy upon me by placing someone in my life that helped me to believe in myself, and to see life beyond the narrow tunnel vision of the streets. Each of you have the potential to be greater than the expectations that you set for yourselves, yet if the three of you don't open your eyes and start believing in who you truly are, then death or imprisonment will become your achievement your achievement, your story, his story, and his story, of which, y'all's actions write the narrative. Moe, will you please stop crying; I'm not going to kill you or hurt either of you."

Sitting on the sofa with his legs pressed against his chest and his face laying on top of his knees, Moe heard his words, but in his mind all he kept thinking of was the words Mr. Johnson conveyed earlier of taking something from them and having his mom. The unsettling thought of her being dead would not allow him to stop crying. He just cried louder to the point of near hyperventilation. As J-Roc and Lil Stunna sat beside him wiping their faces and trying to regain the natural balance of their composure, Moe sat there thinking only of how his actions cost his mom her life. "What is that unusual odor?" Mr. Johnson questioned lifting his hand to cover his nose. "Smells like one of you needs to be wearing a diaper!"

"Definitely ain't me."

"What smell?" Too embarrassed, J-Roc slyly asked.

"I know you smell that shit, shawty. It damn sho ain't me!"

"Travis, Jamal, Montavious look at me," Mr. Johnson commanded with a sense of comforting resolve in his voice. "Listen. As black men, our greatest weakness is self-fear. Who are you? We like to take the easiest route to achieve nothing and blame the white man, whoever he is, for our shortcomings instead of accepting our own responsibilities and putting forth the effort to make a difference. My father's generation struggled, fought, bled through constant torture, and died as one united body for the cause of freedom, equal rights, and equality. Yet here I now sit within a generation completely divided, stripped of self-value, our worth, respect, appreciation and love for one another all for the greed of dead Presidents.

"If you have no integrity, then you have no identity. If you have no purpose, then you'll forever be lost upon a destination of no arrival. There are too many kids in jail or dead because many in the society prefer the financial kickbacks that they receive for sending you to prison than rendering any effort to get you to discover who you truly are. Instead of killing the three of you or having you all sent to prison merely to waste away your lives by sitting in a room and staring at the walls, I'm going to give all three of you jobs, only under the condition that each of you go to school, maintain no less than a C average, and help me give other kids treading the wrong path the opportunity of being exposed to a better way of life. Do we have a deal?" Mr. Johnson asked while extending his hand for the young men to shake.

Detailing his agreement, Mr. Johnson raised the machete in the air, all three detainees' eyes shifted to the door when they saw it open and two of the Rottweilers walked inside the loft and sat beside Mr. Johnson as he motioned with his hand.

"Excuse me sir, can I ask you a question?" J-Roc said, standing up.

"Sure!" Mr. Johnson acknowledged with full attention given as he sat in the lounge chair and massaged the head of each dog.

"I respect what you're saying, and it brought back memories of sharing conversations with my father. You are sparing our lives and acknowledging that you're willing to help us to establish a better one. I don't know how Moe and Lil Stunna feel at this moment, but how do you truly expect me to accept your offer knowing that you killed my mom. I took money from you, but you got most of that back, and you got your Maserati back too," J-Roc cried with the sincerity of his emotions being heard in his tone. "How do I know I can trust you? How do you know you can trust us? Yes, I want to live and yes I'd love to make something of myself in life, but my mom's life to me was worth more than the money we took from you and the life you want to give to me."

Hearing J-Roc's words caused Moe and Lil Stunna to reflect upon their mothers instead of his agreement as they sat silently upon the sofa and the thought of their moms being dead as a consequence of them robbing him began to make them feel as J-Roc was expressing.

"So, you're saying that no life can be equally exchanged as retribution for what you boys did?" Mr. Johnson questioned.

"Yes, that's clearly what I'm saying," J-Roc muttered, standing there with his emotions starting to envelop him again. "I'd rather you had taken my life than my mom's," he admitted with a tear dribbling from his eye.

Motioning with his hand, the Rottweilers rose up beside Mr. Johnson and started looking attentively at J-Roc. Seconds after making another motion with his hand and the dogs executing no command at all, the door opened at which moment Moe, Lil Stunna and J-Roc couldn't believe that not only were their mother's alive, but they were being escorted into the loft with the other two Rottweilers chaperoning them. Wanting to leap across the room, yet not knowing how the dogs would react to their sudden movement, all three just stood standing side by side in disbelief because they thought their moms were dead. Motioning for the dogs to come sit beside him, Mr. Johnson instructed the boys to go hug their moms, and they jumped at the opportunity instantly.

Hugging and being kissed on the forehead by his mom caused Moe to cry even more out of joy because he never thought he'd see her again. "I'm sorry," was all he could whisper while crying in her arms.

"I thought you said you killed our moms sir," Lil Stunna said in a puzzled voice while squeezing almost all the air out of his mom's lungs. "But I'm very grateful that you didn't, sir."

"I never confirmed those words. I only acknowledged that I had your moms picked up and I took something from you, which I was referring to your time and time with your moms and not the lives of your moms. You cannot get back these hours of frustration that I've taken from your lives, nor the peace of mind that each of you lost as a teaching method."

"Thank you, sir! Thank you, sir!" J-Roc cried as he hugged his mother in her wheelchair as if this would be their last.

"What is that smell?" His mom inquired while caressing his head in her arms.

"I was so scared, I crapped on myself by mistake," he mumbled, not caring that everyone now knew because the only thing that mattered to him was that she was alive.

With everyone now laughing and joking that Mr. Johnson needed to have his men take J-Roc outside and pressure-wash him, Mr. Johnson stood while trying to stop laughing and surprised everyone.

"Jamal, I know you want to be the man who supports your mother's needs now that your father is no longer here to be the provider, but you can't do it making careless decisions that will remove you from her life. Same for you, Travis and Montavious.

Mrs. Armstrong, Mrs. Jones, and Mrs. Campbell, I can't leave here today without us all having a significant reason to smile. Each one of you ladies touched my heart dramatically when we talked. So, to say thank you for granting me the opportunity of trying to make a difference in your boys' lives, I'm willing to give each of you a new home in this building once it's completed, with your monthly expenses never exceeding one hundred dollars. The homes will be yours to buy at the building cost instead of the market value price, but not for rent. Ms. Jones, I want you to no longer worry about your medical bills or your treatment. I want all of you to come work for me, and I will give you an increase of twenty percent in your salary. I have drivers waiting for each of you downstairs to take you all home, but Jamal, you will have to walk 'cause you ain't rubbin' that stuff against my seats! It will cost too much money to shampoo them bad boys and get that stank out. No sir, buddy! You have already cost me enough money as it is," Mr. Johnson joked.

"Mom!" J-Roc lifted his head and muttered.

"Mom, nothin' boy, Mr. Johnson has spoken and I don't want to be smelling yo stankin' behind all the way home anyway," his mom said humorously pushing him away from her. "Back up off me, you stank boy, ouuuwee! It makes no sense for you to be this old and still need a damn pamper." They all roared with laughter at that one.

CHAPTER 10

Jogging through the neighborhood was meant to be no more than a physical cardio exercise to stimulate his heart rate while helping to keep his cholesterol levels balanced and to make sure that visceral fat doesn't form in his abdominal area. But in his pursuit to maintain good and stable health, Randle noticed a family of ducks walking across a yard en route to the pond, and the beauty of their unity caused him to reflect upon life.

It's so intriguing how they follow an unbreakable order of obedience. "So distracted we are within ourselves that we often bypass the magnificent wonders of God's creation," he thought to himself. The fascination of their synchronous quacking caused Randle to stop jogging and just admire the blessing of existence in its true aspect. Watching the mother taking the lead position while surveying the area for danger and the ducklings chasing her footsteps with structure, unexpectedly brought to mind the significance and worth of a woman. Instead of continuing his jogging when the ducks were no longer in his sight, he opted to walk home while lingering in thought and admiring the unbelievable creation of life as a whole.

Hearing the door alarm monitor beep but no Randle in sight or audible reply from him as she repeatedly called his name, brought a sweeping aura of worry that had Sheri feeling as though someone was mysteriously watching her walk downstairs. Noticing that the back door was open and Randle still not answering as she called out for him, Sheri grabbed two butcher knives from the knife rack on the kitchen counter. Tightly gripping one in each hand made her wish that she hadn't declined her father's security team combat training. She eased to the back door as silently as she could while trying to carefully listen for any distinctive sounds that seemed out of place. Using her right foot, she eased it closed, seeing nothing suspicious in the yard as she looked through the glass door. "Wham!" Trump slammed into the wall as he tried to dash through the crack before she closed the door in its entirety, startling Sheri,"Aiiiiiih," and she screamed at the top of her lungs while dropping both knives to the floor and scrambling to move her feet out of the way. With her heart beating like pistons in a 1969 Plymouth Roadrunner, and Trump now jumping against her leg excitedly, Sheri could do nothing but lean against the wall with her hands covering her mouth in astonishment.

"Hey baby," Randle greeted, suddenly walking through the door into the house and removing his Beats by Dre headphones with the music still blasting. "Are you okay?" He asked, noticing her position against the wall and the two butcher knives laying on the floor.

"I'm blessed, baby," Sheri breathily responded, pressing her hands against her chest while regaining her composure before bending down to pick up the knives.

"Given that you have two knives in your hands, and you have this look on your face like you saw a gremlin before I walked into the house, do I need to ask your permission to kiss you?" Randle asked jokingly.

Leaning forward without answering the question, Sheri kissed Randle until she felt the stimulation was starting to cause him to get a hard-on. Pulling away by squeezing his bottom lip with her own, Sheri seductively whispered, "Ouuu, I need some of him," as she turned away to go put the knives back in the rack.

"If that's true, then you shouldn't have stopped doing what you were doing, but since you seemingly just wanted to tease him, now, you have to work for it," Randle expressed with humor in his tone and cackling.

"Whatever! I'm a horny black woman with two extremely sharp butcher knives in my hand. I don't have to work or ask for nothin'," Sheri snapped looking over her shoulder, as she was trying to be intimidating with her serial killer facial expression.

"Is that your 'Set It Off,' I dare you face?" Randle inquired while bursting into laughter. "You actually look constipated. Seriously though baby, will you come into the yard for a moment? I wanna show you something."

"I hope you're not about to show me a snake or something?" Sheri warned while walking over to him. "Because I definitely will come back and grab all of these damn knives."

"No, baby," extending his hand to secure the softness of her own. "I won't play with you like that."

Guiding her into the yard where they sat in the lounge chairs on the deck while Trump acted as though he was securing the perimeter, Randle tried to get her to see the beauty of God's creation beyond a typical casual glimpse without taking true notice. For a moment, Sheri thought Randle was literally losing his sanity by seemingly trying to be a naturalist until she allowed her mind to open to his words and realize that God created life more intriguingly than the mind can actually comprehend. Sitting there pondering on how a bird actually flies, a bee produces honey, the trees absorbing our carbon dioxide but releasing oxygen for us to breathe, or the fascinating ability of clouds to hover in the sky and produce rain that cultivates life had them both admiring the mysteries of God's perfect creation and bridging a bond of affection that had seemingly been lost for the past few months.

Sheri couldn't remember the last time they truly enjoyed a moment where they listened and shared each other's thoughts. The sun's heat felt as though it was baking the leaven bread of her swelling face, which she endured without complaining. There was no wine, music, or food between them, yet the atmosphere was endearing and a bit romantic, given that their conversation was intellectual, and Randle was massaging her feet. Trump observed with a look of jealousy in his eyes as if to say he wanted a paw massage too.

"Sheri I'm sorry," Randle said in the midst of talking about the miraculous benefits of the sun to the body.

"Hmmm?" She replied, mildly confused and caught off guard, not truly knowing what he was saying he's sorry for.

"I'm sorry for the way I've been disrespecting you lately, neglecting you, and constantly taking you for granted as though I can replace you by merely walking outside the front door. Lately, I've noticed that the chemistry between us has not been as electrifying and spontaneous as we once were. I used to see light in your eyes from the moon's glow and rays of the sun. Now, I only see your eye color as you sit here beside me and I love you enough to say — I'm sorry."

The magnitude of his words caused tears to fall from her eyes, which Randle wiped away. Sheri was starting to feel as though she was at a forked road with love and didn't know which fork to take, especially with her father announcing his intentions. She wanted to say so badly "I love you; I forgive you, and I'll never stop fighting for our love." But she found herself so astounded with the words falling off of his tongue that she just listened.

"Baby, I don't want to be a loser like my father," Randle confessed. "I love him for giving me life, but his barbaric ways caused him to lose the greatest blessing that God had bestowed upon his path of travel. My mother! And under no circumstance do I want to lose you. My father physically abused my mother while growing up. The constant nights I spent at the hospital sleeping by her bedside and missing school, her broken arms, ribs, jaws and the three miscarriages. But she didn't break the yoke of abuse and leave him until I graduated from college. Her sacrifice, she once told me, was to assure I succeeded in getting an education. The knowledge of that truly weighs heavily on me because my mom showered me with so much love, and here I am dishonoring her in every aspect of my life. Sheri, you are the first black woman I've ever dated and the only woman I've ever surrendered my heart too. I read a few interracial relationship books hoping that I could strengthen our bond significantly. The authors of those books said that black women like alpha males and like to feel dominated within their love, which is why I've tried to love you by walking in my father's shoes these past few months instead of loving you by walking in my own shoes." Randel continued, "I am not him; I will never be him, and I wish to never exist as him. Sheri, I love the strong extraordinary woman that you are. The way you bite your lip when you're lost in thought turns me on. The way you blink your eyes in your sleep or the way you secretly position yourself under the water in the tub and just let it fall upon your clitoris until you climax. Watching you without you knowing turns me on in a massively appealing way that's quite unique. Baby, I notice everything about you, from the distinctness of your smell, your taste, and your movements solely because I love you and I never want to exist without you."

Burning with unleashed emotions due to the feeling of sincerity in his words, while also blushing that he knows of her tub secret, Sheri leaned to the side and kissed Randle as he tried to ask for her forgiveness from the deepest part of his heart. Placing her hand on the side of his face while closing her eyes and becoming one breath with him, "I love you, Trump," she said pulling away and staring deep into his retinas to see the reflection of herself. "I love you!"

"What!?" Randle shouted in disbelief. "I just opened my heart to you and you mistakenly call me another man's name? The damn dog at that."

"No baby, definitely not the dog," she recanted with authority while rolling her neck. "You said our President is a pimp, so respect the Kool-Ace song, '*Pimpin' Ain't No Illusion,*'" mildly laughing, she reaches down to share a little affection with Trump before returning her full attention to him and acknowledging that his words serenaded her heart in ways that he could never imagine.

"Randle, my love belongs to you," Sheri assured. "I have completely forgiven you and do know that I thank God every day for placing you in my life. Baby, I accept you for who you are, and that is not your father. No love is without sacrifice."

For the next few minutes, Sheri sat silently just basking in his words as Randle ran in circles with Trump chasing him in the yard. She thought more about the fact that her cycle is late and wondering how their life would completely change if she eventually had his baby. Rising from the chair smiling, Sheri told Randle that she was about to go inside and cook something to eat for them, but he shocked her by asking her not to.

"Baby, given the fact that my selfish ignorance caused you not to be able to go to your father's cookout at the park today, let's do our own cookout here," Randle said. "And, to add a little spice to our mix, let's play any three games in which you feel that you have an equal opportunity or advantage, and the loser must be the other's servant the entire day. Meaning that the loser has to do whatever is commanded without resisting, otherwise another day is added."

"Bet accepted!" Sheri vowed with a sneaky grin expanding on her face as she walked back into the house to fix them something refreshing to drink.

Randle had no clue that Sheri had become a PlayStation fanatic, due to the kids that she mentored. They'd taught her how to play all the popular video games and shared a few of the cheat codes that gives an extra advantage. She allowed him to pick two 'PlayStation' games just to comfort his ego, but 'Connect Four' being her only game of choice.

Randle found himself constantly thinking of the numerous things he was going to have her do once he won: wax his car, clean all his shoes with a toothbrush naked while listening to heavy metal, cut the grass, cook naked with only a scarf adoring her neck, etc. Randle couldn't wait to be crowned the king.

With the rules being made, one must win two games from each of the three that they picked out in order to be considered the winner. Sheri initially pretended to be clueless as to how the controller worked, faking her frustration as Randle celebrated his boxing victory and tormented her with his laughter after winning the first game.

Concentrating to make her moves effective, Sheri dominated the next two boxing matches in embarrassing fashion and laughed as he thoroughly checked the entire system to make sure that his controller was working properly, which Randle claimed she disconnected somehow without even touching it.

Following the same routine in the Madden game that they played next, in which Sheri selected the Atlanta Falcons, she noticed that Randle was literally looking as if he was about to cry. Never did he expect to lose at a game that he plays so often and has never seen her play once. No longer was he fantasizing of the things she would do for him, he was now wondering in depth what she would command him to do, dumbfounded as to how his plan to stand as a dictator had backfired.

Knowing fully well that Sheri could not command him unless she won two from all three games, Randle played Connect Four as though his life truly depended on it. Drawing the first five games, Randle asked for a truce and acknowledged that they could serve each other respectfully. Yet, Sheri declined out of amusement because she was only toying with him. Connect Four was her favorite game in the world. The only game she truly felt as though no one could beat her on, not even the game's developer.

She quickly secured victory by winning the next two games in commanding style. Disappointed and embarrassed, Randle immediately jumped up claiming he had to use the restroom as a way of trying to avoid her celebration for a moment. But he was completely caught off guard when Sheri commanded him to use it on himself if he truly had to go.

"What? Stop playing, baby. I seriously have to use the restroom. I'll be right back," Randle insisted while holding himself and trembling as though his bladder was about to explode.

"No! Rules are, you follow the command of the winner. So, whatever you have to do, piss, vomit, or shit, just go ahead and push it out like a big boy because you will also be cleaning it up servant boy," Sheri effused while bursting out in laughter.

"Baby, stop playing because this is not a part of the agreement. I would never do you like this," he professed as he slightly bent over and now holding his stomach as if he was in pain beyond comprehension.

"Honestly, I don't know what you would do in my position right now. Probably make me clean the gutters with a toothbrush. But I know if you have to use the restroom, then you're going to use it on yourself, or I receive another day. I'm tired of seeing you stand and talk. Come, get on your knees, take off your shirt, and piss or shit on yourself if you have to, 'cause I don't care, servant boy. What I do know is, I need my toes sucked right now," Sheri purred laying back into the sofa smiling and raising her right leg seductively.

He truly could not believe he had lost all three games, but he knew that he had to be a man of his word. Randle obliged the command by giving her a massage as he intimately licked and sucked the toes of both feet. Sheri enjoyed every minute of her newly awarded dictatorship. Instructing him to wear only his Speedo's with the raccoon prints, Sheri started by making him wash her car, sweep the entire driveway, then made him run in place, do push-ups, and jumping jacks on command for twenty minutes as she sprayed him with the water hose like a drill sergeant. Utilizing her dictatorship wisely, Randle was instructed to clean the entire house wearing a red tie, some Polo briefs she cut into some embarrassing thongs, a pair of dress socks pulled to his knees, and the plastic slippers she received after getting a pedicure a day prior.

Sheri never thought it would be so exhilarating seeing him sanitize the bathrooms, polish the hardwood floors on his knees, clean behind the major appliances, wash clothes, fold them as they came out of the dryer, and iron things she would usually just fold away. With the desire of having another day of supreme power, Sheri instructed him to stand naked in front of the fireplace, to seductively slap his butt, and twerk like a male stripper. Thinking that he would resist or not know how to twerk, undoubtedly awarding her another day of immeasurable satisfaction, Randle surprised her by slapping his backside hard while twerking without complaining. Moving with the natural rhythm of an erotic dancer was his hidden secret. He made sure that she knew with certainty that her smile was his priority.

With the house now spotless in every room, and Randle marinating the beef tips and chicken to be placed on the grill, Sheri had him go into the garage, remove all his clothes and fasten a tool belt to his waist. With the new title "*The Butt-Naked Handy Man,*" and obeying her selfish request, he carried her upstairs, bathed her, and sucked on her nipples whenever she commanded as she soaked in the tub water massaging her clitoris to the exploding peak of unimaginable pleasure. Afterwards, he dried her by patting her gently with a Dove sponge, moisturized her body gently with the deep firmness and expertise of a masseur then dressed her while remaining on his knees the entire time. Sheri was deeply in love with being Queen Bitch!

Never had Sheri felt more appreciated and loved in all her life. So, mentally governed by the pampered affection that Randle had been granting at her command, she was oblivious to Trump chewing on her new Louis Vuitton strap hanging off the table as The Butt Naked Handyman carried her back to the sofa to surf the internet. Lifting her eyes from the screen to admire Randle through the window, grilling, now wearing her super tight Victoria's Secret housecoat with nothing on beneath it and barefooted, Sheri could do no more than smile observing how cute he looked. The soothing comfort of it all was allowing Sheri to understand a little of what the rich endure in everyday life.

Of the two years they'd dated, never had Randle talked to her about his father's abusiveness or the effects which it had upon him, mentally. Listening to him earlier warmed her heart and made her feel as though they were achieving new boundaries within their love. The thought of his mom enduring so much abuse for the benefit of him achieving an education caused Sheri to begin wondering what could and would she endure for the love of her child. How deep is her love? Would she maintain a household so that her child could actually be raised with a father or would she walk away from an abusive relationship for the safety of herself and try to be a strong single mother? At what point can being abused not be forgiven, she wondered? So lost in thought, she didn't even notice Randle bringing the food in the house.

"Baby!"

"Yes, Randle?"

"Baby, did you know that when a silkworm eats a mulberry leaf, it produces silk, when a bee eats of that leaf it produces honey, but when a deer consumes the very same leaf, then musk is produced? Now, tell me that is not intriguing."

Wanting to respond as he walked into the living room but unable to stop laughing at the amusement of how her housecoat flashed the bottom of his pink cheeks, Sheri instructed him to go shower off the smoke and put on some good clothes. Mad that she didn't capture a picture of Randle's flat cheeks being exposed to show Naomi, Sheri jumped off the sofa after hearing Tyrese's *"Best of Me"* blast from Alexa in the bedroom moments later without her having given him permission to play music which then filled her with new desire to have a little fun.

A boot camp type workout in a cold shower is all that came to mind as she was en route to the bedroom to chastise his arrogance. Sheri's love for music opened her ears to the words of the song, and with each step, it brought her closer to her destination. Not only did she realize Randle was talking to her through the song, but she found herself no longer wanting to punish him for his disobedience entering the room.

Unexpectedly seeing the water splash and drip from his body as she stood in the bathroom doorway began to turn her on in a different way. Even though Randle never acknowledged her with his eyes, the fact that he kept stroking himself intimately with the washcloth as though he was trying to get his dick OSHA certified, assured her that he was aware of her presence and trying to be enticing. With Randle being so submissive and obedient all day, Sheri's internal desire and weakness caused her to walk over to the glass.

With unsheltered lust, she opened the door and stepped inside without caring to remove any of her clothes. Kissing his neck and back with heated affection while reaching around him to secure his erection with her left hand, Sheri began stroking him while lowering into a squat as she turned him around and placed his dick in her mouth. Using only her neck to spiral herself back and forth, Sheri massaged his balls with her left hand while caressing his thigh with her right to keep herself balanced. Sheri stimulated the most sensitive region unrelentingly, by twirling her tongue in a circular motion, which heightened the affection of pleasure each time she slid him out of her throat. The way her tongue brushed the base of his hardness side to side, had Randle repeating her name as he tried to grip the tile with his toes.

Removing him from the warmth of her throat, Sheri massaged the sides of his erection with her lips while rubbing his head with her thumb and index finger increasing the blood flow and stimulation. His cries of satisfaction turned her on far more than she had expected. Even though she was in the shower, she felt her own wetness dripping. Engulfing him again, Sheri forced it all in her throat slowly until she began to gag. Bobbing with more intensity and adding a little more pressure with the brushes of her tongue, Sheri could tell that Randle was elevating to the point of ejaculating and she wanted to please her man, so she stroked his hardness with twisting spirals as she pulled it out of her mouth. Sheri kept flicking her tongue upon the base of his head until she caused Randle to ejaculate on her face and tongue, sensuously outlining her lips with the semen seeping from his dick before kissing it and rising to kiss Randle with intimate affection.

"I love you, Randle."

"I love you too, baby," Randle whispered, holding her in his arms as the water splashed upon them, soothing their intensity, yet elevating the romance within their passion.

Laying her head upon his chest and hearing his heartbeat, Sheri smiled, knowing so well that within the pillars of his heart, the blood cells had her name upon them. Breathing against Randle had her feeling like there was no end to their love. Removing her clothes to cleanse herself again after Randle got out of the shower to go prepare the food, Sheri stood under the water and closed her eyes, basking in her serenity and thinking more about having a baby, getting a tattoo, and feeling Randle deep inside her.

Feeling herself, she adorned a Victoria's Secret short set that hugged her curves as though the fabric was painted on by Picasso or Rembrandt. The mere sight of seeing her awakened fascination, and Randle didn't downplay how hypnotic and appealing she looked sauntering into the room with the grace of a swan ballerina. Frozen in the heat of the kitchen watching her every movement, her exotic sexiness caused him to briefly feel as though he was suspended in time.

He liked how the wet strands of her hair laid across her face. Her breasts seemed to have more definition in the bra she was wearing, and he wanted to suck on her nipples, but once again he was hypnotized. The edges of her booty revealing itself in her shorts and how her stomach tightened with the rotation of her hips was causing him to stiffen even more as his erection became more pronounced, and he sensed that Sheri noticed, given she lifted her legs slowly and seductively as she sat on the sofa. While caressing her stomach sensuously, she arched her back and suspended her legs widely apart in mid-air as she began to tease the camel's toe pussy print lining the lace shorts between her thighs with the index finger of her left hand mistakenly enticing even the thin air rushing across her. Even Trump wallowed across her midsection lying upside down while Sheri blew kisses at the erotic statue frozen in time.

Conjuring the strength to break away from the intimate dream she had him suspended within, Randle fixed their plate hoping her actions meant her dictatorship was over. Walking out of the kitchen thinking that they were going to sit on the sofa and watch a movie as they ate, Sheri stopped teasing his eyes as he placed their plate on the coffee table. Licking the wetness from her finger as he watched her every move, she then waved her arm like a witch casting a spell, reminding him that she was still in control. With the authority bestowed upon her, she summoned him to dice all the meat on her plate and feed the entire meal by kneeling between her legs without touching her. "Every time you disobey me, then I receive another day," Sheri asserted as she laid back into the sofa cushion and eased her fingers back inside her panties.

"May I eat now my Queen?" Randle asked still kneeling before her with his gaze directed to the floor. He had fed Sheri and washed all the dishes as commanded. Looking at her hungry servant in his state of obedience had Sheri wishing that their bet was for a lifetime, not just for a day. She never wanted this to end, why would she?

"Yes, you may eat servant boy," Sheri uttered with hidden intentions. "Where are you going?" She immediately questioned as Randle stood and grabbed his plate to walk away.

"I'm going to eat, my Queen, now that you granted my request," he confirmed. "Do you command that I walk as a dog to the kitchen to eat my Queen?"

"I acknowledge you may eat, but that does not entail you getting off your knees to go anywhere. Now, get back on your knees servant boy," Sheri demanded while spreading her legs wider.

Following her every request, yet truly hungry, Randle kneeled and crawled back between her legs imitating Trump. From her right ankle to the left, Randle was instructed to bathe her with his tongue, seductively, only to kiss the inner thighs. Teasing her beyond the measures of her own expectations with every lick forced Sheri to arch her back and gradually slide forward in an attempt to grant wider range to taste her without discomfort. Creating a hook with his tongue and using its strength to slide beneath her panties to massage her clitoris, Randle made her cum with an unbelievable flicking technique. Wanting to feel his oral cavity and lips intimately upon her body, Sheri instructed him to remove her shorts and bra. Climaxing to his tongue always caused her to feel as though she was skydiving without a parachute, and she was addicted to the adrenaline rush as any addict in denial.

Laying on the sofa and spreading her legs, Sheri inserted her index finger and middle finger into the wetness of her pussy, then put it in her mouth to suck on as Randle lowered to kiss her clitoris and parted her lips in a unique way that triggered muscle spasms arching her back in uncontrollable pleasure.

"Hmmmmmmmm," she whispered while biting into her own bottom lip.

The rapid slaps against her pussy with the tip of his tongue had Sheri gasping for air that seemed unavailable to her lungs. Every stroke created a new wave of ecstasy exciting her body overwhelmingly, sparing no pleasure in any aspect. Sliding his finger inside to stimulate her G-spot as he vibrated his tongue on her clitoris caused Sheri to grip onto the sofa cushions as she climaxed, calling out his name repeatedly in Pig Latin.

Easing out of his Polo boxers and sliding his tongue up the body to her nipples, Randle stroked himself while teasing her, yearning to be loved by sliding the head of his dick up and down between her lips without inserting it, coating the head of his dick with the viciousness of her cum and wetness.

Sheri wrapped her legs around Randle as he sucked on her nipples, placing her hands on his cold cheeks and rotating her hips as she slowly pushed him into her. Randle gently eased inside of her tightness, and she arched her back to elevate the pleasure between them while trying to push him deeper and deeper with each stroke as her clitoris screamed of passion with every stroke. With Randle now applying gagging pressure to Sheri's neck and thrusting himself inside of her as she held her legs suspended, Sheri climaxed and desperately begged him not to stop until she climaxed again as she was no longer able to hold her legs in the air though her back remained arched.

Randle loved the way Sheri's pussy gripped his dick. He loved the way she rode him reverse rodeo style and bounced her ass by just lifting her hips and looking over her shoulders while sucking a finger coated with her own nectar. He loved even more the way she twirled her hips in a circular motion when he stroked it from the side and leaned over her body kissing the softness of her lips. In between Sheri's whispers of enchanted passion, the sound of her tightness accepting his dick and releasing it could be easily heard, and it turned Randle on. With Sheri's hands now pressed into the floor and her knees pressing into the sofa cushions, Randle slapped her ass every few strokes and the stinging sensation seemed to ignite new waves of passion inside of Sheri because her pussy got even wetter than what it already was.

"Fuck me baby! That dick feels so good baby! Fuck me baby! Oooooh Randle Fuck me! Oooooooooo baby Fuck meeeeee," Sheri cried as Randle's strokes became more rapid and he deep dived in her wetness without stopping.

So captured in the trance of love making, Sheri began feeling the words of India Arie's "*That Magic,*" squeezing her ass cheeks for support and using them to push and pull Sheri on his erection which intensified the sensation, thereby causing Randle to erupt inside of her warmth like an ancient volcano. Becoming more and more sensitive with each stroke, yet not wanting to stop the feeling they both were enduring. No longer able to push himself beyond the limit, Randle eased out of her slowly and fell back into the sofa cushion feeling like the king he initially wanted to be. Rising from her awkward doggy style position, Sheri placed him in her mouth so that she could taste the mixture of their love. So sensitive and unable to sustain the potency of her throat, Randle pulled her onto the sofa to lay in his arms.

"Sheri, I love you," Randle cajoled, tightly squeezing her while simultaneously trying to make sure she was unable to fiddle with him in any way because he literally had nothing left to offer.

"I love you too, baby," Sheri replied. "Now, get up servant boy. I command you to go fix me a hot bubble bath, then come back to carry me to the tub. You may finally eat as I soak and relax my body. But the very moment you finish, I command that you come bathe me, moisturize my skin, and dress me again. Afterwards, you will come back downstairs to fix me a fruit plate that consists of strawberries, white grapes, peach slices, and mango. You're then instructed to bring me the plate and feed me the fruit while massaging me front and back, servant boy."

"Are you kidding me, baby? I just had you climaxing all over my tongue and dick and you still desire to treat me like a peasant" Randle queried.

"Fuck yes, servant boy, now get your ass up!"

CHAPTER 11

Cruising down Moreland Ave., while listening to the ol' school radio station, Mrs. Johnson couldn't help but smile as she drifted in thought. Memories flashed of the unbelievable weekend spent in New York her first time when they played *"Purple Rain."* So caught in thought, she didn't even notice that she was running the traffic light when crossing the bridge at I-20.

"Purple Rain" always caused her to remember how Gip sent her to Manhattan, thinking that she was merely going to shop for a new ensemble and handbags. Upon reaching the Waldorf Astoria, she was astonished to discover forty-eight long stemmed red roses and a V.I.P. backstage pass to a Prince concert enclosed in the card laying on the bed in her suite. A dream gift unable to be topped by anything other than Gip's love until she was granted the joyous pleasure of Prince personally inviting her onstage after his intermission wardrobe change where the two of them danced together during the song. It was one of the greatest nights of her life.

She loved how her husband always listened to her words even when it seemed like his attention was governed by business and how, after thirty years, he had never stopped defining the fact that his main priority in life was her happiness. Turning into the Grant Park entrance, she drove around before parking sideways next to an ice cream truck. Mrs. Johnson was in awe, stepping out of the AMG S 65, donned in the new Serena Williams Nike gear, and seeing how Gip had the cookout looking like a mini theme park. Even though this was just a family and friends gathering, Gip always extended his generosity to make sure that everyone was comfortable, be it kids, strangers, or adults. Especially, those who come to events with the selfish intention of fixing to-go plates for their weekly meals instead of centering their focus on strengthening the union between family and friends or networking in order to open new doors for themselves.

Walking across the park, Mrs. Johnson showed her respect to the food servers inside the two tents, the cooks from Fo Yo Soul and Eatery, the security members, all the hired entertainment workers, and the kids enjoying themselves on the party jumpers before rendering her full attention to the friends and family that had already arrived. The union of family is something the Johnson's nurtured with utmost sincerity and held with great honor by accepting and respecting everyone for who they are without judgmental or hypocritical views, nor did they allow an individual's selfish choices or bad decisions to bridge a barrier between them. The Johnson's stood on the principles of understanding and forgiveness. Understanding that God created no one to exist by their own expectations and understanding, that one must learn to look past the actions and characteristics of others to receive greater portions of God's mercy. How can one seek true forgiveness for their sins when they refuse to forgive others?

Mrs. Johnson walked back and forth, mingling and sharing laughter, before having a dance battle with Gip's niece, Reanna. She assisted in painting a few of the kids' faces, won one of the bubble blowing contests with Gip's niece, Cadence, and enjoyed playing a couple of games of spades, referring to which, she felt that she was untouchable by anyone in this lifetime. Mrs. Johnson was off the chain! She paid two kids to distract her husband's contracted seafood chef from Eatery while she stole a plate full of his personal sautéed tiger shrimp and two lobster tails from the grill. Sneaking back to her tent with the plate hidden beneath a covering plate of potato chips, Mrs. Johnson was startled when she walked inside and witnessed Mama Lewis and her two granddaughters, Reanna and Cadence, laying on portable tables receiving treatment from three individual masseuses.

"Excuse me, I think I'm in the wrong tent or may have walked through a time portal. Is this the Royal Spa, ladies?" Mrs. Johnson asked jokingly.

"Hi Auntie," the girls greeted and raised their heads while blushing at her words.

"With the Shiatsu finger technique she's using, Yara, it definitely feels that way," Mama Lewis chimed in as Mrs. Johnson lowered to kiss the forehead of both girls before sitting behind the tables, so she couldn't be initially seen.

"You want a massage too, sugar?"

"No Mama Lewis I'm just shocked to see the three of you receiving personal spa treatment at a cookout," Mrs. Johnson exclaimed. "But, given that I had to show Reanna that these fifty-five-year-old hips still rotate like a high school varsity cheerleader, I can understand why she begged you for some body nurturing. Reanna, girl, you dance just like your mother," she laughed while reaching to tickle Reanna's foot.

"No, I don't Auntie, I dance better than my mother," Reanna proclaimed while lifting to turn her head around and smile. "And you know I definitely out-danced you earlier. You know you couldn't compete against me with those old Soul-Train moves." Laughing, as she laid back down.

"Chil', please." Mrs. Johnson retorted while rolling her eyes.

"Yara, I wish I could get pushed around in the grocery store and Walmart with a personal masseuse attending to me. Hell, I've walked enough in life," Mama Lewis interjected, making everybody giggle. Sugar, the girls were supposed to spend the weekend with me, and we were going shopping, to get our hair done, spend the day at the spa, and had intended on going to the gun range before getting our nails painted. But, given that the girls made all A's on their report cards again, your husband is sending Reanna to California in the morning to spend time observing production on a Hollywood movie set, since that's the field she plans on majoring in at college. And Cadence is kicking me to the curb for a trip to Rock City in Tennessee, since she's fascinated with caves and waterfalls. So, given that grandma can't spend time with her babies, we are getting a massage and our nails done here at the park."

"I will never kick you to the curb, grandma, whatever that is," Cadence insisted, raising her head. "I love you grandma." So cute, what she said was truly heartfelt, but she missed the meaning of the idiom that Mama Lewis metaphorically stated.

"Grandma loves you too, baby."

"Congratulations girls, Auntie is seriously proud of you two," Mrs. Johnson stated as she relaxed in the chair, stuffing another shrimp in her mouth. She elected not to say anything about the gun range statement since she didn't feel that a debate was appropriate in front of the girls.

"Thank you, Auntie" the girls replied laying there and enjoying their massages.

Seeing other people smile has always brought an indescribable sense of joy to Mr. Johnson. Being fortunate enough to have money never stripped him of integrity, self-worth, or character. Unlike some people who, following the prideful footsteps of Iblis, accumulate wealth and begin considering their existence more superior to those who are less fortunate, having learned nothing from Fir'aun's arrogance that ultimately led to his death in the Red Sea, they spend extravagantly just to be seen by individuals who offer them nothing beyond worthless attention.

Mr. Johnson has always tried to use his blessings by helping others to effectively reinforce their foundation to be structurally sound, never allowing necessity of money to pose as a bi-product of greed, nor ever losing focus of God's words that he has tattooed on his back as if it were a skin of parchment:

'When God will come in His glory, and all the holy angels with Him, then He will sit on the throne of His glory. All nations will be gathered before Him and He will separate them from one another as a shepherd divides his sheep from the goats. And He will set the sheep on His right hand but the goats on His left. Then the King will say to those on His right hand, come, you blessed of My creation, inherit the kingdom prepared for you from the foundation of the world: for I was hungry and you gave Me food. I was thirsty and you gave me drink, I was a stranger and you welcomed me. 'I was naked, and you clothed me, I was sick and you visited me, I was in prison and you came to me.' Then the righteous will answer Him, saying 'Lord, when did we see you hungry and feed You, or thirsty and gave You drink? When did we see You as a stranger and take you in, or naked and clothe You? Or when did we see You sick, or in prison, and came to You? And the King will answer and say to them, 'Assuredly, I say to you' inasmuch as you did it to one of the least of these of My creation, you did it to Me.' {Matthew 25: 31-40}

Bobbing his head to the music of Kool-Ace performing on stage as he stood beside his brother, discussing the horses at the ranch with a cousin's child in his arms, Mr. Johnson noticed an entourage of ladies walking directly towards them whose faces he did not clearly recognize. He brushed against his brother with a fake laugh to gain his attention, since he seemed to be eyeball raping the women playing volleyball before them in their bikinis. His brother took notice, rubbing his hair and face while straightening his posture as though he was momentarily invisible to all eyes and looking in a bathroom mirror.

"What are you doing? Grooming yourself to go on a date with Tiffany Haddish?" Mr. Johnson asked humorously while shaking his head at his brother's playboy antics.

"I wish! Now that's a dream within a dream bro," he whispered sincerely as the women slowly approached. "I'll retire all the gators to walk barefooted beside her and follow your path of loyalty for Tiffany."

"Please don't do that because I honestly don't think I have enough political persuasion, or money, to bond you out of jail if you were to walk around barefooted bro," Mr. Johnson conveyed, bursting into a casual chuckle. "They would charge you with a war crime, and I definitely don't think Tiffany would talk to you if she saw your feet without socks or a NASA issued protective boot."

"So, you're a stand-up comedian now?" His brother asked while allowing himself to laugh at his words. "And for the record, I'll soak these bad boys in jet fuel day and night if that's what it will take to have Tiffany standing at my side."

"Nothing but a chemical induced dream will ever grant the fantasy, playboy!"

"Excuse me, which one of you gentlemen is Mr. Johnson?" Tina asked politely with her eight girlfriends standing beside her, all attentively shifting their eyes side to side to see which one was going to acknowledge he is the mysterious gentleman she's inquiring of.

Speaking without hesitation, and trying to sound debonair, as his eyes caressed every measure of the women standing in front of him, "We're both Mr. Johnson," his brother admitted while reaching out to grab her hand as a gentleman. Kissing it gently in his uncensored act of being urbane. "If you inform me which one of you ladies, they call Irresistible, then respectfully the Mr. Johnson you seek will no longer be unknown."

Blushing and giggling amongst themselves, they openly acknowledged that they were all called "Irresistible," which Mr. Johnson's brother seemed to unquestionably agree. Granted, he was unable to conceal his lustful attraction, gazing among the entourage.

Lingering upon the extraordinary tale she had heard about the man, Mr. Johnson, and how his appearance was always a pleasurable sight, Tina carefully observed the stature of both gentlemen. She noticed one was wearing a pair of Maison Margiela slacks, an Ermenegido Zegna Couture jacket, a Ralph Lauren tank top, and a pair of Gucci loafers whereas the other was wearing Dolce and Gabbana shorts, a V-neck white tee, and a pair of all white Air Force Ones. Feeling as though her conclusion was the right judgment, she turned to his brother and taunted that they were all vegetarian as there was nothing in the food tents to supplement for them. It was a test his brother would fail by merely opening his mouth.

Unable to stop laughing, as his corny reply centered upon trying to take her and the ladies to a five-star restaurant as compensation, her actions caught both Johnson's off guard. Turning toward the unspoken Mr. Johnson, Tina openly apologized for laughing at his brother's unacceptable Casanova approach, which was amusing, yet unwarranted. "I knew he wasn't you, sir, due to his attire and demeanor. I asked that question to give me confirmation because I was told your compassion for others is quite sincere, yet his reply was motivated by selfish intention."

"There's nothing selfish in appreciating the beauty of a woman, nor seeking the pleasure of getting to know someone, realizing some opportunities are not given twice in a lifetime," his brother immediately countered.

"True sir, however, a man approaches a lady like she's a lady whether it's with his eyes, his body movement, or tongue," Tina replied. "Especially when he respects her and sees the qualities in which he finds appealing, not as an object of thrill or momentary excitement. My father was a pimp, so I recognize recycled game without rendering any attention, sir."

Laughing respectfully at her words as he looked at his brother, "Do I need to call your insurance company so that they can have AAA come help lift your face?" Mr. Johnson chuckled. "I never thought I'd witness a young lady putting you in your place bro, but you must admit, she's absolutely correct. Your game is old and outdated." Smiling as he turned his attention back to her. "How may I help you? Do I seriously need to advise the cooks to prepare some vegetarian plates?"

"No sir! Mr. Johnson, we wanted to thank you in person for inviting us to the cookout and for the full day spa treatment and dinner invitation to your wife's log cabin mountain resort for helping you get your car back. You have no idea how the smallest gesture of kindness brings upon so much joy when you're a college student. If you don't mind, we have something for you, as a respectable way of showing our appreciation for your generosity."

"Young ladies, you all never have to thank me for anything," Mr. Johnson uttered, now recognizing who the entourage of women were. "All thanks and praise belong to God for granting us the ability of enduring His mercy. What school do you all attend?"

Allowing her Asian friend Cindy to speak, she pointed out those who attended Clark Atlanta University and those who attended Spelman, while also stating each individual's name and major as well.

After discovering a little more about the young ladies and their plans after college, which his brother hung on every word spoken while seeking a passageway to gain the attention of any one of them, they presented Mr. Johnson with a unique present, one that softened his heart in a way no material item could. It was a dance routine that was not only unexpected and unbelievably sensational, but so electrifying that even though Kool-Ace and Tru Dillinger had people bobbing and dancing throughout the park as they performed on stage, the young ladies were commanding the eyes of everyone in the park that were fortunate enough to witness their creativity. A choreographed mixture of in-sync salsa, stepping, acrobatics, street, and tribal movement that was beyond mesmerizing, those who were able to record them with their cell phones were uploading their performance to the internet before the young ladies could regain their breath afterwards.

"Baby, that was amazing. Who were those young ladies?" Mrs. Johnson asked Gip as he walked inside the tent moments later with a plate of barbeque beef ribs, grilled shrimp, and three grilled lobster tails.

"College students that assisted Aaron and the guys the other night, love," Gip replied. "I didn't know you were watching them perform. I assumed you would have used that unbelievable distraction to steal more of my shrimp from the grill." He joked as he took a bite of the rib.

"Whatever! What's yours is mine, and what's mine is mine, baby. You belong to me, and never forget that. So, what do I look like stealing from myself?" she effused, giggling as Gip looked at her and shook his head.

"The fact that those young ladies took the time to rehearse that and came here and performed solely for me was unbelievable."

"They truly were baby. I definitely like how the Asian girl and chubby little white girl ended with those tribal moves," Mrs. Johnson continued. "I might try that on you tonight," she leaned to the side and whispered in his ear, words that sparked a stare of heated affection and love between the two of them.

"Sheri called and said she will not be able to make it. Her and Randle are doing their own cookout."

"What? That doesn't make any sense!" Mrs. Johnson roared. "What sense does it make to have a personal cookout when your family is having a gathering? She knows I dislike that no good freeloader she considers a man because of the way he blatantly disrespects and abuses her on the regular, but I accept him out of respect for her. I literally can't believe she would do this," Mrs. Johnson cried, allowing frustration to build inside of her, while adverting her eyes and reaching for her phone to call Sheri.

Realizing that his wife had allowed the news to upset her, he placed his plate on the table and leaned over to her as she attempted to dial Sheri's number. Gently grabbing her hand and caressing with affection, he pulled her into his arms and kissed her on the forehead before whispering, "I love you and that's all that matters right now. Baby, Sheri is grown, and we have to respect the decisions she makes. Under no circumstances do I accept their relationship, because as a father, I cry internally as do you."

"But baby this is family, it's bad enough he verbally and physically disrespects our daughter, but now he is trying to bridge a wall between us as well, it seems. This is unacceptable!"

"Yara, we can't fight her every battle, especially her love life. Sheri must learn to love, respect, and appreciate herself in a manner that parental love can't teach. Everyone loves differently and requires to be loved differently. Scolding her is not going to get her to open her eyes to see what is before her, nor constantly ridiculing Randle or her regarding that matter. Baby you know this because you have supported too many women groups on abuse."

"I know baby, but when it's your own child, then everything seems so different. The emotions become more overwhelming and that's what I'm having a constant issue with. I wanted her here today, especially given the fact that Penélope invited this remarkable artist from Chicago, named Jelani, to meet her."

"Yara, do you feel that?"

"Feel what, baby? You know I don't even feel it when you be huffing, puffing, and sweating." Mrs. Johnson joked, slightly confused, and wondering if he was trying to be sexual by not feeling him pressing or rising against her.

"My heartbeat, Yara! It's saying I love you and I'm all you need. Baby our greatest weapon is prayer, and to support her without conditions or judgmental views. Sheri and I talked, I told her how I feel about the situation, so I'm pretty sure she just decided to enjoy the precious time in which they have left together."

The given weight of his words caught Mrs. Johnson off guard as she breathed within his arms smiling and wondering if that meant what she thought it meant in regards to Randle, given that Yara knew her husband so well.

"Baby, look around for a moment. Everyone has forgotten about their everyday responsibilities and stressful issues. There's no significant value in being upset for any reason because there's so much love here. Look at how my sister is over there entertaining with those girls as though she's still the Queen of double Dutch, your cousin is playing dodgeball even though he's too drunk to stand, or the homeless strangers in line receiving plates. Even more so baby, my wannabe gunslinger mom is pampering the girls with spa treatment and hasn't shot any one thus far, and you know she has spy guns probably hidden in her bloomers." This actually sprouted laughter in both of them as she pressed her head into his chest.

Rising with his wife and grabbing a lobster tail from her plate, Mr. Johnson startled Mrs. Johnson by slapping her affectionately on her booty and blowing a kiss.

"I need a three-dollar bump of that, baby." He whispered in her ear.

"The way I feel right now, you probably wouldn't get but two strokes before you exploded," Mrs. Johnson joked sarcastically, murmuring and rolling her eyes, before eyeing her husband with a devilish look of seduction for trying her with his statement. "So, go out there and do something safe before you find yourself walking around here looking as you do at home."

Smirking to himself, "Well, I had something unforgettable planned for you, but since you want to talk trash but can't stand on it and secretly linger in sorrow over our daughter desiring to be with her boy toy instead of us, then I'll just wait till some other time to try and put a smile on your face," he expressed while walking out of the tent and trying to hide the smile that was widely visible.

"Baby! Gip!" Yara yelled while chasing after him like a child on the playground.

Mrs. Johnson followed Gip across the park repeating the words, "Stop playing baby, I want my gift." creating laughter, as others stared at them playing.

Mr. Johnson continued to playfully avoid responding to his wife as he headed to the stage, smirking while she teasingly pushed his shoulder, popped him in the head, and grabbed his arm even though she wasn't strong enough to stop his pursuit. Out of love and true playfulness, Mrs. Johnson jumped on Gip's back and covered his eyes with her hands while he stumbled about and refused to expose his secret.

"Reanna! Cadence! Come get your auntie!" he yelled while laughing and pulling her hands away so that he could clearly see.

Neither niece came to his rescue; with their nail polish being wet, but they enjoyed the silliness as much as all the others who watched and laughed, as they allowed their love to be a spectacle of joy. Walking up the stage steps, Mr. Johnson secured his wife in the proper carrying grip so as to prevent her from falling. Signaling for the microphone after releasing his wife and requesting that the DJ silence the music, Mr. Johnson spoke into the mic requesting the attention of all family and friends, thereby birthing wandering thoughts in everyone, especially his wife, whom remained clueless of what he was about to say and the type of surprise he had for her. The purity of his love is all she needed, but she wanted whatever gift he had for her as well.

"I'm glad to see that everyone is enjoying themselves," Mr. Johnson spoke into the microphone as he walked back and forth across the stage while scanning the park. "Nothing is more important than family, and true friendship is a branch of family as well. Seeing you all utilize this time to strengthen our relations with one another, while at the same time strengthening our bond of love, respect, and appreciation for one another without discord is priceless, awe inspiring. Everything I do in life is to show God that I'm thankful for all His uncountable blessings, especially, the irreplaceable one that He bestowed in my life thirty years ago. I walked on this stage to acknowledge in a special way how much I love my wife, but seeing you all have inspired me to acknowledge and show that I love you all as well."

A few minutes after texting something on his phone a black Mercedes-AMG G63 Yachting Limited Edition with insane decadence began to drive across the park grass as Mr. Johnson spoke, stopping by the stage, as it birthed curiosity in everyone. Was Mr. Johnson about to give this to his wife as a new gift or was he about to give it away out of pure kindness? Unable to see inside, due to the heavily tinted windows and the angle it was parked, Mrs. Johnson stood on stage smiling with more intensity than everyone and imagining herself driving the new toy through the city. She had assured herself that the G-Wagen was her new gift, even without Gip acknowledging it.

"For those who are very fortunate to know me closely, it's no secret that my 1961 five window Corvette is my pride and joy, much like a precious collector's red diamond but not because of its rareness, its speed, or unique body style. I'm not going to say that Yara chased me like a Roadrunner thirty years ago because she wanted to be seen in the car, yet for those who assume that view as their theory, then it's okay, because we know the truth. But in all honesty, this was the first car of mine in which Yara rode in, kiss me in, and in that car, she revealed her love for me the very first time. We were at the Starlight drive-in trying to … you know … Uhmmmm talk," Mr. Johnson toyed, with a hint of sexual emphasis as the crowd of grown-ups who caught on erupted in instant laughter.

"After thirty years, I no longer need to hold on to this sentimental attachment, because I have the priceless jewel itself, and that's your amazing love, baby," he cajoled slowly turning around to face his wife. "I love you. So, before I show my wife how much I love her, I'm going to give away the only baby I have that's replaceable in my life. And no — You don't have to worry about packing your bags love," Mr. Johnson addressed to his wife jokingly as laughter burst out again. Turning again to gaze upon her, "You're IRRE-placeable, not RE-placeable!" Which caused Yara to illuminate the park with her smile as the sun's rays reflected creating a laser show of spectacular proportion. Reaching into his pocket and raising the keys to the Corvette in the air, "The car goes to the first person who can tell me the name of the individual in the scriptures who discovered the Zamzam well, and how it was discovered."

Mr. Johnson was very surprised to see so many scripture quoters among his family and friends looking around clueless, as if he just asked them to name the eight angels holding God's throne, especially, his auntie who spends every given moment at church or talking about the bible. Watching individuals gossip in groups, while some attempted to google it on their phones, and devoted church members guessed out of a complete lack of religious knowledge was starting to have him wonder what people were actually doing when they go to God's house for bible study or worship.

Bursting out of the tent barefooted and not caring about her freshly polished toes or the plate of barbeque ribs she knocked out of a strangers hand, Reanna ran toward the stage as though she was being chased by three Australian terriers, yelling at the top of her lungs, "Uncle, I know the answer." Hoofing and puffing like the unseen but manifestation of Thoroughbred horses' legs and hooves in her lower extremities, Reanna yelled, "Hagar (may God be pleased with her)," as she reached the top of the stage steps and fell into auntie Yara's arms without moving any further.

"Uncle the answer is Hājar (may God be pleased with her). She was the second wife of prophet Ibrahim (may God be pleased with him) and Ishmael's (may God be pleased with him) mother. She was the first lady of history to use a girdle. The first wife, Sarah (RA) asked prophet Ibrahim (RA) to get rid of her, and he guided them to a sacred valley and left them. After all the stored water for her and Ishmael (RA) was used up, she ran between the two mountains As-Safa and Al-Marwah seven times looking to see someone who may help to assist them in food and water. But after never seeing no one, God revealed an angel to her, and the angel started digging the earth with his heel and his wing, and the water spouted up from the ground. The water still flows today, it has no source origin and is considered the purest water on earth."

Not believing that his sixteen-year-old niece just answered his question out of all the people in the park, Mr. Johnson walked over and hugged her. Then he joked by saying, given that she doesn't have a license at the moment, he would just buy her a monthly bus pass for the year. Seeing the reaction on her face was priceless to him, he just kissed her forehead and fulfilled his promise by handing her the keys.

Smiling like a president on new money, Mrs. Johnson was waiting for the key fob of the SUV to be placed in her hand. A woman of patience, she was, generally speaking, yet being anxious for a big girl toy was also a strong attribute that she possessed. Being cool, calm and collected about a gift that she anticipated just wasn't her strong suit. With Mr. Johnson walking towards her after escorting Reanna off the stage and whispering in her ear, "I love you," she couldn't believe that after thirty years of loving a man who has surprised her in every way possible, butterflies still fluttered inside.

"Yara, I love you," Mr. Johnson promulgated into the microphone as he pulled her into his arms.

Without saying another word, as though his statement was the signal, the white smoke of dry ice creeped across the stage, covering their lower legs and feet, synchronized with dancing multicolored lights, and the Kenny Lattimore song "*If I Lose My Woman*" started serenading clearly with the aid of Peavey and Earthquake Sound DJ-Quake 4x4-inch Array Speakers. Two phenomenal dances ascended the stage, moving in perfect harmony to every word, defining the essence of love through their theatrical movements as the words were cried over a melody.

Mrs. Johnson couldn't hold back the tears of joy that were falling upon her face. It was so spectacular and compelling that many in the park dedicated the performance to their mates as they stood in awe, even as Mr. Johnson was opening more of his heart to his wife.

She hugged and kissed him as though they were on the shores of Bora Bora before saying, "I love you." Mrs. Johnson had never heard that song before and literally couldn't believe that Gip had her crying in such a way that she couldn't stop. "Baby, that was beautiful and as long as God grants me life to praise Him, you will never lose me," she assured breathing upon his chest as family, friends, and strangers in the park continued to applaud the beauty of what he just displayed for Yara.

"I love you too, baby," Mr. Johnson expressed, guiding her out to the center of the stage. "Quite fortunately, I'm not finished yet," he stated into the microphone, which caused the clapping to slowly stop. "Back up please!"

As commanded, the G-Wagen began to roll backwards until it was directly in front of the stage. Mrs. Johnson was still unable to clearly see inside, due to the way it was parked. All four doors of the vehicle opened, and four silky cream legs donning black stilettos stepped out, revealing four beautiful Russian models wearing white semi-sheer one shoulder women's cut out bodycon mini dresses, combing their hair with their fingers, as they all walked to the back of the wagon and stood side by side.

Racking her brain for answers she didn't have, Mrs. Johnson stood on stage trying to figure out what her husband was up to, and why he selected four young hot toothpick size heffas to escort her new toy. Why not four half naked oiled up muscle builders for the women? Why did they park so far away, when she could have climbed in at the steps?

"Yara, for thirty years you have been the light and breath within my heart. My strength and my pillow. To me nothing of life can measure up to you, nor replace you. I ask God every day to guide my footsteps and to nurture me with the ability of constantly proving without failure that I'm grateful of His mercy and the pleasure of being able to love you." Falling to his knees and causing Mrs. Johnson's eyes to stretch wide from shock, surprise, and appreciation, he continued. "Baby, you have given me thirty years, and I ask that you marry me again and give me the joy of loving you an entire lifetime."

Shocked, and not caring about wiping away the tears that were falling from her eyes, "Yes! Yes," Mrs. Johnson cried as Gip rose from kneeling to hug and kiss his wife.

Turning her to the G-Wagen and raising the microphone to his mouth, Mr. Johnson asked the four ladies to bring his wife's gift.

Smiling at the thought of having another wedding and getting a new prestigious SUV, Mrs. Johnson felt as though she was suspended in a dream. She assumed her new ring was hidden in the back of the SUV, given that Gip didn't reveal it as he was kneeling, and the ladies opened the rear door after being advised to bring her long awaited surprise. Mesmerized by the enormity of it all, Mrs.

Johnson didn't even notice the two guys standing behind her holding twenty-four long stemmed roses each. One held red roses and the other all white. Yara had no idea that when the rear door opened, her first-born son, who had told her a few hours earlier that he was in London, would be the gift in the G-Wagen.

"I love you," she purred to her husband, seeming to squeeze the air out of his lungs until Terry ascended the stage.

So, engulfed in the sight of him, she cared nothing about the ring box in her son's hand. All she wanted at that moment was him in her arms. "I've missed you so much, Terry," Mrs. Johnson said while squeezing him with every measure of life inside of her.

"I've missed you too, Mom!"

CHAPTER 12

Hearing the enchanting sounds of a foreign tongue as he opened his eyes, Terry smiled seeing Svetlana in the glares of his peripheral standing beside the bed while sliding on her green lace thong panties. Turning his head to admire the beauty of her long silky suntanned legs, small pink nipples, and skin that seemed to radiate in the sunlight piercing through the shades was by far more enticing than the membranes of the retina.

"доброе утро, Terry," Svetlana said good morning with her sexy Russian accent. Standing before him resembling the essence of pure magnetism, "The girls are in the shower playing if you have the energy to join them."

Terry rose up in bed, stretching as he responded to her greeting and lingering in thought on the limits of ecstasy in which the girls took his body beyond last night, before falling asleep in satisfaction. Playfully pulling her into his arms, he placed his mouth on the soft curve of her tit and started vacuum sucking her nipple while birthing internal waves of bliss as he moved her panties aside and pushed his index finger straight into the depths of her jewel box. Dripping into his palm with every gentle stroke, her whispers echoed in the morning silence, intensifying the desire to feel him pulsate inside her tightness. Svetlana pushed him back into the bed, quickly retrieved a condom from the box on the nightstand while stroking him to an erection that needed not her touch to stimulate, then seductively adorned it using her mouth before mounting him.

With the thickness of Terry's dick expanding the tight walls of her foreign pussy, Svetlana rocked back-n-forth slowly until he was completely inside of her, deep inside to the point it felt like he was making a new passage in her stomach. Grabbing his wrist with a tight grip, she raised them above his head using her body as leverage to press them into the bed as she rapidly bounced on his erection, smacking her cheeks against his thighs which each thrust. Controlling with a sense of dominance that seemingly caused more blood to flow into his erection, she could feel the growth in his width and length.

Pushing him deeper and deeper as though she was chasing the essence of a cocaine high, she stared him in the eyes without allowing him to kiss her in any manner or nibble on her nipples that dangled before his mouth as she stroked his dick with even greater intensity. When she noticed from their reflection in the mirror that the girls had gotten out of the shower and were now standing in the doorway watching her mimic the voluptuous hip movements of an urban stripper as she was reaching the tipping point of her climax, Svetlana then let go of his wrist, placed her hands on the sides of Terry's face, and kissed him passionately as her nectar splashed upon the rapid submergence of his hardness.

To Terry, Svetlana was the most exotic of the four models. It wasn't just her eyes that lured him into lust or the fact that her curves had more definition than the others that had him gravitating to her body, rather it was something about the way her skin felt, her wetness smelled, tasted so exotic, and the way she sounded when he was inside of her was so distinct that it was an igniting aphrodisiac. They intimately kissed with his hardness still massive and submerged inside of Svetlana as her viscous nectar gradually oozed onto his balls.

Turned on and unable to continue watching as an admiring onlooker, Valentina dropped her towel to the floor, leaving the bathroom doorway and easing her tanned slender sexiness onto the bed between his legs and pulling Terry's erection out of Svetlana. After removing the cum soaked condom with her mouth, she opened her throat to all of his hardness, savoring their passion with gagging strokes while getting turned on even more by watching Svetlana's pussy drip like a leaky faucet onto Terry's stomach.

With seven hours to spare before Ethel, Svetlana, Valentina, and Helena were scheduled to board their flight back to Omsk, Russia, they were once again entwined in an orgy that puts a ménage a trois to shame and rewrote the dictionary's definition of pleasure. With the room sounding like Kitty Paradise, the girls climaxed repeatedly on his lips, tongue, fingers, and dick as though they were playing musical chairs. Whether Terry was causing one to climax by rodeo, bouncing her in the air, doggy-style on the bed, floor, pressed against the wall with one leg vertical, allowing one to ride him, or being on top himself, he fantasized about Demi with everyone except Svetlana. With her, their chemistry ignited passion that didn't feel like a passing sexual throb.

After showering, he treated the ladies to a historic breakfast at the Busy Bee Cafe on Martin Luther King Jr. Dr., before escorting them back to the Ritz Carlton to secure their property and drive them straight to the airport. A selfish part of Terry wished Svetlana didn't have to leave. He wanted to explore a deeper realm of pleasure with her mind and body. He liked the way her oral sex made him squeeze his cheeks and arch his back with her strokes.

Promising to fly to Russia for a visit within a week or to fly her back to America, Terry kissed Svetlana as the girls stood outside the SUV, blushing with admiration. He eased his hand beneath her sundress and thrusted his fingers inside of her one last time before she exited his vehicle because he couldn't get enough of her exotic taste.

Now that everyone knew he was back in the city, his phone was blowing up, vibrating to the extent that it had become a mobile massager in his pocket. It felt good hugging and seeing certain family members at the cookout that he hadn't talked to or seen in six years. He hated lying to his mom about still being in London, but he couldn't spoil his father's surprise, and the expression on his mother's face upon witnessing him was priceless.

Pulling into Pikes Nursery to grab the flowers he ordered for his grandma, Terry texted Demi, *"May I have the pleasure of laying rose petals beneath your feet today?"* Constantly checking his phone each time, it vibrated until he reached his grandma's house. Terry was a little disappointed that she never responded to the text.

Grabbing the marsh roses from the back of the SUV, and placing them on the flower bed wall, Terry smiled seeing Mama Lewis walking down the porch steps looking like an urban diva, donning a pink Nike T-shirt, black Nike jogging pants, and a pair of pink Air Max's.

"Heeeeeey baby," Mama Lewis greeted while opening her arms to hug her grandson. "You're earlier than I actually expected. How are you feeling?"

"Hey grandma! I'm blessed, granted God's mercy," Terry replied while squeezing her with a gentle bear hug. "I'm just happy to see you again and I hope you baked me one of your pineapple and mango cakes, because my stomach misses it almost as much as I miss you."

"Baby, you know I have." She admitted loosening her embrace.

Grandma, what's that?" Terry queried hitting something hard against her back waistline as he released her from his hug.

"Just my Beretta Px4 Storm, baby," Mama Lewis answered, gradually turning to the side and lifting her shirt to show him her new husband with no benefits.

"Your what!?" Terry shouted back in disbelief, not believing he just heard those words come out of her mouth without a sense of thought given.

"Baby, with an unethical President like ours and these kids senselessly shooting up buildings merely to see who can become the most famous child killer of this generation, I'm staying strapped! You must have forgotten — this Atlanta, boy, and you can make bail for anything, so I'm shooting first and bonding out later," Mama Lewis vowed, being completely serious regarding her intentions for survival, while grabbing a tray of flowers.

Laughing just at hearing the words flow from her lips, Terry was seriously wondering had his grandma taken the wrong medicine that morning.

"Grandma, give me that .40 cal before you hurt yourself," Terry insisted while attempting to remove the gun from her back waistline, only to have his hand slapped away with a defensive strike which she learned from One Eye that caused a jolt of pain to shoot up his arm.

"Boy, you better stay in your place before I go IP Woman on you. Grandma can teach you a few tricks these days. Boy, I can take this gun apart, clean it, put it back together, and unload the clip before you could load bullets in yours. Don't make me take you to the gun range and embarrass you, baby."

"Whatever, Grandma," he yapped rubbing his wrist. "You couldn't outshoot me if both hands were tied behind my back and I was double blindfolded," Terry boasted, bursting into laughter and not believing his grandma was acting gangster now.

"Terry, things have changed since you were last here," Mama Lewis informed, walking into the house. "You better get you a flame thrower and stop thinking you're the Teflon Don, 'cause these new generation kids have lost they damn mind. There's no more fist fighting for respect like in my days of growing up, all they do now is shoot. The fact you look like a Marvel action figure won't intimidate them. They are senselessly robbing and shooting for cellphones now, not money, baby. Hell, the way you are walking around here looking, one of 'em may rob you for your body," she smirked as she walked toward the house holding a tray.

Spending time with his grandma had always been an enjoyable and unpredictable one. There's never a dull moment in her presence. Terry was flabbergasted to learn that the woman who used to spend her time at home cooking personal meals for the homeless three days a week and was an advocate for abused women, sometimes paying out of her pocket to shelter those who truly wanted to escape from their barbaric mates, was now talking about how the police rolled up just as she was about to shoot a guy in the grocery store parking lot for accidentally hitting her car when he was trying to run over a couple gay guys. And then there's the incident where she emptied an entire magazine in the air for fun just to scare away two drug addicts who tried to break into her shed.

Since Terry hadn't visited his grandma in years, even though they video chatted regularly, he had made it a priority to spend quality time with her, suspending and rescheduling his time with others. Bringing a change of clothes, he worked in the garden with her as he did while growing up and helped to plant the marsh roses beside her elephant's ears. After showering, listening to her speak about things that have been going on with the family, of which had been kept secret, witnessing the unbelievable licensed mini-arsenal lying beside her bed, and eating a quarter portion of the cake that she baked fresh with milk for his delight, he then took Mama Lewis up on her gun range challenge.

He had always considered himself a marksman but lost three-thousand dollars underestimating his grandma at the gun range. Confused at how a seventy-six-year-old lady can hit constant head shots at thirty and fifty yards away without blinking, using special glasses, or any laser devices had him even more puzzled about her transformation. Was this truly his grandma or a robot clone playing the part for some particular reason?

Noticing that Demi hadn't responded to any of the three text messages which he sent as they exited the highway en route to the ranch, Terry called out of developing a sense of concern, immediately after hanging up with his sister. He utilized the SUV's voice feature of the infotainment system instead of placing the phone to his ear.

"Alrighty, Terry?" Demi answers the phone with her sexy accent, teasing the frequencies as her distinct voice traversed as though she were within breathing range of Terry.

"Now that I have the pleasure of hearing your voice, I can suppress my worrying thoughts and smile instead," Terry continued. "I'd honestly feel a lot better if I could breathe the very air that you breathe."

"Terry, every woman wants a man who's charming, yet we also desire a man who's sexy just by being genuine. I told you that you're accustomed to women that fall for the ideal of you. I'm a woman, not a groupie," Demi pointed out.

"If I didn't see you as a woman, then I wouldn't open my thoughts to you nor strive for the pleasure of knowing who you are. Everything I say and do is quite genuine."

"Cute, but you sent me text messages instead of picking up the phone and calling, which — a gentleman would have done," Demi rebutted. "I can't teach you the etiquette of approaching a woman or holding a woman's attention like a man, but I can advise when you're falling short. A woman wants to be a man's lover, not his mother."

"Given that I know nothing of your schedule or routine, and sleep is precious, I was trying to be respectful by not invading your time because you worked last night," Terry assured that he was being considerate. "But given that you're on the phone now, may I have the pleasure of seeing you today? Would you like to come to the ranch and ride with me?"

"Now that's intriguing, Terry. You were respecting my time by texting, which kept waking me up instead of calling which would have done the very same. Earlier you expressed laying rose petals beneath my feet. Whereas now, you are just asking to see me. Intriguing, but unfortunately, I'm using this time to escape from everything, everyone but myself. I had a long night and have to work tonight as well," Demi proclaimed.

Not expecting to hear those words, and not wanting his genuineness to be taken as a repeated line of charm, Terry acknowledged that he understood and would check in on her later before disconnecting the call. Mama Lewis sat in the passenger seat of the truck laughing like Mike Epps was performing and snapped pictures of him.

"What's so funny grandma? And why are you taking pictures?" Terry asked while glancing at her and parking the G-Wagen on his aunt's zoysia sod at grandma's command, just so that she could laugh at her daughter's facial expression and hear her go off while blatantly forgetting her religious principles.

"I'm laughing 'cause I didn't raise you to be a cry baby for a woman's attention. I raised you to be a man. It seems like you've gotten so caught up in those trollops falling for the idea of you and your body that you have forgotten a woman's worth. You spoke to her with no self-confidence, no backbone, and I took the picture to post on Penélope's social media page so everyone can see how an international playboy looks when a real woman strips him of his identity. I like her!"

"Stop playing, Grandma," Terry uttered as they both exited the G-Wagen and walked across the perfectly groomed lawn to the door. "No woman can strip me of anything."

"Boy please! You sounded like your boneless father when he was chasing after your mother, more like an uncontrollable meth addict. Now that is something, I wish I had on video 'cause he was a sweet pussy," Mama Lewis said while laughing as she lingered in memory. "I don't know why you won't settle down with Penélope and give me some grand babies instead of traveling the world and having sex with every no-good hussy who smiles at you. There comes a point in life when you should want something that's irreplaceable, something money can't buy, Terry. Keep on and you're going to be on one of those health videos talking about how you're a proud recipient of the blue waffle disease or something incurable. Grandma loves you, baby, but you definitely not coming in my house with one of them walkin' dead zombie infections," giggling as she brushed against his arms with genuine affection.

"Grandma if things were different with Penélope, which you know exactly want I mean, then I would have married her a long time ago, but we cherish our closeness and respect one another with understanding."

"Whatever chil'! The both of you are into that new age nasty shit, so I don't see what the problem is," Mama Lewis exclaimed while ringing the doorbell. "You lay with all them women, and she got a girlfriend, so the two of y'all nasty asses can share and give me a grandbaby. Both of y'all love women, so I don't understand what the problem is, especially since her little lick-me partner is a cute young lady who, by the way, just happens to be your type. Sounds like a match made in heaven to me. I want some grandbabies, boy. You get with both of them, and Grandma gets a two for one, you hear me? You may think I'm kidding but let me ask you a question. Do you even know what you really want besides some Amoxicillin to cure a venereal disease?" Mama Lewis hinted, wondering why the disconnect and bursting into laughter.

Terry stood laughing and shaking his head at the words of his grandma as his little cousin Cadence opened the door and jumped in his arms, excited to see him. "Yes, I know what I want," Terry answered, following his grandma in the house while squeezing his little cousin with love. "I've missed you Cadence."

"I've missed you too, Terry," Cadence replied laying her head on his shoulder and asking if he will ride with her before they leave.

"Yes sweetie! Grandma, I want her to be a virgin who is wise like a married woman or a married woman who is innocent like a virgin. She should be sweet when she is near and splendid when she is at a distance. She should have lived a life of luxury, then afflicted with poverty so that she could have the manners of the rich and the humility of the poor. When we gather wealth, we should be as the people of the world, and when we become poor, we should be as the people of the Hereafter."

They stopped as they entered the living room only to be surprised to see no one present besides Reanna, who was trying to dance like Beyoncé on some video game. Mama Lewis turned to him, raising her right hand to grip his chin with a sense of aggression while looking as serious as possible into his eyes before stating, "I'm not into that incest stuff, Terry."

"What, Grandma?" he stated confused while laughing at Reanna's uncoordinated movements.

"The woman you spoke of wanting boy, is a reflection of me. And seeing as how there ain't no replica of grandma on this earth, you can't have me because I ain't into no incestuous mess." Mama Lewis doesn't care what comes out of her mouth, straight talk with no shame, laughing and sitting on the sofa to admire Reanna bouncing around like she was born with Nohipsatall syndrome. "Reanna, I don't know where you and your mother received y'all's rhythm from, seriously. Both of you dance like a white woman with no hips who grew up on a farm in the backwoods without a television and grooved to the sounds of a John Deere tractor as though it was country music. Instead of dancing to Beyoncé, you should try to imitate a walrus, given the fact you move exactly like one," Mama Lewis joked while laughing as Reanna giggled and paid her no mind.

"Whatever Grandma," Terry defended while choosing not to indulge in her silliness. "Where is everyone Cadence?" He asked, escorting her out of the room and into the kitchen with her still in his arms to fix them both something to drink.

"Everyone left about thirty minutes ago," she answered. "They left in my mom's car, but I don't know where they went, I was playing in the pool at the time. Terry, while you were away, your mom bought me a horse, and I named her, 'Eye of Paradise' because her eyes are so pretty. She's an Andalusian breed. You can ride her if you want, I don't mind."

"That's a very unique name, sweetie. I like it," Terry complimented as he placed her on the kitchen counter.

Reaching for his cellphone, he dialed his mother's number. "Melody of my Heart was the name of my first horse. She was a Shire breed with midnight black hair that looked like Persian silk in sunlight, and the hair on her legs was black. She was beautiful — annnd fast, but not as fast as you," he stroked her ego, kissing her on the forehead, while attempting to tickle her. "I was in love with Janelle Monáe, and I wouldn't disrespect her by directly naming a horse after her, so I named her that because her voice was the melody of my heart, but I called the horse 'Melody,' for short."

"I don't know who that is, but it sounds like she's a star in your eyes. That's cute, but you're not in love with the melody girl anymore, so, who do you love now?" Cadence asked as his mom answered the phone.

"I love you," Terry whispered in her ear, shifting his attention to his mom and pouring them some cranberry juice.

Pleasantly surprised, "I love you, too," she whispered back.

"Mom, why did y'all leave the ranch?" Terry asked. "Grandma and I are here. Is everything okay?"

"I called you twice, but your line went to your voicemail both times," Mrs. Johnson advised with a sense of sadness that could be distinguished in her voice. "No, everything is not okay. We're at Piedmont Hospital right now. Your uncle girlfriend's son was brutally beaten and repeatedly burned in the face with a cigar this morning. We were told that he was wearing a kufi with his outfit, and three cousins of the young lady he was dating assumed that he was Muslim. So, as it goes with hate crimes, they beat him to a pulp and a state of unconsciousness, before leaving him to die. An elderly white man walking his dog found him lying beside the apartment dumpster and brought him to the hospital. He just came out of surgery, so we're waiting to talk to him ... WHAT!? Terry, let me call you back, the police just walked in and they are talking about arresting him for assault for some reason."

"What the ...! Okay, Mom. Keep me posted. I love you," Terry said, hanging up, but his mom was already disconnected.

Sharing the news with his grandma seemed to ignite something intoxicating inside of her because the blood vessels in her eyes seemed to burst, and without her moving any muscles in her face, one could clearly tell that she was very angry without expressing any thoughts. Not having a connection to the young man or his family to garner any type of true emotional feelings besides a sense of sorrow, Terry and Cadence spent the next hour riding the horses through the trails and mildly galloping through the field.

Being that this was the first time he had been on a horse in six years, he wanted to run his father's horse, Sunshine, like old times after giving Cadence back her Eye of Paradise, sensing she really wanted to stretch her legs. But with Cadence being so young, he couldn't risk putting her well-being in jeopardy, especially with the setting of the sun on the horizon becoming visible and her not being strong enough to maintain a sense of balance if the horse got spooked or lost its footing.

Before returning to the house to show him the science project which Penélope helped her to receive an A on, Cadence allowed him to enter the secret cave her and Penélope built, behind the stable, made with a six person occupancy Coleman tent. It was the same stable where Penélope had carved on the wall that she loved the both of them more than anything. These elements caused his heart to cry without tears falling.

Driving Mama Lewis home, Terry never expected that she'd scold him the entire way about settling down and being the respectable man she raised him to be instead of continuously traveling the world, wasting time chasing heffas that can never wear the shoes of a real woman, housewife or not. Listening to her speak of a woman's virtue, honor and worth caused him to ponder in ways he had never opened his mind to. Realizing the fact that she was actually correct that no man could achieve the true definition of himself without being nurtured and cultivated by a good woman, Terry cruised through the city while thinking in-depth about his life.

Terry felt a sense of loneliness after being admonished with her stern words. Exploring the depths of ecstasy with different women was always a pleasure in and of itself, even when masturbating would have been more stimulating. Yet he questioned, how a man could define true love and happiness, success in life, or moralistic pleasure without a family?

Demi's innocence was spellbinding. Discovering the woman within the beauty of an angel was riveting, but wrestling with the thought of having to wait 'til marriage to taste her sweetness given her vow that her body was on reserve for the exclusive pleasures of her husband, had Terry subconsciously asking God if she was worth giving everything up for. Was she truly a woman of moral beliefs or just speaking like many others who disregard their principles once you show them some attention? Only she'd vowed to die before dishonoring her family of strong cultural and moral values with such shame. Lacking a destination, Terry cruised through the twilight while lingering more and more on the thought of having someone to love him for who he was and what he offers as a whole without discord. With the essence of his true love only being exposed to Penélope, the thought of bridging something undeniable and unbreakable with a woman of Demi's virtue became more intriguing than the mystery of what her hidden lips would taste and feel like.

The more he drove through the city observing the activities and gauging the feel of the nightlife with no particular place to go and reflecting on Demi each time he viewed an appealing woman standing in a club line or sauntering on the sidewalk, Terry realized Mama Lewis' words had him feeling sensitive and vulnerable. Sitting at the red light as an entourage of ladies crossed the street with their heels sounding like trotting horses against the concrete, he spoke openly to God while caressing their bodies with his eyes.

God, if it's time for me to grow up and be the man you gave me life to be, then allow me to be invisible to these beautiful women you created. But if you desire for me to be the joy of these women tonight, then allow at least one of them to notice me, and by Your will, I'll make their night unforgettable. All seven women sauntered past his G-Wagen Yachting Limited Edition without raising their eyes to even see who was inside to his disbelief, so he drove home, wondering if that was just coincidental or truly an answer from God. Terry had put out a fleece with God, assuming that God still interacts with us as He did in the Old Testament.

For the first time in life, Terry found himself sitting alone beneath the stars and staring at his own reflection under a moonlit sky. Unable to stop pondering on what transpired after speaking openly to God, he cooked some lamb and ricotta meatball subs while imagining what life would be like with Demi. Terry had always hidden his loneliness in the acceptance of women but couldn't channel his thoughts to a desired plateau. With an aimless mental disposition, he sat alone in his living room with the realization that he had no one of genuine sincerity to truly talk to and appreciate him for who he is. He had no one to talk to if he wanted to escape the trials of life's realities. A feeling in which he only felt subconsciously, acting as a comforting pillow for everyone else, had him feeling sad and realizing it was time to change his ways.

The playboy lifestyle allowed him to exist as an eidolon, but he actually wanted to know what love was beyond the pillars of a dream. Janelle Monáe and Penélope were all his heart cherished and registered true unconditional love for, yet neither was truly a significant part of his everyday life. Unable to stop thinking of Demi, listening to *"I Don't Want To Be A Player No More"* by Joe, surprisingly playing on the Quiet Storm, Terry went to his closet and put on his Georgia Bulldogs jersey, grabbed and turned his Georgia hat to the back so that the dog face logo was visible, then he Facetimed Demi hoping she'd pick up.

"Hi Terry! This is definitely a surprise," Demi grinned while observing him in his gear. "I assume you consider yourself very snatched right now."

"Snatched?"

"Cute."

"Oh ... No, I consider myself blessed because I am so fortunate to witness myself in your eyes, even if only momentarily."

"Well that's cute too, but to witness and existing are two different things, Terry. Many witness themselves in my eyes every day, but they spark no meaning or significance for me. When you actually exist as my true reflection, then, at that moment, consider yourself blessed because everyone would see you, even though they're only looking at me."

"So smooth, crafty, and effortlessly stated from the heart. That's refreshing. Enough said. I called because I want to talk openly to you without hiding behind a persona. Yes, I'm everything you may profile me to be, but I want to prove that your trust and acceptance, I'll never trivialize or betray. Demi, I recognize the extraordinary woman you are without opening my eyes, hearing the soft whispers of your voice, or being so fortunate as to breathe in your ambiance, because your grace is timeless; and your integrity bridges life with a deep, strong river of meaning. I desire to see you because actions cannot be measured by words. I want you to look in my eyes when I convey why I'm man enough to be the one who electrifies your smile, streams your interest and attention span, cultivates your inner weaknesses, and never neglects your needs.

"If I must crawl, then know it's inevitable that one day I shall stand. I'm man enough not to fail at making sure you are the most significant priority within my path of travel. I'm asking to see you before you go home because I recognize your worth. I want to hear you, I mean really hear how your day started, what you endured mentally, and how you'd like for it to begin when the sun rises. I'd like to share the same with you concerning my day. In order to take a step forward, I need you to look backwards with me for a moment."

"I'm going straight home after work Terry with no detours or guests. Your past, I'm not concerned with because neither of us can change anything of the past. Plus, no ex of yours can stand in my shoes. I see you and accept you for who you are in this moment. Yes, I'm mindful of the fact that you can blink your eye and a woman may appear, yet it doesn't seed me with immaturity or cause me to feel insecure. The depth of your intellect sparked my interest in you, not the charm of Casanova you were trying to personify and maybe still are. Terry, as I've made it clear to you, my mind, heart, and body will only be given to my husband. So, only your actions right here and now matter, not those of yesterday. If you want to see me, then you'll make it happen without me holding your hand and guiding you step for step the entire way to my foyer. Women love a gentleman who's respectable and considerate. Yet, we also find it appealing when he's assertive with his actions, void of always seeking permission, and consistent. You've been a dog with two dicks for so long that it seems you have forgotten certain essential elements. I have to get back to work now but do know that your Georgia Bulldogs shirt and hat has cost you to lose more points, Frenchie," Demi snickered, disconnecting the call.

Quickly showering and checking himself out in the mirror before leaving, Terry couldn't help but admire his own suaveness, looking snatched. Rehearsing in his mind the things he was going to say when he got to her workplace, "I want you to teach me how to love," slipped out grabbing the Polo Purple Label oil as three drops fell into his hand before rubbing it on his neck. The words made him wonder if the challenge of holding her hand as a real man was causing him to become internally weak. Walking out the door, Terry selected a T.I. song on his iPhone to get his mind off the emotional instability regarding his future life, his future wife.

CHAPTER 13

A scending the glass, cylindrical Westin Peachtree Plaza Hotel, on this particular occasion, Sheri's solo liftoff with strangers had her feeling queasy. The only thing that she had hoped wouldn't occur, since it would definitely be the ultimate embarrassment, would be for her to vomit on the silk Lilac Georgette drape dress she wore and possibly spewing on those rocketing up to the Sun Dial in the elevating capsule as well. Usually, when dining at the rotating Sun Dial, Randle is her safety net with such great heights and motion. He always ascended with her, therapeutically massaging her hands as she stood facing his chest, eyes closed.

She would silently chant the lullaby her brother would always calm her with as a child, "Alouette, *gentille alouette, Alouette, je te plumerai..." solely* to escape the dreadful thought of the capsule free falling, reaching terminal velocity at 9.8 m/sec^2, prey to an unyielding concrete reflecting a pillow without comfort. In her thoughts, she'd rather be on the ground and prey to men who think her gender and ethnicity is beneath them. Unfortunately, this was the choice of a prominent politician, and her Sparticus was not there to protect her, therapeutically or otherwise.

The illuminating rays of the sunsetting horizon scintillated on her immeasurable beauty and hid not the pulsating disbelief spontaneously combusting across her face. A few individuals entered the elevator at the last minute in the lobby, unintentionally forcing Sheri to step back against the interior glass, which granted a spectacular elevated view of Atlanta and it's skyline as they propelled to solar bliss. But with Sheri's eyes momentarily closed, she cared nothing about the city's beauty nor the unwanted stranger on her side trying to mack her attention by assaulting her nasal passage with lethal whispers of chemical warfare.

"How ya doing shawty? Whatcho name is, sexy lady?" He asked, contaminating her lungs with his southern ghetto swampy swag.

"I know this fool didn't just call me shawty, and, in addition to that, actually say, 'Whatcho name is?'" Sheri thought to herself while skirmishing with the air for a breath of less toxic molecules. So toxic, the carbon rolling off his coated tongue visibly discolored the air in her space. She actually wanted to open her eyes, and tongue-lash him without losing her character while sincerely advising that before he approach a woman again, he needs to thoroughly scrape his tongue and throat with 220 grit sandpaper twice, marinate both with JP-5 jet fuel before lighting a match since it burns so clean. Then utilize the downtime to educate himself on how to approach a woman who's not a trap Queen. Yet with her inner body mildly reflecting a Raqs Baladi dancer as she gripped the gold-plated arm rails with all her strength, Sheri simply remained silent.

Ironically, she held her breath as the lids of her eyes squeezed tighter and tighter with each rising second. With the toxic smell of the stranger's breath lingering as a water buffalo's musk in extreme dry heat, Sheri could honestly say for certain that this was the first time in her life that she started praying to God that this noxious odor emanating from his mouth would not dissolve her like salt to a snail. She silently feared the angel of death calling for her soul in this manner with the unbearable stench exacerbating her nauseous state to the point of gastrointestinal eruption.

Reaching the restaurant level, Sheri did not shield her cries of praise, impulsively executing a double Dutch hop to separate herself from the curiously offending stranger with lethal Viking breath, who should have been arrested upon retraction of the doors for terroristic fumes released in an enclosed vessel in American airspace.

Unexpectedly mumbling aloud, "O God, I love you," as fresh vented oxygen filled her lungs, causing those around her to turn and say "Amen to that sista!"

"How are you today?" The hostess inquired as Sheri approached the concierge desk. "Welcome to the Sun Dial Restaurant Bar and View. Do you have a reservation ma'am?"

Mildly snickering at her own actions while savoring the pleasant sweetness of fresh oxygen, Sheri illuminated the atmosphere with a smile more sparkling and sensuous than a Christopher diamond, immediately upstaging the ambiance, selfishly hypnotizing all onlookers while saying in a low tone of voice, "I'm blessed, thank you for asking. And yes, ma'am, I have a reservation for two, the Mayor and I. My name is Sheri Johnson — the Mayor here yet?"

"Ms. Johnson, your reservation is confirmed," the unusually tall Puerto Rican hostess acknowledged. "The Mayor has requested to change the reservation from two to four and to dine with a spectacular view. We were able to make the accommodations, Ms. Johnson. Unfortunately, he's yet to arrive with his party. Kim, here, will be your waitress and shall escort you to your table."

"Oh, did he mention who the other guests were?" Sheri inquisitively wondered.

"No!" The hostess observantly replied.

"Thank you." Sheri responded turning to follow Kim's footsteps, before glancing over her shoulder suspiciously to see her toxic mouthed admirer, whose eyes were focused on her every step.

The sight of seeing him in an all yellow pin-stripe suit with purple shoes made her immediately cover her mouth to keep from openly bursting into laughter.

Displaying a menu as Sheri pulled her chair from the table, Kim inquired, "Would you like something to drink while you wait for your guests to arrive, Ms. Johnson?"

"Yes, I'd like a glass of coconut water, no ice, with a side dish of sliced cherries and thick wedges of lemon, please." Sheri politely and precisely requested, removing the strap of her elm burlwood briefcase from her shoulder, laying it in the chair beside her.

Sheri glanced out the window to see what the skyline revealed as the restaurant revolved at one revolution per hour. The Atlanta area landscape was breathtaking as usual, but nothing out of the ordinary. Not expecting to be thrown back to the days of her childhood, Sheri momentarily went back in time as her eyes shifted from the Mercedes Benz Stadium over into the Vine City neighborhood where she joyfully spent a lot of her childhood years. Soothing memories of her step-grandmother began to envelop her thoughts. She wished Fannie was still alive, for the moments in her presence were always like a fairytale. A smile blanketed Sheri's face as warm memories of how her grandfather's girlfriend would make her grandfather sleep on the sofa while she and Naomi slept in the bed whenever they visited and how she would have him cooking, shopping, entertaining them like a jester, catering to their every need as though they were royal princesses.

Startled, a palm imprint placed gently upon her shoulder by the Mayor invoked reclamation while deeply entranced within her thoughts as he announced his arrival, "I apologize Ms. Johnson. I didn't mean to jolt you. You must have been somewhere special in your mind travels," the Mayor declared while extending his hand.

"No! No need for an apology." Sheri affirmed soothing the awkward moment with a million-dollar smile and rising to formalize their greeting. "Excuse me," she grinned, "I was lost in a precious memory of yesteryear, childhood moments I wish I could relive."

"Meaningful memories of yesteryear will always have you wishing the hands of time could be rolled back," the Mayor opined, flashing his baby face smile in between giving Kim his attention, introducing his intern and his young Italian assistant upon whom Sheri's eyes didn't even blink as his hand caressed her arm.

Without extending any gesture of greeting to his assistant, Sheri pierced the Mayor's eyes with a cold stare that would freeze time and seething as she turned toward his assistant, "Excuse us for a moment, please. If you don't mind, I need to discuss a few important business issues with him without your presence as a distraction."

Completely caught off guard, the Mayor acknowledged to his assistant with a nod to grant them a few moments of privacy to conduct business. With her hand enveloped by his own, he kissed her gently on the cheek, at which time she then turned and walked to the bar with his eyes following every step.

Whispering to the extent that only the Mayor could hear her words, "I can't believe you're parading that jezebel in front of me like it's acceptable. Mayor, we are not friends, and this is respectable business. You may find it acceptable to disrespect your wife, but you will respect me, sir."

"Understandable Ms. Johnson. Can we keep this between us? I apologize if I offended you." The Mayor exclaimed, not knowing that she was going to take offense or even notice the affection between them. "Ms. Johnson, afterwards, I have to be a King, a guest at a tea party, a mannequin for their artwork, a baker, and storyteller to my three daughters. Do you have kids Ms. Johnson?" The Mayor asked trying to redirect her thoughts as she listened.

"No, no sir, no kids. Well, not in that sense, just my inner-city kids." Sheri replied hastily.

"Quite novel of you. You know, the only thing I'm able to process once they close their eyes is, I love them. Given that the other members of my staff had engagements, I asked my intern to attend and take notes, if you don't mind, Ms. Johnson."

"Given the weight of responsibilities, Mayor, I think it's a good idea. But I believe it would be more resourceful if he used his phone to record our conversation instead of taking shorthand notes with a pencil. I don't want to have to keep stopping for him to sharpen his pencil or catch up and lose my train of thought." Sheri lipped in a humorous tone that erupted in laughter between them.

"You definitely won't have to stop Ms. Johnson." The intern assured while secretly gazing at her beauty and wondering does a woman that sexy taste better than a woman you have to creep with at night when the streetlights are broken.

As she unzipped her briefcase to remove an iPad and her black leather signature binder with documents enclosed, Sheri asked, "Would you like to get started or order first?"

"Ms. Johnson, we should go ahead and order, and then we can begin, if you have yourself together. I'm seriously intrigued to learn why you're seeking my help to champion the old city library for an after school tutorial program for inner city kids when the city has no room in the budget to gamble or sponsor any new educational programs. Especially, to furnish even greater capital by renovating a building that's years behind on code and structural maintenance, Ms. Johnson. I'm meeting with you out of courtesy to your father. But I honestly don't think we will achieve anything today because the educational budget is already subjected to more cuts this upcoming quarter."

In the process of waiting for the iPad to power up, Sheri passed the Mayor a few power point documents outlining the basics of her objective. "Mayor," Sheri addressed, staring at him directly for the second time and trying not to laugh at the fact that his toupee was on backwards. "The name of the afterschool program that I am advocating and presenting to you is 'Unity After School Center.' I'll refer to it as 'Unity.' Our goal is to have centers throughout Metro Atlanta, and we have a modest schedule to get six more centers up and fully operational over the course of the next two years, that's a responsible and reasonable pace of at least three centers per year. The base essence of the Unity program is to bridge our youth with the most essential elements in which they are void of mainly because of being raised in a home that's governed by a child raising them instead of an adult and stuck in a overfilled classroom that's justified by so-called 'budget cuts. Now, the educators only teach the basic curriculum to sustain a job, and many could care less if the child fails to comprehend any aspect of it. The decline in the yearly test scores is evidence of just that. Unity is centered on cultivating each student's mind with critical thinking skills and life values plus other essential elements lacking in today's school system that also awards them college credit points."

"Ms. Johnson, you're absolutely correct," the Mayor interjected, "Yet going before the city council with a proposal to teach kids life skills after school when the public schools are funded for that exact purpose is a waste of time. Kids today are not interested in going to school during school, much less school after school for that matter. Ms. Johnson, I admire your zeal and desire to awaken our youth, but have you given this any serious thought beyond self-admiration and selfishly feeling as though you made an accomplishment in some child's life at the end of the day?"

Looking at him with the same heated discontented stare that she gives to male chauvinists who try to play upon her intellect because she's a woman, she tapped the table a few times to gather her thoughts before continuing with her argument.

"Yes, as a matter of fact, I have, Mr. Mayor! This program gives our children a leg up in society and in Universities, and our top students may even be able to compete with Ivy League scholarship candidates. Every time I turn on the news and view another senseless death at the hands of a child, I think of it, sir. Every time I witness the results of them applying themselves against the mental restraints of others, I think of it, sir. Until we all partake in a beneficial sacrifice for our kids and not our accounts, then there's no question that things will get worse. But with the Unity program, their lives and our society have the potential to get exponentially better. Sir, we both know that critical thinking skills are absolutely vital in the real world and must be learned for one to succeed. We also know that real world application of critical thinking is key to successfully overcoming many of life's challenges. Social media can't teach it. The reality shows that are now on every channel rail against it. A child raising a child in an unstable home is against the odds of teaching it. The harsh reality of our young black men becoming statistics presents that the attempt to master it by turning to the streets and finding a sense of identity is alarmingly dismal. And crime rates are up, not just injustice from the police force, but black on black crime, so we're left with the horrors of genocide. There's overwhelming research which supports the contention that learning in today's society is mostly information oriented and based on providing ready-made answers, rather than challenging people to think creatively and critically which would help them understand key life issues better, make more intelligent choices, and resolve many problems that critical thinking enables."

"Excuse me. Not to cut you off, Ms. Johnson," leaning forward to take another bite of the wood roasted salmon while glancing at his assistant and speaking. "The government already has millions of dollars invested in programs of this nature with greater resources to accommodate the need of every child, no matter the challenging environment, their living conditions, or learning ability. Ms. Johnson, public schools are losing enrollment and funding from every fiscal budget review, of which I can't change, nor will your program. That's why I can't see myself infringing upon city resources and money to outsource a building for a program that's no different than the ones developed through legislation. Especially in an urban community where crimes and student dropouts are at an all-time high."

Looking over his shoulder again to briefly admire his assistant, the Mayor was ready for this meeting to come to an end, so that he could embark on something more stimulating and pleasing with his time.

Snickering internally to herself as she shook her head with a brief glance at the Atlanta skyline, she sipped her coconut water. Sheri couldn't believe that the man who so aggressively campaigned for the cultivation of urban community centers and the education system was actually sitting right before her reflecting no more than just another nonchalant egotistical politician. Re-enveloping her sense of zeal, Sheri mentally extracted herself from the equation and decided to correspond with the Mayor while using the same heated enthusiasm that she used when debating with lawyers and art brokers, which always crushed the opposition against her.

"Mayor, the one thing I witness daily, whether I'm going to one of my centers or just opening my eyes to life without a blindfold, is the benefits of those ineffective government programs that cultivate no child's mind nor the community in any respect. No disrespect to you Mayor, but I witness this happening every day."

"The backlash of an incompetent politician who thinks the answer to everything is implementing laws that open loopholes for them to steal more of the tax payers' money while claiming that they're making budget cuts that benefit the people by sending kids, all the while, to prison for every simple infraction. The modern-day replacement tool for education instead of investing in the broken system to make it better. While in essence, the real criminals of this life like the child molesters, the rapists, the corporate embezzlers, and the lobbyist-controlled politician, etcetera, get slapped on the hand without recourse for their crimes."

"I see more kids under the age of sixteen lose ten to twenty years of their life for committing a crime that didn't even merit one hundred dollars, a crime committed so that they could put food in their stomach, while the same city councilmen, which you say you can't go before for the benefit of turning a child's life around, merely gets suspended probation for the millions that they've swindled through the so called tax cuts. Then there's the repeated sex offenders who are merely punished by having their name placed on a public list as though it's supposed to be detrimental."

"Mr. Mayor, you should know first-hand, given your upbringing in the Lakewood Village housing community, that a classroom filled with individuals whom have been breastfed from the interest of greedy government officials warrants nothing but excessive lies and empty promises. Your family was blessed to move into a better housing area in your early teenage years Mayor, yet your initial upbringing grants you the ability of relating to the adversities of those public school kids whom are forced to share meals with insects and rodents as a normal way of life under the guise of survival and lack of proper government aid. A key element of life's problem today is that people literally forget where they come from, excluded by rusticating views, vision, and policy."

"Today's generation is structured by kids having kids who internally possess no sense of understanding, no sense of direction beyond what the society considers acceptable, no sense of purpose, and no sense of value or self-worth. The 'WHY' is that the colonialists' mindset of old still thinks that life has remained trapped in time and has no need of transcending status quo as it were in their upbringing. Instead of cultivating new teaching methods and materiel, they just sit in offices wasting tax payers' money by implementing the same rustic, non-beneficial programs, just disguised under a different name, solely to reap more kickbacks lining their pockets and swelling their foreign accounts from programs and fiscal budget cuts, Mr. Mayor, of which you are no stranger to, sir."

Seeing the intern cut his eyes at the Mayor with a distinct look of suspicion taking possession of his face as she spoke, Sheri knew for sure that she had punctured his ego and knocked on a door with some detrimental secrets behind it. To her, his ego had no value, but bridging a difference to help kids' lives — immense value.

"You see, Mr. Mayor," she continued staring at him as he chewed the salmon and selfishly looked over his shoulder neglecting the documents. "My program is not seeded by political ambition or an ego to amass personal or hidden account profits. My program is seeded to eradicate the root of the cancer that suspends our kids on empty dreams. Unity transforms boys into men, girls into women, and trouble minded kids who once seemed lost into sound minded thinkers. A platform on which the constricted minds of the government's elite are losing the battle."

Wiping his mouth while sitting up firmly to take a sip of his Pinot Grigio as her words penetrated his thoughts, the Mayor silently began to wonder if she had knowledge of his illegal investments or the programs he was embezzling from and was using this meeting as a psychological front. Observing the room to see if any eyes were gazing upon him, not wanting to make his sudden discomfort to her constant mentioning of stolen money and accounts seem noticeable.

"Ms. Johnson," the Mayor inquired, "What makes your program more significant and different? How will it mold a child internally and externally?"

"Our teachers are the difference, to clearly answer your question Mayor. Plus, the incentives that we provide for greater motivation," Sheri answered with a sense of arrogance.

"Your teachers?" The Mayor asked sarcastically, turning to his intern with a smirk on his face, not believing Ms. Johnson mentioned teachers as though she had imported the best from all over the world.

Glancing over his shoulder, lustfully admiring his assistant, the Mayor wondered should he just get up and leave, given that she was sitting all alone instead of breathing heavily in his arms. She was looking more enticing to him right now than this proposal for some uneducated ghetto kids. But when he noticed the stranger with the neon yellow suit staring, he immediately turned around, not knowing that he was actually eyeing Ms. Johnson.

"Yes Mayor, our teachers! The sincerity of our commitment bridges the respect and love that's not found in their lives. Our teaching methods are quite different than the public, private, and charter schools which is why all of our students score higher on every curriculum test. The incentives we provide are a major boost of inspiration and dedication. Mayor, if you turn to page nine, you will clearly see that research was conducted by three private agencies which the government uses to conduct all their studies. And what's most interesting is that all three of them acknowledged that ninety-eight percent of all educational programs that the government implement for inner city kids don't even measure one percent in making a difference."

"My program has been in effect for eighteen months now, and other small city council members and principles are calling my office seeking to take part in expanding our program into their districts. We are currently tutoring in four after-school locations. Students that are selected by the schools are those considered as the basic problem child for every behavioral category. Whereas those I select with the approval of all the Fulton County judges, are those who come into the courtroom with charges which the county judges can remit, using the program as an alternative."

"We currently have enrollment of one hundred and sixty-four extraordinary students. Prior to Unity, forty-three were twelfth grade dropouts. Now, twenty-seven are preparing to graduate this year with higher GPA's than many of the school's honor students. Eight have received scholarships from Universities, and the others have all enlisted in junior colleges with the intention of transferring later. No student in our program has below a C average. Many of our students are from one of the eight public schools participating in the program, students who were once considered malignant to the classroom and neighborhood."

"Now, each student is just as extraordinary as those that I've already spoken of, passing without selfish ignorance spoken against them. Mayor, all of our students are a mixture of middle and high school disciplinary problems that are no longer being viewed as disruptive adolescents. We work as one group to properly nurture each other. One unified body. If one fails, then we all fail. Pride, street identity, and arrogance are suppressed upon entry. Of the one hundred and sixty-four students we oversee, twenty-three are on probation and their supervising officers commend the change in their character, speech, and thinking. The difference in our teaching method, Mayor, is that we don't seek Yale or Stanford graduates to lecture from a textbook. I employed teachers whose upbringing relates to the common struggles our students are facing, something you seem to have once lived, campaigned on, yet dismissed the day you were elected."

"Excuse me?!" The Mayor interrupted defensively, slightly adding a little bass to his tone.

"You're excused, sir." Sheri countered without breaking stride. "Whether it's abuse, homelessness, drugs, alcoholic households, or any number of issues, our teachers know what it's like to walk in their shoes. This creates a thirst to help them, which is purer from the heart, and centered upon understanding. Our kids bridge a greater sense of comfort with our teachers than with public school teachers who are underpaid, overburdened, and don't have the ability or time to focus on the learning comprehension of each student. The only thing in which they focus on is getting through the workday. Our students have someone who sincerely shows they understand them without looking over them, and someone who enlightens them with creative solutions and alternatives to open their developing minds to."

"Mr. Mayor take any school's top three students, and I'll allow your intern and your jezebel to pick any three of our students, whereupon my kids will surpass them on any critical thinking test that you or your staff can provide, which you and I know is what matters in life. So, the ultimate difference in our program, Mayor, compared to your government programs and the public school system ... " Sheri began with a sense of sarcasm in her voice, "is that my program is one hundred percent effective, whereas the government's is no more than a hub to shell illegal corporate money and cares nothing about the students."

"Ms. Johnson, I must admit, initially I was not interested. But now I'm definitely impressed, and you have my full, undivided attention. If the numbers from these documents are accurate, then I truly commend you and your team for such a remarkable accomplishment. Yet again, taking taxpayers money to renovate a building for an after-school tutoring program is a mountain to climb," the Mayor insisted while scanning the room for onlookers.

"Mayor, my program is funded by donations from the same taxpayers that you keep speaking of trying to protect. But do you really protect them sir with your decision making?" Sheri asked while looking at him as though she was trying to read his reaction. "The people would rush to vote on something that shows true promise in their kids' present and future educational standing far quicker than a hard stance bill advocating to send them to prison for the rest of their lives for no significant reason or to fund something a lobbyist who donated to your campaign chose for you to advocate."

"My program currently has 2.6 million dollars on hand to purchase and renovate the old city library by we, donations that all came from the very same tax payers, sir. I'm not seeking the government's revenue, Mr. Mayor. You campaigned talking the talk, so I wanted to see if you were actually a man of your words. I offered this opportunity to see if you and the government for once wanted to prove that a child's education is more important than personal financial gain. People will never cry over a sacrifice for cultivating benefits, especially an obstacle my program has already conquered. Changing the life of one child is a blessing, Mr. Mayor. Granting us the old city library expands not only our kids' future, but it would bring back the respect Atlanta once flourished in but lost long ago in regard to our education system."

"Excuse me," Kim politely said approaching the table gracefully, "The gentleman in the neon yellow suit has elected to pay for your meal Ms. Johnson, and he sent you a bottle of Dom Perignon ma'am. Would you like for me to open it for you Ms. Johnson and pour you and your quest a glass?"

"No, thank you Kim, you can place it on the table." Sheri responded, while laughing internally at the sheer audacity of him thinking this was worth the price of subjecting her organs to what his breath offers. "Kim, I will be paying for my own meal. Also, I will not accept this bottle, but what I will accept is that you take the money for this bottle and what he is going to pay for my meal as an added tip."

"Thank you, Ms. Johnson," she cheered, smiling in disbelief.

"If you need me to inform your manager of my request, I will," Sheri politely informed. "And will you please advise the gentleman that the Mayor and I said thank you?"

"Yes, Ms. Johnson." Kim replied before walking away, smiling.

Realizing now that the gentleman was not a field agent watching him, the Mayor began to breathe with a sigh of relief. "Ms. Johnson, I'm following your every step and you have my true support. Yet, I still do not see why kids would want to come to your afterschool program rather than going home and doing the ordinary things they do once school is out."

"Mayor, I'm beginning to feel as though the only benefit of our meeting was the braised ox tails I ate. The questions you should be asking, you're not. And even though you're the Mayor of Atlanta, I waste my time with no one. To answer your question, nothing besides the kids' true desire to learn and achieve, make something worthy of themselves. Also, from what I have openly shared, the documents entail that we provide musical artists for the students to meet, sports athletes, spontaneous trips, and epicurean delight at select restaurants to experience. Several Fortune 100 and 500 companies have signed on to sponsor us with incentives. All donations from taxpayers go towards ensuring our kids excel in life, not to selfishly elevate the Unity staff's lifestyle. Every two weeks, the kids are doing something they only dreamed of doing and meeting famous individuals they never expected to be able to meet. Our kids earn these incentives by engaging in focus and hard, consistent work and dedication to the betterment of themselves."

"Ms. Johnson, I applaud what you are doing with those kids," the Mayor uttered nonchalantly. "Yet, given the direction the city is moving in right now, I honestly don't feel that outsourcing a government owned building for your program is one the city can invest time and resources in at this time."

No longer feeling that Ms. Johnson had knowledge of his dealings and using this meeting to position herself, the Mayor motioned for his assistant as he rose from his seat. "Maybe during the next fiscal budget review, Ms. Johnson, we can actually work on a bill that will help the inner-city kids. But unfortunately, not at this moment. The city is focusing on improving energy."

"Mayor, ...," the intern attempted.

"Hold on." the Mayor interjected raising his hand as a gesture to stop as he continued without taking his eyes off Ms. Johnson. "Again, I respectfully hope that we can keep this meeting between us professional."

Staring at him as their eyes interlocked, she found herself laughing instead of desiring to say anything. Here, he was standing before her being nonchalant and arrogant, yet asking her to hold his affair secret. Unbeknownst to him was the fact that so many of his prominent supporters were sponsoring Ms. Johnson's program and advocating for her to seek his help. Reaching for her phone as the Mayor walked away affectionately caressing the hand of his assistant with his intern following, Sheri made a phone call and stated no more than "Buy the building" when they answered, before hanging up and turning her head to gaze out through the window into the Atlanta skyline.

CHAPTER 14

Yara surfed the internet on her tablet, browsing for wedding dress designs while laying back into the sofa receiving a therapeutic foot massage from Gip. The crackling from the fireplace had become the percussion track for her balladic monologue. The jitters and excitement of renewing their vows had her feeling more like a woman marrying her soulmate for the first time than a Nubian Queen who had been the breath and backbone of her King for thirty years. Gazing at pictures of designer dresses worn by elite celebrities and the decor of royal weddings in South Africa had Yara openly speaking of romantic islands, Lagunas and majestic inland destinations surrounded by fresh water lakes where they should consider renewing their vows, people she'd love to attend whom she's never met, her ideal vision of paradise for the wedding, and the hypnotic dress which she wanted June Ambrose to design that would undoubtedly be the topic of conversation in the midst of so many.

Listening to his wife twitter from topic to topic without once soliciting his opinion, granted Gip the assurance that Yara was not only happy, but traveling upon a path of ecstasy within her own world. Metaphorically imitating a masseuse as she spoke of pavilions, calla lily petals, and white horses on the shores of the Mauritius Island or Zanzibar being the most beautiful wedding of a lifetime. Gip was shocked to be the servant in her presence while discovering that Yara was never openly conveying her expressions to him.

The entire time, Yara was using her Bluetooth to share the details of her thoughts with a girlfriend before grabbing the iPad to share photos for her girlfriend to pick between a custom lace mermaid gown with sheer lace back paneling designed by Givenchy Ricardo Tisci, a line dress custom made by Vera Wang with three layers of Chantilly any lyon lace, and a 1920 chic inspired glamour effortless bias cut gown made by Dior designer, John Galliano. "Women and their superstition," he thought, "were making him irrelevant!"

Realizing that Yara was going to try and keep everything a secret other than the cost, and not wanting to hear the two of them argue in regards to who's the best exotic designer between Oliver Rousteing and June Ambrose, Gip decided to give some of his attention to a few business affairs and leave them to reminisce as women do. Sensuously kissing the bottom of her feet, then rising from the sofa,

Gip began slapping and blowing heavily on his tongue as though he was trying to clean it while rubbing his lips in a circular motion.

"Baby, have you bathed?" He joked holding a straight face and fake coughing as he inquired.

"What? Gip, don't play with me," Yara snapped back looking at him with that distinct glance of a female lion observing her prey.

"Baby, you taste a little sour like you haven't bathed in three or four days," Gip teased as he turned to walk out of the room. "I hope my tongue and lips don't bump up or get infected! You are worrying about dresses, but forgetting the essential of scrubbing your body."

Not caring that she was now video chatting, Yara began a neck-roll, swirling her neck with the grace of a black mamba as Gip slightly turned his head around to interlock their eyes in an intense stare down.

"I bathed an hour ago when I baptized your mouth with my holy water," she piped sarcastically while standing up to throw a pillow that hit him in the back. "If anything, I hope I don't get an infection given that you brushed with the same toothbrush I used to clean all my toys last night, and given the fact that you just massaged my feet. The question is, what have you been doing with your hands, 'cause that's the only thing you taste and will be tasting tonight? Excuse me girl," Yara popped off and apologized, rolling her eyes at Gip and turning her attention back to the tablet. "Gip trying to audition for Amateur Comic View it seems, girl or visit the ER trying me."

Laughing at her words as he walked out of the room and into the hallway, Gip couldn't help himself from shouting as he scrolled through the kitchen en route, "I touched you. That's why my hands are sour." Of course, he kept on playing, knowing there would be consequences.

Yara's strength, integrity, compassion, sense of humor and fierceness has always been the seed of his love for her. He liked the fact that no matter how strong their bond got, they never allowed one another to become complacent or comfortable in the mere essence of just loving each other. Everyday seemed to be a new reminder of why each is significant and how joyful love is when respect, communication, and trust are unwavering priorities.

Scanning over documents while sitting in his office, secretly eating Yara's freshly baked banana bread, Gip noticed an envelope that was laying beneath a book at the corner of his desk, "Stories of the Prophets" by Ibn Kathir. That book had given him more insight on the prophets of God and their contribution to life than spending a lifetime attending Bible study. Grabbing the envelope and flipping it over, he was astonished to see Reanna and Cadence written on it.

Opening it, Gip's smile blossomed like a daylily, seeing the card the girls had made. On one side, Cadence drew a stick figure of him, Yara, Reanna, and herself seemingly hiding in a cave. It reminded him of the days when Sheri was young and would always draw the family. But even more shocking were the words Reanna wrote on the other side of the card.

"Among the signs of Faith is that one does not look to please others and incur God's anger in that process. One avoids praising others for the sustenance that they have received from God (the Exalted) and also refrains from blaming others for the sustenance that he has not received from God. His distribution of provision is not increased for a recipient by the amount of greed or ambition that he shows, nor is it blocked by his hatred or envy. God, in His infinite wisdom and justice, grants provision and contentment for those with strength of Faith and satisfaction with what is divinely ordained. Likewise, misery and discontent are for those that live with doubt and anger. Let us be satisfied with His will.

Love,

Reanna and Cadence"

"Yara! Yara, will you come here for a moment please, Gip hollered, excited by the unexpected artwork of compassion and pondering deeply on Reanna's words?

Entering his office, still video chatting, without knocking, Yara flopped down on the sofa chair and finished her brief makeup artist discussion before ending the call to render Gip her full attention. "Yes, baby?"

"It's respectful to knock before entering a room with a closed door, Yara," Gip scolded, playfully, while looking at her.

"I'm not knocking on no damn door in my own house, are you crazy? Especially when you don't have any guests," she retorted with a spice of attitude in her tone. "It's respectful to do exactly what I did, which was walk in. I bet you're not man enough to tell Mama Lewis to knock before entering," a statement of fact that caused them both to start laughing.

She scanned the entire room, not observing anything out of the ordinary except the disbelief of seeing slices of her freshly baked banana bread on his desk.

"Yes, baby?" she asked again, eyeing him, but no response.

Noticing him signal her attention by waving the card in his hand and assuming it was one of Sheri's childhood cards he cherished, Yara walked around the desk and pulled his chair back enough for her to ease into his lap before completely removing it from his hands.

"Oh baby, this is so cute," she proclaimed admiring the card with a little animosity. "Why does Cadence have my head so damn big, my head ain't that big, baby? She is wrong for that. And look at your feet!" She giggled in pure amusement. "Baby, this is too cute, I love it! Boy, I'm glad your toes don't resemble her artwork. Can we frame it or get some t-shirts made with the drawing on the front and Reanna's words of wisdom on the back? When did they give this to you?

"Now that's interesting!"

"What, babes?" Yara asked turning to look at him curiously.

"Whenever you go to Saks Fifth, Neiman Marcus, or Bloomingdale's at Phipps Plaza, you don't ask my permission to swipe the platinum card, but you ask my permission to frame the creativity of this card or to get some t-shirts printed. Interesting ... " Gip denotes, shaking his head.

"Whatever, I'm grown!" Yara mouthed while rolling her eyes and looking back at the card as a smile appears, instantaneously.

"Yes, true sweetheart," he concurred, "I just found the card on the desk, so one of the girls had to have put it there the other day. We have to do something special for them because this is just too touching and thoughtful. We should buy them a puppy which you know Cadence would love."

"Cadence is wrong for making my head that damn big, it takes up half the page."

"Yara!"

"Yara, nothing! I'm serious, baby, I'ma get her pumpkin-head butt for this. Your damn head should have been that big, not mine. Baby, do you remember when Sheri painted us on your new Mercedes and threw her yellow paint on the hood to resemble the sun?" Yara reflected while falling back into his arms and bursting into laughter.

"Now that wasn't funny at the time, but how can I ever forget that day?" Gip replied joining in on the laughter as the memory of their daughter painting the new Mercedes S600 he bought off the showroom floor the first day he drove it home. "Yara, even to this day I still don't understand what she was honestly thinking to do that, and how Sheri had paint all over the car and garage floor but not a single drop on her clothes.''

"Because we Johnson ladies are clever like that," she concluded turning her head to kiss his lips before placing her free hand on his mouth and aggressively squeezing it with all her strength, while shaking his head side to side. ''Who told you that you could eat my damn banana bread?'' She questioned with authority in her voice, allowing her alter ego to emerge.

Chuckling as he stared at his wife, ''My stomach,'' Gip intoned within her grip, elevating his laughter while blowing fish kisses and extending his hand to caress her face with a sense of gentle affection.

Batting away his gesture of affection by raising her arm defensively, Yara released her grip, shot Gip three quick, playful punches to the chest, and tapped the bottom of his chin with her hand causing his head to slightly tilt backwards as she jumps out of his lap and secured herself in the fighting stance that One Eye taught her in training.

"Don't touch me," Yara growled. ''You ate my bread and talking about I stank. You're on punishment! I should teach you a lesson for trying me!''

Observing and laughing at how his wife was mimicking a bad version of Kung Fu Panda, ''Baby, how many times do I have to show you that the things the guys teach you, my mom, and Penélope in training is not effective on me?'' Gip reminded, inquisitively, while still laughing and reaching for another slice of the banana bread. ''Baby, I'm water and you're just paper.''

"Practice makes perfect," Yara pointed out while throwing a right hand jab to his chin that Gip caught in motion.

With his hand gently securing her fist, he placed the bread slice in his mouth, and rose from his seat, chewing without a sense of concern for Yara's combat skills.

"Paper can never affect water my love. Kiss me," he taunted still holding the fist of her unsuccessful punch.

"No! Now let my hand go before I really give you some smoke."

Pulling her closer using his grip as an advantage, ''Kiss me Yara!''

"No and I meant what I said. You're on punishment until my batteries go dead since you want to say I taste sour and you stole my bread."

"Stole your bread! One can never steal from themselves, what's yours is mine and what's mine is mine" Gip insinuated jokingly, repeating her words. ''Seriously though, kiss me.''

"No, and that's my slogan, not yours, copycat. Now let me go before I call Mama Lewis and tell her that you plan on breaking in her house and confiscating all of her guns."

Releasing his grip from her fist, Gip sat back into his chair as Yara reached for the last slice of bread while giggling at his reaction. Kicking his feet on top of his desk, Gip grabbed his phone while leaning back like a boss and called the head of his security, James.

"Yes sir, Mr. Johnson?"

"How are you doing, James?"

"I'm blessed, sir, and I pray that all is well with you, sir."

"James, I have you on speaker. My wife has placed me on punishment and refuses to give me a kiss. Do you think it would be wrong for me to try and buy my wife's affection with a gift to say "I love you" or should I just be genuine and render sincere actions to gain back her affection?"

Standing there chewing and listening to Gip's words, Yara knew her husband was up to something sneaky and she had no idea what it was. So, she tried to play on his intellect by leaning down to kiss him while seductively caressing him as though he was no longer on the punishment. Gip turned his head and raised his hand as though to indicate he rejected her advance, which she slapped away playfully.

"How are you Mrs. Johnson?" James inquired.

"I'm blessed as well James, and thanks for asking. Just trying to see where all of this is going," she grinned.

"Well, sir, in all honesty, I've learned from watching the two of you over the years that love is a compound action measured by the tongue and limbs of the body. To buy a gift would be disrespectful to Mrs. Johnson because her worth exceeds the value of material items which can never define her, nor cause her to surrender her integrity. Mr. Johnson, you have shown me that a man's sincerity is priceless and there's nothing wrong with patiently crawling to gain the forgiveness of someone, for actions out measure words."

"Thank you, James for your kind words," Yara praised.

"Always, Mrs. Johnson," he replied. "Just speaking the truth."

"I truly appreciate your advice James. And you're absolutely correct in acknowledging that it would be disrespectful for me to try and cater to her smile in any manner with a gift of love or a genuine gesture of appreciation, no matter the sincerity of the intent. So with that being said, if you don't mind James, will you call the dealership and have them send someone to retrieve the SUV. Advise them that I no longer want it at this time, please."

"Yes sir! I'll call them now."

"What SUV?" Yara yelped, forcefully pushing his chair with her hip and snatching the tablet from his desk as though her life depended on her defusing a nuclear bomb before she would blink again.

Yara inserted the password and hit the icon for the surveillance cameras with the quickness of a Summit computer, and in seeing an all-black AMG G63 Yachting Limited Edition identical to her son's parked in front of the house with a large red ribbon attached to it, she turned vicious.

"I'll burn Mama Lewis' flowers and tell her you did it, James, if you pick that phone up! Yara yelled kicking off her slide-in slippers, before running out of the room and house like Florence Griffin Joyner, barefooted, screaming "I love you, baby! I love you! I love you! I love you!" Repetitively.

With both of them laughing at Yara's words, "James, hold back from giving her the keys for a moment," Mr. Johnson instructed, teasingly, "I'm going to act as though I'm still sending it back 'til she takes me off punishment and give me some sugar."

"Sir, I work for you, and I respect you highly," James replied. "But when it comes to your wife and Mama Lewis, I don't joke with either. I will accept being fired for disobeying your request if she asks for the keys, sir. I wouldn't be able to deny her request."

"What!?" Cackling at his words. "A man is not a King in his own castle," Gip joked. "And you're a trained force recon marine yet scared of two women?! Wait until I tell the guys about this, James."

"Sir, all the guys will repeat the same statement. Your mom and wife only shoot head shots during training, not body," James informed. "You should honestly see them in action at the range, especially Mama Lewis. They have been working on new combat exercises with One Eye and Aaron lately, sir. Respectfully, I can't gamble, taking that compromising chance, especially with Mama Lewis."

"Okay then James, give her the keys since you all have trained an old Harley Quinn and a Catalea Columbiana that you're now afraid of," Gip concluded, laughing as he disconnected the line.

Admiring her new G-Wagen like a Star Wars fan, she was no longer mad at the fact that she thought her son's vehicle was a gift from her husband at the cookout. Yara took a few selfies for her social media page, then called Sheri, Terry, and her girlfriend to share the news. Desiring to cruise through the streets of Atlanta a little, she went back into the house to shower before putting on a Divina crop top, and jeans with her open toe Louboutins. With nothing particular in mind as she walked toward the front door, she lingered upon the girls. Gip called out to her from the kitchen of which she initially paid no attention, given the way he was calling her name. Just to satiate her curiosity, she turned on her heels just to see what he wanted, seeing as how he wouldn't stop.

"Baby, you look so beautiful," Gip flirted leaving the stove, where he was steaming some crab legs, to walk over to Yara.

Spreading his arms to embrace her for a hug, Yara took a step back and defensively threw up her hands as though she was about to attack.

"Don't touch me," she commanded slightly bouncing on her heels. "Nothing has changed in spite of my gift. You are still on punishment. Just because I said thank you and I love you don't grant you some affection."

"Yara, stop playing and give me a hug. I need to feel you in my arms right now," he pleaded taking a step toward her.

Trying to be intimidating, she lifted her leg and did a kakato otoshi geri kick, and then a jab that was followed with a tomahawk bow to halt Gip's movement. "The air just felt all of that, but you can experience it as well if you'd like," Yara barked, "I'm serious Gip. Didn't James tell you that it would be disrespectful for you to try and buy my forgiveness, 'cause my worth exceeds the value of a gift?"

"Yara, I gave you that Benz because I love you," Gip countered sincerely and trying to be emotional by producing his sad face as though it would soften her heart. "Baby, I'm sorry, but I need to feel you in my arms before you go."

"How many times must I reiterate that you won't feel me until my batteries die off," Yara exclaimed while erupting with laughter. "I'm too sexy to play with you right now sweetheart, but I will carve 'punishment' on your lips with my heels if you try to hinder me from leaving," she assured, turning on her heels and walking toward the front door. "Enjoy your punishment smart mouth, because you won't be enjoying none of this black magic tonight."

Stopping as she looked over her shoulders and spoke her words, Yara smacked herself on the ass while bending over and allowing the definition of her curves to be enticing to his eyes. "All of this soft pecan sweetness belongs to Mercedes right now, baby. Sorry, but I'm a woman of class and I don't share my goodies," she taunted and blew him a kiss as she walked out through the front door, giggling and chatting, "I'm Mrs. Johnson-G63 now."

"Ain't nothing soft or sweet about you," Gip mumbled as the door closed. "You're sour and old!"

"And you're definitely sleeping on the damn sofa tonight!" Yara surprised him by opening the door and yelling. "I heard your smart mouth ass!"

Completely shocked that she heard his mumbling, Gip burst into laughter as he attempted to blow a kiss that was halted by Yara quickly closing the front door again and yelling, "I'm coming, my new husband."

With Toni Braxton's raspy flavor breaking in the G-Wagen's elite sound system, the wind lifting the curls of her hair as it circulates into the sunroof, and the Cartier sunglasses protecting her eyes from the UV rays, Yara picked up Reanna and Cadence. She couldn't stop thinking of their card as they cruised through the city. After treating the girls to lunch at a restaurant on Piedmont Road, they went to Lenox Square Mall and swiped the American Express card without calling Gip for permission.

CHAPTER 15

Feeling sexy in her Navari cotton wrap blouse, blue jeans, and Louboutin stilettos, Sheri sprayed on her Daisy Love by Marc Jacobs before admiring herself one last time in the oversize floor mirror. Grabbing her purse from the bed and mistakenly kicking one of the Salvatore Ferragamo loafers, which she bought for Randle a few days earlier, in the process, caused Sheri to wonder if it was a sign that she should stay at home instead of going out with Naomi. Randle was out with his friends and had no knowledge of her plans. As if she was granted psychic ability and knew her current thoughts, Naomi called while Sheri was sitting on the bed trying to dial Randle to get his permission.

"Gurl, have you left the damn house yet?" She could hear Naomi hollering before lifting the phone to her ear.

"No, I'm ready Ms. Impatient, but give me a few more minutes to get in touch with Randle and I'll call you back," Sheri vowed, trying to sound excited.

"Girl, you mean to tell me that you have to ask permission to walk out of your own house now or to be a damn woman?!" Naomi teased. "You said the same thing thirty minutes ago. If you're not coming then just say it, 'cause I'm not gonna keep sitting around waiting while you try to find your lost pony in an open pasture, Sheri."

"Whatever! Its respect when you're in a relationship, Naomi, to do things your man accepts and is aware of," Sheri clarified. "I'm coming, just give me a minute."

"Before I let a sorry no good muthafucka or some dick control me like a heroin hooker, I'll just buy me a rabbit or a bullet," Naomi insinuated. "Do what you have to girl. I will either be at Bowleg's Bar & Grill or Charles Sport Bar on Marietta Street if your master releases you," she jokingly stated with a southern tone while laughing at her own impersonation. "I love you Sheri, but you are fuckin' pathetic."

"Naomi, don't do that. Just give me a minute," were her last words before she realized Naomi had already disconnected the line.

Since dialing Randle again and again and again for the next hour, Sheri found herself calling his mom, the hospital, and the county jail given that he wouldn't answer the phone, respond to text messages, nor return her call. Walking into the bedroom to retrieve his friend's number off the caller ID box, Sheri glanced at herself in the mirror and decided that she was looking far too sexy to be sitting around and playing an insecure detective while Randle was out with his friends, paying her no attention. After taking a moment to touch up her hair and makeup again, Sheri made sure Trump had extra water in his bowl, the house was secured, and a note detailing where she was going and whom she would be with was visible for Randle whenever he came home.

Trying to get her mind off Randle and in tune with the climate of the nightlife in Atlanta, Sheri injected the canals of her ears with Nicki Minaj and T.I. until she pulled into the sports bar parking lot. Exiting the car and noticing heads turning to admire her beauty, the definition of her curves instilling selfish infatuation, and the enticing sway of her hips that had her stilettos tap dancing on the concrete as she headed toward the entrance, Sheri wouldn't allow herself to feel sexy because she felt it was disrespectful for a man to desire another man's woman.

Electing to utilize the V.I.P access instead of standing in line, to make it seem as though the sports bar is one of the hottest spots in downtown for the night, Sheri was clueless of the fact that entry required cash. Until she approached the door with her debit card in hand, politely declining a gentleman's request to pay her entry out of courtesy. Feeling embarrassed after being denied entry, she texted Naomi, before turning around and began walking back to her car wishing she had stayed home and waited for Randle, only to halt her pursuit after hearing her name being called.

"Sheri! Sheri!" Naomi called out from the door, waving with a power play goal glass in her hand and a gentleman on each side of her as though she was precious treasure. "Gurl, I can't believe you thought you could swipe your damn debit card to get in!" She yelled in Sheri's ear with the music blaring as one of the accompanied gentlemen gave the security guard twenty dollars to pay the entrance fee. "You are too damn bougie," Naomi yelled out, laughing while grabbing her hand to escort her through the door and to their section. "Gurl why didn't you let one of those men pay your entry fee like every other woman do?"

"Cause I'm not every other woman, Stank," Sheri asserted, sitting in her chair "And I'm not disrespecting my man like that."

"Bitch please! You sound like one of those religious cult women raised on a Fort Weirdo isolated compound." Turning to the 6'3" caramel skin toned gentleman to her left who looked like a linebacker in training camp, "This is my homeboy Kellogg, Sheri. He's a personal trainer for athletes and promised to help me tone my body like Liya Kedede, which would add more seduction to my curves." Naomi emphasized while sliding her hand provocatively down her body to squeeze her butt, giggling. "And this is my homeboy, David," Naomi introduced, turning to her right to acknowledge the 6'6" gentleman who looked like preserved African chocolate from the Thembu tribe. "He's a global strategist and eager to talk to you about how he can help with the teaching of the students, and also help you to expand the Unity program." Leaning close to whisper into Sheri's ear, "He also thinks I'm Naomi Campbell's sister, so don't say nothing to spoil it," Naomi grinned. "He wants me to fly to Greece with him next week just to attend a dinner banquet for high echelon investors."

"I'm not lying for you," Sheri voiced with a serious look on her face.

"Gurl, when you find my best friend, tell her to come back because she lost up in there somewhere, and tell her she is GREATLY missed," Naomi bellowed, turning her attention back to the two gentlemen and sipping her drink.

After ordering the dirty bird, some pecorino and black pepper popcorn, plus a shot of Gold to drink, Sheri sat there gazing at Simone Biles compete on one TV monitor while glancing at the Atlanta Hawks on another so as to pass time as Naomi seemed to network and act like she was the light of the night. She was flirting with every individual who seemed to pass by looking sexually enticing. As men approached with the desire of breathing a breath of Sheri's air, not one was able to inveigle or ignite a spark of her interest.

"I have a boyfriend," she openly advised with authority to every gentleman who kindly walked over to the table and said hello or offered to buy her a drink of which she declined.

"Sheri, why are you here if you're not going to enjoy yourself?" Naomi queried, walking over to whisper in her ear. "People get out to escape the reality of their lives, yet you're sitting here texting and calling Randle like a lost whore searching for a pimp."

"Naomi, I'm just worried about him 'cause he's not answering his phone," Sheri admitted with sincerity. "And I don't have to be disrespectful to my relationship to enjoy myself. I'm good," she conveyed while starting to bob her head offbeat to the music.

"Whatever girl! I never want some dick that causes me to lose myself in the process," Naomi uttered while rising out of her seat to dance with David beside the table. "He might not be answering 'cause he's out with another woman, since he realizes he got a Sesame Street puppet at home. All he gotta do is hit the remote-control button to turn you on and turn you off. Run Sheri Run. Hop Sheri Hop. Suck Sheri suck ..."

Looking at her friend as her hateful words echoed in her mind, Sheri rolled her eyes and began to wish she had never come. It had been more than a year since Sheri stepped out into the Atlanta nightlife, something her and Naomi use to do often. Even though she defined in everything she did that her heart was governed by Randle, he was still insecure and jealous of other men admiring her. Sheri loved to dress up and dance but decided to stay away from the social atmosphere as a sacrifice to show that her love for him was sincere. Yet, she had no problem with him going out two or three times a week and staying out all hours of the night without picking up the phone to assure he's okay.

"Would you like another drink, Sheri?" Kellogg asked as he instructed the waitress to bring another round for the table.

"Yes, but I will be paying for my own drink," she alerted the young waitress who giggled in a sense of disbelief as she took Sheri's card and shook her head at how bougie this lady was acting.

"I'd like an On-base Percentage this time please," Sheri ordered.

"Sheri, I mean this with all due respect," Kellogg shared lifting a buffalo wing to his mouth and admiring the thick plus size sister standing behind her bouncing to the music. "Whoever the man is that has your heart is a blessed individual. And respectfully, I don't say that because of your features. I acknowledge that because I was raised in a home with six sisters, and my mom molded the essence of a woman's worth in them until God claimed back the soul, He bestowed on her. Yet, never have I ever witnessed a woman so committed to love that she extracts herself from the equation of life as you. Men have spoken tonight just to mingle, and your only words without raising your eyes to them is, I'm in a relationship. I come out to network, which my woman has no problem with, and to escape, not to try and disrespect my sisters by seeking to serenade their ears with lies for a quick moment of selfish pleasure."

"Well that's nice of you Kellogg, but most individuals do have hidden agendas and I don't have time to entertain their egos," Sheri opined defensively, sitting in her seat, watching Simone Biles run through the competition like she's actually practicing in the gym to have fun, really not paying him any attention.

"You should never judge without the credible facts to back it up, Sheri," he countered. "Here you are an art dealer and a woman trying to help give kids a better option at life, yet you have sat there since the moment you came in acting as though you are the spotlight of attention and refusing to network or socialize with the very people who can help you."

"Excuse me," Sheri exploded, seemingly goaded to respond while cutting her eyes to him with the heated desire of putting him in his place. "I don't know who you think you are talking to," she roared waving her finger with aggression.

"Sheri! Sheri what's wrong!" Naomi interjected walking back over after hearing her.

"Your damn friend thinks I'm one of those simple-minded sisters he can say whatever to."

"No Sheri, I apologize if my words have offended you in any manner," Kellogg informed with sincerity, slightly raising his voice, and leaning closer. "I will never try to disrespect you, nor judge you. And again, I do apologize. The only thing I'm saying is regardless of the love you have for your man, utilize your time to have fun and introduce yourself to the people of your industry."

"Please don't tell me how to utilize my time," Sheri barked. "I've achieved a lot thus far without your wisdom and following your regimen of health, wealth, and success," she professed while rolling her eyes and caring not what he thought.

"Sheri, chill tha fuck out, gurrl, he's right! Here you are since the moment you walked in, looking like a hen in a snake pit. There are marketing advisers here, models, entertainers, athletes, and artists who would probably love to assist with Unity, if not just buy your art. But you're sitting here acting like you are too superior to socialize. That's narcissistic and arrogant. Sheri, you are my best friend, but that pussy of a man you love has caused you to lose the essence of who you are, and that concerns me. You've changed. And for the worse, and that's not healthy, I don't care how you blend it, juice it, slice it or dice it. I don't even recognize you anymore."

"I haven't changed Naomi, I've grown up. We can't act like misguided teenagers forever. I have businesses to run and an image to uphold that inspires our young ladies. I can't be reckless and act like a slut because you consider it acceptable."

Enjoying herself and not wanting to get into a heated argument with her best friend in this manner, Naomi declined to reply as she stared at Sheri wondering what had happened to her friend, her sister from another mother. Reaching into her pocket and retrieving a small bag of single wrapped chocolate bars, Naomi gave David and Kellogg one after placing one in her mouth, then laid the bag on the table without offering any to Sheri.

Noticing her actions, Sheri felt a little offended that her best friend actually offered chocolate to two strangers then left her at the table all by herself with them without saying a word as she walked across the room to flirt with someone at the bar. Reaching to grab the bag from the table, given that chocolate is her favorite candy, Sheri obliged herself to the decadent chocolate as well. With the flavor unlike any she had tasted before, Sheri ate another bar before putting the bag back on the table.

Not realizing the unexpected change in her demeanor, Sheri slowly synchronized her body with the music, bouncing in the seat like the instruments were in her veins and arterial canals and riding the track as though she was the recording artist. When the DJ played one of Nicki Minaj's songs, Sheri could no longer stymie her groove. Sliding out of her chair to stand beside her table, she started dancing and liked the way she saw the men looking at her, especially those who were in the presence of another woman.

With her stilettos creating sparks on the wood, Sheri moved and bounced as if she was barefoot on carpet. Riding on a wave that she had never surfed, Sheri didn't object when a few gentlemen began dancing with her, each secretly competing for her attention and the chance to grind against her body.

Naomi couldn't believe she was seeing what she saw after returning to the bar from the lady's room. Realizing that Sheri wouldn't oblige the gentleman looking like a young Blair Underwood dancing to her side the chance to vibe with her beyond this magical moment, Naomi bounced, leaping at the opportunity of her fantasy of waking up reverse rodeo on his face coming to fruition.

"Gurl, where have you been?" Sheri asked Naomi as she imitated the way Rihanna makes her booty bounce by pressing on the toes of one foot and rotating it side to side.

"Trying to find me a new baby daddy," Naomi boasted, caressing the new gentleman's face seductively, while sliding her other hand down into his chest, as she squatted in front of him and started bouncing her booty more provocatively than a stripper in hope of stealing all of his attention away from her girlfriend.

"Girl, you have never even been pregnant before," Sheri uttered before erupting into laughter. "You have the Depo Provera shot, stupid."

"Don't knock the fact that I have game and men are too simpleminded to think beyond their testicles," Naomi conveyed while laughing and shaking her butt against her new admirer more teasingly than before. "Girl, men be so caught up in themselves, they never take time to learn about you. So, you can tell them anything."

Ordering another drink at her new admirer's request and sitting down as the DJ switched songs, Naomi noticed that Sheri's eyes were barely open as she rode the wave of the music.

"Sheri, did you eat one of these?" She asked grabbing and holding the bag of edibles out for her to see.

"Yes, I ate two," she replied with a giddy laugh while reaching her hand out requesting another one.

"Stupid, these are edibles, not store-bought chocolate. They have THC in them! Gurrrl, you're high as hell right now."

"I don't care what's in them!" She yelled slinging her hair while bending over and grinding on the guy who was enjoying the feel of her body, as they danced like two teenagers seducing each other with foreplay. High for the first time in her life, Sheri was on the ceiling, a floating cloud of ecstasy, free of all thoughts and trapped inside the music. Never before seeing her friend so into the moment and dancing with men in such a sultry and provocative nature, Naomi stop twerking and grabbed Sheri's arm.

"Come sit down girl, you ate too much, and you are waaay out of character right now."

"Naomi, I'm good," she insisted pulling away to continue grooving with the gentleman who was now smacking her on the ass.

Repeating her efforts, since she didn't like seeing her friend treated like a trap Queen, Naomi pulled Sheri back to the table while giggling internally and interlocking their arms as they sat.

"Loose booty, you can't get pregnant by me," Sheri shouted between laughter. "So, can you let me go? I don't want no baby mama drama."

"Hell, the way you were just grinding with that fool and allowing him to feel on you, it seems like you could already be pregnant though," Naomi analyzed.

"Whatever girl! I was just teasing him, allowing him to rub that big hard muscle against me, while fantasizing about being inside of Randle's pussy."

"Well fuucck, he almost was, Stoni. Earth to Sheri, Girl you in the stratosphere. Sheri gone! You a real stoner right now!"

Bobbing her head as thoughts raced through her mind, Sheri never knew that edibles would cause her to feel so indescribable. The slightest touch sent chills through her entire body and had her clitoris tingling. Now that she was accepting drinks, Kellogg bought a round for the table as they sat laughing and joking amongst each other.

"Stop lying," Sheri and Naomi yelled at Kellogg as he told his story of how he spent the night under a woman's bed that he was having sex with, but stopped due to her fiancé coming home.

"Seriously, I'm telling the truth," he replied. "The worst part of it all is that I spent the entire night pinching my nipples and stroking myself, then I'd stop before ejaculating each time just to keep me from falling asleep because I snore. Listening to them have sex while pushing the bed boards into my body was quite crazy. The messed up part of it all though is that the woman seemingly forgot all about me because she not only fell asleep in his arms after their two-hour tango, but she left for work the next morning without saying anything and turned the damn alarm on. I pissed on her carpet three times waiting for my opportunity to leave. Hearing him snore like a hibernating grizzly bear competing in a Winter Olympic Half-pipe Snowboarding event, I took my chance and eased out of there, triggering the alarm as I descended the stairs. I ran like the brother in Roots after struggling to unlock the front door," Kellogg said as everyone giggled.

"So that's why your nipples have seemed to look hard all night," Sheri asked as Naomi laid in her arms laughing.

"Now that's some of that dick I want. That forget everything dick," Naomi mentioned causing everyone to laugh more.

"Hell, all dick causes you to forget," Sheri asserted lifting her drink to sip while giggling at the look Naomi gave.

Bouncing to the music like he was at a Caribbean festival, David interjected, "I believe you masturbated to them having sex at least once," which almost caused Sheri to fall out of her seat due to her laughing so hard. "Yet, I have one that's crazier," he continued lifting his glass of Hennessy to sip on. "So, a few years ago, I meet this white girl at the 511 club in Kingsland, Georgia, right? I think she was a medical corpsman for the Navy or some shit like that. So, ok, not trying to just settle for the unbelievable deep throat affection she gave me in her car, my horny, dumb ass wanted to be intimate with a white woman so bad, since I've heard the stories of how they pussy feel, taste, and smell from my uncle. After she swallowed every drop of me like a thirsty nomad in the desert, I crawled my hot dick ass in her trunk so that she could sneak me on the Kings Bay Navy Base to spend the night with her. I wanted to brand that pink camel's toe with this hammer so bad. Yet, once we were on the base, they called an immediate lockdown due to a fake bomb threat and she fuckin' ... she just fuckin' panicked, and instead of letting me out of the trunk, I stayed in there for forty-eight hours in the freezing fuckin' cold with no food or water. She never even returned just to allow the heater to warm me for a moment knowing it was freezing cold. I could have died out there.

Never in my life had I ever been so scared. A foreigner illegally on a Navy Base, I was quieter than frozen ice, yet shaking like a shipment of vibrators. I almost caught pneumonia laying in constant wet clothes. I had some degree of frostbite 'cause I couldn't feel my toes or my hands the entire time. And when she finally released me instead of offering a little compassion, she dumped me on the side of the road a mile from the base and pulled off as if I never existed. To make matters worse, the police found me and locked me up, thinking I was a homeless man trying to sleep on the street."

"Damn! What if your dick would have gotten frost bitten or you had caught gangrene?" Naomi blurted out jokingly. "Would you have had surgery to put a metal dildo down there or just walked around with a nub?"

"What!? Naomi you crazy as hell," David retorted. "But seriously, I would have tried some type of experimental surgery and allowed them to give me an inflatable prosthetic dick. I love the way pussy taste, but I like the way it feels more than anything."

"You would have never stuck that in me with your nasty ass, unless it vibrated like a rabbit," Sheri added, with a neck roll and snapping her fingers.

"As bougie as you are Sheri, your man probably has to soak his dick in ammonia, then wipe it with a bleached cloth before you let him stick it in you with a condom on," Kellogg blurted out as he made a toast to sterilized pussy.

"Wait! Hold up y'all," Sheri hollered trying to gain their full attention after the toast and sharing of a few more bad sex memories. "Do y'all see that guy at the bar with the Polo soccer shirt and jeans on?"

"Yes," David and Kellogg replied.

"I definitely see his sexy ass, and the fact that my nipples are starting to get hard actually means he want to taste Snapperrrr," Naomi joked seductively.

"Snapper! Girl, your booty looser than a rim on an axle with no lugs," Sheri blurted which caused everyone to laugh but Naomi. "If Naomi can get him to kiss her, then I'll kiss any man in here you choose David. But if she can't, then she has to tongue kiss that guy sitting by the window with the neon green fish outfit on."

Everyone looked to see who Sheri picked, except Naomi, whose mind was lost in the thought of feeling her prey's tongue in her mouth. Swallowing the remainder of her drink in one gulp, Naomi rose out of her seat and walked over putting more sway in her hips, not caring that her last admirer wanted more of her attention, which she brushed his hand off her arm as she walked by.

Laughing as her girlfriend paraded across the floor imitating the sensuous fierceness of Joan Small on a runway, Sheri advised David and Kellogg that the individual was a married gay man who rejects women and still hiding in the closet, because he's a professional football player. The thought of Snapper losing had them all laughing and eyeing with anticipation.

Watching Naomi dance to gain acceptance was so amusing. Sheri never expected Naomi would be able to pull his head onto her neck enticingly as she grinded on him, or to grip his ass while pulling him into her as though they were hunching. Yet, seeing Naomi's hand caress the side of his face as they kissed with what seemed like heated passion, Sheri literally thought she was dreaming and about to lose her mind. The thought of her having to kiss someone she didn't know was disgusting and an aspect of cheating.

"Who's the baddest Nubian boss bitch born in Atlanta since Chanel Iman?" Naomi bolstered returning back to the table smiling as she gave high fives to Kellogg and David before blowing a kiss to Sheri and sitting down. "I've never kissed someone with a tongue so cold, long, and fat. Gurl his tongue is fatter than some dicks I've had in my mouth," she whispered in Sheri's ear.

As they both laughed in secrecy, David began clearing his throat loudly in a silly manner to gain Sheri's attention. She tried to act as though she couldn't hear him due to the music.

"Naomi," he called out as he stood up doing the Bankhead bounce and reaching to grab her hand.

"What, silly?" Naomi said not believing he was doing the bounce of all dances, looking more like a seizure patient choking.

"Sheri challenged your pimpin' and lost, so it's time for her to fulfill her end of the agreement," he expressed in complete amusement.

"Shut up David. This is between my girl and I, not you," Sheri shouted while rolling her eyes. "A joke is just a joke!"

"You made me a part of the agreement when you said I can pick the person for you to kiss bougie bear," he taunted laughing. "Naomi, since she advised us that the guy in the neon green fish suit has breath that makes a bloated dead whale smell like an exotic men's fragrance, and she wanted you to kiss him if you lost, then I pick Mr. Decaying Turtle mouth for her to kiss as well," David declared while doing the cabbage patch dance.

"I'm not kissing that vulture vomit smelling mutherfucker!" Sheri lashed out as her mellow temper became anger. "You have lost your damn mind!"

"Yes, you are kissing him," Naomi interjected cutting her off in the middle of speaking. "Fair is fair, gurrl! You lost and your stank ass tried to be funny. If we have to hold you down like a psychiatric patient, trust me," she said acting silly as she rolled her neck like a hula hoop and playfully pressed her index finger into Sheri's nose imitating a child being bullied. "You will kiss him, with yo stank ass!"

"I'm not kissing him," Sheri hummed while starting to look as if her windpipe had been crushed.

"Don't make us represent Vine City up in here Sheri," Naomi spat, taking a sip of her drink. "We trying to act civilized for once instead of hood. Either you take a shot to the head and go kiss him with your eyes closed, or put this whole pack of gum in your mouth and kiss him like he's Ghost," she advised reaching into her pocket to retrieve a box of Juicy Fruit and wishing she could abuse Ghost's entire body outside of her dreams. "Regardless, stank, your hard booty ass is about to taste that caviar tongue, baby. Better yet, Kellogg will you go get him please?"

"No! Kellogg, nooo!" Sheri pleaded as he rose from his chair, laughing without caring about her begging, and walked across the room to the gentleman who needed to make this a special, unforgettable night.

With each step as they made their way back to the table, Sheri searched her mind for a way to escape, not believing she was in this situation. Just seeing him smile as they approached made her want to vomit, and the thought of his tongue flopping around in her mouth made it worse. "There's no telling what type of contagious bacteria he has in his throat to cause his breath to smell far worse than a chemical spill," Sheri thought aloud.

"Excuse me, everyone," Kellogg politely stated returning back to the table, chuckling. "This is Highlight, everyone, and he has advised that it would be an honor for him to kiss someone as gorgeous as Sheri."

"Shawty, ya mo gorgeous than a heavenly angel to me!" Highlight expressed caressing Sheri intimately with his eyes. "I don't know if ya remember, but you and me was in the elevator about a week ago going to Sun Dial. I tried to spit some pimpin' to ya, but I could tell that ya ignored me 'cause you was scared o' heights. 'N it jes ... see ... seem lack y'all up der in ya mind thankin' ... ya know ya keep ya mind focus on whatever y'all was focusin' on up der in ya head so you kin escape da moment, ya dig?" Highlight ran it down to all of them, and everybody but Sheri burst out laughing just listening to him, while placing their hands over their nose.

With his breath literally smelling worse than a rotten durian pear, everyone eased themselves behind him with tightened faces so that they no longer had to smell the toxic vapors directly, especially Naomi, who was making it worse by covering her nose with one hand and fanning with the other. Sheri felt like she could smell his breath just by looking at him, even as she was holding her own. Sitting there observing the disgruntled faces of her entourage, while seeking a fresh passage of air, Sheri wondered as she dipped her finger in Kellogg's Hennessy, and placed the dripping finger beneath her nose, if she fell out the seat acting as though she fainted, would the staff of the establishment be able to rescue her before Naomi encouraged him to bend down and kiss her lips like a prince in every girl's fairytale.

"Naomi, we need to talk," Sheri insisted looking directly at her, while now pressing the palm of her left hand against her nose.

Laughing as she stood behind Highlight imitating them passionately French kissing, "No, stank, 'cause we have nothing to talk about," Naomi ranted back as if there was heated tension between them.

Throwing her hands up to hit Highlight in the chest as he unexpectedly moved closer, "Hold on. What are you doing?" Sheri exploded defensively and trying not to breathe.

"I wah jes tryna kiss them soft purdy sweet lips o' yo's, shawty," he stated speaking in his bedroom voice. "Ya boy rat chere said you was ova here, ya know, fantasizin' 'bout o' Highlight, ya dig. All in ya feelin' 'bout puttin' yo lips on mine. Iz jes ya didn't know if that was my woman sittin' rat der nex tuh me or not, and he was tired and jealous o' hearin' ya whisper 'bout me. But if I wanted to kiss on ya, then all I hadda do was walk on ova chere'n, shawty, ya feel me? So, here go'n be da Highlight o' ya night, bae," he presented, delivering with his perfect suave broken Ebonics, smiling while spreading his arms as though the spotlight was highlighting him, seemingly expecting to be hugged.

"Do you see a mutherfuckin' shawty in front of you?" Sheri cursed with veins now popping up in her face. "Say with your CDC wanted ass, 'cause I damn well don't see one whenever I look in the mirror. I'm a woman not your damn shawty, nor someone who would ever fantasize of kissing you, let alone breathe your air."

Even if she tried to run, the three of them were not going to let her out of this unnatural freak show. Aggravated at herself, the entire situation, and not listening to Highlight's response, Sheri swallowed the remainder of everyone's drink at the table before slamming her hands forcefully into Highlight's chest and aggressively snatching him into her body as she closed her eyes, prayed, and kissed him. On the count of three in her mind, she shoved him backwards while jumping out of the seat mimicking one trying to vomit, as she sprinted through the crowd to the bathroom.

"You the boss, homie," David cheered embracing Highlight. "How does it feel to kiss those soft sexy lips, homie?"

Producing a smile as though he just had the pleasure of eating a chocolate covered strawberry from Jessica Parker Kennedy's lips, "I feel like a pimp bein' crowned a King in heaven. Um floatin' in a dimenstional loop of ecstasy rat nigh," Highlight proclaimed, before exchanging a few more pounds and walking back to his table licking his lips.

"Naomi, you need to go check on Sheri. It's been almost twenty minutes since she's been gone now, and I'm starting to worry," David expressed, sounding a little concerned, while still laughing at Highlight's clothes and actions.

After being found in the bathroom, scrubbing her tongue with wet paper towels, she began screaming angrily at Naomi. Professing how kissing that Viking breath mutherfucker has her entire mouth numb, and now tasting like she thoroughly chewed before swallowing a year-old decayed chicken. Irritated that Naomi wouldn't stop laughing, she threw a hand full of water into her face.

"Throwing water on me stank ain't going to remove that gross sewage taste from your mouth, heffa," Naomi joked, sticking out her tongue while reaching to grab a few paper towels from the dispenser to pat her face.

"Bitch you have no idea what his tongue has me tasting right now! I hope that son-of-a-bitch hasn't infected me with something." Sheri barked soaking more paper towels with water to scrub her tongue with.

After listening to Naomi detail the hilarious story of how she won a $5,000 dare bet by giving a coma patient some head in the hospital to see if she could make him ejaculate as a way of trying to enlighten the moment, Sheri struggled, retrieving her phone given the laughter was causing her to gasp for air.

"I love you, but you trifling as hell." Sheri exclaimed as Naomi admired herself in the mirror.

"Whatever! Gurrrl, trifling are those who suck dick for chicken boxes."

Ignoring her best friend's ignorance, Sheri called her father to advise him that she needed him to make sure that everyone got home safely, and to secure their cars because she decided to enjoy the rest of the night as though tomorrow wasn't promised, merely to escape the thought of what occurred.

CHAPTER 16

The thought of a big steak omelet with extra mushrooms and no tomatoes from IHOP, after doing a CrossFit workout, had Terry craving like an addict for some particular reason. Instead of showering at the gym to wash away the sweat that looked like oozing glitter on his face, neck, and arms, or to remove the sweat drenched tank top that seemed as if it was no more than cellophane wrap vacuum sealed against his muscles, Terry jumped in his SUV caring not about lubricating his leather seats with perspiration and headed up Peachtree Road to Buckhead.

Paying no attention to his appearance since his appetite was dictating without words, Terry got out of the SUV to stretch after parking in the lot. He walked into IHOP as though his mission was to instill lust in the eyes of every female bystander given his appearance. Kindly being escorted to his seat, Terry gave the waitress his order without needing a menu and paid no initial attention to the book club members sitting in the center, admiring his glistening physique. As he casually strolled down the aisle texting his financial advisor, the elderly ladies were no longer discussing their views of the book they had read, but the appeal of his bulging muscles until one of the senior citizens shocked him and her attentive associates by aggressively grabbing his entire left butt cheek and squeezing with selfish intentions, as three fingers slid between his crack.

"Excuse me, sunshine," granny grinned, while staring intently into his eyes as though to arrogantly say, "I'm too much woman for you baby-boy," and giggling in unison with the other ladies at what she had boldly done. "I just wanted to see if you have muscles back there as well sunshine or was it soft and flabby like mine." They all died laughing.

Startled on account of her actions, Terry didn't know whether to feel violated or honored standing there given that she was an elder in a wheelchair, yet smiled as he eased into the booth a few steps away from the entourage. Unable to hear the continuous whispers amongst them after inserting his ear buds, their eyes clearly acknowledged he was the star attraction and topic of discussion. Sitting there and staring out the window, he raised the volume on his phone to listen attentively to a business lecture on how to effectively create a marketing campaign to attract new customers. Terry couldn't help but wonder what Mama Lewis would have done if she had been present. The thought of her waving her gun like an outlaw had him laughing as he answered the incoming call.

"What's so funny Terry?" Reanna curiously asked.

"Just a crazy thought I was having of Mama Lewis, Sweetie. What's good with you?"

"My girlfriend, Roz, and I are on our way to watch the Clark University drumline practice on the field before checking out the fraternity step show competition. I'm calling to see if I can drive the car Demi call a Demon," Reanna requested with politeness and saying "please" with so much desire that it would soften the Grinch's heart.

"Sure, as long as you know how to drive and have your license. Didn't my father just award you a new car?"

"Well my dad keeps promising that he's going to teach me how to drive, but he seems to always be too busy spending his free time with his girlfriend's kids. And you don't drive a rare collector's antique just anywhere, Terry," Reanna voiced in her persuasive tone. "I have my Georgia ID but not my license."

Laughing at the frustrated and nearly defeated sound of her reply. "Girl you are too silly and definitely will not be playing bumper cars with my new baby. Do you want me to pick the two of you up in the Challenger and drop y'all off at AU?"

"Noooo, I need to be behind the wheeeeel not in the passenger seat, so like, but if you not gonna let me floss just this one time," she continued while giggling. "I mean, the real reason I called is because I wanted to know if my mother drops us off at the college, will you come pick us up with the ceilin' missin' once it's over with, please?" Reanna asked.

"Sweetie, you know I will always be there for you without hesitation. I was talking to Demi about you last night. Just call me whenever the two of you are ready and I promise I'll teach you how to drive this weekend."

"Okay! Thanks! I like Demi, she reminds me so much of Carmen who you use to date from Cleveland Ave. I hate that you messed up with her because she was my friend and always sweet to me. And what were you saying about me Terry, something good or bad?" She inquired.

"Always good, sweetie, I'll never belittle you to anyone. I showed her one of your mini films and was advising her of how much promise I see in you. While you're at the college, be careful and don't lose sight of the things that I've shared with you. You will be surrounded by older boys who will try to manipulate your thoughts in every selfishly errant aspect just to gain your acceptance. Do not drink from anything you didn't break the seal on, nor buy from a store yourself. Seriously, those boys' intentions do not center upon who you are or helping to cultivate your inner potential. So, don't allow their words or gestures of goodwill to hypnotize your mind."

"Terry, the one thing I do is listen when you talk to me. My focus is not on boys right now. I'm not foolish enough to believe that you don't know what you be talking about, when I see all the things you be advising me of with the boys at school. My dreams are more important to me than the acceptance of individuals who offer my life nothing at this moment but selfish desires. I don't want to take detours merely to be considered cool by my peers, when my straight and narrow path is clear ahead. We are not going up there with the intention of trying to mingle with anyone. We are honestly going to watch the drumline practice on the field and the girl's fraternity step show," Reanna admitted.

"I trust you, Sweetie. Just call me when the two of you are ready, but I also need you to make a promise to me."

"A promise of what?" Reanna asked as curiosity swept into her mind.

"I need you to promise me that if anyone, and I mean anyone, ever touch you in a way you feel disrespects your honor, you come to me knowing I will not judge you but will be there to comfort and support you. Sweetie, as a man, I know we do many foul things out of selfish ignorance, which is why I share this with you. I never want you to feel afraid of anyone, fault yourself for their aggressive actions, or feel as though you will be ridiculed and not believed. Your body is your treasure, and no one has the right to violate that treasure, even with a simple kiss to your cheek. I never want you to take sexual abuse lightly or be afraid to come forward to express what happened and how you feel as a result. It's never your fault!"

"I promise, Terry! I understand what you are saying, and I truly promise," Reanna assured. "It would be nice if you promised to let me drive the Vert when you pick us up," she intoned while laughing.

"I promise to let you drive any one of my vehicles when you learn how to drive and get your license, sweetie," he replied before saying I love you, hanging up the phone, and finishing his breakfast.

Leaving IHOP, Terry had nothing more on his mind other than taking a shower and changing into some clothes that didn't have him looking like a struggling Chippendale dancer. Yet, when an associate called seeking his help because she was stranded not too far from his location with a flat tire, being a gentleman, he couldn't refuse. Pulling up behind her car and jumping out of the SUV, Terry couldn't help but wonder if she was giggling at something personal or the fact that he was out of character being seen in public with wet workout clothes on. After sharing a formal embrace and greeting that sparked a conversation, Terry quickly removed the spare and car jack from her truck, laid the tire on the ground by the right rear flat and attempted to start jacking the car after loosening the lugs.

"One of these days you will open your eyes to realize that seeking only to benefit from a man financially will not grant you true happiness," Terry predicted as he pulled the rim off the axle.

"Fuck emotional happiness! Having my bills paid, being pampered, and receiving luxury gifts is what makes me happy," she uttered nonchalantly with her Puerto Rican accent.

"You sound simple minded and stupid, making that statement as though you have no true self value," Terry replied.

"Whatever, you see me boo'ed up with this shiny new badass Porsche 718 Boxster, and you say I have no value," she exclaimed attempting to roll her neck savagely and sucking her teeth.

"Value exceeds material things which should never define your worth," Terry added, untightening the tire lugs, "when it should be integrity and character. The fact of the matter is, compassion has me out here changing your tire instead of a AAA serviceman or your so called man whom you claim had the audacity to say he was too busy to come help you or even make a call to get you some assistance."

"That's why I got friends like you, mi amigo," she purred, humorously.

"You know I will always have your back," Terry voiced while lifting the spare to put on the axle. "But you have to learn to stop taking yourself for granted. It's sad when you allow men to do it 'cause they give you a few dead Presidents, yet it's much worse when you do it to yourself. Define your worth by your mind, not your body!"

"Who the fuck is that white bitch in the car with him?" She shouted, causing Terry to look up at her and peer through the car windows as curiosity surfaced in his mind. "Terry, my boyfriend just pulled up, act like we don't know each other please. You're just some stranger helping me out of generosity, given that I was stranded, Okay, papi?"

"What!? Damn, you gonna disrespect me like that, chica?!" Terry piped in total disbelief of the words that just rolled off her tongue. Laying the spare back on the ground beside the flat one, he stood up and began walking back to his vehicle without saying a word.

"Terry you're not going to put the tire on for me?" She yelped aloud.

"Your man is here so you no longer need the help of an unappreciated stranger," he stated sarcastically while opening the door and stepping up inside the G-Wagen, not clearly understanding why so many women surrender who they are for a man's acceptance that offers them nothing as a whole.

Sitting there staring at someone he considered a friend act like a puppet to a man whom probably has his wife or another one of his side chicks in the car caused him to shake his head as he started the SUV. The disappointed look on her face bothered him as he pulled off, especially seeing through the rear-view mirror that her so-called boyfriend did the same without stepping out the car to say a word or physically assisting. Noticing a sign that said Big Donny was performing at the comedy club as he drove down Marietta Street, Terry called Demi to see if she was up to attending a show, given that they had reservations at Benihana's later.

"I don't mind as long as he's funny," Demi acknowledged. "But if he doesn't make me laugh like Jessica Moore, Bruce, or Lavell Crawford, then you have to treat your little cousin Cadence and I to an entire day of doing whatever we desire since you wasted my time."

"Our time can never be wasted in each other's presence because we are blessings to one another. But I will accept your deal. Hold on, my mom's calling."

"Tell her that I said hello," Demi mentioned before he switched lines.

"How are you doing, ma?"

"I'm okay baby," Mrs. Johnson answered, "I was on the way to check on Sheri, but the artist Mario Edison the Mafesto just called to inform he's finished with the portrait I asked him to do for Mama Lewis, called the '*Keeper of the Storm.*' So, I'm asking that you ride by and check on your sister, if you can baby because I have to meet him shortly."

"Demi's on the other line ma and she sends her greetings. Is everything okay with Sheri?" He asked with sincere concern being heard in his voice. "Has something happened?"

"I like Demi, Terry, I hope you don't mess things up with her. I honestly think she's the backbone that you need to define who you truly are in life. She's strong and knows her value as a woman. Give her my greetings as well. Yes, I think Sheri's alright, just maybe embarrassed and still recovering from being sloppy drunk and high for the first time in her life," his mom pointed out to ease his thoughts. "Her and Naomi went out two nights ago and got drunk like it was 1999. Your father had One Eye and a few of the guys pick them up and take them home. I just wanted to make sure that she's okay given no one has heard from her and she hasn't been answering her phone since then, that's all.

"I'll ride by there," he assured before they said goodbye and he switched back over to Demi. In the past few weeks, the two of them have spent every day learning more and more about each other. She liked how Terry tried hard to be genuine and had no problem stepping out of his comfort zone as a playboy to show a different more responsible side of himself. The fact that he truly took the time to discover who she was internally beyond the words she openly conveyed to him impressed her, because most men settle for whatever just for attention and access.

"What are you doing right now?"

"On my way to my sister's house to shower then I'm going to go chill at my grandma's house because I promised Reanna I'd pick her and Roz up when the step show competition is over."

"So, you mean to tell me that you're riding around looking like a ligger and smelling like your mum raised you in a pig pen?" Demi inquired while giggling.

"No, I'm riding around smelling like I hugged you and looking like I had to fight you off from trying to kiss me," Terry voiced jokingly.

"Interesting you said that, because I was contemplating allowing you to kiss me tonight for the first time. However, that just wouldn't be proper since I stink apparently, and have rapist tendencies, according to you, chap. So just to be clear then, just know that's no longer an option and a quite distant thought."

Wanting to yell out the words "I'm sorry," but deciding to say nothing at all, Terry drove shaking his head at how she likes to tease him by denying her affection while also wondering if she would change her mind.

"Come get me and I'll ride with you," Demi offered. "I'd like to go to the fraternity step show. I've never seen one in person."

"Well, do me a favor which would save us some time. Run up the street to the mall right quick, if you don't mind please, and grab me some Polo boxer briefs, a tank top, some socks, a Polo outfit, some cologne you'd like to smell on me, and a pair of Polo skippers or all white Air Force Ones from Footlocker. I will give you your money back once I pick you up," Terry promised.

"Is there anything else you need, Boss? Since I'm your personal assistant now," Demi spat jokingly.

"Yes, I need you to make sure you bathe and brush your teeth, 'cause I don't want to smell like this anymore, nor do I want to kiss you with your breath smelling like moose breath," Terry chuckled.

"Laugh now, cry later wanna be T. Kirkland. I guarantee that your comedian jokes will not have you laughing when you can't touch me," she added before hanging up the phone.

Terry liked the way Demi would try to define her strength between them or be sassy in a charming way. She commanded her sense of respect, which was appealing, but the way she teased with her affection seemed to get inside his head, something only Janelle Monae's voice has ever achieved. Cruising along the expressway, Terry wondered what life would be like to exist in the rays of Demi's smile. To be governed with her love. He likes the way her footsteps are an aphrodisiac to his mind and the way she seemed to inspire him even in her absence.

Exiting the expressway, Terry noticed a little Asian lady selling roses and balloons on the corner at the traffic light. So, he turned into that gas station to fill up even though the fuel gauge registered half full. Assuming that surprising Demi with something unexpected may suppress her desire to punish him, he walked over before leaving the station and purchased all six dozen roses in which she had in her possession.

Deciding not to blow the horn as he eased into a parking spot and shifted the vehicle into park, he texted Demi to let her know that he was outside. She could not hide her smile stepping out of her apartment, and seeing him stretched across the hood of his SUV, as though he was posing for a Maxim or Sports Illustrated Valentine's Edition cover with three dozen roses hiding his face.

"These roses are beautiful and I'm thankful that you thought of me. Yet, they do not get you a hug," Demi sassed approaching with a sense of authority as Terry rose to give her the roses, which she took back in the apartment to insert them into a vase of water.

"You are more beautiful to my eyes every time I'm blessed to see you." Terry openly acknowledged anticipating a hug as she returned.

"Boy please! Business before pleasure," Demi insisted returning and holding the bags in her hand.

Cackling at her words, Terry stood admiring Demi in her wrapped halter dress and stilettos. The way she was wearing her hair in a layered bob, seemed to make her attractiveness more seductive and exotic, paired with her hips causing her stilettos to rhythmically clap against the pavement. Terry stood suspended in time with his eyes caressing her entire body in awe, for it seemed every time he was granted the pleasure of existing in her moment, she was more captivating than before. Opening the G-Wagen door and reaching into the center console for his wallet, Terry removed five one hundred-dollar bills and handed it to Demi who inspected each bill for authenticity before releasing the bags. "The extra is out of respect for your gas and time," he mentioned before she could ask, "I see you don't trust me!"

"It's not about trust Terry, it's business, and the extra doesn't grant you any additional points," Demi clarified, inserting the bills into her wallet and stepping into the vehicle as Terry closed the door behind her. "A co-worker's mother was arrested for trusting her daughter's son. The young man gave his grandmother several hundred dollars in counterfeit notes, which he collated with real notes, and the last thing she would ever expect is for any of that money to be counterfeit. And this especially given that it came from her grandson whom she had blessed with so much, and it was actually supposed to be the same notes she withdrew from the bank personally and asked him to hold onto a few hours earlier. By her not checking that currency in his presence, she was later arrested for trying to spend it, which I can only imagine is the most embarrassing thing one could ever imagine. So, to protect myself, I check all currency that's given to me because I'm not getting arrested for anyone else's selfish greed."

Disconnecting Terry's phone from the infotainment system as they pulled off, and connecting her cellphone without asking, Demi selected Monica on her playlist then leaned back in her seat like a lady of prominent stature and bounced all the way to Sheri's house.

Pulling into the driveway, Terry called Sheri's cellphone twice and received no answer before grabbing a dozen roses and his bags from the rear seat while exiting the vehicle with Demi. Reaching to hold her hand in a gesture of affection to see how she would respond while walking up the steps, Demi slapped Terry's hand.

"Touching me caused you to smell like a wet bull remember," Demi reminded him. "Even though you always smell like a bull wrestler."

Laughing at her words and the fact that she smacked him like one who disciplines a child, Terry turned to her and voiced as he pressed the door bell, "Don't make my sister come out here and show you how a southwest Atlanta woman acts when you hit their brother."

"Don't let the pretty looks and mannerisms be blinders to your pupils, 'cause there's nothing soft or airy-fairy about a woman raised in Stockwell, London. Your sister better knows how to throw her hands like Cecilia Braekhus and bob and weave like Mayweather. Otherwise, she'll bloody well spend days hearing bells and seeing stars, and I don't mean Hollywood," Demi barked with assurance in her voice without laughing.

"You not 'bout that life," Terry joked pressing the doorbell again. Setting the bags and flowers down, Terry dialed his mom to inform her that he was at Sheri's house, but she wasn't home.

"Baby, she's there, I'm sure probably sleeping," Mrs. Johnson replied. "I'm surprised that freeloading boyfriend of hers is not there with his sorry ass. Given the way she was drunk and high off edibles, it would be uncharacteristic of her to be out doing anything, knowing she went against her principles. Baby, it's even more of an insult that he's not there taking care of her. Walk around the garage side of the house and lift the rock in front of the statue by the fence. There's a door key underneath and the security code is your birthday backwards."

"Okay mom, I'll call you back in a few minutes," Terry informed her before hanging up the phone to dial his sister's number again while pressing the doorbell a few more times as the phone rang. "I'll be right back," Terry advised Demi when the voicemail recording came on.

Walking around the house to retrieve the key, Terry peered through the garage window and noticed that her Lexus was parked. He began to assume that she was sleeping or out with her boyfriend but couldn't stop feeling more so that something wasn't right.

"Sheri! Sheri! Sheri!" He yelled hoping to gain her attention as he approached the front door again after retrieving the key.

"Terry, what are you doing?" Sheri tried to yell from her bedroom window as Terry was about to insert the key into the lock. "Why are you here?"

"I'm here to check on my drunk ass sister because I love you," he responded with every measure of his heart. "Why haven't you been answering the phone?" He yelled, looking up at the window, but unable to see his sister. "Come and open the door, Sheri."

"I haven't answered the phone 'cause my head has been throbbing and I don't want to be bothered by anyone. I'm not in the mood for any company right now, Terry. I'll call you later," Sheri attempted to shout, still unable to open her mouth wide enough while standing, not quite visible in her window.

Hearing her muzzled tone, he became more adamant, "Sheri, come and open the door. I have some flowers for you," he acknowledged while sensing that something wasn't right.

"Terry, I'm not coming to open the door 'cause I don't want to be bothered right now. Respect that Terry, please," she voiced as though she was about to cry instead of speaking in the tone of one who's being direct. She knew Randle wanted no one in the house and she wasn't about to defy his command.

Turning his gaze to Demi for a brief second, "The way she sounds has me feeling something isn't right," Terry said. "My sister is acting strange."

Securing his bags in his left hand and raising his eyes to her window again, "Sheri, are you going to come open the door?" He asked one last time.

She replied, "No, Terry, no," causing him to insert the key into the lock, granting himself entry as she cried aloud, "Please leave."

After noticing the alarm was not even activated Terry escorted Demi to the living room, dropped his bags on the sofa, and handed Demi the flowers while instructing her to put them in water. He then ran upstairs to his sister's room, only to find her bedroom door locked. Hearing her beg him to leave the house prompted him to dial his mom back to tell her what was going on.

Terry's mind went blank hearing his mother say, "She may be acting that way because Randle has beat her again. Naomi is on hold, and she's concerned as well. Sheri is also ignoring her texts and calls. Naomi says that Randle would certainly become hostile after seeing ..."

Cutting his mom off, ending the call without saying goodbye, Terry kicked the door open without saying a word or knowing if Sheri was against the door listening to their conversation. The literal thought of someone having the nerve to hit his sister had unbridled rage consuming every inch of his body.

The sound of Terry's foot smashing against the door startled Sheri and caused alarm for Demi as the door split from the lock and flew open. Seeing his sister standing before him just footsteps away, looking as though her face was used as a punching bag to relieve anxiety, instantly caused a tear to fall from his eye before a word could be spoken and before he could lift his arms to embrace his fragile, bruised, and battered sister with a comforting hug.

"Terry, is everything alright?" Demi called out from the living room.

"No, it's not Demi. Just wait downstairs, beautiful. Where is that muthafucka, Sheri!" Yelling, he commanded, then attempting to embrace her.

She pushes away, "Terry, please leave my house," she stood there begging as she lowered her gaze to the floor to keep herself from looking into his eyes and allowing all of her bruises to be visible.

"You have lost your damn mind to think I'm about to leave after seeing your face like this!" Terry scolded. "Now, where is that muthafucka, Sheri?"

Their vocal exchange caused Demi to disregard his request and ascend the stairs. "What's going on, Terry?"

"Terry, leave him alone. It wasn't his fault."

"What the hell you mean, it wasn't his fault, Sheri? What you saying, he mistakenly beat you while he was sleep walking? There's no fucking excuse for any man to raise his hands to a woman. Especially my muthafuckin' sister! Now, tell me where that bitch muthafucka is?" Terry again commanded, walking over to look in the bathroom and closet. "Demi, I'm looking for her coward ass boyfriend!
"

"Terry, I went out to a bar the other night with Naomi without his permission and mistakenly ate a couple edibles and did something I know I shouldn't have which led me to get sloppy drunk. It's my fault, so please leave my house." Sheri begged, before trying to scream out of frustration, but the swelling in her jaws wouldn't allow her mouth to open that wide.

"I don't wanna hear none of that bullshit, Sheri! Gip Johnson is your father, not Randle. What the fuck you mean you didn't ask his permission to go out, like you're a child?! I'm not going to ask you again, where is Randle? Demi, tell me if he shows up downstairs. He has beaten my sister like she's not even human!"

Closing her eyes in frustration, the only words that seemed to resonate with her tongue was, "Terry, please leave my house."

Sheri are you alright?" Demi questioned, but received no reply. "Walking back downstairs, visibly escalating in frustration, she couldn't believe a man could beat a woman so maliciously that she faults herself. "Oh my God Terry, I'm so sorry! Is she alright?

"I'll get to the bottom of this. She looks so awful. Would you please pour her a glass of juice, if you don't mind," Terry spoke through the pain and frustration, while escorting her back to the kitchen to crush some ice that he wrapped in two towels before running cold water over them.

"This is horrible, Terry. Sheri is traumatized and embarrassed, so you've got to take a different approach to get her calm, then she will talk. How bad is it? Is her face totally disfigured?" Demi said with an increased heart rate.

"I can't even recognize her, Demi. This guy is an animal. He doesn't belong here. He needs to be mummified and he will be caged." Terry decreed.

"Ok, listen to me. She needs your love right now, not your bravado. Right now you're in attack mode, so please try to calm down and be very very gentle and loving with her. Appeal to her senses and ensure that she realizes that we're here to support her, not attack the man that she loves and is defending. She's literally making excuses for him. I heard what she said. So, breathe deeply, count to ten, and suppress your anger for now. Can you do that?" A clear minded Demi guided.

After listening to Demi's advice on how to communicate with his sister, Terry walked back to her room with the juice, towels of crushed ice, and a greater sense of communicating with his battered and bruised precious sister, yet dismissing even the thought of any reason that would justify a man striking a woman.

"Sheri, we are one heartbeat. You know I love you incredibly. Excuse my reaction to seeing you like this. I brought you a glass of juice. Here, see if you can drink it." He exclaimed extending it out to her.

She tried, but it dribbled down her face. "I can't right now."

"Ok, I'll take it and set it on the nightstand."

Let's put these ice packs on your face, but I need you to lay down first, sis" Terry calmly suggested to Sheri as he set the juice on the nightstand, observing her trying to peer through the window.

Knowing the distinctive look in her brother's eyes and hearing the not quite so calm tone of his voice, she obliged without saying a word. Folding one ice packed towel to rest across her eyes and placing the other towel against her jaw, Terry just stared at his sister in complete disbelief.

"Sheri, tell me what happened."

"I don't want to think about it," she mumbled as though there was a choice.

"I wasn't asking you Sheri," Terry scoffed, starting to sob as her words finally became relevant to his ears.

"Daddy's security guys, James and One Eye brought me home. Randle said nothing as he stood watching James carry me from the SUV to the bedroom and laid me on the bed with Randle present. Yet, once they left, he started yelling about how I disrespected him by going out without seeking his permission first. Then, he started accusing me of being a slut and hitting me 'cause I was drunk in James' arms, but he knows pretty well that they work for our father. Terry please don't do anything to him. Randle didn't mean to do this to me. He was a little drunk himself, and I enticed it by not effectively communicating with him. I'm serious Terry, don't touch him."

"Who the hell are you?" Terry questioned staring at his sister in complete disbelief. "My sister is a woman who knows her self-worth, not a puppet whose only value is to be a puppet and a punching bag. I'm baffled! I can't believe you're laying here making excuses for him. You are unbelievable! Where is he right now, Sheri?" He attempted to control the anger accentuating his demeanor and speech.

"I don't know Terry, and I wouldn't tell you if I did," Sheri answered with a sense of arrogance in her voice.

"I respect that," he admitted rising from the bed and walking toward the door. "Get you some rest, I'll be downstairs."

Sharing the news with Demi as they sat on the sofa, all Terry could really think of were the bruises upon his sister's face. "I appreciate you Demi. Thank you for waiting, patiently. The nerve of him beating her like a man, and all because she went to a sports bar with a friend?! Highly unacceptable on every level." Internal frustration had Terry refusing to retrieve the vibrating phone from his pocket as his mother and father repeatedly called. With Randle seemingly lost in the wind and Sheri finally resting after an hour of complaining about the pain in her face and chest area, Demi talked Terry into taking a shower.

The water was therapeutically beating against his body, but Terry couldn't erase the vision of his sister's face from his mind. Dressing, Terry leaned down and picked up his phone as it vibrated in his sweatpants on the floor and noticed it was Reanna calling.

"Are you ready sweetie?" He asked raising the phone to his ear.

"To drive the Vert, yes I'm ready," she joked while starting to giggle.

"Girl what's up with you and my Vert?" Terry asked out of curiosity and chuckling along with her.

"Demi told Cadence and I that driving a muscle car gives a woman an adrenaline rush that's indescribable and have you feeling invincible. I want to feel it," Reanna confessed. "She also told us how you were seemingly about to wet your pants when you allowed her to drive. She said that you were squeezing the door handle, making cry-baby faces, and squinching like a girl."

"Now I know you don't believe no crazy tale like that sweetie," Terry tried to save face while walking out of the bathroom and peering into Sheri's room to see her still sleeping.

"But no, we not ready. I was calling to say that we will meet you in three hours in front of the entrance on James P. Brawley Drive," Reanna informed him.

"Okay sweetie. I will be there," Terry assured before disconnecting the line and calling Demi a snitch as he approached the sofa looking and smelling like a new man. "Why you tell the girls that boldfaced lie, saying I looked like I was about to wet my pants when you drove my car?"

Rolling her eyes, she centered her attention back on the movie Reanna encouraged her to watch, called "B12ck Cocoon." "I don't lie nor did I lie," Demi responded. "And don't insult my character 'cause your ego won't allow you to openly admit the truth. You and I both know that if I had pressed my stilettos into those horses' necks any more, we would have had to pull into Walmart to grab you some wet wipes and pampers," she boldly quipped while bursting into laughter. "You were scareddddd, scaredy cat ..."

"Is that so?" Terry questioned without cracking a smile and walking into the kitchen. "I'm about to cook her something to eat, would you like something as well, Demi?"

"It depends on what you're about to prepare," she replied without moving her eyes from the TV screen and getting a little emotional watching the movie.

"A quick lemon pasta with shrimp," he stated in his Italian voice.

"It really depends Terry," turning to give her full attention to him. "If you want to stay here to comfort your sister then my answer is yes, 'cause I understand

and respect it. She really needs the support right now, and I'm here for the both of you. But if stepping away helps you to suppress the tension you have built inside for Randle, then I say no, I don't want any, and let's keep our arrangement." Terry just allowed a smile to form upon his face staring at Demi. She was a breath of fresh air in a house that seemed to have no ventilation.

With the food prepared, Terry walked her plate to the room, then sat on the bed to feed his sister, after waking her. The act of sincerity reminded him of their childhood days when he would treat her like a Queen and act like a servant at her command, feeding her meals at the table which would always cause his father to look at him crazy because his mom would request to be treated the same way.

"Sheri, I love you — never forget that. This is not acceptable to me, and this toxic yoke, you have to break. Whatever you are going through, I'm here for you. There is no love in abuse."

"Terry, I love you too, but please believe me when I say Randle didn't mean to do this. He is going through a lot right now, and I should not have been selfish. He has apologized and promised that it won't happen again," Sheri cried, trying to convince him that her words were genuine. "Please respect my privacy and don't mention this to dad or mom! Please!"

Staring at his sister without responding as she was speaking to deaf ears, Terry couldn't conceal the tears that raced down his cheeks while staring at her bruises in disbelief. "Do you need me to stay here with you?" He asked as Sheri reached out and gently wiped the melting emotions from his face.

Not wanting Randle to know she had guests in the house without his permission, "No Terry, I'm okay," she insisted laying back into the pillows and looking up at Demi standing in the doorway with an expression on her face as though she was viewing a ghost, having never physically witnessed someone so battered. In reality, it was too late for her ploy to keep guests a secret.

"I don't want the two of you to worry about me. Demi you are looking too good in that outfit to be sitting in this house for any reason," Sheri stated, pressing the ice pack into her jaw, while praying they would leave before Randle returned.

Without saying another word, Terry walked into the bathroom and started running bath water so Demi could assist Sheri before leaving if need be. Terry went downstairs to wash all the dishes and finally answered one of his father's calls, "What's good Daddy?"

"I'm trying to see what's goin on and where you're at mentally, son."

"Dad, I'm in control. The actual sight of seeing Sheri like this has honestly broken me internally, and to hear her make excuses for his actions as though it was her fault has me baffled."

"Son, I will address the situation, but I need you and Demi to leave without you making a rash decision. Aaron will be on his way when he finishes the arrangement he has with Harley Quinn."

"Harley Quinn?" He questioned in complete bewilderment.

Chuckling to himself before responding, "Your grandma son," Mr. Johnson informed before sharing a few more words and disconnecting.

He listened to the remainder of the lecture as he sat on the sofa relaxing with his eyes closed. The gentle touch of Demi's hand upon his head to acknowledge her presence sent stimulating chills through his body like a slight jolt of electrical current. Opening his eyes, and removing his ear buds, Terry never expected to hear Demi scream as she did.

Unknown to everyone, Randle had returned and was hiding behind the wall in the den trying to figure out if Terry was one of her father's security guys or a guy that she was seeing on the side that she called over to protect her from him. Never had Sheri ever sought outside assistance when his rage overpowered him, and he apologized before leaving as he always did. From his hidden position, he was unable to see the entire room clearly, yet able to view Terry sitting alone on the sofa. Wearing a dress that hugged her curves and having identical skin complexion to his eyes, Randle assumed Demi was Sheri. When she caressed Terry's head with what seemed like gentle affection, Randle realized that it wasn't one of her father's guys. The sight of her touching another man engulfed him with anger. He lunged from behind the wall as rage enveloped his senses.

"Bitch, I'll kill you!" He hollered, startling Demi, as he grabbed a hand full of her hair with his right hand and yanked backwards with unyielding force. It caused her to stumble before falling against the wall and sliding to the floor. Jealous and outraged, He paid no attention to Terry as he turned and thrust his foot into her stomach while repeatedly yelling, "Bitch, I'll kill you!"

Acrobatically, Terry leaped over the back of the sofa without standing as though it were a pommel horse. His right hand created the sound of a M-800 firecracker exploding as it connected with Randle's jaw, instantly lifting him off the ground like wet paper, and colliding with the wall. The sight of Demi laying there crying as she held her stomach infuriated Terry as he lifted her off the ground and sat her on the sofa.

"Are you okay, baby?" He asked; peripherally seeing Randle squirming and hearing Sheri call out to Randle as though he was the victim.

Terry walked over and hit Randle with a left hand hook directly to the ribs, which was followed with a right elbow to the base of his chin that tilted his head as he leaned forward in excruciating pain. Exercising a combination of quick powerful jabs that lacerated his eye and mouth upon impact, Randle was bounced against the wall unable to block Terry's assault with anything but his face. Every hit seemed to be timed with precision and sounded like iron was slamming against plywood.

"Stop Terry! Terry, stop hitting him!" Sheri begged as Terry repeatedly engaged his knuckles into the blood drenched texture of Randle's face.

With blood splashing with every collision and sensing that Terry wasn't going to stop crushing his face, Sheri ran into the kitchen and dialed 911 on the wall phone.

"Please help!" She cried when the operator answered. "My brother is going to kill my boyfriend. Please send help!"

"Terry, that's enough!" Demi shouted while touching his shoulder. "Seriously that's enough."

Not truly caring for Randle as he laid on the floor gasping for oxygen and bleeding from multiple lacerations his fists had caused, "If you ever touch my sister, or any woman again, I'll snap your fucking neck you low life coward." Terry growled, while open handedly slapping Randle one last time and rising to look at Demi.

"I'm sorry," he whispered before pulling her into his arms. "I despise cowards who beat on women."

"Baby! Baby! What have you done Terry!?" Sheri screamed falling to the floor to cradle Randle in her arms, caressing him with every measure of her twisted affection. "Baby, it's going to be okay. I'm sorry Randle. Baby, I'm sorry."

The actions of his sister had Terry at a complete loss for words. Here he was fighting for her honor and respect, yet she's consoling Randle as though he's a saint, wrongly accused.

Hearing the sounds of the sirens moments later and seeing the lights flash through the window, Sheri laid Randle down before jumping up and running to open the front door while urging, hurry, hurry, hurry to the paramedics as the ambulance pulled into the driveway behind the police.

"He's right here," she stood in the doorway pointing and granting entry to the officers first.

With the two paramedics attending to Randle's condition, the officers tried to investigate what happened. Demi couldn't believe she was hearing Sheri give an in depth account of Terry's actions, yet denied that Randle laid a hand on her, claiming she fell down the stairs trying to reposition the books she was carrying. Wanting to interject to expose that the fight ignited because Randle attacked her out of nowhere, pulling her hair, slamming her forcefully against the wall, kicking her in the stomach and making terroristic threats of killing her, thinking that she was Sheri, which caused Terry to leap to rescue and defend her, Demi held her tongue, fearful for some reason and simply questioned, "How can you stand there and lie like that against your brother, Sheri?" Demi queried with anger visibly written across her face. "You're telling on your brother, knowing you're only telling a half truth, while protecting the man who treats and beats you like a whore. You are truly a disgrace, a disrespect and dishonor to all women, and I mean all women, not just those of color."

"Excuse me ma'am," the officer turned to Demi and questioned.

"Did you see him hit her?"

"No sir," she replied, "But what's obvious requires no explanation."

"Did you witness the altercation between these two gentlemen, ma'am?"

"No sir, I didn't."

"Ma'am, how do you know the injuries to Ms. Johnson were caused by this gentleman?" Indicating Randle as he pointed.

"With all due respect officer, my eyes didn't witness anything that transpired under this roof, but Ms. Johnson can clearly answer that question," she stated cautiously, never admitting the terroristic threat and vicious attack on her, personally.

"Can I go with him?" Sheri asked turning to the paramedic as they strapped Randle onto the stretcher. Her concern for his health elevated dramatically seeing him so battered and helpless, now resembling her.

"Yes, ma'am. You can ride in the back," the paramedic affirmed. "Does he have insurance, ma'am?"

"Yes, he's on my insurance. I will grab the card and identification from my wallet," she stated as the officers advised Terry that he was under arrest for assault and battery, plus trespassing.

Reading him his Miranda Rights, the officer searching Terry handed Demi the key fob to the Mercedes he retrieved from Terry's pocket at his request. Observing the lack of concern his sister had for his wellbeing, while seeing the tears upon Demi's face, crushed Terry as the handcuffs were placed on him.

"Officer, can I advise her of something please?" Terry asked politely.

"Yes sir," he replied.

"Take the G-Wagen and pick up Reanna in front of Clark University in an hour, please. Her and Roz will be waiting on the James P. Brawley Drive side. The flowers in the back go to them. A dozen each. I also ask that you call and ask my father to contact my lawyer, please," Terry conveyed looking at her with overwhelming sadness in his eyes.

"Okay," Demi agreed, wanting to hug him and assure with open words that she had his back.

However, she kept quiet not knowing how the officers arresting him would act. This seemed to be the theme for Demi in this situation, proceeding with caution, careful of what she exposes and does. Demi just couldn't believe that she just witnessed someone turn against their own family member for tainted affection, and maybe for that reason she elected not to tell the authorities the whole story of how she was attacked. Would Sheri turn on her too?

"I guess contaminated sewer water is thicker in your heart than blood," she said strolling past Sheri, who was following the paramedics out of the house.

Walking out to the car, Terry looked again at his sister who continued to render no compassion for his circumstances. All of her love and focus was on the care of Randle.

"Mr. Johnson, neither of us are fools," the officer stated as they stood at the back door of the police car. "We know this incident probably occurred because you were reacting to what he did to your sister. My partner and I would probably be in your shoes if the table was turned. I definitely know I would be," the escorting officer asserted while turning to look at his partner. "We just want you to know that we're doing our job by arresting you, which is unfortunate, and this is not personal. Your sister claims you came over, kicked in her bedroom door and attacked her boyfriend which makes her a witness to the assault. We are going to write the report as though the altercation started because he hit you first and give notation of the domestic abuse. Domestic violence is a case that very seldom goes to court because the woman always forgives the abuser. Given the ass whipping you put on him between us, true justice was served tonight."

Staring at Demi as the police car pulled away, Terry couldn't help but wonder if he would ever hold her in his arms again.

CHAPTER 17

Admiring the way the students were working together to analyze, seek information utilizing their notes, apply logical reasoning, and transform knowledge between themselves to solve the critical thinking problems as one united body gave Mr. Porter the idea to see if the students could challenge one another by telling stories that illustrate life's meaning beyond the phrase which he gave.

Every Unity After School Center was comprised of ten dynamic teachers from different areas who educate out of love for the purpose of cultivating a child's mind and the sincerity of wanting to make a difference in their lives. There was a teacher for each general grade class from sixth to twelfth so that the students could clearly focus on their curriculum without getting confused and the teacher having to overwork themselves in trying to teach multiple grade levels in one room. Three additional teachers circulated around the classrooms to assist in one-on-one tutoring as needed.

"We are all equal" is the standard mindset at Unity. No egos! Only the attributes of character, self-discipline, and humbleness elevated one above the other. Knowledge has no value if it isn't recognized in your actions. There was no worldly identity of self, for every male student was called King and every female was called Queen inside the classroom. "As one, we achieve together" is the motto, and if one failed, then it meant the entire student body failed.

Mr. Porter was very creative and unique with his teaching methods, not the typical lecturing as most teachers elect to do, standing before a classroom, which often results in a child not completely understanding the lesson. Many may become confused and neglected due to their learning styles or, sometimes, disabilities or losing focus altogether out of boredom. He effectively helps the students comprehend their lessons by teaching through music, games for curriculums such as algebra, and classroom plays of which the students act out.

A bachelor since losing his wife to a sepsis infection during her pregnancy three years prior, teaching became his therapeutic way of escaping the irreplaceable loss. Mr. Porter was raised in the Pittsburgh Housing Community of Atlanta by a mother who was a prominent lawyer before becoming a crack addict, due to a guy diluting her drink with cocaine in a club after she refused to dance. At a very early age, spawned by his mom's uncontrollable addiction, she often pimped out her son, Mr. Porter, sexually exploiting him to support her habit, which in essence taught him firsthand about neglect, abuse, sex trafficking and sexual assault. These essential factors now helped him resonate with those who hid within their secrets and used disciplinary action as a way of escaping reality.

Even though Mr. Porter was a very handsome individual whose Caucasian tone seemed to always glow like a nightlight, and his physique would render pleasure to the eyes of any woman, teaching was what fueled him with love, and books are his beloved children. Knowledge is what many seemed to believe he now accepted as his second wife, because he utilized every free moment of his day to discover more than what he already knew. As a seeker of truth, he rejected ancient myths that have no linkage to the messengers or prophets of God and advised his students never to be a blind follower to passed down folktales. Every child of Unity was blanketed with the gentle affection of his heart.

Standing before the class, wearing an embroidered collar salwar kameez and a pair of Kenneth Cole loafers, Mr. Porter loved to show the students that one could look attractive and presentable without spending hundreds of dollars on designer clothes to feel accepted or considered cool by the standards of society. Looking over the class and seeing how attentive they were, sitting in their seats, Mr. Porter advised that was the last math problem for the day then walked behind the desk, grabbed his messenger bag from the floor, removed two large bottles of Cîroc and a pack of cups before placing the black bag back in the spot where he lifted it from. Without saying a word, Mr. Porter laid one bottle of black raspberry on his desk, then opened a bottle and poured himself a cup, of which he sipped to his own pleasure.

"The Georgia law imposes that the legal age for one to drink is twenty-one," he stated as everyone listened while he sipped his drink. "Yet, society advertises underage drinking and condones it as a cultural tradition in many respects. Even the music artists of today promote it in their songs and videos, whereas many of you as well as your friends adopt their characteristics with blind acceptance.

Given that each one of you have the ability of making a choice and thus far, has used your choices to climb the mountain of self-achievement, I want to celebrate by making a toast because I applaud the turn around you all have made in your lives. So, whoever would like to drink some Cîroc with me and toast to your own accomplishment of self-growth, then raise your hand, and I'll pour you a drink. But remember one thing, we are each other's keeper."

With only five of the sixteen students raising their hands, Mr. Porter poured each a cup and advised the three Queens and two Kings to come get their drink then they toasted to self-awakening and self-value. Turning to address the class after the students sat back down, Mr. Porter turned to the young Queen sitting before him and asked why she didn't choose to toast with them given that she loves Cardi B who openly displays that she drinks as well.

"Mr. Porter, I choose to reject the celebration because of the symptoms you taught us about alcohol. Study shows that drinking effects the mouth, throat, and esophagus. It has the ability of causing a burn that could eventually kill our body tissues. With prolonged and heavy consumption, alcohol can lead to the development of various head and neck cancers. So, with that thought in mind, Mr. Porter, I pass," Queen Sandra explained with her northern accent. Rolling her neck to emphasize her point, "I need my mouth, throat, and esophagus sir. The world wouldn't be the same without my voice. It would be like New York without my Yankees or the King himself, 50 Cent."

"Understandable, and true, the world would not be the same," Mr. Porter chuckled and turned his head to address the King sitting beside her. "Why did you deny the opportunity of drinking with us?"

"Sir, I rejected the invitation because my mom's ex-boyfriend drank, and I promised myself that I would never strive to be a reflection of him on any level. The thought of drinking reminds me of how he would make my sister and I stand in front of him like scarecrows until he was tired of looking at us, and occasionally he'd beat us for no reason other than self-humor while my mom watched silently. So, I rejected and will always say no," King Carl expressed, seemingly getting emotional.

"I'm sorry about that King," Mr. Porter expressed with sincerity.

"It's okay sir, being a part of the Unity family has helped me to understand that life is a test of constant adversity and challenges. Every event is a life lesson to make us stronger and to bridge our current state to greater understanding."

"True King, and I applaud you still, without the toast. Again, I'm sorry. What about you King Toonk?" He asked referencing the flamboyant young basketball phenom who touched everyone's heart, when he declined several out of state academic scholarships to prestigious colleges to attend college close to his paraplegic little sister.

"Mr. Porter, I refused like Queen Sandra because of the symptoms you shared with us that it brings upon the body. Like for instance, the stomach. Drinking alcohol can increase the stomach's acidity and irritate its protective lining. That irritation, when experienced chronically, can lead to corrosion of the stomach lining. Even moderate alcohol consumption can give rise to or exacerbate existing stomach and intestinal ulcers.

"Mr. Porter, you all encourage us to face life through the windows of reality and not delusion. To understand that every individual is different and never to view ourselves through the eyes of others. I see people who seem to be able to handle the ability of drinking and many that can't. I don't want to be one of those who can't handle the effects and become addicted. So, I've elected to stay away altogether because my stomach is too precious to me. A life without being able to eat fried chicken or my uncle's BBQ would be a form of torture. And the consumption of alcohol also affects the heart, which is a major problem for me, sir, because I need every fiber of mine to share between Zendaya and Keyshia Cole once I graduate."

"Hold on now King," Mr. Porter insisted while bursting into laughter at the amusement of his words. "What makes you think that two strong and extraordinary women such as those two irreplaceable gifts of life will allow you to share their heart without stilettos, bottles, fists, and other items being thrown at your head?"

"Because every real woman needs a real man to define her true happiness, and given that I will bring both of them quantum happiness, they will be willing to accept sharing the blessing I am in order to keep them from wasting their time with all those fake men who give them momentary joy but don't complete them as a whole," King Toonk answered. "My last name is Love, which means I have the juice."

"Interesting King, very interesting," Mr. Porter said as the room erupted into laughter. "Well, do me one favor King when you embark on that nuclear path of no return."

"What's that sir?" He asked, canvasing a smile as though his dream had become reality.

"Inform me, so that I can take a million-dollar insurance policy out on you with every company possible. That's an investment I'll pawn the family jewels and dog to benefit from," he continued while breaking out in a casual happy dance. "Because you are trying to disrespect two women with one heart that you tryna split into two, and they will have you unable to be analyzed by a crime scene investigator for playing with their hearts.

"So, you're the modern-day Mack, is what you're saying. Well class, I see right now that the heart of a woman needs to be a topic that we should address before some of you seriously get in trouble thinking that pimpin' or Casanova mackin' is how we show our love and appreciation for the blessing a woman is, 'cause it's definitely not. A woman should always be honored, respected, and reminded of how significant she is to the existence of life, whether they're in your presence or not. Carry on though King Toonk while you still can move your jawbone," Mr. Porter instructed.

"Okay! Like I was saying, alcohol also affects the condition of the heart. Whether you drink alcohol long-term or binge drink, the consumption itself negatively affects your heart rate. It disrupts the heart's rhythm by causing it to speed up or beat irregularly. Mr. Porter, something is not right," King Toonk implied pressing his hand against his chest and making the facial expression as though he was in pain.

"What's not right King?" He inquired, now sitting on the desk pouring himself another cup from the Cîroc bottle and noticing his actions of discomfort. "Just so you know, neither one of your imaginary wives are here. So, don't fall out 'cause I'm not putting my mouth on you to resuscitate you King," Mr. Porter joked, causing all the students to laugh.

Some yelled, "Me neither."

"King, all I'm going to do is pump your double life heart with my foot until the paramedics arrive, which would actually be the compassionate version of those two women kicking your ... butt ... symmetrically split aortas," continued Mr. Porter.

"You're supposed to pump the chest sir," he corrected. "And to finish what I was saying, alcohol causes the heart rate to speed up and beat irregularly, but mine speeds up even greater and occasionally skips whenever I think of Zendaya or Keyshia," he said looking serious and sincere, while starting to act as if he was literally having a heart attack.

Laughter erupted to the extent that Mr. Porter's actions caused the class to join in out of the act of him sliding off the desk and onto the floor, holding his stomach.

"What's so funny Mr. Porter?" One of the Queens asked while slightly giggling, herself.

"King Toonk just mentioned his heart speeds up and skips occasionally just by thinking of them. I'm just wondering how fast and irregular his heart is going to beat when they take turns slapping him with their red bottoms for trying to be the Casanova of Atlanta or spank him while he's handcuffed to something. And I'm pumping your double heart, King, 'cause the stomach does not supply the brain with blood or oxygen, the heart does, which you seriously need right now," Mr. Porter informed.

"Well sir, when you see us sitting together at the awards show and their heads resting on my shoulders and their hands on my heart of hearts as a sign of our love, just remember I told you so," King exclaimed.

Looking at him directly in the eye as he spoke, "I definitely will remember King, but I will still make sure that my insurance policies are active. I will still pray for your safety and smile wholeheartedly at the sight of your accomplishment," Mr. Porter replied while lifting his head and turning his attention to the female student sitting behind him.

"Queen, why didn't you toast with me?" He inquired.

"I'm too young to drink Mr. Porter, and I didn't want to get you in any trouble," she answered so politely that Mr. Porter smiled with pure affection.

"I respect that Queen, and I appreciate you for caring enough. We are each other's keeper!

What about you Queen Regina?" He inquired, addressing the student sitting beside her.

"I didn't accept because I'm a diabetic, sir, and alcohol affects the bloodstream, so I can't take that chance with my life."

"How does it affect the bloodstream, Queen?" Mr. Porter asked, since she did not expound to re-enlighten the class of its effects.

"Alcohol's presence in the bloodstream can have adverse effects on the body's ability to fight off illnesses or infections because it diminishes white blood cells' ability to battle bacteria or other foreign pathogens, and that makes it easier for you to get sick."

"That's correct," Mr. Porter concurred while smiling at the way she presented her statement with a sense of authority as though her point had to be made. "But can someone advise what a pathogen is so that everyone understands what Queen Regina just shared, he asked, sipping from his cup. "Go ahead King," he acknowledged by pointing to a student in the back of the class.

"A pathogen is a bacterium, a virus, or other microorganism that can cause a disease," King acknowledged.

"Correct," he confirmed, while writing it on the chalk board, as he spoke. After listening to a few more constructive reasons as to why they chose not to accept his invitation, he chose one of the students who accepted his invitation to toast.

"Why did you drink with me Queen Emilia?"

"I accepted your invitation because I used reasonable judgement to consider the evidence. There was no true relevancy in your argument, and I clearly noticed that you laid the extra bottle down while concealing the top as you twisted open the one that we drank from without removing the seal wrapping first. Mr. Porter you educate us on the fallouts of drugs, alcohol, sheltering abuse and pain. So, given that you advise us to apply critical thinking to everything, I accepted the cup of juice because I didn't think you would give us alcohol when you don't drink yourself, sir," Queen exclaimed.

"Excellent analogy Queen. And you are absolutely correct," he admitted as he began pouring cups for everyone. "I used this exercise just to examine the choice each one of you would make, and I'm proud of the way you all responded. Not only did each of you implement sound thinking skills, but you all rendered judgement that elevates your growth. The key is to apply critical thinking in the circumstances that really matter and not just in the classroom. Remember that a strong critical thinker demonstrates self confidence in one's own ability to reason. Can someone advise us of some of the skills needed to be a critical thinker?"

Observing the room of raised hands, "Go ahead King," he acknowledged by pointing to the young man sitting on the front row of the class.

"Some of the skills needed are observation, interpretation, reflection, evaluation, inference, explanation, problem solving, and decision making," he answered.

"Correct King. And I ask that you and the Queen Regina come and pass these cups of juice to everyone, please. While they pass them out, can someone enlighten the class of other ways alcohol affects the body? How about you Queen Stephanie?"

He acknowledged by pointing to the young lady on the second row. "Is everything okay? Because you've been a little quiet today, and that's very unusual for you."

"Yes sir, I'm fine," she replied, "I just have something on my mind."

"If you'd like, I'll ask someone else to answer the question, if you'd like to remain silent or talk privately?" Mr. Porter asked looking concerned.

"I'll answer the question Mr. Porter. I'm okay," she assured. "I'm just thinking of how I can help this autistic student at school who gets picked on because of his condition."

"Challenge yourself to make an influential difference, Queen," Mr. Porter advised while panning his eyes across the entire room to acknowledge that his statement is for everyone and not just for her. "Bullying is never acceptable, and the best of us extend a hand of support. If you don't mind Queen, I'd like to discuss the issue with you later, before we address it openly to the entire class."

"Yes, sir," she responded rising from her seat to walk to the chalk board. Queen Stephanie grabbed a stick of chalk and wrote out her words as she spoke, "Alcohol also affects the brain which many people don't know. Alcohol depresses brain centers, enhances the effects of calming agents on the brain, while also slowing down the rate at which information travels down the brain's expressways. This is what causes the disorienting effects as well as deterioration of motor skills and judgement. If one drinks too much alcohol, these brain centers can become so severely impaired that you could fall into a coma or die."

"Another body organ drinking effect is the pancreas, class. Alcohol causes the pancreas to produce toxic substances that can eventually lead to pancreatitis, a dangerous inflammation, and swelling of the blood vessels in the pancreas that prevents proper digestion. Alcohol also affects the way the liver metabolizes toxins, thereby making it less effective. This can cause scarring to the liver, add fat to the organ, and trigger chronic inflammation, which leads to liver inflammation, steatosis or fatty liver, alcoholic hepatitis, fibrosis, and cirrhosis." Turning to the class so as to render her attention after placing the chalk down.

"Drinking alcohol affects the body in numerous other ways," Queen Stephanie advised. "It raises a woman's risk of breast cancer, causes mood swings, loss of coordination, it accelerates the rate of bone deterioration and increases the risk of bone fracture and osteoporosis. It affects the central nervous system, the colon, and causes you to vomit, among other symptoms as well. Without trying to clarify every exact issue, the bottom line is that none of us have to apply the elements of critical thinking to recognize that drinking alcohol is a choice we should all stay away from. Many try to make it seem cool to drink, but the effects are not worth the risks just to be accepted by society. Like Ms. Johnson constantly advises us, the best path to follow is the path of someone who leads by example. And by standing upon that path, we become better and more rightly guided as a whole."

"Well said, Queen," Mr. Porter complimented as she walked back to her seat blushing and trying to hide her smile. "Well said! Cool is what each and every one of you are without the acceptance or acknowledgement of anyone individual," he stated while starting to erase the chalkboard. "A leader thinks, whereas a follower never does. Which are you?" He asked the class.

"Leaders!" They chorused.

"Which one?" He inquired jokingly and looking as though he was in doubt.

"Leaders!" They repeated.

"Okay, I was just checking, given that it sounded like y'all were being a little unsure," Mr. Porter acknowledged as he got up from his chair to remove the radio from the cabinet and sat it on the desk.

"Listen class, I need your undivided attention for a moment. Last night, I spoke to the artist, Trill, about allowing those of you who aspire to be rappers instead of corporate executives or entrepreneurs, to come and record a track in the studio as a means of inspiring you a little more. He did not only agree to the suggestion but said that he will consult with his sponsor to see if they would be willing to donate a pair of shoes to each of you for extra motivation, in the pursuit of y'all achieving your education. He would also like to do a video with all the students of Unity." Listening to them celebrate as though T.I. walked in the room with the Grand Hustle team, caused Mr. Porter to smile.

"Okay class, calm down for a moment, so that I can finish spelling out his terms. Trill wants a girl against boy dance battle, so you all have until mid-terms to choreograph something that's pleasing to all of you as a whole, but also electrifying. Keep it fun, and don't make it personal because this is not a competition against one another. We shine as one body, not through the actions of one student. Trill has acknowledged that each student will receive one hundred dollars, but only the students who receive no lower than a B minus on their mid-term grades can participate. So, if any of you would like to spend a weekend at the Boardwalk Resort in Virginia Beach, Virginia, then get in your books and no excuses will I accept."

Bobbing in excitement to the sounds of the radio station, they moved their desks to the back of the room so that there would be enough open space for them to bounce around without hitting anything. Mr. Porter couldn't help but admire how they communicated amongst each other before trying to do anything.

"Mr. Porter," King Toonk yelled as he separated himself from the group and stood by himself in a little open area on the floor. "The first time I have the chance to kiss Zendaya on the Mediterranean and her fingers touch my face, this is how my heart will be dancing," he uttered before doing a combination of street dances that ended with him doing a one handed handstand.

"As you all say, that was lit, King," Mr. Porter expressed as the students clapped and embraced him with hugs after his mini performance. "Seriously that was nice, and I can't wait to see what you all come up with. But King, what about Keyshia? Is your heart only going to dance for Zendaya, or will it do the same thing for her as well?" Mr. Porter asked with humor in his tone.

"No, sir," King immediately responded before breaking out into a completely different dance routine, as though his body was sending a personal message to Chris Brown, acknowledging that he wanted a shot at the title. "Mr. Porter that's how my twin heart will shake the first time she kisses me beneath the stars in Venice."

"King, I can't deny the fact that you have some serious talent besides basketball, and I hope you pursue a career in choreographing after you graduate instead of trying to be a Casanova," Mr. Porter encouraged as the other students surrounded him. "You have big dreams, and I mean big dreams. I just hope that you take the time to learn how to bob and weave like a professional fighter, when you're not studying or critiquing your craft, or at least sign up for the North Korean Army. Because the very moment your legs are no longer as fast as your upper body movements, you will need all the help in the world you can get for blatantly trying to gigolo those two hearts," he chuckled.

After watching them dance for the next thirty minutes, as though they had bullet ants in their veins, Mr. Porter instructed them to arrange the class back to its proper order since it was almost time to leave. It was exciting to see them bring out the best in each other's creativity, while also working together to establish a routine. "Class, before we leave for today, Queen Sandra wants to share a short story with you that I need you to ponder over tonight because we will discuss the wisdom behind it tomorrow," Mr. Porter informed them. "We are ready when you are Queen."

Rising out of her seat on the first row, Queen Sandra walked to the front of the room and began reciting a story she seemed to have memorized, as a jewel of self-motivation, once assured that the attention of the class was completely upon her.

"The story I'm going to share with you all is called 'His Dedication to Knowledge.'"

"Muzani said that it was stated to Imam Shafi'i, 'How do you lust for knowledge?'
He replied, 'I hear a word of knowledge that I have not heard of before and each one of
my body parts wishes that it had the faculty of hearing so that they could as well enjoy
the pleasure of hearing what my ears enjoy upon hearing new knowledge.' It was further
put to him, 'Describe your eagerness to attain knowledge.' He replied, 'It is akin to
achieve pleasure through hoarding wealth.' It was then asked, 'How do you seek
knowledge?' Imam Shafi'i responded, 'I seek it like a weak woman seeks after her only
child.'

"Rabi' said, 'I heard of Imam Shafi'i saying during an illness that of all the books
he had compiled, he wished that all of the creation learned of what those books contained
without them being ascribed to him."

"Very enlightening Queen," Mr. Porter complimented as she walked back to her seat. "I need each one of you to ponder over the passage she just shared and write down three things you gained from it. Tomorrow each of you will share your insight the moment we finish with the class curriculum. Unfortunately, our time has expired, I will see you all tomorrow," Mr. Porter proclaimed as he dismissed the students. He put the radio back into the cabinet as all the students exited the room, except Queen Stephanie whom he asked to remain. After listening to her speak from the heart concerning her dislike for how her peers treat the autistic student, he conveyed wisdom on how to get the kids bullying the autistic child to stop. He also ensured her that he would contact the school administration because the issue was too delicate to ignore.

Excusing the young Queen from his class, Mr. Porter was then shocked when he turned around to see one of the young male students from a lower grade class walk in the room, slightly holding his head down with sadness blanketing his face. "King Marcus, is everything okay?" Mr. Porter asked walking over to him and gaining no immediate response.

Placing his hand upon his shoulder he guided the young boy to a chair, pulled another one beside him, and sat down while again asking his question.

"Mr. Porter, I have a problem and I don't know who to turn to," King muttered as tears began falling from his eye. "Ms. Johnson didn't come today and you are the only other person I feel I can trust."

Getting up to close the door and listening without interrupting him, Mr. Porter found himself starting to get emotional by just witnessing the genuine rawness of his actions.

"Mr. Porter, can I tell you something and you promise not to tell my mom?"

Hearing the seriousness within his voice, and needing to know exactly what was bothering him so that he could try to help, Mr. Porter said, "Yes, I promise not to say anything to your mom. We are each other's keeper," he acknowledged while giving him a pound for assurance and a sense of comfort.

"Mr. Porter, I feel like my mom's new boyfriend is touching my little sister like grown-ups touch each other, and I want him to stop, sir," he cried, leaning over to be comforted as tears flowed more rapidly from his eyes. Sniffling, he tried to formulate his next sentences. "The days my mom works her night job during the week, I've been noticing that her boyfriend has been going into my little sister's room and staying long periods of time with the door locked. I know this 'cause I banged on the door once and tried to open it, but he beat me, and my mom grounded me for my actions, so I no longer try. Each time he goes in there, I can hear her crying and him mumbling. I press my ear to the door hard each time, but I can never clearly make out what he's saying to her, because the TV be up too loud.

"I have asked her several times what they be in there doing, yet she refuses to tell me. The look on her face says it all which gives me the suspicion that she has a secret that's bothering her because she always holds her head down, and I can see her slightly shaking due to whatever she's thinking of. Sometimes, I try to hold her to reassure her that I love her, but she pushes me away defensively and just start crying. I told my mom what her boyfriend has been doing. I even asked her why. I told her how my little sister is reacting when I approach her now, when the two of us used to be so close. We was like, inseparable, so that's how I know something is really wrong, and it hurts 'cause I can't help her. My mom just told me to mind my own damn business, close my eyes harder at night, and stop trying to make her lose her man before she sends me to live with my father.

"Mr. Porter, I don't know what to do. I'm supposed to protect my sister, but she won't talk to me," King Marcus muttered sniffling as he wiped tears away from his face. "I've even tried sleeping in her room on the nights my mom works at night. But he makes me leave every time, after slapping me for playing like I'm sleeping."

"How old is your sister King?" Mr. Porter asked, trying to maintain his composure as his eyes moistened.

"She's only ten, sir."

"Does your mom work tonight, King?"

"No, sir."

Sitting there advising King of his plans to help him, he could see that his words blanketed him with a sense of comfort. After brushing off a few teachers who sought his attention, Mr. Porter told King a few stories of his childhood misfortunes and how he overcame it mentally. With King now smiling again, Mr. Porter collected his things, and they exited the room pounding each other and throwing up the three with their fingers before going their separate ways.

CHAPTER 18

Hiding in her secret cave watching the "Birds" episode of the Netflix series, "Life" on her iPad, Cadence sat crying, due to the news of Terry getting locked up, more so than her mom washing her thick wavy hair. Pouting and not caring to be bothered, she acted like she didn't hear Reanna calling her, even when she stuck her head inside the cave's entrance.

"Girl, I know you hear me calling your big head butt," Reanna scoffed, nonchalantly invading her space as she looked around admiring how things were neatly arranged in the tent.

"Get out of my cave!" Cadence screamed at the top of her lungs. "I didn't say you can come in here. Get out before I tell mom on you. Get out!" The cave was her secret hideout, a portal to a land of fantasies, and the only other person allowed to enter besides Penélope was Terry.

"Girl, whatever! Mama wants you in the kitchen," Reanna relayed, rolling her eyes before retracting her head and walking over to the stables to caress the Gypsy Cob that she loved more than anything, but never rode.

Scooping some raisins from the container in the food supply room to mix with a few apples and two hand full of hay, she poured it into her horse bucket, then caressed him as he ate. Reanna admired the look of her horse within the sun's rays beaming through the window. The mesmerizing beauty caused her to capture the sight with her phone. The thought of having one of Sheri's associates paint a portrait replicating the picture, to hang above her bed, is all that lingered in her mind as she stood there feeding Lady Legacy from a bucket.

Not wanting to leave her cave nor stop watching the bird documentary on Life, but knowing fully well that she would get in trouble if she didn't, Cadence got up to see what her mom wanted while allowing the sight of Reanna sticking her tongue out to irritate her even more. With nothing but grass available to throw, she continued walking, wiping away her trickling tears.

Smelling the intriguing aroma as she opened the door caused Cadence to flip the channels of her troubled mind making the episode of being upset a distant show of emotion. All she could think of now was that sweet familiar and satisfyingly enticing aromatherapy of heated brownies, her favorite. Licking the icing before dipping one in some milk and scarfing it down instantly snatched first place in all her thoughts, evaporating all tales of tears.

"Yes ma'am?" She beamed walking into the kitchen and eyeing the brownies that her mom was removing from the pan with 20/10 visual acuity, flaunting a smile that clearly acknowledged that she had hidden intentions of sneaking into the kitchen later that night to eat more, if any were left.

"Are you still mad at me sweetie?" Her mom inquired while gazing at her as she bit into the last brownie that was in the pan. "Hmmmmm, this is so hot, and the icing is sooo good," she hummed teasingly, slowly chewing her food with pleasure so as to antagonize Cadence a little.

"I'm not mad at you, Mom," she reassured, trying to be convincing as droplets of drool began to formulate in the corners of her lips.

With every bite her mom took, Cadence involuntarily licked her lips as her retinas followed every movement but still kept the plate of frosted chocolate tart brownies secured in her purview.

"Sweetie, of the many blessings God bestowed upon you with His mercy, one of them was hair of which to beautify you with. I know you want to wear your hair like Penélope's, but she doesn't have an oily scalp like you. And even with that, she still shampoos and conditions her hair to cleanse, removing the dirt build up. You don't want to be walking around with your hair dirty, filled with dandruff, or smelling like a horse, do you sweetie?"

"No ma'am!" Cadence exclaimed, showcasing a smile, waiting patiently for the acknowledgement that she can grab a brownie off the plate, 'cause that icing was teasing and tormenting her tongue's thirsty taste buds and her anxious palate.

"A princess defines worth through her grace as well as her character and beauty. Yet, cleanliness is an essential quality that can never be neglected or subjected to laziness. I'll make you a promise sweetie," her mother declared while trying to establish eye contact with her, but the plate of brownies was more attractive to Cadence. "I promise to bake you a pan of brownies each time we shampoo and condition your hair, if you don't cry."

"Deal," she vowed smiling as though she knew her mom's next words would be "you can have a brownie." Or better yet, "You can satisfy your palate with a plate of brownies." Orrrr somethin' to that effect.

"Well, since you cried this time and your hair still needs to be moisturized, we will start our agreement the next time I have to shampoo your hair. So, all these brownies are miiiine," her mom teased while grabbing the plate as though she was about to walk away, just to stimulate a laughable reaction.

"MOM!" she shouted in pure surprising disbelief. "MOM ..."

Eyeing her mother with the saddest eyes one could muster, Cadence crossed her arms and stood there unable to shield the disappointment of her mother's words or actions from her face.

"Mom, I'm sorry," were the only words she could think of, as she walked around the center counter in the kitchen and hugged her with all of her affection before saying, "I love you. Please share your brownies with me. I promise not to cry again."

Cadence's affection exhibition was always comforting to her heart, and a weakness, like the look in Reanna's eyes when she wants something.

"Go ahead and eat you some brownies, sweetie," her mom gestured while handing her the entire plate. "I love you, too. Take Reanna some as well."

Without hesitation, she placed the brownies back on the counter and washed her hands in the sink. The warm feeling of the brownie in the palm of her hand was almost more exciting than the taste on her tongue. Stuffing her mouth with sensation that she could endure for a lifetime; Cadence couldn't help but wish that her cousin Terry and friend Penélope was present. Scurrying to grab her iPad off the living room sofa to video chat, Cadence could do nothing but smile, walking back into the kitchen when Penélope's face appeared given that her oral cavity was filled with the sensation of melting chocolaty goodness.

"Hey munchkin! What is that chocolate stuff all over your mouth?" She asked while smiling in between a giggle.

"Mama made me some frosted ... choco ... chocolate tart brownies ... I mean brownies," she struggled to convey with her mouth looking like a black hole. "When are you coming over again? I miss you! I'll save you some brownies, if you want me to."

Cadence was a double blessing to Penélope; she was like the little sister she never had, since her mom only gave her four brothers to love, and the child she always wanted, but she wouldn't commit the purity of her soul to Terry. She refused to harbor the yearning until her girlfriend energized her entirety with new love. Penélope didn't want her child to endure any of the growing pains and childhood misfortunes she encountered or to follow her ways of intimacy. A comfort she accepts in order to suppress the pain within her heart from being repeatedly molested by her stepfather.

"Well, munchkin, I was going to surprise you by picking you up from school today and take you to the movies, but I had some unexpected things transpire at work and I don't know what time I will be able to leave the office. Save me a few, and I promise to stop by tomorrow to ride with you, okay?"

Smiling like a newborn baby with no teeth, hearing those words, Cadence inquired about the enjoyment of her resort getaway while finding prize-worthy humor in retelling how she slapped Reanna while playing the pause game. The fear of her getting some get back had caused her to hide all the remotes in the house.

"Penélope, Terry promised never to leave me again," Cadence complained with a sigh of sadness that could be heard loud and clear in the tone of her sweet small voice, after hearing her mother call his name in the background. "Please don't let him stay in that place. Help him, please, so that we can all be together again."

"Munchkin, don't worry yourself about that, okay? Terry will keep his promise to you, and I shall as well. I see you washed your hair. You look like a mermaid princess. Are you going to help me shampoo and condition mine so that we can look alike?"

"Yes! My mom did mine 'cause a princess has to define her grace through cleanliness, character, and beauty. I wanna be a beautiful Queen like you and my mom when I grow up."

"That's true, munchkin, but you are already more beautiful than us, combined. You have to compete with Reanna," she jokingly cajoled while bursting into laughter. "Don't forget to put me a few up for tomorrow, 'cause I know you! You'll eat 'em all up. And don't be licking my icing off either, gurrrl."

"I promise to save you some or half of one without touching it," Cadence giggled with a devilish look on her face. "And, I love you."

Penélope replied by singing, "I love you too," and blowing kisses through the phone before disconnecting the line.

Cleaning up after herself and putting a few in the refrigerator to save for tomorrow, Cadence placed four brownies on a saucer, poured a glass of milk, and walked to Reanna's room hoping she didn't want any of the brownies she had on the saucer.

Lifting her head from the monitor, "Come in!" Reanna yelled, hearing the soft taps at her door.

"Would you like some brownies and milk, sis?" Cadence offered, walking into the room as though it was her own and looking to see who she was chatting with on her laptop. "Hi Roz!"

"Hi, Cadence," Roz responded from the monitor. "Where are my brownies?" She questioned seeing the saucer in her hand.

Cadence knew that she would not share the ones she put aside for Penélope and herself under any circumstances with Roz.

"You're too late, Roz. I ate the rest of them. Can we watch some of those funny videos on the Internet when you finish chatting with Roz, please," Cadence asked while waving goodbye to her.

"You don't have to leave. We can watch some now if you want to," her sister extended causing a smile to expand on her face.

Reanna's love for her little sister was something she didn't hide, nor did she take her for granted. She playfully teased and aggravated her at times, but there was nothing she wouldn't do to reassure her that she's the light within her heart. To Reanna, Cadence is truly her best friend, and no matter what transpires in life, the well-being of her little sister will always take priority over all other things.

"I know you really want me to say I don't want any of the brownies just so your greedy butt can eat'em all by yourself, but I'll split them with you," Reanna acknowledged, which caused Cadence to smile even more as she eased into the bed to lay beside her sister.

The two of them laid back against the pillows laughing as they viewed video after video of people and animals doing silly things. Reanna thought Cadence was going to giggle herself into a mental institution, the way she was rolling on the bed and laughing uncontrollably — until she noticed Cadence crying after clicking on a picture of a man holding prison bars that read: *The World is a Prison for a Believer and Paradise for a Disbeliever.*"

"What's wrong, sis?" Reanna asked trying to find out what's bothering her so she could give comfort.

"This picture made me think of Terry," she proclaimed, wiping her tears away. "I don't want him to be sleeping in jail. Do those bad people in there brush their teeth and bathe?"

"Neither do I, but he is okay, and yes, they do. He will be home soon, Cadence. He wouldn't want you to be sitting here crying, and neither do I. Just pray for him, and God will protect him as He protects us."

"Pray? What's that?" Cadence asked looking confused by the fact that she had no knowledge of what prayer was or meant. "How do I pray?"

"Prayer is when you call on God for forgiveness of the bad things we do, understanding regarding things our knowledge doesn't comprehend, guidance, mercy and protection from the evil whispers and followers of the devil, strength to overcome our inner weaknesses as well as to help us become more discipline, more humble, more generous, more obedient to His commands, and more sincere in our acts of worship, etcetera. When you pray, you allow your heart to talk to God without holding back."

"I want to pray for you, Terry, mom, and Penélope, but who is God? Do we have to get mom to take us to Him? Will you call Him for me?" Cadence asked, reaching for Reanna's phone on the nightstand.

"No, we cannot call Him using a phone or go to Him," Reanna clarified as she sat there trying to figure out how to explain to her little sister who God was so she'd understand. "God is the creator of all things that exist in the heaven and the earth. We don't have the physical ability of seeing God with our eyes as we see one another, but He grants us the mercy to witness His signs in life. Like the air we breathe, the water we drink, the animals you love to watch documentaries of, the stars in the sky at night, the angels, even you and I, God created them all. Cadence, it's kind of hard explaining who God is to you in a way that you will understand."

"I think I understand what you are trying to say," Cadence stated while typing on the laptop. "You're saying we see God with our heart and recognize His signs in everything He created. It says right here on this website: *He is the Self-Sufficient Master whom all creatures need. He neither eats nor drinks. He begets not nor is He begotten. And there is none equal or comparable to Him.*"

"Correct," Reanna concurred, smiling. "God has no human replica of His creation. There is only one God, so never associate partners to Him. He is greater than His creation, and don't need to lower Himself to our comprehension merely to make us happy. He is the only one who can forgive you of your sins and bestow blessings on you."

"Well, can we pray? 'Cause I want to pray," looking at her sister attentively and eager to learn how to talk to God.

"Yes, we can," Reanna grinned getting off the bed. "Come on, we have to wash up before we pray."

"Why? I'm clean," Cadence nonchalantly informed her, trying to understand all these new things which Reanna was sharing with her.

"God commanded Moses (May God be pleased with him) in the Bible, to clean himself before approaching Him and Jesus (May God be pleased with him) clearly acknowledged that he came to fulfill the law and not change them. So, it is important for us to follow the proper teachings of the rightly guided ones in order to gain God's love and extended mercy."

"Who are they?"

"Prophets and messengers of God, but I'll explain later." Escorting her into the bathroom, Reanna showed her sister how to wash her hands, mouth, feet, etcetera, before praying which became a memorable moment that Reanna would never forget. Cadence argued about the importance of cleaning inside the body as well. So, she washed her face before swallowing a handful of water to clean her throat and stomach instead of just gargling and spitting it out. She washed up to her elbows instead of merely her hands, and she thoroughly washed her entire leg instead of just cleansing her feet.

Prostrating beside her sister on the floor because Reanna claimed this was how Jesus (May God be pleased with him) prayed, as did all the other prophets in the Bible. Cadence closed her eyes and opened her heart to God.

"Excuse me, God. I don't know if you're busy or not, but as You hover above Your throne, I need you to pay attention 'cause it's important that you listen. Please protect my big cousin, Terry, from those bad police officers who like to beat people and bring him home to his family so that I can hug him again. He is sorry for whatever he did wrong, and I ask that you do not punish him by making him stay in that place forever. Please let him go, God. Please let him go."

"I will stop using my sister's toothbrush, whenever she makes me mad, to scrub beneath the toilet seat and inside the bowl if you let him go. I promise! God, I pray you also protect my sister, mom, and Penélope in all that they do and let them know I love them very much. I pray you help me be like my sister when I get older, but prettier and smarter, please. I don't mean to make her mad at me when I do God. I just be wanting her to play with me, 'cause I have no one but her. I'm sorry! God, please protect my mom and Penélope from all evil and the devilish person everyone be talking about, and I thank you for allowing her to be a part of our life."

"God, my mom is very pretty, can cook good brownies, and a clean woman, but she doesn't have a boyfriend like other women of her age. I know I'm asking a lot my first time praying to you, but I ask from my heart with sincerity, God, that you please send her a husband so that she can be happy. I end this prayer by saying that I don't know you, but if you fulfill my request, I will love you with all my heart, always. I also would like for you to send me a puppy, protect everyone in my family, and make sure Penélope comes tomorrow. Thank you for allowing me to pray to you, God. I pray that you are happy, God, and I ask that you allow me to be your new friend. I just don't share my brownies, but I'm a good friend, God."

Feeling a little better now that she had talked to the Most High, Cadence hugged Reanna before kissing her on the cheek and whispering, "I love you."

After allowing her mom to moisturize her hair, Cadence watched more videos on the laptop to pass a little time before dinner. The urge to eat Penélope's brownies was throbbing, but with her mom in the kitchen cooking, she knew it was impossible. With time to spare as the pot roast heated in the oven and everyone sitting in the living room, Cadence sparked a dance battle on their Wii game, of which their mom tried to compete but kept coming in last.

"Mom, grandma was right, you can't dance," Reanna professed, observing her move like a board of sheetrock.

"Whatever! The two of you are only jumping around like y'all have trampoline springs in your ankles. Girl you wish your hips could pop like mine," she retorted, walking from in front of the TV set to go check on her food in the kitchen.

Bouncing to an Xscape jam she hadn't heard in a while, Reanna was shocked to hear Cadence say when their mother was completely out of the room, "I think I have a way that we can trick mom into buying us a puppy."

"Seriously?! How is that?" Reanna asked rendering her full attention because she wanted a little Yorkshire Terrier.

"Mom always says she's a woman of her word, and our word is a reflection of our value, right?"

"Yes!"

"Well, mom doesn't curse, right?

"Uh huhn."

"Soooo — if we can get her to agree that she will buy us a puppy if one of us ever hears her say a curse word, then she has to buy us a puppy, and I want a Yorkie just like you." Cadence said giggling.

"How will we get her to curse; that's impossible?"

"No, it's nooot," Cadence responded while giggling harder.

Scurrying to her sister's room and returning with her laptop, she asked Reanna to insert her code, then lifted the device and walked over to the sofa. Giggling endlessly as she typed, "Come look at this," Cadence called Reanna over after locating the YouTube videos of these girls playing pranks on one another.

"Cadence are you crazy? You have lost your ever-loving' mind!" Reanna shouted while unable to hold back her laughter at what she was seeing. "I'm not doing that! Mom would kill the both of us."

"Not if we make her promise as part of the agreement not to punish either of us for causing her to curse. Let's do it Reanna. It will be funny, and I will let you pick out the puppy."

"As long as she promises not to punish us, otherwise I am not down."

"Okay," Cadence exclaimed jumping around in excitement. "I will get her to make the promise. Yes! Yes!"

"You make me wonder about you sometimes. I can't believe you even thought of this. I see now that I will have to keep my eyes on you at all times because you are sneaky, and I truly hope that you were lying about using my toothbrush to clean the toilet."

"No, I wasn't lying, but I'm sorry and promise not to do it again." I just want a puppy. I got this sis, she said, smiling and rubbing her hands together. "Mom!"

CHAPTER 19

Entwined upon the coral reef as one breath, the thrust of the North Atlantic's current smashing against the shore sounded like repeated thwops of a whale echoing in her mind as she sensuously whispered his name in the moon's glow. Every spraying blanket of cold mist seemed to elevate the passion of their secrecy. Spreading her legs in the darkness to feel him deeper within her vaginal cavity, the cat's-paw had her body feeling like a bed of geysers with each pulsating stroke of his hardness inside of her. Yearning to feel his tongue against the hardness of her frozen nipples, or to feel him bite into the base of her neck, as she intensified the stimulation by syncing the rotation of their hips with his movements.

"Make love to me," she purred while gasping as the sight of the white rose, he was biting into reflected in and out of the twilight. The waving tightness of his abs turned her on more and more in her pursuit of unlimited ecstasy. "Make love to me."

"Excuse me, Ms. Johnson! Excuse me, Ms. Johnson," the nurse said, tapping her arm to wake her, as she tried to steal some sleep, now that Randle was finally napping after three days of continuous crying about his condition.

"Yes?" Opening her eyes while removing the hospital sheet covering her face and sitting up on the sofa to render the nurse her full attention. Wiping her mouth as she glanced at her watch, Sheri was very disappointed that she had only gotten twenty-five minutes of rest after countless hours of verbal torment from Randle and mental exhaustion.

"I apologize for waking you, ma'am. And I know you requested complete privacy," the nurse acknowledged. "But there's a woman in the lobby who is insistent on speaking to you. I can notify security and ask them to escort her out if you'd like."

"No, it won't be necessary, tell her I'll be out there shortly, please," Sheri informed, trying to get her thoughts together while looking at Randle rest to evade the pain. Realizing that it could be no one but her investigative mother whom she really didn't want to see right now, let alone have a discussion with, she pondered upon not going to see what her mom wanted. For the past few days, Sheri had extracted herself from the equation of life, contacting no one after arriving to the hospital and turning off her phone. She immediately had Randle transferred to a private section of the hospital under an alias after his surgery. Instead of going home to grant someone the ability of trying to persuade her to rectify the decision she made out of love, she contracted a car service to drive her to buy a few changes of clothing from Walmart along with her basic hygiene necessities. Emotionally deciding to sleep and shower with Randle, so as to define the sincerity of her commitment to their bond of union.

Looking at herself in the mirror after brushing her teeth, and washing her face, Sheri caressed the healing 2-inch laceration on her lip adjacent to the frenulum with her finger and wondered if her and Randle should just get away from it all: Sell her company and start a new life in another state away from everyone where they have only themselves to focus on at all times. Walking back into the room and kissing Randle on the lips before exiting, Sheri whispered, "I love you," in his ear and hoped he truly realized that.

Walking down the hall and seeing her mom pacing in the lobby with an enormous bouquet of purple trimmed white Star Lilies in a clear crystal vase granted none of the usual excitement she felt when in her presence. Without embracing to show their affection as usual or to share their complementary European bougie kiss, they both stood eyeing each other as though it was a standoff to expose the other's inner weakness.

"How are you, Sheri?" Mrs. Johnson asked, breaking the silence between them while extending her arms to give Sheri the flowers, as she observed the swelling and bruises on her face for the first time.

"Thank you, Ma. They're very beautiful, and I'm good," she replied nonchalantly, while standing there staring at her mom with a sense of cold emptiness for no apparent reason, damming the warmth and love usually abounding that had always made them inseparable.

"Why are you not answering your phone, Sheri? Your father and I have been worried about you. Terry wanted me to tell you that he understands and still loves you."

"Cause I haven't been in the mood to talk to anyone. I'm just focusing on Randle right now," Sheri uttered in a sassy tone.

"So, you're saying that we're not entitled to know how you are mentally or physically, given the entire situation. Our feelings are no longer important enough to be part of your focus?" Mrs. Johnson questioned in an elevated tone while staring intently at her daughter. "Does family mean anything to you anymore? Does your company or those kids mean anything to you?"

"Randle is a part of our family, and he's the most significant priority in my life right now," Sheri stated with a little aggression. "I'm not concerned with other people's feelings, nor the obligations of my company. I'm sorry if that offends you and father, but my focus is on him, and only him. The same way your focus would be on father if the tables were turned."

"That piece of shit is not a part of my family, and I'll never accept a man who has no respect for a woman to be embraced with open arms. I don't know who you think you're talking to, but you need to correct your tone before I knock all your front teeth out making dental inclusions in this hospital lobby, granting you the sick pleasure of lying in bed beside your master, at least that's what your actions dictate. I'm not your child! You and that waste of life may disrespect each other for stimulation, but you will always respect me regardless of how you feel," Mrs. Johnson roared, taking a few steps forward and defining her seriousness by standing a mere breath away from Sheri with her finger pointed in her face.

"And you're wrong to ever think that I would be looking like a stray dog at your father's side if he were to put his hands on me. I'm a woman, and definitely not an insecure puppet with no sense of self love or value. I don't accept abuse nor make excuses for a man's lack of tolerance. Never, and I mean never, will I stand at a man's side who degrades my worth and treats me anything less than an irreplaceable blessing. God gave me life to be a woman and nothing beneath that. I love your father with all my heart, but I love and respect myself more."

"I'm not a stray dog, Ma, nor an insecure puppet. I do love myself just as I love my man," Sheri expressed defensively while not raising her tone, even though she felt offended by her words. "Mom, I'm not in the mood to have a discussion with you right now. Will you please leave so that I can go back in the room and try to relax?"

"Then, when will you be available to step away from your master and lend a moment of your attention to something other than kissing his ass, or acting like a woman with no dignity?" Mrs. Johnson questioned while raising her voice and not attempting to hide her unbridled frustration. "Do you have any idea of what you have done? You are hiding up in this hospital, devoting all of your time and energy to the very man who has your face looking like afterbirth because you didn't ask his permission to leave your damn house — Your House! Like he owns you, his modern-day slave where the slave pays the master, provides for him, submit to being raped and disfigured like your face and body is the constant host for a demolition derby. He has obviously beaten you senseless, chil'! He doesn't even treat you like he loves or appreciate you, but you reward him for your brutal life of servitude under the obscure color of love. You haven't given a single thought to your brother, or your family! I'm beginning to wonder if you're actually my daughter. What has happened to you? Are you suicidal? While you're in here trying to play Hawthorne and probably begging for his forgiveness, have you once taken a look at yourself in the mirror? That's scary Sheri!!

"Think about Terry for what?" Sheri asked while getting a little heated at her mother's trues, sadly coupled with her insensitivity to Randle's physical condition. "Do you have any idea of what Terry has done? I didn't ask him to come to my house, and I begged him repeatedly to leave. Yet because of his arrogance and rage, Randle sustained a broken nose deviating his septum with 100 percent occlusion on the right side. A zygomatic maxillary fracture and bilateral orbital fracture due to multiple blunt force trauma to his face and head. He doesn't deserve that. So, whatever Terry is going through, he brought it upon himself. And I'm not begging for his forgiveness. I'm here showing the sincerity and commitment of my love for My Man! Now if you will please leave because there's nuthin' else for us to talk about."

Withholding no measure of compassion from her action, Mrs. Johnson slapped Sheri so hard with her right hand that she shrilled, stumbling backwards two or three steps before regaining her balance, and almost dropping the vase of flowers, while spilling half of the water on her top, which gained attention from the staff.

"Everything ok?"

"Yes! I just lost my balance and spilled a little water on the floor." Sheri answered.

"I'll take care of it." The staff member promised walking past the door.

Quickly resuming, "How dare you stand there and say what a man doesn't deserve for raising his hands to a woman. Are you even a woman? Or just a junkyard tramp?" She questioned with aggression in her voice. "This man beat you, then left you at home without a disturbing thought. Open your eyes, Sheri! His troll doesn't give a rat's ass about you or your womanhood. We taught you better than this. Yet, you're hiding up in here, crying because your brother beat his bitch ass on your behalf — and Demi's for that matter! Terry fought for your honor — your respect, the honor of women, something you seem to have allowed Randle to strip you of."

"And I've spoken to the arresting officers, Sheri. How, in your right mind, could you give a verbal statement against your brother, of all people, knowing how much he loves you, and, in the same breath, lie to protect the very scum who abuses you whenever he needs to feel like he's worthy of desecrating what is sacred? I'm starting to believe that you like being treated like a whore and discarded like project trash."

Rubbing her face while she stared at her mother, Sheri wondered why everyone wouldn't just leave her alone to love Randle without their belittling opinions. Really though, what did it matter what they shared between each other if it didn't affect them in any way? No one knew what Randle was going through, internally, and when you love someone, you face adversity together. Only problem was that her face currently personified adversity. But if only people would learn to mind their own damn business instead of trying to dictate the course of avoidance of the path of inevitable self-destruction for someone else, maybe the world would be a better place. Dementedly, Randle made her feel complete, and her mind and body were possessed by his hypnotic tongue, which were the only things that essentially mattered. How could she not forgive him when her twisted love was dialed improperly to unconditional?

"I protected Randle because it was my choice. He is my baby's father," rubbing her stomach hoping to create a sense of compassion within her mother. "And when you love someone that's what you do. He was wrong, and he apologized to me for losing his temper."

"And if and when he kills you, all he has to do is apologize to your corpse, sound about right?" A near fatal shot, rifled by her mom. "Can you honestly count how many times he has apologized to you now, seriously?

"Look Ma, I called the police so that Terry would stop punching Randle and leave my house. I begged him, but he just wouldn't stop, he probably would've killed him if I hadn't. So no, I'm not sorry for what I did. I mean, what else could I do? What is the issue? All he had to do was bond out, which is far less than the physical trauma, the torture he put Randle through or the torment he's battling now, not to mention the exorbitant medical bills we're burdened with because of him. Terry's fault — he's the animal."

She wanted to hit her daughter with a combination of jabs, followed up by a right hook to the jaw, sparked by her words. But instead of giving Sheri a concussion, which it currently looked like she had sustained several, spawned by Randle's commitment to controlling her, Mrs. Johnson just stared in overwhelming disbelief.

Growing up, women fought to define their respect, stood upon unwavering integrity, allowed their strength to be witnessed in their grace and weren't afraid to believe in themselves. Now though, it seemed like today's generation distinguished a woman's worth by degrading themselves for some twisted neurotic sense of empty acceptance and submitting as a battered puppet with clipped wings and frail strings to be a meaningless thought.

Retrieving her phone from her purse to see who was messaging her, Mrs. Johnson burst into laughter, which was needed to puncture the wall of tension that spanned between them as her eyes scanned the unbelievable words of Reanna's text. "I'm confused, Sheri! You stated the reason you lied to protect him was because that's what you do when you love someone. So, I assume you only gave a detailed statement against your brother because you don't lie to protect those who love you unconditionally and would sacrifice all that life has to offer for your happiness. You love the chaos, manifested in Randle, whom you met a little over a year ago, more than your actual brother, whom is not just family but has proven, the purity of his love, and whose loyalty has been vested in you for twenty-six years." Mrs. Johnson analyzed, now shaking her head.

"That's not what I meant," Sheri tried to deflect before getting cut off.

"Shut da fuck up, Sheri," Mrs. Johnson commanded with sternness in her voice. "Because your actions clearly acknowledge that's what you meant." Realizing that coming to talk to her daughter was a waste of time, she took one last look at her before walking past Sheri, pausing at the lobby entrance without turning around as she spoke, "The two of you deserve each other. How do you expect to have a healthy baby at all with a low life that beats you every time you blink an eye? There is no celebration in your acknowledgement or joy birthed when you have my son unable to be bonded out due to him sacrificing his life out of unwavering love for you. But, apparently, that has no weight, no value or significance to his parents' caringly reared daughter. You're correct on one thing at least — nice Star Lilies."

Watching her mom leave without either one saying goodbye, Sheri seemed to admire the silk turndown collar, long sleeve, belt blouse her mother was wearing along with the double bonded leather culottes, and the open toed stilettos, far more than mentally digesting the words she sprayed as a means of extermination.

Noticing the card inserted between the flowers for the first time walking down the, Sheri removed it while smelling and admiring the unique beauty of the Star Lilies. Shocked by the inkling on the card, she unintentionally dropped the vase in mid stride to the room after reading its words: *"Not because you're beautiful, extraordinary, or more magnificent than a flower. Just a reminder that you are irreplaceable as a whole. 'Paradise lies beneath your feet.' Sincerely Abdul Waahid."*

"I'm sorry," Sherry iterated.

"No worries, the janitor is already on the way to clean up the mess. Be careful not to cut your hand on the glass," one of the nurses asserted as she approached to help.

Kneeling to carefully collect the forty-eight Star Lily stems from the floor as two nurses volunteered their assistance to aid, Sheri couldn't believe the audacity of her mother to present her with Abdul Waahid's flowers, knowing so well that Randle would attempt to kill her for accepting them. Who was this Abdul Waahid, she wondered? And why does he keep disrespecting their relationship by sending a bouquet of flowers each week, as though there's chemistry or a foundation of friendship between them? There is no sweetness in another man's kind gesture when your heart already belongs to someone. Sheri only felt disrespected. Part of her wanted to tell Randle that she's being stalked, but she didn't want to make matters worse. Not seeking to anger Randle in any way, Sheri offered the flowers to the nurses but requested that they didn't mention anything to her man regarding them. They promised and accepted, which seemed to brighten their day as they smiled and repeatedly thanked her.

"Where have you been?" Randle asked as Sheri walked back into the room with a look of emptiness plastered upon her face.

"Just walking around to stretch my legs before stumbling and wasting my cup of water on me, baby," Sheri uttered approaching the bed to run her fingers lightly across his chest while looking into his eyes, "How are you feeling?" She inquired, trying to divert his attention, given that he advised that none of her family was allowed to visit.

Using the remote to raise the head section of the bed, Randle instructed Sheri to get him some juice from the vending machine and to request a shot of Morphine from the doctor because the pain in his face was becoming unbearable. As the throbbing irritation caused him to reflect heavily upon what had happened, all Randle thought about was how he was going to retaliate by pressing charges and suing the Johnson's to get him some money, thus exiling Sheri from her family.

Grabbing her cell phone and some money from her purse, Sheri left the room to do as Randle requested. She hated seeing him in the condition he was in and promised herself that she would do whatever it took to gain his forgiveness, for his love was all that mattered at the moment. Turning on her phone as she walked down the hall, she wondered why her mother said Terry couldn't get a bond. She couldn't believe that there were eighty-four text messages waiting for her to read and her voicemail was full.

Being extracted from life, she had no knowledge of all the things that had transpired in her moment of isolation. Scanning through the messages, she began erasing many of the unimportant texts. Reading Mr. Porter's heartfelt message, she immediately realized the detrimental affects her absence caused and a greater sense of sadness began to envelop her mood. Randle was her everything, but those kids nurtured her serenity. Purchasing a few juices in case Randle required one later, Sheri responded to a few messages regarding business before googling the county jail number.

As she headed back to the room, she called to inquire on the status of her brother. She was clueless as to why a simple assault charge would prevent him from bonding out when he has no criminal record. Hearing the jail clerk say that Terry Johnson was charged with simple battery and felony murder and has no bond flabbergasted Sheri as her movements began to reflect that of a zombie. Who has he killed, when, and for what reason?

Walking back into the room as though she was drifting in a trance, she absentmindedly handed Randle a juice without opening it, or giving him a straw to insert. Sheri then sat down while being unresponsive to his words. Trying to find answers in a mind where there were none while wondering who had her brother become in his six years of absence.

"Sheri! Sheri!" Randle repeatedly uttered until she finally snapped back into focus, turning her head towards him without opening her mouth to speak. "Bitch, what in the hell are you thinking about that I have to keep calling your damn name as though you are fuckin' deaf? Get your slutty ass up and come give me the straw so that I can drink my juice," he demanded through wired jaws instead of simply lifting his arm to grab it from the tray hovering over his chest.

She frantically searched her mind for someone to call for answers, as she obliged his request. Grabbing her phone after sitting back down and dialing Penélope's number, given that she felt Demi wouldn't inform her of why Terry was charged with felony murder, and she didn't want to talk to her parents.

"Bitch, who you calling?" Randle barked while looking intently at her.

"Penélope," Sheri replied as the phone was answered on the second ring.

"Hang the damned phone up!" He exploded aggressively. "I can't believe you are calling that bitch, while I'm laying up in here looking like this. Fuck them. You don't have no reason, or need, to call her nor anyone in your damn family. It's either us or nothing. Now hang that phone up, bitch! You talk about loving me and making things better, yet you're betraying me by reaching out to the very people who constantly try to pull us apart. How can I trust you when your actions say you're undermining me? Hang the fuckin' phone up before I seriously get mad in here."

Realizing that the things he was saying were correct and not wanting to anger him any further, Sheri hung up the phone as Penélope's voice could be heard advising her not to hang up as she was listening to Randle speak. How can she show she's truly worthy of his trust when her actions clearly confirm she's betraying and undermining him? Who knows what her brother has gotten himself into? But sitting there staring into Randle's eyes with complete submission, the one thing Sheri knew was that she was not going to let anyone come between them.

He looked so helpless staring at her and she clearly understood that the true completeness of his love could not be achieved without sacrifice. Randle was only the way he was because of his upbringing, and she was determined to help him transform into the man she believed he had the ability of always being. A man of compassion, sincerity, understanding, discipline, and one who would one day love her without abuse or neglect. Turning her phone back off, Sheri dropped it in her purse as she rose to stand beside the bed. Grabbing Randle's hand, she lowered to kiss his lips before locking their eyes and acknowledging that her heart and mind belongs to him.

"I'm sorry, Randle, for what my actions have caused to be afflicted on you. Baby, all I want is to prove that I love you. If you'd like, we can move away and start a new life somewhere else. As long as I have your love, then nothing else in this life matters to me. It's you and me baby, just you and me."

Laying there looking into her eyes, all Randle thought of was how much he wanted to stick his dick in her mouth, so that she would stop talking, and maybe alleviate his mind from the pain. His face was hurting too bad to continue laying there listening to her blab about her emotions, which he honestly didn't care about at the moment. Retaliation and getting paid was what granted him a mental sense of relief.

Sliding her hand beneath his hospital gown to tease his softness, "Lock the door," he commanded as she began caressing him. "Show me your word's sincere by sucking my dick instead of talkin'."

CHAPTER 20

U nable to sleep, Terry had to endure his bunkmate snoring at the unbelievably, extraordinary decibel level of a tiger pistol shrimp's hydro-claw, louder than a fighter jet taking off, and then there's the freakin' paper-thin bunk mat that the jail issued to lay atop a steel bunk that had every bone in his body aching. It felt as though it was no more than a thick plastic tablecloth on the cold steel bunk, which he paid an inmate for the comfort of laying on. Otherwise, he would be on the floor given that the jail was overcrowded and those at the helm assigned him to a spot on the floor as if he were a refugee. Terry laid motionless, thinking of Demi as he stared at the subtle darkness of the wall, realizing that reality couldn't be measured.

Never in his wildest dreams did he ever expect to find himself looking at life through a window of suspended time. He was now subjected to having his freedom completely stripped and his integrity spit on without justification. For a man who was raised to adapt to adversity, face life with footsteps of patience, and apply understanding to all things, Terry felt as though he was mentally suffocating by existing in a cell house that contained twenty beds overrun with thirty-seven detainees altogether.

The cell was a dungeon of torment that was literally no bigger than a one-bedroom apartment in a government housing complex and less clean than a public restroom at an industrial truck stop. Terry had heard many jailhouse stories over the years from distant cousins and associates, but never truly expected this experience would be so ignominious nor this mentally tormenting — unimaginable.

The lingering memory of standing in a crowded room full of naked men, during his booking process, kept running through his mind. To be verbally assaulted by guards just to have him in-processed (fingerprinted, mugshot etc.) and then be instructed to share a three nozzle shower station with nineteen other eye gazing individuals while systematically rotating to shampoo their bodies for lice had him feeling violated with his dignity being stripped away and life as he knew it being a distant reality. After degradingly being forced to bend over in a crowded room of detainees, spread his butt cheeks with his hands and cough repetitively as one of the disciplinary detention officer's stared into his anal canal with a flashlight while inserting a lubricated latex index finger to ensure there was no illegal contraband stuck up his ass had him feeling sexually abused. Mental unrest granted no ease as the days passed, because Terry couldn't stop wondering if the officer was secretly gay and found extensive pleasure in violating him with the body cavity search procedure.

"Chow call! Chow call, inmates!" The detention guard yelled while repeatedly slamming a hard plastic cup against the steel door of the unit to wake everyone.

Unhygienic detainees rose from their beds within the pod without brushing their teeth or washing their face, chemically assaulting one another with bad breath while lining up to retrieve their morning breakfast tray. Since being arrested, Terry passed eating every meal due to its less than aesthetic appeal and smelling like compost. No matter the nature of a person's wrong doing, he couldn't understand why those blacks in authority would treat them with malice intent for mere selfish pleasure that amounted to nothing, while the white officers did no more than their job and spoke with kindness. It wasn't enough that the black detention officers verbally and physically abused some of the detainees for cheap entertainment amongst themselves or that it seemed the jail kitchen staff made sure that molded bread was mandatorily served with every meal as though they were scum sheltered in a border refugee camp. The vegetables resembled a blended smoothie at best, and all the meat products had chameleon colors like it was developed as a lab experiment.

Hour upon hour, Terry laid lingering in thought while observing the characteristics of those around him. Intrigued at how individuals were making cooking bombs out of tissue to heat their coffee or fry the chameleon meat that was labeled "turkey ham." Some acted like extremely hungry scavengers by scrapping and eating the food from the thrown away trays in the trash. Not a single individual seemingly gave thought to thanking God for granting them another day to seek his forgiveness besides the Muslim who slept across from him, or cared to submit a moment of their time to nurture their hygiene.

Those who didn't go back to sleep after eating to momentarily conceal the invisible toxins in their mouth played spades, dominoes and told grotesque lies with no consideration of utilizing their time more effectively. Actually, proving that the Muslim, who was currently sitting on his prayer rug reciting in a low tone, was correct when he said the night before that Surah Al-Asr in the Qur'an clearly describes the conditions of these individuals:

"That by time, verily, man is in loss, except those who believe and do righteous good deeds, recommend one another to the truth, and recommend one another to patience."

The dormitory initially smelled like a septic tank, and the toilets and showers seemed as if they were molded with bio-hazardous bacteria. So, Terry placed five hundred dollars on a detainee's account, under the agreement that he would clean the restroom area twice a day for a month using only a bath towel cut into four pieces and a few bars of Dial soap purchased from the commissary, all because the facility wouldn't supply sanitation chemicals. The inmate scrubbed the entire bathroom until there was no visible fungus or mineral deposits on either of the two sinks, the toilets, the floor and shower walls, which had them resembling surfaces carrying contagious diseases worthy of being quarantined by the CDC. The urine odor from the two toilets was no longer assaulting their nostrils with lethal vapors like the intolerable mustiness emanating from the sweaty detainees who seemed to be allergic to free water.

Struggling to receive a moment of proper rest, given the bed had him feeling as though arthritis had been secretly injected into his joints and the isolation had him feeling as though he was suffocating, Terry began feeling the need to talk to someone outside those walls. Stretching as he stepped out of bed, Terry walked to the bathroom to groom himself before going to the phone and was disturbed to once again see two men forcing themselves on another in the shower. The sniveling sounds of plaintive cries had part of him wanting to interrupt their sexual exploitation with some punches, knees, and elbows, especially given the fact that the two predators were in visitation with him the day before telling their women how much they loved and missed them. But Terry understood that only God had the right to judge, and this had become the new norm and acceptance of today's society. Clearly knowing he didn't need any more assault altercations, given his situation, he elected to mind his own business.

Dialing his mother's number, given that neither his father, aunt, nor grandmother would answer the phone in his attempts to call collect, Terry hoped that they could share a conversation without her crying the whole time and saying "I love you" repeatedly as though he were a child in the Marine Corps leaving for war in the Middle East.

"Good morning, baby," Yara greeted after accepting his call. "How are you feeling today? I was just talking to Demi about you before she left the house. I invited her to breakfast this morning and was shocked to discover just how extraordinary and intellectually inclined she is, regarding world views and social injustice, to be from Stockwell, London. But her mother's circumstances are so sad."

"Oh yeah, she wanted me to inform you the moment you called that you shouldn't think that your footsteps have ceased running through her thoughts. She hasn't been able to answer your calls 'cause that job has her living off the wall — workin' day and night, and you seemingly call the very moment she steps away from her phone. Plus, she hasn't come to visit you, considering she doesn't want to see you looking like an entrapped slave behind a plexiglass window."

"Demi is currently on the way to your lawyer's office for me, given that I have to oversee the arrival of the Lois Mailou Jones and Faith Ringgold paintings this morning at the gallery, since Sheri's only priority seems to be catering to her pathetic lover, and shirking all her responsibilities now. I can call Demi on three-way if you'd like baby, but she did ask that you call anytime tonight after six."

"No, I want to talk to you, and I'm blessed, mom. How can I not be when I have your love and support," Terry convincingly stated, trying to comfort her with a sense of assurance. "I just called to check on you and to mentally escape the confinement of these walls for a moment. The television grants you a surface view of physical life behind these walls, yet one would never truly imagine how dreadful it is to the minds of those not mentally fit and up to the challenge of existing both day and night for extended periods of time in this type of isolation."

"I know, baby, and I pray for you constantly throughout the day. You have no idea how greatly I worry about you. I don't need you to lose your sanity being caged like an untamed animal."

"Mom, relax because I'm not a weak minded individual," Terry boasted calmly. "These walls can never contain my mind in any aspect, nor am I worried about someone trying to do something to me physically. Please stop worrying so much and remember I'm a Johnson, not a Sandifer."

"Boy, shut up," Yara retorted with a little sternness in her voice. "It's within a mother's warmth to love and worry about her child when their care is out of her reach. Until you are free of those slave chains and God calls for your soul, I'm going to worry, cry, and pray for you, boy. Especially with women killing men these days for playing with their time and emotions. Your father has been worrying about you as well, even though he may not say it, openly. Last night, he cried at the thought of you being in there, and he kind of blames himself, failing to intervene in their relationship the first time Randle broke Sheri's arm and blacked her eye, which she claims was a result of her falling down the stairs due to her heel breaking."

"Mom, it's no one's fault that I'm in here, but my own. I'm not sorry for my actions, and I never will be when it comes to punishing someone for puttin' their hands on my sister or any woman for that matter. God gave us the companionship of woman as a gift of His mercy and a blessing not to be abused like a barbarian showing ungratefulness."

"You are right baby, but men have been in error since the days of Noah (May God be pleased with him) and you can't become the vigilante for your sister and every woman who openly accepts abuse as a merit of love. I saw your sister yesterday, and you know what she had the audacity to tell me?"

"What?" He queried to play along, while shifting on the concrete bench that was starting to numb his butt.

"That she only lied to protect Randle because she's pregnant, and that's what you do when you love someone," Yara exclaimed. "Bullshit! I wanted to test some of my combat training out on her mouth as those senseless words rolled off her tongue, but just looking at how pathetic she was, standing in front of me while showing only concern for her precious Randle, infuriated me. So, I left, because I'm far too sexy to be your bunkmate, and I was too disgusted to stay any longer.

"Mom, everything is okay, and I'm not mad at Sheri for the choice she made. You misunderstand where she is mentally, which is not her fault because he is at the helm within her mind. You know clearly that words and fear can psychologically control a woman, especially when she's insecure within herself. For those very words can have her walking blindly on heated glass barefoot without caring about the effects, solely to define and distinguish her sincerity. It's not love she harbors, unfortunately, of which we both know. Their bond is psychological, a toxic yoke that is far more detrimental when the puppeteer is a mindless and abusive control freak. Just be patient and supportive of her. In time, she will open her eyes and realize her true value. My circumstances may be a misfortune, yet the blessing is within her womb, and I forgive her, a characteristic you groomed within me."

"Whatever, I will always forgive the both of you for the actions y'all commit, but everything is not okay, because you're in there," Yara expressed with a little hostility in her voice. "There is no understanding in accepting disrespect to sustain a sense of affection, and definitely not when it entails going against family. How can I become excited about having a grandchild when he beats her like a Navy Seal invading a Middle Eastern ISIS compound? She is subject to have a miscarriage by just brushing her teeth, or merely laying in the bed breathing that coward's funk. No baby wants a father with the compassion of an inland taipan."

"Mom!"

"Mom, nothing!"

Realizing how passionate his mom can get when talking about certain things, Terry knew it was time to change the subject before she allowed her anger of the entire matter to be the justifiable reason to go slap Randle and Sheri, which in essence would cause him to break Randle's neck for saying something disrespectful to her or doing something as foolish as retaliation.

"Mom, the guy that sleeps across from me is a Muslim who is very knowledgeable regarding his religious beliefs, it seems, and of Christianity. From what I observe, he is actually the only other individual in here, besides two silly elders, who has character, seemingly common sense, and portray having a sense of direction within their lives. I've been chatting with him a little just to pass time, and he has shared some very intriguing things I never knew."

"Things like what?" Yara eagerly replied, inquisitively.

"Religious theology, I never opened my mind to because I was too busy blindly following things that I had no clear knowledge or understanding of, while at the same time, allowing the news media to fill my mind with propaganda. He asked me a question before walking away to pray last night that I honestly find myself unable to answer ..."

Curious of what the question may be and not trying to wait in suspense, "What did he ask you?" Yara rushed as Terry tried to continue talking.

"Maybe he asked me how come my mother has no patience," he chuckled.

"I see why Demi calls you Lil Bow Wow now, boy!"

"Whatever, Ma! He asked me if I strive to model my character and life from Jesus' (may God be pleased with him) footsteps, who states in the Bible: 'Him without sin cast the first stone.' Then why do I harbor judgmental views of Muslims, when it's the very individuals of my Christian faith and all other religious faiths as well within our country robbing, murdering, raping, molesting, and abusing one another, etcetera? How can I forgive them, allowing nothing to weigh in my heart for their actions or character, yet consider Muslims terrorists and the worst of mankind for believing in God, the very way the Bible commands all of us, wholeheartedly without associating partners to Him or loving anything of His creation dearer than Him?

"In all honesty, I've never looked at it that way, and he has a valid point," Yara admitted assessing his statement. "Terry, what's all that noise?"

"Just two individuals arguing over a biscuit," he reported, while shaking his head at their pettiness. "They playing spades and bet their breakfast biscuit on the game."

"Spades at this time of morning?" She questioned. "Those biscuits must be fluffy and buttered down. Shouldn't they be reading a book or reflecting on the mistake that got them there? I hope you don't waste your time arguing with those guys, especially with that Boy's Club spades game you have son." Yara couldn't stop herself from erupting into laughter at her own punchline. "You know, another assault charge, you don't need, baby, but I do know you have to protect yourself from those booty snatchers."

"I don't know what you find so funny about your comment Ma. Johnson's don't dip or get dipped, and my game is light-years ahead of your recycled senior citizen spades game. I could beat you and whoever you select as a partner any day of the week with Cadence as my partner, of all people."

"Boy, please! You sound like your father, dreaming of one day beating me at basketball," Mrs. Johnson blistered as the phone recording advised that they only had one-minute remaining for the call. "Terry, call me right back so that I can tell you what happened."

"Okay mom," he agreed, hanging up and redialing the house number while eyeing the individual walking past his bed looking suspicious. The one thing he despised more than anything was a petty thief, especially given that all one had to do was ask.

"Terry, do you need me to put money on anyone else's account while I'm thinking of it? Do you have everything you need for the moment?" Mrs. Johnson asked after accepting the call.

"I'm good for the time being Ma. Just waiting on them to bring the commissary so that I can stop walking around with no underwear on and have some more snacks to eat. I've bought almost everyone's snack bag in the entire dormitory, because under no circumstance will I eat the food they serve at this facility."

"You better not be in there advertising the Johnson's goodies for those men either, boy," Mrs. Johnson said jokingly with silly laughter. "I noticed how tight that jumpsuit was squeezing your little butt cheeks at visitation, and you don't have on any underwear? Baby — got to be more careful! You know how some men get when they see something tight and sexy."

"Don't play, Ma!" He retorted. "By God's will, I will never be like these men who act straight when they're on the street around family and so called friends but come in here and explore their curiosity with or without hesitation. They would definitely be crazy to try me like that."

"You just don't because they don't make red bottoms in your size," Mrs. Johnson conveyed erupting in laughter.

"Whatever Ma! What did you have to tell me?"

Laughing even more as the thought of the incident came to mind, Mrs. Johnson struggled to get herself together as Terry's voice repeatedly echoed from the receiver while asking what's so funny.

"Baby, I love you and Sheri with all my heart. But I acknowledge that I would put aside all measure of compassion and stick my foot in both of y'all asses if either of you were to ever prank me like the girls did their mother the other day for a damn puppy."

"What!?" Terry exclaimed sounding a little bemused.

"Reanna and Cadence wanted a puppy, which Robin had been refusing to buy, given the fact that they really don't show any interest in caring for their horses. So, Cadence went to her and asked if they were to cause her to curse one time — knowing how religious and proper her bougie ass try to be — would she agree to buy them a puppy. Under the agreement she could not punish them for their efforts, of which she agreed to like a damn fool. But I'm telling you now — and I'm speaking with clarity — that darn agreement would not have mattered to me because I would have transformed into the Tasmanian Devil on both of them," she warned with a menacing facial expression. If only Terry could get the full effects.

"What did they do, Ma?" Terry queried with even greater curiosity developing. "You know the phone calls are only fifteen minutes."

"So! Even if they were just three minutes, you can't rush me. You don't have nothing better to do at the moment than to hold the phone in your tight sexy jumpsuit and hear the loving sounds of your mother's voice. God has blessed me with the ability of being able to afford your collect calls. Now be quiet so I can finish," she commanded authoritatively.

"Like I was saying before I was so rudely interrupted by your manner less curiosity, the girls have family night each week on Wednesday. So, Reanna makes the smoothies, and Cadence pops the popcorn. This time they chose a two-hour movie to watch. Reanna mixed half a bottle of lactulose with Robin's smoothie. From what I was told, they all used the restroom downstairs before they started watching the movie. Sneaky little Cadence acted like she needed to get her teddy bear just moments before they were about to play the movie so that he could watch with them. But her excuse was no more than a damn boldface lie to step away so she could secretly seal her mother's master bathroom toilet bowl with cellophane wrap.

Then about 2 o'clock in the morning, the lactulose hit Robin, and she jumped straight up out of her sleep fully awake 'cause her bowels were feeling like a volcano about to erupt. She ran to the master bathroom to sit on the toilet without even turning on the lights, so, she was unaware of the plastic wrap. She sat down on the toilet seat as normal, letting go without a second's hesitation. Surprise! Her hot shit and piss splashed back on her, the wall, the toilet, and the floor."

"Cursing like a drunk sailor mixed with an uncensored trap Queen with splashes of shit everywhere, even after she reached between her legs to punch a hole in the plastic so she could finish clearing her intestines directly in the toilet, it still wasn't enough I'm told to stop the splashing, and now it's on her hands too! Gross! With her panties seemingly plastered to her ankles and a shitty shirt sticking to her booty as she slid her feet across the cold tile, Robin said she dripped shit to the shower, only to discover that the water knobs had purposely been removed. Hearing the girls giggle like hyenas in her bedroom, Robin said, had her unbelievably furious as she stood in the shower, cold with piss and shit sliding down her legs and dripping from her butt. The disgustingly funniest part is that she said her stomach was bubbling so bad that she couldn't stop her initial flow as she sat on that toilet with the stench of shit out of control."

Laughing uncontrollably with a grimacing face as he listened to his mother tell the story, Terry noticed that several eyes were now gazing at him in curiosity as every muscle in his stomach throbbed as though he was experiencing body bending abdominal cramps. Wiping the tears from his eyes, Terry inquired about the girls while still chuckling and wondering if they received a spanking or punishment for their actions.

"The girls are okay," Mrs. Johnson acknowledged with a sense of dryness in her tone and a smug face. "Neither of them received a punishment for the prank, and they now have a pretty Yorkie named Precious. Robin is a much better woman than me because I would have made the both of them bathe me like a royal Queen, clean the bathroom without wearing any gloves to wipe up the shit, then stuck my foot up both their asses without taking either of them to the hospital afterwards. They could have crawled or walked to the emergency room for all I would have cared," she scowled.

"Ma, you silly as hell," Terry uttered before she cut him off.

"No, I'm dead ass serious," she retorted with authority as her eyes widened. "I joke but you don't play shit pranks on me! So be mindful that if you ever try me, there will be consequences to follow once the laughter ceases. My agreement is my promise, so don't be foolish."

"I love you, Ma, but we not kids anymore, so you never have that to worry about. Them days are long gone," Terry professed as the one-minute recording came on. "Hey Ma, please make sure that Mrs. Richardson at the bonding company is ready if the judge gives me a bond, 'cause I'm not tryna stay here a second longer than I have to. This place is for the new generation who have no sense of direction in life, not me!"

Hanging up, Terry called and laughed crazily with Reanna about their prank then made a few additional calls to associates. Walking back to his bunk, he found himself getting a little frustrated, reflecting on his situation and the harsh reality of it all. Living isolated like an animal was one thing, but being forced to eat sweets and packaged tuna in order to sustain strength because the food being served looks as though it's contaminated with biohazardous waste definitely couldn't escape being construed as cruel and unusual punishment.

Sitting on the bed with nothing to do other than linger on the possibility that he may never be granted his freedom again, and his sister is too psychologically yoked to care, Terry was stricken with the pulsating urge to work out to alleviate the mounting tension but couldn't because the onesie type jumpsuit he wore was his only clothing. Agitated that he couldn't masturbate to release a little pressure, lacking privacy in the unit, Terry laid back on the bed, closed his eyes, and fantasized about feeding Demi cherries and mango slices beneath the stars on the shores of Praslin Island, Seychelles.

Resting for a few hours for the first time, Terry opened his eyes, stretched, then sat up in bed and turned his attention to Abdullah, the Muslim on the bunk across from him after noticing the book, "The Ideal Muslim" by Dr. Muhammad Ali al-Hashimi, propped against his own pillow.

Laying on his bed, reciting the Qur'an in a low tone as Terry eyed him with a befuddled look on his face, Abdullah knew what he was thinking before he even spoke his first word.

"No, I'm not trying to convert you into Islam by giving you that book to read. The title is no more than the description of a role model for his progeny, but the book defines in every measure of life, the characteristics that one should adopt to be a prominent figure within himself, his family, and society. God tells us in Surah 2 ayat 30 of the Qur'an that *'man is the vicegerent of God on earth.'* But the question is, how can one be when he has no significant identity, nor purpose beyond the illusions he bridges for himself? In order for you to be a leader, Terry, one must know how to follow well. But for one to make a difference in life beyond his dreams, then one must have complete understanding and awareness of oneself. I shared the book to extract your mind from your problems and to get you to reflect internally on yourself, not to convert you. The book will enlighten you of what a man is and how he should breathe upon this earth. Often times, we focus on all the things in life that we are deprived of when God sits us down instead of seeking a path that will strengthen our bond with him. Always remember, 'he who God guides, none can lead astray, and he who He allows to go astray, none can guide.' No matter your hardship, Terry, there is ease," Abdullah expressed convincingly.

"I respect that," Terry replied while laying back on the bed reading the table of contents of the book, so intrigued to discover what the book had to offer. Knowledge of self and life, he loved to submit his mind to. After more than an hour of reading without a care for his surroundings, Terry briefly glanced over to Abdullah, before turning his attention to the dormitory door being opened. Hearing the officer indicate it was lunch time, he sat up to observe the characteristics of the detainees getting in line to receive a lunch tray; for he was interested to see if anyone was going to brush their teeth or wash their hands this time. Unfortunately, the only thing his eyes witnessed were individuals walking into the urinal stalls and leaving the bathroom without sanitizing, instead allowing the dirt and urine drops on their hands to add flavor to the food's contamination as if it's like peeing on a jellyfish sting to make it better.

"Abdullah," Terry called out turning on his side.

"Salam, Terry," he greeted, looking up from the book.

"If you don't mind me asking, how come someone mentally disciplined like yourself is in here?"

"Because it was God's decree."

"What!?" Terry retorted looking slightly confused.

"Everything happens in life by God's will and command. No leaf falls from a tree without His knowledge. No bird blinks without His awareness. You and I are here at this very moment talking because He decreed for our paths to cross."

Placing his book on his pillow to render the completeness of his attention as he sat up on the bed with his feet on the floor, "Terry I'm in here by choice, just as you are here by choice," Abdullah conveyed without a sense of remorse in his tone. "I killed a pedophile."

Bobbing his head slightly while taking in his words, Terry asked the one question he never expected to fall from his tongue given the nature of the person he mentioned.

"Was it worth it?"

"In all honesty, yes," Abdullah responded. "And before you start saying in your mind that all Muslims are terrorists like the news media tends to propagate in order to instill fear in people for ratings, the reality of that is not true. I don't regret what I did, but I have asked God for forgiveness because I took the life of His creation without following the commands which He legislated. I only feel overwhelming sadness in my heart because I fear God's wrath if I'm not forgiven, and it extracted me from my daughter's everyday life for life."

"The individual that my ex-wife was dating molested my daughter. As a father, your initial reaction is to react without a conscious mind, but I exercised discipline, initially, and went to the police with medical proof which her mother, literally, cared nothing about. Terry, the one thing I never wanted was for my daughter to ever feel unprotected by me. The courts may as well had slapped him on the wrist; they gave him just six months to serve in the county jail for sticking his tongue and finger inside of her and making my seven-year-old baby suck on him."

"That's fucked up," Terry growled with deep sentiment.

"Unfortunately, no it's not, Terry," Abdullah continued. "What's fucked up is that even with the medical proof of his wrongdoing, my ex-wife still maintained her love for him. Not only did she visit him while he was incarcerated, but she honestly allowed him to move back in once he was released. She kept that part from me for four months and told my daughter that she would spank her if she told anybody. But my daughter did talk when he touched her again and threatened to whip her if she said something to me about him trying to penetrate her. He broke her hymen. So, given the fact that the court indirectly acknowledged that his actions were acceptable and of no real consequence, I took my daughter to my mom before going to my ex-wife's house and shooting him in the head for violating her body and life the way he did. My punishment from the court was a life sentence with no possibility of parole, so here we sit, Terry."

He truly had no idea what to say as they sat there eyeing one another. Just listening to his words touched Terry emotionally trying to digest that he'd been forever removed from his daughter's life, physically, for trying to protect her, given that neither the courts nor her mother did.

"I'm honestly at a loss for words right now, Abdullah, and need to lay down and clear my mind of everything after hearing those words." Laying there contemplating his life and Abdullah's situation, Terry couldn't help but wonder if his outcome would be the same. Will the court sentence him to life in prison as well? The reality caused a tear to caress his face, as sleep slowly alleviated his mind from everything.

CHAPTER 21

It was a starless night that seemed frozen in time, void of any of the normal sounds of nature or wind breezes to rustle the trees. Ready to render their verdict without the procedures of the judicial system, Aaron, One Eye, and Mike exuded the characteristics of an owl as they patiently waited in the Porsche Cayenne for the flashing light signal.

Wearing tailored Mandarin black suits instead of black tactical camouflage gear and unable to channel their frustration of what may be occurring, internally triggering the release of adrenaline, neither said a word, or seemingly blinked an eye as they bobbed their heads to the 'Lost' album by Eightball.

The notion of patiently waiting almost eighteen minutes past the initial time seemed like 12 strenuous hours, mentally, and One Eye couldn't bear another moment of the disgraceful torment that might be happening inside the residence.

Noticing the carport light suddenly flickering on and off as advised, "Let's move," Aaron instructed while pulling the latch to open the driver's door, as One Eye and Mike exited the SUV with him.

The footsteps of havoc were all one could hear in the night, as they walked on the pavement side by side en route to the door. Tightening the straps of his Breacher combat gloves while ascending the driveway, One Eye knelt down in front of King when he reached the doorstep.

Demanding the silence of little King Marcus, given the significance of a surprise entry, One Eye pressed his index finger to his lips as King peered at them through the door crack. Reaching forward to gently grab his tiny hand, Mike slowly pushed the door open, then pulled him out onto the porch, whispering at a low volume that only the four of them could hear.

"Blink your eyes, Lil man, if you did exactly as we advised you on the phone."

Looking a little puzzled by their professional attire as he stood in the glow of the moon, blinking to acknowledge their orders were followed, he couldn't understand why they were wearing suits. King had assumed the men would have their faces painted like tribal warriors, if not covered with masks, and they'd be dressed in military tactical clothing, brandishing machine guns or hand crafted knives, given that's what they wear on television, or at least some sort of sports gear to grant more comfort and flexibility with their movement. Never did he expect to see three men looking like the corporate executives he often saw on Peachtree Street whenever Ms. Johnson took the students to the ESPN Zone or a restaurant.

"Lil man, there's an Oculus Quest 2 Headset and cellphone on the back seat of the Porsche to occupy your time until we return," One Eye whispered while pointing to the Cayenne that was parked across the street. "Lock the doors once you get inside, and under no circumstances should you leave until we return. None!"

Nodding to confirm he comprehended the instructions clearly, he, unexpectedly, squeezed Mike's hand before turning to hug One eye around the neck while whispering "Thank you, sir," in his ear. Hesitant to let go, due to the excitement of them granting him his wish, he lowered his arms, then walked straight to the SUV, occasionally looking back as they stood watching his every movement before entering the house.

Closing the door behind them, Aaron, Mike, and One Eye briskly walked through the kitchen and living room that were adjacent to the hallway. As instructed, King left his school bag by the door to mark his sister's room. Hearing only the voices of actors coming from the television inside the room, they positioned themselves outside the door as initially planned. At Aaron's nodded command, Mike kicked the door open with one thrust. Exposing what they feared, yet neither could honestly believe the actual sight before their eyes.

Startled by the sudden invasion of privacy, the mother's boyfriend, Carl, tossed King Marcus' little sister aside like a ragdoll, whom was sitting on his chest, crying, given that he was forcefully attempting to defile the innocent purity of her body.

"What the hell!? Get the fuck...!" He exploded in fury. Clueless to their intention, or who the three strangers were standing before him in suits, interrupting his sick pleasure, he tried to rise from the bed in a defensive manner with the intention of trying to regain a sense of control. Unfortunately, his statement was yielded by screams of pain, due to Aaron's lightning quick left hand which created a 5cm laceration from his left jawbone to his ear on impact, thereby causing him to flip off the bed as blood squirted like a water nozzle, which immediately caused him to feel as though he was going into shock.

Swiftly stepping around the belaboring assault, Aaron and One Eye was instituting to the pedophile's body, Mike grabbed the top bed sheet and wrapped it around King's traumatized little sister. "You're safe now," he whispered before lifting her into his arms and walking out of the room to console her mind.

Using his body as a lethal weapon to release the anger he couldn't contain after witnessing what he did, One Eye followed every strike Aaron imposed, with a precise blow of power himself. As disciplined and merciful as One Eye normally was, for the first time in combat, he had no pity and cared not about taking the individual's life. After stomping the pedophile in the chest and ribs a few times, One Eye trusted a heavy kick to his genitals to get the job done in damaging him permanently. They strategically delivered an execution of force with such dramatic impact and precision that after they broke his jaw with a combination of hammer fists and jabs, King's stepfather hadn't an atom's measure of strength to cry for mercy as blood leaked from his gashes. He laid on the floor, incapacitated, curled up like a fat fetus.

With his scrotum throbbing with excruciating pain, he held his gonads with no faculty to have any concern for the pain that was emanating from every quadrant of his face. Aaron commanded One Eye to stop, which he did by raising his right foot and colliding with one last explosive stomp to his chest that fractured two of his ribs upon impact.

"Please stop! Pleeeeease ...!"

"You have one minute to put your clothes on, starting now," Aaron interjected aggressively, while stepping forward to press the heel of his boot into the Adam's apple of the pedophile. Quivering beneath his foot, naked, Aaron desired nothing more than to crush his windpipe as he selfishly crushed her right to stay an innocent pearl and free of trauma induced by sexual perversion.

A pedophile deserves every measure of punishment life could offer, the three of them wholeheartedly felt without speaking it aloud. Every individual has an inner sickness in which they can reorient from, yet to Aaron and One Eye, only the extraction of a pedophile's life would help instill true meaning back into existence.

Conjuring every measure of strength possible in between the grunts of indescribable pain and gasping for air, he crawled over to the chair on the other side of the bed. Not trying to be subjected to another dose of their brutality, he cried to God and fought internally for strength to follow the command, struggling to clothe himself. His facial lacerations were blood donors, soaking his now crimson shirt as if it were a paper towel. And the internal pain seemed to become more pronounced with every movement. Without removing his eyes from either of them, the worrying thought of what was to follow began to blanket him with frightening images.

"Please don't kill me! I've never hurt her whenever I touched her. I promise, I'm sorry!" Carl cried aloud as gasping breaths of fear entered his lungs and his jaw twisted more with his words. "I don't want to die like this! Her mother said it was okay for me to play with her whenever she worked late as long as I paid the bills and promised to remain a part of her life. Please don't kill me!" He cried on the floor, shaking, while trying to slide into his pants.

Repulsed by his cries for mercy, "Say another word, Carl, and I will walk out of the room, closing this door behind me," Aaron calmly stated looking over his pathetic disposition, knowing One Eye would love to execute more punishment for his disgrace.

"Secure him," Aaron instructed, once he was finally dressed. Removing the zip ties from his jacket's inner pocket and handing them to One Eye, he thought of smashing his face one more time with his foot, but knew it would cause One Eye to react as well, so he suppressed the urge.

Not caring about the pervert's hemorrhaging or external injuries, One Eye slammed his hands into his chest with unyielding aggression, gripped his shirt and lifted the 247lbs of wasted lifeform from the floor like a featherweight cotton stuffed animal. The slithering perpetrator's cries of pain hovered above all other sounds within the air of the night, as One Eye threw him on the bed and pushed his arms up into his back purposely to bind his wrists with the handcuff style zip ties.

Assured that his assistance was no longer needed, Aaron walked out and stood in the doorway of the living room, silently admiring the words of comfort Mike was sharing with King's little sister to awaken her smile and dispel her worries and fear. Being childless and a single family military brat, Aaron knew he lacked the ability to effectively comfort a child who may become suicidal due to post traumatic stress disorder (PTSD), develop neurotic reactions, self-injurious behavior, lose trust in all men for the rest of their lives, or become mentally yoked with fear of being touched, due to their innocence being wrongfully taken away. How could a man be so selfish in his desire for pleasure?

Nodding without saying a word as Mike glanced up at him standing in the doorway, signaling to acknowledge that they were ready to move, he asked her to insert his ear buds into her ear after retrieving them and the cellphone from his jacket's inner pocket. With nothing but Sade and Anita Baker albums on his playlist, Mike knew very well that a love song would be inappropriate at the moment, so he pulled up a talking shark video on YouTube to entertain her for a moment. He hoped that would hold her attention as they removed the pedophile from the house without her having to witness him again, especially in his gruesome condition.

Escorting him out to the SUV without her noticing, Aaron secured him at the rear as One Eye gained King Marcus' attention who was momentarily lost in whatever he was doing with the Oculus Quest 2. Removing the headset, King was a little flummoxed by only seeing One Eye as he opened the rear passenger door. Hearing the whimpering cries of the pedophile, King tried to turn his head toward the rear of the vehicle to see what was going on and what his stepfather looked like to be making those unusual sounds. But One Eye stopped the movement of his head by quickly placing his hand on the side of his face gently and standing beside the Cayenne to block his view as he instructed him not to bother himself with the cries coming from behind the SUV.

"Did y'all beat him up, sir?" King asked energetically, throwing air punches before laying the headset on the seat as he prepared to step out. "Can I see what he looks like? Is my sister okay?"

Unable to mask his facial expression at the eagerness of his words, One Eye earned an even bigger smile from King's face when he attempted to dodge his questions with an uninhibited telltale cheesy grin, then he advised him that Mr. Johnson bought the headset and phone for him, and the unopened one in the bag on the floor was for his sister.

"For real?!" King exclaimed, illuminating the night with his smile, like a human neon light, quickly grabbing everything not allowing One Eye the chance to even think about changing his mind.

"Yes, for real little man," he assured him, beaming a smile, himself, as King threw everything back in the bag and stepped out of the SUV to hug One Eye again.

"Please tell Mr. Johnson I said thank you, and I promise not to break it," King uttered while squeezing him.

Walking back to the house, King wanted to turn around to confirm if that was actually his mother's wretched boyfriend making those grunting noises behind the SUV, and how severely he was beaten. But he was asked not to look back before crossing the street. And given the fact that Mr. Johnson had fulfilled his word by sending someone to remove that cancer from their lives as he had promised when he spoke to him the following day in Mr. Porter's office, he didn't want to anger him by having One Eye reveal that he didn't follow instructions.

Calling out to his sister as he entered the door, he was overwhelmed with endless joy to see her sitting on the sofa giggling beside Mike as she watched something attentively on the device in her hand.

"Look at what Mr. Johnson bought for us!" He interrupted with a jovial heart and energetic excitement while dropping the bag in front of her and reaching inside to retrieve her new identical Oculus Quest 2 box and cellphone. "You didn't ask me if you could wear my favorite shirt, but it's okay because you're smiling, and I love you, sis," King said before hugging her.

"Sit down for a minute, little man," Mike instructed him rising from the sofa as King was giving his sister her gifts, yet slightly feeling some type of way about wearing his airbrushed T-shirt of Tiffany Hayes and Natasha Cloud hugging him inside a heart. "Your sister's safety is forever your responsibility, and never allow anyone to force either of you into being silent. She's going to be okay, but for her to be better, always remind her that butterflies have beautiful wings even though they can't see how lovely they are." Handing him two cards with his name and number on them, "Put these in a safe place and call me if either of you ever need me," Mike insisted before turning to leave the house.

"Sir, what do we tell our mom when she comes home and asks about him?" King asked.

"Tell her the truth," Mike informed them. "He left with three guys in a white SUV, and completely leave it at that. Okay? Neither of you have any knowledge of who they were or where they planned on going."

"Yes sir," King said smiling while following Mike to the door so he could lock it behind him. "Thank you, sir, for helping us. Do you think I can thank Mr. Johnson tonight, also?"

"Yes! I'll always have your back lil man, but you never have to thank me for anything. Like Mr. Johnson always says, 'All thanks and praise belong to God and God alone,'" Mike apprised while shaking his hand, before exiting and closing the door behind him.

Dialing Mr. Johnson's number as they drove down MLK Drive, a part of One Eye wished that he would permit them to do whatever they wanted with Carl, yet he knew for sure that no matter a person's evil, Mr. Johnson still treated them fairly, because he feared God's wrath for being an oppressor or acting like a tyrant.

"Sir, we have Carl Griffin," One Eye advised as he answered the phone.

"Good! How's the little girl?" Mr. Johnson inquired with a compassionate tone.

"She's good, sir, and little King Marcus would like for you to call so he can thank you. We got there in time, but unfortunately not before the initial act of defiling started."

"Okay! After Aaron finishes video recording him openly confessing to his acts of child cruelty, I ask that you upload the video to every social media outlet that you can, then call me back, please. I would like to talk to him before you all drop him off at the jail. I've already spoken to the District Attorney regarding the matter, so the shift supervisor on duty is aware that you will be dropping him off.

"Yes sir," One eye said, hanging up and hitting the pedophile with an elbow so forceful that it fully broke one of the ribs he had already cracked earlier.

CHAPTER 22

Occasionally pacing in his jet black pinstripe, double breasted suit before the group of investors, encircling the table in the conference room of his Dunwoody office, Mr. Johnson began to feel like the presentation was remotely falling on deaf ears, as he tried to highlight his objectives on the projector board using a laser pointer. Motivated to make a difference, he used this business meeting to pitch his idea of opening a rehabilitation facility, supported by donations, that would provide healthy food, clothing, shelter, and homeless individuals the benefit of receiving adequate medical care for free.

Mr. Johnson expected his business associates to be elated at the opportunity of doing something enormously positive and beneficial for the redevelopment of the society, especially since their investment would stem from a GOP tax exemption loophole that takes funding from the lower class and redirects the incentives to wealthy Americans, money that he actually intended to sow back into the communities. Instead, he was bombarded with skepticism and mild laughter as if he was not only asking them to invest their personal capital, but to offer physical labor out of sheer compassion that they weren't about to exert.

Sitting in awe at the head of the table, Mr. Johnson couldn't believe that a group who spends so extravagantly upon wasteless things for the acceptance of others and has always talked about doing something to benefit those that are homeless and physically disabled, now sat arrogantly before him with such audacity to scoff at the idea. Blatantly acting as if there was a correlation between social status and human worth, he became infuriated, hearing them refer to those considered beneath them as low life peasants, scum, worthless and unworthy of being helped. The group questioned why they would want to spend money investing in the rehabilitation and health of dysfunctional lives when they could benefit from far greater tax breaks and return incentives by donating to other causes.

Rising from his chair, he panned his eyes back and forth on each individual sitting at the table as they reflected the characteristics of Fir'aun. "It offends me to hear the five of you speak as if you have no reverence for life and it has no value, when profit is not and should not be the sought objective," Mr. Johnson voiced sternly with no signs of resentment in his tone. "Each of you sit here acting like misers, and as though those who are less fortunate are maggots, devoid of value, foreign to the air that we all breathe, and undeserving of compassion. Do y'all realize, even maggots have value to an open wound. Word of advice to each of you: never allow arrogance and greed to elevate your ego to a level you feel that God can't strip you of the very meaningless things you cherish, far more than being grateful for the countless blessings He has bestowed upon you. Who are we when we lose all sense of appreciation for His blessings and think only of greed that will not profit any of you when your bodies lay covered with soil and absent a soul or the faculty to intake oxygen and exhale CO_2?

"There's not a person in this room that hasn't quadrupled their net worth since I introduced each one of you to Mrs. Martinez at Nazadina Consultants. Yet, you come into my office and disrespect the very essence of people we all have a sense of connection to in some respect. Especially given the fact that two of you were once homeless yourselves, which makes your actions an even greater atrocity, bigotry! It highlights you with the neon glow of hypocrisy, an ingrate. It's an insult to me and you should feel embarrassed. On the one hand, it's acceptable for someone to offer you an act of kindness, but on the other hand, your heart is void of compassion, incapable of offering the same hand of generosity. Sincerity follows the same rules as forgiveness in the eyes of God. No one is deserving; however, you will not be blessed with that which you are stingy or reluctant to give, or am I missing something?"

"Mr. Johnson we're not bashing your idea. Actually, each of us applauds the concept, yet half of a million dollar investment every year that yields no return is not an investment," his female associate, who made her fortune importing and exporting cosmetic jewelry, cautioned, looking at the others for support of her statement.

"Moral values will always be a priceless investment," Mr. Johnson countered. "You just paid three hundred thousand to have a sauna and a computerized play area built in your house for your dog! And while I'm not downplaying God's creation that has intrinsic value to so many disciplines, your dog does not contribute to your financial wealth. Yet, you consider it degrading and a waste of free cutback money which could be used to help someone who has fallen and needs a little support to stand erect again. Are you serious?!" He inquired with so much aggression in his tone that veins became visible in his forehead. "You slept in your car for seven months, that is until you received an extension of God's mercy, so what's the difference here?!"

"Well, I beg to differ, sir. I am immensely grateful, as I think we all are. It's just not like that Mr. Johnson!" She exclaimed defensively as if her words were truly sincere.

"Ok, whatever. Not only will this facility help to improve self-awareness, stress management, self-esteem issues, and counsel drug addiction, but the medical treatment is just as significant, given that hospitals refuse to treat them without insurance or it being an extreme medical emergency that forces them. The ROI is the acknowledgement that it will bring an evolutionary change to others' lives, which is more pleasing to God than a financial kickback that merits nothing. I don't want to waste anymore of your time or my own. I respect that all of our schedules are very hectic. Truly, I thank all of you for coming and granting me the opportunity to share my vision. I encourage all of you to always remember the words of a wise man who once said: *'You will never believe until you have sincere compassion toward one another. The people then said, 'O' Messenger of God, all of us are compassionate.' He said, 'It is not the compassion of anyone of you toward those you love but yet compassion toward the common folks."*

After switching off the projector and placing the laser back in the box on the wall, they chatted amongst themselves about other issues before leaving. Mr. Johnson found new reasons to smile when his lawyer called as he strolled down the hall to his office and advised that the purchasing deal for the library was now completed. He assured that he would stop by in the morning with the papers for him and his daughter to sign. Realizing how happy Sheri would be at hearing the news, he tried calling only to receive her voicemail, which has been the only sound of her voice that he has heard since she brought Randle home from the hospital a week prior. Face Timing his wife after leaving another message, Mr. Johnson couldn't help but feel the desire to physically show his wife how much he appreciated her for being the blessing within his life.

"Hey baby," Mrs. Johnson greeted. "Did everything go well?"

"It depends on what angle you wish to look at it from, love. I've decided that instead of offering others the opportunity of being a light within someone else's life, I'm going to pray and ask God to grant me the ability of doing this project solely for Him. Yara, it's sad when people treat those less fortunate than them as if they're dirt beneath their feet. When in God's eyes, only our submission to Him without associating partners and piety separates us from one another."

"You're right baby, but don't allow the shallowness of others to dampen your mood or to burden your mind with unfruitful thoughts. Pray as you said, and God will provide. Which of the blessings of your Lord will you deny?"

"Yara, when I have life's greatest jewel as a wife to love, how can I ever deny a blessing from our Lord? Baby, I was actually calling to advise you that the library deal is now finalized, and I love you! I tried to call Sheri, but she's not answering the phone."

"Don't allow that to bother you baby, she'll open her eyes pretty soon. All we can do is pray. I love you too baby, and that's wonderful news," Yara complimented with nothing but joy in her voice. "The kids are going to be excited. We should take them all out bowling for them to celebrate."

Listening to his wife express her excitement and articulate her ideas for the new center caused Mr. Johnson to smile at how compassionate she was for those kids and the effort as a whole. She did no teaching in the classroom but still contributed hours of volunteer assistance. Yara made sure that the students received countless incentives for their hard work, provided them with free school supplies, and made sure that they felt loved over all things.

"Baby, I often express my love for you through words and by giving you gifts, but I want you to know that I appreciate you for your sincerity, your inner warmth, and your strength, which is the core essence of your integrity. Your smile, I cherish because, other than God's love, it's the only jewel of life that's irreplaceable to me."

"I love and appreciate you too, my King," Yara reciprocated, blushing at the sincerity of his words.

"I have a couple meetings, but I should be done by three. I plan on stopping by the jail for a moment, then I'll be right home afterwards. Be dressed, because I'm taking you to Fannie's tonight and a surprise venue afterwards," Mr. Johnson informed and requested before receiving Yara's dictatorial instructions of what she needed him to pick up on the way as he blew her a few kisses then ended FaceTime.

Not intending the land development negotiations to carry over an additional hour, Mr. Johnson realized, looking at his watch while exiting the office building, that he wouldn't have time to visit the jail before the next visitation hour was scheduled and be able to pick up the Coca Cola cake from the West Egg Cafe before they closed as originally planned. Wanting to see his son, yet knowing that he gave Yara his word, Mr. Johnson elected to pick up the cake and called his brother to see if he could visit for support.

Riding through Cabbage Town always seemed to bring back a painful memory for Mr. Johnson no matter his state of mind. Thirty-six years had passed, yet the resurfacing images of his friend's suicide made it seem as if it was just yesterday that he was wiping away tears as he stood before the cold, breathless body of his childhood best friend, who killed himself out of fear of going to prison. His friend was wrongly accused of raping a white cheerleader of an opposing school as a prank, merely to exclude him from playing in the high school championship football game. Precious life, they took for a meaningless trophy! Pondering on stopping to purchase a bouquet of Calla Lilies while sitting at the light after picking up the cake, Mr. Johnson couldn't help but admire some of the graffiti adorning the landscape.

One drawing in particular was very unique, yet the inscribed words gave it a greater sense of meaning, so, he captured it on camera and forwarded it to share with Yara, *"Do not let the temporary and little charms of this world distract you and entice you ... and do not say tomorrow and tomorrow, for indeed you do not know when you will be heading to God."*

Pondering on life as he pulled into the driveway, Mr. Johnson parked, stepping out with the cake and vase. He almost dropped the cake when his dogs ran up to him with unbridled excitement, but he instantly commanded them to sit, knowing that if he were to drop Yara's cake, he and the dogs would be in the ICU for an extended period of time. Forget being in the doghouse! He placed the box and vase on the roof of the car before apportioning a few minutes of his time to share some affection. Commanding them to run off after about fifteen minutes of caressing, playing, and training, Mr. Johnson sanitized his hands using the EO Botanical hand sanitizer gel that Yara keeps in all of the vehicles' center consoles before retrieving the items from the roof of the car and walking into the house. Inhaling mixed aromas of food as he walked through the house, grooving to the soft melodic sounds of Toni Braxton had Mr. Johnson a little perplexed — especially after entering the kitchen and seeing his wife in her red and black ombre robe stirring the charred broccoli with lemon and parmesan in a cast-iron pan with her right hand, while using her left hand to sauté the honey walnut shrimp.

"Yara, I asked you to be dressed because I have a surprise for you after Fannie's," he appealed moving close to kiss her lips as she turned her head to welcome his affection.

"I know," she responded without showing any signs of concern.

"Then, why are you cooking and not dressed?" He discontentedly challenged while allowing his eyes to caress her body with wanton lust as the aroma curiously taunted his nostrils, only to have his hand slapped for trying to grab a broccoli floret from the pan. "I paid for that," he yapped jokingly.

"That you just did a second time, and if I hit you in the mouth, you will have to pay for the stitches and wiring as well," Yara piped sticking a broccoli in her mouth to tease him. "Now, get out of my kitchen so I can finish cooking for you."

"Baby, what are you doing? We have reservations!"

"Then cancel them. I'm cooking 'cause I just want to spend some time alone with you," Yara confided while flinging her hair back and cutting her eyes to add a sense of enticement with her attraction.

"But I have a surprise for you," Gip added, staring at the broccoli while contemplating pushing her aside so that he could grab one or two florets and run.

"There's nothing in life you can surprise me with. I have everything my heart has ever prayed for right here. Now, go take a shower and get ready for yooourrr surprise. Tonight, is about you, not me," she commanded seductively while grabbing another small floret of broccoli and sucking it in her mouth with heated enticement.

Moving close to caress Yara's back with his left hand while lowering to kiss her on the neck in pursuit of pleasure, she had his body calling for her affection as she stood there hiding the jewels of his addiction behind silk fabric. Gip never expected Yara to hit him in the stomach with an elbow which she quickly followed with two playful jabs to the chest, as the spoons fell into the pans.

"I'm serious, get out of my kitchen," Yara snapped while giggling. "Which of the blessings of the Lord will you deny? I know you're trying to distract me so you can grab a broccoli. Get out my kitchen!"

"You hit like a butterfly," Gip joked walking over to the refrigerator to grab a handful of white grapes while chucking and rubbing his chest in secret. "I'll show you how to hit, if you were to stop cooking and get on the counter."

"Who told you that you have a sledgehammer, Mr. Make Me Yawn?" She teased raising her voice as he walked out of the kitchen after washing off a hand full of white grapes. "I'm not in the mood to fake an orgasm just to stroke your ego."

"Whatever! If only you honestly knew what I fake for the awakening of your smile." He joked, sarcastically. Yelling at the top of his lungs with passion while climbing the stairs, "I'm the King," Gip stressed humorously, repeating himself in his African tribal voice when he reached the top of the stairs. "I'm the King!"

Laughing at his silliness, Yara just shook her head and smiled as she stood there preparing his meal and lingering upon the surprise that she had planned. Removing the bouquet from the counter and placing it in the center of the table along with his plate after putting the cake away, she took a picture and uploaded it to her social media with the caption: *"When a man proves by actions that you are appreciable and irreplaceable. A Queen reminds her King that he's a significant value to her heart as well."*

Turning off the Ontario lights and lighting two vanilla scented candles on the table to illuminate the darkness, Yara turned on some classical jazz once she saw Gip on the monitor, exiting the bedroom. Perched like a swan in her seat, seductively caressing her lips as Gip walked into the dining room, wearing his white linen pajamas and slippers, she leaped to give him a passionate kiss that caused the muscles in his body to stiffen.

"You have to earn the pleasure of tasting more exotic chocolate," she cajoled seductively biting his bottom lip as she pulled away, and guided him to his seat by resting his hand on her butt. "Follow me my King."

Stepping out of her slide-in-stilettos and grabbing his plate off the table, Yara straddled him, initially teasing his neck with a few kisses, before feeding Gip the entire meal while occasionally rotating her hips to stimulate his yearning. Laying the plate back on the table, Yara unbuttoned his shirt while nibbling on his ear then caressed the sides of Gip's face with her hands before she kissed him with every single atom of love in her body.

"I love you," she purred biting into his bottom lip again while pulling away.

"I love you more," Gip whispered staring at the highlights of her beauty in the candle's glow.

Standing to entice the thirst already stirring in his veins, she grabbed the remote from the table, switched the music to Mary J. Blige's *"I Found My Everything"* and started dancing sensually between his legs. Gradually, she brushed her softness against his thighs enticingly, while slowly loosening her belt and opening her robe to reveal the custom made Atlanta Falcons eyelash lace splicing bralette pierced lingerie bra set she was secretly adorning beneath for his eyes only. With his fingers gently surfing the soft ebony fibers of her stomach, Yara lifted her right leg to place her foot on his chest, as Gip sensually caressed her calf.

"Suck my toes," she whispered while sensuously rubbing her fingers across her body and staring intimately into his eyes.

"I'm not putting your damned toes in my mouth," Gip exclaimed humorously while chuckling at Yara's amusement and sliding her foot down, given that her toes were already getting close to his face. "I'll put something else in my mouth."

"I'll just wait until you go to sleep, as always then," she mischievously stated while removing her foot and closing the robe. "I guess you are going to deny your blessing." Turning away to begin clearing the food from the table, "Baby, you had your chance to make me your play-toy."

"Whatever, Yara! This is my kingdom!"

"Say another word and we'll see where you'll be sleeping in your so-called kingdom," Yara said while looking over her left shoulder. "You say that you love me but won't even suck my toes.

"Not even if my life depended on it," he sarcastically stated while chuckling.

"We'll see smart-ass! But seriously baby, I want to play a game that Reanna advised me of earlier. I want to know how well you actually know me?"

Laughing at the comical nature of her words, "I know you better than you know yourself," Gip answered humorously while rising from the table to help his wife clean the kitchen and changing the music to Prince's *"Somewhere Here on Earth,"*

"Shut up!" She shouted while playfully throwing a broccoli that hit him on the lips as he turned around. "You don't know nothin'."

"If you say so! You've been my wife for thirty years and I've cherished every moment, so don't try me. Reanna called and had me answering questions about her and Cadence earlier as well. If I made a perfect score on both of them, then what do you think I'll make on you sweetheart?"

"Only your participation will answer that question. But I'm adding some sauce to the questionnaire. If you want me to remove all my clothes tonight and let you taste the candy box, then you must get eight right. Nine and I'll make you cry like you did the first time I gave you some of this black honey," she implored caressing her body seductively. "But if you are fortunate enough to get all ten correct, then I'll allow you to eat fruit off my body as I lay in your massage chair wearing only my heels after I climb off the pole tonight, and spread my falcon wings to your command for a week. However, if you fail to get eight correct, then you shake dance on my command for a week. I mean anywhere!"

"Well, you might as well spread your wings right now on the stove. Better yet, I want some honey baked wings so climb in the oven." He insisted with confidence in his tone, chuckling as he walked over to the oven and opened its door.

Paying his silliness, no mind, Yara continued to clean while pondering on the questions she intended to ask. She wanted to win because the thought of having the ability of making him dance in public was starting to become increasingly and comically appealing.

Grooving before his wife to the sound of music as if the spotlight was shining on him, Gip had Yara gripping her stomach in laughter, as he danced imitating someone with two left legs and no rhythm. Not wanting the smell of the shrimp shells or broccoli to linger in the air overnight, Gip took the trash out, returning to the echoing calls of his wife calling out to him from the game room intercom system. Resetting the alarm and washing his hands, Gip paraded through the house and down the stairs like a pledge for a fraternity.

Yelling repeatedly, tickling his own comedic senses, "Spread yo falcon wings! Spread yo Falcon wings!!" while mixing the A-town Stomp dance with the Atlanta Falcons celebration dance as he entered the entertainment room door.

"You're stupid," Yara joked humorously while standing on top of the pool table's leather cover with her stilettos back on, black furry bunny ears on her head, and a Calla Lily stem in her mouth, which she removed to laugh at the unorthodox movements of her husband. "I'm calling a psychiatrist in the morning because I should be getting a check for you."

"Don't worry my love, 'cause I will definitely give you a checkup after you spread your falcon wings on the fireplace mantle," he promised while putting an extended emphasis on his words when he stated them.

Using the remote, she dimmed the room lights, lowered the retractable stripper pole from the ceiling, and turned on the audio system for the purpose of syncing her body with the music to help entice him. Trying to block out Gip's continuous attempt to annoy her by doing the dirty bird dance, Yara closed her eyes to shield herself from his distractions and danced sexily to Karyn White's "*Superwoman.*"

"Baby, sit down," she demanded sternly opening her eyes to see him still bouncing around like a fool. "And stop acting silly before you make me fall."

She shook her head as he did the dirty bird dance and the A-town Stomp over to his personal massage chair. Leaning back and crossing his legs as he surrendered his full attention, Gip smiled at Yara's beauty. He was endowed with the fact that he was blessed to have her and her graceful movements on the pole.

"Damn, I love this woman," he whispered to himself while admiring every feature of his wife as she performed enticingly. "The King has a suggestion, my Queen," Gip said, using his Zamunda voice.

"What, baby? Yara inquired moving to the groove of the music.

"For every one of your questions I get correct, you have to give me a thirty second strip tease. And every one I get wrong, I'll suck your toes for one minute," he vowed to Yara who responded by rotating her hips as she lifted her leg and curled it around the pole, bouncing her booty like a young stripper 360 degrees.

"Let me stop before I have to call and ask James or Aaron to pick you up some Huggies from the store," Yara chortled, swaying her upper body side to side as the sounds of Milestone filled the air. "Who is my favorite designer?"

"For clothes, it's Tracy Reese and Ituen Basis. For shoes, you love Fendi loafers, and when it comes to stilettos, you love Saint Laurent more than Christian Louboutin," Gip announced without taking a moment to surf his thoughts.

Acting as though they were in a Dancer's Club VIP lounge, he reaches into his pocket for his wallet, he pulled out every one of his credit cards, then threw them on the pool table as he started bouncing like a happy client, looking at his watch to time the grace of her mimetic exhibition.

"Name my five favorite celebrities," she asked after she finished dancing.

"Jada Pinkett Smith, Regina Hall, Angela Bassett, Taraji P. Henson, and my other wife, Halle Berry," he rattled off, while looking at his watch.

"I'll kick both y'all's ass if you ever try me again," Yara exploded with heated aggression in her voice. Mama Lewis is on speed dial, just so you know. With each question Yara asked, Gip not only showed that his wife was truly his reflection, but his eyes and ears were her keeper. Turning up the heat being few degrees sexier with the movements at every loss, Yara honestly couldn't believe he answered every question without hesitation as if he was reading her thoughts before she posed each question. Biting her lower lip teasingly, then lowering to lay provocatively on the pool table, staring at him, she lifted and held her legs, before starting to shake them, with the intention of making her booty clap for his appeal. Yara was eager to reward his smooth work on the exam, but really what she needed and wanted was her toes massaged with his tongue after all the dancing she was doing.

Not only was he knowledgeable of her menstrual cycle changes, remembered the breed of her first childhood dog, the name of her first teddy bear, the name of the college book she left at the movies on their fourth date, her secret guilty pleasure, and her new gynecologist's entire name, but he even remembered line for line the first poem she wrote him and quoted it, to Yara's disbelief.

Standing on the pool table dancing against the pole had Yara desiring her husband far more than he was yearning to breathe as one with her. The tingling sensation stirring internally had her body feeling as though it was on fire, roiling like an estuary. She wanted to feel his hands and tongue caressing every silky strand of her cellular fabric. Yara asked her last question, knowing he couldn't answer because her thoughts, she had shared with no one.

Watching him in anticipation as he caressed her body intimately with his eyes, Yara lifted her right foot and wiggled it while asking, "Are you ready to suck these toes?" With only a smile warranted from her husband, she imposed her unanswerable question. "What date have I set for us to renew our vows?"

"Of all the challenging questions you could have asked, love, this truly is the easiest one. I expected you to at least ask me what's your pet peeve about me or what are you most proud of. Because your smile is my priority, I'm going to intentionally answer it wrong just to suck your toes, since you deserve it, desire it, and your love is my pillow," Gip said rising from his seat and walking over to the table to grab her foot, intimately massaging it as he stared into her eyes. "The wrong answer is tomorrow and that is the official answer I give. But the truth is that as long as our son is confined behind bars, there is no date or time frame set. You want him to walk you down the aisle," Gip stated before sliding her toes into his mouth. The heated spark unleashed every ounce of their passion, bridging an awakening of love that left memories on the pool table, his massage chair, the stairs, and Jacuzzi throughout the night.

CHAPTER 23

F eeling as though she's suffocating mentally, confining herself within the walls of her house and the limitless needs of Randle to prove the depth of her love is greater than words, Sheri decided to go to work after a three week absence and arrived at the Art of Life two hours prior to when the doors are normally unlocked. Not expecting anyone to be in the building, she could free her mind and lose herself in the viewing of the new art without the presence or words of anyone invading her serenity. Sheri was surprised to see Naomi's BMW M4 convertible parked in her spot with her office lights on. Backing into her reserved spot and sitting with Keyshia Cole's *"Heaven Sent"* on repeat, Sheri sat thinking about her life while listening to the song three more times before turning off her ignition, sliding her sunglasses on, and stepping out of the car.

With no meetings scheduled and focused on her initial intention of just going to the office to mentally escape, Sheri wore high waisted ripped blue denim skinny jeans with a striped polo sweater and air max cross trainers for comfort instead of the usual professional attire that causes onlookers to admire her ensemble, exotic beauty, and the tailored definition of her curves. Walking into the building felt like crossing a portal into a new world. Instantly, the depressing thoughts that were yoking her mind like a spider web to an insect were suppressed as her smile expanded as she scanned the room.

Suspending her attention in admiration of the new art, gracefully moving through the gallery observing every previously unseen canvas as though she were an aestheticism, Sheri found herself marveling over a Gwendolyn Knight painting. She seriously contemplated removing it from the wall and having it hung above the mantle of her fireplace. Selfishly taking a picture to use as her screensaver, Sheri walked to her office and cropped it for the perfect fit. So, engulfed in the creative beauty resonating with her spirit, she never noticed that Naomi was standing in her office doorway watching her as she strolled around the corner and went up the stairs without a word spoken.

Sitting in the dark, Sheri googled Gwendolyn Knight, wondering if others of her works were just as beautiful and caused her to feel a sense of empowerment as well. Lost in time, Sheri couldn't believe two hours had passed so quickly when Heidi buzzed her on the phone's intercom to greet and welcome her back. After enlightening her on what's been going on in her absence, what's scheduled for the upcoming week, and ordering her a crescent turkey bacon breakfast ring, Sheri instructed Heidi that she didn't want to be disturbed by anyone. She spent the majority of the morning addressing the pile of mail in her basket and responding to emails that seemed like annoying advertisements on a social media page.

"Excuse me, Ms. Johnson," Heidi courteously beckons, buzzing on the intercom.

"Yes, Heidi?" She answered while trying to figure out why $147,000 was suddenly missing from her account.

"I know you acknowledged that you didn't want to be disturbed, but your father is here to see you."

"Tell him I'm busy," she ordered, looking back at the monitor, confused.

"Excuse me, Ms. Johnson, but your father says this is an important visit, and he needs to see you."

Leaning back in her chair, she was unable to think of any business engagement they may have that would warrant a visit from him.

"I'm sorry, but I'm extremely busy catching up on things and have no time in my schedule to see him," she nonchalantly countered, releasing the intercom button to call the financial manager and inquire about the unusual withdrawal transactions.

Picking up the phone to dial the bank, "Yes?" Sheri responded to the knocks at her door, assuming that it was the intern bringing the financial records she had just requested from the business office. "Place the documents on the desk please, and thank you," she informed candidly without turning away from the window, as she silently rocked back and forth in her office chair, holding for a bank manager.

Presuming the loud classical music blasting in her ear through the receiver was the reason she didn't hear the door close to the intern's departure, Sheri turned around and was shocked to see her father sitting cross-legged before her, resembling a snowman in his sport jacket, turtleneck, traditional fit tailored pants, and black expensive loafers.

The calmness of his presence dominated the room without a word puncturing the essence of silence. Staring at him, Sheri couldn't help but admire who he was and missed their closeness. But Randle and the life developing in her womb were her only family now that she promised to cut off all connections to prove the sincerity of her love belonged only to him. Realizing that her sunglasses were not on, Sheri got a little defensive as though she was talking to a staff member instead of the man who seeded her mom with life by God's will and was once her best friend in a sense as well.

"Why are you in my office?" She objected with a low tone of hostility in her voice. "Will you please leave and respect the fact that I'm busy?"

Without losing his demeanor or uttering a single word, Mr. Johnson sat there wondering if he had lost his daughter completely. Had she allowed Randle to manipulate her thoughts to the extent of separation, instilling fear into the realms of her love and playing upon her low self-esteem to the point that she finds it acceptable to be disrespectful?

"No good morning, not how are you doing, or even I miss you daddy?"

The look in her eyes saddened him because he never expected that a moment would come in his life where genuine love would be absent in the retinas of his precious little angel.

Speaking with authoritative directness as he stared into Sheri's eyes, "Not even one with diplomatic immunity is too busy to see me in a building I own. Business exceeds the priority of comforting your personal emotions right now," Mr. Johnson stated rising from the chair to lay the leather binder on her desk, while distinctly observing the newly formed bruise and swelling around her left eye.

"The land development deal and library purchase were completed weeks ago. I've been patient and respected your privacy Sheri. But, as I've repeatedly informed you, I need your signature on the six documents with the sticker tabs. If you're still too busy to offer anything of yourself to life other than your reprehensible womanizing partner derailing you from the course of family for selfish gain, I truly understand. I'll complete the project and deal for the kids without you."

With her head slightly lowered in embarrassment of her newly swollen black eye, Sheri couldn't believe how far detached she had gotten from her priorities, surrendering her time, loyalty, and attention to Randle. The purchase and development of the library for Unity was important to her. How could she have allowed her obedience to Randle, to be so submissive that she became detached from the shopping center development and the kids altogether? Eyeing the cover document without moving, typhoon-like thoughts began swirling through her mind. Sheri wanted to say, "I miss you daddy, I'm sorry for the character I've been portraying, and I love you." Instead, she turned away arrogantly from the desk to gaze back through the window as if his presence merited no respect. Her loyalty to Randle was a priority and all she focused on.

"I'll send the documents to the business office so my lawyer can look over them when I get a moment," she expressed nonchalantly.

Desiring to scold his daughter for her unwarranted arrogance and to share the things he has been denied in her three-week absence from everyone, Mr. Johnson just rose out of the chair and turned away while whispering, "I love you," loud enough for her to hear his words.

With no response, he turned back, opening the door, slightly brokenhearted, seeing his daughter so mentally and physically battered, detached from reality as she momentarily viewed life with no vision.

"Sheri, raising you, I never expected that one day your mother and I would be expelled from your love for any reason. I remember the first time you said 'I love you' to me and wrote it on your bedroom wall with mustard and ketchup. Can Randle recall the first time you conveyed it to him or share something personal to your heart? When you drop the documents off with your lawyer, you should also take time away from your busy schedule as you claim and have a doctor examine your eye, because it looks like you may have an orbital fracture. I promised you that I would address the situation the next time he raised his hand to disrespect you. Unfortunately, you allow me to realize there's no need to defend your honor because you love him far more than you love yourself," Mr. Johnson advised then closing the door behind him, leaving her staring arrogantly out the office window, trying to figure out how to return to the right path of travel.

"Heyyy, Mr. Johnson," Naomi greeted, extending her arms as he descended the stairs. "I didn't expect to see you here today."

"Serendipity is the beauty of life, Naomi," he exclaimed, reaching the last step and embracing her with a comforting hug.

"I was just about to call your wife, but I'm glad you're here. Do you have a quick moment so that I can show you a surprise?" Naomi queried with a devious look in her eyes.

"Yes, Naomi," he calmly replied as she smiled against his chest, squeezing wrinkles into his clothes.

Cuffing their arms to escort him through the gallery, while enlightening him of the new modernism, cubism, and abstract art on display, the theme for the women's "Awaken Your Soul" luncheon tomorrow night, and the fact that she needs a raise so she can vacation in Borneo for a month to find her a jungle man, one that she can bring back to America and who would love her faithfully due to his desire not to return to the butt-naked, barefooted jungle life she rescued him from. That one caused them both to burst into laughter, walking through the gallery without a care in the world.

Opening her office door, Naomi saw Mr. Johnson fixated as his pupils suddenly dilated and the rosiness abandoned his cheeks as if the gloriously shining sunlight ethereally refracted the image of an ifrit jinn seen only by him. The pale traumatic look on Mr. Johnson's face made Naomi feel a bit uncomfortable because she had never seen him project such a lifeless expression.

Walking into her office, Mr. Johnson sat down, carefully supporting himself, without saying a word while shifting his eyes back and forth as Naomi closed the door and sat behind her desk. Wondering if there was a punchline to this joke of a surprise, Mr. Johnson just stared until the chilling silence turned the room into an icebox.

That which was seemingly a celestial rendering finally broke the ice with a simple ice pick, "How are you doing, sir?"

"What are you doing here?" Mr. Johnson retorted with serious aggression in his voice that instantly sent cold chills through Naomi's body as she sat silently, trying to understand why Mr. Johnson wasn't smiling as she expected, given the surprise she revealed.

"I'm attempting to take Sheri and Naomi to lunch, but Naomi claims she doesn't want to be in Sheri's presence right now."

"Don't insult my intelligence nor play with me. What are you doing here?" Mr. Johnson reiterated with increased frustration in his voice, while gazing intently without shifting his eyes or blinking.

Rising from his seat, he walked over to the window to gaze out before turning back around. "Terry wrote me Mr. Johnson, and I can't let him stay in jail for something I did sir. You gave me a new life and have always protected me. Yet, you also raised me to be a man of honor, integrity, and one who is a guardian of family, something I would be defying by not coming forward and speaking the truth. I love you and respect you beyond words, Mr. Johnson, but I can't continue to stand aside and let your son, whom is my brother, regardless of blood relations, lose his life for my selfish ignorance. I also can no longer allow Mrs. Johnson to suffer emotionally when my confession would grant her heart ease."

"Boy sit down," Mr. Johnson commanded sternly. "So, I assume the plan is for you to walk into the police station and openly confess to a crime you can't prove was justified, whereas you expect them to just release Terry under the blind assumption that there would be no further investigation, and you'd just spend the rest of your life in prison?"

"Yes, sir, and I can live with that," he affirmed, trying to keep his composure without getting emotional. Still looking like a hologram as the spectrum of sunrays bathed him through tempered glass windows, "I've lived every day thinking about the consequences of my actions, and it's time I unyoked myself of this burden and faced the truth. I promise you that I'll never say anything about you. I'll never betray you, Mr. Johnson."

"You're betraying me by being here. You have betrayed me by your thinking, and your plan is not the plan," Mr. Johnson concluded, staring at Naomi as he rose from the chair and fixed his clothes. "What do you expect to happen when they start questioning you about the incident that unfortunately has us where we are now? Or what if they thoroughly investigate your ability to elude them for all these years, living so comfortable without having a job or an inheritance to fund your college tuition, your condo, and the company you now oversee, what then? You seek to be a hero, but what will you say happened to the evidence and bodies? You honestly think they're not going to ask or investigate? Neither of you have any knowledge of what's going on, and I expect both of you to stay out of the way, without trying to fix what neither of you can. You're grown now Stewart, and I can't command you to do anything, but turning yourself in would not only complicate everything, but destroy it. The both of you have betrayed me, and it breaks my heart to see that after raising the two of you with the genuine love I give my own, neither of you trust me," he calmly spoke, turning to walk toward the door.

"I do trust you, sir," Stewart reassured instantly.

"So, do I," Naomi repeated sounding more sincere.

"But how can I stand and accept myself as a man without doing the right thing — an attribute you've ingrained in me my entire life? Character and the will to sacrifice for family, you said, is what distinguishes the core essence of a man's heart, and you all are my family," he mumbled as tears began falling from his eyes.

"The right thing, Stewart, is for the both of you to focus on building a better relationship with God, strengthening the foundation you stand on, and continue allowing me to be the shepherd for all of you," Mr. Johnson stated, exiting the room while dialing numbers on his cellphone.

"I told you this was a bad idea," Naomi hissed to Stewart as Mr. Johnson closed the door behind him. "You probably just messed up my chance of getting a raise, stupid."

"Whatever! I'm not wrong for wanting to do what's right. Terry shouldn't be in there, subjected to watching men scratch their backs with toilet brushes and covering their body with shit to elude prosecution, by being considered psychologically incumbent."

"What!? That's disgusting."

"In the letter he wrote me, he enlightened me of a few unbelievable things that transpired within his dormitory. He said there's a white guy that uses the toilet scrub brush to clean the bathroom with during the day, and, at night, he sits on the bench scratching his back with it. There's also a guy that walks around with rings he has made from potato chip bags interior foil on each toe as though it's a new fashion for male sexiness, plus he also uses his T-shirt to wrap around him like a diaper because he has no boxers.

"Stop laughing silly so I can finish," he exclaimed, chuckling, himself. He also wrote about a man who covered his entire body with shit, and then stood on the table naked until the guards came to escort him out of the cell. Supposedly he was locked up for trying to rob a bank, dressed as James Brown. He covered himself with his own shit because he intended to plead mentally incompetent to stand trial and needed to act the part."

"That's crazy and disgusting! I can't even imagine what else goes on behind those walls. Stewart, I understand what you're saying, but neither should you be incarcerated," Naomi replied defensively, while taking selfies at her desk. "Those men were wrong to make your father watch as they took turns raping your mom then poured ammonia in her vagina in an attempt to hide their DNA. All life has value, but yet a part of me doesn't fault you for what you did, even though killing them wasn't right nor suppressed your inner suffering. I applaud you for wanting to free Terry, but I seriously think you should let Mr. Johnson handle this, Stewart, before you make things worse by trying to be a savior."

Staring out at the landscape through the window, confused and afraid, he knew so well without saying a word that she was correct, but the right thing had to be done. Stewart Giles was Terry's childhood best friend and never missed a meal in the Johnson's' home after connecting with Terry. Even though they had no resembling features, many still considered them twins growing up. They were inseparable whether on the sports field, the classroom, talking to girls, or spending time with family. With his naturally wavy hair, pecan skin tone, bowlegged feature, and 6'2" muscular physique, he had a commanding presence upon entering any room just as much as the handsome Terry. Growing up with no father in his life and no mother after her accident when he was a young teenager, his attachment to Mr. Johnson became more like an adopted son than a mere friend of the family.

"I'm hungry even more now, Naomi," he turned to her and professed. "What are you going to do? I eat when I get nervous."

"I'm not going out to eat with you if Sheri's going," Naomi reiterated, seductively exposing her tongue for a selfie.

"Seriously though, do you think I should go to the jail right now and advise them of what truly happened so they could release Terry?" Stewart asked with a hint of sadness creeping upon his face.

"No, super stupid. The fact Terry assaulted Sheri's stray dog is still an issue within itself. I think you should let the lawyers do what Mr. Johnson is paying them to do. He was right. If they start looking into your life, then you bring unnecessary attention to him. Why can't you just chill and stop trying to be a modern-day hero? What you are forgetting concerning the entire matter is the fact that Terry is an accessory to the murder by law because he kept your actions a secret. Oh! My! God! — which ... which makes me one as well. So, listen, you! Don't start acting all saintly or holy, because I will hurt your bowlegged ass, Stewart, I mean it! And I promise you, I will haunt you about my freedom. I'm far too sexy to be in some nasty jail, fighting some toothless woman with muscles about my pussy."

Flopping down in the chair, Stewart laid his face in his hands. "I am so confused! I don't know what the two of you have going on, but I'm not going to starve myself over an argument that's probably about some shoes you didn't return or a handbag. What office is Sheri's? I'm about to go see if she's hungry or not, because I definitely am."

"Well don't come back to my office asking me what's up with her, when I already warned you repeatedly that she has changed," Naomi warned as he walked toward the door.

"Each one of us goes through a tough phase in our lives. A true friend will never turn their back because of characteristics we don't like. Yes, we get upset seeing someone we love being abused. But without someone to comfort with understanding and support instead of judgmental views, Naomi, it will always be hard for them to break the yoke that's constricting rational thought and action. Every individual has a different desire and a different pursuit of pleasure. We can only accept people for who they are, not by the selfish expectations we often set as though a true friend's acceptance has entitlement," Stewart administered, walking out, leaving the door open.

Laying on her sofa while streaming a rerun episode of "Orange is the New Black" on her iPad, Sheri didn't want to be bothered and tried not to pay attention to the knocking at her office door, yet whomever it was persisted in annoying her.

"Who is it?" She yelled for the third time with no reply.

She was hoping that they'd walk away until the knocking started again, more insistently. With irritation stirring inside of her, Sheri slid her sunglasses on and walked to the door so that she could fire whoever it was for being so aggravating and playful. Snatching the door open with her flamethrower tongue ready to light a fire under some soon to be ex-employee, Sheri couldn't believe standing in front of her was the one person she never expected to see again in her lifetime. It was her brother's best friend and her first childhood crush. Stuck with her mouth agape as excitement enveloped her, Sheri felt like she was visited by a ghost as she began to drool.

"Where have you been?" She asked sensuously, wiping her mouth before embracing him with an affectionate hug and inviting him in.

"I've been in D.C., building a prominent life for myself since moving away from Atlanta. I graduated top of my class from Howard U., against all odds, which you should already know. And now, I have my own sports marketing company," Stewart expressed while observing the room.

"Congratulations, Mr. Educated! The last time I saw you, my mom made you and Terry wash cars and rake the leaves in every neighbor's yard on our street for cutting school to go meet some hot-tail girls that tricked the two of you by stealing y'all's clothes and phones while in the hot tub drinking wine at a vacant mansion." Sheri stated, while laughing at the memory vividly flashing in her mind of the police picking them up naked. "Now you're a boss!"

"So, what brings you back to Atlanta?"

Chuckling at a memory of the past, "Yes! Your mom nailed a string to the rakes, and she tied the loose ends to our wrists. She made us sleep, shower, and eat with the rakes for a week! Those were the good old days," Stewart chortled. Taking a deep breath, then sighing, "My conscience brought me back, Sheri, and the desire to see you in the flesh, rather than the images you post."

"Whatever," she sassed sarcastically. "That is a lie you can save for the girls you meet at the gas station. If you wanted to see me, then you would have called, sent me a ticket, Mr. Boss Man, hit me up on social media, or visited at some point between the ummmm....eight years you have been gone and today."

"It was complicated," he blurted sitting in the seat in front of her, interlocking their eyes for the first time in ages.

"Nothing in the world is that complicated. Especially with social media, but seriously, why are you here? Are you moving back to Atlanta?"

"Honestly I'm here in your office trying to take you and Naomi out to eat, but she won't go if you're going."

"What? Why?"

"That's for the two of you to discuss, Sheri given that neither of you are paying me for my counsel. But I'll oblige you this, free of charge; nothing and no one should ever come between true friendship. Would you like to have lunch with me or not, 'cause I'm hungry?" Stewart declared, rubbing his stomach. "At this point, I'd sacrifice my mucosa and eat your cooking, which is a terroristic act."

"Boy Please, I'll have you on your knees begging to lick the pan I buttered the toast in," Sheri boasted while rolling her eyes. "Stewart, I can't go out looking like this."

"Girls stop damn frontin'. You'd burn water if given the opportunity. And, looking like what, the prize of every single man's dream?" He voiced. "There's nothing wrong with you, but I do understand. I don't need my social media followers to assume I've lowered my standards."

"What!?" Sheri snapped.

"Sheri, look at me — now look at you." Stewart joked while rumbling inside with laughter at her facial expression. "Seriously though, never allow anything or anyone to take away your halo. If you don't feel comfortable allowing the world to witness the true grace of a woman, then let's have lunch in your office. My play-sister, Diamond, is a Grab-n-Drop driver now and will pick up whatever you desire.

Do you remember that time you cooked your brother and I some Ramen noodles? They were so damn hard; we couldn't even chew them or stick our forks in them!"

A distant memory that caused Sheri to smile. "You talking about Diamond who use to cut y'all's hair growing up?" She inquired.

"Yes, the one and only," he replied with a chuckle.

"Oh my God, boy this is too much," Sheri confided bursting into a light laughter. "Do you remember that time we all went to Applebee's and she was crawling under people's tables without saying excuse me, pushing their legs out of the way, and knocking over chairs looking for a socket so that she could charge her cellphone?"

"How can I ever forget that night?" Stewart continued holding his stomach in amusement. "She was higher than three Jamaicans with one lung, trying not to miss the phone call from some Spanish guy who paid all her bills."

"Oooooh yeah, the midget man who liked her to sit on his face wearing a different animal mask each time because he had some beastie fetish, and she was the only woman who was able to give him an erection! You have to give me her number so I can call. I really miss her Stewart. To be honest, I really don't have a taste for a gourmet meal right now. I want a Chick-fil-a number one and some sweet lemonade."

"Well, why are you talking instead of grabbing your things?" Stewart said, standing up and motioning toward the door as her eyes followed his every movement behind the sunglasses.

Since opening her heart to Randle, she hadn't eaten alone with or entertained any man on a personal level outside of business.

Stewart was like her brother to a degree, which made him family. But it was also considered disrespectful and deceitful to do something without him knowing, an act that got her in trouble before. The urge to call Randle and run her intentions past him was stirring greatly inside of her, especially given the stiff penalty of him finding out on his own.

Staring at Stewart, Sheri couldn't help but open her eyes to the magnificent bowlegged sexiness standing before her in the Jordan jacket that was firmly squeezing his biceps and pecs so attractively, the Levi's that were hugging his butt like it was delicate treasure, and the retro 6's she wanted to buy Randle whom doesn't wear Jordan's because he's a Larry Bird fan.

"I can't go out like this," Sheri apologized, removing her sunglasses and lowering her head in shame. "My boyfriend hit me this morning."

Embarrassed at being seen with her eye so swollen, she wished she would have just awakened and given Randle some head as he requested instead of trying to sleep a little longer.

"Sheri, when you're beautiful, there's nothing that can ever stop you from being beautiful. No matter how a red diamond is cut or graded, it's still magnificent and worthy of appreciation. Let me show you something," he said reaching out for her hand as he guided her to the mirror on the wall.

Not knowing of the soreness to her ribs which was an injurious consequence of her defiance, he uttered "I'm sorry," with genuine compassion after she growled in pain when he gently touched her side to straighten her posture. "Please forgive me!"

Placing his hand beneath her chin, he stood behind her inhaling the sweetness of her aura, secretly yearning to kiss the soft fibers of her neck.

"Look at the reflection you see," he whispered in close enough proximity for her to inhale his minted breath which gently blew her hair against her ear. "Open your eyes to the beauty of who you are. Not the bruise, but the reflection of an extraordinary woman. That bruise can't take away your inner strength nor your worth to God. If you never witness the light within you, then life will always be void of significance. Sheri, what you see is irreplaceable and irresistible no matter the damage to the exterior. Don't fear the creation, fear God. If you fear Him, He will be enough for you so that you don't need people. And if you fear people, they will not satisfy you in the least in terms of your total dependence on God. Beauty and sexiness are measured from within. Appreciate and love yourself, no matter the challenges you endure."

His words were like melodies to her heart. Randle never called her beautiful nor sought to comfort her insecurities unless her sadness was an effect of his abusiveness. He didn't ask who disgraced her honor or why. Stewart just said God made you irreplaceable and irresistible, which she never felt anymore. Looking at self, Sheri couldn't help but wonder who she had become since opening her heart and womb to her Dumb. She had become a woman so engulfed in ~~love~~ loath that she accepted abuse, neglect, and abomination, without contesting the tyranny of it all in the evacuation and prolonged hiatus of happiness. Turning around, Sheri had to take a step backward, as only a thin layer of air was separating their lips, and his presence was already causing her to feel vulnerable, nostalgically.

"Okay, I'll go. But you have to drive, and I'm not going in under any circumstances," Sheri gave in, smiling at the spark of confidence she was feeling.

"No problem, a gentleman always caters to a lady's request," Stewart humbly exulted by making a unique gesture with his hands, as Sheri donned her sunglasses, then snatched an all-black Atlanta Falcons skullcap from the shelf. She pulled it over her head to shadow the swelling, without caring about the effect on her hairstyle.

"Excuse me, Ms. Johnson," Heidi chimed in from the intercom. "You have a delivery that just arrived by FedEx," she acknowledged after Sheri responded. "Would you like for me to send it up ma'am?"

"Yes, Heidi," she replied looking at Stewart who was standing with his hand on the doorknob, awaiting her footsteps, so that they could go eat.

Strolling over to open the door and peering out in anticipation of her package, Stewart never expected to see Naomi ascending the stairs, entering the room with a gentleman holding an enormous box, which he placed on her desk and left upon the complement from Sheri, while Naomi stood momentarily just eyeing her as neither said a word nor embraced.

"Because of Stewart's words, Sheri, I'm here to say I miss you, and please believe that most people wouldn't even bother to give you the opportunity of hearing those words or anything remotely close. I hold no ill feelings towards you, and Lord knows I should, given the disrespect that you've shown our friendship the past several weeks. I was worried about you and cried to your mother's comfort several nights. Yet, you didn't have the decency to send me a text in the least to acknowledge you were okay, given that you avoided me and my phone calls."

"I'm..."

"Hold up, don't say nothin'," Naomi interjected throwing up her hands and cutting off Sheri's attempt to speak. "Who you've become, I must admit without caution, is a disrespect to all women, but I love you, and I have to respect that only you can define your happiness. I can't judge you but know that I will always be present if you need me.

"It hurts to see you allowing this man to not only strangle the life out of you with fear and strangle you physically, but to strangle the life out of every meaningful relationship that you have ever known, separating you from everyone who loves and cares for you, every bright spot that has ever shined upon you. And maybe the toughest thing for all of us is that you have scales covering your eyes, a blackness that blocks out your vision so that you cannot, on any level, see Randle for who he really is: a selfish, insecure, abusive, sick coward. We've been part of each other's life since we were four, Sheri, and until recently, I truly thought that meant something to you. Stewart pointed out in my office that there are no expectations to friendship, only genuine love and appreciation for who that person is, regardless of their character. He's right, but there is also respect. And without it, there's nothing, and I'm not sorry for having said about Randle what I said — and you call that love. You have the nerve to call him your king?! He's a real big kink, a royal fuckin' Kink! Wake the fuck up, girl, look at you! He's a dick! A puny one at that! No, he's a diseased, disgusting dick. He's a scrawny, ruthless coward-ass wannabe dictator that you get dicked, kicked and kinks by. King, my ass!" Naomi emphasized turning away.

"Naomi, wait, you're right about our friendship and I'm sorry," Sheri declared. "Please don't leave!"

"I've never left Sheri," Naomi reassured over her shoulder. "Unfortunately, you did the very moment you stopped loving yourself the way your mother and step-grandmother groomed us to. I will always be here," she vowed turning to face Sheri directly. "But sometimes you have to fail in order to appreciate what truly matters. I'll never turn my back on you. I'll never allow anyone to come in my life and sever the bond we've built over the past twenty-two years — 22!! Nor will I ever be fake."

"Naomi! Naomi!" Sheri yelled watching her best friend walk out of her office, so detached from the closeness that has always been was hurtful. "Whatever then," she whispered to herself.

Randle had already poisoned her mind that the jealousy of their love would be the factor everyone tried to use to distance themselves, influencing her to hold fast, maintaining her composure without allowing the given situation to dent her emotions or remove the blinding scales from her eyes of darkness — and swollenness.

"Are you ready?" She questioned Stewart, catching him off guard, while using her scissors to slice the tape securing the box. "Why are you looking at me like that? I'm not going after her if that's what you expect. She'll be okay. She's the one in her feelings for no reason. I was tending to my man, and I don't care who doesn't like it or what they call him. He's always going to be the King of this ass," She chortled followed by a teeth sucking. When I don't desire to be bothered, I mean just that." Removing the wrapping from the crystal crest that was inside the box and laying it on her desk, Sheri couldn't believe the exquisite beauty before her eyes. She opened the lock and lifted the lid to reveal twelve hand crafted red eternity crystal roses, trimmed in gold with her name scribbled on each stem in gold as well.

"This is so beautiful," she said reaching for the card as her smile illuminated the room.

Even though Randle has never sent her any gifts and a not so secret admirer has been doing so recently, still, an unsuspecting Sheri found herself believing it was from him as an apology offering for abusing and raping her body as he did earlier that morning. But in her defense, her mind was twisted, especially given the fact that she was just looking at crystal glasses with him lying beside her a few days earlier. Opening the card, Sheri momentarily forgot about Stewart standing in her office. All she could think of was reading his words and going home to apologize for her selfishness earlier.

"I'm nosy, what does this card say?" Stewart asked, stealing her away from the fantasy she was losing herself in.

Engulfed by the excitement of reading Randle's words, while admiring the roses greatly, Sheri lifted the card and read the inscription while trying to become one with him mentally and romantically. *"The best woman is the tallest when she stands, the most prominent when she sits, and the most truthful when she speaks. She is the one whose anger subsides quickly, and whose laugh is a beautiful smile. When she does anything, she does it well. She is honored among her people, yet insignificant in her own mind, affectionate and fertile, and everything about her is a blessing."*

"That was priceless! I applaud your man for those words, yet still there is no respect or acceptance awarded to abuse." Stewart proclaimed as Sheri flipped the card back and forth. "What's wrong?"

"It doesn't say who it's from," Sheri blurted looking bewildered, desiring to see "Love always, Randle" scribbled somewhere.

"I believe the only reason your mother took you to school every day when we were younger was to shield you from the ridicule of being seen riding the short bus with a helmet," Stewart joked while chortling at his own amusement. "Silly woman, you have allowed yourself to be taken for granted far too long. In a gift of this exquisiteness, they always insert two cards. One for the message and one to acknowledge the sender as a touch of class."

Reaching into the box to retrieve the additional one, which was taped to the plastic, Stewart opened it as Sheri tried to snatch it from his hand.

"So Abdul Waahid is the lucky man in your life," he uttered teasingly after reading the name card and imitating Sheri as though she wanted to kiss it.

"Oh, my God will he please stop!" Sheri screamed, crumbling the message in her hand before throwing it back inside the box with aggravation and frustration billowing from a volcanic hot spot stoked by this named but mysterious romantic continuing to disrespect their bond of union or rather, bondage of pinion to be exact. Disappointed that neither the crystal roses nor the angelic passage were from Randle, Sheri's demeanor did a 180.

"Let's go," she demanded, knocking the crystal chest and roses off her desk with a swing of aggression as she stormed toward the door. The sight and sound of them hitting the floor and shattering did not halt but quickened her pace.

"Is everything okay, Sheri? I apologize if I offended you by reading the card," Stewart uttered looking confused by her unexpected reaction, while following her footsteps that seemed to increase in pace with each step. "Why are we speed walking?"

Sheri spoke no words until they were outside, not even returning the verbal greeting of those she raced past. A simple head nod is all she returned.

"Which car is yours?" She muttered nonchalantly, standing with her arms crossed and scanning the parking lot without moving her head.

"That beautiful mystic sea blue Reliant Robin you see in front of you. Don't act like you don't recognize it, you know there's no one in this building with enough sauce to drive something that sexy and classic," Stewart beamed with enthusiasm, smiling as they meandered their way onto the lot.

"Are you serious?" Sheri questioned in immeasurable disbelief, slanting her eyes as she burst into laughter. "You mean to tell me that you're still driving the car you begged my grandfather to buy from his friend in high school, Stewart? I'm not riding in that unstable Flintstone antique. If I felt like walking, I'd go to the track."

"Stop frontin'. Everything in that car is brand new and the interior is custom by Distinctive Upholstery. My car is considered a collector's classic now, and she feels like a Maybach on the road. Sheri, my iron will stand up against your fiberglass any day," Stewart insisted in defense of his baby.

"Whatever let's go please," Sheri said, throwing him her keys. "I'm not putting my life at risk in that garbage. I literally can't believe you're still wasting your money on that thing instead of buying yourself something new. You own a sports marketing company but you driving a car that didn't even make the hot wheels collections. This is too much for one day."

No longer smiling or talking, the disappointment had her feeling emotionally broken. Granted, she had surrendered and sacrificed so much of herself with no reason to smile in return. Staring silently out of the window en route to Chick-fil-a, Sheri found herself pondering heavily upon their union. Why couldn't Randle love her as she loves him? Why couldn't he be gentle, romantic, and compassionate as others are with their mates? Will he ever change as he has promised time and time again?

Removing her glasses to caress the swelling around her eye, the mental flashes of him abusing her for his sexual pleasure caused a tear to fall, which she wiped away to hide from Stewart. She was tired of depriving herself of life, only to be treated as though she's invisible. "Let's go to Paintball in Atlanta or shoot a few games of pool," Sheri proposed while ordering her meal. "I need to have some fun."

"Say less. Show me the way," Stewart sanctioned as Sheri located it on her GPS system while he paid for their meal.

Not knowing of the skills she had gained from the students who attended her program, Stewart talked trash with absolutely nothing to back it up. For the next several hours, Sheri's mind was free of everything that consisted of her everyday life. She smiled, talked, and laughed with substance that reminded her of what it's like to exist. Running around in the paintball center, imitating a Don Dada, had Sheri feeling like she was a modern-day Stephanie St. Clair, the new Queen of the streets! Being with Stewart brought back so many loving memories of their childhood days and in a way, elevated her spirit.

After nurturing their appetite at the Nicolais Roof restaurant, they returned back to the Art of Life. Sheri found herself not wanting to go home for many reasons. She was missing Randle but didn't want to be in his presence.

"Sheri, Can I ask you something?" Stewart asked as they sat in the car reminiscing about old times.

"Yes," she replied.

"Is everything okay with you?"

"I'm good, why do you ask?" Sheri inquired.

"For one, you have a swollen eye, yet keep referring to him as your man. Earlier, you received a gift from a gentleman, or admirer I should say, that had you smiling like an angel until I read the name and you realized it wasn't from the one who takes you for granted. While out with me today, you resembled a sparrow with wings of joy, yet now you sit here looking as though you have no sense of direction."

"The gift was not from my boyfriend or someone I'm secretly," Sheri corrected, turning her head around to gaze out the window. "I don't know who he is, and I wish he would stop being disrespectful."

"What do you mean?" Stewart asked lowering the volume of the music.

"I have a man is what I mean," Sheri dug in, remaining firm with a bit of heated passion in her voice. "It's inappropriate and a blatant sign of disrespect, for a man to flirt in any respect with a woman who's in a committed relationship. Especially, when he's coming across as a stalker. I have not given whoever Abdul Waahid is any reason to think of me."

Stewart laughed at her words and position of naivety shrouded by humor; slightly hurting Sheri's feelings given that she was expecting him to console her with wisdom instead of making her feel even lower.

"I don't see nothin' funny," she barked punching him playfully and commanding him to get out of her car.

"Sheri, I apologize if I hurt your feelings, but you just confirmed you actually did ride the short bus going to school," he stated while still chuckling. "Listen, every individual that is fortunate enough to cross your path, even if it's merely a picture on social media, instantly birth the natural desire of wanting to know who you are. Not because you're successful or physically sexy. If you open your eyes, you'd see how beautiful and extraordinary you are, which is why desire is seeded in Abdul Waahid and every other man who witnesses your grace. You shared with me earlier that your man does nothing to blossom your smile. Nothing! Yet, you have a secret admirer who takes the time to think of you respectfully and put forth the effort merely to acknowledge that you are appreciated. Truthfully that's not disrespect.

"I applaud him for trying to remind you of how significant you are, especially when the man you commit your heart to only wants to control your mind and body. Often times, we get so caught up in looking at things from a negative perspective that we bypass the beauty within the given. I witnessed your eyes smile when you opened that chest and saw those crystal roses earlier. But every time you've spoken of the one you so-call consider your King today, your body became tense and the look in your eyes were more of fear than anything that resembled true love."

"If you truly want your black knight to stop reminding you of how meaningful you are to life by just existing, then find out who he is and tell him. Just like you want to stop being taken for granted and abused, you have to stop allowing it. Whoever Abdul Waahid is you can't get mad at him for wanting to hold the hand of a blessing. You should be mad at the one who spits on your worth arrogantly and yourself for allowing it to continue, when you know it will only get worse. Sheri, you are only as strong as you allow yourself to be, and only you are your own weakness. Don't allow love to destroy you when it's supposed to elevate you. You are the first woman I've ever met who gets irritated when someone appreciates her, but blossom of love for the one who neglects and abuses her."

Hearing his words brought to mind her exclusive moments of quality time with her grandfather, whom she missed greatly, and how he always tried to nurture her insecurities and remind her of how beautiful she was, even though she didn't see or feel it within. She hadn't thought about discovering who her secret admirer was but felt Stewart was right; It was about time she did just that.

Seeing Randle's name appear on her phone as she was about to lean over and give Stewart a hug, given that he had to leave, sent chills through her body like an ice bath in the ocean with the polar bear club, only she felt alone. Scanning the parking lot and not seeing him or his car, she wondered if he was watching her from inside the building.

"Hello?" She answered nervously placing the phone to her ear.

"I need you to come home and cook something to eat, 'cause I'm hungry, bitch!" Randle yelled through the phone.

"Okay, baby," Sheri went along within the fuck shit, not trying to aggravate him because she could tell by his voice that he wasn't in a good mood. "Randle, have you been removing money from my business account by any chance?"

"Why bitch?! What, you accusing me of stealing or something?!" Randle insinuated elevating his voice as he spoke.

"No, t..th..that's not what I'm implying," Sheri replied trying to be assuring because she didn't want him to take his aggression out on her again.

"Just bring your damn ass home," he commanded. "Click." He rudely and abruptly hangs up the phone.

Not knowing what to expect upon returning home, Sheri turned to Stewart and said goodbye, shocking him as he hesitantly stepped out of the car and she walked around to the driver side without giving him a hug before getting back in.

"Is everything okay, Sheri?" Stewart questioned out of concern, not liking the lifeless look upon her face and wondering if he should follow her.

"Yeah! Everything's okay," she lied closing her door and lowering her window. "Stewart, you still haven't answered my question," Sheri stated looking at her watch.

"What question, Sheri?" He asked placing his hands on her car door.

"What brought you back to Atlanta?" She revealed, pressing push-to-start. "You mentioned your conscience, but never elaborated on what that meant."

Licking his lips while staring into her eyes, angry at the fact that she's committing herself will to someone who does not value her worthwhile abusing her for the enjoyment of control. The look in her eyes made him feel as though he failed at keeping his word to her brother and their late step-grandma when he promised Terry to always protect her, yet some battles can't be fought with physical strength.

"I'll call you," Stewart advised reaching in to squeeze her hand on the steering wheel before stepping back and watching her pull away.

CHAPTER 24

Basking in the ambiance of the cold secluded darkness, he never knew that making love on milk crates in a grocery store walk-in cooler would allow him to feel the distinct changes in her heartbeat each time his hardness embedded the intoxicating lining of her throat. "Prove to me dis yo dick," he struggled to whisper as she forced him deeper without gagging and the warm sweetness of her nectar mimicked thawing ice droplets upon his face. The pulsating effects of her deep throating was causing him to feel vulnerable and wanting to scream, "I love you." Trapped in the waves of passion and the burning desire to taste more of her climax as she slowly extracted his hammer from her mouth to sensuously stroke it while teasing his balls with her other hand, he intensified the thrashing engagement of his tongue.

Cupping her lower back with his arms to prevent her from lifting off his mouth, she casually rotated her hips to magnify the sensation that he was causing to spiral throughout her body. "Ooooooh did yo pussy daddy!" She purred so seductively. Resembling a hummingbird feeding on a Red Columbine, with its crimson spurs and bright yellow stamens, he caused her body to define the essence of euphoria by bouncing his bottom lip against her pink pearl, while using an irregular licking pattern to bath the mouth of her arousal. His tongue flicked back and forth within her pool of moisture like a mass oscillating at the end of a spring, thus, miraculously causing her to cry of ecstasy, while climaxing with so much passion and pleasure enveloping her vibrating body that she stopped stroking him and hid his entire erection back in her throat. Squeezing and brushing her tongue against his massive hardness to stimulate their chemistry, she was so turned on by the way he was exploring the depths of her sexual delights that she started sucking him as though his dick was a fruit favored pacifier.

"Your moaning is turnin' me on and making me so fuckin' wet." She purred to the head of his dick as if it was a microphone, after slowly removing him from her titillating tunnel of warmth, while still teasing his balls with her fingers. Yearning to feel the width of his hammer stretch her tightness and create new depths, she eased off his oral playground. Dragging her pussy down his chest, which left a trail of nectar droplets, she stopped stroking him and began patting his hardness against the sensitive softness of her vertical smile before rubbing the head of his erection between her lips and sliding down on it with slow perfection. Resting her hands on his knees to balance herself, she looked over her left shoulder to witness his facial reaction while starting to rapidly thrust, pushing him deeper and deeper up into the depths of her precious wet treasure.

Hearing the door of the cooler open as light punctured the darkness, the thought of someone seeing them pursue love through incongruous affection seemingly turned her on more and more as her cries of ecstasy rang out. Turning it up a notch as she observed the store worker standing in the doorway through the stacked crate cracks, she oscillated her hips like a pendulum in a grandfather's clock, swaying them back-n-forth, back-n-forth. Spreading her legs to grant him greater terminal depth, the enhancement of pleasure caused him to start smacking the cold fibers of her ass each time she lifted off his erection, which propagated uninhibited heat waves throughout her body that intensified the chemistry between them.

With them both ignoring the repeated question of the worker, "Is someone in here," after stepping into the cooler to load a few crates on his cart and hearing the whispers of love making, she reached down and tickled his balls in a unique fashion that caused him to fertilize her garden in the very instant she climaxed herself. Feeling the thrust of his super-hot cum fuse with the sensitive walls of her canal sent her body into a convulsion of stratospheric proportion spawning unbridled pleasure.

Sheer ecstasy enveloped her entire body causing it to violently palpitate while her teeth chattered as though they were on the fault line as a quake was felt with the shift of tectonic plates beneath the crates of their sexual transgressions. Yielding to the effects of raw sex and love, the tremors from her trembling caused their bed of passion to shift as well, which sent them both tumbling to the frigid frost coated stainless steel floor.

Seemingly unphased by the store worker now peering over other stacked crates at them, the unsanitary environment, or the instantaneously chilling shockwaves the cold steel was sending through their bodies, they laughed while pealing their sweaty nakedness from the floor as their skin's detachment from the frigid floor could be heard with Bose clarity. Noticing the way, the worker was now caressing her nakedness with his eyes and no longer speaking, she began stroking her baby once he rose to his feet. Repositioning herself after teasing the observing eyes by bouncing her butt a little, she squatted then started rotating her hips seductively as she eased his dick back into her mouth to taste the potion that was the culprit of their love bizarre.

"Terry! Terry, get up. A deputy is calling you to the door," Abdullah informed while tapping him gently upon the ankle. Knowing, in his experience, that waking an individual in jail from a heated erotic dream is very tricky because the mind doesn't know if someone is trying to rape them for the pleasure of conquering a new virgin, beat them, stick'em with crudely fabricated knives (shanks or shivs), or merely centered upon killing them due to something that transpired on the streets.

"What?" Terry mumbled, opening his eyes while stretching and looking around the entire room.

"Eey, a deputy sheriff at the door calling for you," he repeated, sitting back on his bunk.

Terry slowly got himself together and walked to the door resembling someone who jogged barefoot on hot sand. For some unknown reason, the dormitory was much hotter that day than any day prior. The fact that basically everyone was walking around in their boxers instead of their jumpsuits indicated the extremeness of the heat.

In the twenty-two days that he had been locked up, Abdullah and Terry had become a little close. Speaking a lot about religion, who they were outside of the jailhouse jumpsuits, and watching each other's back respectfully, became the norm of their daily routine. Terry was intrigued to have learned how to fry his food using bombs of tissue, boil cups of water by using crudely constructed water immersion heaters built from different gages of wire and lock components, how to sit on the toilet naked in front of men as a precautionary survival technique when using the restroom, shower without lathering the face and sleeping on top of the covers instead of beneath them. The atmosphere that seemed like a subway station central hub had become fascinating in a peculiar way to Terry, yet mentally draining as well. Within a short period of time, Abdullah's presence had become a beacon of enlightenment for him.

He listened attentively when he spoke and liked the way that he challenged him to view life in ways he had never opened his eyes or mind to. Initially, talking on the phone all day was Terry's way of escaping the reality of his situation. But the more he read the Qur'an and sought to bridge a connection with God, the more he found himself looking at his reflection in the mirror and wanting to strengthen his character as a whole.

Being from Arkansas and incarcerated for killing someone from Henry County, Abdullah was a targeted outsider to those who sought jailhouse credentials and preyed heavily on the weak. Whenever a new detainee enters the dorm, he is challenged to either fuck or fight to survive. But at 6'3 and 304 lbs. of unleashed aggression, everyone knew upon sight that it would require more than just a few of them combined and plastic knives that they formed out of the spoons to take his virgin chocolate. Fear of his very presence was enough to suppress even the thought of them trying him up, especially now with Terry standing at his side.

Seeing Terry go to the phone after speaking to the deputy and embark upon a heated conversation unlike any he had ever witnessed before was startling — seemingly unsettling. "Is everything okay, Terry?" Abdullah asked out of sincere concern once he returned to his bed with some certified court documents in hand.

"Yes, everything's fine Abdullah," Terry responded while scanning through the documents angrily. "I just had to fire one of my lawyers. I mean, the guy is so in the dark about everything and seemingly has a solution to nothing. The deputy sheriff at the door just served me a damn subpoena. I honestly can't believe this fool is trying to sue me for six million dollars, claiming punitive damages and mental anguish. He beats my sister, gets her pregnant, turns her against her family, and have the audacity to sue with the intention of trying to get paid for his work. I should have snapped his fuckin' neck."

"Suppress your anger and don't allow yourself to entertain those unfruitful thoughts," Abdullah advised, lowering the Al-Nawawi's forty hadith book that he was reading to render his full attention. "Never allow yourself to react to the ignorance of someone's actions with hostility seeded in your mind or coming forth in your actions, because it makes you a reflection of them. Terry, anger is like a kindled fire on dry land which you can't possibly combat by using sparks of other engaging fires to pour upon it. Instead of extinguishing it, you'd be creating something massive that has the psychological ability of swallowing you up. Humility, mercy, forgiveness, and understanding gives structure to your character, yet anger will always damage and tarnish your image."

"I listen to you Abdullah, and I value your insight it's just crazy to be in this awkward situation. I physically have no control over my life right now. I'm forced to spend my days enduring mental torture, being isolated with countless unstable characters, not eating properly, can't see the one woman who literally causes me to not think of Janell Monáe when I'm in her presence, and now I may be subjected to pay this fool for being an abuser to my sister. I truly understand what a major corporation CEO feels like right now in the sense of when someone tries to sue their company for falling in their establishment due to their own clumsiness, or intentionally wasting something on themselves claiming that their drink was too hot or cold, 'cause they weren't paying attention."

"Terry, God advises us in the Qur'an not to cling to the amusement of this temporary life or the things He momentarily bestows on us out of His mercy, for the Hereafter is the eternal goal for those who truly seek His closeness. He tests us continuously with family, loss of property, and wealth. To see the measure of faith within our breast and to purify our hearts. Don't buy the life of this world at the price of the Hereafter like many have, purely out of delusion, because the reward is an endless punishment within the Hellfire. A place where ten mountains the size of Everest sheltering an endless supply of colorless cultivated diamonds couldn't ransom you from. We are given life only to worship God, not ourselves nor individuals we say we love. Find benefits in these momentary moments and utilize the given grace to strengthen your identity because only then will failure not be witnessed within your footsteps Terry."

"There's almost never a moment that you don't share a little of the wisdom you have obtained in your spiritual awakening. I find myself wishing our paths could have crossed prior to the hell and torment of these walls," Terry stated while rubbing his face with his right hand as he laid the documents on his pillow with his left.

"It may have been nice, but nothing would have ever changed. You and I would still be sitting here as we currently are," Abdullah vowed while reaching in his property bin beneath his bed to retrieve a bag of tropical trail mix. "We all are granted the ability of choice, yet nothing transpires without God's knowledge or will, for everything that occurs in life is already written in a book called, Al-Lauh Al-Mahfuz that is preserved and protected by God."

"I truly believe that" Terry concurred while removing his jail issued shower shoes.

Laying back onto his bunk to read more of the "Do You" book by Renesha Acosta that Demi sent him to read, a part of him wanted some revenge with Abdullah on the dominoes table. After competing last night with the understanding that the loser had to drink a twenty-ounce bottle of water per game, which he became the recipient of twelve unflavored cups to Abdullah's six. But the way Ms.

Acosta spoke about moral values and the fundamentals of self-worth from a woman's perspective that even resonates with men had him intrigued to explore more of her insights and discover how he could challenge himself to strengthen his character from a woman's intellect.

With his earbuds pushed in deep so he could effectively drown out the noise within the dormitory and become mentally lost in the words of the book as he laid on his side facing the wall, Terry did not hear Abdullah advising him it was count time, nor did he have any knowledge until the officer kicked his bunk, shouting at the top of her lungs like a military drill sergeant.

"Count time, inmate. Count time! Get yo big ass out da bunk before I send you to isolation for disrupting my count! Get up, asshole!"

Turning over to witness an endomorphic black woman wearing a cheap curly Drag Queen sky blue wig like a kippah on her head with platinum extensions literally super glued to the left side of it and a blond bang sewed to the front with purple sewing thread made him laugh unintentionally while rising to stand at attention like everyone else.

Terry's unexpected reaction caused the officer to no longer feel sexy, rather irritated and angered now that he reacted by laughing after opening his eyes to her presence instead of smiling to make her feel admired. To her, the disrespect was unacceptable and warranted the abuse of her authority, which gave her pleasure restricting the privilege of the unit's television and phones for the remainder of her shift. Upon her leaving, many within the cell house began eyeing Terry with heated resentment. He initially listened to Abdullah and paid the disgruntled detainees no mind as they whispered aloud and secretly amongst themselves about the dislike of losing their privileges for nothing.

Some of them began turning their attention back to playing chess, dominoes, spades, reading, working out, or trying to rest, due to the fact that there was no television to watch or phone to use. All except one particular individual, new to the dormitory, who just sat on his bunk licking his lips seductively and eyeing Terry as if he resembled the exotic breathtaking beauty of Greta Onieogou some kind of way. The irritation and disrespect bothered Terry, and the thought of not addressing the stranger seemed to affect him increasingly as the silent whispers of the Shayatin blew in his ear.

"Do you have a problem?" Terry asked looking directly at the stranger, which caused Abdullah to turn over to see who he was referring to, given that his voice had elevated and was filled with tension.

"Yes, I have a muthafuckin' problem," he exploded rising off his bunk with aggression, distinctly with the tonality of a Spartan, thereby causing many to shift their eyes in curiosity of seeing who he was speaking to. "You just caused me to miss the ending of the movie I was watching on Lifetime bitch and the Little Women Atlanta episode that comes on next. So, I feel you need to do something to make me feel good, given the fact that you have taken that away with yo sexy Georgia peach lookin' ass. You walk around like you're untouchable, but I'm definitely about to feel that soft caramel skin of yours with the entertainment I got on my mind."

The words of disrespect ignited something in Terry that shielded his ears from everything Abdullah was mentoring, and the instigation being yelled across the dormitory. His vision narrowed until all he saw was the figure of the detainee walking toward him step by step. Abdullah tried to encourage him to ignore the stranger's selfish ignorance, yet how can he discipline his body and humble his mind when this individual is challenging his manhood. As he eased out of his shower shoes to enhance stability and foster precise movements without slipping on the concrete, Abdullah pleaded with him to stay calm and not allow the man's words to dictate his actions.

Terry just remained silent, while exhibiting a martial arts horse stance and watching him approach sounding like a defective radio that can only be turned off by pulling the plug. His 6'5" muscular physique aroused no intimidation in Terry, who reacted the very moment he was in striking distance with a powerful jujitsu strike centered from his inner chi to the stranger's throat seemingly paralyzing every function in his body, instantly. Gagging and gasping for air as he leaned forward with both hands gripping his throat, Terry parted the wind with timeless execution using a left uppercut elbow that broke his nose on impact. Shifting his body as if he were dodging a punch that was never executed and moving inwardly toward his victim, Terry landed a double spinning elbow to his chin that caused the unsuccessful attacker to stumble uncontrollably backwards, colliding with the bunk bed on the other side of Abdullah.

Inhaling as he stepped forward, Terry swung from his hip and torso to generate power. Throwing a devastating right hook to the stranger's liver section which caused his eyes to close instantly as he silently fell to the floor dreaming of feeding Ms. Juicy Baby oysters and pomegranates on the shores of Maldives. Regaining a sense of consciousness after his face fossilized itself with the concrete, he scrambled to get back to his feet as blood oozed from his nose, and he spoke recklessly of raping Terry's body after first carving his name into Terry's chest.

With excruciating pain spiraling throughout his body and his pride hanging by invisible threads of a spider's web before the eyes of the dormitory, he reached inside his jumpsuit and pulled out a thirteen-inch jolly ranchers' waistband. Slicing the air to elicit fear as he sought an opening to make his move supposedly insured there was no possible way Terry was going to escape without being stabbed, carved up, and raped for breaking his nose. In his mind, he was already casting images of taking Terry's virginity. Even more so, hearing him scream for mercy as he choked the life out of him while forcing his hard-dry erection inside of Terry at the same time. Raising the jolly rancher shiv above his head to bring down like a hammer as he lunged at Terry which seemed with all indications to be a well-timed deadly strike to his face. Terry sidestepped with the skillful technique of a Krav Maga, then threw up his left arm to block his motion, while spinning inwardly with the grace of a danseur to land a smashing downward elbow to his eye. Ducking as he swung the jolly rancher shiv again towards his face, Terry pushed off his right leg with all of his strength. Lunging with the physical explosiveness of a Tsar Bomba, Terry immediately grabbed his head and pulled it forward to connect with his left knee. The impact was so devastating that it not only knocked him out for a second time but broke his jaw in two places while also causing him to bite off the tip of his tongue.

As he fell and laid on the floor snoring like a blue baby whale, Abdullah immediately informed Terry to go rinse the blood off of him before the officers came in.

Grabbing a pair of clean clothes from his property bin beneath his bunk, Terry removed the jumpsuit he had on and gave it to the dormitory laundry man to wash. Walking to the shower, as Abdullah followed to protect his back by standing guard just a few feet away just in case, the slugged out aggressor recovered with the intent of squirreling Terry or another inmate approached to defend the sleeping giant's honor. Neither said a word while entering the shower area, yet couldn't believe that the young guy everyone in the cell house joked about looking like a bad bag of rotten duck gizzards was still sitting on the toilet, masturbating to the facial pictures that he cut out of the newspaper and glued on the cardboard of a writing tablet, using toothpaste, three hours after he initially started.

Taking a quick shower to rinse off the blood that had spattered on him, Terry stepped out of the shower and put away his things just as the detention officer re-entered to do her security check. Seeing the blood and the detainee still laying on the floor snoring peacefully, she immediately grabbed her walkie talkie on her belt holster while shaking nervously as she called for assistance and medical personnel, then she commanded everyone to sit on their assigned bunks.

Forcing the detainees to line-up around the dormitory wall, whereupon their hands, feet, and faces were thoroughly examined, as the medical staff strapped him on the stretcher, she was flabbergasted not to discover a single bruise or drop of blood on anyone. With the fear of being Terry's next victim or being labeled a snitch, no one said a word. And with no cameras to answer the questions that the routine body examination didn't, the detention officers just left the dormitory verbally threatening that they better not have to return.

Now with a glimpse of Terry's combat training executed on someone bigger than himself and far more intimidating by physical presence, the atmosphere within the dormitory had quickly and drastically changed. Instead of all the loud talk, the inmates were whispering moderately and constantly glancing at Terry as if he was the new UFC champion.

Laughing amongst themselves regarding the incident, Abdullah still lectured Terry on the importance of being disciplined and suppressing all measure of anger, *"For the messenger of God (may the peace and blessing of God be upon him) said, the strong is not one who overpowers another with his strength, but suppresses it when faced with adversity."*

Pondering his words, as he lay on the bunk, staring at Demi's picture, which he used toothpaste to stick to the bottom of the bunk above him, he thought about how she would feel if he was to do something to derail his chances of receiving a bond by gaining in-house assault charges. He knew fully well that she was not the type of woman to suspend her life for an emotional dream. The possibility of losing her altogether, under the same circumstances his cousin lost the love of his life years ago, bothered him heavily. The reflection of his cousin's actions wasn't something he wanted to mirror, especially before discovering what they could build together and the measure of happiness they could attain, assuming the pure acceptance of each other's heart prevailed. Just the beauty of her eyes festered deep desire for her, and he hated feeling like an outsider to her moments and thoughts.

"If you're going to take a nap Terry, tie one of the towels around your mouth, given that we don't have a muzzle, because I'm trying to read this book. It's literally quiet in here for a change, and I don't want to hear you moaning nor see you over there making a world's funniest video with your pillow," Abdullah pleaded, bursting into laughter.

"Go 'head on man," Terry chortled. "I see you got jokes, right now. Don't make me grab the dominoes."

"No, I'm serious," he interjected imitating Terry kissing his pillow. "I don't know who you were dreaming about earlier, but I definitely know she's pregnant given the way that you were whispering and hunching like a dog in heat. Hell, you may be the first black man to get a pillow pregnant," Abdullah joked, laying back into the bunk, laughing.

Unable to deny that was funny, naturally, Terry erupted in laughter, lingering in thought of his heated fantasy with Demi. "Do you ever wish we had the ability of turning back time, Abdullah?"

"Honestly, I can't answer that question as you wish for me to," allowing his mind to drift in thought. "As a Muslim, we learn that looking through the window of "what if" I would have done this or that, assuming maybe the given status would be better, is an aspect of shirk al-khafi, which is a form of inconspicuous shirk, the type that implies being inwardly dissatisfied with the inevitable conditions that has been ordained by God."

"Everything I have endured in my pursuit to discover the true essence of myself has helped to mold me into a more distinctive man before God, society as a whole, women separately, and my daughter. Truly, I have no regrets for any of my shortcomings. My failures, I have learned from God's mercy and my inner weaknesses that He has allowed me to strengthen. Would I have liked for my daughter not to have been mentally and physically exposed to what she was so selfishly and irreverently exposed to? Yes, by reason of negative psychological effects. I'm human, and no true parent wants to see their child suffer in any respect. But within the essence of my faith and the pillars of my heart, I smile because we are advised by God in the Qur'an that our patience and faith will be tested like those before us. We cry over the very little things that we are afflicted with, yet who do you know could endure what prophet Lot (May God be pleased with him) did and sustain true sincerity without once blaspheming God."

"Many of this life only believe in God by tongue, Terry, and not by heart, because if truly by heart, then their actions would reflect it. There is a saying of the beloved Prophet (peace and blessings of God be upon him) that acknowledge, '*our calamities are a means of expiration of our sins and raise one's status. There's nothing that befalls a believer, not even a thorn that pricks him or her, but God will record one's deeds and will remove one bad deed from them.*' One of my favorite sayings regarding calamities is, '*trials will continue to befall the believing man and woman with regards to their children and their wealth, until they meet God with no sin on them,*' God has a purpose for our misfortune, *Terry, so I can never wish to tu*rn back the hands of time."

"I understand! Well, is there a woman of your past that you sometimes linger on?" Terry asked, no longer lying in bed.

Realizing Terry wasn't going to allow him to read his book in peace, and, unfortunately, the dormitory may never be this quiet again. "Yes," Abdullah said, placing his book on top of his pillow as he sat at the end of his bed. "Once, I had a woman in my life named Nikki. I met her pulling up to her mom's house to apologize for shooting it up a week or two priors."

"What!?" Terry uttered not believing a love connection could bridge considering something so bizarre.

"Yes, I know it sounds crazy," Abdullah mentioned, echoing Terry's sentiment before continuing. "When I pulled up to her mom's house, she walked out of the front door cursing and waving her hands like she was about to put me in a chokehold or intended to slap the shit out of me. Deep down, I truly feel she was waiting day and night for my return so that she could meet me. I mean, I never even blew the horn or expected to pull up as I did. Coming out of the house like that, I think was just a premeditated performance to get my attention. I was so captured by her smile, and her long sexy legs that I probably would have allowed her the pleasure of slapping me a thousand times in that very moment just to feel the softness of her touch over and over again. Truly, I think that we both got caught up in the moment, being in the presence of one another, because when she was in breath's length of me, her mind wasn't on me shooting up the house in my attempt to kill her mom's boyfriend. She was focused on getting to know who I was, and my desires were aligned with hers.

"With all misfortunes that transpire in our lives, there's something to gain, Terry. In shooting up her mom's house, I was bestowed the blessing of falling in love with a remarkable woman, whose acceptance I abused because I was childish and selfish at that phase of my life. Unable to stand before her as the man I was given life to be, I didn't know how to love beyond mere words, and, to be blunt, I was too blinded by self-pride to suppress my arrogance and ask her to teach me.

"Terry, everything about her, I cherish because her sincerity was never hidden, and she believed in me when I didn't know how to believe in myself. Eventually, she moved away to strengthen her foundation, but she offered me one last opportunity of being the one to cultivate the chambers of her heart. Yet, I was so caught up in chasing empty dreams, and trying to redefine a broken gigolo's image that I said goodbye to her and her daughter Destiny whom I had become just as fund of. Taking her for granted was a mistake I may never get over, but I accept my misguidance, because it was God's will. When I finally opened my eyes to see life as it really was intended and reached out to her, it was too late. The seed I recklessly planted had already matured in her mind. So, my late awakening stood no chance against her preconception of which I had sown. Oh, I mean, she came to visit, sure. But she left, believing, in her eyes, I was still asleep, which was one significant reason I called on God's help to change my character. Years have passed, and we have traveled in different directions, but if I had just one more chance to feel the softness of her hands — truthfully, I'd love her greater than the benchmark of expectations etched in her heart. God knows that I fear standing before Him again as a failure."

The thought of taking Demi for granted kept Terry silent as he sat there staring at Abdullah, digesting his words and thinking of how easy it is for one to dismiss a person's true worth with nonchalant acts of selfishness. He never wanted to come across as being ungrateful for the blessing of being able to walk within her thoughts or telegraphing insensitivity to her feelings. Many bonds fall apart because mutual respect and understanding is foreign and their core is not the seed of true love, unconditional friendship. He didn't know Demi in depth, yet he knew enough about the way she made him feel that losing her altogether wasn't a card he was willing to play. Thinking of the first time she allowed him to kiss her, the thought of her wanting their first kiss to have a sense of unforgettable significance made him smile. Thinking of how she chose the rain, which she cared nothing about her hair or clothes getting wet, acknowledging how the water purified their togetherness also purified his thoughts, cleansing his desire for any other woman.

"Abdullah, I've been a playboy my entire life," Terry confessed, breaking out of the trance that had him suspended in thought. "Because the two women that my heart cried for, neither could I have to myself. One can't quench her thirst for another woman's nectar, and the other is a fantasy that my desires made appear real."

"Mannnnnn, don't tell me that we go'n have to fight for Zahra Lari or Ibtihaj Muhammad's attention, 'cause I'm definitely ready," Abdullah said, standing up and getting in the Karate Kid's crane stance while trying to imitate Dragonfly Jones' voice. "I'll die fi sabi lillah for either of them," He vowed while watching Terry laugh, totally unraveled. "Damn, Am I that funny to you?"

"No, I'm not laughing at you, Dragonfly Jones," Terry clarified while pointing. "I'm laughing 'cause he finally got off that toilet after masturbating for four hours! Now, he's walking like every muscle in his body is asleep. Turn around and look at him."

Turning his head, Abdullah burst out laughing while seeing the young man move across the room bent over and sliding his feet without lifting them from the floor.

"Someone needs to get medical down here, 'cause I know he has blisters after jacking for four hours. Look at him walking like a rescued seal."

"I can't fight you laughing," Abdullah declared while sitting back on his bed. "If he can sit on a toilet for four consecutive hours, staring at black and white pictures on a cardboard, whatchu think he'd do to a woman if he had the chance?"

"I hate to imagine anything so traumatic being done to a woman," Terry responded. "What I do know is that he just gave me a business idea, because he's definitely not the only man with that type of sexual sickness. Many are married to women who accept it because the idea of being alone and starting over terrifies them."

Reaching into his property bin to grab a pen and pad, Terry began writing out his thoughts, which granted Abdullah an opening to enjoy the calmness of the atmosphere and read his book. With the words of Abdullah lingering in his mind and those from the "Do You" book, Terry wrote a sincere letter, centered upon understanding, trust, and respecting one another without judgmental views, after detailing his idea. Sitting on his bed and sealing the envelope, he looked around, observing the individuals that were surrounding him, finding a sense of amusement in characteristics that should be monitored by a psychiatrist instead of just sitting them in a room to flop around like birds.

Watching the military guy leave the spades table after every hand to perform an inventory on his property, merely to assure that no one stole anything, the guy who doesn't consider himself a homosexual, finding solace in that his wife is transgender after having surgery is quite amusing. But to have the evolved homosexual perform karaoke to "her" pictures, scattered across his bed like an audience was absolutely hilarious. It caused him to think of the story he read in one of Abdullah's books about the man who went to Ibn 'Aqeel and said, *"whenever I plunge myself two or three times into a river to take a bath, I am not sure whether the water reached every part of my body and am consequently unsure whether I have purified myself. What should I do?"*

He said, "Do not pray."

"Why do you say that?"

Ibn 'Aqeel answered, "Gods messenger (peace and blessing of God be upon him) said, 'the pen is raised from three: from the child until he reaches adulthood, from the one who is sleeping until he wakes up, and from the insane man until he regains his senses.' And whoever plunges himself into a river once, twice, and then a third time, yet still feels that he has not taken a shower is insane."

Turning his head to face Abdullah, who seemed to be deep in concentration reading his book, the thought of disturbing him, which he hated, became a little bit amusing.

Closing his eyes and pulling his pillow into his arms, Terry began moaning, grinding, and whispering softly, "I love you baby! Don't stop kissing me. You are the breath of my heart ..."

Laying his book down and jumping out of bed, Abdullah snatched the pillow from Terry's arm and hit him in the face with it, playing around.

"Get up," he commanded, throwing up his hands defensively, indicating that he was ready to fight. "Seriously, get up, I told you that I'll die to prove my love for Zahra. You go'n wear this ass whipping for disrespecting my Muslimah."

Holding his stomach while laughing at the comedic actions of Abdullah, Terry couldn't believe the fact that he was actually looking like Dragonfly Jones in his fighting stance.

"There you go laughing again, trying to discourage me from upholding her honor, but your laughter is not going to work this time." Grabbing the pillow to hit him again, "Get up!"

"Abdullah, I'll never disrespect you, a Muslimah, or the woman you love," he conveyed while sitting up in bed. "I was honestly joking about fantasizing again. Seriously, I could never fight you over a woman, because I feel that's beneath me, but I will make an exception for Regina Hall's acceptance," he vowed, jumping out of bed and raising his hands to fight.

"Terry Johnson, attorney visit," the officer yelled through the intercom as they challenged one another by sparring, throwing a few punches.

"God saved you because I was about to write Regina's name on your lips with my knuckles," Terry chuckled, turning away to go groom himself in the bathroom.

CHAPTER 25

Leaving the jail with heated aggression stirring internally after seeing her grandson through a plexiglass window like a peep show feature, and hearing the two white officers entering the building upon their departure say, "I'd like to spank that monkey," in reference to Penélope, caused Mama Lewis' brewing hatred to intensify for Randle, whom she fantasized night after night about having One Eye wrap his hands and feet in wet rawhide, then throwing him in a pin of feral German Shepherds after the sun dried it out.

Turning around to confront the two officers for their racial disrespect, Penélope immediately grabbed Mama Lewis' arm easing her through the doors before she could release the venom that was foaming on her tongue. A confrontation was the last thing they needed at the moment, especially with Terry's bond hearing in Superior Court scheduled just days away. Observing Mama Lewis' release her frustration by throwing spear hand strikes across the parking lot and in the car, which she claimed were intended for both officers' mouths. Having been snatched through the doors like a recalcitrant hoochie and denied the ability of practicing her new skills against police training, Mama Lewis had Penélope feeling as though she was being granted a personal session of comedy hour, driving through interstate traffic, heavily feeding the horses in her Infinity Q60.

They arrived at Lennox Mall with the intention of adding more charms to their Pandora Bracelets before meeting her son at his office to discuss whatever surprise he required their help to fulfill. Mama Lewis, couldn't bypass the opportunity of going into the Nike store, given that they were only footsteps away.

Most ladies define their sexiness by wearing stilettos and revealing their legs in designer raiment's. Yet, after being the diva of attraction for so many glorious years, Mama Lewis now finds comfort wearing Air Max and Jordan attire, which she claims is the new sexiness she's defining for older women.

A casual browsing to see what new gear had arrived turned into two hours of royal treatment once the manager was informed that Mama Lewis was in the store. She was not only provided a private dressing room to try on all the new accessories yet to be stocked on the floor, fed a Mauritius Island redfish with sparkling antioxidant tea the manager requested from The Food Kitchen, allowed to preorder

Nike merchandise not available to others but also submitted two Air Max color styles to the main office for production approval.

Sauntering through the mall generating sparks with every soft click of her heel against the granite floor as Mama Lewis was being catered to like Cleopatra, Penélope's exoticism was commanding the awakening of lustful eyes of every bystander that was fortunate enough to see her in the skinny jeans that hugged her hips like vacuum sealed plastic and the smiley tie front, silk blouse that highlighted the arch of her cleavage. But neither diminished the allure of her almond shaped eyes, attractive beauty, or the funky side braided hairstyle she was rocking with the pink dip-dyed ends.

Stepping into Bloomingdale to purchase some new fragrance for Reanna and Cadence, Penélope couldn't believe the sight before her eyes at the makeup register as she approached the perfume counter. Instantly grabbing the cellphone from her purse, she took a few pictures using the front camera so her actions wouldn't be noticeable, and onlookers would clearly assume that she's taking a selfie. The desire to approach was fueling her curiosity, but she knew so well that Mama Lewis would never forgive her if she went into combat without her.

Heading back to the Nike store, now that Mama Lewis sent a text to acknowledge that she was finally ready, Penélope wondered how she would reveal the pictures. Should she wait until they left the mall so Mama Lewis couldn't stampede her way to Bloomingdale's like an outlaw waving one of her guns, or just show her now? The thought of being the headline story on the news with their mugshots flashing confirmed that she should wait.

The store manager instructed one of the male employees to assist with Mama Lewis' bags, which made Penélope smile because she did not want to carry seven additional bags while Mama Lewis walked to the car holding no more than her purse, claiming that she couldn't carry heavy objects 'cause she's a senior citizen. Cruising down Peachtree Street, listening to a relationship discussion on the FM radio station, V-103 and noticing that Mama Lewis kept glancing suspiciously at her without saying a word, Penélope was completely caught off guard when she yelled out, "Bitch please," as if she was literally talking to someone.

"What?" Penélope wondered slightly confused cutting her eyes to see what Mama Lewis was doing because it's always something unexpected. She hoped that Mama Lewis wasn't engaging in passenger seat road rage, threatening to shoot someone for looking at her.

"The woman on the radio was saying that a man must be willing to cut ties with all other female associates to gain her full devotion, loyalty and acceptance because she needs to be assured beyond words that she's the only true desire standing in his eyes," Mama Lewis repeated while shaking her head.

"That's cute, don't you think? She wants all of his attention without having to share it with anyone. I can clearly relate to what she's requesting."

"No, that's selfish. She honestly sounds like a woman void of her own self-worth, and a woman who doesn't know how to love herself without the acceptance of someone else to make her feel sufficient," Mama Lewis insinuated, assuring her gun's safety was on as she inserted it back into her side holster. "Women cry openly about wanting to be respected and treated like Queens. Yet, they constantly degrade themselves to attract the attention of a man who offers them nothing. Nothing! They accept being abused, neglected, verbally disrespected, considered no more than a distant side chick to someone they suspend their life surrendering empty dreams for, and extract all measures of moral integrity for attention that offers them nothing. The sad thing is it has become the new norm. Fortunately, that doesn't apply to all women, but it definitely applies to a high majority."

"There's nothing wrong with having a relationship in which the two individuals center all of their attention on each other, Mama Lewis. That keeps a lot of confusion from developing. Yes, we do have some very trifling sisters and arrogant brothers who literally uphold no value when it comes to chasing their lustful desires. But it's a comfort of joy when your mate truly becomes your best friend, sharing any and all things in that you don't need to depend on anyone else morally, opposite sex or not. I don't need the suffocating effect, but I understand and support what she's desiring. Especially, when men constantly try to treat a woman like a simple-minded chicken head and expect royal treatment in return. Women are devious when it comes to their desires, as you know Mama Lewis, so you can't say that she's selfish and insecure for protecting her heart."

"A man can do no more than what a woman allows him to do, but only boys take a queen's acceptance for granted. If that's the type of bond she wants to yoke her heart with, then the two of them should move to Alaska and live like Eskimos, secluded from civilization. Because in reality, it's quite impossible for anyone to exist without a thought or dreaming of the opposite sex. Hell, every night I close my eyes, I think of Billy Dee Williams with the body of 50 Cent feeding me white chocolate covered pineapples while holding me, whispering in my ear with the voice of James Earl Jones but spiced with the accent of Idris Elba."

Laughing uncontrollably at Mama Lewis' unbelievable combination, Penélope couldn't muster the words to respond.

"Women irritate me with their double standards," Mama Lewis continued while gazing through the sunroof at the plane flying over. "They don't want him to think of anyone else, yet when he doesn't have that stallion dick, then it's okay for them to fantasize about someone else to have an orgasm."

"Mama Lewis," Penélope chirped while slightly giggling at her words. "No woman in her right mind is going to stay in a relationship like that. You are too funny."

"Girl, please. You are living in a lick-me bubble, so you wouldn't know," Mama Lewis protested which caused them both to laugh. "Women stay with men for all kinds of meaningless reasons these days, and they fantasize more than men, yet they try to act sooo innocent. Chil', seven out of ten women think of another man to climax. Denzel and Idris have more kids than the population of China."

Exiting the expressway, Penélope laughed and listened attentively, yet couldn't help but imagine how funny it would be if Mama Lewis had her own television show, giving relationship advice to women. Hearing a caller on the radio station speak about wearing booty pads and regretting having her lips done to please a cheating ex-boyfriend almost caused Penélope to briefly pull off the road because Mama Lewis was cracking hilarious duck jokes regarding her lips. But listening to the next individual who called seeking advice on how to effectively love someone who treats her like a queen in every aspect: pays all the bills, has no female friends, unbelievable in bed; yet, she complains about her boyfriend refusing to stop clubbing every other weekend with his fraternity brothers, playing video games occasionally in his spare time, and his unwillingness to attend any church but his own seemingly threw new fuel on what was extinguished," Penélope thought as Mama Lewis counseled without a microphone.

"See, Penélope, that is exactly what I'm talking about," Mama Lewis prefaced her lecture, following the caller's words. "Many women of today have become so self-centered and have gotten so caught up in trying to construct a meaningful relationship by taking advice from books, pastors who have more side mistresses than congregation members, and radio DJ's. As though they have the insight of God that the true measure of love has come to be lost instead of trying to build a relationship upon friendship, communication, trust, and accepting one another for who they are. Changing him is all they focus on now. Every individual is different, so how can someone instruct you on how to love a man or a woman they have never met? Impossible! Yes, one can profit from insights, yet, how effective would their wisdom be when applied to someone not of those characteristics nor has the same internal grooming?"

"This man respects her, treats her like a queen, and proves that her happiness is his greatest priority. Yet, she is complaining 'cause he enjoys doing things in his own free time that doesn't consist of submitting more of his time to her. Now that's selfish! I was married for forty years, and I never tried to change him, which so many women of today dedicate every moment to. I never went through his phone out of curiosity, asked him to stop doing things that gave him a sense of fulfillment, or dictated that he couldn't associate with other women like I was needy or insecure. I loved him without trying to mold him into the image of what I thought a man was, due to my father's actions or someone else in particular. My husband laid the blood of his heart beneath every step that I took, and I'll never stop honoring him for showing me what true unconditional love was through his eyes. How can a woman tell a man how to be a man when she has never existed as one? A man respects a woman without the words having to be spoken every ten minutes, but he understands as well when he has a puppet in his presence, someone he can dangle on a string because she's searching for her self-worth."

"Mama Lewis, you say some of the craziest things," Penélope opined, turning into the parking garage and pressing the button for a ticket. "I can see your side of reasoning, and I do believe she's being a little selfish to a degree. Claiming she's feeling a certain type of way because of what he desires to do in his spare time without her. I wonder, though, what she's offering or sacrificing to have the perfect King on the throne. Many men of today lack family values and do not hold the sanctity of family as close to the vest as maybe your generation does. She better try to find a measure of compromise before she loses the pleasure of being treated like a queen and discover what it feels like to be neglected, taken for granted, and maybe even forgotten."

"Truth is truth, and time has nothing to do with anything, girl! Women and men talk about self-empowerment, but instead of cultivating the mindset that caused the misguidance, they find self-gratification in uncovering and exposing the faults of someone else instead of looking in the mirror. If only they knew that when a servant does not cover the faults of another servant in the world, God will not cover their faults on the day of Resurrection."

"Well, I definitely believe that's true," Penélope concurred while eyeing herself in the rearview mirror.

"Then you have the women who stand on the simple motto, 'I'm going to do whatever for my man, 'cause what I won't do, another woman will.' So, they allow their man to turn them out with selfish ménage a trios and orgies to comfort his ego, when in return, he won't even pay a damn light bill. Penélope, I remember reading an article about a woman saying the way to keep a man is by giving him some bomb ass head or pussy on-call."

Penélope reacted, "Mama Lewis!!" as Mama Lewis reacted with a little aggravation in her tone. "I literally thought that was the most degrading statement a woman could make. Sex has never kept a man, and the countless single mothers giving their sweat and tears upon the earth proves that to be true. Unfortunately, you can't advise certain women of that because they're too busy claiming there's something hypnotic and toxic between their legs, even though there's no man in their lives."

"A woman's intellect, disposition, and integrity wins his attention Penélope, when a woman defines in every breath that God grants her that there will be no name calling, no forgiveness for cheating, no abuse, no mistreatment of her kids, and no selfish or childish games. That man will applaud, respect, and treat her on every level as the Queen she truly is. My husband was a king, but I was the Queen, if you truly understand what I mean by that. It's the very same way with Yara and Gip. You can never allow yourself to get too comfortable because the words 'I love you' are spoken openly and privately. Women lose sight of that essential element, then want to complain when the flowers stop, and boredom sets in and becomes equivalent to the efforts of his desire to remind her what love actually is. When a woman shows a man that her affection is replaceable, what significant reason is there for him to hold on? Especially, when there's a knockoff or cheaper carbon copy at the dollar store."

"I must say, you're honestly right for once," Penélope conceded after stepping out of the car and approaching the building as Mama Lewis scanned the parking area, eager to find something peculiar or out of place.

"Please! I'm always right."

"Whatever, but regardless of our opinions, we have to continue to nurture one another and support the platforms that give us a voice in this society, Mama Lewis. It isn't possible to have everyone on one accord concerning love or anything, really, but the good experiences and misfortunes of others gives us wisdom. Yes, women cry aloud regarding all the wrong that men do," Penélope declared as they entered the elevator, only to turn around and shake her head observing Mama Lewis licking her tongue at a security guard.

"I've always admired Terry because he rendered no characteristics of a playboy. Always a gentleman and he has always been completely honest with me. Because of his gentleness and sincerity, I now value myself no matter what comes my way. It's hard for a woman of integrity to find a real man or just be willing to waste time allowing unworthy prospects to get close when so many other women are fulfilling their fantasies with no strings attached. Mrs. Johnson once told me that Paradise is at the feet of a woman, while Hellfire is between the legs of a fool and upon the tongue of a hypocrite, which I completely understand now. She said that when she met with Mr. Johnson, he was a prominent thug in the streets. Yet, under no circumstances did she ever lower her standards for his attention or affection. By defining a woman before his eyes, he recognized that she was irreplaceable and did what it took to keep her, qualities I stress to young ladies."

"Relations between men and women seem to be headed back to the 'Time of Ignorance', Penélope," Mama Lewis surmised, exiting the elevator. "There are far too many kids having kids and raising them without any sense of true guidance, to feel there will be change on the horizon. That's why I keep one of my newly elected husbands close at all times because even though I know it's not the fault of today's young men that moral values are not groomed internally, I want them to fully understand the consequences of not trying to be more in life than a blind follower of their environment when they cross me and my path at the same damn time with ignorance. Emptying my clip is the compassion I share to let 'em know they're trying the wrong one on a slippery slope."

With Penélope shaking her head at those words walking into the office, they greeted Mr. Johnson's assistant who immediately notified him they had arrived. You're my grandma, and I love you, but I truly understand why your son established a million-dollar bail bond policy with Angels Bell Bonding Company. You need to be mindful, there's no Stand-Your-Ground self-defense law in Georgia for combat, Mama Lewis," Penélope reminded her while grinning and walking toward Gip's office.

"I don't care about no damn state law, federal law, or world law for that matter. They need to be concerned about how accurate I am when I pull the trigger and how fast I can load another clip." Mama Lewis piped sternly, eyeing Penélope as her son opened his office doors. "Shoot first, bond out later is my motto. The politicians have messed up our society with all these 'Get Tough' laws that are imposed only for blacks to comfort the lobbyist instead of giving convicted felons a constructive alternative to providing for their families once they are released. So, since they have excluded them from the equation of life, the only option I have for them trying to invade my space is some hot Black Talon coming from one of my husbands."

"Seriously, ma? Is there even an ounce of compassion left in your heart?" Gip wondered, releasing her from his arms to embrace Penélope, whom he closely stared at after hugging gently and leaning forward to whisper, "Should I be saying congratulations?"

"Yes, there's compassion in my heart," Mama Lewis rifled back, pushing him aside, so that she could sit in his customized massage chair behind the desk instead of the guest chairs or the sofa. "I care enough to see Reanna and Cadence as much as possible, since tomorrow isn't promised to us. Hopefully, Terry will plant a smile in my heart before it's too late. So, I'll err on the side of caution and defend myself before I allow someone to hurt me in their quest to feed their family." She grinned arrogantly while caressing her husband with teasing affection.

Chuckling at her unending entertainment and her constant defiance of bringing a gun to his office, Gip sat beside Penélope in the chair without demanding his mom to move out of his own. He placed his hand on top of hers, as it rested on the arm bar, then spent the next half hour dining, listening, and laughing as they detailed their activities for the day, before enlightening them of the surprise he had in mind. Gip was appalled and outraged by hearing the words that demanded everyone's silence as they turned their attention to the wall-mounted television. But he was not shocked to hear his mom speak recklessly about shooting the boyfriend. The news reporter had just broadcasted that a guy brutally beat his girlfriend's three-year-old daughter for eating the last piece of red velvet cake and that the child's mother waited two days before taking the baby to the hospital for treatment.

"Look at the baby's face," Penélope emotionally whispered as her picture flashed on the screen before the reporter tearfully spoke of the baby sustaining a loss of four teeth, a broken right leg, dislocated vertebrae, multiple contusions, and an ecchymosis with the eyes' bilateral inability to open. "How can someone be so cruel to a baby?"

"And y'all have the audacity to wonder why I keep one finger on the damn trigger," Mama Lewis ranted, removing and laying her husband on Gip's desk, only to pat him with affection. "Where the fuck is the baby's father is my damn question? That senseless coward would never have had the nerve to even think of raising a hand to abuse my child."

Sitting at a loss for words, Mr. Johnson couldn't believe a baby's life was literally subjected to that amount of trauma, merely because she ate a piece of cake. Trying to continue was emotionally hard, given that the little girl's picture kept flashing in Gip's mind, Mama Lewis wouldn't stop talking about what she'd do to the boyfriend if granted five minutes in a room with him, and Penélope was implementing unusual characteristics with her movements.

Calling his assistant into the office, Mr. Johnson informed her of his desire to pay for the child's medical care if her mother had no insurance, and to instruct James of his request to have a close family member of the baby standing before him in the morning. Grabbing his cellphone from the desk, Mr. Johnson called Yara, for no other reason than to soothe the anger stirring internally with the softness of her voice and to say, "I love you." But she sent him to voicemail. Then texted a moment later to acknowledge that once she and some of the kids from Unity finished taking social media selfies with his Mercedes 300SL Gullwing and the dogs, she'd return his call.

"Mr. Johnson, I have a question," Penélope interjected while giggling at the fact that he turned around and caught her trying to steal another one of his coconut curry shrimps.

"For someone who usually nibbles through an entire meal, but just finished eating a spicy Thai lobster soup and a portion of my mom's tempura soft-shell crab with Asian sauce, it's really amazing how you won't stop stealing my shrimp," Gip observed. "Do I need to call security or call back to Fo Yo Soul and advise Mrs. Linda that we need some more food sent over?"

Giggling profoundly with her hand covering her mouth as she chewed, "No, Mr. Johnson," Penélope simpered. "Your shrimp are just so good, and you have enough for all three of us to share, so I just thought you wouldn't mind me indulging myself to a few of them."

"So, you assumed! Well, stop acting like the Pink Panther with my shrimp. Enjoy yourself," he urged while grabbing two more and sliding the plate closer to Penélope, who was already reaching for another. "And I answer yes to whatever you are about to ask me, also," Mr. Johnson exuded with a smile on his face, as though Yara was standing in his view.

"What? My question doesn't require a yes or no, sir, unless I can request a million dollars," Penélope deflected while turning to look at Mama Lewis who was momentarily scrolling through the Grab-a-Gun website on his laptop. "We were discussing relationships in the car because a woman on the radio stated: 'A man must be willing to break off relationships with all other female friends in his life in order to gain her full devotion, loyalty, and acceptance.' That is because she needs to be fully assured beyond words that she's the only true desire reflecting in his eyes. What's your opinion?"

"No one can truly define love for everyone, Penélope, because the principles I stand upon may not cause someone else to smile. Some may consider her method a true form of commitment, whereas others may feel she's naive and insecure. I myself do not have female friends, even though my wife has never dictated such a request. Every woman is not conniving but upholding my wife's honor is my responsibility. So, I open no doors because failure or disrespect is not an option. Yes, I have female associates in business and those that I've known my entire life, but there is no calling, texting, or hanging out just to see how each other is doing. If for some particular reason I'm needed for anything outside of business, then Yara and I will address the matter together because a friend never turns their back on you. But my wife is the only friend I need in life.

"However, even if a man severs all ties with his associates, it doesn't mean that their togetherness will become a symbol of love. Without compromise, sacrifices, understanding, patience, and true dedication to their bond of union, nothing is long lasting. When a woman needs a man to awaken her self-confidence to feel the butterflies of love in her heart, then she has an internal weakness that only true self-reflection can strengthen. God created and bestowed woman upon life as a blessing. Nothing or anyone can take that away. In giving my opinion, a relationship structured upon those merits will truly manifest into endless happiness, unless her need for him to sever ties with his female associates was personal, in which case, she will continuously demand more of him to satisfy her insecurities. There is no love without trust and no trust without acceptance. Penélope, I truly feel that the only way to experience lasting enjoyment is to accept your mate for who they are. Changes are to strengthen an internal weakness that may exist, something of which hinders their potential from blossoming and elevating the foundation on which they stand, not to soothe the lack of self-appreciation that one may have for oneself or the fear that jealousy stirs.

"Penélope, every relationship has differences, and a conversation concerning love has no end because your views or opinions may only have substance in your eyes. Women must understand that as long as they demand no self-respect from a man, then she will always be treated less than her worth, unless a true gentleman crosses her path. It's easy to say, 'I love you,'" Mr. Johnson administered while get up to pour himself a glass of water. "But to cultivate the fibers of a woman's heart, nurture it, and elevate the seeded elements to become meaningful requires communication, acceptance, understanding, respect, friendship, and trust, more than anything. Some consider being mentally and physically abused a form of love, just as some think that submitting to a man entails making his needs more of a priority than their own. There are many different ways people require their hearts to be nurtured, but, in truth, no one can distinguish true love without loving themselves first and foremost. I applaud the woman for having principles. More should."

"So, you assumed my son was going to say something other than what I said earlier," Mama Lewis yelped to Penélope while leaning back in the massage chair like a mob crime boss. "Who do you think groomed Terry to be a Casanova and my son a gentleman, even though Yara has him pussy-whipped." Mama Lewis slammed her hand on the desk, chortling at her own humor, while slightly rolling her neck, arrogantly. "I've been an international Mack Diva all my life, Penélope. I am one of the founding madams of game, which some label as pimpin', not primpin'."

"That's not what you said," Penélope barked.

"Ma!"

"Boy, don't Ma me," Mama Lewis sassed at Gip. "Your father knew I was a mack, and I walked through shower storms in his heart, barefoot, without ever being touched by a drop of blood. How come you think I was able to get a man of his caliber to love me wholeheartedly without an atom's measure of floss in his game? I'm the reason Kool-Ace and UGK wrote that song 'Pimpin Ain't No Illusion.' Penélope, babygirl, I used to make all them jig-a-boos kiss my pinky toe instead of my hand."

Gip silently stared at his mother with endless love as Penélope called out Mama Lewis for lying and shared her reasons as to why she asked Mr. Johnson the question. His messages ringtone, set to the Four Tops' 'Ain't No Woman like the One I Got,' began playing, but Mama Lewis grabbed the cell phone from the desk before Gip could and opened the text message out of curiosity. Seeing her start to giggle while repeatedly saying, "Nasty, just nasty," he hoped Yara hadn't sent a lingerie picture to acknowledge what he was missing out on, being in the office instead of at home in bed.

"Harley Quinn, hand me my phone, and please stop being nosy," Gip demanded with a little amusement in his tone.

"Yara's message says there are three doors," Mama Lewis yapped arrogantly while continuing to read the text message without paying his request any attention. "Behind door one is a black Victoria's Secret dream angels crisscross babydoll lingerie set laying on a pillow. Behind door two is a pink strappy eyelash lace teddy laying on almond coconut bubbles. And behind door three, is a red dream angels plunge garter baby doll set covered with mango slices. Pick the right one, and you will receive the treasure of a King. Pick the wrong one, and Vaseline will rock you to sleep."

"Mrs. Johnson keeps it sexy," Penélope chimed in while smiling and watching Mama Lewis text something on Gip's phone. "I like that, and I'm definitely going to steal that one."

"Y'all just nasty!" Mama Lewis expressed while giggling.

Standing to reach across the desk to retrieve his cellphone as Mama Lewis texted and giggled, Gip couldn't help but ponder his wife's words. With time being of the essence, and a very important meeting scheduled with his lawyers, he resumed the engagement of their meeting by advising them of the surprise that he was planning and how their help was required.

Mama Lewis impishly raised her eyes from the monitor, while contemplating tricking Gip into purchasing the UMP and Scorpion EVO 3 she just added in her shopping cart. The particular way he was eyeing Penélope's awakened curiosity.

"Gip, why are you looking at her like that?" Mama Lewis queried. "You've been eyeing her suspiciously ever since we walked in your office. Stop looking at her for a moment and let me see one of your cards, please. Better Homes and Gardens has a sale on Hellebores, and Asiatic Lilies I'd like to plant in my garden beside my roses and elephant's ears."

"Cause I'm wondering when she's going to share the good news with us," he replied, smiling, interlocking eyes with Penélope, while retrieving the American Express card from his wallet and handing it to her.

"Tell us what?" Mama Lewis asked with curiosity stirring within while she focused on typing in his credit card information before he decided to see what she was truly ordering.

"I guess your attention only gives awareness to guns now Harley Quinn," Gip speculated. "Just look at her, Ma, you don't see the distinct glow in her face. When she hugged me, the sensitiveness in her breast caused her embrace to be different than her normal squeeze. Plus, she's eating like someone who was just released from a refugee camp who was only fed rice. I pay close attention to things Mack Divas don't, it seems, Harley Quinn."

After completing the purchase, she opened her eyes to Penélope for the first time since noticing her glow in the car but got distracted by the radio callers. Mama Lewis couldn't believe that her mind had been so occupied with other things that she didn't notice the change, but she was extremely annoyed and upset that her babygirl hadn't shared the good news with her.

Lowering her head while slightly blushing at the thought of life developing inside of her, "Yes, I'm pregnant," she confirmed, looking at Mr. Johnson, before turning her attention to Mama Lewis.

"Oh my God! Oh my God! My baby is having a baby!" Mama Lewis erupted, rising from the chair to walk around the desk to hug Penélope, as Gip grabbed his phone and acknowledged he was about to call Yara.

"You don't have to call Mrs. Johnson because she already knows," Penélope proclaimed, shocking the both of them with her statement.

"What!? You told Yara before you told me?!" Upstaged, Mama Lewis quipped with an offended expression on her face, pushing her head playfully with her fingers out of jealousy. "Betrayal and treason!"

"Be quiet, Ma," Gip joked, yet not believing Yara didn't tell him about the pregnancy, knowing fully well that the excitement would add comfort to his heart. Smiling with nothing but endless joy in his eyes, Mr. Johnson was embracing the thought of having a grandchild by both of his kids. Spoiling his grandchildren with the wisdom of life and affection, while at the same time awakening new jealousy in Yara given that she would now have to share his attention.

"I didn't betray you," Penélope stated, giggling at her jealousy, while shaking her head. "How can my actions be treason? You sound like the President. I sought Mrs. Johnson instead of you, Mama Lewis, because I needed some constructive advice regarding a decision I was contemplating and a sense of comfort in regard to suppressing memories that still haunt me. I needed a mother's warmth and not the insight of a grandmother's love. Please understand that I asked Mrs. Johnson not to say anything for personal reasons that I'm still adapting to. I smile in front of you, yet I cry inside. I'm seven weeks right now."

"Seven damn weeks, and you are just mentioning the fact that my great grandbaby is breathing inside of you? Seven weeks?!" Tapping Penélope's head with her fingers again as she spoke in intimidating fashion, "Girl you better be glad there's something in your womb right now, 'cause otherwise I'd Superman punch you in the mouth for your betrayal," Mama Lewis admitted. "You're in my house every damn day eating my damn food and training with me. Yet, your secretive ass hadn't said nothin'."

"Have you let Terry know yet?" Gip asked, massaging her hand as he sat beside her, smiling.

"Yes, he knows I'm pregnant, Mr. Johnson. I honestly don't think I would ever have realized the level of happiness I'm experiencing now if God hadn't blessed me with him in my life to help me break down the walls I allowed others' influence to cause me to build. Actually, Terry acts like he's happier about the pregnancy than I am. He was very supportive of me making the decision," Penélope affirmed while smiling.

"I'm only going to forgive you because you're pregnant and that I need my little great granddaughter to come out healthy. But if you ever betray me again, I will tango on your lips with my knuckles," Mama Lewis vowed, while hugging and kissing Penélope on the forehead. "If the baby comes out looking sexy like me, the very least you and Terry can do to acknowledge y'all's love is give her my name."

"Are you serious, Ma? Surely not," Gip protested while bursting into laughter. "We do not need a baby Harley Quinn walking around with guns instead of dolls, trying to be a reflection of you. I love you, but definitely not, Ma."

"Unfortunately, the baby is not Terry's, and I'm hoping for a boy, not a girl," Penélope clarified, causing a blanket of heavy silence to fall upon the room. "Ok, yes, he is the only man I love, have ever consensually been with, and may ever love for life. But because I can never commit to him faithfully as he deserves to be loved, then I could never be selfish and bring a blessing into this life just to bridge our life together. My girl and I are planning on getting married once she receives her doctorate degree in the spring. Having a family is something that I couldn't take from her because of my fears.

"Several months ago, she was diagnosed with endometriosis and uterine cancer. The doctor advised us that after the surgery, she'd no longer be able to have kids. So, given that she was initially going to be the surrogate for one of my oocytes as a way of saying the depth of her love for me is immeasurable, I elected to be a surrogate for one of hers. We spent a lot of time at the fertility clinic talking to counselors and doctors before undergoing the in-vitro fertilization procedure. I'm truly finding solace in my decision, thanks to Mrs. Johnson and Terry. The decision was extremely hard for me to make, but it was a sacrifice I made because I love her and because there's no selfishness in true love."

"You truly just touched every measure within my heart, Penélope, and you know the family is here to support you however you need our assistance," Mr. Johnson assured.

Squeezing her hand, he couldn't help but miss Sheri and their closeness. The thought of her pregnancy caused him to pick up the phone and order her some dipped cheesecake trio and chocolate covered strawberries, hoping that she would shatter the wall she was apparently building between them for no reason.

Being escorted to the elevator, Penélope listened attentively as Mr. Johnson advised her to contact his financial adviser, Mrs. Martinez, and have her establish an IRA investment account that would be beneficial for the baby. So, engulfed in the excitement of revealing her pregnancy, learning of his surprise, and trying to remember his words, Penelope didn't remember her initial intention of showing Mr. Johnson and Mama Lewis the pictures she took at Bloomingdales. It wasn't until her girlfriend sent a text, acknowledging that she had just purchased her an outfit and some tickets for them to go to the Jill Scott concert, that she remembered. Walking through the lobby of the building, Penélope grabbed Mama Lewis' hand and stopped as they intended to enter the door of the parking garage.

"We need to go back to the office for a minute. I need to show Mr. Johnson what I'm about to show you. Mama Lewis, I witnessed this at the mall earlier," she pointed out, extending her arm so that Mama Lewis could see the screen.

"What the fuck!?" Mama Lewis gasped while shielding no measure of her emotions as her eyes captured the person within the picture.

CHAPTER 26

Galvanized by his anger and to alleviate the frustration of having to physically chastise Sheri for offending him by disturbing his sleep to question if he removed an additional thirty-eight thousand dollars from her account without her permission, after refusing to acknowledge what the $147,000 he withdrew was used for, Randle stepped out, seeking to intoxicate his mood in the downtown Atlanta nightlife. For it was better than remaining in the presence of a worn love he was starting to despise. Seeing the queue of club-goers standing outside Voltage as he cruised down Ponce De Leon, grooving to the sounds of Bruno Mars in his Audi A7, the urgent need for a sip of whiskey compelled Randle to park and blend in with the club atmosphere.

Sliding the door security fifty dollars to bypass the line, Randle eased through the crowd and sat at the end of the bar to exclude himself from the need to socialize, momentarily. He was intent on scorching his throat with shot after shot of Crown Royal Black before panning the lounge for a slut that he could pay for some parking lot head and maybe a quickie if she was sexy enough. Slowly relinquishing all ill vibes as he sat alone, bobbing to Post Malone blasting through the lavish entertainment speakers and enjoying the UFC fights on 5 different TV monitors, Randle couldn't stop reflecting on the high from his adrenaline rush, racing through his veins while playing Russian roulette with his .357 revolver in Sheri's mouth to teach her a lesson, just prior to leaving the house.

The fear in her eyes psyched him out, giving him power and control that made him feel even more like his pimp President, basking in the enjoyment. To ensure that Sheri had not left the bedroom as he dictated, he retrieved his phone from his pocket and logged into the security camera he left as he ordered another glass. The sight of her laying across the bed watching a rerun episode of Game of Thrones awakened a smile that made him feel as though he truly controlled her now. She was obeying his command in his absence, 'cause she knew he would be monitoring.

"Excuse me sir," the waitress approached, placing a double shot of Remy in front of him and advising who it was from.

Raising his eyes from his cellphone screen, "tell her I said thank you," Randle informed the wiry waitress who he paid no attention to all night until she brought him a drink paid for by a woman sitting alone at a booth table, wearing a provocative, black sheer lace, wide leg jumpsuit. The sight of her waving stirred something inside of him, which caused him to walk over and introduce himself. Tipsy and enjoying the flirtatious conversation that rewarded him with free drink after drink, Randle drifted through the night forgetting that Sheri existed.

Awakening to a sensual embrace as if he were a rare jewel, Randle struggled to squeeze out an exhaling morning stretch. The soothing caress of a temple massage and a therapeutic heartbeat thumping against his face was medicinal to his throbbing headache, courtesy of his excessive drinking throughout the night. Randle slightly turned his head to the side to kiss the soft textured skin, fragrant with Eternity Air billowing a fresh aromatic scent of lavender, infiltrating his lungs and meshing with the silk threads of satin sheets. The intensely cradling masseuse's movements physically replicated oceanic waves smashing against his body with the therapeutic current of a cool Caribbean breeze. Desiring to catalyze morning sexual stimulus to eradicate his now medicinally soothed but yet lingering mild headache and as a way of saying he was sorry for gambling with her life so nefariously, Randle sought to awaken the innermost passion of Sheri's throat. Knowing so well that Sheri's weakness is her clitoris, Randle began rubbing his hand along her inner thighs, that is, until he touched her magnificently swollen clit. At the touch and sheer size of Sheri's unnatural extension, his eyes went from moping to a wide opening in point two seconds! Something wasn't right; this was unusual and highly unexpected. He shouted, "OMG!" Further stretching his eyes and dropping his jaw in complete horror, while leaping out of bed without hesitation, into the piercing sun rays, naked, confused, and clueless of last night's events.

"Who the fuck are you?!" Randle shouted, gazing intently at the stranger sprawled across the bed, looking like an unhygienic swimmer in sewage while observing the splatter painted Tinkerbell decor throughout the room. "Where in the hell am I?!"

Reaching from under the covers, she seductively massaged her over-bulging beer belly that was no longer compressed by tummy tucking shape wear as she sat up in the bed gloating, just thinking of their night of incredulous intimacy.

"With passion marks on your body like that, Snowflake, how can you honestly forget that I'm the one your rabbit stroking ass had calling out your name in three languages last night?" She argued.

Staring at breast implants which seemed to have been done experimentally in a drug store bathroom and thinking of what his hand just touched, "No fucking wayyyy! Arrrrrrrgggh! Please tell me you're at least a fucking hermaphrodite!" Randle implored nervously, shocked by the sight of hickeys visibly seen all over his neck, chest, stomach, then turning in the mirror, his lower back and ass, screaming while still not truly believing the presence before his eyes nor trying to digest the fucked up and humiliating situation he was in or the words he just heard.

"Don't disrespect me like that, Snowflake. I know you were a little tipsy last night, which is no excuse, but I proved to you in more ways than one, all over your body, that I'm all woman even though I haven't had my operation yet," she boasted while trying to reach out and caress Randle's chest.

Feeling as if he were going into a state of shock and hyperventilate, he literally could not believe that he was standing naked in an unknown place before a fucking transgender, wannabe transsexual, truck driver wearing a green drag queen wig, extra thick glittery eyelashes, with a tattoo of pink mermaids swimming with dolphins on its breasts who was rudely claiming that they created magic with their unsettling intimacy and him with the blemishes to prove it.

"Don't fucking touch me, you mother-fucker!" He rebuked, and Randle swung, softly connecting his fist to the stranger's jaw, as the fingertips of the transgender brushed against his stomach to rekindle the unprecedented passion. Randle's lashing out did no more than unleash the bridled anger of a raging bull.

Tired of men waking up in her bed after a night of partying and acting as if they were clueless of the delish passion shared once it's discovered that they crossed over to the other side of ecstasy, she tossed aside the sheet which was covering her legs and jumped out of bed with x-rated vengeance flowing through her veins like hot lava. Standing at 6'4" and a trained 264-pound kick boxer, she torpedoed Randle against the wall with all of her force, aggressively pressing his neck with her forearm, denting the sheetrock with his body's outline as Randle gagged for air. Touché, he now experienced what he so often did to Sheri.

Reacting swiftly with her offensive attack to keep Randle from being able to counter, she threw a left jab that connected with his eye socket which sent him tumbling like weightless matter to the floor in excruciating pain. The raging stranger bent over to grab a firm handful of Randle's butt cheek and the back of his neck, lifting him like one of those Caterpillar off road truck tires while doing her workout. She slammed Randle on the dresser, paying no attention to the pleading cries that he gave through wired jaws as he slithered off onto the floor. Hammering her foot into his stomach while yelling offensively at the top of her lungs, Randle strained through the pain and loss of air to beg for mercy.

Trying to protect his jaw and ribs over all other things, "I'm sorry! I'm sorry! I'm sorry!" Randle cried until she straddled his chest like a saddle and gripped his neck with a force that seemed as if the stranger was going to strangle him and crush his windpipe. Staring into his eyes with tears leaking from the corners and his heart rate elevating with every breath, "Please! Please, don't hurt me anymore! I'm sorry!"

Emotionally disappointed that Randle used her to explore the dark side of the abyss in his drunkenness, but not wanting to kill him, "Get the fuck out of my house!" She shouted with uncontained aggression, after lowering to selfishly kiss Randle's lips one last time.

Releasing her grip from his neck and rising to hover over him, she pressed her foot into his dick. It amused her to know that he was getting an erection from her abuse, and she contemplated giving him some head and riding him one last time, just so the memory would never evade his thoughts. But the disappointment of his words extracted the attraction she had for him moments before. Sauntering over to the bed to sit cross legged after sliding into the high-waist boy shorts she retrieved from the floor, she watched how Randle secretly glanced at her as he struggled, slipping into his clothes. Curiosity of their involvement was eating him up inside, which she could obviously tell from the look in his eyes, and it caused her to blush.

"Just so you know, I have a video if you ever wanna see our artwork, Snowflake, confirming those hotspots radiating all over you." Still blushing.

"What!?"

Hearing those words sent inexpressible shockwaves through Randle's body, causing his hands to tremble while attempting to slide his shoes on. No one could ever know of their entanglement. No one!

After lifting his jacket off the floor and discovering an open tube of anal heat plus and some un-sanitized deluxe vibro balls in the pocket. Randle began to hyperventilate while struggling to say, "Name your price. What do you want for the video?"

"Calm yourself Snowflake, because I don't need you dying up in my shit. Passion Mark #101 is not for sale, but you're free to come watch it with me anytime," she drawled, pulling on the Newport bouncing between her lips. "It's my only memory of you, Snowflake, since you're leaving and acting like last night was a black out to you. I'll email you a copy if it will cause you to come back to me."

"Passion Mark #101 my ass! I can't have you uploading that video to an internet site. I'll give you ten thousand dollars for that video right now," Randle shrieked with sincerity, looking a little neurotic as he stood surfboarding the waves of his mind for a flash of last night's memory.

Did they truly indulge in a sexual affair blacked out by an over-indulgence of whiskey? Does this aloof intimacy now classify him as gay or bisexual? The bag of prescription pills on the table and the once mild throbbing headache that seemed to intensify with his breathing had him wondering if he was drugged. Constant thoughts were flowing through Randle's mind like an electrical current, but all that seemed to matter was finding a way to secure that video.

"Snowflake, if you have ten thousand dollars to throw away that easily, then you are telling me that our recorded travel through each other's Milky Way is more significant to you than the reason I cherish it."

Walking across the room of the loft style apartment, she stopped before reaching the entrance to retrieve Randle's cellphone and car keys from her Pink and yellow fanny pack hanging on the chair.

"You really made me smile last night, Snowflake, and a part of me hates that your feelings are not mutual," looking over her shoulder to talk while combing the shiny thick hair of the wig with her fingers as she acknowledged once again that their evening of pleasure was not for sale.

The way she blushed with a devilish smirk upon her face deepened Randle's anger.

"Snowflake, the taxi company has just sent a text acknowledging the driver I requested to take you back to your car has arrived," she uttered while opening the door. "I programmed my number in your phone under Crispy Crème, just in case you ever desire to use drinking as the excuse to explore my creamy filling again, watch the video with me, or merely curious to know how you act when my tongue is searching for your anal G-spot. Just so you know, I make a salmon ranch garlic parmesan pasta that will have you licking your fingers, the plate, and me for a second serving," she teased while grinning to her own amusement.

Knowing that there was no way that he could actually overpower the mammoth of a stranger standing before his eyes and there was nothing visible that would grant him the ability of striking her and of taking the video, wherever it was,

Randle walked out of the bedroom and started to exit the apartment, furious at Sheri for putting him in such a compromising position, so angry and frustrated that he had no control and began visualizing the brutal affliction that he was going to impose on her for this embarrassment.

Turning around after crossing the apartment's front door threshold and attempting to be persuasive, Randle offered one last pleading cry for mercy, only to be granted no more than a kiss in the wind blown from blemishing lips and the door being slammed in his face with a kick. The thought of going to get his gun lingered as he descended the stairs. What if there was actually no video and the stranger was only trying to get into his head? The blemishing hickeys all over his body had Randle outraged at the thought that a transgender had sexually abused his body so fiercely: An ugly and bad body one at that.

Riding silently in the back of the taxi, clueless as to what to think or do, Randle began texting his cousin who was a jack of all trades when it came to being a crook. Paying him to confiscate the video became a priority, no matter the cost involved. Stepping out of the taxi in the sports bar parking lot, Randle retrieved his phone and logged into the security camera he mounted in their bedroom and observed Sheri peacefully resting, which aggravated him even more. Calling and talking to her without an iota of compassion in his voice, Randle verbally assaulted her with his words then commanded her to get up and go to work because he didn't want to see her when he arrived.

The constant reflection of Randle putting his gun in her mouth three times and spinning the cylinder that contained two bullets, had Sheri petrified of him killing her in time. Opening her heart and womb to the toxic elements of his love was a choice she was starting to feel she should never have made. Running to the arms of her father was all she contemplated, but how could she ever live with herself if she betrayed her child by allowing her father to do something that would take Randle out of its life forever? The psychological trauma wouldn't allow Sheri to stop shaking as she moved through the house.

Taking an ice-cold shower before leaving the house to ease her anxiety seemed to be more worthless than her drive to the office, listening to the meditation audio she googled and downloaded. After sacrificing and offering so much to love, Sheri couldn't understand why she was feeling confused, now at a crossroads without a direction of comfort to turn to.

With only one meeting scheduled for the day, Sheri sat in her office listening to Nicki Minaj on her laptop. The creativity of her music seemed to be the only therapeutic sound that was able to penetrate her sadness as she stared out the window, gently caressing the only crystal rose she didn't break. Basking in the moment that only granted a breath of peace, Sheri bobbed her head, while trying to find answers in the characteristics of the family of Kingfishers living in the tree adjacent to the building. She admired how they were free of the endless drama attached to human life: Well, hers anyway.

After declining Stewart's request to have lunch at Pappadeaux to avoid further potential conflicts, Sheri tried to find a sense of solace away from the birds by focusing her attention on the library development. Making essential calls to double check everything seemed to ease her mind and became a great benefit, given that the construction crew had started hanging drywall in a section of the building where the wiring wasn't complete.

Leaving her office to attend the meeting scheduled, Sheri was caught off guard seeing the florist's delivery driver enter the building while holding a bouquet of colorful tulips as she stood at Heidi's desk discussing the paintings that she needed wrapped and transported to the buyers. Initially, she assumed the flowers were from Abdul Waahid when the driver asked for Ms. Johnson. But after discovering that they were from the Mayor, who all of a sudden had been praising her program in his public campaign speeches and wanted his constituents to think that he was a strong supporter of the Unity movement, Sheri threw the card in the trash without reading it. Concurrently, she politely advised Heidi that she could have the bouquet of flowers or give them to someone worthy of a smile. Seeing the enthusiastic look in her receptionist face as Heidi tossed them in the trash beside her desk shocked Sheri as she started to turn and walk away.

"Why did you do that?" She questioned Heidi, perplexed.

"Because the trash was worthy of a smile. The Mayor's being a sycophant, and I'll never disrespect you or our sisterhood by supporting someone with his characteristics."

Sheri could do nothing but smile while walking away and admiring her unity for sisterhood. Approaching the conference room, Sheri noticed an abstract painting of a man feeding a baby girl through a window as the mother slept on the bed holding a torn picture of him. For reasons she couldn't explain, the artist spoke to her heart with his creativity. Miraculously, it caused her to develop an urge to call Randle and apologize for confronting him about withdrawing an additional thirty-eight thousand out of her account without asking. A family is what she wanted far more than a life of separation for their child.

It dawned on her that her love for him couldn't possibly have had true value, and she now understood how he was correct to say she was wrong to question him, when she already openly acknowledged her full commitment to their relationship and willingness to share everything. If her money was off limits to him to use as he felt, especially in the sense that she had not established a discretionary spending account separately for him, then how can her love be genuine? Warped but rationalized, she retrieved her phone from her purse to dial Randle's number, so she could tell him that whatever he used the money for was his business and that she was sorry for offending him with her questioning. The only thing important now, she felt, is that he knew she loved him. Unlocking her screen, Sheri noticed that she had a text from, James, the head of her father's security team, acknowledging that he received her voice message and will look into discovering who Abdul Waahid is for her.

"Sheri! Sheri, come on, everyone is waiting on you!" Her project coordinator stated from the conference room doorway before stepping back inside as Sheri hesitantly followed.

Listening to her staff's ideas regarding their new strategies for marketing was more intriguing than Sheri truly imagined. Maintaining the core values of art and relevancy while, at the same time, developing a platform that would inspire young artists to be innovators by opening new doors of creativity went over quite well with Sheri. Remaining relevant, a visible light in the art world, was challenging, which is why Sheri applauded her staff for their impact in the Art of Life's growth and stability by compensating everyone with a ten percent pay raise that seemed to ignite and awe to everyone's delight.

Silently sitting next to one another without a single word spoken, Naomi massaged Sheri's hand the entire meeting, as if she knew Sheri was crying inside and needed a shoulder to lay her head upon.

And then, the silence was broken, "I need to talk to you," Naomi expressed while grabbing Sheri's arm in her attempt to leave after the meeting had adjourned. "Do you have a moment?"

"Yes!" She replied lingering more upon the portrait and Randle.

Depriving herself of Naomi's companionship was more torturous to Sheri than words could elucidate. Trying to make Randle happy had been the focus of her priority, but it was starting to seem like he wanted more so to wreak havoc in the form of control and fear upon her, mentally and physically. Apologizing for the characteristics she had been portraying, Naomi and Sheri knocked down the invisible wall that Randle forced her to construct, while reminding each other that their love is unbreakable, inseparable. Sheri has never been able to hide her secrets from Naomi, who knew for sure that something was wrong by the look in her eyes. Instead of spoiling their reunion by dissecting her thoughts, she just smiled at the fact that they were talking again.

As she escorted Sheri to her office, she no longer felt deprived of discussing the affairs of her life until now, baffled by their silence. Naomi was compelled to tell the story about the guy she met at the grocery store who tried to hide the fact that he had erectile dysfunction due to cancer, so he used a strap-on to selfishly defraud her eyes, attempting to impress her by trying to make it seem as though he had a sledge hammer between his legs.

"Gurl, I thought he was a real Mandingo," Naomi stressed while showing measurements with her hand. "You could see his bulging print even when he was sitting down. In the days after our first date, I would go to sleep fantasizing about what it would feel like to have something that enormous expanding my coochie and sliding it back and forth in my throat. I had no damn idea that he was walking around with a damn strap-on fastened to his body just in case the opportunity presented itself, gurlllllll.

"The room had to be completely dark when we had sex and there was no caressing him or grabbing his ass, even after I told him that I get wetter by squeezing his cheeks and spreading my legs whenever he's on top. Sheri, all type of red flags went up when he blatantly refused to let me ride him or give him head the first time, which was crazy coming from a man, because not only can I move my hips like the pistons in a big block V8, but my jaw suction is what damn vacuum companies try to replicate!

"The first time, he tricked me because I was satisfied by the way he used his tongue and the way he had me so open, I climaxed five times if not more. He had my pussy calling for that dick in my sleep. Sheri, I like to throw these hips, gurl, instead of just lying there like a doll, she purred while imitating her movements. The second time, I lifted my head to suck on his nipple, given that he was diving so deep and I wanted to intensify our passion. By coincidence, I looked down to see how wet my pussy had his dick, which turns me on even more. To my surprise, I saw the straps around his waist and the muthafucker was using a white dildo instead of a black one!" Naomi exclaimed as they giggled to her every word. "I waited 'til I couldn't take it anymore, 'cause the way he was touching my body and stroking my pussy had me chasing crazy waves of stimulation. Driving home the next morning, I felt so embarrassed, knowing that I was climaxing so heavily to a damn plastic dick instead of the real thing. Not because I liked the way he had me feeling and I wanted some more, but in truth, real dick has never felt that damn good," as they erupted, dying laughing.

Laughing at Naomi's freaky tales was more therapeutic than sharing the details of her own thoughts.

"Are you going to see him again?" Sheri coaxed just to see if Naomi was going to lie or tell the truth. With her eyes slightly shifting to the left as they do whenever she tells a lie, Sheri bursts out laughing as she yelled out, "That plastic dick gotcha sprung bitch!"

"No, the way he treats me like a lady and the fact that he's a petroleum engineer is what has me slightly sprung," Naomi clarified, rolling her eyes. "I feel like the plastic has its own benefits outside of a selfish nature. If I were to lower my standards and accept it, then at least my pussy would constantly know what true pleasure feels like, and I'll never have to worry about catching any STD's, gurrrl. Hmn. Soooo ... How is Terry holding up in there by the way?"

"You're not just nasty bitch, but you're stupid! I don't know how he is Naomi. I haven't spoken to him since they locked him up," Sheri admitted realizing what just came out of her mouth was more shameful than the reality of what caused him to be there.

Sheri was speechless when Stewart exposed the truth of why he returned, but not as much as she was right now. The thought of her brother spending the rest of his life in prison because of her was hard ... no, impossible to swallow. She tried to find comfort in Randle's arms, but he had no sympathy regarding the matter. Changing the subject to keep her from getting emotional at the fact she betrayed him for love that seems more like torment, Sheri started venting about fashion, which Naomi considered herself the guru of style. Forgetting about their responsibilities for the day, they sat in the office laughing and catching each other up on the things they had missed out on in their separation until Naomi broke the ice.

"Sheri, the last thing I ever want to see is you hurt in any way, so it's not even possible for me to hold back on denouncing anything detrimental to you." Reaching out to grab her hand as they sat side by side on the sofa, Naomi found herself getting emotional, staring into her eyes.

"I spent the night with an old friend of mine who likes to soak my feet in Sweet and Sour Asian Hot Sauce, then lick it off. Gurl, his dick may literally be the half size of my pinky finger, but I swear his tongue is long like a tamandua's, yet thick and heavy like a giraffe."

"Are you serious Naomi?" Sheri effused with a little hostility and humor in her demeanor.

"Yes! I'm sorry, but I definitely have to tell you about him later," she added, unable to stop smiling. "Aneewaay, I creeped out of his apartment this morning so I could get home and shower without being late to the office. In opening the door to his apartment, which you know I peep out thoroughly before exiting, I saw Randle exiting the adjacent one, which belongs to this super crazy, but cool transgender name Crispy Crème. I didn't see them hug or kiss, but I did hear Randle begging her for some video. I started to stop by to inquire what he was doing over there, but instead of being nosy, I felt I should inform you first out of respect, to give you the chance of talking to Crispy Crème, unless you already know what's going on."

The devastation upon Sheri's face in hearing her words, clearly acknowledged she was clueless of any connection that Randle may have with a transgender person. Was he cheating on her? Was she sucking dick that had been in a he-she's ass?

"Are you sure it was Randle?" Sheri asked, clearly knowing Naomi wouldn't lie to her in this fashion, and he did stay away all last night without answering his phone or calling.

"Yes, I'm sure it was him," Naomi insisted reaching to grab her cellphone from the table. She scrolled through the gallery to reveal the pictures she took. "I can also call her for confirmation if you'd like Sheri."

With tears starting to fall rapidly upon her face, staring at the picture of him wearing the clothes he left home in, Sheri sat motionless. What was she doing wrong that would cause her man to seek affection from a sissy? Is it the head, her personality, or the fact that she won't try anal sex? The abuse and physical detachment was acceptable for the baby, but cheating crossed the line of no return. The thought of catching a sexually transmitted disease began to terrify Sheri as she lingered in thought. Is that where Randle was each time he stepped out and refused to answer his phone? Is that who he spent her money on?

Laying in Naomi's arms, Sheri began to realize how foolish she has been. Forcing herself to be blind to his actions because she didn't want to be laughed at and considered a failure by others. How could she have turned against the ones who love her for someone who had forgotten how to even respect her and make her smile? Caressing her stomach, Sheri wanted to believe it was all a lie and that Randle loved her faithfully. Knowing how much Naomi hated him, and disliked the fact that they hadn't been talking, the thought of this all being a deceitful act to push Randle from her heart began to make Sheri regain a sense of composure. Wiping the tears from her face, Sheri began asking questions as though Naomi's jealousy of their bond was the driving force behind her motives.

"You have literally lost your fucking mind to assume I'd Photoshop a picture and plot some wicked shit like this merely to get your attention. I love you," she vowed rising from the sofa, "But I'm starting to believe that he has beat you so much that you can't think straight and you fear spreading your wings and opening your eyes beyond anything that don't consist of him. The woman you are has so much promise, but you fail to accept that there's no benefit to contaminated garbage, toxic waste. The audacity of you believing that I'm lying to you is a very clear confirmation that y'all two are miserably insane and you belong together," Naomi stated, emotionally, as she got up and stormed toward the door without stopping at Sheri's plea not to leave.

"Naomi! Naomi!"

CHAPTER 27

The sharpness of the last rays of the sun illuminated the pecan skin tone of Demi as she stood against the glass patio door in her rose lace tea-length applique slip, while casually drinking a bottle of Zamzam water, and getting lost in the irreplaceable beauty of the horizon. Fascinated by how the light created a haze amongst the clouds, she patiently watched until the sun was no longer visible. Such a hypnotic spectacle is commonly overlooked by those often chasing the pleasures of this world. Admiring the true beauty of life, Demi wondered if she would ever be granted the pleasure of witnessing the glory of the sun or the moon's luminescence upon Terry's face again. The lawyer seemed to have no definite answers regarding his situation, only possibilities that gave her heart no comfort.

Desiring to kick her feet up on the sofa and watching a re-run episode of Homeland, Demi decided to check her phone first to assure herself it wasn't on vibration mode. Two hours had now passed beyond Terry's usual scheduled calling time, and she was starting to wonder if something happened in the unit that caused the inmates to lose their phone privilege as a result. Trying not to step on her Shih Tzu which accidentally ran into her foot as he played with his chew toy, Demi stumbled in the process of reaching for her phone and mistakenly knocked the mail off the counter while trying to regain her balance. Reaching down to tickle her little prince briefly before picking up the mail off the floor, she noticed a letter from Terry, inserted between the pages of the newspaper that she was unaware of.

Unable to hide her smile from the angels, Demi grabbed the letter and went to her room to lay across her bed instead. Desiring to smell a sense of his masculinity, Demi held the jailhouse made envelope to her nose and inhaled, wishing the fragrance he was wearing the day they first met was exuding from the paper. Opening the envelope, the creativity warmed her heart to the extent that it weakened her desire to actually open it, solely to preserve the artwork. Unfolding the letter, Demi's eyes scanned over his words with the keenness of a linguist, trying to feel the magnitude of Terry's heart, as though he was actually laying in her lap, speaking and her hand was caressing his chest.

"Dear Sylphina Angel,

I can't sleep at the moment, for all I keep wondering as I lay here repeatedly engraving your name into the wall beside the bed with my finger, is why did God grant me the pleasure of meeting an extraordinary woman such as yourself, then isolate my eyes from the beauty of your smile. Am I being punished for my years of childish deception by portraying a gentleman openly, merely to nurture the selfishness of my lust? Or is this my road to redemption as Prophet Joseph (may God be pleased with him), time granted for me to face myself in the bricks constricting my footsteps. Isolation to allow me the opportunity of breaking the yokes that deny me the joy of holding your hand without failure.

I ask God to forgive me for any and all wrong that I have ever done. But I thank Him wholeheartedly for allowing me to witness the blessing you really are. Truly, I now understand that my purpose in life is to worship Him and not to seek the enjoyments that have prevented me from achieving the true definition of a man. For without God's mercy, the latter can never be rewarded.

Demi, there are moments these walls have me feeling as though I'm seeing illusions and trapped in a window of time that doesn't exist. I stare at your picture to remind myself that succumbing to the whispers of Shayatin and finding solace in my weakness is not an option. You are the reason there is no darkness in my day, even when the lights are cut off and my eyes are closed.

I never imagined that being isolated would allow me, by God's will, to discover myself. I used to be afraid of my reflection because the feeling in my heart seemed to be limited to empty dreams. I dreamed a few days ago that you broke into the jail to kiss me, then we walked over to the wall and smashed out a window, in order to wrote each other's name upon a star to give us meaning beyond words. Demi, I asked God to bestow upon us the pleasure of witnessing the sunrise in the retinas of one another. The beginning of us striving to be each other's last first kiss. Besides my prayers and dreams, all I have is your picture to keep me from losing my sanity and to remind me of what life actually is. Internally, it's no secret that I'm currently afraid of losing your acceptance and never knowing what it feels like to be loved by you outside of a selfish fantasy.

Sometimes, I wonder do you hear me calling out your name in between the obtrusive snores of my bunkmate in the twilight or feel me trying to hug you each time I squeeze this so-called pillow the jail issued. I miss witnessing the way your bottom lip slants slightly to the right whenever you smile, lowering my gaze to honor you in public and the way you caress my hand when I'm driving. I miss you, and I realize that even though I pray several times each day, for my sins to be forgiven and to breathe the sweetness of your air again, being granted the pleasure of freedom will mean nothing if I don't better myself as a whole. I can't offer you branches of Terry which I've exposed to those of my past. My every weakness, I'm strengthening and my every vice, I'm internally shattering. I want to share the truth of myself with only God and you.

Before I end this letter, my Sylphina Angel, I want you to know that I applaud the magnificent woman that you are. Truly! I've never met a woman with the confidence and self-assurance that you possess. Nor a woman who intrigues me so much mentally that I'm having to take notes and study them in order to preserve every measure of your preciousness. I had a very shocking visit today, as my grandmother and Penélope advised me that I'd be a fool to take you for granted in any respect.

For future references, my grandmother cannot hold water. Even with gorilla tape on her mouth and a muzzle welded to her lips, loose words will still flow off her tongue. Grandma Lewis informed me of the secret meeting you established with Penélope and my mother to bridge some understanding and respect, given that she is strongly connected with my other family members. The way my grandmother and Penélope spoke of you was highly remarkable. It's interesting how some women would try to define themselves by imposing automatically or being brusque regarding the entire matter of Penélope and I. Yet, you defined a woman of grace and character by having an open dialogue with her.

Your trust, I will never dishonor! I may not be able to feed you papayas before the fireplace, see you lick your fingers after eating my cooking, or traverse the earth, touched by the warmth of the sun and admire God's creation with you right now, but I have faith that one day our paths will cross again. Desires, I hold with my molar of witnessing your smile in my shadow, but I can prove beyond the given power of words that you are sincerely thought of and appreciated. Call your mother!

I miss you, my Sylphina Angel,

Terry"

After reading his letter two times, Demi squeezed her pillow and thought about the bonfire picnic on day lily petals that they both shared the night before his arrest as she gazed out her bedroom window blowing him imaginary kisses. No day has passed whereas she hasn't wished they would have bypassed going to Sheri's house. Paying no attention to the time, Demi rolled over to grab her phone off the dresser and dialed her mother's number, only to receive the voicemail on both attempts.

306

Very curious to know what the unexpected surprise was that she needed to call her mother for, but even more intrigued to know how Terry was able to get her mother's number and what they talked about. Scrolling through their pictures in her gallery to see his eyes, the sight of Terry covered in mud on one picture as though he'd been mud wrestling with a bull, caused her to laugh until joyful tears began to fall from her eyes. The memory of him being thrown from his horse, because it saw a field mouse in the rain, will always be a hilarious moment she'd cherish.

Easing off the bed to slip on a pair of jogging pants and a jacket, Demi took her Shih Tzu out to relieve himself after he entered the room and alerted, he had to go. She extended their usual itinerant to the pool area due to the cool breeze creating a soothing atmosphere. Imitating the fierceness of a lion, he barked at everyone in the complex, as though he was reassuring without doubt this was his territory. Her little prince transformed into a lifeless statue upon seeing the enormous size of the Great Dane crossing the parking lot, as one of her residents was walking by. No longer making a sound, blinking, and refusing to move, Demi lifted her little protective prince into her arms as the bystanders joined her in laughing at his actions. Feeling the cellphone vibrate, she put him back down, given that the Great Dane was gone, and her little prince had suddenly regained his heart.

"Hey, mom," Demi uttered, answering the call without looking to see who it actually was.

"This is not your mother dear," Mrs. Johnson corrected chortling. "If I was, then you owe me back years on my income taxes."

"I'm so sorry, how are you Mrs. Johnson?" Demi queried, finding humor in her statement. "I assumed you were my mom, given that I just called her."

"I'm blessed, granted God's mercy, dear. I bought a book today my girlfriend referred me to get, called Mirror Mirror on the Wall by Ms. Asiya Nasir, which I think you would love."

"Yes, I've heard of her through a few of my associates, Mrs. Johnson. She's an exceptional writer and speaker, I'm told, who strives to empower young ladies with the inner essentials of womanhood," Demi related while noting in her phone the name of the book so that she could order it. "Thank you for referring it to be read because I just finished with a motivational book by this foreign male writer that was a complete waste of time. The entire book uninspired me, which is definitely a challenge for anyone to do. I was tempted to forward a copy of Renesha

Acosta's book to his office, so that he'd discover what a motivation book is supposed to read like."

"Yes, girl! I can't thank you enough for referring the "Do You" book, which I still find hard to put down when I'm not reading *Mirror Mirror on the Wall*," Mrs. Johnson revealed. "I've read it three times already, and plan on reading it again after this one. Sweetie, I do apologize if I disturbed you in any way by calling so late."

"No, ma'am you're okay," Demi assured while unlocking her apartment door. "Feel free to call anytime, I wasn't sleeping. I'm actually walking back in the house after taking my little scary prince out to do his business."

"I love your little baby. He's so cute," Mrs. Johnson effused after listening to Demi tell her about his audition to be a Transformer, when he saw the Great Dane.

"Sweetie, the reason I'm calling is because there's been a little incident at the jail. Terry's friend Abdullah called me a moment ago and advised me that Terry was stabbed twice by this young boy trying to join a gang for protection."

"What!?" Demi screamed, becoming a little hysterical in the thought of someone hurting him. "Is he okay? Have you spoken to the doctors at the jail yet?" Unable to calm herself, the rareness of her emotions brought tears to her eyes as Mrs. Johnson tried to assure her that Terry was truly okay.

"Demi, I feel your distress, but please stop crying before you cause me to start crying. Yes, I have spoken to the nurses on staff at the jail and they report that Terry is well. He received seven stitches to close both wounds, but they are keeping him overnight in medical isolation for observation. Abdullah said the young boy waited till the officers came in for count and stabbed Terry twice in the side, before running to the officers so Terry or him couldn't retaliate. The plastic spoon he used didn't damage anything internally, but the nurse on staff did say that Terry's lucky the knife wasn't sturdier because otherwise, the second insertion to his side would have punctured his kidney."

"Oh my God," Demi babbled, covering her mouth in disbelief. "I knew something was wrong, given that he didn't call tonight. I'll be glad when this is all over, Mrs. Johnson because I can't stop worrying about him no matter what I do. One of my cousins went to prison back home and lost his life to a gang fight. Many have no idea what they actually go through to survive mentally and physically within those walls, daily."

"You are so right, Demi. But please don't worry yourself about this. Abdullah said Terry was not directly targeted by the gang members. Terry was the closest to the young individual during count, and given that their backs were turned to him, naturally, neither had the chance to stop his cowardly act. But they will definitely be on the lookout from now on. Terry should be back in the unit tomorrow, but I'm going to the jail in the morning and will call you once I leave, sweetie."

"Thank you, Mrs. Johnson," Demi stated before hanging up, wiping her tears. Unable to regain a mental sense of comfort after learning about Terry's incident, Demi paced throughout the apartment before finding a sense of solace, by flopping onto the sofa and just stared out the patio window as her prince stared at her.

CHAPTER 28

Jogging on the rubber flooring track at the gym, Sheri tried to maximize her endurance so as not to think of Randle, but the fact that he had physically avoided her for three days couldn't escape her thoughts. Unable to maintain the high cardio tempo of Mama Lewis and Penélope, she broke her stride to speed walking at a moderate pace. Pridefully trying to maintain, Sheri secretly desired to request an oxygen tank from one of the staff members for the half lap that she had run behind them, which had her lungs seeking an infusion.

"'Gurl, you speed walk like a baby turtle," Mama Lewis jabbered while playfully pushing Sheri off the track and up against the wall due to Sheri being in her lane, and she didn't want to go around just to pass.

Unable to figure out how a woman of her grandmother's age could have so much energy and stamina, Sheri continued on the inside lane for another quarter lap before granting the muscles in her legs some relaxation and therapy by willing herself to the lower level sauna as the aspiration in her breathing was heavily pronounced. Pouring some water on the hot stones in her attempt to raise the temperature, Sheri strolled over to an empty section on the bench, closed her eyes, and pondered for the thousandth time on Naomi's words. Randle's sudden detachment to care for his father the past three days illuminated curiosity behind her draped eyelids, and his despicable, apathy for his own child's life within her womb nauseated Sheri. Living through constant stress, torture and psychological trauma to sustain the closeness of a developing family, as Randle's mother had once done, is not what she envisioned for love.

At the sound of the door sensor beeping, she opened her eyes to see Penélope approaching the bench. Sheri motioned her to sit directly beside her, so that she could chat without being heard by the others. Overwhelmed with joy in exposing her secret and gaining Penélope's assistance to uncover the hidden truth, Sheri hugged her with genuine affection, before kissing her on the cheek, then saying, "Thank you," and acknowledging she'll text her once in the car.

Rising from the bench smiling, Sheri couldn't help but wish that she possessed the inner strength and fierceness of Penélope as she exited the sauna room and wasted no time scurrying to her locker. Hearing the frantic, loud screams of a woman's voice coming from a nearby area and the sound of things slamming against the floor, undoubtedly implying that someone was being attacked. Sheri grabbed her cellphone and ran out of the locker room to notify a staff member without donning her shoes.

Curious to know who was fighting, she followed the 6'2'' muscular female personal trainer and two security guards back into the lounge, as the screams seemed to echo louder in the hallway with each approaching step. The sight of a chair flying across the room, as one of the security guards opened the door of the lounge entrance, had everyone assuming that the altercation was intense between the two individuals. Yet in stepping inside to assist, they discovered Mama Lewis standing against the wall caterwauling with vengeance cast in her eyes, while attempting to throw a napkin dispenser at one of the two small spiders crawling on the floor preventing her exit.

The sight of her in a karate cat stance caused Sheri and others to burst out in laughter, before truly noticing the room's disarray, as one guard killed the spiders and the other one escorted her safely through the door and to a chair in the lobby.

Sheri advised the manager entering the room that she would cover all damage expenses and respectfully tip his staff for cleaning up her grandmother's mess, which he declined with a genuine smile plastered upon his face.

"Grandma, are you okay?" Sheri inquired walking toward her.

"No, I'm not Sheri," Mama Lewis emphasized lifting her arm for the gym physician to check her heart rate, while trying to regain her composure. "I almost had a heart attack in there!"

"Grandma, you boast of there being no MMA professional woman capable of beating you with their hands because you're a lethal assassin, and you champion that shooting bad people should be a seasonal hunting sport. But how can you expect people to take you seriously, when you're deathly afraid of spiders?" Sheri queried, giggling at the amusement of her grandmother's face when they walked in the room.

"Girl, you better leave me alone right now before I get up and kick your ass," Mama Lewis piped, snatching her arm from the physician. "I'm okay, little man, you don't have to keep feeling on me like you tryin' to arouse my damn interest. I'm not seeking a spelunker to explore my cave of wonders. So, go help someone else, please." Mama Lewis declared without saying another word as the physician gathered his equipment and left. Seeing the bewildered look on a bystander's face sitting across from her, Mama Lewis leaned over and hugged her granddaughter. "I love you, Sheri."

"I love you too," Sheri replied squeezing her hand and momentarily laying her head against Mama Lewis'.

"Why haven't you been returning my calls or coming by the house to see me?" She asked, pulling away. "What's going on with you, babygirl?"

"I'm sorry, Grandma, I've just been a little busy the past few weeks," Sheri lied while looking down at the floor.

"If that's your excuse, then I will accept it, but you know I'm the one person you never have to lie to for any reason. I hear you haven't spoken to your mother, father, or brother either," Mama Lewis noted as she massaged her hand. "Listen, I'm not going to hold you, given the fact you have an OBGYN appointment this morning. But I need you at my house tonight at eight, so that you and I can talk — no excuses."

"Unfortunately, I can't tonight, grandma."

"Fortunately, you can, and if you know what's good for you, you will be there," Mama Lewis insisted slightly applying pressure to her hand as she spoke. "You see, Sheri, I have a clear idea of what's going on, and it's about to stop. If you're turning against your entire family to have a life with your child's father, then I wish you all the best. Yet, you should honestly rethink your decision because without a foundation to stand on, everything you build will crumble. But if he's applying force to make you exclude us from your life, as I know he is, then know I'm serious when I say Randle's reign of terror is over. Look at me," she demanded as Sheri tried to turn her head away. "Are you in on the six-million-dollar lawsuit he has filed against your brother?" Studying the movement of her eyes closely, as she replied no, "You better be glad that you're speaking the truth, otherwise I was about to punch your ass in the mouth. I'm not playing with you, Sheri. If you're not at my house tonight, then know that One Eye and I will be at yours."

Knowing that Randle was not going to let her go, given that he had strongly dictated that she stays away from everyone and he was definitely not going to allow her to have family over for company. She sat clueless of what to do. The last thing she wanted to be was the cause and victim of his anger.

"Okay, Grandma," Sheri nodded, trying to deflect the conversation from her demands and scurry away before she was spotted by Randle or someone he may know. Sheri lived in fear of Randle as he monitored her every move through cellphone tracking, and she was not all that good at disguising it. One could see the visible look of fear in her eyes which were distress signals covertly.

The fear of him forcing and subjecting her to Russian roulette, placing the pistol in her mouth again, terrified her. And with a very important art investor luncheon scheduled for her to host in a few days, she wasn't trying to have any type of altercation with Randle. Walking to her car, she wondered if Mama Lewis was playing about the lawsuit, and if not, "What is Randle up to," she thought to herself.

Swerving through traffic to get home so that she could shower before heading to her OBGYN appointment, Sheri was shocked to see Randle's car in the garage as the door raised for her to back in. She seriously contemplated pulling off to avoid being in his presence. The thought of him assuming that she had something to hide, caused her to immediately think against her gut feeling of driving away. She sat for a moment, bracing herself for the worst, given that this is her first time seeing him in three days. Sheri walked out to grab the newspaper from the driveway before strolling back and hitting the button to seal the garage as she entered the house.

Hearing only the clicks of her heels walking through the foyer, Sheri realized while touching the stair rail that she was shivering and becoming even more nervous with each step toward her bedroom. Knocking on the door instead of just entering, the sound of Randle telling her to come in felt like the cold breath of death upon her neck. Twisting the knob, pushing the door open, Sheri hated that she was feeling so petrified and intimidated in her own home.

"Hi, sweetheart," she forced out with caution, while walking into the room, opening her arms to embrace him for a hug. "Is your father feeling better?"

"Yes, he's doing much better, baby," Randle acknowledged turning to squeeze her with gentle affection, before sparking heated passion with a light kiss that caused Sheri's nipples to harden. Raising his hand to caress the side of her face with the back of his fingers, while looking into her eyes. "I love you," he expressed, before bending to kiss the bare softness of her stomach and whispering, "I love you too, little Trump."

"Trump!" Sheri repeated in complete disbelief.

"Yes Trump, if it's a boy," Randle affirmed, caressing her stomach. "How can I not honor my pimp President by naming my son after him?"

The inside of Sheri's stomach felt like hot ice after Randle kissed it. Puzzled by his cordiality, when his demeanor had been terroristic as of late and clueless as to why his eye was bruised, Sheri stood silent, momentarily, watching him fold the collar of his shirt. His actions came across a little eccentric, given that she had never seen him wear a turtleneck, and the weather was too warm for lamb's wool.

"You look nice baby," she cooed, while turning to walk into the bathroom. Randle followed, causing her to get very nervous as he sat watching her get undressed.

"I've been doing a lot of reading and thinking at my father's house the past three days, and please know that I've missed you," Randle claimed while helping to unfasten her bra.

Sitting on the edge of the tub, watching Sheri open the heavy glass door and enter the shower, his eyes were unable to shield his vivid exploration of every inch of her body.

"Baby, I read up on the diets you should be on at each trimester, the signs of preeclampsia, pregnancy warning symptoms, complications to watch for, amniocentesis to check all these symptoms, and how being pregnant can affect your mental and physical health. Also, I can't wait to sign up for Prenatal Care classes as your supporting partner and feel you doing Kegel exercises on my hardness. Sheri, I want to be a significant part of your pregnancy without you ever feeling as though you're alone. I have a business engagement scheduled this morning, but if you want me to attend the OBGYN appointment with you, then I'll cancel it, baby, 'cause the two of you are my priority."

Perplexed at how to actually respond to his words, and literally not believing he was being so sweet, Sheri lathered one last time seductively while eyeing him before rinsing off and stepping out of the shower to be pampered with affection that he has never shown.

"Baby, you don't have to cancel whatever you have going on. We can FaceTime, which would allow you to be in two places at once," Sheri declared as he softly hand patted her body with the towel.

"Okay, baby," Randle agreed while kissing and laying his head against her tummy, gently. "Given the effect of the radiation process, will the anatomy scan affect the baby in any way, Sheri? If so, then I ask you to decline the procedure."

"Yes, it's safe," Sheri answered, grabbing his face and bending down to kiss his lips. "The baby will not be affected at all," sharing sensitive conversation as she dressed seemed to alleviate a thin layer of tension, but her fear still ran deep.

"Sheri, I promise to attend counseling for my anger," Randle continued, while walking her to the car. "I promise to prove with my actions that I respect and appreciate you. Baby, I promise to bring no discomfort to your pregnancy, no stress, and I shall give my all not to raise my hand in any manner. I love you, Sheri, and I know some actions can't be made right. Yet, I promise to make all my wrong a pinnacle of joy, for you and the baby."

Kissing Randle before getting into the car, Sheri tried to get a little affectionate but was stopped in her pursuit. Her fingers had begun caressing his neck in the manner that turned him on and would expose the passion marks if he allowed her to continue. Assuming he was trying to make sure she made her appointment on time instead of falling weak to sexual temptation, Sheri dismissed his odd reaction and closed the car door. Can she believe his words? Is he sincere regarding his promise to change? Driving to her appointment, Sheri wondered how much of a change the baby would actually make in him. Would it be temporary relief from his anger or just empty words spoken for the moment?

The jitters and excitement of having her first trimester exam was more emotional than Sheri actually expected. She kept wiping away endless tears of joy the entire time. Even though Randle was on the phone observing the ultrasound transvaginal procedure and asking more questions than a researcher, when the doctor advised that they were having twins and showed them the heartbeats on the monitor, she couldn't stop wishing he was there holding her hand and saying "I love you."

Hearing Randle tell the doctor to send him a certified copy of the ultrasound by a same day courier so that he could tape their heartbeats to his chest and be reminded upon every breath how much of a Common Nightingale Sheri is to his life, melted the ice that had begun to form within the arteries of her heart. She wanted to kiss him and be in his arms at that very moment. Fastening her clothes after the procedure, the thought of her mother and father being estranged from her pregnancy and their grandchildren's life began to weigh on her. She wanted nothing more than to hear their voice and send them a picture of the ultrasound, but she had made a promise to Randle and feared the wrath of his anger for betrayal.

Driving to the office with a smile on her face and only the reflections of her twins' heartbeats channeling her thoughts, Sheri allowed herself to bask overwhelmingly in the moment. Occasionally lifting the ultrasound picture to kiss, while caressing her stomach, "I love the both of you," she whispered, trying to feel any aspect of movement.

Sheri couldn't wait to plan her baby shower or learn their gender and discuss names with Randle as she sipped on an iced chai tea latte while pulling into the office parking lot. The name Trump for her boy, she was not accepting. Seeing Naomi stroll across the parking lot to a blue Astro van beside a guy wearing a wrinkled Testival three-piece suit, excited such a wave of curiosity that Sheri parked strategically and waited patiently to explore. Stepping out of the car as the van pulled off, smoking up her parking lot, the expanding smile on Naomi's face intrigued her even more to discover who the new Mystery Guy was. "Good morning, stank!"

"Good morning, my gorgeous, pregnant sister from another mother," Naomi politely greeted with a gentle hug and snatching the ultrasound picture out of her hand. "So, what did the doctor say?"

"Girl, you better not tear my damn picture," Sheri scoffed while pushing her playfully and pointing to the spots on the paper to indicate the twins' heartbeats. "I'm twelve weeks, and the twins are forming in my uterus without complications."

"Gurl you are having twins?!" Naomi blurted ecstatically as she turned and squeezed Sheri out of joy. "I hope you have boys, so I can teach them how to make a woman cry out of one eye when they choke her and penetrate that pussy with slow strokes from the back, standing up." To tease Sheri, she raised her leg, rotating her hips to illustrate. "I can't be teaching no little girls how to suck dick."

"Bitch you have lost your damn mind with your nasty ass. There is no way possible I will ever leave my kids alone with you," Sheri giggled into the building. "I can only imagine the charges the Department of Social Services and District Attorney would read off to me. Who was that in the van?" She queried. Gracefully turning to greet her staff members in the foyer.

"He's just a guy I met at the post office a few minutes ago. I had a flat and didn't feel like waiting on the repair service. So, he agreed to bring me if I agreed to give him a personal tour of the gallery. I know he was referring to my pink canoe, but I gave him a tour of the art gallery instead. He's very nice and owns a mobile wig wash-n-repair company," Naomi announced as Sheri fell into her market advisor's arms, laughing.

"Girl, you meet the most unusual men in life," Sheri teased, trying to stop laughing. "Yesterday, you introduced me to an organic onion grower, the day before that you had dinner with a guy who gives private dances to midgets, and today it's a male seamstress. I can only imagine the next title."

Sharing the news of her having twins with everyone in the office, seemed to make the moments of her day far more pleasant, especially with Heidi taping the ultrasound to a wall in the gallery and labeling it "Heartbeats" by Sheri Johnson.

She was unable to stop Naomi from turning the office into a disco hall, to celebrate the heartbeats of the twins. Heidi blasted music on Alexa as Naomi danced throughout the building more provocative than a desperate stripper, which others joined in like falling dominoes. Instead of allowing the excitement to completely deter her from her responsibilities, Sheri snuck away to her office to bask in her own serenity. She couldn't stop contemplating decor ideas for the twins' nursery, while wishing that she knew their gender so that she could go on a shopping spree.

Browsing the net, watching hilarious videos of baby incidents, Sheri hoped the babies weren't affected in any way by her uncontrollable laughter. The thought of waking up to the twins' powder painting her entire kitchen with flour and cornmeal, only to claim they were trying to make pancakes or to discover them trying to have a ketchup and mustard fight after drawing on the cabinets with peanut butter and spilling all the cooking oil on the floor, encouraged Sheri to have some child prevention locks on cabinets and gates added to the house once they started crawling — Especially, after seeing the video of one child putting hair relaxer in his drunk mother's hair as she slept.

"Come in Naomi," she uttered recognizing her distinct knock at the door.

Holding a brown sugar peach cake with a number two candle burning in the middle, Naomi entered, smiling and poised to discover what Sheri's been in her office doing, while everyone else is dancing, drinking, and enjoying the food from Eatery.

"Are you okay?" She questioned, setting the cake on her desk and cutting them both a slice.

"Yes, I'm fine. I really haven't begun to experience the symptoms of pregnancy other than a little nausea at times, but I'm trying to prepare myself, mentally. Hmmm, this is so damn good, Naomi. My babies are going to have cavities in the womb," giggling at her own comedic hysterics without missing an opportunity to stuff her mouth with another piece of cake.

Chewing and eyeing her best friend, Naomi sat before her wondering how she truly could be smiling after exiling her mother and father from their grandchild's life.

"I called your parents and advised them of the good news," she confessed while observing her reaction. "Both said congratulations and that they love you as well."

"That wasn't your place Naomi," Sheri scolded nonchalantly. "I understand what you're trying to do, but please don't. Randle and I are at a good place right now, and I don't need you complicating things even though your intentions are good."

"You are a successful businesswoman, yet Randle has no job besides his abuse upon you. You have your own house, but he lives with you and owns nothing. Your parents groomed us to stand upon unity of family, forgiveness, love, and respect. Whereas his parents are more of a mystery than he really is. He abuses you, neglects you, constantly takes you for granted, and undoubtedly shows in all of his actions that you are only a priority when he needs something. Sheri, this is a very joyous moment, but the truth is something a blind man can see wearing a blindfold. Randle offers you nothing besides some tongue and dick, which you can buy better ones online at a discount under my membership. Yet, you are willing to separate all ties with your family for him," Naomi lectured. "Why?"

"Sheri, you know I love you, and you know in your heart the decision that you're making is not right. How do you think your parents feel being outcasts to you right now, and for no other reason than for you to please a barbaric man? Especially, given that you're the first of their kids to grant them a grandchild. How would you feel if your twins did you the same way? Karma is a bitch!"

"Please leave my office if this is what you came in here for Naomi, because I'm not in the mood to have a discussion about my affairs. If you weren't too busy jumping in the bed with every shade tree entrepreneur that laid eyes on you, then maybe you'd experience the taste of love," Sheri implied with a sense of aggression in her tone. "Stop trying to judge me as though you are pure and innocent. "."

Staring at her friend in disbelief and not wanting to get into a heated tongue-lashing, Naomi wondered if it was truly love, fear, or psychological trauma due to the aftereffects of abuse. Rising to cut another slice of cake before turning toward the door, Naomi began caressing the crystal rose she had sitting on the shelf, then eyed the Johnson family portrait hanging above it.

"If love means losing all aspects of myself, my family, and existing as a prisoner within my relationship, then I'd rather stay the simple-minded whore you consider me as. At least I have my dignity, sanity, self-respect, love of family, and freedom of my mind and body," Naomi defended eloquently while walking out of the office and slamming the door behind her.

Seeming as if she heard not a single word, Sheri cut herself another piece of cake and turned her attention back to eye shopping the internet for baby beds and clothing. She was excited to discover Randle's taste in things and to show him a few videos of what to get prepared for when their babies climb out of their cribs at night. Not realizing how lost in time she had gotten with browsing; Sheri made a few essential calls before gathering her things to leave the office. Walking into the gallery to retrieve her ultrasound photo, the sight of it taped next to a very prestigious painting and reflecting the greatest art of life, Sheri decided to leave it with the intention of framing it later.

After jumping into her car and exiting the parking lot, she called to see if Randle wanted a home cooked meal or requested for her to pick up something, but he didn't answer. The instant desire of surprising him with something special to celebrate the twins began to warm her heart. Not knowing if there was enough baby spinach, mushrooms, and scallions to make the meal she had in mind, Sheri stopped by the store and ended up full-fledged grocery shopping instead of grabbing the few items intended. The romantic sight of a couple walking across the parking lot holding hands as she loaded her trunk with the grocery bags stirred the notion of love in her heart. She walked back to the car lingering in thought of sharing that type of affection with Randle. Bobbing to Camila Cabello as the wind circulated through the sunroof, causing the strands of her hair to tickle the sides of her neck, Sheri started to fantasize as though the movements of her hair were Randle's fingers. She wanted to kiss him, sit on his mouth backwards and feel him ejaculate inside of her, while spanking her, doggy-style.

Sheri was slightly upset, arriving back home and unable to pull into the garage due to some unknown car being in her spot. Parking in the driveway instead, Sheri grabbed the bags out of the trunk without any assistance from her white Knight and sat them by the door in three trips.

"Randle!" She yelled opening the side entrance door and walking inside with a few bags in hand. "Randle!"

"Bitch stop calling my fuckin' name." He warned in an aggressive tone without lifting his eyes.

"Sheri couldn't believe her eyes when she discovered he was sitting in the living room with a guy, ignoring her pleas for assistance while struggling. "Randle, can you help me with the bags please?" Sheri reiterated, passing him en route to grab some more, without a response given.

Knowing from his silence that it wouldn't be wise to press the issue for his assistance again, she made the remaining trips quietly, and began preparing dinner without saying another word. Noticing the stranger in her house constantly looking at her lustfully instead of rendering his full attention to Randle, she went upstairs to shower after putting up the grocery and seasoning her meat. Wearing a pair of oversized jogging pants to hide the curves of her body and an extra-large T-shirt instead of the lingerie she had planned for Randle's eyes only, Sheri walked back downstairs to cook their dinner and was deeply disturbed to hear the stranger say to Randle, "You got a bad fuckin' bitch, cuz. Does she swallow?" as she passed them en route to the kitchen, and he answered "yes" instead of correcting the stranger for his disrespect.

"Who are you calling a bitch?" Sheri challenged, interrupting their conversation. "I'm not a bitch, and I want you out of my house if you can't respect me."

"Bitch, shut the fuck up," Randle warned aggressively without lifting his eyes from the laptop monitor, shocking Sheri with his words and sparking a sense of fear, for she knew the repercussions of his anger. "You're my bitch, so you are a bitch, bitch. Now, take your damn ass in the kitchen to do whatever bitches s'pose to do or take your stupid ass upstairs."

Speechless, embarrassed, and confused, given that just hours ago he had promised to love her without a hint of abuse, Sheri eased back in the kitchen trying to hold her head high. But for him to chastise her in front of a complete stranger for defending her own honor, brought to mind everything Naomi had said prior to storming out of her office.

"It's not here. The fucking video is not here," Randle cursed turning to his cousin.

"Are you sure, cuz? 'Cause these were all the discs that were in the apartment," he acknowledged, rambling through the bag to ensure there was not one he missed.

Randle began to wonder if there was actually one at all.

"Yes, these were all the CD's I saw, and I went through everything, thoroughly, before I torched dat muthafucka. Because of you, I saw and accidentally touched shit I honestly wish my eyes were forever blind to. Well, cuz, just look at it this way — If it's not here, then it's definitely burned in the blaze I ignited. Nothing survived that work of art, not even a damn demon." He vowed extending his hand to initiate their secret handshake while cackling.

Lingering on his words, Randle began to smile at the thought of the mysterious video being forever destroyed. If only he could get some additional get back for the physical abuse he sustained. Seeing and hearing that mother-fucker cry and bleed beneath his feet is all he could envision. "Let's go to the strip club to celebrate," Randle stated, pounding his cousin, as he rose jubilantly off the sofa.

"Sure, as long as you pay me first," his cousin demanded while holding out his hand. "Business before pleasure, cuz. Why go out when your bitch in there cooking? I'm hungry as hell."

"Fuck that. We can grab something on the way or at the club. I'm about to shower right quick," Randle declared while walking out of the room.

Tasting the spinach to see if it was to her perfection, Sheri was startled when she turned around to see the stranger leaning against the wall, licking his lips, and watching her every move. Wanting to say something but afraid it may unleash a fit of rage in her unstable Randle, she continued without voicing her thoughts.

"You sexy as fuck, babygirl," he cajoled, causing chill bumps to blanket her entire body. "I must say, cuz is one lucky Georgia cowboy. What 'cha name is sexy lady?" He coaxed, walking over to the stove to grab a large pinch of sautéed spinach out of the skillet without washing his hands or asking, while trying to brush against Sheri.

Stepping back from the stove to avoid his scandalous advance, Sheri noticed Randle was no longer in the living room, and the stranger's presence had her feeling extremely uncomfortable.

"Damn, bitch. So, you're not going to introduce yourself to me?" He queried, taking a step closer, and gently caressing Sheri's hand as she tried to avoid him. "It's cool, sweetheart, there's no need to reject me. Randle and I share everything, and I'm definitely hoping it's you tonight after we get drunk."

Not knowing how to react, given the fact that Randle's an irascible individual, and not wanting to be sexually abused, Sheri stepped to the side as he advanced a third time without allowing their eyes to connect. With no way to grab a knife due to the way the stranger was standing, terrifying images of Randle sanctioning and watching the stranger rape her with abhorrent approval and twisted pleasure only to beat her afterwards for allowing it to happen, flashed and flickered in her mind. Sheri switched the stove off, scraped everything into a glass serving dish to keep from burning the meal or starting a fire by leaving it simmering. Grabbing her cellphone off the bar counter over the sink, she thought of calling her neighbor to invite them over as a means of protection, given Randle never excluded them but realized she'd been too isolated to mingle.

Attempting to leave the kitchen, Sheri batted his hand away as he reached and grabbed the firmness of her butt. She was overwhelmed by nervousness that elevated her heartbeat, causing her hands, legs, feet, and arms to start tingling. Sheri bolted down the hallway without paying any further attention to the stranger, whom was now standing in the center of the kitchen's floor, flicking his tongue, touching himself, eyeing her body with desire, and still waiting to learn her name. Stepping with a sense of urgency, her phone's sudden vibration slightly startled her as she reached out to touch the stair rail.

"Hi Penélope," she greeted, trying to shake the phobia his words and presence had excited within her body.

"Are you alright, Sheri?" Penélope asked recognizing the timorousness in her voice. "Do I need to pull up?"

"No, I'm good, girl! I promise I'm okay," Sheri assured, taking deep breaths going up the stairs.

"Listen, the concert is about to start. I don't have much time to talk. I will come by the office tomorrow morning to inform you of what Crispy Crème shared with me. The apartment surveillance cameras show Randle parked in the parking lot, waiting as some white guy burglarized his apartment before leaving with a blue book bag and torching the place with gas, they're alleging. I just sent you a video Crispy Crème forwarded me just moments ago. You really need to watch it girl. Make sure you have it before I hang up."

The thought of that very bag sitting on her table downstairs terrified Sheri. What if the police traced the stranger or Randle's car back to her house, and why is this video so important that Randle and this stranger not only burglarized his home for it, but burned it down because of it?

"Alright, hold on," she replied, checking her message.

Pressing play as she walked into the bedroom unwittingly without knocking, Sheri almost dropped her phone as she did her lower jaw. She couldn't believe Randle standing before her with nothing on, but a towel wrapped around his waist and fading passion marks all over his chest, neck and stomach. Everything, she surrendered to him: her breath, dignity, and every ounce of her will. Yet, in return he had repaid his appreciation with abuse and betrayal. So physically numb to the sight before her eyes that she didn't hear Penélope's voice repeatedly calling out to her in between Randle yelling "Get the fuck out, bitch," as he stood in the closet doorway. The fact Naomi was telling her the truth the entire time made her feel so stupid. Standing there as if life had literally stopped, the video started playing and nothing could be heard more distinctively than Randle's voice repetitively saying, "Show me you're a dolphin girl."

"What the fuck you have in your hand?" Randle asked while walking toward her with fury and shock pulsating throughout his body. Hearing the unbelievable words his voice was slurring, and the name Snowflake being called confirmed his nightmare wasn't over.

She briefly looked down at her screen in disbelief of what she was hearing, as Randle reached out to secure her wrist aggressively. The sight caused her to vomit on his towel, as he snatched the cellphone from her hand.

"Bitch, where did you get this from?" Randle cringed as his face began to resemble an inferno flame. Grabbing a handful of her hair, Randle yanked Sheri's head back as she tried to wipe her mouth. "Bitch, I know you heard me," he huffed through wired jaws, while viewing the contents in disbelief.

With no form of response coming from her mouth, but whimpering, Randle slapped her across the eye with the phone as he repeated himself. Knocking her to the floor and caring not that her head smashed against the oak doorframe, "Whore, you set me up!"

Leaning down to backhand her with a forceful swing, the sounds of the video intensified his anger. Randle lifted Sheri off the floor by tightly grabbing and pulling her hair, only to punch her in the jaw as she tried to straighten her legs beneath her. Sheri was unable to completely fall due to Randle's grip of her hair, of which strands were extracted from their roots each time he yanked her head.

"Bitch, I can't believe you'd do this to me!" He shouted, punching her again and again in the face until he unclenched the bundle of hair, releasing her weakened body to tumble to the floor.

Removing his towel after scanning the entire room finding nothing suitable to beat her with, Randle wrapped it around her neck and began strangling Sheri, bashing her head twice against the wooden bedframe.

"Bitch, I'mma kill you for betraying me like this."

Barely able to see with so much blood dripping into her eyes and faintly conscious, gasping for air, "Please, don't kill our babies," Sheri managed to whisper in between her choking.

Lifting her off the floor by the towel, strangling her slowly, Randle hook punched her in the face before letting go and kicking her in the base of her back, a precisely timed assault that caused her to lunge defenselessly head first into the wall before sliding up against the nightstand. Randle's anger seemed to intensify with every excruciating strike he exacted upon her.

"Bitch, you're going to pay for your betrayal today," he promised, moving closer with immeasurable fury stirring in his veins, slightly slipping on blood droplets while trying to throw another punch that missed.

In an act of desperation, Sheri grabbed the crystal lamp on the nightstand and smashed it against Randle's head in his attempt to turn around to hit her again. The collision knocked him out on impact, which caused him to fall like a tree snapped from its roots. Struggling to stand on her own as she dropped the remains of the lamp and pushed herself off the wall, the sudden rage of her anger caused her to start stomping him in the face in retaliation, aiding her attempt to escape and stopped when she could see that he was not moving and felt it was safe for her to exit.

Conjuring the will and strength to move her legs, she stumbled across the bedroom floor. Using her blood drenched shirt to wipe some of the tears and blood from her eyes, Sheri hoped it would grant her greater visibility in her attempt to escape, at which time she looked at his body, peppered with passion marks even on his ass. "Oh God, oh my God, how could I be so stupid." She turned, crying, and noticed her phone laying in front of the door as desperation became her survival. Unbeknownst to her, Penélope had heard the entire altercation and was still listening on the other end. Sheri picked it up, stopped the disgusting video, and then disconnected the call while dragging herself against the hallway wall.

Reaching the bottom of the stairs, she thought of nothing but the lives within her womb, while dialing the only number that instantly came to mind. The taunting sound of Randle's voice faintly echoing throughout the house as he regained consciousness, caused her entire body to quiver while yelling, "Please help me!" Into the phone.

Standing in the foyer, listening to their commotion attentively and fantasizing about being inside Sheri's tight sexy ass, he wondered if Randle would be in the mood for a ménage a trios after he finished chastising her for whatever reason had sparked his anger. Hearing the stumbling and crying coming through the upstairs hallway, he hid himself behind the foyer wall after seeing Sheri, so as to observe her movements. Physically battered and dragging herself with each step, this was his chance to explore the inner depths of her ecstasy, and he wasn't about to let it slip through his hands again. With Randle out of sight and audible range, he stepped from behind the wall when Sheri was within close proximity, touching distance. The shock of his sudden appearance widened her eyes as though a ghastly shadow figure materialized before her as an ominous premonition evoking fear pervaded her senses.

"Help me, please!" She cried as if to say, even though you're evil and satanic, spare me from what I fear is about to happen. Take pity on my already violated and bludgeoned body.

"Dick help to the rescue, bitch! I see you, ahhh, primed and ready to let me feel that tight ass of yours after all," he cackled, throwing an uppercut to her stomach so devastating that she regurgitated before buckling and dropping to her knees. "Get up, slut," he goaded, kicking Sheri in the breast driving her backwards, then forcefully kicking her in the stomach with the heel of his shoe, doubling her forward, dropping face down to the floor and curling up. "I don't want your mouth this time, just that sweet tight ass of yours."

Ignorant of the fact that she was pregnant with twins and caring not that she was drenched in blood and curled in the fetal position, crying and in pain, Randle's cousin flipped her on her back, snatched off her jogging pants, and eased between her legs before her feet landed back on the floor. Massaging her lace panties with one hand while brutally slapping her twice with the back of his other hand. He then grabbed both of her wrists and secured them above her head, pinning them to the floor as she struggled with the little strength she had.

Lowering to satisfy his craving of having her tit in his mouth and being the sadist that he was, he bit into Sheri's breast, inflicting excruciating and unexpected pain, she screamed as if she were in a warzone being tortured in a P.O.W. camp, expelling every ounce of air in her lungs as he fumbled to unfasten his pants. The blows he initiated to her stomach still had her powerless, stripped of any defense. After sliding his index and middle fingers inside of her and removing them to taste her sweetness, "My, my, my, damn that's some good shit! That's exotic flava, bitch, and you were go'n deny me of tastin' somethin' so heavenly, and it's already naturally cooked up?!" He was eager to feel the tightness of her brown sugar, slippery walls squeezing his sick hardness. Using his thighs to spread her legs further apart, as he engaged to force himself inside of her, the voice emanating from Sheri's phone caught his attention as he attempted to part the lips of her pussy and insert the head of his dick in her oil slick canal.

Shifting his eyes slightly to the side to view her lit screen, he noticed the person she cried help to and whose voice was currently coming through the speaker, was the 911 operator. He jumped off of her with the quickness of a first responder to a crisis, an emergency. While looking around, he noticed that there were no lights flashing and no blaring sirens yet. So the need to finish what he already started fueled his desires, especially with his hardness primed in hand and the taste of her wetness intensifying his yearning, but knowing that the police were en route had him slightly conflicted, spooked to be exact. He had only been out of prison a few months and he wasn't trying to go back so quickly.

Stomping her in the stomach once more, before grabbing Sheri by the hair after sliding his fingers back inside of her to taste her heavenliness once more, he dragged her weakened body to the top of the stairs, upon seeing Randle stumble through the bedroom door holding his head with blood dripping from his face and arm.

"Cuz, wha what the fuck happened to you?? Bro! Bro we need, we, we need to get the fuck outta here. Ya bitch done called twelve! She done dialed 911 an.. an..and the police bro, I'm telling ya, they're on the wayyy!" he stammered, rushing to assist him down the hall.

Seeing Sheri try to pull herself up by the stair balusters as he lifted his head approaching the stairs, "It's not over, bitch," Randle muttered while lifting his foot to kick her in the chest.

Watching her tumble backwards down the stairs, mentally injected him with an adrenaline rush, the desire of seeing it again peaked, but his vampirish hunger could not be satisfied because he knew time was of the essence and the police would be pulling up soon, given the neighborhood. Spitting on Sheri as they walked by, Randle cared nothing about her condition, as she laid motionless in a puddle of blood. He cared only that she kept her mouth shut regarding what happened, and he made it clear to her temporarily deaf ears before closing the garage door behind them.

"Why are you driving so damn slowly, suuuga'?" Anxious to arrive at Sheri's house so that she could test out her new AUG A5 on Randle's rabid body. "I need you to drive this SUV with a little bit more urgency in your foot, please. I want to catch that sucker before he leaves. These kids video and post everything nowadays, so I want to video him chewing a fully loaded magazine," Mama Lewis arrogantly stated, sliding an additional extended clip in her side pocket, while making sure the Glock 19 on her hip had a bullet in the chamber.

Releasing the safety switch on her gun, rounding the curve to Sheri's subdivision entrance, Randle pulled into the intersection, following his cousin while adding torque to his acceleration. Recognizing the distinctness of his Audi, she threw her gun in front of One Eye's face to shoot out the driver window as he attempted to pass, which he instantly batted down before she squeezed the trigger.

"That was Randle you just passed and caused me to miss out on covering the asphalt with his blood!" She exclaimed turning around in her seat to fire a few shots through the back window that impacted Randle's trunk and shattered his rear window, causing him to swerve slightly before rounding the curve.

"It would have been our blood covering the asphalt as well, Mama Lewis, if you would have fired. The muzzle flash would have burned my entire face causing us to probably flip," One Eye stated while turning on Sheri's street. "James and Aaron are not too far behind us. Call and advise them he's approaching, but under no circumstances are I allowing you to kill him while I'm present."

"Whatever! Fuckin' with my grandchild, I'll kill him on camera in front of the damn courthouse."

Pulling into the driveway with the sound of sirens heard approaching, Mama Lewis jumped out of the SUV like a military soldier engaging in combat and ran into the house through the garage, given that the doors were already raised. Seeing her granddaughter lying motionless on the floor in a puddle of blood, instantly brought back the dreadful memories of her husband's death. "One eye! One eye! Help my baby, please!" Mama Lewis screamed at the top of her lungs, lifting her head into her lap. "Please, don't die on me, baby!"

"Her pulse is very weak," One Eye announced, releasing her wrist and laying her body out properly to perform CPR. "Call to make sure the ambulance is en route because they need to get here fast."

Seeing the police lights flash through the windows as she dialed 911, Mama Lewis dropped the phone and ran outside to inform the officers pulling into the driveway about the urgent need for the paramedics. Standing in the garage doorway hollering hysterically at the top of her lungs. "Hurry! Hurry! She needs help!" Mama Lewis was not conscious of her disposition. Her only focus was getting help for Sheri.

"Freeze!" "Freeze!" Is all she heard as officers jumped out of their cars simultaneously drawing their guns.

CHAPTER 29

Anxious to scream, while sitting patiently in the back seat of the car, watching the jet slow to a complete halt. "Subhan Allah," Demi shouted aloud, jumping out of the car ecstatically upon seeing the halo of her heart appear in the doorway of the charter jet, smiling. Exposing the tone of her thigh muscles to the sunlight in her asymmetric hem, flower print, slip dress, Demi sprinted across the tarmac of the Charlie Brown Airport with her peep-toe stilettos in hand, as if she was being chased by a pit bull of the razor edge bloodline. Reaching the stairs in the very instant that her mother was trying to plant her foot on American soil. Demi embraced her with a smothering hug so inundated with love that it seemed as though time froze for the both of them. I love you were the only words recorded in the wind as their heartbeats synchronized with each breath.

They walked back to the car with their arms entangled, smiling and holding hands while Marcus retrieved her mother's luggage. Demi wished she could look into Terry's eyes at that very moment and express the immeasurable depth of her gratitude before kissing him with unsheltered passion, never exposed to another man. Bringing her mother back into her life was the greatest gift and act of kindness God could have allowed Terry to bless her with. Riding in the back seat reminiscing on the new developments in each other's lives and the things they were going to do once situated, Demi was a little baffled noticing Marcus bypass the interchanging expressway ramp that led to her apartment.

"Marcus, where are you headed?" Demi asked, curious to know why he was taking an unexpected detour without advising her.

"Respectfully, I've been instructed not to inform you of anything, Ms. Laconette, until we reach our destination," Marcus answered, looking at her through the rearview mirror.

Gently squeezing Demi's hand to soothe the nervousness that was beginning to stir because of his words, "Is everything alright?" She whispered in her daughter's ear, not expecting her return to America to start off mysteriously.

"Yes," Demi assured before leaning in to kiss her on the cheek. "Just relax, mum, everything is fine. Knowing Terry, he's probably having Marcus chauffeur us to an exotic restaurant as another welcome to Atlanta gift for you. I had planned on cooking your favorite meal tonight, but now that it seems he has taken the initiative of catering to us, I'll just let you rest when we return home. I know you're tired from the flight."

"Baby, I'm not tired at all. The excitement of being here with you has me feeling like I've been injected with an experimental adrenaline drug. I could cut the rug with you and a group of teenagers right now, whereas all of you would sit down before me. I'm just overwhelmingly anxious to meet this mysterious man who has flown me across the world, merely to make you smile," her mother simpered, massaging her hand and gazing out the window in admiration.

"Demi, Terry sounded so debonair when he called and persuaded me to come back. Which I thought was a joke until a lawyer contacted me the next morning, advising that he has been instructed to pay off all my debts, plus fifteen thousand dollars had been deposited into my account for relocation expenses, and the scheduled time the jet would depart."

"Neither can I, mum, he's truly unique and the definition of a gentleman in every respect," Demi confided while admiring the bounce in her mother's hair and pointing out historic landmark buildings as they cruised through downtown Atlanta.

Assuming her mother would be staying in the guest room until she was financially able to move out without assistance, Demi went out of the way to prepare it for her comfort, given that she was only granted a seventy-two-hour time frame after reading Terry's letter and discovering his surprise from her mother. Her mother was so ecstatic about reuniting their love, she had spent her last thirteen hours in London sitting patiently in the airport and waiting on the pilot of the jet to arrive. She was the only passenger and was not trying to miss her flight.

"Blimey, these homes are sooo beautiful!" Mrs. Laconette purred as Marcus entered the gated log home community.

Demi had no clue why Marcus was pulling into the driveway of such an awe-inspiring house, or why he was stepping out to open the car door for their exit. With no cars visible, and no one coming out of the house to greet them, Demi became even more baffled seeing Marcus open the trunk to remove the luggage.

"Now, can you please tell me what's going on?" Demi insisted while looking at him walk toward the house carrying her mother's things and politely instructing them to follow him.

Standing before the door on the porch, and yet to say a single word in response, Marcus retrieved some keys from his pocket. Inserting one particular key into the lock, before extending his arm to place the additional set in Mrs. Laconette's hand, "You may have the honor of opening the door to your new home," Marcus stated watching her eyes expand in disbelief.

Demi and her mother were in shock and couldn't honestly believe Terry had gone so far out of his way. Paying off her debts and covering her expenses to relocate her mother back to America was one thing, but to give her a luxury log home was completely going overboard.

"I can't accept this," Mrs. Laconette protested politely reaching out to grab Demi's arm, as Marcus clicked the garage opener to acknowledge the car keys attached to the house keys in her hand were for the BMW X1 inside.

"Respectfully, it's now yours to do whatever you desire, Mrs. Laconette," Marcus confirmed. "The house is in your name, which you will find all the appropriate documents inside. Your signature is required on each page where there's a blue sticker tab. Mr. Johnson wanted your relocation to be a comfort for the both of you without the joy of your presence adding new responsibilities or burdens to Demi's life. By unlocking the door, you will see that everything I've advised you of is true ma'am."

"I can't accept this! None of this is necessary, I'm very appreciative for all that he has done, but I'd feel more comfortable being with my daughter," she acknowledged attempting to turn around and head back to the car.

"Open the door, mum," Demi encouraged while smiling and admiring the beauty of the landscape. "At least walk through the house, given that we are already here. You never know what to expect when a Johnson is involved."

Hesitating slightly before turning back around and raising her hand to turn the key, Mrs. Laconette looked over her shoulder at Demi one last time for assurance before finalizing her decision. Walking into the house, they both felt like kids, admiring the decor and contemporary construction. Every room was astonishing and a masterful work of architecture that kept the both of them in awe. Demi found clawed feet, jetted Jacuzzi tubs in each bathroom, and the handcrafted log frame for the passageway throughout the house that enriched its rustic charm, fascinating. Whereas Mrs. Laconette was mesmerized by the tongue and grove pine on the interior walls and ceiling filled with knotholes in the master bedroom, but was even more blown away by the walnut stained alderwood cabinets trimmed with Vulcan 3/4" gold granite counter tops that gave greater visual panache to the kitchen.

Unable to contain her emotions any longer, while standing on the cedar deck admiring the house's mixed stonework and Engelmann spruce with oversized prow windows, "I change my mind! I change my mind, Marcus! I'm completely on board with this. It's magnificent!" Mrs. Laconette ecstatically shouted, while trying her best to cover the radiant beauty of her smile within the palm of her hands and looking at Demi as if she was about to cry. "I love the house and I will accept it only if it's okay with you, Demi."

Stepping forward to hug her mother, who was glowing as though the sun was shining on her in the shade, "Yes, it's perfectly okay with me. I'll never shield you from happiness."

Escorting them back into the living room area of the house, Marcus retrieved the documents from the fireplace mantle, and pointed out where her signature was required as she sat on the sofa in Demi's arms, smiling. With overwhelming excitement, Ms. Laconette scanned over the documents where the inking of her signature was required as Marcus retrieved his phone from the car and sent out a few text messages. Walking back into the house and seeing the way the both of them were smiling, he couldn't help but admire the man Terry had grown to become. Approaching the table, to oversee and assure she signed all the appropriate documents before inserting them neatly back into the folder, he then handed her a manila envelope that contained the security instructions on how to set her password for the house alarm, a Georgia driving manual, and a letter from Terry that she opened without hesitation.

"Ms. Laconette, there's nothing more precious than family, for a mother's warmth gives significance to the breath of air we breathe. Each time I looked into your daughter's eyes; I could see the emptiness that existed because of your absence. A void that sheltered the true measure of her smile from me. Asking you to return to America was selfish, and I sincerely apologize to you, but I'd be less than a man if I took any aspect of Demi's smile for granted. My actions were not centered upon gaining greater depth within Demi's heart. Honestly, this is my way of saying thank you for giving my life a blessing so magnificent and raising her to be a woman of character with unwavering integrity. Forgive me for desiring to see the both of you smile, as only the angels of God have. I know that was selfish of me, but far too often we take time for granted and undervalue the true union of family. Life has no purpose beyond worshipping God and no meaning when our moments can't be shared with our mother, whom is only a breath's length away.

The Woman Who Pleads

To help you in your transition, Mrs. Laconette, a driving instructor will come by each morning for the next two weeks at nine o'clock and tutor you for an hour in driving until you're able to pass the exam. During this time, I have elected for Marcus to be your personal driver, so that Demi won't be constrained while trying to focus on her responsibilities and making time for your personal needs and desires. I also arranged for someone to come by at a time of your convenience and tutor you on property management because you can't start work until you're familiar with the policy and procedures. Anything you need, just advise Marcus, and he will take care of it for you. Hopefully, the house gives you a sense of tranquility, and know beyond words spoken or written, Demi loves you, and again, I thank you for having given life such an irreplaceable blessing."

Sincerely,

Terry

Turning to look at her daughter after reading the letter Mrs. Laconette hummed, "I love you too, baby," causing them both to smile and embrace.

Standing between them with his professional demeanor, Marcus advised that a chef from Eatery was en route to cook dinner, and to just call on him if they needed his assistance for any reason.

"In the instance you all wish to ride around without me, then know that the SUV has a license plate, Demi, and the insurance card is in the center console. Once you obtain your driver's license, Mrs. Laconette, the SUV will be transferred to you as well," he affirmed and assured before heading out.

"I am so happy, even though I don't deserve all of this," Mrs. Laconette exclaimed to Demi, as she stood before the fireplace caressing the mixed stonework in complete admiration. "I've never had or even been in a house this big."

"You do deserve it, mum," Demi reassured while walking over to hug her. "You have sacrificed your entire life for the benefits of others, now it's time for you to bask in the glory of your own ambiance. No more scrubbing floors, cleaning up bowel movements of others, or having to endure brutal hardship to survive another day. This is a new beginning for the both of us. You just don't know how happy I am to have you in my life again. I truly never expected this."

Even after all the trials and tribulations she had faced over the last ten years, Mrs. Laconette was still internally strong within her 5'4" petite frame and more beautiful than women half her age. Drinking a gallon of water, a day and eating fresh vegetables from her garden was her physiological secret for maintaining healthy brown skin that always looked exfoliated and moisturized even when dry. After marrying an influential Italian businessman while in college, Mrs. Laconette gave birth to Demi, dedicating her life, after dropping out of her junior year, to raising a daughter governed by Islamic moral values but centered upon education. Suppressing her dreams to be the perfect wife and mother, everything seemed to crumble when Demi's father, whom she was separated from, died and the insurance policy wasn't enough to pay off the extensive amount of debt he had accumulated, trying to live triple lives secretly, creating the reality of hardship that became her responsibility, as she was forced to leave Demi and return to Stockwell without a degree or career skill. Saying goodbye because of her late husband's infidelity abounding with selfishness and neglect, was the hardest decision she ever had to make, which is why she promised God that she will not take this second opportunity lightly.

After feasting on a meal so epicurean that they both secretly craved to lick the Eatery chef's pans, Mrs. Laconette elected to relax in her new Jacuzzi and unpack a little, thereby allowing Demi the opportunity of driving home in the meantime to retrieve some overnight necessities.

So engulfed in her feelings, and needing to express her thoughts openly, Demi detoured from her initial intentions and did something she never expected. Waiting fifty minutes in the febrific temperature of the lobby before being allowed to go upstairs, to sit an additional twenty minutes, Demi felt like she was viewing life on a television screen seeing Terry approach the glass window to sit before her. Within his arms, she wanted to breathe and feel the thumps of his heartbeat against her face. Watching him clean the phone with his jumpsuit sleeve, before placing it to his ear, she couldn't help but wish Terry was caressing her the same way with his fingers.

"How are you, my Sylphina Angel?" Terry greeted, while pressing his hand against the window, in request for Demi to do the same.

The desire to feel her touch was so intense, Terry held his breath and concentrated to see if he could feel the vibrations of her pulse through the window. Staring at her reminded him of how precious life is, and the reward one is granted when their character and actions are obedient to God.

"I truly don't know how to explain the true measure of my happiness right now!" Demi exclaimed while holding her hand on the glass and staring into his eyes. "You honestly didn't have to do what you did for my mum, but I had to put aside my feelings and come here to say thank you in person instead of obscurely acknowledging my appreciation by phone."

"There is no need for you to ever thank me for anything, Demi," Terry revealed in his sexy voice. "All praise and thanks belong to God who tests us with the blessings He has bestowed. Having money means nothing if it's not used to make a complete difference in someone else's life. A miser gains God's wrath while trying to define their worth through Forbes, whereas one who gives solely for the sake of God, will always be abundantly rewarded in this life and the hereafter. Why should your mother spend her remaining years struggling and sacrificing to pay off the debt of a man who stopped appreciating her worth long before he passed? Demi, depriving her of seeing the blessing that you are is pure negligence I will not accept. She deserves to spread her wings and enjoy a foundation of tranquility?"

Demi allowed herself to get a little emotional, looking into his eyes and listening to the words flowing from his lips. His compassion for their feelings softened her heart. Yet, no matter how hard she tried to suppress the thought she couldn't stop wondering, to a degree, was he trying to buy her acceptance by doing so much, so early? She liked him, applauded the way he stimulated her mind, and represented a gentleman in every aspect, but her demand for self-respect outweighed everything and she refused to ever be looked at as a possession.

"Why did you give my mum a house and a SUV when your generosity of bringing her here was enough?"

"If I have offended either of you or caused you to feel that my intentions were selfishly motivated and not sincere, then I truly apologize, for my actions were never meant to be taken as though I'm motivated by anything other than seeing the both of you smile. By now you should know that I'll never disrespect you by trying to use money as a means to gain any measure of your affection. If that's the reason you're asking me this question and why you truly came today, then extinguish the whispers of Shayatin. With every home development my family constructs, we give away three homes to individuals we feel will appreciate a new start with monthly expenses that do not exceed one hundred dollars. Whether it's a battered woman seeking to escape her past, a family who has lost everything for all the wrong reasons, or an elderly person we can provide for without the extensive medical amenities that only a licensed facility can accommodate.

I gave your mother the house and exempted all expenses because she deserves her own house after all she has endured in life. Plus, my mother hired her as the property manager for the new subdivision, of which would have awarded her a log cabin at a reduced monthly expense without my assistance. Your mother didn't come back to be a burden to your growth, Demi. She came to redefine herself as well, and whether I am endowed with the fortune of holding your hand or spend my life dreaming of what could have been, I'd still help her without seeking anything from you or her in return because the purity of her love came at a cost. You make me smile by just thinking of you. Your mother is the core essence of your smile, so it was incumbent upon me to make her smile by showing that God heard the countless supplications she cried in secret. As I've advised you before, family is everything."

"You are too much, Terry," Demi grinned before blowing him a kiss. "What am I going to do with you? Just so you know, my mother accepted your offer, and she truly loves the house. It's so beautiful!"

"I know, my Sylphina Angel, I talked to her prior to coming out here. After saying thank you more times than I've heard in my life, she instructed me to hurry up and come home, 'cause she wants to fill my stomach with some Stockwell dishes, and she needs some grand babies to share the house with,'" Terry revealed, cackling."

"What?"

"Mrs. Laconette said that she's going to spend her first night staring into the stars from the lounge chair on the deck, while drinking Zamzam water and thanking God for wiping away her tears. All I could say was Al hamdulillahi!"

"I see Abdullah is teaching you some Arabic," Demi effused. "Well, until I'm married, no man will ever have any rights over my womb. So, the two of you need to talk about something other than my body next time because my purity is not a topic of casual discussion. The nerve of the two of you," she spat, rolling her eyes in distaste.

Due to you advising her of your favorite ice cream and cookies, I now have to stop by the store on my way back to grab her some peach Breyers ice cream and a pack of Archway oatmeal with raisin cookies. Better yet, I'll also pick her up a doll set, since she needs a baby to play with all of a sudden," Demi sarcastically stated, which caused them both to laugh.

"You are so silly. I wish you had the ability of seeing your face as you were just speaking. It seemed as though your alter ego was about to emerge. Don't make me call my grandma and tell her you are talking sassy to her baby! She just got out of the can, so you know she's 'bout that life."

"What's the can, Terry?"

"It's slang for jail, sweetie."

"Whatever, Terry. How is it that I get some flowers you bought on the side of the road and my mum gets a house? You talk to me about community planning and the things you discovered traveling the world, yet my mum calls to acknowledge her sincere appreciation and all of a sudden a baby conversation is sparked between the two of you. The both of you have some nerve, but you need to step up your game before I trade your jailbird ass in for someone at the care home." She joked causing them both to burst into laughter. Bloke call your grandmother. I've advised you before, there's nothing internally soft regarding a Stockwell woman. She's trained to be confident within her heart, but it's within my blood. I was born 'bout dat life as you Americans say."

So engulfed in one another's presence, their thirty-minute visitation seemed like only five minutes of borrowed time, and neither wanted to say goodbye. Staring and blowing kisses as the officer escorted him away, reminded Demi just how significant the moments are that God allows us to share with one another.

Riding back to her mother's house, while being unable to stop thinking of Terry and all he had done, she began to pray and thank God for His many blessings, which she hasn't done since her mother was forced to leave her side, years prior. Walking back in her mother's house and discovering the soft ballad mix sounds of DJ October blasting through her phone speaker as she laid beneath the stars breathing so peacefully, Demi retrieved a thin blanket from the guest bed and covered her with it, given the fact that the breeze was calm but still could be felt. Selecting the Sade collection on her playlist, Demi moved like the Pink Panther and switched their phones while kissing her on the forehead. With the sounds of DJ October grooving her body and being therapeutic to her mind, Demi found solace in the jetted tub for forty minutes before stepping out and laying on the bed, where she fell asleep while trying to read another chapter of "Mirror Mirror on the Wall".

CHAPTER 30

Blushing as she walked out of the side entrance of the school building, she was holding hands with the young man that she'd been keeping a secret. Reanna was so caught up in the admiring whispers of her classmates commenting on how cute they looked together and speculating whether they would attend the homecoming as a couple that she never noticed Cadence standing on the sidewalk watching her attentively with hidden intentions stirring.

"Reanna! Reanna!" Cadence called out at the top of her lungs, exposing a devilish grin, due to the hilarious movements of her sister's shocked reaction.

Letting go of her boyfriend's hand after nonchalantly saying goodbye and depriving him of the hug and kiss he sought by walking away like a stranger, Reanna maneuvered swiftly through the crowd not knowing what to expect. Gradually approaching her little sister, whose presence was mysterious, Cadence grinned, mimicking a videographer.

"Why are y'all here?" Reanna inquired curiously while extending her arms to embrace Cadence for a hug. "Is everything okay?"

"We're here to pick you up stupid, duhhhh. What other reason do you think mom would be sitting in the car waiting on you? Don't be trying to act innocent now," Cadence hinted, arrogantly brandishing her phone to reveal the recorded video of her prior affection. "Now, you know mama disapproves of us having a boyfriend until we're old enough to make conscious minded decisions without being influenced by peer pressure. If you want me to erase our new secret, then you need to buy me two bags of Double Bubble."

Spoiling her mood with blackmail that was never expected, "Deal," Reanna accepted immediately, while stopping her to secure their agreement before they reached the car. Extending her pinky finger, while acknowledging "I promise when we get our allowance to give you the money for two bags, or I'll ask mom once we get in the car to stop by the store and buy them whenever she gets the chance. Now, delete the video."

"No deal," Cadence countered without hesitation as their mother blew the car horn for them to stop standing there talking and come on. "I will accept my money from your coin bank when we get home and buy the bags myself. Mama

Lewis told me to be firm regarding all business agreements in life because money out of sight will always start a fight, so I need mine today."

Interlocking their fingers to seal the deal, Cadence kind of wished that she had demanded more but still felt like she achieved a major victory in getting Reanna to agree to her terms so easily. She didn't want to erase the video without her money in hand, but when it came to fulfilling a promise, she'd never question her big sister. Their mother raised them to stand upon their word and to always relay the truth, even if it's against self.

"Hi mom," Reanna spoke, getting into the car and leaning over to kiss her on the cheek before securing the seatbelt.

"Hi baby," she responded as her phone started ringing and she reached to answer.

Riding to the hospital without clarity of Sheri's condition or any knowledge regarding Mama Lewis's circumstances, Robin felt a little discombobulated and offended that the news was only shared with her an hour before by text instead of someone calling the night before when everything occurred or at some earlier point of the day. She dodged through traffic while ignoring Reanna's constant pleas for her to slow down a little.

"What is so funny, Cadence?" She questioned a second time while lowering the volume of the gospel music station and looking in the rearview mirror, curious as to why she wouldn't stop laughing.

"Terry is on the phone telling me about the man in his dormitory who sleeps on the nasty shower floor in his underwear because it psychologically makes him feel clean, and about the man who makes baby noises all day, yet prepares his covers to sleep like he's camouflaging himself for warfare," Cadence related.

"Well, tell him I said hello, to make sure he prays, and call me later tonight," Robin interjected, switching lanes to exit the expressway.

Humming her favorite church song until they reached the hospital's parking garage, Robin started waving her hands and speaking in tongues as she felt that her spirit was receiving communications from the Holy Spirit. Ignorant of spiritual matters, therefore fearful and embarrassed of her mother's interaction, Cadence jumped out of the car without hesitation the very moment Robin shifted the gear into park because her ritual always brought to mind those possessed by demons in the scary movies.

"Hold up, Cadence!" Robin yelled while exiting the car, demanding her to stop running toward the building and come back to grab the fruit basket.

"Mama, look, isn't that uncle sitting in his car over there?" Reanna assumed while pointing in his direction.

Noticing that it was in fact her brother, Robin instructed Reanna and Cadence of Sheri's room number and that she would follow after checking on him. Walking toward his car, she called Naomi to inform her that the girls were en route and to have someone looking out for them in the hallway. Unable to see his face as she approached from the passenger side, instinctually, she just knew that something was wrong, given that he was sitting by himself, listening to the Curtis Mayfield song 'New World Order.'

Constantly tapping the window for his attention, which he initially ignored, Robin felt her knees weaken while standing there, finally seeing her brother raise his head as if he had no strength and witnessing the tears drip from his chin, simultaneously. In all the years their hearts have been joined, never had she seen him so emotionally distraught. Easing into the car after getting the door unlocked, Robin sat for a moment before extending her hand to wipe a canal of tears and inquiring of why he seemed so broken.

"I feel like the Prophet Job (may God be pleased with him) in a sense right now, Robin, and my heart is atrophying. God says, *and among mankind is he who worships Him as it were upon the edge (in doubt): 'if good befalls him, he is content therewith, but if a trail befalls him, he turns back on his face (revert to disbelief). He loses both this world and the hereafter. That is the evident loss."*

"Robin, within my heart there is not an atom's measure of contentment in my acts of worship. Everything I do is for His sake and His sake alone without seeking any praise or glory from others. Yet, I sit here lingering upon those words while realizing how greatly my faith is being tested through my kids."

Therapeutically massaging her brother's hand, Robin listened attentively without wiping either of their tears, as he unburdened his chest, admiring him for his discipline, piousness, compassion for others, and honor of family as she always have. Yet, even emotionally broken, Gip still found a way within his sorrows to impact her with his words and give new meaning to the essence of a man.

With a son fighting to regain his freedom in the county jail and a daughter unconscious, fighting to sustain her life in a room footsteps away from daddy, Gip seemed more worried about strengthening the weaknesses that God may consider

340

exists in his faith and the pain all of this was causing Yara than how it was silently strangling him.

For the first time in Robin's life, she recognized greater character in her brother than she ever witnessed in their father, and it tore deep into her heart seeing Gip so far removed from the realm of calmness that is usually evident in his demeanor. Not knowing what to effectively say to comfort his sadness, given that the circumstances surrounding his kids and Yara's smile weighed heavily on him, she removed the USB cord from his phone to stop Curtis Mayfield from playing. Robin then leaned across the console, snuggling in his arms like in their younger years, to hum the Sam Cooke song "A Change Go'n Come," the exact way their mother would always sing whenever one of life's issues was in God's hands and she had no ability to make a clear difference with her actions.

Trying to regain his composure after noticing Yara approaching, Gip started wiping away his tears to disguise his sensitivity because his strength is what she relied on to maintain the balance of her serenity. Stepping out of the car to be greeted with a kiss and the gentle brush of her hand upon his cheek, Yara stared deep into his eyes while seeking the assurance he was okay.

"Baby, we all have our moments when we must step outside of ourselves and allow our emotions to bleed. You more than anyone, my love, given that you wear the weight of everyone upon your shoulder, when God has advised that only He and He alone is the provider and the sustainer for all that exists. I need you to hold back your tears for me right now, and we will cry in each other's arms once we are home, luv. There's a detective standing outside of Sheri's room whom requesting to speak with you, baby," Yara informed, once more caressing his face with gentle affection.

Grabbing his hand as she does when they stroll through the park, Yara escorted them through the hospital. She advised that Mama Lewis had been released without being charged for carrying a concealed assault rifle and a fully loaded extended magazine, due to her having a license for the weapon, but the police department is still holding her gun until the ballistic report comes back and clears it of being used in a crime.

"The law was infringed when they granted her the license to bear arms. I pray that she hasn't shot someone with her commando antics," Gip cackled.

"What's so funny?" Robin queried, exiting the elevator on Sheri's floor.

"I'm just visualizing our Harley Quinn mother from the description that One Eye gave when he told Yara and I the story of how she almost blew off his face and shot up the back of the SUV in her attempt to shoot Randle."

"What?" Robin gasped. "Gip, we all know mama is stubborn, but you seriously need to have something done about those guns before someone gets hurt. I love the fact that your men keep her actively working out and energetic at her age, but this newfound gangster aggression scares me."

"One Eye is constantly with her just for that particular reason, but I am going to make some changes," Gip promised approaching the detective, whom he advised to give him a moment before walking into the room and instantly being smothered with Cadence's affection over all others.

"I miss you," she proclaimed, immediately lifting her phone to show him a few pictures of their dog in her cute outfits.

"She's almost as cute as you," he expressed, before kissing her hand and moving closer to Sheri's bed while greeting the others in the room.

Staring at the swelling and bruises on his daughter's face brought upon vindictive thoughts he'd suppressed since leaving the streets. "I love you, babygirl," he whispered, while lowering to kiss her forehead. "I failed you once out of compassion, respect, and mercy to your feelings, but I'll never fail you again."

"Gip, baby, come speak to the officer right quick," Yara requested, placing her hand on his arm and wiping away a layer of his fallen tears.

Pulling himself away from the bed, Gip grabbed his wife's hand and walked out of the room with her.

"How are you, Mr. Johnson? I'm Detective Reed, and I've already introduced myself to your wife, respectfully," he stated while extending his hand for a handshake. "Sincerely, my sympathy is with you and your family during this unfortunate ordeal, for I am a father as well. I hate to disturb you all, given the circumstances, but there are formalities within my job that often compel me to present myself as though I have no virtue for compassion or understanding. With your daughter being in her situation and the house legally assigned to you, I'm here to ask a few questions if you don't mind."

"I understand procedures, Detective Reed," Mr. Johnson articulated, while putting his arm around his wife for support and comfort. "How may I assist you, sir?"

"I noticed in my walk through of your house, a carry bag in the living room containing videos stolen from an apartment that someone set on fire some hours prior to this incident. I also noticed there are interior and exterior surveillance cameras, but the hard drive was removed. I suspect..."

"Let me stop you right there, detective," Mr. Johnson interjected. "My daughter had no involvement in the burglary or the arson fire to the apartment, and I can confirm that by several credible sources, including the apartment occupant himself. I meant herself, sir, excuse me." He averred. "The hard drive is in the trunk of my car, of which is in the parking garage at this moment. I had it removed by my security because I wanted to view what transpired in the house with my own eyes. If you'd like, I can walk down with you to retrieve it or you can go on your own," he suggested while extending his car keys.

"I would prefer to walk with you, which would allow us to cover a few more questions, Mr. Johnson," Detective Reed concluded.

After assuring that she didn't need anything, while electing to stay behind to observe Sheri, Gip wiped tears away from her face, kissed her upon the lips, and told her he'd return shortly. Looking back as he was escorted by the detective, the visible pain in Yara's eyes gave confirmation that Randle and his cousin was going to answer for suspending her smile.

Traumatized by it all, she stepped back into the room with her head slightly lowered. With nowhere to sit due to family support, and declining for anyone to relinquish their seat, the sight of Sheri laying so despondent caused Yara to remove her heels apprehensively, climb in bed, and close her eyes as her salty tears dripped as if rivaling stalactite and stalagmite formations. It had been years since they breathed so peacefully in one another's arms, and the present bonding had her drifting off to sleep, while lingering on the family camping trip they took to Mount Cook National Park in New Zealand.

"What are you doing, Cadence?" Naomi asked as she watched her remove one of her ear buds from her ear and insert it in Sheri's.

"I'm allowing her to listen to the new Nicki Minaj album," Cadence answered, shifting her eyes to notice the doctor walking into the room with an Asian nurse following in step. "She always listens to Nicki when she's not feeling well."

"Don't do that right now sweetie, how about we take it out for the time being," Naomi politely pleaded. "Let's wait until she's feeling better, okay boo?"

"Why do you talk to me like that? That's not even how you talk, and I'm not a baby, and why do you want me to stop making her happy, Naomi? I saw Buttercup do it one time to this girl who was sleeping just like Sheri, and it made her open her eyes," she yapped a little defensively in declaring but with sincerity and genuine compassion that caused the doctor to smile while approaching the bed.

She chortled slightly at the amusing nine-year-old child referencing the actions of a cartoon character to nurture her loved one.

"The music is okay for her to listen to. Only if you agree to be my little assistant, then you don't have to remove the ear bud," the doctor proposed, looking at Cadence and lightly touching Naomi to let her know that she appreciated her concern.

"I agree," she promised hastily. "Do I receive an assistant name tag and coat like yours?"

"The coat will be too big for you precious, but I will see about getting you an assistant badge," the doctor advised while admiring her humor. "Just keep the volume low when playing the music. Can you do that for me?

"Yes, doctorrrrr ...? As she looks closer at the name tag. "Kasper?"

"Kasper, Yes, I'm Dr. Kasper." She confirmed.

"Dr. Kassssperr! No wonder you're so friendly!" Making reference to Casper the friendly ghost. And they all laughed, including an overridingly slight chuckle from Mrs. Johnson who was still weeping. "I'm gonna do that rigggght now." As she lowered the volume, instantaneously.

"Well great! She's adorable. Besides the given circumstances, how are you, Mrs. Johnson?" She asked as Yara stretched but still tearful. The nurse with Dr. Kasper handed her a few tissues from the Kleenex box on the counter.

"Thank you! And I'm okay, Dr. Kasper," Yara responded while easing off the bed with her husband's assistance, whom was literally just walking back into the room.

"Did I miss something with the laughter I heard and all these smiles?" Gip eagerly inquired."

"Yes. Cadence compared Dr. Kasper's bedside manner to Casper, the Friendly Ghost! She's sooo silly!" Said Reanna.

"Am not," retorted Cadence.

"Are too," rebutted Reanna.

"Mom!" Cadence reached out for a referee.

"Girls." Robin commanded them to chill with a glaze that would frighten a lion.

"I mean it in a funny way." Said a calming Reanna.

"Better," coaxed Cadence.

"Just your adorable nieces' baby," Yara said turning back to Dr. Kasper. "I feel like I'm mentally trapped in a maze that has me locked in a room without a door."

"The best healing remedy is patience and prayer," Dr. Kasper encouraged, scanning Sheri's medical chart while reaching out to gently grip Yara's hand in comfort as Mr. Johnson obliged her request and escorted the two of them out of the room so that they could learn of their daughter's condition in private.

Unable to contain her emotions, as strength vacated every measure of her body, Yara fell into Gip's arms as she listened to the diagnosis of her precious babygirl.

Speaking calmly as if she was practicing in a mirror, "Sheri received a frontal cortex hematoma due to sustained blunt force trauma to the head," Dr. Kasper stated. "X-rays revealed no crack in her skull, and the CT scan reports no internal damage. During surgery, I was able to suction out the hematoma and relieve the pressure mounting in her brain because of the bleeding by performing a craniotomy. She also sustained a broken pelvis and started leaking amniotic fluid, which caused a placental abruption, where basically she starts hemorrhaging because the placental detaches from the wall of the uterus and that's how a baby gets their nutrients, breathing, etcetera."

"So, are the babies okay?" Mr. Johnson asked.

"Some experiences are more traumatic than actually losing a child. We performed an amniocentesis, and unfortunately, the environment was grave enough that the twins couldn't be saved, Mr. and Mrs. Johnson," Dr. Kasper solemnly yet professionally emphasized while sharing more details. "To save Sheri's life, and stop the internal bleeding, we had to do a caesarean section, removing the babies. The laceration to her left eye required three stitches, and the gash to her head required five, but overall, your daughter should heal without any complications beyond the mournful loss of her fetuses, mentally or physically."

"Auntie! Uncle! She's awake!" Cadence shouted ecstatically, while opening the door and running out to them. "Sheri's awake, doctor! I knew that doing what Buttercup did would help. I'm a good assistant right, Dr. Kasper?"

"Yes, you are, precious," Dr. Kasper avowed motioning to the room following the Johnson's.

Flicking her eyes, Sheri tried to mentally access what was going on as everyone surrounded her with whispers of love and compassion.

"Excuse me! Excuse me," the nurse appealed as Dr. Kasper made her way to the bed. "Can everyone step back, please?"

Dr. Kasper introduced herself, then conducted a series of tests while asking conscious minded questions, which Sheri responded accordingly even though the pain medicine had her a little woozy and caused her to slightly slur her words. She was very intrigued by the fact that Sheri kept asking for someone named Randle, whom she discovered wasn't present in the room. She advised the family that they could visit for a moment, but she needed her rest.

Seeing Sheri's eyes open brought overwhelming joy to Gip's heart, which was atrophying at a rapid pace. His entire family was crumbling before his eyes, and not being able to control or help anyone had him endlessly wondering if God was going to punish him to the extent of Job (May God be pleased with him) before allowing him to smile again.

With Yara easing back into the bed to caress their princess, Reanna kneeling beside the bed massaging her hand, and everyone taking turns kissing different parts of her face while acknowledging their love. He stood at her feet, silently repeating, "I love you," until a tear fell from Sheri's right eye, and she mumbled it herself.

"Free at last! Free at last! Mama Lewis is free at last," she sang while walking into the room with James' and One Eye's footsteps behind her. "Grandma loves you, baby, and need you to get your strength back." She whispered in Sheri's ear after pushing Robin aggressively out of the way to stand by her side. Happy that her grandbaby was alive, she kissed Sheri gently on the cheek then blew a kiss to Yara. Witnessing her granddaughter's face in such an abused state caused her to close her eyes as she whispered more into her ear. "I am so sorry, Sheri. I am so sorry! I love you so much! Baby, I promise to make that bastard eat a whole clip for you."

Noticing the bulge at her back as she leaned across the bed to caress and whisper to her granddaughter, Gip grabbed his mother's arm and escorted her into the bathroom. "Mama, what is wrong with you? Are you going through a midlife crisis? Do I need to admit you to a facility for a thorough psychiatric evaluation or something? Because I can't wrap my mind around why you're carrying another gun when you were just released a few hours ago. Not only are you disrespecting me right now, but you're putting my daughter's health at jeopardy, given that it's against hospital policy for you to be carrying on their premises. Where did you get it from?" Gip asked while staring intently into her eyes, demanding an answer.

"I wasn't charged with anything, since you're all in my damn business with your nosy ass, and I'm carrying 'cause I'm a grown ass woman. I'm not about to get into this with you right now. I'm your mother, not your damn child, boy. What's disrespectful is the fact you had the audacity of going to my house and confiscating my artillery while I was being held for questioning, which it seems I was smart to hide a few pieces. A part of me wants to slap the shit out of you and dare you to feel some type of way. But my granddaughter needs us right now far more than my ears need to repel your words or my desire to exercise with you in this bathroom. The hospital won't know that I'm packing unless you snitch, and you love your mama too much to do that sweetie pie, and our bloodline don't produce rats, so fall back before I knock your ass back." Mama Lewis bickered, rolling her eyes while shifting her neck. "Bring back my guns, Gip, or it's going to be you and me in the worst way," Mama Lewis spat aggressively, while slapping his hand off the door knob, and reentering the room to Reanna's gentle affection.

Laying in her mother's arms as she did in her youthful days felt so good. It was comforting seeing everyone that Randle forced her to alienate. Yet, all she lingered on with the intent of soothing the pain ricocheting in her mind was the childhood memories of them holding each other beneath the stars and playfully arguing about who loved her father more.

Slanting her eyes to interlock with Yara's, who was wiping fallen tears in the process, "I love him a million times more," she whispered, to her mother's surprise.

With Nicki Minaj in one ear and Yara's acknowledging, "We both love him a trillion times more in her other ear," Sheri momentarily considered herself in paradise until the Asian nurse walked back in the room carrying a bouquet of yellow roses and handed them to One Eye to sit with the others before checking Sheri's vitals. She removed a heart shaped card from her pocket and placed it on the tray stand beside the bed, which Cadence pleaded to read aloud, given that it had puppies on the front of it.

Removing the ear bud, so that Sheri could clearly hear her playfully imitate the voice of Mama Lewis when she stands before her bedroom mirror, rehearsing her street Oscar acceptance speech for being a Boss OG, Cadence read as though

347

from a teleprompter, "Sheri, *Love is what we dedicated our hearts to. Love is what I feel. Love demands us to have mercy and to be forgiving. Remember my promise bitch, and know I'm watching you. I'm sorry....*"

Recognizing that the words were written by Randle, Gip swiftly reacted by stepping around the bed to pull Cadence in his arms playfully, before she could utter another word. Looking into his daughter's eyes, noticing the words resonated and how she was beginning to shake, Gip knew his action wasn't quick enough.

The audacity of him to send flowers was one thing, but to add magnesium to the fire he had already kindled caused Yara to witness a look in Gip's eyes that she had never seen before, and it scared her.

With Randle's words "I'm watching you" echoing in Sheri's mind, the relapse of fear of him playing Russian roulette or beating her again for her defying his commands began to consume her all over again. She didn't know if he had walked by the room and saw everyone in his attempt to bring the flowers or just wrote it on the card to fuck with her mind. A part of her wanted to see him, but a part of her felt like God was trying to open her eyes to something greater than the perception of love. After turning to see the look in her mother's eyes as tears caressed her face, the one thing she knew for certain was that she didn't want to endure any more of his anger and cause something to happen to their babies.

"Get out! Get out! Get out!" Sheri screamed at the top of her lungs, against their pleas for her to calm down. Tears began to fall rapidly from her eyes and the elevation of her heart rate caused the electrocardiogram to beep, signaling stress. "Get out! Get out!"

Yara sent Reanna and Cadence to retrieve the doctor as Gip respectfully asked everyone to leave the room, which Mama Lewis slightly hesitated before obliging, given that Sheri wouldn't let Naomi's hand go and demanded that she stay behind.

"I love you," Yara said, leaving, as Dr. Kasper entered the room.

Sitting beside the bed rubbing her best friend's arm to calm her emotions as the doctor finished her observation, Naomi could no longer hold back the tears that she was restricting in her attempt to be strong. Looking at the bruises on Sheri's face and how swollen it was, she couldn't understand how a love so pure and genuine could literally be subjected to an act so malicious.

"Truthfully, I don't know what to think at this moment," Sheri whispered, while straining to wipe a fallen tear from Naomi's face with her finger. "But I do know that I don't want you to leave. You are the only person I can turn to right now."

"I will always be here for you girl," Naomi assured, with a gentle clasp of Sheri's hand.

"I apologize for however my actions may have ever offended our friendship. Truly, I'm sorry Naomi."

With nothing but tears and the air they were breathing separating them, Sheri opened her bosom after the doctor left, to how she truly felt about Randle, and how her pride allowed her to endure the abuse, which Naomi remained silent upon hearing the wholeness of the truth.

"Naomi, I never wanted to be the first in my family to raise kids in a broken household. I fought to generate his happiness because I fear him far more than I could ever love him. And due to my pride forcing me to stay, I surrendered my will by trying to help him break the yokes of his upbringing somehow, while internally hoping his character would change. I know my staying with him has looked foolish and naive beyond reason, but when you're on the outside looking in. You can't possibly see the full picture, there's so much that you're not privy to, so much unknown."

Speaking, as Naomi wiped both of their faces with Kleenex, Sheri didn't know it would feel so good to unburden her heart. "I tried to love him and understand what love was with him. The greater part of me stayed, not because of mere stupidity or the fact that he's possessive, but more so because I know he's extremely vindictive. I couldn't imagine looking over my shoulder my entire life, wondering was he in the grocery store, hiding beneath my bed, sitting in the parking lot, all sorts of crazy thoughts, and for good reason. Naomi, he put a gun in my mouth and made me bite down on the barrel. When he pulled the trigger on three separate attempts without knowing whether or not a bullet was in the chamber, it truly let me know at that very moment, Naomi, that Randle holds no value for my life. I make excuses for being afraid of him, and I know beyond all other things, I'm a hypocrite to go against the very principles I instill in others for healthy growth and to stand firm on. I don't want my kids raised in an abusive household, nor do I want my kids raised void of a father. The one thing I do know is this can never happen again. I'm a mother now, and my love for them exceeds any measure of fear he can seed or induce. I refuse to raise my kids, subjecting them to mental and physical trauma."

With the falling tears soaking the sides of her face, Sheri released all the pain trapped in the fabric of her heart.

Comforting her friend drained all internal strength because Naomi never expected to discover such devastating news. Learning some of the insensitive reasons Randle had abused Sheri for his pleasure was emotionally impossible to digest, and it helped Naomi to clearly understand why she was so committed to loving him when there was actually no love at all.

Forcing her to take provocative pictures to store in his phone for sexual amusement by whipping her with a fan belt in the head to hide the bruises was one thing. But hearing the heart-breaking revelation of how Randle played Russian roulette with her life, merely to instill fear, caused tears to flow from Naomi's eyes just as rapidly as those falling from Sheri's.

Emotionally shattered, Naomi climbed in the bed to hold her friend. Never before had she truly understood what her best friend had endured to maintain a sense of serenity. Within her mind, she commissioned to doing nothing less than informing Mr. Johnson of his actions once free of Sheri's presence because no amount of fear is worth sacrificing your life for.

"Togetherness is a complement that should magnify internal joy, and not become a bed of endless torture." Mustering enough strength to wipe away her tears, Naomi opened another box of Kleenex to absorb Sheri's pain as memories of Sheri's late step-grandmother came to mind. "We have shed our last tear gurl, now it's time to regain every measure of your identity because neither your step-grandmother nor your mother raised a puppet," Naomi stated, gently squeezing Sheri's hand, as she rose on the bed to establish eye contact.

"You have always been my rock, now it's time I truly show my appreciation and love for you. Randle tries to control your mind by fear and fear alone, but we will shatter the pillars of his manipulation together. I love you, Sheri," Naomi expressed while kissing her hand. "I love you, gurl, and I promise we will get through this together."

Placing the Kleenex box back on the tray stand, she glanced at the sealed manila envelope James had asked her to give Sheri once she was conscious and thought against it at the moment, given the height of their emotion and the fact that she had no knowledge of the contents.

"We love you as well, girl," Sheri purred, lifting Naomi's hand and laying it on her stomach.

This simple act paralyzed Naomi and awakened new tears because she knew Sheri was going to be devastated when she discovered the babies were no longer in her womb, as she did eavesdrop on the doctor's conversation. Realizing she couldn't expose her to the truth, Naomi laid back next to Sheri, closed her eyes, and just held her friend closely.

CHAPTER 31

Terry beamed from the excitement of realizing the fact that he was about to put a dime on Abdullah, skunking him in the process, which constitutes two cups of water he must drink this time instead of just one. "Domino!" He exclaimed laughing, while slamming the bone on the table with enthusiasm. The competitive act momentarily extracted him from the equation of life beyond the walls of the jail cell, thereby allowing him to relinquish his sheltered anger, and bask in the enjoyment of it.

"That's enough for me right now," Abdullah calmly admitted grabbing his cup to go fill it with water, while urinating in the process. After observing Terry lament for the past three days following the devastating news which he received about his sister and feeling as though he was mentally suffocating. Given the facility placed their unit on phone and visitation restriction due to a detainee masturbating off his girlfriend and another trying to obtain some drugs, Abdullah reverted to using reverse psychology to re-cultivate his perspective and to remind him that God said, *"Verily, along with every hardship is relief."*

Forcing him to get out of bed and go shower, virtually escalated into a shoving match that Abdullah's discipline and humbleness combatted by reciting ayats of the Qur'an in Arabic which caught his attention and seemingly appeased his aggression. Contemplating ways to alleviate his mind of the things he had no control over, Abdullah elected to persuade him into playing a few games of dominoes for a cup of water per game, while fixing him a bowl of tuna fish to eat once out of the shower. Knowing fully well that Terry was fixated on beating him for once, but out of compassion and understanding, he chose to let him win every game.

Standing at the sink in the bathroom, preparing to drink his eleventh cup of water, "Subhan Allah! Al hamdulillahi! Allahu Akbar," Abdullah couldn't pass up whispering to himself as he looked at Terry compelled to glorify God for bestowing upon him the will and sincerity to help puncture the bubble of mourning he was allowing to engulf him.

Hearing some chuckling coming out of the shower as he attempted to leave the bathroom, but noticing only one person beneath the non-running nozzle and not smelling any cigarette or Kush smoke, Abdullah peered around the wall out of curiosity to see what was actually going on. Initially, he wondered after witnessing what he did, if drinking all the water caused him to become a little delusional.

Strolling back to his bed to lay down instead of stopping at the table, Terry observed the look on his face and paid it no mind at all. He just assumed the excessive drinking of water had him feeling as though he was about to vomit instead of thinking of it as actually being an issue. A part of him wanted to leave the table and annoy Abdullah with his boasting, but the seductive voice and captivating beauty of Max kind of intrigued him to watch the rerun episode of Black Sails with the others instead.

Noticing Abdullah laying on the bunk in an unusual manner without a book in his hands or hearing him recite a surah he's trying to memorize, as he approached a hour later for count time sparked curiosity far more than true concern, given that Terry assumed it was the effects of the water bothering him.

"Are you okay, akhi? Don't tell me the water has you feeling as though you're a seasick pirate," Terry taunted, posting up beside his bed so that the officers could conduct their count.

"Subhan Allah, I'm good," he responded, scurrying to the bathroom to relieve his bladder of water for the umpteenth time, once the officers left the dorm. Curious to know if he'd witness the same thing or something different, he peered into the shower again after performing istinja and wudu. Realizing it was time for him to offer the maghrib prayer walking back to his bunk, he grabbed his prayer rug from the foot of the bed and could only smile while uttering, "Al hamdulillahi," noticing that Terry had gone into his property bin and selected The Sealed Nectar book by Safiur-Rahman Al-Mubarakpuri to read.

"Abdullah, can I ask you a question before you go offer your prayer?" Terry inquired, sitting up on the bed as he was turning away.

"Na'am!"

"Earlier, I pushed you very aggressively into the bed, which I'm truly sorry for allowing myself to step out of character with you because I recognized your intentions of awakening me from my mourning was sincere. I was ready to fight you for no reason, but instead of combatting me with the same measure of ignorance, you started reciting the Qur'an and just stared at me. Why? What were you saying?"

"Character, discipline, and humbleness are essential attributes of a Muslim and man, regardless of his religious beliefs. Most of mankind, who openly embrace

Islam do not truly comprehend the reality of the meaning of the first fundamental principle, *La ilaha illallah, Muhammadur-Rasul-Allah:* Which as you know means none has the right to be worshipped but God, and Muhammad (may the peace and blessings of God be upon him) is the Messenger of God. My pledge and covenant with God, distinguishes that I will strive sincerely to be obedient in all manners without transgressing the limits when they are contrary to my own desires.

"I'm in check with my emotions Terry, so hitting you in the mouth would not have achieved anything. A true believer is commanded to be unlike the people in character and actions, which is what caught your attention. There are many people who claim to believe, yet their speech and walk reflect those who are considered hypocrites and mockers, which allows one's true religious principles to be unseen and ridiculed because people tend to view and judge religion through their shortcomings. Look around as we sit here, and you see individuals reflecting patients in a psychiatric facility instead of being reminded that we're in jail.

"The beloved Prophet (may the peace and blessings of God be upon him) said: '*Whoever seeks the pleasure of God at the risk of displeasing the people, God will take care of him and protect him from them. But whoever seeks the pleasure of the people at the risk of angering God, God will abandon him to the care of the people.*'

"I avoided your temptation because knowledge without action is fruitless, and believing or worshipping God by tongue instead of within the heart, grants no merits. To translate the last ayat of Surah Al Baqarah I recited in that moment says: "*God burdens not a person beyond his scope. He gets reward for that (good) which he has earned, and he is punished for that (evil) which he has earned. Our Lord! Punish us not if we forget or fall into error, our Lord! Lay not on us a burden like that which You did lay on those before us Our Lord! Put not on us a burden greater than we have strength to bear. Pardon us and grant us forgiveness. Have mercy on us. You are our Maula (Patrón, Supporter and Protector) and give us victory over the disbelieving people.*"

Pondering on the magnitude of his words as Abdullah walked away, Terry laid back into the bunk and began pontificating on his own character instead of returning to the book. Feeling the urge to write out his thoughts so he could properly reflect later to measure his growth, Terry leaned to the side to reach in his property bin for his writing utensils and was flabbergasted by witnessing nasty ear wax coated cotton swabs laying on the floor beside the bed, as though it was the garbage can. Irritated and disgusted at the constant squalid conditions caused by his bunkmate, Terry banged forcefully on the bottom of his bed to gain his attention.

Startled and confused as to why Terry was waking him in such a manner, he rose up to look around, assuming it was count time or they were feeding, but obviously discovered neither was transpiring.

"Yo, what's up, shawty?" He responded leaning off the bed with a passage of dried slobber on his face, mucous in his eyes, and the breath of a bison.

"Did you throw these Q-tips on the floor?" Terry asked sarcastically.

"Yes, I didn't feel like getting out of bed and walking over to the trash. I intend to take them when I get up for breakfast, unless you wish to use them for candles."

Not believing that he had the nerve to give such a senseless reason for his actions and insinuate something so stupid, Terry jumped out of bed with the intention of reviling him and maybe snatching him out of bed for being so disrespectful and nasty. Yet, he caught himself in the process when his eyes glanced upon Abdullah praying, and he acknowledged the measure of disrespect that it would be to disrupt his prayer with an altercation. Especially when suppressing his anger and exercising the mind is something Abdullah constantly conveys to him. Staring at his bunkmate, he immediately checked his emotions and spoke politely, even though a part of him wanted to roar like a South African Mapogo lion.

"I need you to get off the bed, pick up your Q-tips, and bring something to disinfect the area after you throw them in the trash, please."

Seeing the look in Terry's eyes, he mumbled something beneath his breath like a disoriented child, then eased the covers off of him and got out of bed. "Shawty, I didn't know you were going to get offended by me throwing them there," he grumbled sarcastically while reaching down to pick up the seven Q-tips he had thrown beside the bunk after cleaning his ears. "I didn't say anything to you, when you made the mistake of knocking my rag off the bed last night, and you didn't walk to the bathroom to rinse it off before hanging it back up."

Staring at him walk away mumbling as Abdullah approached, he couldn't help but contemplate just how precious freedom was and how much he missed the simple things. The audacity of him to compare the two incidents or use a mistake to justify his nastiness, was ludicrous in Terry's estimation. Images of slapping him for being disrespectful began to make Terry smile, but he knew the man would tell the officers out of fear.

Learning of what just transpired, Abdullah flopped into his bunk laughing hysterically, which seemingly annoyed Terry who didn't think it was that funny. He snatched Abdullah's pillow from beneath him and slapped him playfully with it.

"I'm not laughing at you, akhi," Abdullah expressed raising his feet off the ground so that Terry's bunkmate could easily mop the space between them as he approached with the jailhouse made cleaning supplies they used to sanitize the dormitory.

"Then what's so funny? Because the appearance of the officer working tonight who always smells like she purchased her perfume from the CDC and glued that ridiculous red bang track to the center of her head to give her a ponytail the mere length of a fingernail is not that funny!"

"I'm actually laughing at your bunkmate, not you, or her Terry. While you were informing me of what happened, he turned around at the trash can, called you a 1-800-janky-joker in that squeaky childish voice of which he speaks in sometimes, stuck his tongue out like a pouting child, then shadow boxed as though he was actually beating you up and hit himself in the mouth throwing an uncoordinated wild uppercut," Abdullah informed while chuckling.

Looking at his bunkmate with the intentions of saying something, a fight erupted at the spades table, which momentarily suspended his attention. They watched in amusement at the two young men who were throwing windmill punches with their heads lowered like women, until other detainees broke it up.

Laughing amongst themselves at what just transpired, Terry was caught off guard when his bunkmate tapped him on the shoulder and apologized for his actions and promised to be more mindful. Unbeknownst to him, as he openly accepted the apology with a nod, was the fact that Abdullah whispered in his bunkmate's ear while the fight had Terry's attention, encouraging him to make amends for his wrong with peace rather than with ignorance.

"That's the growth in you, Terry, whether you recognize it or not," Abdullah stated reaching in his property bin for his Qur'an.

"What do you mean? I wasn't going to put my hands on him, even though I did want to shake some sense into his nasty ass," Terry responded as he was flopping down on his bed and raised his eyes to scan the dormitory.

"The small measure of discipline you exercised with your tongue is what I'm referring to. Yes, it was clear you wanted to revile him, even as he stood before you and apologized for being so thoughtless in his actions, but you didn't. God says in the Qur'an, Terry, "*Verily, the most honorable of you with God is that (believer) who has Tawqa (piety, righteousness, the fear of God, etcetera).*"

As I've enlightened you using wisdom and different literature, the key to true awakening is learning to accept people for who they truly are and their characteristics without allowing their actions to affect your emotions. You can't stop viewing everything as a test to strengthen your faith, your discipline, your understanding, your patience, or your humility, because life is a test and God has commanded that He will test you.

To survive mentally within these walls means that your relations with people once you're free in sha Allah will have greater sustenance. The hypothetical, as well as the judgmental views you'd break. Your tolerance for others' selfishness or ignorance will suppress the urge to spark anger, and your understanding would become a light for them to witness, learn from, and guide.

With Abdullah flipping through the pages of the Qur'an as he was searching for a particular note he inserted, Terry commented on the words he shared. Starting to acknowledge the fact that he understood, until Abdullah interjected to relate a statement, Umar bin Khattab (may God be pleased with him) once said: "*If you have religion, then you have honor, if you have a sound mind, then you have dignity, if you have knowledge, then you have respect, otherwise, you are on equal footing with donkeys.*"

Terry, take the time to observe your surroundings properly with more attentiveness when you're not hunching that pregnant pillow of yours, and fantasizing as though you were fortunate to share an unforgettable love affair with Daenerys Targaryen. You are a man of great potential, but you will never achieve who you truly are by walking in the footsteps of your past and blowing kisses to Demi's picture every moment you are on your bunk. The moment you break the yoke of trying to live up to society's identity of you, your mind will open to greater understanding of what I'm saying and life altogether."

"Earlier, when we finished playing dominoes, I witnessed those two individuals," Abdullah indicated by pointing them out to Terry, "Literally sitting in the shower playing casino and eating cookies from the same bowl while that white guy over there danced naked in the shower. In visitation last week, that young man right there told his girlfriend the diamond he just got tattooed on his neck reflects the precious jewel she is in his heart, and it's the signature symbol of his love for her. But you and I know that tattoo signifies his love for the guy named Diamond he creeps in the shower with each night. Now, to give an even greater example, the young guy who sleeps on top of the one who sings karaoke to his wife's pictures."

"Who?" Terry interrupted, while looking around to see exactly who Abdullah was referring to, chuckling while thinking about his words and the characteristics of those who are around them.

"The white guy who cried the other day, silly man, because the barber cut his bangs off."

"Oh yeah, the one who said a white man looks like a woman without his bangs!"

"Yes! He claims the reason he uses meth to stay awake is because he hates dreaming of little fairies raping him whenever he falls asleep. People are people, Terry, so develop no expectations because only to God do, we have to answer. He created everyone unique and perfect. So, learn to look over their faults without allowing it to awaken your emotions. Abud-Darda (may god be pleased with him) said: '*The signs of the ignorant one are three: self-conceit, much talk in that which does not concern him, and forbidding others from something that he himself commits.*'

"Terry, instead of allowing the unstable characteristics of those around us to spark a reaction within you, utilize this free time to focus on reconnecting your relationship with your sister, or even surprising me with another visit from my daughter, one that I wholeheartedly praise and glorify God for bestowing in your heart the compassion to do. Your focus should solely be on using this isolation time to strengthen all your inner weaknesses and calling to remind Sheri that your love for her is unbreakable. As a playa, you know what she's going through, and as a brother, your love is what she needs."

"I do get what you're saying, akhi," Terry acknowledged, openly conveying how he felt regarding the entire matter and quoting a scripture from Psalms, he was shocked to discover Abdullah knew of. After sincerely thanking Abdullah for forcing him to get out of bed earlier and discussing life for the next hour or more, Terry developed the urge to workout, given that it effectively helps to sort his thoughts when a lot is weighing heavily on him, mentally. He stretched before unfastening the upper portion of his jumpsuit to tie around his waist, as Abdullah prepared to go offer his 'Isha' prayer. Terry walked to the table area of the dormitory to perform some incline push-ups and was caught off guard by the whimpering that he heard coming from beneath the blanket of a young man, who was forced to sleep on the floor in the day room area due to the overcrowded conditions of the jail.

With others' concerns only on themselves and unable to suppress his compassion, "What's wrong, lil man?" Terry asked, kneeling down and tapping his arm to gain his attention.

Easing the blanket from his face with the slowness of an ice cube melting in room temperature water, he gazed intently at Terry before wiping his face and sputtering the truth, "I'm scared, and I miss my mom!"

Having a sense of understanding to what the seventeen-year-old was mentally enduring as a result of being locked up for the first time, Terry encouraged the young teen to sit up, allowing him to ease beside him on the bunk., whereupon he listened and consoled him more with the genuineness of a big brother than inmate to inmate. So caught up in trying to escape these walls mentally since arriving, while using Demi as his rock and rope to pull him through that Terry subconsciously channeled the core essence of his sensitivity until the young man cried on his shoulder regarding the mistake he made prior to his being locked up. Terry found it hard to hide his frustration, after learning that the court imposed a twenty-year sentence on the young man to serve because he robbed someone for a cellphone and nothing more. Yet, three child molesters have entered his dorm and been released within the twenty-four days of his incarceration.

Needing to mend a bruise within his own heart that was long overdue instead of rising to begin his workout after promising the young kid that he would help him get through this new challenge in his life, Terry walked over to the phone to see had their restriction been lifted. Shocked to hear a dial tone and not complete silence, he called Reanna and had her call his sister on three way.

"I love you," were the first words he expressed, hearing Sheri's voice, before embarking upon a conversation that embedded his face with tearful joy.

CHAPTER 32

The awakening sun piercing through the window shades, illuminated their entanglement, as they laid beneath the sheets playing footsies and looking more adorable than teenagers in love. Sensuously, she slid her leg against his, while staring into the depth of his eyes and caressing the glow of his face with her hands. Unexpected tears began falling from Yara's eyes that Gip leaned forward and kissed until she spoke.

"Baby, you sacrifice so much of yourself to guard and fight for my happiness. You are the light of my darkness, and there's no way my love for you could ever be measured."

"I love you too, my love, but, baby, what's wrong?" Gip inquired, while softly scribbling I love you across her chest with his index finger.

Gazing intently with tears dripping on her pillow before breaking the silence between them, Yara closed her eyes as her heart wavered between the stress of a mother's pain and the duties of a wife.

"Even though my heart is atrophying because of our kids' circumstances and there's no physical way for you to suppress my sorrow in the breaths of your own emotional vulnerability, you still give your all to comfort me. Right now my tears reflect the joy of our togetherness, and how I appreciate the fact that you never stop cultivating the core essence of my intent, allowing nothing that falls upon our path of travel to become a weighing factor between us."

Leaning forward to kiss her lips, as his fingers wiped away a passage of joyous tears, "I thank God every day for granting me another moment to witness the extraordinary woman that you are, by His mercy, and to prove your happiness is my priority."

Gip woke Yara up by teasingly eating cold white grapes off the lace satin camisole covering her back to explore the bounties of love making after tip toeing back in the house that morning. Thus, momentarily extracting them both from the equation of life, Gip focused on the significance of their heartbeats with tearful spoken words being the only way to define his appreciation as of late, due to the overwhelming circumstances of their kids' misfortunes which had denied them quality time outside of crying in the comfort of each other's arms. Respecting her grieving, but not wanting to allow the loss of their grandkids and Sheri's inconsolable heart to completely shatter the realm of her tranquility, Gip used this moment to remind Yara that she was his queen. Her smile was his pillow, and the tears that were descending in her heart, which he could only see when they fell from her eyes, he intended to nurture, even though he couldn't wipe them away.

Laying beneath the sheets, while reminiscing in whispers, as though they were hiding from life, Yara tried her best to exist in the moment without opening her mind to the growing repugnance she had for Randle, what he caused and the fact that he was still free. The way Gip outlined her lips with his finger while speaking in French to momentarily console her pain with charm brought to mind the reflections of their first entanglement of love when Gip had the entire bed covered with Apricot-pink rose petals and the sounds of New Edition to stimulate her passion, whereas now, the difference is that he was only using his heart.

"Why are you gasping for air as though you need an inhaler?" Yara teased, lifting back the sheet covering their faces, while sitting up in bed.

"I...I..."

"What? Do I need to contact your doctor and advise him I just exposed yo old ass to this high octane, which now your aspiration has you wheezing like one having an asthma attack? I knew I shouldn't have given you something you can feel." She jokingly questioned, before starting to sing some Aretha Franklin, while walking her fingers down the center of his chest before bursting into a light laughter, tickled by his facial expression.

"High octane! Something I can feel! Ha! Baby, I haven't felt tightness in yo loose booty or any type of octane for over twenty years. I'm gasping because I held my breath the entire time, we made love," Gip effused, reaching up to caress her back with gentle affection.

"What?" Cutting her eyes to him with the distinguished look of a curious tiger's stare, while seriously wondering if he was trying to be a smart ass because of her statement or was he actually trying to practice a technique he read in a magazine to maintain greater stamina.

"Baby, I woke you and dropped the King's hammer without allowing you to brush your teeth first. So, I held my breath to keep your halitosis from intoxicating my respiratory system," he joked in his Black Panther accent, briefly closing his eyes, while cackling at his own corniness.

Playfully slapping Gip in the chest for his unfunny remark, Yara slid out of bed and into her slippers while looking at him as one does to a child for curiosity's sake. "To correct you, I experimented by not stopping to go brush my teeth because I know you have a secret fetish for nastiness, whereas I was hoping that the odor would turn you on and awaken the stud of your younger years, because the phalloplasty surgery and pills are only producing a thumbtack nub for a hard on, one that I often have to hold my damn breath and concentrate even harder just to spark any iota of stimulation," Yara rebutted, rolling her eyes while laughing on her way to the bathroom.

Gip loved his wife's feistiness and the sense of humor which she never deprived him of, no matter how she was feeling internally, just two of the many essential attributes that help to nurture and sustain their perfect bond of union.

Throwing a pillow that she dodged, Gip blew her a passionate kiss, then mumbled beneath his breath playfully like a kid, "You're right, which is why I married your nasty butt," Gip chuckled, assuming that she didn't hear his little nasty murmur.

Surprising him by stopping in her tracks at the bathroom threshold, she hit the control monitor on the wall to retract the curtains. Reflecting the beauty of an angel in his eyes, standing in her nakedness as the rays of the sunrise illuminated the atmosphere, Yara briefly gazed out at the beauty of their landscape through the window before turning around and proving once again that a woman's hearing is keen like a pussycat.

"Being nasty is not why you cried like a spoiled toddler on the shores of Riviera Maya when you proposed to me, or when you were standing at the alter weeping aloud over the pastor's voice. You married me because I'm a woman! The only one to cross your path, whom you recognized was strong enough to build a foundation with you without crumbling, allowing material things to complement my worth and who's trust would never derail. Unfortunately, my nasty side, you've never seen, my king," Yara asserted, leaning back on her legs, while combing the hair from her face enticingly and shifting her weight to one hip. "Because I've always had you were sprung by keeping my affection sensuous as only a lady can. I perspired like a wet seal during my workout at the gym last night and didn't bathe prior to going to bed because I fell asleep reading with Demi, so ask your mouth who's nasty, nasty boy or better yet, what's nasty now." She said sarcastically, fiercely projecting her tongue between sensuous lips. Scratch that — sticking her tongue out.

Knowing fully well that her husband couldn't counter her remarks, she kissed the tips of her right fingers, then gently tapped her hypnotic punani, turning around and commanding Alexa to play Lauryn Hill's Miseducation album as she opened the glass door to the shower, activating the body spray jets and rain shower.

Retrieving the TV remote and his phone from the nightstand, Gip checked CNN for any breaking news while attempting to dial a number. A text came through that dictated the need to make the call from his office, given the importance he'd attached to the information. Bottom line, Gip had to insure that the conversation escaped Yara's extra sensory gland having witnessed her catlike hearing. Rising to slide on his pants and house shoes, Gip walked out of the room with a sense of urgency in his step.

Securing a sim card to insert and dialing his associate's number from the encrypted burner phone he keeps in his office safe, he proceeded to sit at his desk, after closing the door. Calmly, Gip spoke of his frustration while strategically voicing the essential things needed to execute his plan, which had to be flawless, because a simple mistake could cause him to lose everything. Gazing intently at a picture of his wife holding their newborn, Sheri, after ending the call, Gip began to send out a series of text messages. His patience was wearing thin, and even though he knew only God could comfort a mother's sorrow for losing a child, comforting and reminding the two stars of his heart that they were loved was his charter and no other reasoning took precedence.

Stepping out of the shower to seal the moisture of her body with coconut oil, feeling more rejuvenated by the affection from her husband and the therapeutic water pressure massaging her body, Yara called the hospital to check on Sheri's condition. After talking to Naomi, due to her daughter crying herself back to sleep, she found an intense urge to pray after engaging in an emotional conversation that was not without Randle's name being mentioned.

Standing in the bay window in her bedroom, donning a silk flounce-sleeve kimono with an all over lace bikini set beneath, Yara threw her phone on the bed, then stared beyond the infinite beauty of cloud layers for the sun while trying not to allow the acknowledgement of Randle sending a five-minute video of himself to Sheri's room to dampen her serenity. The audacity of him begging for her forgiveness, promising never to make the same mistake again, while claiming he'd do anything to have her back. On impulse, Yara kneeled to the floor and opened her heart to the Highest.

"O' my Lord, you gave me life to worship You, but I am suffocating as a mother right now. Carry me, for my sorrow is depleting me of strength. Comfort me, for my pain is weighing heavy on my spinal cord, and only to You do I bow. Please remove my suffering, O Lord, for I am emotionally drained of life preservers and drowning in mourning. I glorify You in all that I do, and I know You are the source of everything, but I'm afraid. I'm afraid of Your punishments for my negligence of worship. I'm afraid of failing to gain the true measure of Your love in this life and the next. I'm afraid of my daughter losing hope in You, but I'm also afraid of losing sight of myself in trying to be strong for my family, when internally I'm withering with each breath I inhale.

My Lord, please send Your angels to cleanse my baby heart of the sorrow strangling it of life, and to reassure that her loss was not a punishment from You, but yet a blessing, no matter the depth of pain her heart cries of. I beg of You to give her the strength to bow to You in humility, raise her arms in mercy, and acknowledge with sincerity that the rope of Your love she's not letting go of. Lay Your hand on my baby O' Lord, for without You, she cannot breathe, see, or feel.

The son of my womb is behind bars and the daughter of my womb is fighting for her life and sanity. I beg of You to bring them both back to me peacefully, so that we may all pursue Your pleasure as a family again. Allow the sacrifice of my unborn grandkids to be the sign that reopens all of our hearts to worshipping You more sincerely, for I beg of You to grant us all another chance to clearly prove that nothing is greater than your love and worshipping You without associating partners, we shall."

Using the momentary seclusion, Gip cultivated his emotions by reading a few chapters from the book of Job to reassure himself of God's love for the believers. One particular scripture forced him to ponder on the depth of Sheri's pain, which he could never truly measure being a man. Noticing the time, Gip got up and headed back to the room while sending a coded voice text to someone he hadn't communicated with in years. Hearing Yara moving around in her walk-in closet as he re-entered the bedroom, he asked her to remove some money from the safe and place it in his tie case once she finished dressing. Jumping into the shower as she assisted his request, he thought of nothing but doing what was needed to see the two stars of his heart smile again.

Therapeutically availing himself of the hot massaging jets and the rain shower head to soothe his tension, the presence of a distraught Yara entering the master bath, voicing what Randle had done and how she truly felt inside cued Gip to step out of the wonder waterworks glass encasement in his wetness vastly shy of his tenderizing goal to console his wife by pulling her into his arms, caring nothing about the designer clothes she was wearing. With his heartbeat massaging her face, the acknowledgement of her sadness literally had him standing there feeling as though someone had taken a dull shaving razor and dragged it forcefully against his skin, carving back layer after layer excruciatingly until his aorta was vulnerably exposed. Yara's pain intensified his anger and taking a cold shower after consoling his wife availed nothing.

Drying off as Yara returned, flaunting in the white, wide leg V-neck plain jumpsuit before every mirror in the bathroom, while gaining a sense of emotional relief giggling endlessly with their son and daughter on a 3-way call, Gip smiled as he dressed but was unable to stop contemplating the words she conveyed to him and the picture Penélope took. With calmness in his demeanor, yet Randle's face infusing his anger, Gip began to think and move with a greater sense of purpose after checking his phone and noticing the recipient of his coded text responded.

"Baby, I've scheduled for the dealership to pick up and service your cars today, while also asking Aaron to chauffeur you. Unless, you'd rather stay in the bathroom trying to find fault in what you're wearing and catch the Marta bus to the hospital," Gip teased while noticing from the look in her eyes that her brain was stirring to say something smart.

"God blessing us hasn't caused me to become egotistical, and by His will, I never shall. I was riding the public bus when you were chasing me night and day like a hungry, lost puppy, in case the synapses in your brain are misfiring, causing you to have a memory lapse," she reminded him as she was walking over to the dresser, initially grabbing the key fob to his Mercedes but switched it with the Maserati's' before openly voicing her opinion.

"I can drive myself, baby," Yara acknowledged, while dropping the key fob in her purse. "Let Aaron and the guys be with their families if the office doesn't have them scheduled as bodyguards for anyone and you're in no need of their assistance. I always appreciate their presence and they know pretty well that we consider them as family instead of just employees, but I don't want him or any of the guys to sit with me at the hospital when he can be enjoying moments with his own kids. I'm not afraid of that little coward, Randle. I want to be alone with Sheri today, other than with you, which is why I've called and advised the family of my request. Naomi will leave and handle the affairs at the gallery once I arrive."

Obliging her request by merely nodding his head, Gip inserted the stack of cash in a leather pouch, grabbed the key to his muscle car, and escorted Yara towards the garage. Strolling through the house with her mind on Sheri, yet speaking of the overwhelming report card accomplishments of the Unity students, Yara was completely surprised to see five dozen Double Delight roses sitting in a vase with I love you inscribed on each rose bud once she opened the door that leads to the garage. Kissing Gip initially was merely to show her appreciation for nurturing her heart with his sincerity, but kissing Gip after following him back into the house to place the flowers on the mantle in the foyer was solely to acknowledge that he would surely need his energy pills and an oxygen tank tonight.

After watching Yara leave, Gip took a few minutes to play with the dogs then feed them before pulling his 1969 Mustang Boss 429 in the driveway as the Mercedes servicemen secured Yara's G-Wagen and car. Generously tipping the driver while advising him to make sure the cars are thoroughly detailed before returning and where to park them when he does, he then jumped in the Mustang and followed him to the expressway. Gip's heart throbbed, while listening more attentively than an award-winning composer to the gritty and thunderous rumbling echoing in his exhaust system like a storm on the horizon.

Maneuvering through morning traffic, the pressure given to his Ferragamo slippers caused the highway asphalt to vibrate as if the 375 horses panting beneath his hood were disturbing the peace of the earth's crust. Gip's libido had him feeling like a younger version of himself, mixing the southern accent of Goodie Mob with the ground thumping roars of American muscle, an ineffable infusion of adrenaline, yet could not out-measure the motivation of rebalancing Yara's smile.

Lowering the volume as he pulled on the site of the condominium high rise he was developing, Gip parked behind a food vending truck then stepped out to greet and thank the construction workers whom he passed en route to the superintendent's trailer. After receiving a detailed status update and a brief walk-through of the lobby area, Gip found out that the new architectural model design of the building not only supersede the computer images that he was presented with initially but was far more captivating than he had initially imagined. He advised the superintendent that he would be in his office for a moment if needed, then walked off alone, knowing fully well that his presence served no purpose to any of them.

Locking the door behind his entrance, Gip removed a duffle bag he stashed in the air duct, nights prior and immediately changed into the labor gear which he had inserted. Folding his clothes neatly to prevent them from wrinkling, he placed everything back inside, pulled the construction hat down over the hoodie he was now wearing, and carefully eased out of the building through an unmonitored back entrance without being recognized by any of the workers.

Walking briskly with his head down, Gip jumped into the Caprice Classic he had parked in between a patch of trees the next street over, and quickly drove out of the area using a secondary route of exit. Tightening the draw string of the hoodie to grant visibility of his eyes only, now that he was driving, Gip donned the pair of aviator sunglasses he had resting on the passenger seat, leaned back and cruised to a secured vacated building in the Midtown area of Atlanta.

Circling the block to survey the area for any unmarked cars that may be watching the activity of his associates, Gip sent a text after witnessing nothing out of the ordinary and pulled up to the security gate so that they would look at the camera without him having to draw attention by blowing the horn. Driving to the back of the warehouse after being granted access inside, he sat patiently until he was signaled in by the wave of an arm through a broken glass window.

Sliding the leather pouch into the hoodie pocket and placing the keys under the floor mat, he stepped out of the car without removing his sunglasses or loosening the drawstring of his hoodie, briskly walking with his head lowered to the door entrance of a building that he hadn't visited in over thirty years. Gip shifted his eyes side to side within the vacant structure, clearly noticing that only the interior paint of the warehouse had changed, as he greeted the toothless, one eared, chubby white man who was standing before him barefooted uttering the code word, "Black Knight."

Hearing the proper response of "Grey Swan" from the guy who stood before him with a stomach that rolled over his waist and rested on his thighs, Gip removed the leather pouch from his hoodie pocket, and then handed it over to him. After looking inside for confirmation, and radioing for instructions, he then escorted Gip up two flights of stairs, down an unlit hallway, through a door that opened to the adjacent building, and into a room that was filled with cheap dominatrix accessories.

Patiently waiting in the seclusion of the room for further instruction, Gip began to browse through some of the accessories on one of the tables and hanging on the walls while sparking curiosity as to their use. Recognizing a familiar accent approaching and hearing the squeaking of the door hinges, he placed the rechargeable magic wand back on the hook and turned his attention to the individuals entering the room.

"How are you my old friend?" A shirtless petite elderly Irishman, who had a baldhead and whose entire body was covered with graphic tattoos, inquired as he was entering the room wearing a smile and followed by two associates with tattoos on their faces and neon piercings in their lips, carrying equipment boxes.

"I'm blessed, granted God's mercy," Gip responded as he and the Irishman embraced for a gentlemanly hug before spending the next fifteen minutes reminiscing about old times and associates that have passed away over the years while his two helpers unpacked their equipment on a table.

With time being of the essence, Gip removed the hoodie and T-shirt he was wearing as instructed, then he sat on the leather stool which the Irishman had dragged from the corner of the room to the center. He then selected one of the six prosthetic masks presented to him and two tattoos. For the next forty-five minutes, Gip rested without speaking a word, as the three individuals worked diligently to transform his face into someone thirty years younger.

Inspecting the finished features in the mirror, Gip was unable to recognize anything of himself, other than his natural eye color and his voice. Choosing a face with the same skin complexion, yet a thick untrimmed mustache and beard, a four-inch razor cut beneath the left eye, dark freckles, and short nappy hair, he knew beyond a doubt that there was no way possible that he could be identified by anyone or facial recognition technology. Fingering the tattoo applied to the latex on his arm, Gip couldn't help but smile at the beauty of their work, even though he could smell nothing but alcohol at the moment.

Rising from the stool, the Irishman handed Gip a garment bag with a uniform and a pair of boots inside. Wasting no time, he changed into the gear, and shared a few words with the Irishman before they bear-hugged goodbye, and Gip was escorted by one of the helpers to an all-black DCS cargo van parked in the garage of a chop shop.

CHAPTER 33

Disappointed that Eatery and FoYo Soul were both booked for the morning, catering major events and neither could accommodate her last minute request to cook the sautéed lemon salmon with butternut squash which Sheri desired for lunch, Yara decided to stop by Organic Health on Peachtree Street to grab a few smoothies for the time being and just delegated the task of FoYo Soul to bring dinner later, which would allow them all to eat together.

Turning into the parking lot listening to Mary Mary's 'Shackles,' Yara lowered the volume, closed the sunroof, and then backed into one of the few available spots. Finger combing the strands of hair that was affecting her vision through the sunglasses while stepping out of the car, Yara briefly scanned the entire area with a panning of her eyes to be completely aware of her surroundings before sauntering across the concrete, sounding like a tap dancer in her red bottoms, accented by the undulation of her hips.

Feeling disrespected by the childish antics, classless cliché comments, annoying cat calling and whistling, Yara paid no mind to the guy leaning against the Escalade nor his associate who sought her attention by beckoning, "Miss Lady, come here," as she approached the shop. The audacity of them acting blind to her glistening wedding ring, speaking to her as though she were a child, yet grown. Yara entered the restaurant as a lady while rendering no thought to either of them or trying to figure out what the girls would probably want in a smoothie.

Patiently standing in queue while observing the menu behind two young Omega Psi Phi brothers, Yara's spirit lifted as she unintentionally listened to them communicate amongst one another on the essential principles of brotherhood and working to uplift the honor, mindset, and character of other young men.

Hearing the door sensor beep, Yara turned her head slightly and noticed in her peripheral that the gentleman who had childishly referred to her as "Miss Lady" was walking into the shop smiling and staring at her body lustfully. Rendering no thought to the stranger, yet cautious of his presence, Yara looked back up at the menu. Stepping forward to place her order, she felt the stranger's hand press into the small of her back, while trying to whisper in her ear as if he had the privilege of her husband.

"Yo sexy, you go'n make me chase ..."

Not allowing him to complete the statement he had probably rehearsed in his mind, Yara forcefully swung as she spun on the heel of her stilettos, painfully delivering a hammer chop to his forearm.

"Don't ever assume you have the granted pleasure of touching me," she exploded, feeling frustrated and disrespected, yet still keeping the character of a lady without raising her voice too loud. "Respect me, even if you don't respect your mother. I'm married, which my ring is not hidden from your eyes, so there's no reason for you to be invading my peace."

As he massaged the throbbing pain in his forearm, she rolled her eyes turning back around to place her order. He couldn't deny that her feistiness elevated her sexiness, and he was compelled to gain her acceptance. Disregarding the seriousness of her words, he arrogantly leaned forward, assuming her bubble of loyalty could be punctured as easily as that of the many other married women his charisma had conquered.

"I.. I apologize, Miss Lady, if I offended you, but I find myself vulnerable ..."

Looking over her shoulder without turning around to face him, Yara was surprised to see and hear the two young fraternity brothers defending her honor.

"Sir, it's sad when a black woman can be appreciated and respected in public by everyone except a black man. She advised you that she's married, so why are you irritating her by trying to press your luck?" The dark complexion athletic brother asked, flexing his strength with his hand resting firmly in the stranger's chest to stop his advancement.

Realizing that the Que Dogs were not going to allow him to spit his game as they stood between him and the sexy Georgia peach, staring aggressively without blinking, and the manager now causing him to overwhelmingly feel embarrassed by asking him to vacate the restaurant. Lusting with his eyes, he caressed Yara's body one last time, before uttering, "It's definitely your greatest loss, bitch," and turning to walk away.

Desiring nothing more than to leave and go be with her daughter, she calmed her emotions by joking with the brothers about how they just caused her to lose out as the stranger claimed. Yara openly thanked the Que Dogs for their support, complimented them for upholding principles, and verbally brokered a bond with Omega Psi Phi Fraternity ($\Omega\Psi\Phi$) to allow them to assist Unity, while declining a discount from the manager who offered the discount to compensate for the stranger's inappropriate advance.

After programming their numbers in her phone, and promising to have someone contact them to see how the fraternity can assist with the students, the two gentlemen escorted her to the parking lot where the both of them stood attentively watching from their car as she walked to her vehicle without the stranger or anyone approaching her again.

Driving off, Yara couldn't help but allow a smile to surface through the unseen pain strangling her heart as she eyed the brothers entering their car. To cross the path of young men, who were morally groomed with respect and principles, which they obviously defined in their actions without seeking to be praised, Yara considered it to be a rare blessing, which she thanked God for.

Trying to alleviate her emotions with the sounds of Regina Belle, Yara drove to the hospital lip syncing the words to every song that played before arriving and entering the parking structure. Pressing the button for a ticket, Yara parked on the elevator level to keep her legs from having to exercise themselves climbing the stairs. Eager to hug her princess, she grabbed the tray of smoothies, exited the car, and walked across the garage deck to the elevator a little more briskly than usual.

Greeting the staff as she passed the nurse's station, Yara was surprised to see Sheri's door open as she approached. Entering with curiosity rising in her soul, she felt relieved seeing her baby resting without tears in her eyes as Naomi laid back in the chair watching "The View. "

"Good morning, Mrs. Johnson," Naomi exclaimed, while stretching before standing to embrace for a hug, and thanking her for the tropical paradise smoothie. Snatching off the lid without hesitation, Naomi turned up the cup and drank the combined fruits and vegetables as if she were more hungry than thirsty.

"Good morning, sweetie. And you're welcome," she responded, while moving to the other side of the bed to kiss Sheri on the forehead, while placing her smoothie on the tray stand hovering over the bed at her waist.

Gathering her things to go home and shower before going to the office, Naomi walked over to Yara as she stood beside the bed looking at her baby's bruises and swelling. She grabbed her hand and shared that she instructed the hospital to change the room number and make it private because Randle had called several times that morning, claiming he was sorry, but threatening her not to tell, effectively threatening that the consequences would be worse. She expressed how Sheri naturally felt broken after losing her babies, embarrassed, and wished that God would have taken her life instead of her fetuses. Naomi also detailed the observation that Dr. Kasper noted and the advice she offered during her checkup on Sheri prior to her drifting back off to a slumber due to the medication given to her.

Naomi firmly embraced Mrs. Johnson, as the aggravating recap caused her eyes to well up. Even after physically traumatizing her baby, Randle was now trying to mentally traumatize her as well.

"I love you," is all she could think of saying to comfort Yara before letting go to kiss Sheri on the cheek, and whispering "I love you, girl" before rising to leave the room.

Closing the door behind Naomi's departure, Yara took a few sips of her dragon smoothie, then removed her shoes and climbed into bed with her princess. Sliding her arm beneath Sheri's neck while securing her hand to massage, as they laid in the morning silence, "I love you so much, baby, and you are not broken," Yara whispered in her ear.

CHAPTER 34

Looking at his watch and noticing that he had been waiting for twenty additional minutes, Stewart tossed the Essence magazine back on the table as he rose out of the sofa seat. Spending thousands of dollars to feel unimportant while trying to do the right thing was really irritating to him and made no sense, he felt. Feeling his cellphone vibrate as he approached the receptionist's desk, Stewart paid it no mind because he wasn't in the mood to entertain someone else's thoughts at the moment.

"Excuse me, I had an 11 o'clock appointment scheduled with Mrs. Thompson. Yet, we're at twenty-two minutes past eleven, and I didn't pay ten thousand dollars to retain her counsel merely to sit in a lobby as though my presence is insignificant or as if I need additional time to contemplate my thoughts," Stewart articulated while staring at the secretary looking so confused, impatient, and restless.

"Mr. Giles, I apologize for the unintentional wait, and Mrs. Thompson is aware that you are present, sir," the secretary responded, feeling a little uncomfortable due to his jittery demeanor. "Unfortunately, she's on the phone with the District Attorney and will be with you shortly. May I offer you something to drink, Mr. Giles?"

"No, I'm good, I just want to do the right thing and get this entire matter over with," he insisted, glancing back at his watch, before strolling back toward the waiting room and eyeing the contemporary African art on the wall.

Since returning to Atlanta and being confronted by Mr. Johnson, Stewart has struggled with his decision to remain silent out of respect instead of clearing his own conscious by going to the police as he initially intended. With Naomi calling every day and lecturing him to be patient, coupled with his feelings for Sheri clouding his judgment, he felt obligated to maintain a sense of loyalty. However, now that the pressure had him going without sleeping and eating properly, Stewart was seriously questioning how he could possibly continue to remain silent to the truth when Sheri's circumstances are adding immeasurable sorrow to Mrs. Johnson's heart.

Electing to retain a lawyer so that he could make a deal which would exclude the court from sanctioning an internal investigation into his past to help prepare the state for a trial, Stewart sought the assistance of an attorney whom Mr. Johnson favored. Remembering the counsel that helped his mother when his father left, he felt there was no better choice. This is someone he felt would help negotiate in his best interest instead of someone seeking to be praised and more focused on nurturing their courtroom stature by being present than effectively playing chess with the law to preserve some portion of his remaining life.

Reaching for another magazine as he sat tapping the arm bar impatiently, his cellphone started vibrating again, which he was reluctant to answer. Uncoupling it from his waist holster, merely to see who it was, Stewart immediately answered then pressed 0 to accept the collect call while recognizing from the caller ID that it was Terry.

"What's good with you, bro?" Stewart asked, once the voice recording acknowledged the call was connected.

"Nothing at the moment. Just chilling and trying to stay mentally free of these walls. I'm reaching out right now because my girl just tried to call Sheri's room for me, but the number has been changed. We tried to reach out to others, but no one is currently answering their phone, and I was wondering have you spoken to anyone?"

"Yes! Naomi called and gave me the new number almost an hour ago, before joking about some male nurse with a prosthetic leg, who had her tempted to sit Sheri on the toilet and lock the room door so that she can show him the real mother of dragons," Stewart mentioned as they both started laughing. "But seriously though, she claimed the number was changed because Randle had been irritating Sheri with his constant calling and threats."

"Threats?!" Terry retorted with heated aggression in his tone.

"Yes! Supposedly he's saying she better keep her mouth shut regarding what happened at the house or there will be further punishment. Naomi said the thought of further retaliation is crushing Sheri's will to exist because she fears he will never let go and, for certain, he'll eventually get angry and beat her again. The number is in my car, which I can't give to you at the moment because I'm in my lawyer's office."

The nerve of Randle threatening his sister merely days after almost taking her life, as he did their kids, caused anger to erupt deeply inside of him in a way he had never felt before. Knowing how devastated and emotionally drained Sheri already was, only made it worse. The ability of causing her to laugh before going to bed las night was a blessing that lifted his spirit, which now felt like an inferno.

"I should have broken that fool's neck when I had the chance."

"Don't start thinking like that, bro, because it would have only made the situation worse. I'm furious too, more so at myself for the selfish choice I made that removed us both from her life. But we have to focus on comforting her and your mom right now, not allowing our anger to cloud our judgment, which is why I'm meeting with my lawyer."

"Honestly Stewart, you're right, but what are you talking about?"

"I'm talking about facing and handling my responsibilities as a man. Your family needs your presence right now more than anything, which is why I retained my mom's old attorney, Mrs. Thompson, because I need to make things right."

"Stewart, have you lost your damn mind?" Terry roared into the phone without trying to jeopardize himself by saying too much. "I have a hearing scheduled in two days and you want to cleanse your conscious now, which could complicate things even worse. What is wrong with you? I thought we talked about this!"

"No, bro, holding on to the truth is tormenting me, Stewart asserted as he was getting a little emotional. I've seen your sister and your mother, as you have not, and both need a reason for a smile to blossom in their heart, especially your mother, considering the countless things she has sacrificed for the benefit of all three of us."

"How can there be a right solution with either of us trapped within this dungeon of hell and torment? Why do you honestly think that would comfort my mom's heart, when she views you as a significant part of our family?"

"Terry, I've wrestled with this far more than you can imagine. I've listened to your father, Naomi, and you regarding this issue, yet my guilt subconsciously has become a burden too heavy to bear. I understand the detriment of my actions, but last night I prayed to God with tears falling from my eyes. The weight of responsibility is too heavy for me to suppress, whereas my love and respect for your parents is more significant than my sorrow. I asked God to ease my hardship and to guide my footsteps so that there can be no wrong in my decision, especially when He says always speak the truth even if it's against your own self."

"Stewart, please leave that office and go home, I'm begging you. I know your emotions are spiraling right now, but how do you think Sheri would feel, given what she is already going through?" Knowing of his secret love for Sheri, Terry tried to seed a thought that would be effective in causing him to suspend his intentions. "Just as you feel my mother needs a relief in her heart, Sheri does as well. How do you think my sister would react, or feel, to lose you right now? Don't you honestly think she has endured enough, mentally and emotionally?"

"Only God can answer that, but I do know from talking to her that you are standing beside her bed would awaken her smile, which this entire ordeal has taken away. Bro don't look at my actions as though they're selfish or of those that will bring greater complications. God is the best of planners and the best mender of affairs."

"Stewart, I hear you, but hear me right now. Please don't do this. Love my family the way you love us all by not making a decision you can never turn away from."

"Terry, my attorney has just walked out of her office and is signaling for me to come over, so I have to go bro, but I need you to respect my decision and find peace in your heart from this profound statement, because I have after reading the book passage of a prominent scholar a few times this morning."

Retrieving and unfolding a piece of paper from his wallet, while informing the attorney to give him one minute by raising his index finger, Stewart started reading.

"Ibn Qayyim (may God be pleased with him) said: *'When the slave wakes up as the night encloses him and his only concern is God and how to please and obey Him, then God takes upon Him to fulfill all of his needs and remove from him all that causes him anxiety. God also makes his heart free to love Him only, his tongue free to remember Him only, and his body free to serve Him only. However, when a slave of God wakes up when the night encloses him and his main concern is the world, God will make him bear the burdens of its anxiety, grief, and hardship. God will entrust him to his own self, and He will make his heart busy, sealing it from His love since it will be preoccupied with love for creation. God will keep his tongue from His remembrance because it will be kept from obedience since it will be enslaved by its desires and services. And he will toil like a beast of burden toils in the service of another. And all who turn away from the worship, obedience and love of God will be put into trial with the worship, service, and love of creation.'* "

"God also says: *'And whoever turns away (blind himself) from the remembrance of the Most Gracious, we appoint for him Shayatin to be a Qari (an intimate companion) to him.'*"

"I don't want Shayatin as a companion, Terry, nor do I wish to keep fighting within myself to please everyone but God. I love you, bro," were Stewart's last words before disconnecting the line, attaching the phone back to the clip fastened to his pants, and walking over to formally greet Mrs. Thompson with a handshake.

"Good morning!"

"Good morning, Mr. Giles, and I do apologize for the unexpected wait," Mrs. Thompson expressed, removing her hand and escorting him to a chair in her office. Arranging a few files on her desk prior to sitting down, she grabbed a handheld portable recorder and pressed record while opening a folder with his name on it.

"This is attorney Shirley Thompson, and I'm currently present with, Mr. Giles, whom I ask to state his name for the record on this date of ..."

"My name is Steward Giles," he confirmed staring at her, while picturing Mrs. Johnson and Sheri in his mind, smiling as they embrace Terry surprised to see him.

"Mr. Giles, I need you to clearly understand that everything you share with me remains confidential and I will pursue the best possible deal I feel the District Attorney can offer. I am recording our conversation to have full and adequate depth of your testimony, so that there will be no weakness on my part in representing you."

"I understand and approve," Stewart acknowledged removing his vibrating phone to power it off, after looking at the screen and seeing that it was Terry calling again.

"Are you currently under the influence of any drugs, Mr. Giles?"

"No, ma'am!"

"When was the last time you drank alcohol, Mr. Giles?"

"A few days ago, three Hennessey shots if I'm correct."

"Has anyone coerced you into coming to my office today, forced you in any way, or promised you anything, Mr. Giles?"

"No, ma'am. I'm here on my own recognizance to convey the truth."

"Now, when we initially spoke, you indicated that you have knowledge of a double homicide that happened six years ago off Campbellton Road, where the weapon used to facilitate the crime is located, who actually committed the two murders, and that someone is currently being wrongly accused for this horrific act, whom you wish to have released with all charges dropped for the disclosure of everything."

"Yes, ma'am. That's correct."

"Well, in speaking to the District Attorney a moment ago, he acknowledged that he would be willing to draft a formal agreement in order to drop all charges and release the wrongly accused inmate you are referring to, granted the wrongly accused had no involvement in the facilitation of the crime, your story is accurate, you provide the weapon used in the murder, the actual perpetrator is arrested, and you testify under oath. At the moment, no precise deal can be made because the nature of the double homicide is unknown, but the District Attorney confirmed a deal will be placed on the table granted you fully cooperate."

"I understand, Mrs. Thompson, and I accept the terms you have presented."

"Okay then. Well, let's start with who was murdered by whom, and all that you specifically know of the crime, Mr. Giles."

"Yes, ma'am! The name of the two individuals are ... "

CHAPTER 35

Lingering in thought on the last images he had of his wife and daughter as the annoying voice of the portable GPS program instructed him to exit the highway onto Tara Blvd., Gip switched lanes and drove up the ramp. Following the directions attentively, turning left and right with caution so as not to make a mistake, he cruised into the subdivision and parked in front of the townhouse that one could tell was owned by a cat lover.

Arriving approximately sixteen minutes ahead of schedule, Gip sat patiently for a hundred and fifty seconds, scanning the homes in the cul-de-sac while faking as though he was checking paperwork. Re-tightening the straps of his gloves as he stepped out of the van, he began strolling around the vehicle with a distinguished limp in his left leg to open both doors at the rear. Wasting time by shifting the boxes that he arranged to have scattered on the floor as if he were searching for a particular package which the delivery sheet attached to his clipboard required, Gip removed one and sat the box on the ground.

Hearing the sound of the neighbor's door close, he turned around and politely greeted the stranger. Speaking with a high pitched southern drawl to disguise his voice, Gip waved the peace sign with his fingers as the stranger strolled toward the motorcycle parked in the driveway while observing him as though he expected a delivery.

"Good afternoon, sir! Are you Mr. Clipper Faggyon?"

"Good afternoon, and no." He replied, waving unlike that of a straight man, yet pointing toward the adjacent townhouse as he got on his bike and inserted the key, "Mr. Faggyon is my neighbor, and from the look of things, he's at home."

"Thank you sir," Gip expressed limping around to lock the vehicle while leaving the back doors open for the neighbor to clearly see that he was alone and there was nothing inside the van but packaged boxes.

Returning to the rear as the stranger drove away, Gip removed an additional small box from the cargo, sat the clipboard on top of them both so that he could easily lift everything without discomfort, then limped toward the house after closing and locking the rear door. Extending a finger to press the doorbell twice without lowering the packages, Gip utilized the time to scan the surrounding area again. With nothing and no one visibly moving or heard besides the birds and the therapeutic sounds of nature, he pressed the bell once more and could hear movement inside as he listened attentively.

"Who is it?" A squeaky voice questioned from behind the blinds of a side window.

Taking a few steps backwards so that he could be visibly seen, Gip turned his head toward the window to his left and politely introduced himself.

"Good afternoon sir," he greeted, continuing to speak with a high pitch southern drawl. "Sorry to disturb you if I have by any chance, but I have a scheduled delivery for Mr. Clipper Faggyon. I'm an employee of Dynamic Carrier Services, and I can slide my identification badge beneath the door, if you'd like to call the office and confirm my identity and the delivery sir."

Seeing the blinds move, and hearing no further words, Gip knew his pitch was effective when he started to hear the clicking sounds of locks being removed and the front door swing open.

"I'm Mr. Faggyon," a slender white pale bodied gentleman acknowledged, while standing in the doorway wearing nothing but a pair of blue and yellow trimmed briefs with a dinosaur print, one black sock, and holding a beer can in hand.

With a burst of adrenaline flowing through his veins, as though he were testing the killer instinct of an Aston Martin AM-RB 003 at the iconic and fatally dangerous Nürburgring Nordschleife Racetrack in Nürburg, Germany, he was poised to drop the packages and break every bone in Clipper's body. On track to rip through Clipper top to bottom, Gip stabilized maintaining his sense of discipline standing before the violator, who had no knowledge that his life was dangling by a spider's web on the most dangerous racetrack in the world. Lowering the boxes to the ground, while listening attentively for the distinct sound of another's presence, he handed Clipper the clipboard to sign the attached document and gazed beyond him looking for the physical or shadow movement of anyone.

Swallowing the remainder of his beer, then throwing the empty can over his shoulder without a sense of concern where it fell, Clipper tried to scribble his name, but no ink released from the pen Gip provided. Curious to know what was in the boxes, given that the paperwork didn't acknowledge any details, he shook the unusable pen, tapped it against the door frame a few times, and rubbed the tip of it against his tongue, but still no ink was extracted.

"I apologize to you, Mr. Faggyon, for the inconvenience and my unprofessionalism, but is there by any chance you might have an ink pen to write with and a picture ID to confirm your identity, which I shoulda requested for in the first place?" Gip disguised inarticulately, watching his every movement.

"Sure, give me a minute," he slurred, walking away from the door without closing it behind him.

Purposely using the inkless pen as a means of distraction to gain greater insight of what may be going on inside, Gip grabbed the boxes and sought entry before Clipper was out of sight as he ascended the stairs for identification.

"Mr. Faggyon, would you like for me to bring the packages inside for you as I wait, sir?"

"Sure, why da fuck not?! Thank you boy! Just place them wherever, if you don't mind."

Easing inside, Gip limped to the living room and sat the delivery on the floor beside a stolen park bench, which Clipper probably considered a sofa that was covered by a green sheet, heavily stained with multiple grease spots. Observing every visible room while waiting, he eyed the countless pictures along the wall, tables, and shelves of the same woman whose smile naturally reflected a visual of heaven and assumed the mesmerizing beauty was his wife as he turned to watch Clipper descend the stairs.

Jumping off the last few steps and into the kitchen, as if everything in between was a bottomless pit of lava, Clipper grabbed another beer from the refrigerator without extending the courtesy and walked back in the living room smiling after taking a few sips.

Needing to make sure no one was present before he made his move, and how to react if someone was, Gip commented on the pictures just to gain a response.

"Mr. Faggyon, I mean no disrespect, but you are a very lucky man, and I hope you don't take your wife for granted like so many of us do. You should call her down to open the delivery, that way you witness her smile in unexpected fashion."

Bursting into laughter as he approached and stopped before Gip, indicating the document was signed, he extended his license with the clipboard. Clipper's entire demeanor changed as he turned his head to gaze at a few pictures on the wall to his right, while transforming as though he was now in a hypnotic trance with the glow of love sparkling in his eyes. With the smile of happiness expanding across his face, and seemingly moving as though he could feel butterflies walking within his body, he pressed the clipboard against his chest and spoke from the purity of his heart.

"I wish a woman was upstairs, let alone that perfect specimen. Oooooh boy, you have no earthly idea how she makes my heart jump, like a 5150 Case Tractor whenever her footsteps tread my thoughts. I love that woman far more than I love my own life. I wish ... I wish, and I literally mean with every fiber of my being, I wish I was married to that grown man's dream in these pictures," he expressed as he was walking over to lift one of the framed portraits from the fireplace mantle as he kissed it before blowing passionate kisses to several others. "Just looking at her exotic ass makes me feel as though I have the world by the tail. I know you may think I'm crazy for having a shrine of Charlize Theron, but how can a man not put his inner demons aside for a woman so ravishing. I'd run through a herd of starving wild boars with a backpack of fresh vegetables just to breathe the air from the crack of her ass. I'm so in love with everything about her that I can't walk into a room without seeing her smile, nor can I look at another woman in any respect without envisioning her altogether, except maybe this one angel of a hot tamale I kinda got a taste of recently that could probably erase every memory in my hard drive of Charlize, but yeah ..." Momentarily suspended in a fantasy, Clipper caressed a portrait on the wall with his fingers, then turned his attention back to Gip as he re-approached.

Receiving the answer, he sought, Gip gazed intently at Clipper extending the clipboard which he made no movement to obtain.

"Dick rescue to the help, bitch!"

"What?" Chuckling at the words Gip spoke as though they were amusing, Clipper had no knowledge who was actually standing before him. Gip's secret intentions, nor the fact he was repeating his own words, although Gip did say them somewhat out of order from his "Dick help to the rescue, bitch!"

"Dick rescue to the help, bitch!" Gip reiterated, vigorously.

Curious to know what the delivery guy meant, repeating the awkwardly offensive phrase, Clipper pondered as he took a few swallows of his beer and advanced a step closer, while still extending the clipboard.

Realizing that he was surfing his thoughts for the exact reason the words were spoken, and his mouth was parting to say something he didn't wish to hear as he stood clueless in precise striking distance, Gip threw a lighting quick right hook that collided with his temple, instantly causing his knees to buckle, as he unconsciously toppled into the glass table that broke his fall. Moving swiftly, Gip ripped open the top box and removed a roll of duct tape before turning to bend down, as Clipper breathed peacefully on the glass with his eyes closed, bleeding profusely, due to the multiple lacerations to his arm, face, and back. Gip cupped his neck with one hand, while grabbing his wrist with the other and lifted him as broken glass particles sprinkled from skin and clothing. Dragging him over to the park bench, Gip quickly taped his mouth shut by encircling the entire head twice to ensure that it wasn't easily removed, and no cries could be heard. Backhanding him with immeasurable aggression until his eyes reopened, Gip removed a picture of Sheri from his shirt pocket and dangled it before his eyes, which expanded as though he had witnessed the Angel of Death before him, recalling that he had actually spat those words in different order to his cousin's bitch before attempting to rape her. "A taste of this angel of a hot tamale, your despicable douche bag?!" Gip rhetorically asked?

Flashes emblazoned his thoughts of the countless tears he had wiped from his wife's face, the immeasurable sorrow stirring in her heart, the physical trauma his princess endured, the emotional distraught of losing her babies which Sheri is cursed with when all she sought was his help. And the sickening fact that he tried to dishonor his baby girl by attempting to rape her, Gip unleashed an onslaught of havoc, throwing fracturing and bone breaking punches to his face as he momentarily drifted into a fugue state.

Begging for mercy beneath the duct tape that went unheard and unable to defend himself against the barrage of punches and kicks Gip was engaging to his body as though he had volunteered to be an experimental torture victim for the CIA, Clipper lost all self-will to exist, while trying his best to say I'm sorry aloud, just loud enough to be understood with his mouth taped and jaw destroyed.

After stomping him in the chest to the extent that it was visibly concave, indicating his ribs were broken, Gip glanced at his watch to make sure he was staying within the timeframe he set for himself. Walking into the kitchen to grab two chairs from the table, as Clipper lay fighting for oxygen, Gip literally couldn't believe this fool had a table cloth, apron, and dish towels custom made with Charlize Theron's picture on them as well.

Dragging the chairs back into the room, he sat them side by side at his feet. Caring not about the cries of excruciating pain bellowed from behind the tape as he secured his arms above his head to the park bench, he quickly ducts taped his feet to the legs of both chairs. With time being of the essence, Gip opened the bottom box he brought in the house and removed a 3L cryogenic container of liquid nitrogen, a hazmat suit, and a pair of cryogenic gloves which he eased on his hands without removing the pair he was wearing. Watching Clipper out of his peripheral, as he set the 3L container of liquid nitrogen between his shivering legs, he could see the fear engulfing his entire body.

"Every woman is perfect, regardless of her physical beauty or characteristics because God created her as a blessing for life to honor, not rape, Clipper," Gip articulated, while staring into his teary eyes with heated aggression. "I refuse to allow you the joyful pleasure of disrespecting or hurting another woman as you defiled my daughter. A man who raises his hand to a woman is just as much a scum to the earth as a man whom attempts to rape her out of selfish ignorance, aggressively defiling her body due to the disease rooted deeply in his heart. The only cure for cancer is to cut it out, which I shall, given that you've caused me to step out of my preferred element," Gip calmly stated.

"Since the woman you and your cousin abused must now spend the remainder of her life traumatized and emotionally broken due to the miscarriage y'all inflicted upon her, Clipper, it's only fair that you spend the remainder of your life regretting the very moment you stopped respecting women for the immeasurable blessing they are."

Speaking not another word as Clipper labored for air, mumbled to deaf ears, and struggled to break free of the restraints to no avail, Gip eased into the protective hazmat suit he removed from the box, covered both of their faces with protective masks, then carefully poured the liquid nitrogen onto Clipper's forearms, hands, legs, and feet. Wasting no time to render the full punishment of his verdict, Gip reached back into the box after resealing the container and retrieved a 12.5" American Eagle Dragon Kukri. Swinging with aggression that seemed as if he was chopping off the hindquarters of a deer, he had frozen, Gip sliced through his pathetic body with the artistic precision of a butcher. Severing both arms an inch below the elbows and both legs precisely the same just below the knee, the malice beauty caused him to banish a smile.

Gip pulled down Clipper's briefs while he was passed out from the shock of draconian pandemonium inflicted. Pouring a full cup of liquid nitrogen into a Styrofoam cup, retrieved from the box, he thoroughly coated Clipper's penis and balls before slicing them using the kukri as well. Moving swiftly to remove the frozen appendages taped to the chair's legs, Gip then laid them side by side executing the distinct charter to shatter each by stomping them with the souls of his boots, pummeling them into oblivion. Feeling no remorse for stopping him from ever hurting another woman but knowing he would have to beg God for forgiveness, Gip stared briefly at his artwork before removing Clipper's ventilation mask. Lowering to slice the duct tape bounding his mouth, Gip strategically extracted his tongue with swift swing of the Kukri, to prevent him from ever speaking another word.

Gathering the clipboard and other items, while stepping out of the hazmat suit, Gip placed everything back inside the big box. To assure he was still breathing, Gip checked the pulse of the coward who would now be known to the world as "Clipped" before preparing to lift the box and leave the house. He was astounded to realize that he was ahead of his own schedule. Checking the time, Gip smiled at discovering that "Clipped" had a highly elevated but stable heart rate. Assured that the toxic waste of life would not bleed out before help arrived, he grabbed two framed pictures of his goddess from the mantle, laid one on his chest and the other beside his head, while mumbling. "No more 'Dick rescue to the help for you bitch!"

Turning the doorknob lock so the door would secure behind his exit, Gip briskly walked to the rear of the van, opened the door and threw the boxes inside. Climbing into the driver's seat, and inserting the key in the ignition, he removed a phone from the center console as he pulled off. Using a computerized female voice from an app he downloaded to the phone, he dialed 911 and informed the dispatch operator of Mr. Faggyon's address and that an ambulance was urgently needed because a man had been viciously mutilated but still had a pulse.

Removing the sim card and battery from the phone after hanging up, Gip cruised back to the warehouse thinking about Randle and the picture Penélope took. Walking through the garage area admiring the new set-up after changing back into his clothes, Gip patiently watched as the worker's pressure washed the color off the van, then strolled over and placed the logo stickers in the same plastic barrel of hydrochloric acid he threw the clothes, phone, SIM card, prosthetic work, and other items he used at the house into.

With his hoodie pulled tight and wearing his Ray ban Aviator sunglasses again, Gip drove back to the construction site the same way he left, while listening to Young Jeezy as icing on the cake to ease his mind as if his masterful work wasn't soothing enough.

CHAPTER 36

Cradled by the smooth fabric of a freestanding hammock with the skies aflame as the morning star broke free of the clouds, Randle physically bathed in the therapeutic rays to achieve the perfect suntan. He rotated his body side to side every twenty minutes, while intentionally paying his ex's son no mind. With the boy repeatedly tapping his arm and cheerfully harassing him to throw a pass, every other solo toss and catch or miss of the football, Randle was starting to feel annoyed. The relaxing Randle had no desire to be babysitting, let alone oblige this pint-sized menace, interfering with his peace at the moment.

Disturbed by the fact that Sheri's hospital room phone number had changed, he no longer had access to any of her accounts or the house, and feeling as though her family was utilizing this time to turn her against him, Randle swung side to side in the hammock, contemplating his next move because continuing to stay with his ex and her autistic son was not an option.

Reaching to grab his beer from the lawn table, he ignored the fact that his cellphone was ringing as he amusingly watched the little one begins to play Falcons football on his own. Portraying the quarterback, wide receiver, and running back, while he seemingly dodged and ran over invisible defenders to score touchdowns didn't revive or resuscitate Randle's boredom. Nor did it inoculate his boredom as a preventive measure of rage. Raising the bottle to his mouth as the child tossed the ball for him to catch, which ended up hitting Randle's leg, impulsively, he leaned off the hammock and grabbed the little man aggressively by the shirt, snatching his lightweight body close, splashing beer on the boy's shocked baby face.

"Go play some damn where else, before I throw you and that ball in the fucking trash boy!" Randle exploded as the boy trembled nervously in his grip.

Not expecting any counteraction from abusively chastising the child, Randle was completely caught off guard when the boy started throwing a barrage of punches that struck the intended target his eye and wired jaw, while screaming at the top of his lungs, "Stranger danger! Stranger danger!"

Shoving him backwards out of frustration after being hit in both eyes and the chin, he tossed the football toward the house instead of handing it to the kid. Realizing from the boy's response and the tears beginning to fall from his eyes as a sign that he had just made a huge mistake, Randle eased off the hammock with the intention of consoling the little one. Sipping from his bottle while wishing the boy would shut the fuck up as he approached, Randle knew he had to mend his wrong because otherwise his mother would be furious and probably put him out after discovering his actions. "Calm that shit li'l man, I'm sorry." Randle stated without sincerity, reaching down to pat his head, but the little one jumped up and began running hysterically toward the neighbor's house continuing to scream.

"Stranger danger! Stranger danger! Stranger danger!"

Hurrying to catch him before he could reach the neighbor's patio steps, Randle cradled him with a swing type lift which caused him to lash out even more, thereby unleashing the uncontrollable rage of his anxiety, as Randle briskly strolled back toward the house, begging him to stop.

"I'm sorry! Calm your ass down, boy. I'll give you some ice cream li'l man," Randle pleaded as he was entering the house and maneuvering toward the kitchen as his tantrum seemingly became more violent.

Struggling to hold him as he kicked, swung wildly, and screamed without an end in sight, he opened the freezer and grabbed one of his Push Pops, only for it to be knocked out of Randle's hand as he tried to offer it to him. Tired of his antics, completely dumbfounded of how to calm him, and seemingly pleading to deaf ears, Randle carried him to his room, tossed him on the bed, and walked out, closing the door behind him without saying another word.

"Stranger danger! Stranger danger!"

Hearing him repeat the same phrase over and over for five minutes, while throwing toys and other objects against the wall in his room, Randle jumped up from the sofa and walked back into the kitchen. He hoped one of the many goodies in the sweets cabinet would calm him so that he could peacefully look at the Troy series on Netflix and finish plotting his plan of breaking into Sheri's house to steal some of her collected art to sell. Gathering cookies, cupcakes, fruit cups, raisins, and a few packs of his chewable gummy bears, he threw everything in a bowl, then walked to the room and tossed the goodies on the bed beside him out of frustration.

"I'm sorry, little man. Please calm tha fuck down," he repeatedly begged as the child began grabbing the items and throwing them at Randle with heated aggression.

"Stranger danger! Stranger danger!"

Tossing snacks with missile-like projectiles from a F-15 Eagle fighter jet, Randle maneuvered out of hostile airspace and closed the door to shield himself from the outrage. Clueless of how to remedy the civil unrest with "peace treats," Randle walked back into the living room debating whether or not to call his ex, given the fact that all the hollering was starting to get on his nerves and he was reaching the point of spanking him and forcing him to go to sleep. Grabbing the TV remote from the table while plopping down on the sofa, he raised the volume to drown out the noise of his tantrum.

Laying back and trying to finish watching the episode of Troy, Randle had no idea of the precautionary measures his ex-had taken to assure her baby's safety in endangering and uncomfortable situations. No longer hearing any noise echoing from the room, he lowered the volume and pondered as his eyes and ears enjoyed the entertainment instead of taking the time to check on him.

Climbing out of the window and down the ladder, as rehearsed with his mother numerous times, he ran back to the neighbor's house without detouring a single step. Screaming with every breath of air inside of him, "Stranger danger," he banged his little hand against the patio glass with no resolution to his actions. It wasn't until the neighbor opened the door minutes later, due to the echoes of his anxiety being unheard as she relaxed in the tub with the headphones on that he found soothing comfort in a gentle recognizable embrace. With his head on her shoulder as she caressed his back, she wiped his tears, kissed his cheek, and then he openly presented his case to her against Randle's tyrannical bedside manner and every impersonal and un-nurturing thing he had heard him say.

Using his phone to see if he still had the ability to log in and out of the security system, which he was thrilled to discover the codes had not changed, Randle accessed all the house cameras. He needed to see what valuables he would be able to broker to a fence quickly without bringing notice to himself, and to make sure Mr. Johnson didn't have someone staking out the property in their absence. Feeling he could easily receive at least a hundred thousand by just grabbing her jewelry box, the solid gold heart sculpture Sheri's father gave her for graduating from Spelman University that sits in between the vintage crystal vases on the fireplace mantle, and a few of the paintings not yet bolted onto the wall. Randle began to smile, knowing fully well that the money would hold him over until Sheri was out of the hospital and back under his control or Terry made a significant contribution with a counter offer that would suffice, motivational enough to settle the lawsuit out of court.

Surfing through the *Dish* channels once the episode ended, he intended to stop after seeing the lions hunt on National Geographic. But mistakenly hitting the channel button as he was laying down the remote, causing the station to change to a Motown documentary where hearing the soulful melodies of "Just to See Her" and "One Heartbeat" by Smokey Robinson had him missing Sheri for the blessing she was instead of the benefits she offered him.

Thinking that the little one had fallen asleep after his anxiety explosion, given that it was painstakingly quiet and the annoying noises of a tantrum had long ceased, approximately half an hour now, Randle grabbed his phone to dial his cousin, yet he received no answer. Needing to rekindle his rush of adrenaline instead of allowing himself to get emotional, he turned to the Bad Blood series on Netflix and dialed his father.

"What's up, Pop?" Randle inquired hearing the grumpy voice mumble on the other end of the receiver.

"Fuck ya callin' me, fo boy? Spit it out 'cause um not in da mood fo ya bullshit right now, and um not loanin' ya any money," his father retorted.

"I just called to get your advice, and hopefully your assistance on something, not to argue with you, Pop. Some very valuable merchandise is about to cross my path in the next couple of hours, and I was wondering if you would reach out to your old connections and fence them for me. I am willing to give you twenty percent of all profit."

"I knew ya wur callin' me with' sum bullshit! Ya don't even call to ask me 'bout me health, even when um in da hospital, ya stinkin' scoundrel. Everything is always 'bout ya sorry, no good ass! Like a fool, I spent all me hard earned money investing in ya college education. Yet, in return, I received nothing but ya incompetence, disrespect, and ya lack of drive to be anything besides a low-level womanizer and baby killer, ya fuckin' ingrate. Fuck ya! Ya are a disgrace to me bloodline, boy, and quite honestly, it often makes me wonder if ya are actually my fuckin' son. How could ya kill ya own babies, your fuckin retard?!! Then you were going to allow ya scum ass cousin to rape ya unborn kids' pregnant mom? What kind of man are ya?! Ya a fuckface demon, ya sissy mutherfucker!"

"Pop, I didn't call you to be ridiculed, nor to engage in a discussion about your feelings. I called to see if you wanted to make some money. So, are you going to help me or not?"

"Fuck ya! Cock sucka, don't tell me what to say out of me damn mouth or when it's appropriate for me to express myself. Kiss my ass ya pathetic piece of shit!" He roared into the phone.

"Pop, please! I need your help," Randle interjected realizing he had no one else to turn to, given that his cousin wasn't returning his calls. He openly apologized and begged his father for the opportunity to bridge a new foundation with him.

"I'll do it for forty percent without any further negotiations, boy. Hell, I oughta make that sixty. And I've told ya stupid ass about talking on these phones," he barked. "Just come to da house when ya have the goods in hand," he stated before hanging up the phone.

Smiling as though he just achieved a major milestone, Randle kicked his feet up on the sofa and began watching the episode, imagining himself as a crime boss while lingering in thought about hotel he was going to go to once he got the money. Lifting the half full bottle to his mouth, he noticed red and blue lights flashing on the wall in the adjacent room. Jumping to his feet instantaneously, he eased to the edge of the doorway and peered around the frame, which allowed him a perfect visual through the den window.

Seeing the four police cars parked on the street, while one officer seemingly gave commands by directing others with the waving of his finger towards the house, Randle turned without any delay in his actions. Grabbing his cellphone from the sofa cushion, he ran out through the back door without a thought given to anything besides getting away after hearing an officer acknowledge his presence while ringing the doorbell and seeing two additional officers walk up the driveway.

Leaping fences and running through yards as though his life was threatened by the original Terminator, Randle's exercise regimen was beneficial in helping him escape the vicinity. Pacing himself, rhythmically breathing, he ran five blocks barefooted with nothing on but a pair of shorts and hid in the dumpster of a mom and pop corner store. With no one to contact but his cousin, yet afraid of being heard, Randle opted not to call, rather repeatedly texted: 'Urgent...Police are after me. Need U! Please help ... "

"Hey, u there?"...

"U there!" ...

"Urgent..."

"Urgent..."

"Help me!"

"Please Respond!!," until a response finally came through almost an hour later.

"What's up? Where you at?" The text message read.

"I'm on the run...Inside the dumpster behind the Pink store on McDonough Road."

"On my way!"

Relieved to get a response and thinking nothing about his ex's son, he waited patiently until he received the most significant text his eyes had ever envisioned: "Come out."

CHAPTER 37

Trying her best to help Sheri alleviate the thoughts of her loss, the reflections of her trauma and the cries of love from a wounded heart, Yara openly exposed her to a childhood secret that only a few knew of. Even though she knew words weren't always effective for healing, she felt it was important to acknowledge how turning to God in the vulnerable depths of her weakness kept her from falling apart. Holding her daughter as she laid staring at the three dozen pink roses her father had a florist deliver just moments ago, as tears caressed her face without wiping them, Yara shared the painful memory of her baby sister being brutally raped by her boyfriend and two baseball players in the middle school bathroom. Detailing how she painfully lost months of her serenity, and blaming herself for participating in what she innocently assumed at the time was a silly prank by luring her sister inside the building instead of a dare request taken too seriously. Yara got emotional while expressing how she allowed her sister's suicide to mentally suffocate her with depression afterwards, something she didn't want for her daughter.

"Why does God hate me, Ma?" Sheri interjected.

"God doesn't hate you, baby. He will never hate a believer!" Yara exclaimed, while squeezing her hand with a little more affection. "No matter the depth of sins you amass against your soul or the darkness within a person's heart, God will always forgive and be your light when you call upon Him."

"Then, why does He continuously punish my body for worshipping Him without associating any partners with the oneness of His Lordship, when He acknowledges that He will not?" Sheri expressed as she struggled to turn over to face her mother. "I no longer feel whole as a woman or have a desire to love. I feel like I'm breathing without any existence. Mama, how can you say He doesn't hate me when He never gave me a chance to hold my babies, kiss either of them, or experience the warmth that blankets a mother's heart when they look at you? How can you say He doesn't hate me when I begged Him every day to soften Randle's heart, yet all I continued to receive was his abuse?" Raising her hands to blanket her face, Sheri asked as emotional frustration began to compel her, "Why did God take away my babies and leave me feeling cold, meaningless, and broken?"

"We all have an appointed time, and God makes no mistakes," Yara asserted while tilting her head to kiss Sheri's face. "Your sorrow, I will never be able to measure baby, but I feel just as you, internally, because your heartbeat is mine."

"I don't feel a heartbeat anymore. I feel nothing at all, not even the desire to live."

Yara felt devastated, personally hearing the gravity of those words falling from her daughter's lips, but she knew only patience, prayer, and gentle support would remind her of how significant to life her existence is, even though the core essence of pain would never be removed. Pulling Sheri closer to herself, she began to share the very things the spiritual adviser enlightened her of during her mourning period, as Sheri's tears dripped steadily into her chest.

"Sweetie, God said, *'O you who believe! Fear Him and keep your duty to Him. And let every person look to what he has sent forth for the morrow and fear the Most High.' Verily, God is well acquainted with what you do.*"

"When anger robs us of our tranquility, we tend to blame God, the so-called white man, or anyone we can point our fingers at for justification. Yet, accepting responsibility for the works of our own hand, we seldom do. God grants us the ability of choice, and when you neglect to make effective choices you can't blaspheme Him, assuming it's a punishment and that He's vindictive as though our life has that much value."

"Then, what else can it be, Ma? He took away my babies!"

"No, He did not take your babies. The selfish choice of trying to love and change a man who showed you his unstable characteristics every day through physical abuse is what has us crying together. Baby, it's not your fault your heart opened to love. Nor is it your fault that you allowed fear to manifest within you. So, never blame yourself or blame God for the actions of a callous human being. You begged God to soften Randle's heart, as Moses (may God be pleased with him) repeatedly pleaded for Fir'aun to do the same, yet you blindly rejected the signs He presented for you to step away from that toxic relationship. Granted, He bestowed upon you the strength, understanding, support, and will. Sheri, trying to rationalize an effect of life will drive you insane, so relax your mind because only the Most High possesses control and can answer your questions beyond theory.

Who's to say your momentary grief is not a bridging for a greater blessing, like in the compelling story of Al-Khidr (may God be pleased with him), when God commanded him to remove a sinful child from a family's life, only to bestow upon them the blessing of a righteous one. Sweetie, I know you are hurting and common words will not soften your heart overnight, but as long as you crawl through the shallow depths of your own tears, then I will crawl beside you until you're able to suppress the pain and find the strength to stand once again. God only removes things from your life to bestow on you greater blessing, and never forget that sweetie."

Opening her heart within the comfort of Yara's arms, provided no true resolution to her sorrow. Sheri felt like an empty vessel, but she was happy her mother was close, and her support meant everything. Internally, a part of her missed Randle, and wished he was there to hold her because he always knew how to awaken her smile and suppress her pain. He was her pillow, but the thought of seeing him ever again disgusted her. She could never forgive him for being a coconspirator, actively contributing to killing the life within her womb.

Realizing that Sheri was getting more and more emotional detailing how she felt, which was therapy in some respects and torment in others, Yara grabbed her cellphone off the tray stand and began showing her pictures: The library's development, the Unity kids that attended the Atlanta United soccer game, those who helped feed the elders at the nursing home, and the video Trill produced of his new song that has the kids' battle dancing against one another. Seeing Sheri smile streamed a breath of fresh air into Yara's heart. She loved her baby and knew the pictures of the kids would awaken something within her.

Startled by the door moving in her peripheral, Sheri lifted her eyes away from the phone to witness the doctor walking into the room with three male assistants following. Staring without saying a word, she was curious to know why one was pushing a Broda wheelchair, while the other two pushed carts.

"How are you, Dr. Kasper? What's going on?" Yara inquired as the assistants were being instructed to move certain equipment, and to load all of Sheri's flowers and property onto the carts.

"I'm good, Mrs. Johnson, and I pray that the two of you are as well. I just wish I was home hugging my baby girl as you are fortunate to do right now," Dr. Kasper articulated while observing Sheri's vital signs on the monitors. "Mr. Johnson and his lawyer called this morning and made arrangements for the hospital to release Sheri for homecare as a surprise gift to the both of you."

Perplexed as to why Gip would jeopardize her health as a seed of joy to uplift their spirit just to make them smile, Yara quickly sat up in bed, reversing the decision as it was unacceptable to her. Yes, she openly mentioned the joy it would give her heart to have Sheri at home during this traumatic ordeal, but knowing the severity of Sheri's injuries needed adequate treatment and attention that only trained medical professionals could offer, she insisted that they halt the process.

"Mrs. Johnson, what's wrong?" Dr. Kasper questioned, confused by her reaction.

"She's not well enough to be released to home-care, and I'm not going to compromise her recovery," Yara retorted while easing out of bed to reclaim authority over the situation. "I thank you for honoring the doctor's orders, given my husband's request, but please place the flowers back and leave us," she politely instructed the assistants. "I reject this decision and you can advise hospital authority that she's not an outpatient — she's staying."

"Mrs. Johnson, I'm Sheri's doctor ..."

"And I'm her goddamn mother," Yara snapped.

"No, pardon me, Mrs. Johnson, please," Dr. Kasper respectfully interjected while reaching out to bridge the confusion with a gentle touch to the arm. "I'm trying to say, as her doctor, I would never make a decision that would compromise the integrity of my career, this hospital, or the full recovery of your daughter's health."

"In consulting with the administrators of the hospital, Mr. Johnson and I have successfully arranged for a section in your home to be transformed into a comfortable, state of the art, recovery facility for Sheri. She will have 24-hour medical care on-site by a rotating team of four certified RN's. Mr. Johnson insists you select with me, the staff members you feel comfortable allowing to work in your home beyond tomorrow, given that you are the woman of the house. I will remain her doctor and shall video chat with you on the days I cannot appear in person. I assure you, Mrs. Johnson, the contracted home-care company comes highly recommended and will not take treating Sheri's condition lightly. In fact, this is exciting and an honor to them as it is for me."

Hearing the words of assurance, Yara smiled as she hugged Dr. Kasper, then turned and granted the assistants the approval to pack her things. Leaning over the bed to kiss Sheri's brushed and swollen forehead while massaging her hand, she purred, "I love youuuu," which Sheri responded with the same reply. Excited about having her baby cared for at home, which would grant her the ability of always being a few steps away and knowing she'd be protected from Randle's selfish deviancy, Yara grabbed her cellphone to call Gip on video.

"Hi, my love," Gip exclaimed answering the phone and seeing his wife and daughter on screen.

"Thank you, baby! Dr. Kasper just informed us of what you did, and we are both so excited."

"I love you, daddy," Sheri acknowledged, then waved and blew a kiss.

"Saying I love you, princess, is an understatement. How are you feeling?" He inquired while walking through the construction site back to his car.

"I'm okay, daddy, just hungry since I declined the hospital's lunch, 'cause mom said you were going to bring me some lemon pepper salmon," Sheri wishfully stated.

"I do apologize, princess, but I've scheduled for two balsamic vinaigrette chicken salads to be delivered to the both of you, once they have you secure and ready for transport, which should be within the next ten to fifteen minutes at best," Gip informed her, smiling. "Mama Lewis is at the house now, with the contracted medical team, making sure everything is ready for your arrival, and your favorite hibachi meal is being prepared by Cadence as well."

"Daddy ..."

Chuckling at the thought of Cadence causing everyone to have their stomachs pumped with her easy-bake cooking, Gip smiled, observing their reaction with overt facial expressions that says it all. "Princess I'm just kidding! Yara, I have to make a stop on the way home, but I should be there by the time Sheri is situated in her room."

"Okay, baby." She cooed, blowing a kiss with their daughter.

As the additional assistants entered upon request and secured Sheri in the Broda wheelchair moments after disconnecting the call, Yara jumped in the bed and laid back as though she too was a patient. Seeing how the medical staff was pampering Sheri as if she were a queen, while handling her as though they were transporting a delicate Lladro or Swarovski crystal figurine treated as an ancient artifact, she playfully demanded they grant her the hospital royal treatment as well. Her humorous antics caused everyone to laugh, even though Yara was serious in her own way.

Easing off the bed and back into her stilettos, while grabbing her things so that they could depart, Yara noticed an unsealed manila envelope stuck inside one of Sheri's gift bags on the cart and retrieved it out of curiosity.

"What is this, Sheri?" She inquired, while stepping in front of the wheelchair to be seen, due to the side blinders protecting Sheri's head.

"I have no idea, Ma," she responded as the assistants received instructions to transport her and the property downstairs.

Following the staff through the hospital and to the transport vehicle, Yara remained silent as her mind swirled with intense curiosity. Assuming the envelope could be something undesired from Randle, which the last thing she wanted to do was stress her baby out by once more causing her to reflect on him in anyway, she folded the envelope and stuck it inside her purse. Electing to ride with Sheri and have her husband send someone back for the car, she climbed inside where they were given their salads once they were both secured.

Attempting to text Gip to inform him of her plan, she noticed a text from Stewart saying he loved her, was sorry for what his actions had caused, and that he was currently meeting with his lawyer so that he could turn himself in and get Terry released. Flabbergasted by the unexpected turn of events, that added even more sadness to her heart instead of the relief he assumed it would bring, Yara's hand shook as she tried to eat and forwarded the shocking message to her husband.

"What's wrong, Ma?" Sheri queried, feeling the vibration, and seeing the tear fall from her eye.

"Nothing! I'm just overwhelmed by the fact you're coming home, and we can be together," Yara claimed, shielding her from the truth but speaking an aspect of it as well.

Streaming an episode of The Tamron Hall show on her phone to alleviate her mind after sending the text, Sheri momentarily escaped the realms of her own sorrow by allowing the phenomenal talk show host to lift her spirit with her wittiness, whose onscreen character seems to always be a beacon of light for many women. Reaching for the phone as the episode ended, which Yara relinquished, assuming she was going to stream another show, Sheri surprised her by raising the volume and bobbing her head while playing YouTube videos of Nicki Minaj. Happy at the fact that her baby was in a state of mental comfort, Yara leaned back without letting go of her hand, and thought of the damage Stewart was about to do all the way home.

Seeing individuals carrying furniture from the house, while additional staff carried medical equipment inside, she smiled, gazing through the rear window. Ecstatic at it all, after the transporters opened the door and assisted her out of the van, Yara stopped one of the workers who was unloading supplies from the truck and joked as the men carefully removed Sheri while still bobbing her head to the music.

"Are y'all turning my entire house into a hospital with all of this equipment?"

"Nooo! No ma'am." He politely replied, chuckling at her statement. "We're just making sure she has everything she needs to properly recover."

"With all of this equipment, it looks like y'all trying to establish a satellite clinic on the low," Yara grinned before turning to escort the gentlemen in the house as the medical staff followed with her daughter.

Walking through the foyer and being greeted with a hug from Mama Lewis, who didn't hesitate in pushing her aside to embrace and kiss her granddaughter as well, Yara immediately noticed that things were out of place but said nothing. Getting Sheri to the room so that she could be comfortable was her main priority. Astonished by how quickly the workers had transformed the mother in-law suite of the house into a home clinic for her baby, she immediately insisted on treating all the workers to a hibachi lunch, while stepping out of the way so that the medical staff could transfer Sheri to the bed and connect her to the monitors.

Needing to advise the chef of her request, Yara began moving toward the kitchen, but stopped before reaching the stairs when she noticed that her Ming vase was missing from its stand and the new Salvador Dali painting Gip had yet to have bolted in the wall due to Sheri's incident. Quickly moving to the bedroom to retrieve her tablet, so that she could rewind the security footage before accusing the workers of stealing, Yara was shocked when she entered and discovered the perpetrator had invaded the privacy of her room as well. Dumbfounded by the fact that all of her husband's watches, cufflinks, the keys to his '67 GTO, and his priceless African tribal mask collection was also taken, yet none of her valuables were touched, Yara reviewed the security video.

Not believing what she was witnessing, "Mama Lewis! Mama Lewis!" She screamed at the top of her lungs, until she entered with her Glock G48 in hand and seemingly ready to squeeze the trigger.

"Chil' don't be screaming my damn name like that. I thought one of the workers was up here disrespecting you, and you were calling me to bust a cap in their ass," Mama Lewis exaggerated.

"No, I'm calling you because I just watched the security video, given that I noticed things were missing...."

"You could have just asked me instead of wasting time scanning footage, Yara, and I would have informed you that I took all the items that are missing, and don't plan on giving them back until your husband returns my guns," Mama Lewis concluded with a devilish grin.

Standing with one hand on her hip and the tablet in her other hand, Yara stared without blinking, while contemplating calling her husband so that he could address the matter, but thought against it given that he was en route, and Sheri was more of a priority than replaceable art objects.

"If you were anybody else, I would step out of character and spank your ass right now, then drag you out to the trash for disrespecting my house as you have, especially given the circumstances surrounding why you're here," Yara retorted, tossing in the tablet on the bed and strolling past her, frustrated and shaking her head in disbelief of her actions.

Mama Lewis knew her combat skills were no match for Yara's, who she respected, admired as a strong woman, and loved like a daughter from her own womb. But she also knew that no matter what she said or did out of arrogance, Yara's internal grooming would never allow her to raise a hand to hurt her. Too prideful to accept and admit when she's actually wrong, Mama Lewis spoke because she refused to allow Yara to feel as though she chumped her off like a sucker without saying a word.

"Chil' you better stay in your place and watch your damn mouth before you be the one being dragged to the trash, while picking my toe nails out yo teeth," Mama Lewis mumbled beneath her breath not intending for Yara to hear.

Stopping in her tracks, Yara turned and locked in a heated stare with Mama Lewis that spoke volumes without words exchanged. Refusing to allow her ego or self-centered antics to deter her from what was important, she rolled her eyes and strolled to the kitchen as she initially intended.

Lured directly to the outside grill by the aroma of blended spices being charred, Yara greeted the Chef with a gentle hug. She wasted no time in filling her mouth with pieces of steak the Chef cut for her to taste before briefly walking away to remove more meat from the freezer so that she could make preparations to oblige the last minute serving request for the workers.

Thinking of nothing besides feeding her baby girl, Yara poured herself a glass of white grape juice, after fixing Sheri's plate, then sarcastically asked Mama Lewis, as she sauntered into the kitchen conversing with someone on the phone, not to steal anything as she grabbed the tray off the counter and headed to the room.

"Chil' don't push me!" She roared without lowering the phone yet portraying a facial expression that insinuated that she truly meant what she said.

"With the way I'm feeling right now!!! — If I pushed you, Mama Lewis, the possibility of you EVER walking or using your hands again is slim to none!" Yara barked, allowing the heated aggression she felt to be manifested in her voice because of Mama Lewis selfish actions, not slowing her pace.

With all the workers fed and gone, Sheri elected to take a nap after eating. The on-call nurses were monitoring her condition from the adjacent room while stocking the supplies in the room transferred into a clinic office. Now that Mama Lewis was en route home, arguing with her husband because she refused to return the items, she took without her guns being given back to her. Yara went out into the yard and fed two of the dogs some of the hibachi mix with their food, then used wet wipes to thoroughly clean the paws of the other two before escorting them in the house to lock in her bedroom so that she could shower comfortably, given that Gip was gone and one of the nurses was a man.

Emotionally exhausted with tears falling like the hot water beating her back from the massage nozzles, Yara placed her hands on the wall and humbly lowered her head to thank God for all the blessings He had bestowed upon her life. Having no desire to move at the moment, for subconsciously she felt as if God was using this moment to deep cleanse her heart and mind, she remained suspended in that soothing position for countless minutes before forcing herself to bathe and stepped out of the shower feeling like a rejuvenated woman. Observing herself in the mirror as she gently patted her body dry with a towel, Yara thought of her mother, which caused her to search her breasts for lumps as her doctor taught. Ecstatic to discover nothing as the dogs laid attentively eyeing her beauty instead of watching the bedroom door, she brushed her teeth, massaged coco butter into her skin, donned some relaxing clothes that didn't highlight her curves, then took the dogs back out and fed them.

The warmth of the sun felt so good that Yara wished she and Sheri were relaxing by the pool, or merely sitting on the steps admiring life as they did before she discovered womanhood and moved out. Hearing the tablet beep in her hand, signaling that the front gate was opening, Yara smiled while looking at the screen and seeing her husband returning home with Aaron driving the car she left at the hospital and One Eye following in a van she assumed contained all the things Mama Lewis confiscated.

Pacing toward the house, feeling free and energetic with her arms extended like the spread wings of a falcon, she answered the phone with the touch of her Bluetooth, which caused an instant burst of excitement within her heart, hearing the voices of her son and Demi. Choosing to surprise him with the news of Sheri's presence by going to the room and putting his sister on the phone instead of revealing it herself then doubling back to meet her husband at the door, Yara struggled in her attempt to climb the stairs, due to the stomach crunching laughter Terry was causing by sharing the unbelievable jailhouse stories about some guy who wigged out on meth after staying awake for nine straight days, then started swinging on people in the dormitory because he psychologically thought they were goblins as well as the guy he claims walks around with toothbrushes and tubes of toothpaste literally attached to every single piece of clothing he wears because he believes it centers his energy with the universe and shields his soul from the Angel of Death.

"Baby I can only imagine the unwritten comedy y'all see within those walls daily. I still laugh sometimes, just thinking of the guy you told me about in the wheelchair. The fact that you said he rolled into the bathroom and swung on a man sitting on the toilet 'cause he felt with the guy's pants down, he had a chance of winning the fight. I love you, baby," she purred while giggling to the thought of what she just said.

Removing her Bluetooth, entering the room and realizing Sheri was no longer asleep, she walked over to place it in her daughter's ear. Whereupon Sheri mildly protested that she was watching Game of Thrones, but paused the episode and switched the channel to the news station while smiling when she heard her brother's voice in the ear piece. Desiring to let them talk in private so that she could go discuss how Stewart turning himself in and confessing to the double murder was going to affect everything now that Mama Lewis was out of their presence, Yara removed the phone from her pocket and handed it to Sheri. But as she turned away and attempted to take her third step toward the door, the sound of her phone smashing against the floor, and the beeping from the electrocardiogram caused her to halt in her tracks, turning her head back, immediately.

Rushing to her daughter's side as the nurses stormed into the room and began checking to see why her heart rate was elevating so rapidly, Sheri pointed a trembling finger toward the TV and mumbled, "That's him! That's him! That's him!" Alerting words that caused everyone to gaze at the screen as they continued to assist.

"That's who, baby?" Yara questioned, panicking while stepping back to allow the nurses to perform whatever procedure needed to calm her baby.

"That's him! That's him, mama! Randle's cousin! The man who tried to rape me," she forced herself to say as the traumatic abuse of that night began flashing in her mind and tears began falling from her eyes.

Entering the room, clueless of what was transpiring, Gip immediately threw his arm around Yara and asked what was going on as a wave of concern rippled through him.

Stepping away from his affection, without responding, Yara grabbed the remote from Sheri's lap to quickly change the channel. A selfish part of her smiled on hearing the reporter detail the horrific things that happened to Clipper, yet as a mother, her heart grew in sadness for his own mother. Watching one of the nurses remove the Bluetooth from her ear, she grabbed it then enlightened Terry, Demi, and her husband of what just transpired, as he picked the phone up off the floor and advised them to call back.

Moving out of the nurse's way to back up against her husband's chest, Gip wrapped his arms around her and whispered in her ear, "I love you, and everything is going to be okay because she's strong like you."

Gradually calming from the unexpected mild anxiety shock that awakened a smile within her heart, while extracting an indescribable sense of fear, Sheri laid motionless as the nurses observed the vital monitors. Gazing at her father intently, as if she knew without doubt that he butchered her abuser with his own hands for her honor, Sheri whispered, "I love you so much," while reaching out her hand for him to grab.

"I love you more, princess," he cajoled, leaning in to kiss her forehead as he wrapped his hand gently around hers and eased onto the bed, granted that her heartbeat was stable again and the nurses were leaving the room.

Seeing the two of them so emotionally connected, touched Yara's heart. Standing there, she couldn't remember how many months had passed since the last time she witnessed them so vulnerable together. Wishing this moment could be forever savored, she snapped a picture and immediately shared it with a few family members with the caption: *'Love Can Never Be Measured by Words!'*

Leaving the two of them to enjoy some alone time, Yara went and thanked the nurses again for their assistance, checked to see if they needed anything while making sure the clinic's refrigerator was full of refreshments and food items which they could eat if either of them got hungry. Desiring to make some banana bread so that she and Sheri could munch on it while watching the movie, "Life," later, Yara wasted no time in heading to the kitchen and displaying her baking skills.

With the two pans of bread in the oven and the dishes properly washed, Yara walked to the room to change her T-shirt, due to water and spots of pudding adding new designs to the one she was adorning. Not wanting to suffocate Sheri with her presence or make her feel as if they considered her helpless and were trying to comfort her emotionally out of pity versus love, Yara went to her bedroom turned on the TV and attempted to lay in bed for a moment instead of going back to Sheri's room, but the manila envelope sticking out of her purse completely caught her attention.

Curious to know what was inside, she eased out of bed to grab it but stood eyeing the package, contemplating whether or not to open it out of respect for Sheri's privacy. Allowing her protectiveness and the thought that it may be something unwanted from Randle to be the reason she peeked inside without permission, Yara unsealed it and pulled out the contents.

Standing there eyeing the enclosed photos of an extremely handsome caramel skinned muscular gentleman after reading the attached letter from James, Yara was at a loss for words, finally discovering the true identity of the charming mystery man who had intrigued her for months. Grabbing her phone from the bed without hesitation, she video chatted Naomi to inquire more about him. But all Naomi could offer besides dominatrix illusions of what he could do to her body with ice cream and a leather bull whip was that he's a respected business associate of Sheri's, one of which Naomi fantasized about whenever he visited the office.

Anxious to know the truth of the matter, Yara stormed towards Sheri's room. Expecting to find them reminiscing or watching TV, she was completely caught off guard by the blasting sounds of Nicki Minaj approaching the door and the unbelievable sight of them sitting on the bed intensely battling at Connect Four and eating her freshly baked banana bread, while the two nurses watched the entertaining grudge match.

"Baby, she should be resting!" Yara exclaimed, sauntering to the top end of the bed to comb Sheri's hair from her face with her fingers, after which she playfully pushed Gip's head back with her hand. "And who told either of you that you could eat my damn bread before me?"

Laughing with the nurses as her father stood up claiming to be the King and needing no permission, she couldn't help but smile at the expression on her mom's face due to his silliness. "I'm okay, Ma. Daddy is the one who should be resting, given the way I'm beating him without thinking and not to mention, I'm drugged up," she snickered. "Ma, I thought you proved long ago to Daddy that a woman's mind is far more lethal than a men."

"Princess, I'm only allowing you to win because your smile is more beautiful that way," Gip boasted, only for Sheri to yell "Connect Four" again to his disbelief.

"See what I'm saying, princess," he chuckled. "Beautiful!"

"Whatever!"

"I am the King, and my word is law." Gip uttered in his African accent, which caused everyone in the room to burst out laughing again.

"But seriously, Mom, I'm okay, and your banana bread is sooooooo good."

"Whatever!" she responded, rolling her eyes to the both of them.

"Beating our so-called 'Peach King' with the horrible African accent is taking my mind off things, and nothing will ever be able to stop me from a Connect Four challenge," Sheri piped while separating the pieces for another game. "You can help your husband if you'd like. Beating the both of you together still won't cause me to have to think or affect my situation," she boasted while high fiving the female nurse and laughing at the expression on her mother's face.

"Whatever chil'. Stay in your league!" Yara was truly at a loss for words. The sight of Sheri being cheerful, truly warmed every inch of her heart, which unexpectedly caused Yara to yell aloud the word Terry taught her whenever she desired to glorify God, "Al hamdulillahi."

"What? What do that mean, Ma?" Sheri queried while dropping her checker into the frame and arrogantly advising the male nurse that he could help her father, given his head movement every time her father inserted a checker, because she had no problem spanking two men or everyone in the room altogether.

"It means all thanks and praise belong to God," Yara responded while removing the pictures from the envelope and laying them in Sheri's lap.

"Excuse me, but baby, do you know this gentleman?"

"Yes," she replied grabbing the pictures with a smile expanding on her face. "He's a warm hearted and a very generous business associate of mine, Ma, who's just as extraordinary as daddy. He owns a software company that has made many breakthroughs in the technology industry, and he spends some of his fortune building free live-in homes for elderlies with disabilities, safe escape living centers for battered women, plus free schools to educate and treat special needs, including autistic kids. Many consider him the walking sun because of his character and his compassion for others. Why, Ma?"

Shifting her eyes to stare at her husband, as he playfully snatched the pictures from Sheri's hand and started looking at them as though he was jealous, Yara was about to verbally answer until Gip caused everyone in the room to laugh with his silly arrogance, speaking in his African accent.

"He is definitely not male eye candy like me, nor a King like me! But, if he's truly a servant of God as you say sweetie, then I'd love to meet him," Gip acknowledged, while trying to slide two checkers into the slot, only to be caught.

"Daddy, are you serious?!"

Laughing at her husband's cunningness to win, the amusement of his words and seeing the way her daughter's eyes sparkled when speaking about the gentleman she considers a respected associate, Yara raised Sheri's hand and kissed it, while comforting Gip's masculinity by agreeing to his statement. "You're right love, he's not the eye candy or King you are." Initially against revealing the truth because of her emotional state, and how the trauma has affected her mentally, but after witnessing the way she naturally smiled and talked delightedly about him, Yara felt no harm could be done in enlightening Sheri of her greatest mystery. So, she handed her the letter from James.

"Oooh my God! Oooh my God!" She purred as she was releasing the letter and covering her swollen mouth with her hands, while looking up at her mother in disbelief and Gip eyeing them both befuddled as to what's going on.

"You mean to tell me he's Abdul Waahid?!"

CHAPTER 38

Randle sat like a mannequin unable to scream or create any other kind of commotion that would draw the attention of the pedestrians trying to figure out who the police were searching their neighborhood for as his panic attack worsened with each passing second. His survival fully depended on him hiding in a dumpster infested with hungry rats. Randle was so freaked out when he received the text, assuming his cousin had arrived that he leaped over the top, tumbling like a boulder off a cliff onto the concrete instead of exiting through the side hatch.

"Ahhhhhh! Fuck! He mumbled, scurrying to his feet, while slapping different parts of his body as though the dumpster rats were crawling all over him. Clueless of who was actually responding to his plea for help and the catastrophic torture awaiting his arrival, he hurried to the vehicle. With sirens blaring and lights flashing from all directions, Randle was so happy to be eluding the police. Suddenly pumped with a new wave of adrenaline as he ran and snatched open the back door, that he paid no conscious minded attention that there were no seats in the van, no windows, a protective wall which hid the visibility of the driver, and the entire cargo area was isolated with thick green plastic. Jumping inside, Randle eased against the side wall and rested his head between his knees.

Slowly regaining a sense of composure and escaping hyperventilation after frantically checking himself to determine whether or not his sustained bodily injuries were mere scratches or bites from rats, Randle tried to hold on for dear life as every careless turn or abrupt stop within the sealed off community caused him to slide and slam against the sides of the van.

"Come on cuz! What the fuck?" Randle yelled after sliding on the plastic and hitting his head on the side wall.

Already disturbed that the assailant had assaulted a mentally handicapped child at the residence of incidence, anger was fueled among the deputies given the child actually helps to feed the K-9's at the precinct on the weekend, the onsite Sgt. wasted no time in radioing the Sheriff. Being granted the authority to establish roadblocks, he immediately directed deputies to secure every entry point to the neighborhood. Male testosterone was looming high on account of the child they had all befriended and treated the situation as though a fellow officer had been abused. Using Randle's clothes from the house to give the K-9s a scent to follow, many of the officers got even more aggravated when they discovered from dispatch that Randle was also wanted for double feticide and aggravated battery.

There was no way to escape the heavy police presence, no matter which street the driver opted to turn onto. With roadblocks and enforced car searches, the driver of the van pulled into the driveway of a vacant home. Parked, he called for further instructions, knowing full well that Gip would be very disappointed by the unfortunate revelation, but not trying to deny him the desire that was yoking every measure of his heart, the Irishman instructed the driver of what to do if there was no alternative routes of escape, then disconnected the line.

Removing the sim card and battery from the phone, he grabbed the butane lighter from the passenger seat and incinerated the sim card. Backing out of the driveway and realizing as he cruised to the end of the block that there were no available exit routes, he parked on the street in front of the corner house. With Randle oblivious to where he was or what was about to happen, the driver stepped out of the vehicle, locked the door, removed his gloves, lit a cigarette, and then began jogging up the street as if he was getting his exercise in.

Sitting in the back of the van with his head between his knees, patiently waiting, Randle lingered in thought without answers. With only silence to comfort him, he tried to figure out why the vehicle wasn't moving, why he could still hear the sound of sirens in the distant, and what were the irritating dogs he could hear barking at. Randle was so greatly shocked when the deputies snatched open the rear doors of the van, guns drawn commanding him to freeze, that he started urinating on himself. Being forced out of the van with his arms visibly raised after confirming that he was in fact the suspect they sought, Randle was instructed to lay on the ground, which he quickly obliged out of fear. Face down on the scorching concrete wearing only shorts, one officer slammed his knee into the center of his back to secure his hands to be handcuffed, without concern for his human rights, as Randle screamed of the ground burning him. Lifting him to his feet with the assistance of another deputy, the Sgt. approached and began reading him his Miranda Rights as Randle tried to interject by reiterating the same statement over and over.

"I need to talk to the detective in charge. I have valuable information to share."

"What?" One of the deputies helping to assist him to his feet asked once the Sgt. finished.

"I can't go to jail, sir," Randle cried, standing before them, shaking as though he was having a standing seizure. "Please allow me to speak to a detective or whoever is in fuckin' charge that can make a deal with me! I know where a lot of drugs are at right now, and I mean a whole bunch of drugs. I know a group of people conducting a state to state forgery scam. My father associates with men who sell multimillion-dollar stolen art and I also know about..."

"Sir that's enough. You will have your time to talk once you get to the precinct," the deputy informed him as co-workers began to laugh at how determined he was to snitch. Trying his best to resist walking given the realization of being arrested was starting to become more and more frightening, Randle refused to stop selling that he had valuable criminal information, as the deputies struggled to escort him to the awaiting police car and secured him in the back seat.

Feeling as if his life was over, even though he didn't know the extent of his charges, Randle pleaded for mercy and claimed that he was sorry during the entire ride to the jailhouse. Assuming the transporting officer could help him elude going to jail as the informants do in the movies, he started spouting names of every crook he knew, the type of crime they were committing and where they operated as the officer assisted him from the car and walked him inside the building for processing.

Placed in a holding tank with countless other criminals, barefoot and wearing nothing but a pair of pissy shorts, Randle was starting to panic, looking around and noticing all eyes were on him. Easing toward the bench to use the phone on the wall with his legs feeling like jello, he sat down and grabbed the receiver while realizing he had no one to call but his mother, whose number he could not recall. Trying his luck, he repeatedly dialed random numbers, yet nothing prevailed from his attempts.

Scared out of his mind, Randle stared at the floor until his name was eventually called for him to be processed. Trembling like a cold, wet dog while following all instructions, through fingerprinting, lice showering, changing clothes, and being screened by the nurse, he asked every deputy he came in contact with to help him because he had valuable information to make a deal with.

Clueless about how to conduct himself and what not to do for the sake of survival, Randle was allowing everyone in his presence to know that he was trying to snitch to avoid going to a cell. Willfully relinquishing whatever necessary, in order to help himself any type of way possible, Randle was completely afraid. He was extremely terrified, and several detainees recognized it as they were escorted through processing. Paying no attention to the gathering of men at the back of the holding tank whispering and eyeing him like a virgin in distress once placed back inside, he elected to bypass sitting on the bench and started doing some yoga stretches to extract his mind from the present atmosphere and his problems.

Randle was so focused on implementing the perfect downward dog while channeling his mind and energy that he didn't see the mammoth sized detainee approach and position himself between his legs. Nor did he initially feel the individual sliding his hand teasingly across his butt, until his fingers caressed his skin, tickling the nerves along the base of his spinal cord, while he grinded and sexually pulled Randle onto his rising erection.

"What...what...what are you doing?" Randle nervously asked, falling to the floor like a helpless but yet vulnerable victim. "Ba...ba...baack up, you're... you're in my space..." he stated sounding like a woman as his lips shivered, while looking up at the muscular Caucasian detainee with a spider web covering his left jaw and neck, more terrified than anyone could ever imagine.

"I'm taking claim to be your jailhouse war-daddy, Pink-Toe, before someone else do, unless you enjoy a struggle to get mmmmmoist," he piped with the look of lust in his eyes as he aggressively stepped forward. Teasingly he licked his lips, while attempting to grab Randle's hair so that he could lift him from the ground, choke him into submission, then drag his limp body to the rear of the cell for some conjugal pleasure.

But he was unsuccessful in achieving his fantasy because Randle immediately started backpedaling to the door while hollering at the top of his lungs, "Help! I'm the victim of an attacking! Helppp! Helpppp!" Which caught the fingerprinting officer's attention?

Removed from the holding cell and momentarily separated for safety, Randle's face glowed like a portable nightlight. The presence of Detective Reed unlocking the door and acknowledging himself gave him hope, especially when he escorted him out of the isolated holding cell and into a small interrogation room with no windows. Because of his persistent cries to the others, he assumed that the detective was there to help him get out of his troubles instead of being present merely to investigate the arson and feticide case that was assigned to him. Reaching into his pocket to remove a small portable recorder, he placed it on the table with a file and notepad prior to seating himself across from Randle. Detective Reed informed him of the charges being filed against him and asked would he like to talk.

"Yes! Hell yes! Is it possible for me to get immunity if I provide creditable information?" He exclaimed without hesitation, thrilled and excited to finally be granted the opportunity.

"I see you watch a lot of movies Mr. Carter." The Detective insinuated, while reaching to press the record button after casually acknowledging the interrogation interview would be recorded. Det. Reed verbally stated the date, time, and purpose of the interview, then openly advised Randle of his Miranda Rights once again before granting him the opportunity to say anything.

Not trying to postpone the interrogation for another time due to him not having a lawyer present, Randle waived his rights and asked the one reiterated question he needed an answer too. "If I tell you all the creditable things I know, will it help me out of this situation?"

"I can't say or promise that anything will help you out of the predicament you have placed yourself in, Mr. Carter, but all information is helpful."

"Please help me, Detective. I can't stay in this place," Randle cried. "Let me work for you, I know people who are selling illegal guns they steal from train cargo. I know about a warehouse that has an underground meth lab ..."

"Mr. Carter, I'm not here for that at this moment," Detective Reed interjected, "I need to know what happened at the Johnson residence on the day in question."

"Sir, if you allow me to tell you about the things I know, I promise to answer all your questions truthfully, Detective. Please, I'm begging you to allow me the ability of helping myself. Honestly, I know a lot. Jewelry store heists, bank fraud ..."

Realizing the volunteered information he was willing to give could probably help other detectives on their ongoing investigations and bring upon more arrests without him receiving any beneficial credit, he leaned back in his chair and instructed Randle to share what he knew if he truly wanted to get out. He was referring to getting out of the interrogation room, but knew Randle clearly assumed otherwise.

"What do you want to know about first, sir, the associates of my father who sell stolen art, the way my cousin steals and smuggles OxyContin from different Tennessee pharmacies for this pharmaceutical doctor in Florida, the woman who

used the names of dead people to file fake claims with medical insurance companies
..."

Not truly believing he was actually hearing all the things Randle was exposing,
Detective Reed stopped him until the video recorder which he texted the front desk
officer requesting was brought in the room by a coworker and set up.

Pressing record and testing the video recorder's operation, he was now ready
to hear all that Randle had to leak. "Mr. Carter, in all honesty, I'd like for you to
tell me everything you know at this moment without leaving anything out. You
may continue with our interview...," Det. Reed announced, after adjusting the lens
and pressing record on the camera.

After giving a five-hour detailed, recorded interview, Randle was released and
escorted to a dormitory, which he never expected. With no officers standing outside
the cell door as those in the booking area of the jail, Randle had no guardian to
protect him. Shaking as he stood motionless, panning and focusing on the detainees
in his new living quarters, his face was immediately recognized as the individual
from the news broadcasting channel moments earlier that caused a pregnant
woman to lose her twins and was also rumored to have assaulted an autistic child.
With individuals angry, frustrated, and stirring with lustful desires that could not
be extinguished, several detainees already assigned to the unit and seeking a way to
channel their aggression, forced him into the shower to defend himself from their
knuckles. The news reporting had them seeking vengeance with no remorse.
Overpowered and defenseless as he laid on the cold wet tile surface bleeding from
multiple lacerations, and trying to mumble, "Help me," with a re-broken jaw,
Randle drifted out of consciousness as a foot smashed into his head in the very
instance that one of the detainees requested another to go get the Vaseline.

CHAPTER 39

Electing to sleep late, after having to work a double shift unexpectedly, Demi wished she had turned her phone off before going to sleep. Not wanting to climb out of bed to put it on silent, the constant ringing caused her to wish she had. Throwing back the sheet and easing off the mattress like a garden snail, she stumped across the room and grabbed her phone from the dresser, then contemplated throwing it out the window but noticed that it was her mother repeatedly calling like the world was about to end.

Debating whether or not to dial her number back, for Demi wasn't in the mood to engage in a long winded conversation, yet was curious to know what was so urgent, she pressed her picture on the screen and climbed back into the bed because she knew her mother wouldn't stop until she reached her.

"As salam alaikum wa rahmatullahi, sweetie!"

"Wa alaikum as salam wa rahmatullahi wa barakatu, mum. What's wrong?"

"Nothing is wrong, baby girl! I was just calling because I sent you three pictures you didn't respond to, and I wanted your opinion on which pair of shoes looks best with the outfit I have on," Mrs. Laconette concluded.

"Mum, you mean to tell me that you called me nine times back to back just to inquire about some shoes?" Demi emphasized without raising her voice, literally stupefied, unable to assimilate how it's even possible that she is being deprived of sleep and comfort just to give an opinionated verdict on some shoes.

"I apologize sweetie. I didn't know you were sleeping, but yes, the 'Tears of an Empty Heart' author is in town having a book signing at a battered women's shelter this evening for his new book, and I want to look nice for the event. I promise to get a book signed with your name scripted inside as well."

Flabbergasted by the thirty-six minute conversation that now has her feeling even more sluggish yet unable to fall back asleep, Demi laid sprawled across the bed thinking of Terry as her little prince rested on his pillow staring at her. Noticing the light on her phone blinking, she hesitated before tilting it to see who was now messaging her, because she was not interested in viewing more shoe pics.

Smiling as the slideshow of Reanna's dog pictures flashed on her screen, Demi forwarded a few of her baby in his rain suit and his sleep wear, then called Mrs. Johnson since it seemed like escaping to another dimension was no longer within reach. Delighted to have received her support for the request she phoned about, Demi playfully muzzled her dog's face with her right hand before sliding back out of bed as he chased her into the bathroom, where she stepped in the stall after getting undressed and shocked all of her senses with a cold shower.

Feasting on the roasted garlic, spinach, and a feta cheese omelet she threw together after sliding on her draped, sleeveless jumpsuit and pulling her hair up in a ponytail, Demi found her little prince's whimpering and begging, licking his chops so amusing as she ate the omelet in his face that she recorded him and uploaded it to her social media page. Smiling, she was pleasantly surprised to see it receive over a thousand likes before they left the apartment just twenty minutes later. "You are famous, honey." She jokingly exclaimed as she walked to the car, playfully lifting him up and down in the air.

Lowering the window so that the wind could blow in his face as she drove through traffic while holding the leash to his harness, Demi was tickled by his jealousy as usual. He bounced playfully in the seat, exciting kids in other vehicles, yet barked aggressively at every man they passed that looked Demi's way. He was her protector and father it seemed in his eyes.

Demi loved driving to the Johnson's estate. The indescribable beauty of the luxury glass homes and multi-million-dollar gated mansions always fueled her with inspiration, never shy of suspending her in awe. Rolling up the passenger window as they were buzzed inside the gate, her little prince's eyes missed not a single movement of the Rottweilers walking toward the vehicle as she parked behind a pink, convertible BMW M4. Not knowing how the dogs would react to her getting out of the car with him in her arms, she called Mrs. Johnson as they approached her car, licking their lips. Stepping out of the front door seconds later, Gip instructed them to back away from her car and sit, which each obeyed.

Demi admired the flowers of their landscape and always took a moment to bask in the tranquility of the scenery before climbing the steps. Greeting Mr. Johnson at the door with a hug, she then handed him her prince as he requested, but his little eyes were fixated on the Rottweilers and not trying to play. Walking into the house and giggling at Gip's silliness, Demi didn't hesitate telling Mrs. Johnson how stunning she looked in the striped halter maxi dress as she entered the foyer from a side entrance door and greeted her with a gentle hug.

Escorting her to Sheri's room so they could all talk, Yara introduced her to Naomi, who was too busy flaunting her curves in a faux suede romper to some Asian guy while video chatting, to properly return the greeting when they entered.

Facing Sheri for the first time since her egregious incident was a bit much for Demi because she was raised by men who honored the breath of a woman, not physically abuse them for control. She remembered their last encounter and her exchange of words with Sheri which added to her emotional storm. The swelling and multiple lacerations in her face sprouted grief in her heart. She stood there not understanding how a man could unleash any remote measure of brutality upon a woman. Compelled to apologize out of respect for allowing her anger to affect her character when their paths last crossed, Demi articulated her words with such sincerity that Sheri reached out and touched her cheek with her fingers as she stood beside the bed and interjected: "You don't have to apologize to me, Demi. My apology is the only one necessary because it was my stupidity, selfishness, and blindness that took my brother from all of us."

"Gurrlll, you know what they say about a white man's tongue," Naomi interjected.

Mrs. Johnson leaped like a leopard at Naomi's inappropriate ramp up, "Naomi! My free consultation advice to you is to shut the fuck up!"

"Well, I know what they say and why they say what they say!" Naomi ignored and mouthed playfully, shaking as though she were experiencing an orgasm, causing uncontrollable laughter to erupt from everyone, Mrs. Johnson included.

"Gurrrrl, I can only imagine what's said about your damn nasty mouth." Mrs. Johnson articulated, continuing to laugh as Naomi rolled her eyes and contemplated what to say.

With the little prince being caressed as he laid across Sheri's stomach, feasting off the hand-fed roast beef slices she requested earlier for herself and the shift of the mood becoming comical, Demi and the ladies veered toward lighter conversation, while attempting to ignore Naomi's x-rated video chatting. They entertained one another by talking about hilarious aspects of their lives, fashion, unforgettable experiences, and their goals.

Laughing amongst each other as Sheri stopped Naomi from telling a dominatrix story she experienced with a man in a wheelchair, Yara couldn't hold back from sharing the story of how Naomi assumed she had supernatural power the first time she had her menstrual cycle. And the story of how Sheri caused Terry

415

to mess all over himself by putting her three pet mice in his bed when she was nine because he made the mistake of leaving her doll in a White Water Theme Park locker and laughed about it.

Shifting the atmosphere of entertainment away from Naomi's chickenhead characteristics that had their abs stricken with intense laughter, Demi decided to enlighten them more about herself. Bridging new relations, she shared personal things about her childhood which she held close to the breast, her beliefs, and why she's compelled to one day open a safe center for battered women and children. Silence momentarily prevailed when Naomi's phone started beeping and instead of saying, "excuse me" to answer it respectfully, she jumped up and started twerking before positioning it to see her body as she pressed the icon to video chat.

"Hi Papi!" She purred seductively, not caring what others thought as they watched her actions in amazement.

Finally arriving to the house after leaving her OBGYN appointment, Penélope sauntered into the room with the grace of a butterfly fluttering in the wind. She politely greeted everyone before showering Sheri with a 24-count box of white chocolate covered strawberries as well as a 24-count box of chocolate covered pineapples then turned around to affectionately hug Mrs. Johnson. "I love this outfit you're wearing, ultra fab. But Mrs. J." She expressed devilishly slanting her eyes to Naomi without turning her head. "I just don't understand how Naomi can be a student of your teaching her entire life, yet always looks like a ratchet doodoo momma whenever in public."

"Let me tell your...." Naomi attempted as everyone burst into laughter.

"Be quiet Naomi," Yara interjected with sternness in her voice, as everyone continued to giggle and she stepped forward to hug her friend, even though Naomi was now acting nonchalant. With Penélope now present and Demi interested to hear everyone's opinion, she clearly acknowledged that they could begin discussing the party they were going to host for Terry, granted he obtains a bond and gets released.

Wanting to do something special for her baby because she seriously missed him and his sincere gentlemanly characteristics, but not exclude his family, Demi inquired from Yara if they could all plan something together which would leave no one feeling unappreciated or as though she were trying to be selfish and have him all to herself.

"Demi, I must applaud you, girl. You're definitely a better woman than me," Naomi instigated, snatching the top box of chocolates out of Sheri's hand and opening it to exercise her incisors on a chocolate covered pineapple, capping off her needling remark and rudely satisfying her sweet tooth simultaneously..

"Gurl, how in the hell are you gonna eat one before me?" An aggravated Sheri reprimanded as Demi's little prince stood on her stomach and started barking.

"Like this," Naomi boasted, placing another up to her lips then slowly placing the whole pineapple in her mouth, while playfully licking her lips and sticking her tongue out at the little prince.

"Okay, you've tossed a bone out there which definitely sparks my curiosity, Naomi. Just what do you mean by that?" Perplexed, Demi inquisitions.

"You invited the ex-lover of your man to consult with us about throwing him a party," Naomi responded. "There's no way in hell my man's ex would have the audacity of being in the same area code as me, let alone in the damn room, unless I'm spanking her ass to let her know who the boss bitch is."

"What man?" Sheri blurted out while opening the box to retrieve a white chocolate covered strawberry. "Girl, you wake up and go to sleep in a different man's bed every day, other than the few days you stay home 'cause you don't like to be bothered when you have menstrual cramps. If the boldface lie you just told was true, then you'd be a prize street fighter, Naomi, because every married and unmarried man is considered your man, as long as they show you some attention," Sheri exclaimed, causing everyone but Naomi to laugh before biting into her strawberry.

Giggling with everyone as Naomi rolled her eyes and teased, tossing yet another chocolate covered pineapple in her mouth, "Naomi! What do you think those are? Poppers, fool?! Ya'll better get some before Ms. Thang devours them all," Penélope asked rhetorically and warned the others.

Just then, Demi looked at Penélope and spoke the truth. "Penélope is beautiful and a blessing to any man, as am I in my opinion, but she can never be my enemy because of what her and Terry shared over the years or what they feel internally for one another though they're not together," Terry is going to make his own choices, no matter what I do or say, and nothing will ever change that. My self-worth and integrity exceed chasing a man or fighting another woman because she gained his attention. Penélope is a part of this family, regardless of the foundation Terry and I build together. So, I would be wrong not to include her.

She still loves him and wants what's best for him and what makes him happy, just he does her, I'm sure. Besides, she's about to tie the knot, and I know that Terry wishes her well, as do I, so I respect that. I believe it's all about empowerment, both mentally and physically. When we learn to put aside our differences and selfish envy that wedges us apart, we begin to prove that we're irreplaceable as a whole, which in essence will compel men to respect us as they once have, which many women no longer demand."

"Bitch please! Pardon me, I'm nawt Bri'ish, but I am territorial, and I demaaand my respect, quite honestleee, especially when that cock can cause you to shed that one tiny bit of a tear at the bloody precise moment you're climaxing," Naomi professed with a British accent, causing everyone to erupt in laughter.

"Not bad, Naomi, but you should probably stick to your day job, devouring cocks and chocolate covered pineapples." Quipped the Lady from Stockholm, complementing the laughter.

Rising from her seat and approaching Penélope as she stood beside the bed pampering the little prince with Sheri. "Demi, gurrrl, if I were standing in your shoes, I would have backhanded her one good time on our bloody first encounter just to let her know that I'm Queen Bitch with a badass alter ego she shouldn't eva wanna meet," playfully throwing up her hand as though she was about to slap Penélope to illustrate for Demi, reinforcing the gravity of what she meant. Unfortunately, Naomi never expected her to block the unintended swing then use an un-choreographed defensive technique to spin her around and lock her in a submissive choke hold while playfully squeezing the air from her lungs and slapping Naomi's booty with her free hand.

Losing the British accent altogether, "Penélope, let me go, girl! Mrs. Johnson, tell her to let me go," Naomi pleaded as everyone laughed and the little prince barked in Sheri's arms.

"I tried to warn you to stick to your day job, Naomi," Sheri reminded.

Tapping Penélope on the shoulder to indicate she had had enough, she released the yoke from Naomi's neck, then squeezed another handful of her booty before falling into Mrs. Johnson's arms laughing.

Transformed back to the gutter Naomi, "Stank, you play too damn much." "Don't be grabbing me like that, I have flashbacks when I'm choked, and you are not Mr. Magic Stick. You need some dick with your strong lesbian ass," Naomi piped rubbing her neck and sitting back down as Demi covers her mouth to keep from laughing so loud.

"I have several of them, and not one of them can infect me," Penelope declared, rolling her eyes. "Naomi, I know one thing, you better learn how to defend yourself instead of trying to be a dominatrix queen. You talk about being territorial for some dick, but I could take any man you claim and your hard butt ass at the same time without breaking a sweat," Penélope expressed while laughing and apologizing for cursing.

Trying to come up with the right party theme, seemed to be a little more challenging than Demi initially expected. Yara wanted an elegant all white event. Penélope believed that they should have a BBQ at the ranch with only close friends and family. Naomi spoke foolishly about having Chippendale dancers and allowing her to jump out of the cake with one of them, which only she considered a good idea. Sheri felt a big party would be the last thing he would desire. Everyone should just eat together, which is something they haven't done in years. And Demi kept looking at Sheri, feeling sad that no matter what they agreed upon, she wouldn't be able to be a part of, given her condition.

"Penélope, will you come help me in the kitchen please?" Yara asked rising from her seat to walk out the door, after they agreed on eating lamb quesadillas.

Waiting until they were downstairs before she started talking, Yara thanked her for being keen on not starting a conversation about her own pregnancy as it would have fueled the trauma of Sheri's preempted pregnancy, and for never exposing her to the picture she took of Randle, his ex, and his son at the mall.

"Mrs. Johnson, she's still devastated internally, and her healing is going to take a lot of time. She and I talked extensively last night, and she awakened my heart when she said that listening to Selma Blair speak openly about the trials and tribulations of her misfortune had given her strength. She acknowledged that you are her rock and the pain she feels for losing the twins, but Sheri also understands that God is testing her faith by removing the very things that she was holding more dear to her heart than Him. I only hate the fact that I showed the picture to Mama Lewis first because you know she's like a woven bucket of Braveheart plaid that a fool tries to fill with water."

"We've talked, and I honestly don't think she will say anything," Yara opined while placing the Korean-style lamb in the pan, "I just think it's sad that Randle doesn't even realize that the little autistic boy is his son. His mom told Aaron that death would come upon her ten times before she'd ever tell him that he's the father, but she wouldn't say what Randle did to make her feel that way."

"That is so sad! I will never understand what gives women the right to feel they have the authority to take that joy, right, and responsibility away from a man or the child. Some women are so delusional and selfish that they never truly take into consideration how a child suffers, mentally, being forced to go through life feeling that their father cared nothing about them," Penélope exclaimed, grabbing the kimchi, spicy mayo, and cilantro from the refrigerator.

Meanwhile, upstairs, "Demi, can I ask you a question?" Naomi uttered while trying to comment on one of Cardi B's social media post.

"Yes!"

"Being that you're from the UK, do the women there teach y'all, growing up, any sexual techniques with the mouth or a position that would drive a man absolutely crazy? Gurl, you have to excuse me, but I'm always trying to elevate my sex game."

"You are the sex game," Sheri insinuated before Demi could open her mouth and respond.

"Fuck you!" Shouted Naomi.

"To answer your question, no, Naomi. The women of my upbringing groomed us to preserve our worth for our husbands and treasure who we are," Demi asserted. "We are taught how to define ourselves as women and how to compliment a man to strengthen the bond of the relationship."

"Gurrrlll, please! You just don't know what you're missing. There's no way possible I can wait my entire life for one man — dick is too refreshing to the soul." An urban poetic Naomi rifled.

"Naomi, shut uuuup!" Sheri shouted, realizing that she was being insensitive and disrespectful, yet honest only regarding herself. "Demi, I applaud you and wish I would have had the same disciplined virtue."

"Both o' y'all bougie hoochies crazy," Naomi insisted while getting up to grab a white chocolate covered strawberry from Sheri's box. Rubbing her left hand across the curves of her body seductively while biting into the strawberry, "I am a man's greatest sex toy and his greatest experience." Naomi advertised with southern authority in her voice, while squatting to rotate her hips provocatively.

"You are a man's greatest reason to get a new prescription of penicillin," Mrs. Johnson articulated, re-entering the room while carrying a tray of lamb quesadillas.

"I'm really starting to believe y'all just jealous of me," Naomi retorted while rising to grab two wrapped quesadillas from the tray and a strawberry lemonade Evolution juice from Penélope. "If I shared with y'all what happened to me last night, then all four of y'all would envy my game and beg me to sprinkle some sauce on y'all. I am the baddest thing on the east coast, besides my girl, Cardi B, of course."

"Alright, well go ahead and claim yo' title, Ms. Easy-n-Nasty," Penélope roasted with sarcasm seasoning, which caused everyone except Naomi to burst out laughing.

Even though Sheri was internally broken as she lay in her condition, she enjoyed every moment of their company. She found it extremely hard for her not to think of her babies with Penélope nurturing embryos in her presence, but she knew it was important for her to remain strong and work on getting stronger. The gentleness and compassion of Demi was a light for her darkness, which is why she whispered in her ear for her to stop by the following day, if she could, so that they could talk alone. She was starting to admire Demi's character and the integrity she bore which defined her.

Not realizing all their joking and talking had caused them all to lose track of time and the new episode of Animal Kingdom was about to come on, Demi made a suggestion and hoped it would gain the approval of everyone after consulting with the nurse in private, regarding Sheri's condition.

"Mrs. Johnson, to have a party would be inconsiderate of Sheri. And in truth, you wouldn't be able to enjoy yourself because you'll constantly be thinking of her. I think all white attire, we can make happen, even Sheri, but I honestly think we should BBQ here instead of at the ranch. We should have a family dinner as Sheri acknowledged hasn't happened at your table for many years. Using the Broda wheelchair, Sheri can be the host, which won't be discomforting for her. But, when she's back on her feet, we can plan an appreciation party for us, whereas we exclude everyone except our mates. Having a big gathering would have people smothering Sheri with affection and I honestly don't feel she wants to be pitied, which would take away from the purpose of the gathering."

"I like that suggestion, Demi, and you're so right, I don't want to be comforted with fake pity nor do I care to be the topic of gossip." Sheri expressed, while asking her mom to turn out the lights because the episode was coming on.

"I don't take sand to the beach, hoochies. Why invite a man anywhere and lose out on meeting someone if the opportunity presents itself? I'm looking for Mr. Right, not trying to imitate a flight attendant holding hands with some yesterday's baggage," Naomi blurted out, being sincere.

"Unfortunately, you are the beach," Yara lipped before walking over to kiss Sheri on the forehead and attempting to leave the room with the little prince, so that they could watch TV.

"She's not the beach Ma, she's yesterday's baggage." Sheri joked tossing a strawberry at Naomi, who actually caught it with her mouth.

Rolling her eyes after catching the strawberry and devouring it, of course, Naomi showed Sheri her bird finger, while sticking her tongue out at Penélope. An act of defiance that caused them to laugh even more.

"You're a riot, Naomi," said Demi.

"A what?"

"Thank you, Mom,! Love you," Sheri purred, elevating the volume on the TV, while starting to giggle with Demi and Penélope, at the face Naomi was making.

"I love you too baby," was her closing sentiment, walking out the door and answering her phone.

CHAPTER 40

B rushing his teeth, while trying to effectively comprehend the wisdom Abdullah just shared regarding the virtue, integrity, and honor of a woman, Terry looked at himself in the bathroom mirror. Staring deeply into his own retinas, he wondered if he could ever truly love Demi with the same devotion and appreciation his father surrenders to his mother or greater. Her purity was a virtue that he had often taken for granted in others. But, the way Abdullah caused him to ponder in depth, concerning Demi's strength within the broadness of her knowledge, personality, loyalty, gentleness, and immeasurable love in the value of her self-worth, caused him to realize how great of a blessing she actually was beyond the essence of her mesmerizing exoticism.

Walking out of the bathroom, he paid no attention to how the majority of the detainees in the dormitory had gathered before the TV to admire the irresistible natural beauty of Kat Graham. All that lingered upon his thoughts was the Muslim referenced hadith Abdullah conveyed by The Beloved Prophet (may peace and blessings of God be upon him) that states: *"Woman was created from a rib. She will never be straightforward and consistent for you in any way. If you enjoy her (or your relationship with her), you will do so in spite of her crookedness. If you try to straighten her, you will break her, and her breaking is her divorce."*

Trying to deeply understand the psychology that one should completely accept the blessing that a woman is as God created her without attempting to straighten her in the traditional ways of a man's ego, was subconsciously challenging. How does one who feels that a woman's full submissiveness is the correct way for her to define the true essence of her love? Wholeheartedly open his eyes to believing that a real man respects her unique feminine nature, be her friend, and turn a blind eye to her common faults, while recognizing that these are parts of her nature as men have their own. Terry wondered as he smiled and imagined Demi breathing in his arms as the white thread of the morning sky acknowledged the sun's awakening — would allowing her to be completely herself, as his father does with his mother, elevate their foundation and closeness or create constant conflict, her feminine strength and values taken into account?

"What is so funny?" He asked Abdullah, arriving back at his bunk and noticing him chuckling while trying to do some sit-ups in bed.

"Just the open-minded awareness that many ethnicities are like the myrmicacin," Abdullah enlightened while baring the pain of straining to do a few extra sit-ups.

"What is that and what do you mean?" Terry questioned, putting away his hygiene items and preparing to pray before trying to get a few hours of sleep, given that his bond hearing was scheduled for the next day.

"The myrmicacin is a genus of the jumping spider, which imitates the ant by waving their front legs in the air in order to simulate antennae which is the very same thing the majority of races are doing because we no longer have an identity beyond the sacrifices of our ancestors. When you look at our race in today's society, you will clearly see that we are imitating the characteristics of every ethnic race, while lack defining our own. We have no unity outside of a political protest that lasts no more than a few hours, nor a true American culture to gain inspiration from or to mold our moral values without studying African tribes that our characteristics do not resemble. The majority of our sisters no longer honor or applaud their natural beauty because they're too fascinated with mimicking someone else's features, and many of our brothers are still structuring their life off the Jim Crow philosophy without a true sense of the black man's worth.

"I was laughing when you approached because the personalities of people are quite funny, Terry," he pointed out while sitting up to massage the burning tightness in his stomach. "I am forever entertained by the characteristics of others without the need of a TV or fantasy novel to escape reality. Do you hear the senseless argument those young guys have going on over there? They waste time and energy every day, as many others around us do, on fruitless conversations instead of striving to strengthen their intellect, their character, or working on their case. Last night, they argued for an hour on who has more money between Jay-Z and 50 Cent, as though it benefits their life in any way. This morning while you were at visitation, they argued about muscle cars neither has ever owned or driven, and now they're standing in front of the TV arguing like women over whether it's Kat Graham's eyes or breathtaking smile that causes her beauty to be hypnotic instead of considering her intellect and character the sexiest quality she offers life or just acknowledging altogether, God created her as a blessing."

Turning around to see who Kat Graham was while attentively listening to their argument, Terry couldn't help but chuckle when he heard one of the young men say, "I'd loved to hand feed her on a picnic with my special recooked

Moroccan seasoned leftover chicken dish that I make with ramen noodles, dried coconuts and the dark meat chicken from Church's."

"And you have the nerve to wonder why I say people are like the myrmicacin. It's not a view of being judgmental, Terry, 'cause we all can discover characteristics of ourselves in other creations of God," Abdullah proclaimed while starting another set of sit-ups. "I'm just saying it's sad that people waste time talking fruitlessly about things that have no value in life while others spend every passing moment striving to achieve the acceptance of someone who grants them nothing."

"I see your point, but it's also like you once advised me, if I'm correct. Someone has to be lost upon a path of no arrival so that God can bestow His light on them and guide them to His kingdom," Terry recalls while grabbing Abdullah's prayer rug to go pray.

"Subhan Allah," Abdullah exclaimed, "but the key is also to learn from your mistakes as well as others."

Walking over to the corner of the room everyone uses to pray or gather to have bible study without the interference of others, Terry laid out the rug and thought of his family as he fell to his knees and cried out to God with his head lowered onto the fingers of pressed together hands.

"O God, You are my Lord! None has the right to be worshipped but You. You created me, I am Your slave, and I am faithful to my covenant and my promise as much as I can. I seek refuge with You from all the evil I have done, knowingly and unknowingly. I acknowledge before You all the blessings You have bestowed upon me and I ask You to forgive me for all my wrongdoings against people that You have recorded, for there are many rights and dues owed to Your servants that I have burdened myself with and for which I am hostage.

O God, I call upon You through Your benevolence, generosity, and abundance of what You aide and help, because without Your assistance, there is no light on my path of travel. Please, grant me Your mercy and the ability of going home to my family tomorrow in sha Allah, so that I can learn more about you, help others for Your sake and Glory alone but more so to prove that I love you from the purity of my heart and not my tongue. I confess to You that I've sinned out of selfishness and ignorance, my Lord, yet I beg of You to let me glorify, honor, and worship You as the servant You gave life to..."

Rising from his prayer, Terry turned around feeling a little different and momentarily stood there observing others in the dormitory before strolling back to his bunk. Neatly replacing Abdullah's prayer rug on the bed rail before sitting on his own, the annoying imitated baby speech of his bunkmate caused him to turn around. Terry was flabbergasted to witness the ex-soldier dancing more provocative than a Chippendale dancer to the imaginary friend he constantly entertains on his shoulder, while repeatedly uttering, "why you, why you, why you make me drop it like daaaat." Instantly realizing even more that this is not the life he wished to exist within, long term, Terry mumbled aloud with conviction in his heart, "God please grant me your mercy."

Laying back on the bed, he stared for a long time at his pictures of Cadence, Reanna, Sheri, and Demi he has tooth-pasted beneath his bunkmate's bed. Terry couldn't help but wonder if any of them missed him as much as he misses them.

"I offer du'a' for you in all of my prayers, Terry, and you have truly grown in the time that the distractions of life were stripped from you," Abdullah acknowledged while interrupting his train of thought.

"Abdullah, it may be sad for one to acknowledge, but I thank God every day for granting me this experience in many ways. He has not only opened my eyes to the greater meaning of life, but He bestowed upon me a new perspective which is priceless. A man is so many things, yet he is nothing without establishing a true worship with God that's held as his first priority, respecting women even when they don't know how to love themselves, and to be a light of hope for those who feel they are unseen in God's eyes."

"I'm going to miss you, Terry, but I do feel you are truly ready to step into the shoes you were given in life to wear."

"My release is something I pray for, yet don't honestly see it happening given the way others have been coming back from court lately." Removing the picture of Reanna holding her puppy while standing beside the horse she never rides, he started smiling, thinking of how he used to babysit her and would always feed her wet Hot Fries to stop her from crying. "Abdullah, your wisdom, inspiration, and presence, I could never stop thanking God for exposing me too. You will always be able to call me as long as I am granted God's mercy to breathe, which I also promise to keep money on your account, have my lawyer look into your case, and make sure you are able to see your daughter more regularly."

"Masha Allah! Al hamdulillahi, but I need you to understand that I accept the judgment that was given to me, Terry. Yes, it is painful to exist as a ghost in my daughter's life right now, but I was wrong to take someone's life as I did, which

I don't regret under the circumstances," Abdullah admitted. "You don't have to waste your money on trying to free me. *'Imprisoned is he whose heart is imprisoned from God. Captured is he who is captured by his desires,'* Ibn Taymiyyah once said. I'd rather you give it to my daughter to make sure she has shoes on her feet, clothes on her back, and food to prevent her from being hungry."

Instead of responding to Abdullah's words, he closed his eyes, knowing she will never have a need as long as he is concerned. Laying there lingering on memories, Terry drifted off to sleep after replacing Reanna's picture and blowing three kisses to Demi's. Being woken up by the jab of a female officer's radio antenna poking him in his side and calling his name, Terry opened his eyes and immediately assumed he was viewing a trailer park version of a cosplay girl with three inch eyelashes that looked like untrimmed walrus whiskers.

"Get ready for court, Mr. Johnson. I will be back to get you in thirty minutes," the officer informed in her bedroom voice while looking at the muscular curves in his chest instead of looking into his eyes.

"Yes, ma'am," he mumbled while stretching.

Looking over to realize Abdullah was not in his bed, he scanned the dormitory and noticed that he was offering his tahujjid prayer in the corner. Grabbing his necessities from his bag to take a quick shower, Terry hurried to the bathroom because he knew the officer's thirty minutes usually meant ten. Seeking a quick therapeutic hot shower, Terry turned the water nozzle and spent the entire time jumping and shaking due to the ice-cold stream never heating up. Stepping out to dry himself and noticing a detainee going to the toilet with the jack pics, he realized that if his freedom was granted, he would never miss being startled by the water temperature becoming a scalding stream every time someone flushed the toilet or being exposed to people masturbating on the toilet all day.

Walking back to his bed to dress and groom himself, Terry tried to imagine it was Demi massaging the lotion into his skin to comfort the moment. The anticipation of seeing her soon was intensifying his yearning, yet the dullness of his touch caused him to stop fantasizing, given his caresses didn't resemble hers.

Brushing his hair as he stood beside his bed, Abdullah interrupted his train of thought and handed him a piece of paper, on which, he wrote a du'a' that he instructed Terry to recite constantly while in the holding tank and courtroom.

"I will," he promised before the doors later opened and the officer stepped inside to call his name.

"Terry Johnson, court call! Terry Johnson, court call!"

"Coming!" He yelled, while throwing his things in the property bin before turning to walk toward the door as Abdullah accompanied him with encouraging words from the Qur'an. Stepping outside of the dormitory door, the duty officer highlighted his name on a docket sheet after commanding him to state his name. Visually checking Terry's armband to assure he was the right detainee, she then instructed him to place his hands on the wall and performed an intimate pat search out of personal pleasure more so than a requirement by policy or an obligated duty of security.

Being escorted with a group of detainees to the elevator, and commanded to face the wall like a child as the elevator operated, Terry assumed they were headed directly to the transfer area of the jail where he'd be transported to the courthouse on a bus. Yet, he had no knowledge of security procedures required for them to be taken to a secure room on a lower floor at one o'clock in the morning to be thoroughly strip-searched, fed an ice cold bologna sandwich with an apple, a frozen solid 4oz carton of orange juice and forced to wait in an adjacent holding cell on concrete until court transportation left at 7am.

Unable to establish a sense of comfort sitting on a concrete bench in the overcrowded room that was smelling like an unventilated chicken coop, Terry shifted side to side for hours as he listened to the others gossip about their cases, the lies they told women for the opportunity to exploit their bodies, crazy drug experiences of their past street adventures, and petty scams they planned to indulge in once released. But nothing was more unforgettable and disgusting than hearing the three guys standing before him whisper about some white guy they've been repeatedly raping like an erotic porn star for abusing a child and how good he was causing them to feel. With the odor of the room seemingly getting worse with every intake of polluted oxygen and the voices around him becoming more irritating than amusing as time passed like a frozen watch with no battery, Terry tucked half his face into his jumpsuit, closed his eyes, and thought of the way Demi's lips tasted and felt when she kissed him in his dreams until the officer started calling their names for transport.

Standing in line to board the bus with shackles now secured to his ankles, handcuffs binding his wrists, and a chain around his waist that attached to them both to limit his movement and ability of escaping, Terry stepped forward by the officer's command as the excruciating pain of the shackles cutting off his blood circulation began numbing his legs.

"Excuse me, sir! Officer, can you please loosen the shackles a notch or two please? The cuffs are very tight against my ankles, sir," Terry informed politely.

Feeling disrespected and challenged in front of his coworkers by being asked to stop what he was doing to redo something he had already done thoroughly in the process of securing the detainees for transport, he slowly removed the expandable baton from his waist band as he approached Terry in a state of frustration. Spitting in his face while speaking like a drill sergeant, he extended the retracted baton with a forceful snap of his wrist and pressed the point of it into the right side of Terry's jaw.

"Boy, don't ever ask me for shit 'cause I'm not your damn friend. I don't care how tight those shackles are around your fuckin' ankles or how you're feeling. You're a prisoner, boy, and have no fuckin' rights or requests. If you ever stop me from doing my job again, every inch of this baton you shall eat willingly while beggin' me to remove my foot from your ass," he yelled. "Are we clear, boy?"

Staring intently into the black officer's eyes as he pressed the baton harder into his jaw with each breath, Terry thought of Abdullah's words of combating ignorance with kindness, and allowed his humility to suppress his anger as the metal ball tip pressed against his teeth. "Yes, sir."

With no officer stopping their coworker from abusing the detainees verbally or physically, now that Terry had aroused his anger, he began forcing the remaining inmates on the bus like cattle by tapping them on the back of the head or back with the baton as he called their names.

Clueless as to why some blacks always feel they have to degrade one another to prove something when working around whites, Terry sat on the bus observing the character of the other black officers and wondered how can we as a race ever truly feel we have broken the unseen yokes around our necks and limiting our minds, when we can't even respect or appreciate who we are without existing in the presence of others like puppets. We hate and ridicule one another for senseless reasons, but claim the white man is racist and our enemy. Pulling away from the jail and cruising through traffic en route to the courthouse, Terry stared out of the window to alleviate his mind from the pain and numbness the shackles were causing.

Arriving at the courthouse in a time frame that seemed as if they pulled out of the garage and drove around to the back of the building, a huge sigh of relief, Terry felt like a baby exhaling after being escorted inside and having the cuffs and chains removed. Placed in a holding cell according to what courtroom their case was assigned to, Terry stood patiently against the wall in the basement hallway with forty-seven others while listening and waiting for his name to be called. Thankful to only have to share a cell with eleven other detainees, and several too anxious to know the unknown ruling of their case to sit down, he laid back on the concrete bench, removed Abdullah's note from his pocket, and repeatedly recited the scribbled words :

"O God, Knower of the unseen and the evident, Maker of the heavens and the Earth, Lord of everything and its Possessor. I bear witness that there is none worthy of worship, but You. I seek refuge in You from the evil of my soul and from the evil of Satan and his countless helpers. I seek refuge in You from a heart that has no love for Your glory or fear of Your wrath. O God, I seek Your forgiveness and Your protection in this world and the next. O God, I seek Your forgiveness and protection in my religion, in my worldly affairs, in my family, and in wealth. O God conceal my secrets from the eyes of everyone but You and preserve me from anguish. O God, guard me from the front of me, from behind me, from my left, from my right, from above me, O Lord, and from being struck down from beneath my feet. I seek refuge in You from the disbelieving people who have no love in You. I seek refuge in You in every calling upon You and being ignored..."

No longer able to read or meditate on the written words in peace, due to the ridiculously loud conversation of the detainee sitting beside him, trying to explain to another the medical benefits of why he saves all his jail food and allows a small portion of mold to develop on it before eating as a means of giving his body natural antibiotics to fight off germs and infections that may develop by being incarcerated with so many nasty individuals, had Terry laughing internally at the thought of someone truly believing there were medicinal benefits in something so stupid. Little did Terry know, it was a hoax, and the loudmouth actually began to wonder if he could convince Terry to try the ridiculous regimen at his amusement.

With only one of the six whom had attended court so far, returning with good news of going home, the others complaining of the judge's refusal to listen to reason and his dislike for violent offenders, Terry began wondering more and more as he waited on them to call his name, would he be forced to stay longer?

Monitoring the movement of the guards through the window, Terry was already standing and approaching the door when he saw him grab his name card from the board before the officer opened it and yelled his name.

"Terry Johnson!"

"Standing before you, sir," he acknowledged extending his arms to have his wrist bound with the handcuffs before being escorted to the courtroom through a back hallway that leads to an elevator where he was again commanded to face the wall as they ascended three floors.

Terry's excitement at seeing his lawyer sitting in an adjacent back room of the courtroom as they exited the elevator was instantly suppressed when he was led inside to sit in the chair across the table from her. Without the usual formal greeting, her first words were, "I'm going to ask the judge for a two week continuance on the bond hearing this morning because I've just been advised that the District Attorney has new incriminating evidence against you, Mr. Johnson, and I'm not yet aware of what it is."

Looking as though his face had just stopped the blunt force of a hickory bat falling from an airplane, Terry momentarily sat frozen as her words echoed in his mind. Distraught by the realization that holding his mother, sister, grandmother, or Demi was no longer an option in the making, he stared at the handcuffs binding his wrist, unable to say a word.

"Mr. Johnson, please don't allow this to discourage you ..."

"You have got to be kidding me, right? He interjected. "Discouraged?! I haven't slept in thirty-four days due to the unbearable snoring in the isolated cell that I'm forced to share with others. I'm constantly surrounded by men who smell worse than gorillas, men who claim to have girlfriends and wives, but nurture the desires of their lust with the physical affection of another man, and men who are more mentally challenged than a mad scientist's human cloning experiment. Yet, you sit here advising me not to get discouraged as though I'm faced with countless alternatives. How can there be some evidence against me when I haven't done anything?" He barked, irritated and flabbergasted by the thought of having to stay longer.

"Mr. Johnson, I know the circumstances may be mentally tormenting and this is unexpected news," she leaned forward stating while twirling the pen between her fingers like a baton. "But I cannot represent you effectively, being in the blind. I will ask the Judge for a continuance, but I'm also submitting a motion to suppress new evidence today which will allow me time to view whatever the prosecutor has obtained and re-strategize accordingly."

Thinking that Stewart turning himself in and maybe mentioning that he concealed the knowledge of his actions was the new evidence, Terry rose out of his seat while staring at his lawyer flip through documents in a folder before her and speaking words that had become inaudible to his deaf ears.

"You will not ask for a continuance," he instructed her, reaching into his jumpsuit pocket to retrieve the note Abdullah gave him prior to leaving. "Read this," he said extending it for her to grab, while watching as she unfolded the piece of paper and her eyes caressed every word. Remembering the words his father taught him to whisper within his heart when faced with adversity, Terry recited a passage from Psalms when she raised her eyes from the handwritten note attempting to speak.

''Give ear to my prayer, O God, and do not hide Yourself from my supplication. Attend to me, and hear me, I am restless in my complaint, and moan noisily, Because of the voice of the enemy, Because of the oppression of the wicked for they bring down trouble upon me, and in wrath, they hate me. My heart is severely pained within me."

"I have prayed," Terry professed as they stared into each other's eyes. "And whatever God's will, no one can alter. I respect your counseling strategy, but I've paid you to represent me for a bond hearing today, not in two weeks, and I'm ready to go inside now without any further delay. I believe in you."

"Mr. Johnson, I pray myself but..."

"Seriously," Terry interjected walking over to the door and starting to knock for the guards, which she immediately advised him to stop before the judge found him in contempt.

Handing Terry back his note after gathering her things and the officers coming to the room, due to the banging causing a disturbance to the courtroom's silence, his lawyer apologized for the unintended noise and informed the officers that they were ready to proceed. Pat searching Terry thoroughly to make sure he wasn't given any contraband from his lawyer, the deputies escorted him ten minutes later into the courtroom and sat him at the table beside her after being notified by the Judge to bring him inside.

Seeing his entire family, except Sheri sitting on the benches behind him whispering, waving and snickering amongst each other at the extreme tightness of his jail jumpsuit, warmed his heart like a child's first day of school. Unable to hide the excitement flowing through his veins, Terry wrote, "I love you," in the air with his fingers, then turned and started blowing kisses to everyone, which his father batted down causing everyone to start laughing.

Being instructed to stop by the Bailiff and then his lawyer, due to court rules and procedures, certainly it was a distraction for the district attorney standing at the podium presenting the case, Terry vs The State, to the court, Terry turned around and gave his full attention to the preceding. After viewing countless courtroom episodes on TV and the movies, Terry had no idea how the actual atmosphere would suspend him upon the feeling as though he was a barefooted funambulist, defying gravity and disaster above the mouth of a volcano without a harness.

Quietly sitting at the table and becoming annoyed by the mountain of lies spoken against him, Terry mentally recited the du'a' Abdullah wrote to calm himself while listening attentively as the district attorney degraded his character as if he was void of morals and values. Needing to make a prolific opening argument to give his theory a solid foundation, the district attorney fabricated a ridiculous story of how the murders transpired, Terry's intentions behind his motive, and the assumption of why he left the country for six whole years, which he argued is a significant reason his bond should be denied as a precaution of classifying him a flight risk and a threat to society.

Pleading not guilty to the indictment charges filed against him, and assuming the judge had already formed a ruling due to the way he was exchanging words with the prosecutor and staring occasionally, Terry began to wonder should he have listened to his attorney and allowed her to request a continuance. With his lawyer now standing at the podium arguing her opening defense and requesting for all charges to be dismissed, Terry was unaware of the fact that Stewart and his attorney had entered the courtroom and were sitting on the bench directly behind the district attorney.

Wanting to turn around to gaze upon the hypnotic beauty of Demi's smile for a sense of assurance as his lawyer combatted the prosecutor's lies and the State's frivolous allegations, Terry thought against it after seeing the prosecutor, peripherally, rise out of his seat and quote something Terry had no knowledge of what it actually meant, demanding that the court deny the defendant's request to dismiss the indictment for the felony murder charge and the request for a bond.

"Your Honor, my office is in the process of bringing forth additional charges to the Grand Jury against the defendant," a statement that caused Terry to lay his head on the table in bewilderment. "The State has obtained a creditable key witness who will testify under oath that the defendant, Terry Johnson, strategically planned how he was going to kill both victims before he carried out the horrendous act of violence. The witness has also submitted a detailed affidavit through his attorney," which he lifted from an open binder on the table and presented to the court as evidence.

Now turning his head to stare at Stewart who refused to establish eye contact, Terry couldn't believe someone he considered his brother even though he wasn't from his mother's own womb had betrayed him in this manner. Lying profusely about turning himself in only to bring his mother's heart peace, only to retain a lawyer to make a deal that seemed to center on helping himself and disregarding the principles of family.

The courtroom was silent as the Judge read the affidavit before having it entered into the records and having a copy presented to Terry's attorney. The sighs of frustration and disappointment coming from his family were starting to disturb the Judge, which caused his attorney to immediately turn around and ask them to contain their emotions when she noticed the way the Judge was scanning their section of the benches.

"My grandson ain't no damn killer," Mama Lewis stood up and hollered, while pointing her finger at Stewart. Angry at what was transpiring before her eyes, and no longer able to hold her silence as lies mounted against her grandson, Mama Lewis caused all heads in the courtroom to turn with her outburst. "That backstabbing coward has betrayed us..."

Gently grabbing his mother's arm and placing his hand over her mouth, while pulling her back onto the bench as the judge pounded his gavel with frustration, Gip couldn't believe what he was hearing nor could he believe Mama Lewis's actions and hoped the Judge would be merciful given her outrage.

"Order! Order in the courtroom," the judge demanded while looking at Mama Lewis as though her ebullition was a blatant disrespect. "Ma'am, if you speak out in my courtroom again, I will find you in contempt and sentence you to seventy-two hours of isolation so you can think about your actions. Are we clear, ma'am?

Glancing at Yara before she spoke, Mama Lewis sarcastically apologized and tried to finish her statement to the Judge, but he interjected as she once again tried to state that Stewart was the actual killer, given that he had betrayed her trust and the loyalty seeded in her heart.

Addressing the bailiff standing on the wall closest to Mama Lewis, the Judge instructed him to arrest her if she uttered another word, even if it's to a family member.

"Yes sir, Your Honor!" He replied.

Resuming the proceedings after the Judge gave his remarks and questioned the district attorney of whether or not the State's witness was present and ready to place his statement on record, Terry was overwhelmingly affrighted when the prosecutor looked over his shoulder without saying a word as if he was seeking confirmation from Stewart. Then, he completely turned around in his seat to engage in a short conversation with Stewart's lawyer who had tapped his shoulder to gain his attention and passed him a note in the process.

"Your honor, may counsel approach the bench, please?" The District Attorney stood up and requested after reading the words on two-page document.

"Counsel, approach," he commanded, while placing his hands over the microphone as they created a new wave of curiosity whispering amongst each other.

Releasing both attorneys, Terry didn't know what to think while witnessing nothing in his lawyer's facial expression and hearing the Judge instruct Stewart's attorney to step to the podium.

"What's going on?" Terry queried as she sat down beside him.

"I honestly don't know, Mr. Johnson," she confessed. "The District Attorney has asked the judge to allow this lawyer to speak. She is acknowledging that she knows where the murder weapon is and willing to present it to the court with a confession. I rejected the request and asked the Judge for a continuance to grant me time to review the evidence and prepare accordingly, yet he denied the request, due to the documents the District Attorney just submitted to him. So, I have no knowledge of what's about to transpire."

"Present your name for the record please," the Judge informed her while signaling for the attention of the bailiff.

"My name is Attorney Shirley Thompson, and I'm an associate of the Fleming, Watkins & Miles Law Firm, sir."

"From what I'm advised by the District Attorney, Mrs. Thompson, you have knowledge of the actual weapon used to commit this heinous crime, its location and you're requesting to give it's whereabouts here in open court instead of just relaying the information directly to the District Attorney or law enforcement. How long have you known about the weapons location, Mrs. Thompson?"

"Honestly, five days, Your Honor, but before I was willing to present such critical evidence before your courtroom, I had to confirm that the ballistics were a match. So, I contacted an associate of mine at the GBI office, who out of courtesy sent out a trained recovery unit to secure the weapon for lab testing, which he also had expedited given the circumstances surrounding this case."

Leaning down to retrieve a sealed manila envelope from her Attaché case, which she extended for one of the bailiffs to secure and deliver to the Judge, "Your Honor, this envelope was given to me directly from the Special Operations Unit Lieutenant himself this morning, and the department's two security seals are unbroken. He inserted the test results inside, and a thumb drive that contains an unedited video recording of the agents digging in a wooded area outside of Stone Mountain and properly securing the weapon under the procedures of the GBI guidelines. There's also an additional recording of the gun being removed from the sealed storage bag it was recorded to have been placed in by the field agents assigned, whereas they fired the weapon, obtained fingerprints, and the test results were all conducted by skillful GBI technicians. Your Honor, when my client retained me as his counsel, his only desire was for the truth to be told so that the family members of the victims can have closure."

With Stewart rendering no attention after betraying the loyalty of his family, an affidavit submitted into records claiming Terry is the actual killer, the District Attorney slandering his character while presenting that there's a key witness, and demanding the Judge deny his bond, Terry felt his life was dwindling before his eyes while listening to Mrs. Thompson speak and his lawyer sitting without arguing against her statements.

Turning the chair slightly to the right to gaze at his mother who was starting to shed tears brought on by the unraveling news and Demi in his peripheral, Terry was too emotionally distraught to hear the assuring words of Stewart's attorney that caused the District Attorney to leap out of his seat and scream, "Objection!"

"Overruled." The Judge stated.

"Your Honor, I urge you not to consider such a decision without a thorough investigation being granted for my office to conduct. The defendant was in exile for six years, courtesy of his family's resources, and who's to say that their connections weren't used to sway the outcome of these unprecedented actions?"

"Objection, speculation, Your Honor," Terry's attorney yelled.

"Sustained," the Judge stated preempting the District Attorney for his wrongful insinuation while voicing his opinion to the fact that he requested attorney Thompson to testify without questioning the extent of her intentions first, and instructing him to change his argument.

"How dare you accuse me of anything other than upholding my sworn duty under the bar to convey the truth," Mrs. Thompson retorted, facing the DA as she handed the unsealed recording's envelope to the bailiff to enter into the records and walking back to her seat.

"Your honor, the State has a key witness who will testify under oath to the fact that the defendant committed this senseless act of violence, once he's medically cleared, I was advised prior to this hearing. The defendant is a threat to our society, and his uncontrollable aggression is evident by the altercation that this arrest stemmed from," the District Attorney argued to the court. "The obtainment of someone else's fingerprints from the weapon six years later doesn't exclude the defendant from actually committing the crime, Your Honor. One can easily assume that another individual could have discarded the weapon after the crime was committed," the prosecutor argued staring at Terry as though his life's purpose was to ruin his own life.

Rising out of her seat quoting case law to support her argument, and not being commanded to cease speaking by the judge, Terry's attorney torpedoed a lethal verbal assault that forced the District Attorney to sit without a word of rebuttal as she defended Terry.

"Your Honor, standing within your courtroom, at the prosecutor's request to convey the truth of justice rather than allow an innocent man to lose his life, Mrs. Thompson respectfully produced the actual weapon which the GBI secured, confirmed the ballistics were a match, and the fingerprints on the gun are not those of the defendant, Mr. Johnson. But she also openly acknowledged under oath without being coerced or forced that her client, Mr. Carl Robinson, who is currently being held in the Rice Street Jail, has openly admitted on video to committing the murders without seeking a deal in return, and the fingerprints from the gun are a positive match to his own. He also acknowledged during interrogation when questioned as attorney Thompson stated that the defendant, Terry Johnson was not his accomplice and he had no knowledge of him. And I don't have to remind you, Your Honor, the recorded interview was done by the GBI's Special Operations Unit, which has no connection to Mr. Johnson. Your Honor, besides ... and ... (Clears her throat) ... Excuse me your Honor. Regarding the affidavit that could have been coerced before written, the State has nothing that proves Mr. Terry Johnson rendered any verbal knowledge in the commitment or concealment of this crime. There's nothing that suggests that because he was away for six years, he offered physical assistance, which undoubtedly proves my client's innocence and warrants a dismissal of the indictment against him.

Being passed a copy of the star witness affidavit from the court clerk as she attempted to sit back down, Terry's attorney could not believe her eyes and roared. "Your Honor, the affidavit which the State obtained from their so called star witness, Mr. Randle Carter, is no more than a desperate act on his behalf to say or do anything that would help him get from under the mounting charges that the D.A's office is imposing on him, such as double feticide, the murder of his own unborn twins, aggravated assault on the twins' pregnant mother, and assault to a handicapped child, for starters."

Shocked by what he heard and looking annoyed by the conveyance of knowledge that was withheld from him, the Judge began questioning the District Attorney on the validity of her statements and why was such crucial information withheld in his pursuit to bring this case before the court.

Taking his time to voice the appropriate words, while shifting his eyes back and forth between the defendant and his lawyer, the District Attorney stood and requested to approach the bench, whereupon he unsuccessfully defended his reasons for not disclosing the open cases against Randle and his lawsuit against the defendant while trying to acknowledge the significant amount of creditable information Mr. Carter had provided to the law enforcement.

"Your honor, the State's witness has committed murder, just as the defendant within your court and my office shall prosecute them both without seeking a deal, regardless of what Mr. Carter has provided. But I also ask that you do not toss aside his willingness to testify, considering the evidence that Attorney Thompson has presented to the court without at least hearing what he has to say, especially given that he claims to have received the information from the defendant's own sister."

"Are we speaking of the very same sister I'm just now discovering was sexually assaulted by the State's witness's cousin and brutally beaten by the State's witness himself to the brink of death, which caused her to lose her twins in the process, before coming forward with his testimony?" The Judge queried with sarcasm and distinction in his tone towards the District Attorney.

"Yes, Your Honor, the very same, unfortunately," he whispered as he was looking down at his shoes, standing right before the bench before being excused to go back to his seat.

Shifting his eyes side to side, while scanning the occupants of the courtroom as though he was searching for someone in particular before addressing the attorneys, the Judge shocked everyone by imposing a thirty-minute recess and demanding the court clerk to follow him to his chambers.

Being escorted to an isolated cell outside of the courtroom by two bailiffs during recess, Terry wondered more about what Sheri may have told Randle regarding the incident than all other things. Staring at the wall as he sat on the cold steel bench, he pondered how would the affidavit come to affect the Judge 's ruling in his case or Stewart's freedom in anyway. He couldn't believe the extent Randle was going to, solely to hurt his family even more, and he wished the opportunity of crossing his path was granted. But even as he lingered in thought of his sister and the detriment her words could cause, he wondered who this mysterious Carl Richardson was, acknowledging he's the murderer and how in the hell did his fingerprints get on the gun? Beginning to pace back and forth in the cell within a time frame that seemed like days before being lead back into the courtroom, Terry found himself thinking heavily about something the Judge said prior to recess and started losing all hope of his freedom, and seeing the additional officers standing against the wall by his table in the courtroom seemed to make it worse.

Rising and sitting to the Judge retaking his bench, the District Attorney tried to speak but was immediately silenced by the Judge.

"In all my years on the bench, never has a case of this magnitude crossed my desk, nor am I familiar with one as this entangled in case law," the Judge articulated. "Mr. Johnson, I'm curious to know more about this intriguing case and your so-called involvement, if any. Which at this point, only you know why the State has a witness who claims your sister confided in him. Yet, hearsay is no longer admissible in the court of law. With the new found evidence being presented, which I have confirmed during recess, was conducted by the GBI and in accordance with their guidelines, along with the video acknowledgement of Mr. Carl Richardson openly confessing to the crime without seeking anything in return but closure for their family. Usually, I would drop all charges and dismiss the case without feeling as though justice has been infringed, but I'm wondering if I should be reluctant to make that ruling today."

"Bullshit! That's bullshit!" Mama Lewis jumped off the bench yelling while waving her hands with immeasurable tension rising. "Bigot, how can you not dismiss the charges and release my damn grandson ..."

"Order! Bailiffs remove that woman from my courtroom now," the judge commanded repeatedly slamming his gavel against the wooden sound block. "Ma'am, you are in contempt of court, and I remand you to the custody of the county jail for seventy-two hours."

"I don't care nothing about no damn jail," Mama Lewis professed being escorted out of the courtroom like a captured tyrant. "My grandson is innocent, and your ruling is bullshit..."

"Another outburst of any sort and I will clear the entire courtroom," the judge insisted, regaining order."

Clearly hearing the Judge say that he's feeling reluctant to dismissing the charges against him, even though there is no evidence beyond Randle's affidavit. Terry sat lingering in doubt of his freedom, until he noticed from the discovery documents his lawyer allowed him to read. Stewart's fingerprint on a Swarovski crystal elephant figurine that one of the men stole when they raped his mother was no longer a part of evidence.

Looking over his shoulder at his father, whom nodded without a sense of concern in his facial expression as though he knew exactly what Terry was thinking, he turned back towards the Judge while removing the note Abdullah gave him and started mumbling it loud enough for him to hear. With the Judge's silence causing him to believe the video confession was irrelevant, and feeling his life was dangling by a single thread, Terry shifted his attention to witnessing Demi's smile for inspiration. In doing so, he mentally blacked out, sitting at the table gazing at her beauty as if it was forever lost to him. So entangled and lost in their gazing into the eyes of one another that the illusion of basking in her ambiance to alleviate himself mentally from the nightmare transpiring in the courtroom literally caused Terry to initially render no attention to the Judge as he commanded him to stand.

"Mr. Johnson! Mr. Johnson," his lawyer whispered tapping his hand lightly to snap his mind back into focus. "The Judge wants you to stand."

Rising out of the chair without removing his eyes from the ground until the Judge spoke, Terry stood shaking against the table and wishing he had allowed his attorney to request a continuance now that everything had fallen apart and the fact that the judge wasn't closing the case, obviously meant he was staying anyway.

"Mr. Johnson, even though I am reluctant to rendering my verdict in your favor, I am going to rule against the District Attorney's request and dismiss the felony murder indictment against you. Mr. Johnson, I am stern in enforcing the law, but I am a man of justice as well. And given the circumstances surrounding this, I cannot render a ruling to keep you incarcerated for a crime you may not have committed merely to waste tax payers money, but definitely let this be a lesson learned. In regards to the simple battery charge against the State's witness Mr. Randle Carter, I will impose a ten-thousand-dollar cash only bond with the conditions that you relinquish your passport, granted that you are able to post bond."

Stating his closing arguments before handing his written ruling to the clerk to record, the Judge was shocked when he asked Terry if he had anything else to say, and instead of saying thank you as others usually do, he recited something in Arabic the Judge was clueless of, "*Ash-hadu an la ilaha illallah. Al hamdulillahi Rabbil 'Alamin!*" and some scriptures of Psalms that one could see his mother reciting with him if they cared to pay attention. "*O Lord, your word is a lamp to my feet and a light to my path. Righteous are You, O Lord, and upright are Your judgments.*"

Witnessing the excitement in his mother's eyes as his family applauded the verdict, exiting their seats, and Stewart nodding his head, smiling as the bailiffs escorted him from the courtroom, Terry's heart overflowed with endless joy while fantasizing of holding and kissing Demi. So emotionally caught up in the moment that he never saw the kisses Demi was blowing or noticed the signal his father was making to indicate he loved him while calling the bonding company from his seat to post his bail.

"Stop beating on the window, ma'am," the guard instructed Mama Lewis, who was beating for her grandson's attention as they placed Terry in the isolated cell beside hers.

"Shut up, boy. I'm old enough to be your damn mother, so respect me," she retorted angrily. "The two of you are so damn pathetic, arresting an old lady without checking to see if I'm claustrophobic or mentally incompetent to be incarcerated, which Matlock clearly proved is against the law, so, free me coward, 'cause I'm calling my damn lawyer. Where's my phone call? I bet neither of you will open this door and raise your voice to me like y'all did initially." She roared while rolling her eyes as they locked the door behind Terry and removed his handcuffs. "Terry forget them, what happened, sweetie?"

"Sir, please excuse my grandmother," Terry pleaded. "I promise to keep her calm, sir."

Amused by the feistiness and smart tongue of Mama Lewis, both officers chuckled amongst themselves and accepted his plea without a word as they walked back into the courtroom.

Receiving the judge's verdict from her grandson before they were escorted downstairs and separated until the bus ride back to the jail, Mama Lewis rejoiced like a high school cheerleader hearing the news that her baby was about to be released. So caught up in proving she was not soft, Mama Lewis verbally challenged every woman detainee who looked at her out of curiosity of knowing why she was being locked up, to try her if they're 'bout that life.

CHAPTER 41

Strutting briskly out of the jail as if he were speed walking on a track to burn calories, Terry was baffled at the fact that no one was waiting on him as he actually expected. Terry had been forced to remain in jail an additional forty-one hours which was more excruciating to him mentally than all of the days prior. All due to two elderly white men fighting over some hot water for a cup of coffee, which caused the privilege of jail phones in his dormitory to be restricted, thereby denying him the ability of calling to advise his mother where to find his passport, Terry stood at the top of the moonlit steps so happy to be free, yet wondering where Demi, his father, or mother was — somebody!

"Mr. Johnson, why are you walking so fast? Slow down," the bail bond agent insisted, raising her voice to be heard as she exited the building steps behind him.

"Ma'am, I'm in a hurry to get away from this tormenting place before they try to arrest me for trespassing on their property or something."

"Relax Mr. Johnson, everything is okay. Your freedom will not be compromised by just standing here or casually walking to my car. Spread your wings for a moment, I know that you're filled with anxiety ... you're ... you're eager to put all of this behind you, I get it. But you're not completely free until you sign the papers at my office, so relax."

Requesting to use her phone to call Demi, the agent obliged, however, Demi didn't answer. As the agent escorted him to the car, Terry was shocked when she commanded him to sit in the back while reaching for the front passenger door handle.

"Are you serious?"

"Yes! Mr. Johnson, you are not my boyfriend and definitely not my husband. People see things and tell lies, so to avoid further drama, that privilege isn't granted to you nor any other man beside my own," she stated with conviction, sliding into the driver's seat and securing her seatbelt as he slumped into the back seat, agitated, but respecting her directive.

Driving around the corner to the bonding company, and seeing Demi exit his G-Wagen while blushing as the bondsman agent backed into a parking spot, Terry didn't hesitate to jump out of the car. Scooping her up in a twirling hug beneath the stars and attempting to bridge their long-awaited affection with a kiss, Demi rejected him by muzzling his entire face with her hand.

"Boy, stop! I don't know where your lips have been, nor if you have scrubbed your tongue," she grinned leaning back from his advance. Playfully covering his mouth with her fingers to shield him from giving a reply as the muscles in his face tightened from the shock of her words. Staring into each other's eyes, and no longer able to contain her yearning, Demi sensuously began caressing his face before passionately kissing him until the bail bond agent interrupted their reunion of ecstasy.

"Excuse me! I want to go home and kiss on my boyfriend like that too," the agent teased by imitating their affection with the wind, then turned around and walked toward the building as they severed their bond and followed the agent while wiping the drooling evidence of their chemistry from their mouths.

Walking inside and sitting in one of the chairs before her desk, Terry and Demi listened attentively as the agent advised of the rules that he must oblige by in order to keep from having his bond revoked before taking two pictures to be added to his file and scribbling his signature on a few documents.

"Now you are free to speed walk outside Mr. Johnson and kiss your baby until you're able to inhale the fragrance from a blossoming tree," the agent said smiling, while rising to shake their hands. Sitting back down as they strolled towards the door caressing one another in a sensuous hug, she couldn't help but admire how the agonies of suffering often awakened the sweetest of joys.

Allowing Demi to drive, since she didn't relinquish his keys when they left the bonding company, Terry laid back in the passenger seat, while enlightening her of his desire to establish a weekend workshop that molds and empowers boys to be men, teaching them moral values, the principles of self-worth, and the importance of appreciating, respecting and honoring a woman instead of degrading her just because the standards of society says it's okay.

Conversing with Demi was always stimulating because she always challenged him to think beyond the narrative of his objective, never failing to help expand his insights. Detouring to grab something to eat to satisfy Terry's voracious appetite, Demi cruised through the night lights on Cascade Ave. and pulled up at The Beautiful Restaurant. Parking on the street instead of in the rear parking lot, they strolled inside, holding hands, and dined at a table by the window. Demi knew that Terry survived in the jail by eating only the commissary purchased food, yet she honestly had no idea his appetite would resemble that of a bear awakening from hibernation and discovering a mountain of honeycombs.

Reminiscing about life and his father's silliness, which caused Demi to burst into laughter thinking of the hilarious things he has said or done to combat Yara's feistiness while in their presence at the house, she spoke of how the bond they've successfully bridged together is an inspiration to learn from and reach for. Challenging, respecting and appreciating one another without allowing their love to become complacent or demanding, Demi smiled, voicing how she admires their bond of friendship and the fact that they don't exist outside the natural comfort of their character to sustain an unbreakable perfect union. She entertained questioning thoughts of could he love her the same.

Realizing from the weight he had lost and the way he was devouring the chicken sausages, scrambled eggs, cheese grits, blueberry pancakes, hash browns and buttered biscuits on the three plates before him, Demi was really starting to believe that he had every intention of regaining the pounds his sacrifice forced him to lose before leaving the table.

Paying their bill and exiting the restaurant, talking about how much he missed Reanna and Cadence, the immeasurable beauty of Demi's smile lit up the night in the glow of the moon. Defining the grace of a lady as they passed an entourage of college girls trying to gain Terry's attention with their childish antics, he lowered his gaze and acknowledged by grabbing Demi's hand to lift to his lips and kiss that she was the only life blessing he desired. The sudden sound of the girls giggling amongst themselves at his action, assured him without doubt that he had made the right decision.

Relinquishing the softness of her touch to retrieve the keys from his pocket, the emptiness quickly reminded him that she was, at this instance, his chauffeur. "Why are you smiling like I just bought you a bar of soap or a tube of toothpaste for the first time?" He joked while reaching again for her hand on the sidewalk only to have it slapped as they crossed the street.

"Because it's sad that some women actually feel that they have to strip themselves of integrity and flaunt their body provocatively for a man's acceptance instead of being admired for their intellect or character," Demi revealed while using the key fob to unlock the SUV. "Their silliness was a compliment to me but confirmed as well that even when you resemble a shade tree Casanova, you're still eye candy for psychiatric patients. Honestly though, I more so smiled in consideration of the respect you showed and the way you redirected your eyes by shifting them away from the girls, which I noticed by watching you with my Spidey vision."

Staring into her eyes without commenting on her joke, Terry playfully leaned over in her seat after getting inside and started looking out for the ladies through Demi's window, only to be introduced to the bare palm of her hand and having his face pushed back as she pulled off giggling with him in amusement.

"I see now that you need some 'Act Right' in your life."

"What's that?" He asked turning on the radio.

"The threads and leather of my heel between your teeth." Demi delivered, which caused them both to start laughing.

Listening to the Quiet Storm for the first time in weeks, Terry tormented Demi's ears, sounding like a braying donkey instead of a vocalist, all the way home. He sang every ol' school song they played, dancing humorously in his seat while occasionally tapping her hand each time she tried to reach for the power button.

Pulling into his garage and parking, Demi wasted no time jumping out of the G-Wagen to grant her ears a sense of relief. "*Allahuma ashkuruk ealaa aniqadhi - al hamdulillahi!*" She cooed as though the momentary silence was therapeutic. Sharing a few words while reaching back into the SUV to gather her things, Demi couldn't help but blush, witnessing Terry's sensitiveness when he realized her intentions.

"You're not staying?" Terry queried climbing out and looking like a fish suddenly hurled out of water. He wanted to wake up with Demi in his arms, but never expected that once she parked his G-Wagen in the garage, she'd basically step out, give him his keys, kissed him passionately good night, then sauntered to her car talking over her shoulder while retrieving the car keys from her purse.

"No! It's unladylike for a woman to grant a jailbird the pleasure of basking in her ambiance to that degree, you're not my husband, and I have a few priorities to handle in the morning."

Watching her tease, him by blowing a kiss before entering her car and driving off, Terry found himself admiring her worth from a new perspective while strolling toward the building. Greeting the new security guard who demanded his credentials to verify his identity and residence before allowing him access to the elevators, Terry politely applauded him for doing his job as he returned his license. He then rode to his floor relentlessly reflecting on Demi's loyalty and love.

Inhaling the mixed essence of scented oils, entering the door, Terry immediately smiled, realizing the beauty of where he was in comparison to the jail's atmosphere he just left. Noticing things out of place while walking through the house and seeing his new comforter set on the bed, which he had actually bought as a gift for Cadence prior to getting arrested, he knew his mother spent more time doing tasks other than just retrieving his passport from the safe. Taking a therapeutic hot shower before detoxing for 30-minutes in Epsom and sea salt while allowing the jets to massage his body, he commanded Alexa to play the Quiet Storm as he soaked endlessly in deep thoughts of Demi.

Enjoying the solitude of being within the peaceful calmness of his own home, Terry air dried by grooving in the bathroom mirror to the soulful sounds of Floetry while brushing his teeth. After cleaning behind himself and fixing a bowl of peach ice cream, he jumped straight in the bed naked and fell asleep without turning on the TV unlike his usual routine.

Awakened by the annoying sound of his doorbell repeatedly ringing, Terry eased out of bed, slid on a pair of boxers, some drawstring linen pants, his house shoes, then swaggered to the front door caressing his face. Not trying to reveal that he was home to possibly someone unwelcomed, he glanced through the peephole without asking who it was, only to snatch open the door after recognizing it was Stewart, disturbing the peace. Perplexed of truly knowing what to expect of this visit, Terry just stood there staring at his friend clueless of what to say to him.

"Aren't you going to invite me in?" Stewart asked holding a box containing two fluffy crab, cheesy mushroom, and spinach omelets.

"My bad, come on in," Terry insisted stepping aside and allowing him to enter. Terry relocked the door and followed Stewart into the living room where he placed the box on a coffee table. Stewart turned and shockingly surprised him with a firm bear hug and expressed his love before letting go to hand him one of the wrapped omelets from the box.

"Why are you here?" Terry asked, lifting the hot wrap to his mouth while peeling back some of the wrapping.

"Hey man, now that ... that is the best omelet you'll taste in da city. The crabs I'm told marinate in a secret sauce for two days. Your mom told me after court that your bond was posted. But knowing you, I assumed that you wanted to spend the night allowing someone to abuse your tongue," Stewart teased, licking his lips while playfully caressing his face projecting the allusion of intimacy. "I decided to wait 'til this morning to come by." Removing a layer of the wrapping to bite into his omelet as Terry, who was just standing observing as Stewart walked around the sofa, grabbed the remote, and sat down.

"Hey Stewart, don't turn the TV on 'cause you need to give me answers I don't have," Terry projected with no trace of humor in his voice, rather sincerity in his demeanor. "You are supposed to be my brother — the one person though not of my own blood whom I felt I could trust and depend on no matter what. Yet, your selfish stupidity jeopardized my life, my father's life and your own as well. You all of a sudden seek redemption which will never grant you peace of mind. I truly felt while sitting in that courtroom that you had completely turned against me to save yourself, which I'm beyond grateful you didn't and apologize for doubting you. But what were you thinking attempting to turn yourself in?"

"I was thinking that sacrificing my freedom for yours was the only way to bring you home to your mother, and you can't be mad at the fact that I love you enough to sacrifice my own life for you. Yes, my decision was hasty and reckless, yet seeing your mother going through the emotional rollercoaster due to your situation and Sheri's, I panicked, assuming my decision was best for everyone."

"Well it wasn't," Terry clarified, walking into the kitchen to throw the wrapper in the trash, then wash his hands and grabbing a bottle of purified spring water from the cabinet.

"Stewart, in all honesty, there's no possible way I can be mad at you for what you did. That's love, but we were not groomed to move off our emotions. We have far too much to lose for either of us to be making rash and drastic decisions like that. You've spent the last six years of your life becoming the man you never expected to be, whereas I've spent the past six years discovering life, manhood, and living solely as the playboy you know me as. Look, with my father forcing you to leave as a way of fulfilling his promise to your mother and a means of protecting you, I didn't leave out of fear of thinking I'd have to face the consequences of your actions alone. With the uncertainty of my relationship with Penélope seemingly going nowhere beyond our sexual entanglements, and my best friend being stripped out of my life, I left to see the beauty of the world and to define my legacy by aiding poverty stricken countries."

Rising to retrieve his tablet off the glass entertainment shelf to text Demi as her smile invaded his thoughts, Terry continued to speak passionately, "Stewart, being raised in America, fortunate as we were, never really granted me a true understanding of life, mercy, forgiveness or sacrifice in the way you tried to offer, until I went to Africa, and selfishly volunteered for a mission abroad to get close to a UN doctor."

"The love and culture Africans allowed me to experience in their everyday hardship compelled me to start a non-profit foundation that helps to establish flowing water in destitute villages, schools for youths who had no knowledge of existence beyond their tribunal customs, and a financial pipeline that allows the women of those villages to support their families by selling their craft at market price. Hey, I even have loyal tribal goons on standby that are ten times more dangerous than the worst ideological terrorist. So, just know from this moment on that the worst mistake you can ever make is jeopardizing my life as you tried because they will come to America and hunt you down like the survival of their tribe depends on it," Terry exclaimed, looking serious as he began doing a warrior's dance.

Laughing as he watched Terry imitate one of the village warriors, Stewart was happy to know his best friend was free and that this door was now forever closed to the both of them. Sipping his smoothie through a straw, he broke the momentary silence by asking the very same question Terry was preparing to ask.

"Who is Carl Robinson?"

"Damn, you literally just read my mind! I have no idea, and I'm still puzzled as to how his fingerprints got on the weapon, when you said you got rid of it. Why did you tell your lawyer about the weapon anyway?" Terry asked while walking back to his bedroom, drinking water and forwarding Demi a sad face picture of himself with the caption: *'the face of an ex-jailbird deprived of witnessing your smile.'*

"I promise you that I never mentioned the whereabouts to Mrs. Thompson. I informed her in detail of my actions, why I did it, what I've been doing with my life since the incident and asked her to make a deal with the District Attorney's office that would release you." Elevating his voice to the extent that Terry could clearly hear him in the other room as he groomed himself and dressed, Stewart suspended him in a state of disbelief, revealing that after the murder, Yara demanded the gun and said she would dispose of it when she found him crying in the laundry room, trying to remove all the DNA from the bloody clothes.

"What?" Terry screamed.

They spent the next hour reminiscing, making phone calls to whomever, and in between, laughing hysterically over Terry's jailhouse stories. But then, Stewart received a video clip from Naomi as they prepared to leave, which then caused his entire demeanor to change.

"Man are you alright?" Terry questioned while noticing the surprised look on his face, but sparkle in his eyes as he stood there doing no more than staring at his phone, breathing audibly. With no reply given, Terry walked over to see what he was viewing that had him entranced. Witnessing the lost love of Stewart's life, he immediately started smiling because she still possessed his heart.

"Damn! Lashun still has that hypnotic effect on you, I see. How is she?"

"I have no idea. We haven't spoken since she moved on with her life."

"What? You mean to tell me that you're still making excuses to hide from the woman you love instead of telling her the truth about everything. Then, how did you get the video," he asked curiously. "Don't tell me you are stalking her now, Stewart."

"No! Naomi is in Vine City and just sent me the video."

"I honestly don't want to know or imagine what she's doing over there. Well, you can't stay here and lust off a video of her all day because I'm definitely not trying to come home to Vaseline stains and butt streaks all over my stuff," Terry chuckled while pacing toward the door with him following as if he'd been shot with a single fatal arrow by Cupid.

Playfully snatching a love-struck Stewart into the hallway and locking the door behind them, Terry never expected that his ears would become the pillow of Stewart's empty heart. The entire time they maneuvered through the hallway, descended in the elevator, and walked to their cars in the garage. He couldn't escape Stewart's passionate cry of love for her. The deep pain he endures each day feeling as if he were a fleeting thought to her, and how he can't date other women without fantasizing about her the entire time. Feeling like he was trapped in a heartbreaking trilogy listening to Stewart beat up his ears in the pent-up space, Terry couldn't help but feel sorry for his friend as he cried from the inner depths of his heart.

"Stewart, you may have been protecting her, but you lost Lashun because of the selfish choice you made, which left her standing alone, holding nothing more than a dream. She's a woman, in case you have forgotten — not a child. If she's truly irreplaceable to you and the only woman you want to prove has a key to your heart, then allow her to witness the man you have become instead of standing here crying as though I'm going to open my arms to hug you," Terry rifled, hitting a nerve and the unlock button on his G-Wagen fob at the same time. "She honestly deserves to know the truth of your sacrifice. You're afraid to be rejected by her, so you won't even give yourself the opportunity to see if love still stirs in her heart as well, which is perplexingly alienating. Stewart, stop tormenting yourself and be a man, because a boy, she definitely doesn't want, I can promise you that."

A breakthrough occurred after being comatose by her video in seemingly an infinite loop, given Stewart hit rewind for the umpteenth time; he managed to raise his head, expressing his greatest fear before embracing his friend and walking towards the G-Wagen door.

"As long as I'm able to dream of loving her once more, sharing with her the elements of my growth, then I can bare the pain that pulsates in my heart daily, even if that means being dead to her. Yet to look in those mesmerizing eyes of hers or witness her irresistible smile and be told I'll never hold her again, darkens my heart," he stated so emotionally that Terry's eyes welled up like a reservoir but no trickle of a tear.

Easing into the SUV and selecting 'Find Me A Man' by Toni Braxton on his playlist, while observing the zombie like movement of his friend through the window, Terry opened the sunroof and turned up the volume so he could clearly hear the words. He then removed the phone from his pocket and called Naomi, who at the moment was being fed beef rib tips by some twins. Seeing Stewart as he pulled off, suspended in time like a video junkie in a hypnotic state, though strange, his efforts comforted him in knowing his intentions were good.

Having set an appointment, he started the day off by stopping at the spa to indulge in a deep tissue massage and a facial treatment with microderm abrasive crystals, then dropping by the barbershop on Sylvan Road to be groomed, now had him feeling more like himself. Terry left the barbershop and drove through the heart of downtown, contemplating doing something romantic for Demi to outwardly show she's appreciated. That is until Sheri called and informed him that she's hosting an all-white dinner party that evening in his honor, prompting him to blaze up the interstate to Perimeter Mall after reaching out to invite his queen, whom indicated that she was already out shopping with his mother. In disbelief that they were hanging out together without him, Terry mimicked Stewart's lovesick behavior, being left in the dark, which caught Demi off guard.

"Terry, wake up, this is a woman's world! There's a lot you will never have firsthand knowledge of. We're trying to define our sexiness without having to nurture our men right now, so we will have to talk later," Demi conveyed before disconnecting the line and starting to laugh with Yara.

Spending two hours, patronizing one department store after another, swiping his credit card for a sundry of unrelated purchases, searching for the perfect attire and complementary kicks for the evening out, Terry was ecstatic. Walking into Footlocker to purchase Reanna and Cadence a few pair of the new Air Max for women, he received a collect call from Abdullah, of which he accepted without hesitation. Listening to him speak inspiring words that caused him to ponder on love, Abdullah didn't pass up the opportunity to remind Terry not to allow freedom to be the distraction or an excuse for him to lose sight of God or his purpose.

Terry honestly wished as they engaged in a meaningful conversation that there was a way he could help him out of his conviction, because his daughter needed her father and he needed a friend like him by his side. Ending the call, Terry pondered heavily on the words of God Abdullah shared as a reminder for him to stay focused: "*And among mankind is he who worships God as it were upon the edge (i.e. in doubt): if good befalls him, he is content therewith but if a trial befalls him, he turns back on his face. He loses both this world and the Hereafter. That is the evident loss.*"

The urgent taste for some BBQ beef ribs after leaving the mall motivated Terry to detour and go out of his way to stop by the Rib Shack on Campbellton Road, since cooking them himself would take too long. Every delightful bite undoubtedly reminded him of the privilege it is to be free, a blessing he refused to take for granted. He was so caught up licking the sauce from his lips while holding a rib with his right and steering the SUV with his knee that he didn't interrupt the moment to answer Lashun's call as his phone vibrated in his pocket.

Arriving home and still implementing the characteristics of a lion, by tearing at the carcass as he parked in the garage, Terry used a half container of wet wipes to cleanse his hands before grabbing his things and exiting the vehicle. Walking into the building and noticing the gentleman before him enter the elevator, pushing one child in a stroller while feeding another in a toddler's carrier, awakened something in Terry's heart that caused him to want to speak with his father, yet noticing the important missed call after reaching for his phone inadvertently put the conversation he wanted to have on hold.

Getting in and putting away his things, before reaching out to the love of Stewart's life, Terry couldn't help but feel like an unappreciated relationship counselor trying to bridge two hearts that should never have been decoupled, regardless of the unexpected circumstances that sometimes befalls a person's path of travel. Terry always admired Lashun because of her unwavering principles, strength, devotion to family, and her determination to succeed against all odds. Yet, when he saw how she became Stewart's light, the inspiration that caused him to start believing in his inner potential and the only woman he respected and loved enough to commit to, Terry felt she needed to know he still loved her and now he's the man he should have been years ago. Whereas granted another opportunity, he wouldn't be likely to fail.

He jumped into the shower after calling Stewart to request that he pick up a very important associate that night at eight and drop her off at The Select Restaurant without informing him whom the associate actually was while providing the address. Terry smiled, knowing that the sight of her was going to elevate his heart rate and probably cause him to hyperventilate, which just might grant him the pleasure of feeling her lips if he fainted. Interested to see what Demi was wearing but, more so, desiring to see her smile as he walked through the house eating a mango and checking himself out in every mirror he passed, Terry tried to video chat with her on his phone, but she sent a text instead of answering.

"A gentleman physically stands before a woman to marvel at her beauty and grace, not video chat, lol."

"Well, a real woman never denies her man the pleasure of the blessing she is to him when he desires her even when substituting physical presence with modern day technology is convenient. Ditto on the lol :-)."

"Boyyy....A real woman?! Convenient? So, I guess I'm just obligated to your every beck and call, huh?"

Thinking of how to respond to her text while walking into the kitchen to grab a bottle of water from the cabinet, Terry smiled as his answer came to mind, and his thumb began tapping the letters on his phone's keypad. "Okay ... Sprinkled by your grace, I cherish and will never take for granted that which you offer freely: you acceptance, your time — in essence, your very being, ... 'cause the blessing of your gift isn't obligatory and therefore promised to no one," he wisely replied.

"Awwwww....The charm of Casanova!"

"No ...The truth of a man."

With no text or call to follow, Terry finished getting ready while processing the enlightenment from Abdullah, cleaned up after himself, then left to shop at Phipps Plaza before they closed.

Video chatting with an excited Mrs. Laconette as he pulled into his parent's driveway, Terry barely could speak a word, given she was so excited that he was free and seeking to follow the ways of the sunnah. So happy to see him for the first time, she initially neglected the reason he called. Mrs. Laconette took him on a visual tour of the house as he punched in the code on the keypad to open the gate. Terry subconsciously felt unbreakable by being apprised of the things he never knew about Demi, receiving pointers from Mrs. Laconette on how to truly appreciate her, love her, and virtually wiping away the possibility of failure. Parking in his garage spot, he sat for a minute after disconnecting the intriguing thirty-minute video chat. Getting himself reacquainted, he quickly scanned the yard and garage before seeing his father walk around the side of the house, apparently training the dogs.

Noticing his mom's new G-Wagen being pulled out of the garage to be washed as he sat texting Lashun and Stewart, Terry was becoming a little bit jealous of the upgrades she had made. Staring at her chrome trimming and the new rims that caused her SUV to look even better than his own, he sucked his teeth with envy in his eyes, while promising himself to come back harder.

Grabbing the bags from the passenger floor as he exited the SUV, while still glancing at his mom's in disbelief, he placed a box from Saks on the hood. Yelling to gain Gip's attention, Terry made him aware of the gift before pivoting to enter the house with the swag of a tribal warrior. Initially, Terry intended to go directly to Sheri's room, but the gourmet food on display was an alluring and inescapable distraction as he greeted the crisply decked out chef, and the serving staff from Eatery while walking past the kitchen. The persuasive delights and delicacies all but twisted his arm and placed a gun to his head to indulge his uhmmm — agreeable stomach.

"Get out of my kitchen!" Yara abruptly exclaimed, startling Terry by playfully slapping the back of his neck as he tried to open the foil to taste the grilled red snapper.

"Ma!" He screamed, while massaging the pain, before opening his arms to give her a smothering hug that didn't fall short of letting her know she was sincerely missed.

Spending a few moments to advise him about Sheri's mystery admirer, Abdul Waahid, while also calling to memory all the things he'd missed out on, Yara was speechless when Terry asked her to close her eyes, which she refused to do because she assumed he was trying to sneak a piece of the red snapper. Realizing his mother was not going to oblige his request, Terry reached in the bag and removed her gift.

Even though his presence was a gift that could not be matched by material things, Yara expressed her happiness and gratitude, by repeatedly kissing his cheeks and thanking him for never allowing her to feel unappreciated. Of course, she couldn't miss out on taking a few pictures with her baby, but that was short-lived due to the incoming call. Noticing that it was Mama Lewis who was interrupting their passionate mother-son bond with a collect call, Yara answered the call, wondering if she needed to inform Terry to call their lawyer. "Hi sweetie!"

"Ma, tell her I said not to drop the soap! And where's Demi?" He whispered as she began to listen to Mama Lewis rant.

Yara slyly and nonchalantly indicated, to his surprise, that Demi was upstairs in his room getting dressed. Apparently amused by whatever Mama Lewis was saying, because she paid Terry no more attention as she stumbled out onto the deck laughing like Big Donny, the comedian, was standing on her side telling a couple of unscripted jokes.

Thinking of Demi, Terry suddenly gained the strength to leave the kitchen on that note, but not before scooping a handful of white grapes from the fruit tray and a piece of the red snapper, with his mom out of the picture. Like a playful child, he darted through the house, ascending the stairs, eager to see the exotic rose of his eye. Feeling unstoppable, He twisted the door knob to his room only to discover it was locked, so he began knocking and calling her name inquisitively, but then ceasing as he felt a really familiar vibration and realized it was her calling after observing the screen.

"Why are you calling me instead of opening the door?"

"Baby, I'm about to shower and get dressed, can I have my privacy please," she gently pleaded.

"Your privacy?!! You're in my room! Demi, open the door so I can see you, I promise not to come in the bathroom."

"I truly see right now that I'm going to have to strip you down and remold you brick by brick, because you seem not to know the difference between a real lady and a girl. Terry, I will not disregard my honor to appease your ego or desires. Respect me, and that will unlock the door to your every desire — but as for now, this door remains as is until I'm finished."

Jokingly, he advised that the rejection was her loss and that he had a gift for her smile, she immediately interjected, countering with, "Not a material girl, so no material gift can outweigh or even measure up to the gift of your acceptance."

He could do no more than zip it with a shocked pause followed by, "Okaaay," before pressing [End Call].

Not knowing that the entire mother-in-law suite had been transformed into a state-of-the-art treatment center for Sheri, Terry called to discover her whereabouts after noticing that she wasn't in her room nor any room in the guest house. After receiving the scoop on where she was, he headed that direction with mixed emotions.

The moment was surreal as he stepped into the transformed suite which had a feng shui vibe. His fervor waned just a bit, but he could feel the strong positive energy flow upon entry. However, it just wasn't strong enough to pillar him for what came next.

For the first time in his life, he saw a once beautiful girl, his sister, now heavily disfigured. This, he just wasn't prepared for as Sheri slowly turned her head toward him. A restrained gasp manifested itself as a deep inhale to avoid offending Sheri, and this first image of his once breathtaking sister brought him to tears as he slowly approached her bedside. Reaching her with anxiety and an increased heartbeat, he caressed what he recalled as the soft radiant beauty of her face with the tips of his fingers ever so gently while squeezing her hand for comfort.

After sharing a sensuous embrace that inevitably caused tears to fall in both of their hearts, reminding one another of their mutual love, and engaging in a conversation that kept them both laughing, Sheri, apologized before opening the wielded doors of her heart. Massaging her hand as she conjured internal strength to break the yoke of fear, Terry listened attentively to Sheri express how caring for Randle always felt like there was a noose bounding her neck, which seemed to tighten with each breath she inhaled.

The torment she exposed to his ears caused Terry to feel as though he had honestly failed to protect her, thereby breaking the last promise he made to their step-grandmother before she died. Somehow, this caring for Randle seemed to allow the abuse to become the accepted norm, and Terry felt responsible for all that happened as he was seemingly begging his sister to forgive him for selfishly leaving her side to endure life alone.

The more he looked at her swelling and the lacerations that were on a steep incline of healing, the more he wanted to show Randle what happens to someone in the Suri tribe that dishonored a woman. One can only imagine the hurt and pain he felt for her and the huge disgust he had for the coward who did this to his sister. But he came to her bedside to console her, so he adorned her with a 3 carat, heart shaped, key diamond studded pendant and chain that was quite identical to the one he had given their mother to symbolize that familial love is one which transcends all — unbreakable and unconquerable.

Surprised by the gift while looking up at the ceiling, Terry laid on the bed beside an emotional Sheri. Rubbing her hand as he did as a child, he convincingly expressed that she and their mom had infinite access to his heart. Speaking on life and love between them, he reminded her of the irreplaceable life blessing she is and the very significance of never allowing her love for a man to strip her of integrity. Especially not to merely satisfy his selfish desires when he offers nothing in return and certainly not to gain and sustain his unappreciated attention as it is not an asset and does not profit your self-esteem or existence. He shared insights that warmed her heart while encouraging her with wisdom that nurtured and empowered her with inner strength.

Focused on bonding mentally and emotionally with his sister for the first time in years, though she did travel to Africa and the UK to visit him occasionally, neither noticed Demi standing in the doorway. She was stealthily like a fly on the wall as she attentively listened to their every word. Speaking of his admiration for Demi and openly pouring out his heart in unsealed secrecy as to how he felt about her and how she caused him to feel, Sheri was overwhelmingly surprised that the playboy was talking as though he had been knocked off his feet. So shocking, it was even more so to Demi, who was so delighted to be that undetected fly on the wall, hearing the unedited, unadulterated version of where his heart truly lies, being shared to one so close to him. Demi, still in the shadows, smiled with warmth and was without a doubt feeling the love and feeling herself in that serenely precious moment. It didn't last long though.

Walking up to catch the last few sentences, Naomi burst out laughing, startling the both of them, then began teasing Terry for seemingly becoming weak in his mackin'. "Bro, please don't tell me that going to jail for a few weeks made you this damn soft. How can you feel that way about some loose booty you haven't even tasted yet? No offense Demi," she drew a pardon card, while turning to face her as she patted her arm and spoke. "I'm just saying, he doesn't even know if you flow like a waterfall or need to be lubed with gel first. And just to be honest, being unbroken don't grant you the USDA vacuum seal tightness and potency like this blue-ring octopus between my legs," Naomi purred jokingly while caressing herself provocatively before leaning into Demi, grinning.

"It only depends on how you classify potency because toxic and beat up are much more appropriate words," Sheri lifted her head to pounce like a snow fox, which caused everyone but Naomi to laugh.

The hypnotic sight of Demi adorned in a white slinky belted wrap kimono maxi dress, innocently staring at him, caused Terry to forget everything Naomi had said just seconds prior. He was so engulfed by her beauty resembling an angel in his eyes that he didn't even realize he mumbled aloud, "I thank God for choosing my heart to love you." Until Naomi stopped him in the process of passing her to embrace Demi, by placing her hands on his chest and purring with seduction, "What about meeeee?"

"Girl, you better stop playing with Demi before she do you worse than Penélope did. And you know damn well my brother don't want no booty the CDC has labeled contaminated and needs to be quarantined," Sheri piped up, rolling her eyes as Terry gently eased her to the side, laughing, to wrap Demi's body with his impatient arms.

"Whatever stank! Your brother is the one who is contaminated and should be damn quarantined, sleeping with those unvaccinated tribal women in Third World countries and God knows who else," Naomi countered, flopping down in the massage recliner and kicking her feet up. 'Gurl, you know I love Terry, but he couldn't get nonna this blue-ring octopus even if he begged me with red diamonds or rubies on his tongue."

"I heard everything you said to your sister, and I also thank God for choosing your heart to love me," Demi whispered in Terry's ear as he held her firmly against his body before kissing him while staring at Naomi. Joking amongst each other as Demi sat on the sofa with Terry laying in her lap as she lightly massaged his head, he amused them with unbelievable insights of what some men do when they are denied the pleasure of a woman's affection in jail. Naomi couldn't help but wonder as she listened to him paralleling the depiction of several men she dated. "Hmmm, were they men from the dark side on the low?" she thought curiously without saying a word.

"Excuse me Ms. Johnson," one of the two male medical assistants said entering the room.

"Yes?"

"Your mother requested that we transfer you to the wheelchair and bring you downstairs,"

"Do you need any help, sir?" Terry sat up asking as they began leveling the bed to transfer Sheri. Her female nurse walked in and seemed distracted by Terry's handsomeness, trying to remove the vital sign monitor cords from her body.

"No sir, but thanks, we got it," one of the male assistants politely assured, hinting at his physique and hoping they didn't make a mistake that would cause Sheri discomfort, compelling her to audibly signal distress, because he didn't want to make Terry angry.

Standing beside the bed and holding Demi's hand, Terry patiently waited for Sheri to confirm that she was positioned comfortably in the wheelchair before grabbing his bag to leave the room. As the assistants strapped her in, Naomi tried to distract the assistant with the dreads whose skin complexion resembled wet brown sugar, by making her booty bounce while lifting her purse off the floor. Caring not for her tramp like antics at the moment, Sheri brushed Naomi to the side as she attempted to seductively insert her finger between her lips after noticing the nurse observing her movements. Knowing from their past that there's no limit to Naomi's provocativeness once she got started and not caring to intoxicate his eyes, Terry walked over to kiss his sister on the forehead then helped the staff carry the wheelchair down the stairs as Demi and Naomi followed.

Seeing the sumptuous assortment of food artistically gracing the table as they entered the dining room and his mother not present, Terry immediately let go of Demi's hand and the wheelchair. Joking as they did when they were kids, "Ma, Terry is in here eating the food before we can sit down together," Sheri struggled to scream due to her injuries, then laughed at his shocked reaction.

Stealing a sliver of delectable gourmet spinach and gruyere stuffed red snapper roll as the assistants eased Sheri up to the table, he quickly stuck the remaining piece in Demi's mouth seductively, though he intended to eat it all himself until his sister tried to get him in trouble by snitching to their mom, while applauding him afterwards for being romantic.

Walking into the room with their father holding her hand and chuckling as Yara scolded Terry for his selfish actions, Yara was so happy to see Sheri out of bed that she ceased chastising him, bent over, placing one hand on the wheelchair, and kissed her cheek.

"I love you, baby!" Yara purred.

"Ma what about me? And that's not true!" Terry denied as he quickly interjected, looking serious, while pointing his finger toward Demi's face as he defended his innocence. "She's the one eating, and the evidence is still in her mouth. Not believing Terry just snitched on her so boldly after trying to be romantic by feeding her, Demi just stood there with puffy red cheeks as though she was not breathing. Laughing with his father, sister, and Naomi at the way Yara was now looking at Demi who was frozen still as a mannequin until he leaned in, attempting to kiss her lips. *Smack!* The mannequin came to life and slapped the innocence off his face instead.

"Terry, don't make me call the Sheriff and see if I can buy a few of those jailhouse trays to serve you instead of allowing you to eat with us," Yara teased, rolling her eyes and patting Demi on the arm. "Sweetie, it's okay, I know he has set you up to deflect the attention from himself."

The images of those trays flashing within his thoughts immediately caused him to stop snickering. "I'd sit here and starve instead," he truthfully admitted, pulling out Demi's chair as everyone took their individual seats.

Assuming his father was about to speak once he finished drinking the bottle of Zamzam water, Demi had brought for them to taste, Terry was flabbergasted when the words that broke the staring and silence among them were those of an accent that serenaded his ears like the melodies of Janelle Monáe.

"Thank you, Mr. and Mrs. Johnson, for making this opportunity possible for us all. I also thank you Sheri, not just for your help in selecting the right menu to please your brother or sharing his soooooo cute baby pictures with me." Demi purred turning to squeeze his cheeks with her fingers. "I thank you even more for allowing me to assist your mother in rekindling the light within you."

Blushing as she raised her hands to hide the captivating beauty of her smile even with a swollen face, Sheri whispered, "All thanks and praise belong to God."

"What about me, girl?" Naomi chimed in, looking a little offended that she wasn't acknowledged for something.

Demi smiled as she stared and pondered her thoughts. "I thank you for being the extraordinary woman you are and for reminding me to always love myself more than a man."

"Always girl! My game is a light of inspiration for everyone to learn from," Naomi exclaimed, grinning, not realizing that Demi just called her a disingenuous trifling whore, politely.

Demi addressed the family by expressing her gratitude for the effort that everyone exerted to pulling off the special and amazing all white dinner. Checking his phone as Demi finished expressing her appreciation, and Sheri sharing that Penélope would not be joining them as she began to talk, Terry smiled seeing the pictures Stewart forwarded of him and Lashun eating together and reading the "I love you brother" text from him.

"Even though we've traveled to distant countries over the years to visit you Terry and dined together, it has been six years since we've eaten as a family beneath this roof, and I cherish this moment more than all others as I cherish my time with each one of you," Sheri acknowledged, panning her eyes side to side. "I now realize that God will test us with good and hard days to distinguish the true faithful believers from the wicked, although He knows the answer before putting us to any test. With you void in my life, Terry, and the dedication to my dreams causing me to feel lonely, I sought attention by trying to commit myself to love solely because I didn't want to be alone and, unexpectedly, became a prisoner in my own mind."

"Mom, Dad, Terry, Demi, and my sister from another mother, I'm sorry for everything I've put y'all through in my pursuit to discover the true value of my own worth. Terry, I jeopardized your life and no matter how much I say I'm sorry, the acknowledgement will always affect me equally as the loss of my babies. For the emotional rollercoaster my actions have caused everyone, I ask that we allow this moment to bridge a new beginning of understanding, trust, appreciation, and love for our family without judgment."

Grabbing her glass of Zamzam water from the table and raising it, Sheri gazed at Demi, and then her father and honored him specially, while proposing a toast for fulfilling his promise of bringing Terry home.

"You are our protector, our rock, and I ask God to let you know even when we fall short of reminding you of how meaningful you are daddy, that you are appreciated and loved beyond poetic words. I love you a trillion and three times more than everyone combined."

"Good to know baby girl, 'cause I love you a trillion and four times more my King," Yara raised her glass, professing, before winking at Sheri and starting to laugh.

With the dinner being for Terry, Sheri asked him to bless the food so they could eat. Breaking their traditional custom of holding hands, bowing their heads and glorifying God for the sustenance, He has provided. Terry briefly enlightened them that God's Messenger (may the peace and blessings of God be upon him) related that saying "*Bismillah,*" which he did looking at Demi, is what pleases God and thanking Him is recommended for afterwards.

"Hold up! Hold up shawty! Now you know damn well I'm from Vine City, so what in the hell do, 'Bismillah' mean," Naomi snapped, raising her hands and waving them aggressively.

Chuckling at her silliness before answering, "It means, In the Name of God in Arabic," Terry articulated. "The wisdom behind saying 'Bismillah' is that God removes all harm from the food. We should always say 'Bismillah' before we place anything into our mouth and be thankful towards our creator."

"Ooooooh…"

Passing dishes between themselves instead of allowing the Eatery staff to serve the food, they laughed and bonded in ways that has eluded them for far too long. The Johnson's were a family again and they promised to never allow anything or anyone to separate their love from one another. Feeling a little jealous, while at the same time admiring the way Gip showed his appreciation and commitment to Yara by feeding her the spicy tomato boiled lobster on her plate instead of eating from his own at the head of the table, Naomi secretly started sending seductive videos of herself eating grilled garlic and herb shrimp to tease the sex store mascot at Teddy Bear Novelty because she wanted to feel special. He was the only man she knew who would be romantic with her, whereas all others only sought to get her drunk.

Imitating the characteristics and gangster girl antics of Mama Lewis, Sheri and Demi had everyone at the table gripping their stomachs. Sheri truly couldn't believe she had called the judge a bigot in open court and said that she was going to slap his old dried up raisin looking ass if she ever sees him on the street. Her being in jail had everyone wondering how she was acting without her guns.

Staring into Sheri's eyes as he rose out of his seat, Terry began tapping his spoon against a glass to command everyone's attention. Seeking to be funny and using the taps as a beat, Gip stood up and started doing the A-Town stomp in front of Yara, of which Terry turned to the side and did the same to Demi.

Noticing Naomi moving in her purview as though she was about to join in and not wanting to see any booty shaking, Yara playfully pushed Gip in the stomach, then started waving her salad fork and instructing them both to sit.

Gazing at his mother and father whom resembled the essence of love, now cuddling each other at the table before shifting his eyes to Sheri then Demi, Terry said something his father truly thought he'd never hear him say sincerely to a woman other than Penélope, while fidgeting with his phone.

"Though our time together has been short lived, you've opened my eyes and heart to how extraordinary you are. You are a blessing that's irreplaceable, and I refuse to make the mistake of taking you for granted. I love you, Demi!" Terry professed, causing everyone to stop and pinch themselves to assure they were not in a dream.

Transfixed by the unexpected expression, Demi blushed as she tried to hide the immeasurable beauty of her smile with her soft fragile hands. "Demi, words will never be able to paint what I envisage in you, nor will words scribe or print the way your presence causes me to cosmically feel — it's as though I'm suspended within my subconscious, dreaming within a dream. Every day, I thank God that my father asked me to come back as a gift for my mother's birthday because in my return, you became the blessing I refuse to deny from God. Being granted the pleasure of existing in your grace has awakened me as a man, cultivated the essence of love in my heart, and allowed me to discover that your light is honor worthy and irreplaceable," Terry artfully articulated while reaching to remove her obscuring hand from her mouth.

"I want to be the shield that protects your smile from the wind. The pillow you lay upon to gaze at the rain through the window. I want to be one of the reasons you fall to your knees and thank God before closing your eyes at night and when you open them each morning. Demi, I can promise you many things by tongue, but I confess from my heart: *Ashahu an la ilaha illa illa-ilah, wa ashadu anna Muhammadan rasul ullah*. And I'll never selfishly dishonor your worth or defy your trust if you grant me the honor of proving that I love you beyond poetic utterances, and though undeserving of you, I truly desire you beyond need."

"Masha Allah!" Gip said, kissing his wife on the cheek before rising to offer a toast that God purify his heart to exist as a true believer.

Reaching into his pocket while falling to his knees, Terry removed a box and held it in his hand right before Demi. Staring into her eyes and saying nothing as the excitement caused a tear to fall from Yara's left eye.

"Bro you stupid! Marriage before..." Sheri slapped Naomi in the mouth to prevent her from completing her inappropriate comment.

As Demi lifted the box from his hand and opened it to reveal a 4 carat Ascher cut diamond ring, Terry asked her to be his infinite future. "Demi, I don't need a lifetime to realize you are more magnificent than words and a gift of God's mercy. Given that pursuing God's pleasure, I seek, and Islam does not condone boyfriend and girlfriend relations. I have taken my shahadah, which is genuine just as my words, and I ask that you teach me how to love without failure. Will you marry me?"

Suspended in awe with everyone patiently waiting for her answer, Demi politely discredited her desire, clearly articulating while raising her eyes from the ring that she could not accept his proposal without the approval of her wali granting him the privilege of holding her hand and guiding her footsteps in accordance with the Qur'an and sunnah of the Beloved Prophet (may the peace and blessing of God be upon him) as a believer.

"What?" Disappointed and confused by her reply, Yara shifted her eyes from Demi to her husband, who immediately whispered in her ear to comfort the sadness that was beginning to envelop her.

"Calm down baby! A wali is the male guardian over her, and she is only advising him that she cannot agree to marry anyone without her wali's approval, regardless of her personal desires," Gip whispered. "Demi's a muslimah and by God's laws, she can only marry a believer with his consent."

"I knew you were wasting your time bru...." Naomi piped before being nudged by Sheri punching her in the arm and advising her to shut the fuck up at the same time.

Flipping his phone over, which was lying face down on the table, Demi was shocked and surprised to witness her mum, her uncle who was her wali, and the Imam of his masjid on video chat. After Terry reconfirmed his shahadah openly, answered a few questions, and was given the approval to prove he would cherish, respect, protect her honor, and nurture her mind and heart with sincerity Demi didn't hesitate in saying, "Na'am, na'am! Na'ammmm!" To his proposal and kissing Terry, as her uncle recited a du'a' in Arabic that only Demi, the Imam and her mother understood.

"What do that mean? A confused Yara asked rhetorically.

"I hope it's not some voodoo word they say where she from." Naomi ridiculously stated.

You need to stop Naomi! Sheri chimed in, snickering. "Seriously!"

With the family gathering becoming an engagement celebration, and Demi promising Sheri that there will be no wedding until she is completely back on her feet and healthy, they finished their meal, watched a movie as a family in the theater, and then went out on the deck to relax beneath the stars, while reminiscing and challenging one another to some karaoke.

Desiring to see her father perform out of character, of which is always an unforgettable spectacle of delight, Sheri requested that he sing "Love on the Brain" by Rihanna for her and "Baby Hold on to Me" by Gerald Levert for his wife.

Inserting the Beats by Dre wireless ear buds in his ear and selecting Rihanna on the playlist, Gip sang and danced for his daughter as if she was a talent scout. Turning his attention to Yara afterwards, he removed his shirt, then begged her to hold on to him in a performance that caused Demi to hold Terry, as Naomi looked on and texted with jealousy.

"Excuse me!" "Excuse me!" The short female nurse interjected while standing in the doorway to gain Sheri's attention.

"Yes!"

"Please excuse my interruption Ms. Johnson, but I thought you should know that your phone has constantly been ringing the past hour, so I brought it in case you may be missing an important call," she informed as she was handing her the phone and walking away.

"Thank you!" She managed to express while laughing hysterically at her father's silliness as her mother and Demi applauded his unforgettable cameo performance. Electing to check her missed calls and text messages while Naomi karaoke performance had the little prince laying in her mother's lap covering his eyes with his paws and whimpering, the dogs howling in the yard and everyone playfully pleading for her to stop singing "Tell me you love me" by Demi Lovato.

Sheri had no idea when Demi stood up to sing. Her voice was so electrifying and melodic. Being challenged to sing 'No More Rain' by Angie Stone, everyone listened attentively as her vocals echoed and serenaded the night with her beautiful accent.

Receiving a call that Demi's voice had her not wanting to answer, but assuming it was Mama Lewis calling collect again, she pressed 0 as the operator instructed, "Hi love! How are you grandma?" She uttered as Demi's voice continued to lift her soul.

"Bitch, why haven't you come to get me?!"

Momentarily frozen by the sound of his voice, Sheri's grip on the phone began to loosen as her arm began to tremble. Dropping the device as if she was standing at the edge of an abyss and unable to stop herself from falling inside, Sheri lost all facial coloring, mortified at the unexpected shockwave.

Yara began screaming at the top of her lungs for the nurses as everyone started to rush to her aide. Shaking and feeling as though she was falling to her death, Sheri sat there staring into empty space, eyes stretched to outer limits.

"Sheri...Sheri...Sheri! Who was that on the phone?" Terry repeatedly questioned, as he became emotional and scared seeing his sister react the way she did.

Bending down to retrieve Sheri's phone from the floor as the nurses scurried from the lower sitting area of the deck to aide her, Yara glanced at the cracked screen before placing it against her ear. "Hello!"

"Bitch, what type of games you playin'?" Randle roared. "You..."

"Muthafucka! Yo bitch ass has crossed the line for the last time..." She growled interjecting, after hearing the horrific threats Randle decreed, assuming it was Sheri's ear he was abusing, if she didn't find a way to get him out of jail.

Moving swiftly, Gip stepped around Demi as she stood motionless, holding the microphone against her chest, observing Sheri. Demanding the phone from his wife as her words began to torch the air around them and the glow of love in Terry's eyes had suddenly become rabid, Gip immediately disconnected the call, realizing that anything said would be recorded. Gaining the assurance from the medical staff that she was only hyperventilating and they were effectively treating her to get it under control, he stepped close to whisper a few words into Terry's ear, then walked to his office without looking over his shoulder. Retrieving the phone from his safe and a new sim card from a hidden compartment in a book on the shelf, Gip walked over to the window to observe his family and dialed a number once the phone powered up.

Seeing his Queen and princess in the illuminated glare of the moonlight reminded him of his life's purpose. Skipping the formalities of a usual greeting, Gip spoke as though he was giving a direct order to the Attorney General and not seeking a favor from a powerful friend. "I need Randle Carter free before a Piranha can chew the flesh off a mosquito's ass!"

إِنَّ الَّذِينَ اتَّقَوْا إِذَا مَسَّهُمْ طَائِفٌ مِّنَ الشَّيْطَانِ تَذَكَّرُوا فَإِذَا هُم مُّبْصِرُونَ ۝

Indeed, those who fear Allah – when an impulse touch them from Satan, they
remember [Him] and at once they have insight.
Surah Al-A'rāf 201.

Every woman makes life significant, but I thank even more those whom God
bestowed in my life to cultivate me. A woman is to be respected, nurtured,
infinitely appreciated, and honored; for anything less is truly unworthy of her
acceptance. Never accept abuse because it's not love.

"Signature Strokes"
Saudia Halim
Calligraphy / Henna Artist
804-433-0596

What Is Domestic Violence?

Does your partner ever....

- Insult, demean or embarrass you with put-downs?
- Control what you do, who you talk to or where you go?
- Look at you or act in ways that scare you?
- Push you, slap you, choke you or hit you?
- Stop you from seeing your friends or family members?
- Control the money in the relationship? Take your money or Social Security check, make you ask for money or refuse to give you money?
- Make all of the decisions without your input or consideration of your needs?
- Tell you that you're a bad parent or threaten to take away your children?
- Prevent you from working or attending school?
- Act like the abuse is no big deal, deny the abuse or tell you it's your own fault?
- Destroy your property or threaten to kill your pets?
- Intimidate you with guns, knives or other weapons?
- Attempt to force you to drop criminal charges?
- Threaten to commit suicide, or threaten to kill you?

National Domestic Violence Hotline
24/7 CALL SERVICES
If anything, you read here makes you want to talk to someone, call us at
1-800-799-SAFE (7233), available 24/7.